FALCO ON H

Lindsey Davis was born in Birmingham but now lives in Greenwich. After an English degree at Oxford she joined the Civil Service but now writes full time. Her novel *Two for the Lions* won the first CWA Ellis Peters Historical Dagger Award.

BY LINDSEY DAVIS

FALCO ON HIS METAL

Venus in Copper
The Iron Hand of Mars
Poseidon's Gold

Lindsey Davis

ARROW

Published by Arrow Books in 1999

1 3 5 7 9 10 8 6 4 2

Venus in Copper © Lindsey Davies 1991
The Iron Hand of Mars © Lindsey Davis 1992
Poseidon's Gold © Lindsey Davis 1992

Arrow Books Limited
The Random House Group Limited
20 Vauxhall Bridge Road, London SW1V 2SA

Random House, Australia (Pty) Limited
20 Alfred Street, Milsons Point, Sydney,
New South Wales 2061, Australia

Random House New Zealand Limited
18 Poland Road, Glenfield, Auckland 10, New Zealand

Random House (Pty) Limited
Endulini, 5A Jubilee Road, Parktown 2193, South Africa

The Random House Group Limited Reg. No. 954009
www.randomhouse.co.uk

A CIP catalogue record for this book
is available from the British Library

Papers used by Random House are natural, recyclable products
made from wood grown in sustainable forests. The manufacturing
processes conform to the environmental regulations of the
country of origin.

ISBN 0 09 940639 X

Printed and bound in Denmark by
Nørhaven A/S, Viborg

VENUS
IN COPPER

ACKNOWLEDGEMENT

Selfridges' Food Hall for supplying the Turbot

ROME

August–September AD71

'The bigger the turbot and dish the bigger the scandal,
not to mention the waste of money . . .'

Horace, Satire II,2

'For me it's "Enjoy what you have", though I can't feed
my dependants on turbot . . .'

Persius, Satire 6

'I've no time for the luxury of thinking about turbots: a
parrot is eating my house . . .'

Falco, Satire I,1

PRINCIPAL CHARACTERS
Friends, Enemies, & Family

M Didius Falco	An informer; trying to turn an honest denarius in a distinctly inferior job
Helena Justina	His highly superior girlfriend
Falco's Mother	(Enough said)
Maia & Junia	Two of Falco's sisters (the madcap & the refined one)
Famia & Gaius Baebius	His brothers-in-law, about whom it is best to say nothing (since there is nothing good to say)
D Camillus Verus & Julia Justa	Helena's patrician parents, who reckon Falco has much to answer for
L Petronius Longus	Falco's loyal friend; the Captain of the Aventine Watch
Smaractus	The landlord Falco is trying to lose
Lenia	Proprietress of the Eagle Laundry, who is after Falco's landlord (or after Falco's landlord's money)
Rodan & Asiacus	Falco's landlord's bullyboys; the seediest gladiators in Rome
Titus Caesar	Elder son and colleague of the Emperor Vespasian; Falco's patron, when he is allowed to be by:
Anacrites	Chief Spy at the Palace, no friend of our boy
Footsie, the Midget & the Man on the Barrel	Members of Anacrites' staff
A prison rat	Ditto, probably

Suspects & Witnesses

Severina Zotica	A professional bride (a home-loving girl)
Severus Moscus	(The bead-threader) Her first husband (deceased)
Eprius	(The apothecary) Her second husband (deceased)
Grittius Fronto	(The wild-beast importer) Her third husband (deceased)
Chloe	Her feminist parrot
Hortensius Novus	A freedman, now big in business; Severina's betrothed (can he last?)
Hortensius Felix & Hortensius Crepito	Business partners to Novus (all friends together, naturally)
Sabina Pollia & Hortensia Atilia	Their wives who consider that Hortensius Novus ought to be a worried man (an interest some might say was worrying)
Hyacinthus	A runabout to the Hortensii
Viridovix	A Gallic chef, reputedly a ruined prince
Anthea	A skivvy
Cossus	A letting agent Hyacinthus knows
Minnius	Purveyor of suspiciously delicious cakes
Lusius	A praetor's clerk, who is suspicious of everyone (a sharp type)
Tyche	An evasive fortune-teller
Thalia	A dancer who does curious things with snakes
A curious snake	
Scaurus	A monumental mason (with plenty of work)
Appius Priscillus	A property mogul (just another rat)
Gaius Cerinthus	Somebody the parrot knows; suspiciously absent from the scene

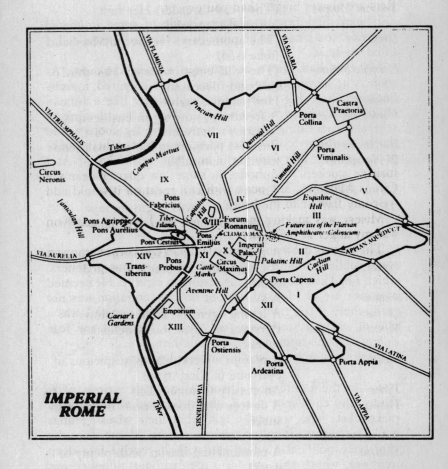

IMPERIAL ROME

Pincian Hill

VIA FLAMINIA

VIA SALARIA

Castra Praetoria

Porta Collina

Quirinal Hill

VII

VI

Porta Viminalis

Tiber

VIA TRIUMPHALIS

Campus Martius

Viminal Hill

Circus Neronis

IX

IV

Esquiline Hill

V

Janiculan Hill

Pons Fabricius

Capitoline Hill

VIII

Forum Romanum

III

Pons Agrippae
Pons Aurelius

Tiber Island

Pons Emilius

Pons Cestius

Future site of the Flavian Amphitheatre (Colosseum)

CLOACA MAX.

VIA AURELIA

XIV

Trans-tiberina

XI

Pons Probus

X

Imperial Palace

Circus Maximus

Palatine Hill

II

Caelian Hill

APPIAN AQUEDUCT

Cattle Market

Porta Capena

Aventine Hill

I

Caesar's Gardens

Emporium

XIII

XII

VIA LATINA

Porta Ostiensis

Porta Ardeatina

Porta Appia

Tiber

VIA OSTIENSIS

VIA APPIA

I

Rats are always bigger than you expect.

I heard him first: a sinister shuffle of some uninvited presence, too close for comfort in a cramped prison cell. I lifted my head.

My eyes had grown accustomed to near-darkness. As soon as he moved again I saw him: a dust-coloured, masculine specimen, his pink hands disturbingly like a human child's. He was as big as a buck rabbit. I could think of several casual eating shops in Rome where the cooks would not be too fussy to drop this fat scavenger into their stockpots. Smother him with garlic and who would know? At a furnace stockers' chophouse in some low quarter near the Circus Maximus, any bone with real meat on it would add welcome flavour to the broth . . .

Misery was making me ravenous; all I had to gnaw on was my anger at being here.

The rat was browsing nonchalantly in one corner amongst some rubbish, months' old debris from previous prisoners, which *I* had avoided as too disgusting to explore. He seemed to notice me as I looked up, but his concentration was not really there. I felt that if I lay still he might decide I was a pile of old rags to investigate. But if I shifted my legs defensively the motion would startle him.

Either way, the rat would run over my feet.

I was in the Lautumiae Prison, along with various petty felons who could not afford a barrister, and all the Forum pickpockets who wanted a rest from their wives. Things could be worse. It might have been the Mamertine: the short-stay political holding cell with its twelve-foot-deep dungeon, whose only exit for a man without influence was straight down into Hades. Here at least we had continual entertainment: old lags swearing hot Subura oaths, and wild swoops of disconcerting mania from hopeless drunks. In the

Mamertine nothing breaks the monotony until the public strangler comes in to measure your neck.

There would be no rats in the Mamertine. No jailor feeds a man condemned to death, so leftovers for the rodent population are scarce. Rats learn these things. Besides, everything there must be kept neat, in case any high-flown senators with foolish friends who have offended the Emperor want to drop in and relate the Forum news. Only here in the Lautumiae among the social dregs could a prisoner enjoy the keen excitement of waiting for his whiskery cellmate to turn round and sink its teeth into his shin . . .

The Lautumiae was a rambling affair, built to house squadrons of prisoners from provinces which were restive. Being foreign was the regular qualification. But any thorn who prickled the wrong bureaucrat could end up here as I had done, watching his toenails grow and thinking harsh thoughts about the establishment. The charge against *me* – in so far as the bastard who committed me to prison had a charge at all – was typical: I had made the fundamental error of showing up the Emperor's Chief Spy. He was a vindictive manipulator called Anacrites. Earlier that summer he had been sent to Campania on a mission; when he bungled it the Emperor Vespasian despatched me to finish the job, which I smartly did. Anacrites reacted in the usual way of a mediocre official whose junior shows any tenacity: he wished me luck in public – then at the first opportunity rammed in the boot.

He had tripped me up over a minor accounting error: he claimed I stole some imperial lead – all I did was borrow the stuff to use in a disguise. I had been prepared to pay back the money I took in exchange for the metal, if anyone ever challenged me. Anacrites never gave me the chance; I was flung into the Lautumiae, and so far no one had bothered to book a magistrate to hear my defence. Soon it would be September, when most of the courts went into recess and all new cases were held over until the New Year . . .

It served me right. Once I had known better than to dabble in politics. I had been a private informer. For five years I did nothing more dangerous than seek out adultery

12

and business fraud. A happy time: strolling about in the sunshine assisting tradesmen with their domestic tiffs. Some of my clients were women (and some of those were quite attractive). Also, private clients paid their bills. (Unlike the Palace, who quibbled over every innocent expense.) If I ever managed to regain my freedom, working for myself again was beckoning attractively.

Three days in jail had doused my happy-go-lucky nature. I was bored. I grew morose. I was suffering physically too: I had a sword-cut in my side – one of those slight flesh-wounds which chooses to fester. My mother was sending in hot dinners to comfort me, but the jailor picked out all the meat for himself. Two people had tried to extricate me; both without success. One was a friendly senator who tried to raise my plight with Vespasian; he had been denied an audience due to Anacrites' baleful influence. The other was my friend Petronius Longus. Petro, who was Captain of the Aventine watch, had come to the prison with a winejar under his elbow and tried the old-pals act on the jailor – only to find himself pitched straight out in the street with his amphora: Anacrites had even poisoned our normal local loyalties. So thanks to the Chief Spy's jealousy, it now looked as if I might never be a free citizen again . . .

The door swung open. A voice grated, 'Didius Falco, somebody loves you after all! Get up off your backside and bring your boots out here – '

As I struggled to raise myself, the rat ran over my foot.

II

My troubles were over – partially.

When I stumbled out into what passed for a reception area, the jailor was closing a heavy drawstring bag, grinning as if it was his birthday. Even his grimy sidekicks seemed impressed by the size of the bribe. Blinking in the daylight, I made out a small, pinched, upright figure who greeted me with a sniff.

Rome is a fair society. There are plenty of provincial backwaters where prefects keep their felons in chains, ready to be tortured when other entertainment palls, but in Rome unless you commit a horrendous misdemeanour – or stupidly confess – every suspect has the right to find a sponsor to stand surety.

'Hello, Mother!' It would have been surly to wish myself back in the cell with the rat.

Her expression accused me of being as degenerate as my father – though even my father (who ran off with a redhead and left poor ma with seven children) never landed himself in jail . . . Luckily my mother was too loyal to our family to draw this comparison in front of strangers, so she thanked the jailor for looking after me instead.

'Anacrites seems to have forgotten you, Falco!' he jeered at me.

'That was his intention, presumably.'

'He said nothing about bail before trial – '

'He said nothing about a trial, either,' I snarled. 'Holding me without a court appearance is as illegal as denying bail!'

'Well if he decides to press charges – '

'Just whistle!' I assured him. 'I'll be back in my cell looking innocent in two shakes of a bacchante's tambourine.'

'Sure, Falco?'

'Oh *sure*!' I lied pleasantly.

14

Outside I took a deep breath of freedom, which I instantly regretted. It was August. We were facing the Forum. Around the Rostrum the atmosphere was almost as stifling as the bowels of the Lautumiae. Most of the aristocracy had dodged off to their airy summer villas, but for those of us at the rough end of society, life in Rome had slowed to a sluggish pace. Any movement in this heat was unbearable.

My mother examined her jailbird, looking unimpressed.

'Just a misunderstanding, Ma . . .' I tried to prevent my face revealing that for an informer with a tough reputation, being rescued by his *mother* was an indignity to avoid. 'Who provided the handsome ransom? Was it Helena?' I asked, referring to the unusually superior girlfriend I had managed to acquire six months ago in place of my previous string of flea-bitten circus entertainers and flower girls.

'No, I paid the surety; Helena has been seeing to your rent – ' My heart sank at this rush of support from the women in my life. I knew I would have to pay for it, even if not in cash. 'Never mind about the money.' My mother's tone indicated that with a son like me, she kept her life savings continually to hand. 'Come home with me for a good dinner – '

She must be planning to keep me firmly in her custody; *I* planned on being my footloose self.

'I need to see Helena, Ma – '

Normally it would be unwise for a bachelor who had just been redeemed by his little old mother to suggest sloping off after women. But my mother nodded. In the first place, Helena Justina was a senator's daughter so visiting such a highly placed lady counted as a privilege for the likes of me, not the usual depravity mothers rant about. Also, due partly to an accident on a staircase, Helena had just miscarried our first child. All our female relations still regarded me as a reckless wastrel, but for Helena's sake most would agree that at present it was my duty to visit her at every opportunity.

'Come with me!' I urged.

'Don't be foolish!' scoffed my mother. 'It's you Helena wants to see!'

That news failed to fill me with confidence.

15

Ma lived near the river, behind the Emporium. We crossed the Forum slowly (to emphasise how Ma was bowed down by the troubles I caused her), then she set me loose at my favourite bathhouse, which lay behind the Temple of Castor. There I sluiced away the stench of prison, changed into a spare tunic which I had left at the gymnasium to cover emergencies, and found a barber who managed to make me look more respectable (under the blood he caused to flow).

I had come out, still feeling grey in the face after being locked up, yet much more relaxed. I was walking towards the Aventine, running my fingers through my damp curls in vain attempt to turn myself into the kind of debonair bachelor who might arouse a woman's ardour. Then disaster struck. Too late, I noticed a pair of disreputable bruisers posing against a portico so they could show off their muscles to anyone who had to pass on their side of the street. They wore loincloths, with leather strips tied round their knees and wrists and ankles to make them look tough. Their arrogance was horribly familiar.

'Oh look – it's Falco!'

'Oh cobnuts – Rodan and Asiacus!'

Next moment one of them was behind me with his elbows clenched round my upper arms, while the other shook me charmlessly by the hand – a process which involved pulling out my wrist until my arm joints strained in their sockets like bowlines fighting their couplings on a galley in a hurricane. The smell of old sweat and recent garlic was bringing tears to my eyes. 'Oh cut it, Rodan; my reach is already long enough . . .'

To call these two 'gladiators' insulted even the clapped-out hulks who usually feature in that trade. Rodan and Asiacus trained at a barracks which was run by my landlord Smaractus, and when they were not smacking themselves silly with practice swords he sent them out to make the streets even more dangerous than usual. They never did much work in the arena; their role in public life was to intimidate the unfortunate tenants who rented homes from him. For me, being in prison had had one great advantage: avoiding my landlord, and these pet thugs of his.

Asiacus lifted me off my feet and shook me about. I let him rearrange my guts temporarily. I waited until he grew bored with it and put me back on the paving slabs – then I carried on downwards, pulled him off balance, and threw him over my head at Rodan's feet.

'Olympus! Doesn't Smaractus teach you two *any*thing?' I hopped back smartly out of their reach. 'You're out of date; my rent's been paid!'

'So the rumour's true!' leered Rodan. 'We heard you're a kept man now!'

'Jealousy gives you a nasty squint, Rodan! Your mother should have warned you, it will drive away the girls!' You may have heard that gladiators trail throngs of infatuated women; Rodan and Asiacus must have been the only two in Rome whose special seediness deprived them of any following. Asiacus got up, wiping his nose. I shook my head. 'Sorry; I was forgetting: neither of you could interest a fifty-year-old fishwife with two blind eyes and no sense of discretion – '

Then Asiacus jumped me. And they both set about reminding me why I hated Smaractus so bitterly.

'That's for the *last* time your rent was overdue!' grunted Rodan, who had a long memory.

'And *that's* for the *next* time!' added Asiacus – a realistic forecaster.

We had practised this painful dance so many times that I soon twisted out of their grip. Throwing back one or two more insults, I skipped away up the street. They were too lazy to follow me.

I had been free for an hour. I was already battered and despondent. In Rome, a landlord's city, freedom brings mixed joys.

III

Helena Justina's father, the Senator Camillus Verus, lived near the Capena Gate. A desirable spot, just off the Appian Way where it emerges from the republican city wall. On the way I managed to find another bathhouse to soothe my crop of new bruises. Luckily Rodan and Asiacus always punched a victim's ribcage, so my face was unmarked; if I remembered not to wince there was no need for Helena to know. A sickly Syrian apothecary sold me a salve for the sword-wound I had already been nursing in my side, though the ointment soon produced a greasy mark on my tunic, blueish, like mould on wall plaster, which was not designed to impress the fashionable residents of the Capena Gate.

The Camillus porter knew me but as usual refused me admittance. I did not allow this fleabag to delay my entry long. I walked round the corner, borrowed a hat from a roadmender, knocked again with my back turned, then when the porter foolishly opened up for what he thought was a travelling lupinseller, I rushed indoors making sure my boot stomped down hard on his ankle as our paths crossed.

'For a *quadrans* I'd lock you out on the step! I'm *Falco*, you muttonchop! Announce me to Helena Justina, or your heirs will be quarrelling over who gets your best sandals sooner than you expect!'

Once I got inside the house he treated me with sullen respect. That is, he went back into his cubicle to finish an apple, while I searched for my princess by myself.

Helena was in a reception room, looking pale and studious with a reed pen in her hand. She was twenty-three – or perhaps twenty-four now since I had no idea when her birthday was; even after I had been to bed with their treasure, I was not invited to share the family celebrations of a senator's house. They only let me see her at all because they cringed from Helena's own wilfulness. Even before she met me she had been married but had chosen to divorce herself (for the eccentric reason that her husband never talked to her), so her parents had already realised their eldest offspring was a trial.

Helena Justina was a tall, stately being whose straight dark hair had been tortured with hot curling rods, though it was fighting back well. She had handsome brown eyes which no cosmetics could improve, though her maids painted them up on principle. At home she wore very little jewellery, and looked none the worse for it. In company she was shy; even alone with a close friend like me she might pass for modest until she piped up with an opinion – at which point wild dogs broke pack and ran for cover all along the street. I reckoned I could handle her – but I never pushed my luck.

I posed in the doorway with my normal disrespectful grin. Helena's sweet, unforced smile of greeting was the best thing I had seen for a week. 'Why is a beautiful girl like you sitting on her own, scribbling recipes?'

'I am translating Greek History,' Helena stated pompously. I peered over her shoulder. It was a recipe for stuffed figs.

I bent and kissed her cheek. The loss of our baby, which we both still felt, had inflicted a painful formality on us. Then our two right hands found and gripped one another with a fervour that could have got us denounced by the pompous old barristers in the Basilica Julia.

'I'm so glad to see you!' murmured Helena fiercely.

'It takes more than prison bolts to keep me away.' I uncurled her hand and laid it against my cheek. Her ladylike fingers were perfumed with an eccentric combination of rare Indian unguents and oak-apple ink – quite unlike the stagnant whiffs that hung around the floosies I had previously known. 'Oh lady, I love you,' I admitted (still buoyed up by the euphoria of my recent release). 'And it's not just because I found out that you've paid my rent!'

She slipped from her seat to kneel by me with her head hidden. A senator's daughter would hardly risk letting a house-slave find her crying in a convict's lap – but I stroked her neck soothingly, just in case. Besides, the back of Helena's neck was an attractive proposition to an idle hand.

'I don't know why you bother with me,' I commented after a while. 'I'm a wreck. I live in a pit. I have no money. Even the rat in my cell had a sneer when he looked at me. Whenever you need me I leave you on your own – '

'Stop grumbling, Falco!' Helena snorted, looking up with a mark on her cheek from my belt buckle, but otherwise her old self.

'I do a job most people wouldn't touch,' I carried on gloomily. 'My own employer throws me into jail and forgets I exist – '

'You've been released – '

'Not exactly!' I confessed.

Helena never fussed over things she believed I ought to sort out for myself. 'What are you intending to do now?'

'Work on my own again.' She said nothing; no need to ask why I was unhappy. My bright plan posed one great problem: I would earn much less independently than my notional public salary, despite the fact that Vespasian's pay-clerks kept me months in arrears. 'Do you think this is stupid?'

'No; you're quite right!' Helena agreed without hesitation, though she must have realised going freelance destroyed any hope of me affording marriage into the patrician rank. 'You've risked your life for the state. Vespasian took you on because he knew just what you were worth to him. But Marcus, you're too good to suffer poor rewards form a stingy employer and petty Palace jealousies – '

'Sweetheart, you know what it means – '

'I said I would wait.'

'I said I wouldn't let you.'

'Didius Falco, I never take any notice of what you say.'

I grinned, then we sat together in silence a few minutes more.

After jail, this room in her father's house was a haven of tranquillity. Here we had rag rugs and tasselled cushions to make us comfortable. Thick masonry muffled out sounds from the street, while light flowing in through high windows on the garden side lit walls which were painted as mock marble, the colour of ripened wheat. It provided a gracious impression – though a slightly faded one. Helena's father was a millionaire (this was not good detective work on my part, just the minimum qualification for the Senate); yet even he regarded himself as struggling in a city where only multimillionaires attracted election votes.

My own position was far worse. I had no money and no status. To carry off Helena on respectable terms, I would have to find four hundred thousand sesterces and then persuade the Emperor to add me to the list of pitiful nonentities who form the middle rank. Even if I ever managed it, I was for her a disreputable choice.

She read my thoughts. 'Marcus, I heard your horse won his race at the Circus Maximus.'

Life does have its compensations: the horse, who was called Little Sweetheart, had been a lucky bequest to me. I could not afford to stable him, but before he went to the horse sales I had entered him in just one race – which he won at amazing odds. 'Helena, you are right; I made some money on that race. I might invest in a more impressive apartment, to attract a better class of client.'

Her head nodded approvingly, close against my knee. She had her hair pinned up with a pantheon of ivory bodkins, all with knobs carved as strict-looking goddesses. While I mused about my lack of money I had pulled one out, so I stuck it in my belt like a hunting knife, then teasingly set about capturing the rest. Helena squirmed in mild annoyance, reaching for my wrists. Eventually she knocked my fistful of pins to the floor; I let her flail around trying to find them while I carried on methodically with my plan.

By the time I had her hair all loose, Helena had repossessed her bodkins – though I noticed she let me keep the one stuffed in my belt. I still have it: Flora, with a crown of roses which is giving her hay fever; she turns up sometimes when I burrow for lost pens in my writing-box.

I spread out Helena's shining hair the way I wanted it. 'That's better! Now you look more like a lass who might agree to being kissed – in fact you look like one who might even kiss me of her own accord . . .' I reached down and pulled her arms round my neck.

It was a long, deeply appreciative kiss. Only the fact that

21

I knew Helena very well made me notice that my own passion was meeting unusual restraint from her.

'What's this? Gone off me, fruit?'

'Marcus, I can't – '

I understood. Her miscarriage had shaken her; she was wary of risking another. And she was probably afraid of losing me too. We both knew more than one bright spark of Roman rectitude who would automatically ditch a distressed girlfriend at a time like this.

'I'm sorry – ' She was embarrassed, and struggling to escape. But she was still my Helena. She wanted me to hold her almost as much as I wanted to. She needed to be comforted – even though for once she shrank from encouraging me.

'My darling, it's natural.' I loosened my grip. 'Everything will right itself . . .' I knew I had to be reassuring so I tried to treat her gently, though it was hard to take disappointment when it felt so physical. I was cursing, and Helena must have been aware of it.

We sat quiet and talked about family matters (a bad idea as usual), then not long afterwards I said I had to leave.

Helena took me to the door. The porter had now disappeared altogether so I undid the bolts myself. She threw her arms round me and buried her face in my neck. 'I suppose you'll run after other women!'

'Naturally!' I managed to make a joke of it too.

Her huge stricken eyes were affecting me badly. I kissed her eyelids then tormented myself, holding her tight against me while I lifted her right off her feet. 'Come and live with me!' I urged suddenly. 'The gods only know how long it will take me to earn what we need to be respectable. I'm frightened of losing you; I want to have you close. If I rent a bigger apartment – '

'Marcus, I just feel – '

'Trust me.'

Helena smiled, and pulled my ear as if she thought that was the quickest way to make our difficulties permanent. But she promised to think about what I had said.

My step lightened as I walked home to the Aventine.

22

Even if my lady was reluctant to join me, with my winnings on Little Sweetheart there was nothing to stop me leasing a more gracious apartment anyway . . . Knowing what I was going home to, the thought of living somewhere else was bound to cheer me up.

Then I remembered that before I was hauled off to prison, my uncashed betting tokens had been swallowed by my three-year-old niece.

IV

The Eagle Laundry, Fountain Court.

Of all the groaning tenements in all the sordid city alleyways, the most degrading must be Fountain Court. It was five minutes off the great road from Ostia, one of the most vital highways in the Empire, but this ulcerous spot in the armpit of the Aventine could have been a different world. Up above, on the double crests of the hill, were the great Temples of Diana and Venus, but we lived too close to see their lofty architecture from our deep, dark warren of aimless, nameless lanes. It was cheap (for Rome). Some of us would have paid the landlord more just to have him hire a pair of competent bailiffs to evict us into the fresher air of a better street.

My apartment was high in a vast, ramshackle block. A laundry occupied all the space at street level; woollen tunics awaiting collection were the only things in our neighbourhood that were clean. Once on, their pristine condition could be ruined by one short trip down the muddy single track that served as both our exit road and the nearest we had to a sewer, amidst the smuts from the lampblack furnace where a one-eyed stationers' supplier brewed stinking domestic ink, and the smoke from the beehive ovens where Cassius our local bread-man could char a loaf to the verge of destruction like no other baker in Rome.

These were dangerous byways: in a moment of lapsed concentration, I sank to the ankle in sticky brown dung. While I was muttering and cleaning my boot on a kerbstone, Lenia the laundress stuck her head round a line of tunics. Seeing me, she bustled out to deride me as usual. She was an ill-kempt bundle who approached with the gracelessness of a swan landing on water: wild writhings of luridly dyed red hair, watery eyes, and a voice that was hoarse from too many flagons of badly fermented wine.

'Falco! Where've you been all week?'

'Out of town.'

It was unclear whether she knew I meant in the Lautumiae. Not that Lenia would care. She was too lazy to be curious, except in closely defined areas of business. Those included whether my filthy landlord Smaractus was being paid his dues – and she only became *really* curious about that after she decided to marry him. A decision made for purely financial reasons (because Smaractus was as rich as Crassus after decades of squeezing the Aventine poor) and now Lenia was preparing for her wedding with the clinical will of a surgeon. (Knowing that the patient would pay heavily for her services, after she had carved him up . . .)

'I gather I'm in credit,' I grinned.

'You finally found out how to pick a woman!'

'True; I rely on the Parian perfection of my face – '

Lenia, who was a harsh critic of the fine arts, cackled cynically. 'Falco, you're a cheap fake!'

'Not me – I come with a certificate of quality from a lady of good repute! She likes to pamper me. Well I deserve it, of course . . . How much has she contributed?'

I could see Lenia opening her mouth to lie about it; then she worked out that Helena Justina was bound to tell me, if ever I had the good manners to discuss my debt. 'Three months, Falco.'

'Jupiter!' That was a shock to my system. The most I ever reckoned to donate to my landlord's retirement fund was three weeks (in arrears). 'Smaractus must think he's been transported on a rainbow to Olympus!'

I deduced from a certain cloudiness in Lenia's expression that Smaractus had yet to discover his luck. She changed the subject rapidly: 'Someone keeps coming here asking for you.'

'Client?' Nervously I wondered if the Chief Spy had already discovered me missing. 'Take his details?'

'Oh I've better things to do, Falco! He turns up every day and every day I tell him you're not here – ' I relaxed. Anacrites would have had no reason to be looking for me until this afternoon.

'Well, I'm back now!' I felt too weary to be bothered with mysteries.

I set off up the stairs. I lived on the sixth floor, the cheapest of all. It gave me plenty of time to remember the familiar smell of urine and old cabbage ends; the stale pigeon droppings staining every step; the wall graffiti, not all of them at child height, of stickmen charioteers; the curses against betting agents and the pornographic advertisements. I knew hardly any of my fellow tenants, but I recognised their voices quarrelling as I passed. Some doors were permanently closed with oppressive secrecy; other families opted for no more than curtained entrances which forced their neighbours to share their dismal lives. A naked toddler ran out of one, saw me, and rushed back inside screaming. A demented old lady on the third floor always sat in her doorway and gabbled after anyone who came by; I saluted her with a gracious gesture which set her off into torrents of venomous abuse.

I needed practice; I was stumbling when I finally reached the top of the building. For a moment I listened: professional habit. Then I operated my simple latch-lifter and pushed open the door.

Home. The sort of apartment where you go in; change your tunic; read your friends' messages; then find any excuse to rush straight back out again. But today I could not face the nightmares on the stairs a second time, so I stayed in.

Four strides permitted me to survey my premises: the office with a cheap bench and table, then the bedroom with a lopsided contraption that served as my bed. Both rooms had the worrying neatness that resulted when my mother had enjoyed three days of uninterrupted tidying. I looked around suspiciously but I reckoned no one else had been there. Then I set about making the place my own again. I soon managed to knock the sparse furniture askew, rumple the bedclothes, spill water everywhere as I revived my balcony foliage, and drop all the clothes I had been wearing onto the floor.

After that I felt better. Now it was *Home*.

Prominent on the table, where not even I could miss it, stood a ceramic Greek bowl which I had bought off an antiques stall for two coppers and a cheeky smile; it was half full of scratched bone counters, some with extremely odd streaks of colour. I chortled. The last time I saw these was at a ghastly family party where my little niece Marcia had seized them to play with and swallowed most of them: my betting tags.

When a child has eaten something you prefer not to lose, there is only one way – if you are fond of the child – to recover it. I knew the disgusting procedure from the time my brother Festus swallowed our mother's wedding ring and pressured me to help him find it. (Until he was killed in Judaea, which put an end to my fraternal duties, there was a tradition in our family that Festus was the one who was always in trouble, while I was the fool he always persuaded to dig him out of it.) Gulping down family valuables must be an inherited trait; I had just spent three days in prison wishing constipation on my feckless brother's sweet but feckless child . . .

No need to worry. Some hard-headed relation – my sister Maia probably, the only one who could organise – had gallantly retrieved these tags. To celebrate, I pulled up a floorboard where I had half a winejar hidden away from visitors and sat out on my balcony with my feet up on the parapet while I applied all my attention to a restorative drink.

As soon as I was comfortable, a visitor arrived.

I heard him come in, gasping for air after the long climb. I kept quiet, but he found me anyway. He pushed through the folding door and accosted me chirpily. 'You Falco?'

'Could be.'

He had arms as thin as pea-sticks. A triangular face came down to a point at a dot of a chin. Above it ran a narrow black moustache, almost ear to ear. The moustache was what you noticed. It bisected a face that was too old for his adolescent body, as if he were a refugee from a province racked by twenty years of famine and tribal strife. The true cause was nothing so dramatic. He was just a slave.

'Who's asking?' I prompted. By then I had warmed up enough in the late-afternoon sunshine not to care.

27

'A runabout from the house of Hortensius Novus.'

He had a faintly foreign accent, but it lay a long way back behind the common lilt all prisoners of war seem to contract in the slave market. I guessed he had picked up his Latin as a small child; probably by now he could hardly remember his native tongue. His eyes were blue; he looked like a Celt to me.

'You have a name?'

'Hyacinthus!'

He said it with a level stare that dared me to scoff. If he was a slave he had enough problems without enduring rib-aldry from every new acquaintance just because some over-seer with a filthy hangover had stuck him with the name of a Greek flower.

'Pleased to meet you, Hyacinthus.' I refused to present a target for the aggressive retort he held ready. 'I've never heard of your master Hortensius. What's his problem?'

'If you asked him, he'd say nothing.'

People often talk in riddles when they commission an informer. Very few clients seem capable of asking straight out, *What are your rates for proving that my wife sleeps with my driver?*

'So why has he sent you?' I asked the runabout patiently.

'His *relations* have sent me,' Hyacinthus corrected me. 'Hortensius Novus has no idea I'm here.'

That convinced me the case involved denarii, so I waved Hyacinthus to my bench: a hint of cash worth being secret-ive about always perks me up.

'Thanks, Falco; you're a regular general!' Hyacinthus assumed my invitation to sit included my winejar too; to my annoyance he dodged back indoors and found a beaker for himself. As he made himself at home under my rose pergola he demanded, 'This your idea of a gracious setting for interviewing clients?'

'My clients are easily impressed.'

'It stinks! Or is this just one of the drop-ins you keep around Rome?'

'Something like that.'

'It was the only address we had.' It was the only address *I* had. He tried the wine, then spluttered. *'Parnassus!'*

28

'Gift from a grateful client,' Not grateful enough.

I poured myself a refill, as an excuse to shift the winejar out of his reach. He was having a good squint at me. My informality made him doubtful. The world is full of straight-haired fools who think curly-tops who grin at them cannot possibly be good businessmen.

'This place has all I need,' I said, implying that to exist in such squalor I must be tougher than I looked. 'The people I want to meet know where to find me – while the ones I may be avoiding are put off by the stairs . . . All right Hyacinthus, I don't issue a prospectus of my services, but here's what I can offer: I do information-gathering of a mainly domestic type – '

'Divorce?' he translated, with a grin.

'Correct! Also investigating prospective sons-in-law on behalf of sensitive fathers, or advising recent legatees whether their bequests involve any hidden debt. I do leg-work for lawyers who need more evidence – with a court appearance if required. I have contacts in auctioneering and I specialise in recovery of precious artworks after theft. I *don't* tackle draftdodgers or debt collection. And I *never* fix gladiatorial fights.'

'Squeamish?'

'Better sense.'

'We shall want to take up references.'

'So will I! All my business is legitimate.'

'How much do you charge, Falco?'

'Depends on the complexity of the case. A solving fee, plus a daily expense rate. And I give no guarantees, other than a promise to do my best.'

'What is it you do for the Palace?' Hyacinthus threw in suddenly.

'I don't work for the Palace now.' It sounded like official secrecy: a pleasing effect. 'Is that why you're here?'

'My people felt a Palace man came ready recommended.'

'Their mistake! If they hire me I'll do a decent job, and be discreet. So, Hyacinthus, are we in business?'

'I have to invite you to the house. You'll be told about the case there.'

I had intended to go anyway. I like to inspect the people who will be paying me. 'So where am I heading?'

'The Via Lata sector. On the Pincian.'

I whistled. 'Highly desirable! Are Hortensius and his relations people of rank?'

'Freedmen.'

Ex-slaves! That was new for me. But it made a change from vindictive officials and the hypocrisies I had run up against with some of the senatorial class.

'You object?' Hyacinthus enquired curiously.

'Why should I, if their money's good?'

'Oh . . . no reason,' said the slave.

He finished his drink and waited for another, but I had no intention of offering. 'We're on the Via Flaminia side, Falco. Anyone in the district will point out the house.'

'If Hortensius is to know nothing about this, when shall I come?'

'Daytime. He's a businessman. He leaves home after breakfast usually.'

'What's his business?' My question was a routine one, but the way Hyacinthus shrugged and ignored it seemed oddly evasive. 'So who do I ask for?'

'Sabina Pollia – or if she's unavailable, there's another called Hortensia Atilia – but it's Pollia who is taking the initiative.'

'Wife?'

He gave me a sly grin. 'Novus is unmarried.'

'Don't tell me any more! So the females of his household are hiring me to frighten off a gold-digger?' Hyacinthus looked impressed. 'When a bachelor has a houseful of for-midable women – and don't tell me Hortensius Novus hasn't,' I growled, 'because you're here behind his back on their behalf – why does he always decide that the solution to his troubles lies in marrying another one?'

'Now tell me you don't do gold-diggers!' the runabout retaliated.

'All the time!' I assured him glumly. 'Gold-diggers are wonderful women: the bedrock of my trade!'

As he left he said, 'If you ever do think of leasing a more respectable apartment – '

'I could be in the market.' I followed him as far as the balcony door.

'Try Cossus,' Hyacinthus offered helpfully. 'He's a letting agent in the Vicus Longus – a dozy pomegranate, but reliable. He has plenty of decent property for men of affairs. Mention my name and he'll be sure to look after you – '

'Thanks. I may do that.' I deduced that Hyacinthus thought his suggestion earned him a tip. I keep a half-aureus sewn in the hem of my tunic, but there was no way I would part with that for a slave. All I could find was a thin copper *as* which no self-respecting latrinekeeper would accept as an entrance fee.

'Thanks, Falco. That should swell my freedom fund!'

'Sorry. I've been out of touch with my banker!'

I tried to make my spell in the Lautumiae sound like a secret mission in Lower Parthia, so he could go home with a good report for my prospective clients.

The freedman Hortensius Novus lived in the north of the city, on the scented slopes of the Pincian Hill. His house stood surrounded by a perfectly plain wall of sufficient height to prevent people peeping over the top, had any of his well-heeled neighbours lived near enough. None of them did. It was an area where the grounds of the private villas were even more spacious than the public gardens which were graciously allowed to fill the lesser spaces in between. If I say that one of *those* was the Garden of Lucullus, which the Empress Messalina had prized so highly she executed its owner when he declined to sell, this gives a fair idea of the scale of the private mansions on Pincian Hill.

I talked myself through the Hortensius gatehouse, then hiked along the hillside on their broad gravel drive. There was plenty of landscape to occupy me. Luckily I had stopped at a sweetmeat stall and made some enquiries, so I was to some extent prepared for the opulence of the freedman's estate. His box trees clipped like winged griffons, his pale statues of broad-browed goddesses, his intricate pergolas swagged with roses and vines, his massive alabaster urns with blush-pink veining, his dovecotes, his fishpools, his marble seats in intimate arbours with views across neatly scythed lawns, were a treat.

I was admitted past the bronze sphinxes guarding the white marble entrance steps into a formal entrance hall with heavy black pillars. There I tapped my boot gently on a white and grey geometric mosaic until a tired servant appeared. He took my name then led me through the delicate ferns and fountains to an elegant inner court where one of the three Hortensius freedmen had recently installed a new statue of himself, in his best toga, looking important and holding a scroll. This was, I decided, what my landing needed at the Falco residence: me in Carrara marble, like a plush prig with lots of money who felt satisfied with his world. I made a note to order one – some day.

I ended up in a reception room, alone. Throughout the house I had glimpsed burnt-out tapers and torches. A faint whiff of stale garlands hung round the corridors, and from time to time when a door opened I caught the sound of last night's dishes clattering. A message came from Sabina Pollia asking me to wait. I guessed that the lady was not yet up and dressed. I decided to reject the case if she turned out to be a rich party-giving slut.

After half an hour I grew bored and wandered off down a corridor, exploring. Everywhere was hung with lavishly dyed curtains, slightly crumpled; the furniture was exquisite, yet jumbled into the rooms quite haphazardly. The decor was a strange mixture too: white stuccoed ceilings, deliciously delicate, above wall paintings of grossly erotic scenes. It was as if they had bought whatever they were offered by every fast-talking salesman who came along, without reference to a design plan, let alone taste. The only thing the artwork had in common was that it must have cost thousands.

I was amusing myself putting an auction price to a Phidias 'Venus adjusting her Sandal' (which gave every appearance of being original, unlike almost every other Phidias you run across in Rome) when a door flew open behind me and a female voice cried, '*There* you are!'

I spun round guiltily. When I saw what she looked like, I did not apologise.

She was a peach. She had kissed farewell to forty, but if she ever went to the theatre she would attract more attention than the play. Her melting dark brown eyes were outlined with kohl, yet even left to nature those eyes would cause moral damage to any man with a nervous system as susceptible as mine. The eyes were set in a near perfect face, and the face belonged to a body which made the Phidias Venus look like an out-of-condition eggseller who had been on her feet all day. She knew exactly the effect she had; I was swimming in perspiration where I stood.

Since I had asked for Sabina Pollia, I assumed this was

33

she. From behind her two burly boys in vibrant blue livery surged towards me.

'Call off your dogs!' I commanded. 'I have an invitation from the lady of the house.'

'Are you the informer?' The direct way she spoke suggested that if it suited her she might not be a lady.

I nodded. She signalled the two flankers to back off. They stepped aside just enough for privacy though near enough to lather me soundly if I tried to cause offence. I had no intention of doing that – unless someone offended me first. 'If you ask me,' I said frankly, 'a lady should not need a bodyguard in her own home.'

I kept my face neutral while madam toyed with the suspicion that I had just accused her of being a common piece. 'I'm Didius Falco. Sabina Pollia, presumably?' I offered my paw for a handshake in a deliberately unconventional way. She looked unhappy, but accepted it. She had small hands with many jewelled finger-rings; short fingers with pale oval fingernails like a girl's.

Sabina Pollia made up her mind, and dismissed the two boys in the Adriatic uniforms. A lady ought to have sent for a chaperone; apparently she forgot. She threw herself onto a couch, rather untidily; the graceful Venus had the advantage of her now.

'Tell me about yourself, Falco!' A risk of my trade: she intended to enjoy herself, interrogating me. 'You're a private informer – how long have you been in that business?'

'Five years. Since I was invalided out of the legions.'

'Nothing serious?'

I gave her a dry, slow smile. 'Nothing that prevents me doing what I want to do!'

Our eyes met, lingeringly. Getting this beauty to discuss my commission was going to be hard work.

She was one of those classic kittens with a straight nose down the centre of a balanced face, clear skin, and extremely regular teeth – a perfect profile, though slightly lacking in expression since the owners of very beautiful faces never need to express character to get what they want; besides, too much expression might crease the paint they never need but always use. She was slight, and played on

34

it – bold snake-headed bracelets to emphasise the delicacy of her arms, and a little, girlishly wounded pout. It was designed to melt a man. Never one to quibble when a woman makes an effort, I melted obediently.

'I hear you work for the Palace, Falco – though my servant tells me you are not allowed to say anything about that . . .'

'Correct.'

'Being a private informer must be fascinating?' She was evidently hoping for some scandalous revelations about past clients.

'Sometimes,' I answered unhelpfully. Most of my past clients were people I preferred to forget.

'You had a brother who was a military hero, I hear.'

'Didius Festus. He won the Palisaded Crown in Judaea.' My brother Festus would think it hilarious that I had gained status through being related to him. 'Did you know him?'

'No – should I?'

'A lot of women did.' I smiled. 'Sabina Pollia, I gather there is something I may be able to help you with?'

These doll-like creatures whip to the mark like artillery bolts. 'Why, Falco – what are you good at?'

I decided it was time to reassert my grip on the situation. 'Lady, what I'm good at is my job! Can we proceed?'

'Not before time!' Sabina Pollia retorted.

Why do I always get the blame?

'If I understood Hyacinthus, this is a family problem?' I asked somewhat dourly.

'Not quite!' Pollia laughed. She gave me the vulnerable pout again, but I had never been fooled by it; the lady was tough. 'We need you to keep the problem *out* of the family!'

'Then let's describe the "family" first. Hortensius Novus lives here; and who else?'

'We *all* live here. I am married to Hortensius Felix; Hortensia Atilia is the wife of Hortensius Crepito – ' Slaves intermarrying: a common development.

'Novus sits among this brotherly triumvirate, still a happy bachelor?'

'So far,' she replied, with tension in her voice. 'But they are not brothers, Falco! What gave you that idea?'

I was thrown off balance slightly. 'The set-up; same names; you call yourselves a family –'

'We are none of us related. Though we *are* one family. Our patron's name was Hortensius Paulus.'

So to add to the normal inconvenience that every Roman is reverently named after his father, as are his brothers and sons, here I had a whole gang of ex-slaves, each bearing their old master's patronymic now they were free. Females too: 'Hortensia Atilia must be a freed-woman of the same household?'

'Yes.'

'But not you?'

'Oh yes.'

'Your name is different –' Sabina Pollia raised the proud pared crescents of her eyebrows, amusing herself at my expense. 'I'm struggling here!' I admitted freely.

'I worked for the woman of the house,' she stated. The words 'belonged to' and 'was freed by' slipped by unsaid. 'I took her title . . . Falco, is this relevant?'

'It helps.' Mainly it helped me hold back accidental insults; I hate to offend my paying clients, in case they pay me less. 'To sum up: five of you were given your release for good service –' Set free by the Paulus will, no doubt. 'You have lived together; married amongst yourselves; worked together, ever since.' As the minimum age for a slave's manumission is thirty, a shrewd glance at Pollia suggested she had been on the loose in society for at least ten years. More, I thought, forgetting to be tactful about the lady's age. 'You have a well-established household; visibly prosperous. I can work out the rest: enter an outsider – who may be a floosie but we'll come to that in a minute – and entraps your one loose end. You want me to fend her off?'

'You're sharp, Falco.'

'I like to eat . . . How far have things gone?'

'Hortensius Novus has had himself formally betrothed.'

'Rash man! Before I take the case,' I pondered thoughtfully, 'tell me why I should believe that you and Atilia are

36

not simply annoyed at this clever operator for disrupting your routine?'

Pollia seemed to accept that it was a fair question. 'Naturally our concern is for our old friend's happiness.'

'Naturally!' I exclaimed. 'Though I gather there's an amount of cash at stake?'

'If Hortensius Novus brings home a bride who has the right motives we shall welcome her.' I found it a marvel that *two* women could share one household, let alone three. I said so. She explained the harmonious arrangements they had devised: 'Felix and I live in this wing; Crepito and Atilia have the far side. We meet for business and entertainment in the formal rooms at the centre of the house – '

'Where does Novus squeeze in?'

'He has a suite on an upper floor – more than ample, Falco.'

'We bachelors have restrained tastes. But if he weds, can you accommodate a third married couple?' I asked, wondering if all I had to sort out here was the normal sort of housing problem that blights family life in Rome.

'Easy enough.' Sabina Pollia shrugged. 'Our architect would build on a new wing.'

'We come to the crunch question then: if Novus taking a wife causes no problems domestically, what is so distressing to you and Atilia about his ladyfriend?'

'We believe she intends to kill him,' Sabina Pollia said.

VI

Informers are simple people. Given a dead body our response is to look for the killer – but we like the body first; it seems more logical.

'Lady, in good Roman society, mentioning a murder before it even happens is considered impolite.'

'You think I'm making this up!' Pollia rolled her magnificent eyes.

'It sounds so ridiculous, I'm taking you seriously! When people invent, they usually choose a story that's plausible.'

'This is true, Falco.'

'Convince me.'

'The woman has had husbands before – three of them!'

'Oh we live in slack times. Nowadays five weddings is the minimum to count as reprehensible . . .'

'None of her previous husbands survived long – ' Pollia insisted; I was still grinning evilly. 'And each time she walked away from the funeral far wealthier!'

I let the grin evaporate. 'Ah! Money lends this story of yours a genuine patina . . . Incidentally, what's her name?'

Pollia shrugged (negligently revealing her beautiful white shoulders between the sparkling dress pins on her sleeves). 'She calls herself Severina. I forget her other title.'

I made a note in my pocketbook with a stylus I kept handy. '*Forename, Severina; cognomen unknown* . . . Is she attractive?'

'Juno, how should I know? She must have something, to persuade four different men – men of substance – to marry her.'

I made another note, this time mentally: *bright personality*. (That could be difficult.) *And possibly intelligent*. (Even worse!)

'Does she make a secret of her past?'

'No.'

'Flaunts it?'

38

'No to that too. She just lets it be known as if having three short-lived husbands who happened to leave her everything were commonplace.'

'Clever.'

'Falco, I told you she was dangerous!' Things began to look intriguing (I was a man; I was normal: dangerous women always fascinated me).

'Pollia, let us be clear about what you want from me: I can investigate Severina, hoping to nail her with her past indiscretions – '

'You'll find no evidence. There was a praetor's enquiry after her third husband died,' Pollia complained. 'Nothing came of it.'

'Praetors miss things. It may help us. Even gold-diggers are human; so they make mistakes. After three successes, people like this start believing themselves demigods; that's when people like me can trap them. Tell me, is Hortensius Novus aware of her history?'

'We made him ask her about it. She had an answer for everything.'

'A professional bride would come prepared. I'll try to frighten her off anyway. Sometimes finding themselves under scrutiny is enough – they scuttle away to prey on an easier mark. Have you considered offering her money?'

'If it will help. We have plenty.'

I grinned, thinking ahead to my bill. I had known rich people who hid their wealth with decent secrecy, and I had known men who owned immense estates but treated it quite matter-of-factly. The open vulgarity of Sabina Pollia's boast made me realise that I had stepped into a brash new world. 'I'll find out her price then – '

'If she has one!'

'She will have! Bound to be less than Hortensius Novus imagines. Realising how small a value she sets on him has helped many an infatuated lover see his beloved with new eyes.'

'You are a cynic, Falco!'

'I've done a lot of work for men who thought they were in love.'

She was looking at my slyly through half-closed eyes. We

were back on the suggestive tack again. 'Falco, don't you like women?'

'I love them!'

'Anyone in particular?'

'I'm *very* particular,' I retaliated rudely.

'Our information was different.' Their information was out of date. 'I ask,' Pollia justified the question with outrageous wide-eyed innocence, 'because I am wondering whether *you* will be safe from Severina's wiles . . .'

'Severina will grant me complete immunity – the minute she learns that the Falco bankbox contains only my birth certificate, my discharge from the legions, and a few suffocated moths!'

I screwed the subject back to business, obtained a few more facts I needed (an address, the name of a praetor, and most importantly, agreement on my fee), then I took my leave.

As I skipped down the broad white marble entrance steps, frowning because they were so slippery (like the householders), I noticed a sedan chair which had just arrived.

There were six carriers in cobalt livery, huge, broadshouldered, glossy black Numidians who could push across the Forum of the Romans from the Tabularium to the Hall of the Vestals without once losing step despite the crowds. The chair had gleaming woodwork inlaid with tortoiseshell, crimson curtains, a lacquered Gorgon on the door and silver finials on the poles. I pretended I had twisted my ankle, so I could hang about to inspect whoever would descend.

I was glad I waited.

I guessed it was Atilia.

She was a woman who wore a half-veil because it made her more attractive; above the veil's embroidered edge glowed dark, solemn eyes of oriental origin. She and Pollia had access to a great deal of money, and evidently spent as much as they could on themselves. She jingled with expensive filigree jewellery. She wore so much gold that such a weight on one woman was certainly illegal. Her dress was that shade of amethyst where the rich tint really looks as if ground-up gemstones created the dye. As she came up the steps I saluted her in a pleasant manner and stood aside.

She removed the veil.

'Good morning!' It was the best I could manage; I was struggling for breath.

This one was as cool as the icecap on Mount Ida. If Sabina Pollia was a peach, the new apparition was a fruit of rich, dark mystery from some exotic province where I had not yet been.

'You must be the investigator.' He expression was earnest, and highly intelligent. I was under no illusions; in the old Hortensius household she was probably a kitchenmaid – yet she had the gaze of an articulate eastern princess. If Cleopatra could raise a look like this, it explained why respectable Roman generals had queued up to throw away their reputations on the mudbanks of the Nile.

'I'm Didius Falco... Hortensia Atilia?' She nodded assent. 'I'm glad of an opportunity to pay my respects –'

Her exquisite face grew sombre. A serious mood suited her; any mood would. 'Forgive me for not attending your interview; I was taking my young son to school.' A devoted mother: wonderful! 'Do you think you will be able to help us, Falco?'

'It's too early to say. I hope so.'

'Thank you,' she breathed. 'Don't let me take up your time now...' Hortensia Atilia gave me her hand, with a formality which made me feel gauche. 'Do come and see me, however, and let me know how your enquiries proceed.'

I smiled. A woman like that expects a man to smile; I imagine in most circumstances men try to avoid disappointing women like that. She smiled too, because she knew that sooner or later I would find an excuse to call. For women like that men always do.

Halfway down the hill I paused to survey their handsome views of Rome. Seen from the Pincian, the city lay bathed with a golden morning light. I loosened my belt, which was making my tunic feel damp against my waist, and cautiously steadied my racing breath while I took stock. Between them Pollia and Atilia had left me with a feeling, which I have to

41

admit I was frankly enjoying, that I was lucky to get out of
their house alive.

The omens were interesting: two glamorous clients whose
vulgar lifestyle guaranteed to amuse me; a fortune-hunter
whose past was so lively there must be a real chance to
expose her where the official magistrate had failed (I love
to prove a praetor wrong); plus a good fat fee – and all of
this, with any luck, for doing nothing much . . .

A perfect case.

VII

Before I staked out the gold-digger, I wanted to explore the Hortensius ménage. People tell you more than they think by where they live and the questions they ask; their neighbours can be even franker. Now I had gained a general impression, the sweetmeat stall where I had been given directions earlier was ripe for a return visit.

When I got there a hen who liked the high life was pecking up crumbs. The place itself was just a shack opposite a stone pine. It had a fold-down counter and a fold-up awning in front, with a small oven tucked away behind. The accommodation in between was so scanty that the stallholder spent a lot of his time sitting on a stool in the shade of the pine tree on the other side of the road, playing Soldiers against himself. When a customer turned up he left you long enough to get excited over his produce, then sauntered across.

The freeholders of the Pincian discouraged shops; but they liked their little luxuries. I could see why they let this cakeman park on their hill. What his emporium lacked architecturally was made up for by his bravura edibles.

The centrepiece was an immense platter where huge whole figs were sunk to the shoulder in a sticky bed of honey. Around this circular dish were tantalising dainties set out in whorls and spirals, with a few removed here and there (so no one need feel reluctant to disturb the display). There were dates stuffed with whole almonds the warm colour of ivory, and others filled with intriguing pastes in pastel shades; crisp pastries, bent into crescents or rectangles which were layered with oozing fruits and sifted with cinnamon dust; fresh damsons, quinces and peeled pears in a candied glaze; pale custards sprinkled with nutmeg, some plain and others cut to show how they were baked on a base of elderberries or rosehips. On a shelf at one side of the stall stood pots of honey, labelled from

43

Hymettus and Hybla, or whole honeycombs if you wanted to take someone a more dramatic party gift. Opposite, dark slabs of African must cake drowsed beside other confections which the stallholder had made himself from wheat flour soaked in milk, piercing them with a skewer and drenching them with honey before adding decorative chopped filberts.

I was drooling over his specialities which were pastry doves filled with raisins and nuts before they were glazed and baked, when he popped up at my side.

'Back again! Find the house you wanted?'

'Yes thanks. Do you know the people at the Hortensius place?'

'I should think so!' The cakeman was a wizened stick with the careful movements of a man whose trade relies on delicate arts. The awning pole that was not labelled DOLCIA informed me he was called MINNIUS.

I risked a frank question. 'What are they like?'

'Not bad.'

'Been acquainted long?'

'Over twenty years! When I first knew that clutch of puffed-up bantams they were a kitchen-sweeper, a mule driver, and a boy who trimmed the wicks of household lamps!'

'They have come on since then! I've landed an assignment for the women. Know Sabina Pollia too?'

Minnius laughed. 'I can remember *that* one when she was a hairdresser called Iris!'

'Ho! What about Atilia?'

'The intellectual! I mean, she'll say she was a secretary, but don't suppose that implies a Greek bookish type. Atilia scribbled the laundry lists!' He chortled at his own anecdote. 'In those days I was hawking pistachios off a tray in the Emporium. Now I'm still vending confectionery – from a booth the Hortensius lamp-boy owns. If anything this is a step down for me; the customers are ruder, I pay that bastard too much rent, and I miss the exercise . . .'

He cut into a tipsy cake, oozing with honey, and gave me a taste. Plenty of people take one look at my friendly visage and find themselves afflicted by dislike. Luckily the other half of society appreciates an open smile.

44

'Ask me how they managed it!' I would have done, but my mouth was full of wondrous crumbs. 'Even when they belonged to old Paulus they were all entrepreneurs. Every one of them kept a jar under the bed filling up with coppers they earned privately. They all had the knack of running special errands for extra tips. If your Pollia –'

'Iris!' I grinned stickily.

'If Iris was given anything for herself – a hairpin or a length of fringe off a dress – she turned it into denarii straightaway.'

'Did old Paulus encourage this?'

'Dunno. But he let it go on. He was pleasant enough. A good master allows his servants to save up if they can.'

'Did they buy their own freedom?'

'Paulus saved them the trouble.'

'He died?'

Minnius nodded. 'By trade he polished marble. There was plenty of work, even if he never made much at it; the will was generous to his people when he went.' Paulus could manumit a percentage of his household by bequest; my clients had the bold look of slaves who would have ensured they were among the favourites he chose for the privilege.

'They soon made good with their savings,' Minnius mused. 'Is there some special scheme for cargo ships?'

I nodded. 'Incentives; for fitting out a grain transport.' By coincidence I had been looking into corn imports shortly before this and was well up on all the fiddles. 'The scheme was started by the Emperor Claudius to encourage winter sailings. He offered a bounty, dependent on tonnage, for anyone who built new vessels. Insurance, too; he underwrote any ships that sank. The legislation has never been repealed. Anyone who knows that can still reap benefits.'

'Pollia had a ship that sank,' Minnius told me rather dourly. 'She managed to acquire a new one quite rapidly too . . .'

He was obviously suggesting it was the original ship with its name changed – an intriguing hint of sharp practice among the Hortensius crowd. 'Had she fitted out the ship herself?' I asked. Under the Claudian scheme a woman who did so would acquire the honours of a mother of four

45

children: what *my* mother called the right to tear her hair in public and be treated to constant harassment.

'Who knows? But she was soon wearing earfuls of rubies, and sandals with silver soles.'

'What did the men do to earn their fortune? What line are they in now?'

'This and that. In fact this, that, and pretty well everything else you could name . . .'

I sensed coyness creeping over my informant: time to back off. I purchased two of his stuffed pastry pigeons for Helena, plus some slices of must cake for my sister Maia – to reward her selfless gesture in recovering my swallowed bets.

The price was as exorbitant as I expected on Pincian Hill. But I did get a neat little basket containing a natty nest of vine leaves, to carry my confectionery home with clean hands. It made a change from the inky papers torn out of old scrolls of philosophy which were used to wrap up custards where I lived in the Aventine.

On the other hand, there is nothing to read on a vine leaf once you've licked it clean.

VIII

Next I risked raising my blood pressure with a visit to a praetor.

In the days of the Republic two magistrates were elected annually (*se*lected, since it was an appointment from the ranks of the Senate so not exactly subject to a free vote), but by my time legal business had increased so much it kept eighteen of them busy, two solely on fraud. The one who had investigated the gold-digger was called Corvinus. The Forum *Gazette* had familiarised me with the ludicrous pronouncements of the current legal crop, so I knew Corvinus was a self-opinionated piece of pomposity. Praetors always are. In the scale of public appointments it is the last civil honour before a consulship, and if a man wants to parade his ignorance of modern morality then being praetor gives him dangerous scope. Corvinus predated the current Emperor's campaign to clean up the courts, and I reckoned the praetorship would be his last position now Vespasian was in charge.

Unfortunately for my clients, before Corvinus was retired to his Latium farm, he had had time to make his pronouncement that poor little Severina had lost three wealthy husbands in rapid succession *purely through bad luck*. Well. That shows you why I think what I think about praetorian magistrates.

I had never met him, and in fact I didn't intend to, but after I came down from the Pincian I went straight to his house. It was a quiet mansion on the Esquiline. A faded trophy hung over the door, commemorating some ancient military show in which an ancestor had been honoured for not running away. Indoors were two statues of dour republican orators, an indifferent bronze of Augustus, and a huge chain for a watchdog (but no dog): the usual tired

47

trappings of a family which had never been as important as it thought, and was now sinking into oblivion.

I hoped Corvinus would be in Cumae for the summer, but he was the sort of conscientious fool who probably sat in court on his own birthday; he grumbled about the pressure of business – yet fed his ego by bungling pleas all through the August heat. A bored porter let me in. Bundles of ceremonial rods and axes were lolling in the atrium, and I could hear a murmur from a side room where his honour's lictors were gnawing their midday snack. In a side passage a row of benches had been provided so clients and plaintiffs could hang about looking pathetic while the Praetor snored off his lunch. Sunlight slanted in from high square windows, but once my eyes grew accustomed to the harsh interplay of light and shade I discovered the familiar crowd of moaners who clog up the offices of famous men. All watching one another, while they pretended not to; all trying to dodge the mad-eyed know-all who wanted a conversation; all set for a long and probably disappointing afternoon.

I avoid sitting around catching other people's diseases, so I strolled briskly past. Some of the hangdog crowd sat up straighter, but most were prepared to let anyone who looked as if he knew what he was doing carry on doing it. I felt no qualms about queue-jumping. They had come to see the Praetor. The last thing *I* wanted was to endure a pointless interview with some tedious legal duffer. Praetors always have a clerk. And because litigants are so touchy to deal with, a praetor's clerk is usually alert. I had come to see the clerk.

I found him in the deep shade of an inner courtyard garden. It was a warm day, so he had moved a folding campstool out to the fresh air. He had a startling tan, as if it had been painted on – possibly the result of a week's concentrated vine pruning. He wore a large seal ring, pointed red shoes, and a glittering white tunic; he looked as sharp as a furnace-stoker on his festival day off.

As I expected, after a long morning up against senators' sons who had been caught peering into the changing rooms of women-only bathhouses and vague grannies who wanted to ramble through three generations of family history to explain why they stole four duck eggs, the clerk was glad to push aside his pyramid of petition rolls and enjoy a chat with me. I introduced myself straightaway, and he replied that his name was Lusius.

'Lusius, some clients of mine are worried about a professional bride. Name of Severina; I don't know her cognomen – '

'Zotica,' said Lusius abruptly. Perhaps he thought I was a time-waster.

'You remember her! Thank the gods for efficiency – '

'I remember,' growled the clerk, growing more expansive with this chance to express his bitterness. 'There were three previous husbands, who had all lived in different sectors of the city, so I had to cope with a trio of disorganised aediles all sending me incomplete local details, four weeks after I required them – plus a letter from the Censor's office with all the names spelt wrong. I ended up co-ordinating the documents for Corvinus myself.'

'Routine procedure!' I commiserated. 'So what can you tell me?'

'What do you want to know?'

'Did she do it, basically.'

'Oh she did it!'

'That's not what your man decided.'

Lusius described his man in two brief words: the usual opinion of a praetor if you hear it from his clerk. 'The honourable Corvinus,' Lusius confided, 'would not recognise a boil on his own bum.' I was starting to have a lot of time for Lusius; he seemed a man of the world – the same shady world I inhabited myself.

'Routine again! So will you tell me the tale?'

'Why not?' he asked, stretching his legs in front of him, folding his arms, and speaking as if he thought anyone who worked as hard as he did deserved time off for anarchy. 'Why not, indeed? Severina Zotica . . .'

'What is she like?'

'Nothing special. But the madams who cause the most

49

trouble never look much to outsiders who are not involved with them.' I nodded. 'And a redhead,' he added.

'I should have known!'

'Imported as a teenager from the big slave market at Delos, but she got there by a roundabout route. Born in Thrace – hence the hair – then passed about with different owners; Cyprus, Egypt, then before Delos Mauretania, I think.'

'How do you know all this?'

'I had to interview her at one point. Quite an experience!' he reminisced, though I noticed he did not dwell on it. In fact his expression became guarded, like a man keeping his own council talking about a girl he planned not to forget. 'Once she reached Italy she was bought by a bead-threader; he had a shop in the Subura; it's still there. His name was Severus Moscus. He seems to have been a decent enough old bastard, who eventually married her.'

'Husband number one. Short-lived?'

'No; the marriage had lasted a year or two.'

'Peacefully?'

'As far as I know.'

'What happened to him?'

'Died of heatstroke while he was watching a gladiatorial display. I *think* he had sat where there wasn't an awning, and his heart just gave out.' Lusius was evidently a fair man (or wanted to be, when he was assessing a redhead).

'Maybe he was too stupid or too stubborn to sit in the shade.' I could be fair myself. 'Did Severina buy his ticket?'

'No; one of his male slaves.'

'Did Severina weep and wail over losing him?'

'No . . .' Lusius pondered thoughtfully. 'Though that was in character; she's not the type to create.'

'Nice manners, eh? And Moscus liked her enough to leave her everything?'

'To an old man, a redhead – who was sixteen when he married her – is bound to be likeable.'

'All right: so far she looks genuine. But did her sudden inheritance supply her with an idea for getting on in life?'

'Could be. I could never ascertain whether she had married her master out of desperation or honest gratitude. She

50

may have been fond of him – or she may have been a diplomat. The beadseller *may* have bullied her – or perhaps she coerced him. On the other hand,' said Lusius, balancing his arguments like a true clerk, 'when Severina realised how comfortable Severus Moscus had left her, she immediately set out to acquire greater comfort still.'

'Exactly how well off was Moscus?'

'He imported agates, polished them up and strung them. Nice stuff. Well, nice enough for senators' heirs to buy for prostitutes.'

'A flourishing market!'

'Especially when he branched out into cameos. You know – heads of the Imperial family under patriotic mottos. *Peace, Fortune,* and an overflowing cornucopia – '

'Everything one lacks at home!' I grinned. 'Imperial portraits are always popular with the creepers at court. His work was in fashion, so his ex-slavegirl inherited a thriving enterprise. What next?'

'An apothecary. Name of Eprius.'

'How did he die?'

'One of his own cough lozenges stuck in his throat.'

'How long had he lasted?'

'Well it took him nearly a year to get her to the priest; she put on a good show of dithering. Then he survived another ten months; perhaps she needed to steady her nerve.'

'The apothecary may have lingered because Severina wanted to acquire a knowledge of drugs . . . Was she there when he choked? Did she try to revive him?'

'Desperately!' We both laughed, certain we had the measure of that. 'She was rewarded for her devotion with three drugshops and his family farm.'

'Then what?'

'Grittius Fronto. He imported savage animals for Nero's arena shows. She was bolder that time. She must have been courting Fronto while the executors were still snipping the tape on the Eprius will. The circus manager only managed to survive four weeks – '

'Eaten by a lion?'

'Panther,' Lusius corrected without a pause. He was as

51

cynical as me; I loved the man. 'Strolled out of an open cage below the stage at Nero's Circus and backed poor Grittius up against some lifting gear. They say the blood was horrible. The thing mauled a tightrope walker too, which seemed a bit superfluous but made the "accident" look more natural. Grittius had been making a lot of money – his empire included a sideline in unusual floor shows for sleazy dinner parties. You know – naked females doing peculiar things with pythons ... Servicing orgies is like owning a Spanish gold mine. Severina danced away from the Fronto funeral pyre with what I estimated at half a million big gold ones. Oh, and a parrot whose conversation would make a galley overseer blush.'

'Was there a medical report on any of the bodies?'

'The old beadseller's heart failure looked too natural, and there was no point calling a doctor to examine the panther's handiwork – not enough left!' Lusius shuddered fastidiously. 'But a quack did see the apothecary.' I lifted an eyebrow and without needing to look it up he gave me a name and address. 'He saw nothing to take exception to.'

'So what put the law onto Severina?'

'Grittius had a great-nephew in Egypt who used to arrange shipping for the wild beasts; the shipper had expected to inherit the loot from the lions. He sailed home fast and tried to bring an action. We made the usual enquiries, but it never came to court. Corvinus threw it out after an initial examination.'

'On what grounds, Lusius?'

His eyes were darting angrily. 'Lack of evidence.'

'Was there any?'

'None at all.'

'So where is the argument?'

Lusius exploded with sardonic mirth. 'Whenever did lack of evidence stop a case?' I could tell what had happened. Lusius must have done the work for the aediles (young local officials, responsible for investigating the facts but keen only on pursuing their political careers). The case had gripped him, then when his efforts came to nothing due to the Praetor's stupidity he took it personally. 'She was clever,' he mused. 'She never overreached herself; the types she picked had plenty of cash, but were nothing in society – so seedy no one would really care if they had met a sticky end. Well, no one except the nephew who was a rival for one of the fortunes. Perhaps Grittius had forgotten to mention him; perhaps he forgot deliberately. Anyway, apart from that slip, she must have been extremely careful, Falco; there really was no evidence.'

'Just inference!' I grinned.

'Or as Corvinus so lucidly put it: *a tragic victim of a truly astonishing chain of coincidence* . . .'

What a master of jurisprudence.

A portentous belch from a room indoors warned us that the Praetor was about to emerge. A door pushed open. A sloe-eyed slaveboy, who must have been the tasty bite Corvinus used to sweeten his palate after lunch, sauntered out carrying a flagon as his excuse for being there. Lusius winked at me, gathering his scrolls up with the unhurried grace of a clerk who had learned long ago how to look busy.

I had no intention of watching the Praetor amuse himself rejecting pleas; I nodded politely to Lusius, and made myself scarce.

IX

I convinced myself it was now late enough to stop work for the day and attend to my personal life.

Helena, who took a stern view of my casual attitude to earning a living, seemed surprised to see me so early, but the Pincian confectionery persuaded her into a more lenient frame of mind. Enjoying my company may have helped too – but if so, she hid it well.

We sat in the garden at her parents' house, devouring the pastry doves, while I told her about my new case. She noted that it was an enquiry packed with feminine interest.

Since she could tell when I was evading an issue I described my day as it had occurred, glamour and all. When I got to the part about Hortensia Atilia being like some dark oriental fruit, Helena suggested grimly, 'A Bithynian prune!'

'Not so wrinkled!'

'Was she the one who did all the talking?'

'No; that was Pollia, the first tempting nibble.'

'How can you keep track of them?'

'Easy – for a connoisseur!' When she scowled I relented. 'You know you can trust me!' I promised, grinning insincerely. I liked to keep my women guessing, particularly when I had nothing to hide.

'I know I can trust you to run after anything in a pair of silly sandals and a string of tawdry beads!'

I touched her cheek with one finger. 'Eat your sticky cake, feather.'

Helena distrusted compliments; she looked at me as if some Forum layabout on the steps of the Temple of Castor had tried to lift up her skirt. I found myself mentioning a subject I had told myself I would let lie: 'Thought any more about what I suggested yesterday?'

'I've thought about it.'

'Think you'll ever come?'

'Probably.'

'That sounds like "*Probably not*".'

'I meant what I say!'

'So are you wondering whether *I* mean it?'

She smiled at me suddenly with vivid affection. 'No, Marcus!' I felt my expression alter. When Helena Justina smiled like that, I was in imminent danger of overreacting . . .

Luckily her father came out to join us just then. A diffident figure with a sprout of straight untameable hair; he had the vague air of an innocent abroad – but I knew from experience he was nothing of the kind; I found myself sitting up straighter. Camillus shed his toga with relief, and a slave took it away. It was the Nones of the month so the Senate had been in session. He touched on today's business, the usual wrangles over trifles; he was being polite, but eyeing our open cake basket. I broke up the must cake I had purchased as a present for my sister, and we handed it round. I had no objection to going back to Minnius' stall another day to buy something else for Maia.

Once the basket was empty, Helena tried to decide what she could do with it; she settled on making a gift for my mother, filling it with Campania violets.

'She ought to like that,' I said. 'Anything that sits in the house serving no useful purpose and gathering a layer of fluff reminds her of my father . . .'

'And someone else!'

I said to the Senator, 'I like a girl who speaks her mind. Was your daughter always so cantankerous?'

'We brought her up,' he answered between mouthfuls, 'to be a gentle, domestic treasure. As you see.' He was a likeable man, who could handle irony. He had two sons (both on foreign service), but if Helena had been less strong-minded she would probably have been his favourite. As it was, he viewed her warily but I reckoned their closeness was why Camillus Verus could never bring himself to send me packing; anyone who liked his daughter as much as I did was a liability he had to tolerate. 'What are you working on nowadays, Falco?'

I described my case and the Hortensius freedmen. 'It's the usual story of the wealthy and self-possessed, fighting off an adventurous newcomer. What makes it so piquant is that they are nouveaux riches themselves. I'll take the commission, sir, but I must say, I find their snobbery intolerable.'

'This is Rome, Marcus!' Camillus smiled. 'Don't forget, slaves from important households regard themselves as a superior species even to the freeborn poor.'

'Of which you're one!' Helena grinned. I knew she was implying Sabina Pollia and Hortensia Atilia would be too finicky to tangle with me. I gave her a level stare, through half-closed eyes, intending to worry her. It failed as usual.

'One of the things I find interesting,' I mentioned to the Senator, 'is that these people would probably admit they rose from next to nothing. The man who owned them polished marble. It's a skilled job – which means the piece-work rates hardly pay enough to keep a snail alive. Yet now the ostentation of his freedmens' mansion suggests their fortunes must be greater than a consul's birthright. Still; that's Rome too!'

'How did they overcome their unpromising origins?'

'So far that's a mystery . . .'

While we talked I had been licking honey off the vine leaves from the cake basket; it suddenly struck me a senator's daughter might not wish to associate with an Aventine lout whose happy tongue cleaned up wrappings in public. Or at least, not associate with him in her father's townhouse garden, amongst the expensive bronze nymphs and graceful bulbs from the Caucasus, especially while her noble father was sitting there . . .

I need not have worried. Helena was making sure no currants from the must cake were left behind in the basket. She had even found a way of forcing the corners open so she could recapture any crumbs that had worked themselves among the woven strands of cane.

The Senator caught my eye. We knew Helena was still grieving for the baby she had lost, but we both thought she was starting to look healthier.

Helena glanced up abruptly. Her father looked away. I refused to be embarrassed, so I continued to gaze at her thoughtfully while Helena gazed back, in peaceful communion about who knows what.

Then Camillus Verus frowned at me, rather curiously I thought.

X

Although I had given up for the day, other folk were still labouring, so I popped along the Vicus Longus to see whether the letting agent Hyacinthus had mentioned was open for business. He was.

Cossus was a pale, long-nosed individual, who liked to lean back on his stool with his knees apart; luckily his green and brown striped tunic was sufficiently baggy to allow it without indecency. He clearly spent most of his day laughing loudly with his personal friends, two of whom were with him when I called. Since I wanted a favour, I stood by looking diffident while these orators dissected the various perverts who were standing in the next elections, discussed a horse, then hotly debated whether a girl they knew (another hot tip) was pregnant or pretending. When my hair had grown half a digit waiting, I coughed. With little attempt at apology the clique slowly broke up.

Alone with the agent, I found an excuse to drop the name of Hyacinthus as if I had known him since he cut his teeth on an old sandal strap, then I explained my yen for up-market real estate. Cossus sucked in his breath. 'August, Falco – not much shifting. Everyone's away . . .'

'Plenty of death, divorce and default!' Since my father was an auctioneer, I knew property moves at all seasons. In fact if I had wanted to buy something outright, my own papa could have put some ramshackle billet my way; but even he kept his hands clean of the rented sector. 'Still, if you can't help me, Cossus – '

The best way to screw activity from a land agent is to hint that you are taking your custom somewhere else. 'What area are you looking at?' he asked.

All I needed was lavish space at a small rent, anywhere central. The first thing Cossus offered was a boot cupboard beyond the city boundary stone, right along the Via Flaminia, an hour's walk out of town.

'Forget it! I must be near the Forum.'

'How about a well-established condominium, no snags, small out-goings, extremely appealing outlook, on the Janiculan Ridge?'

'Wrong side of the river.'

'It comes with shared use of a roof terrace.'

'Can't you understand Latin? Even if it comes with Julius Caesar's riverside gardens, Cossus, it's not my area! I'm not some damned itinerant matchseller. What else do you have?'

'Courtyard outlook, shaded by pine tree, opposite the Praetorian Camp – '

'Rats! Find a tenant who's deaf!'

'Ground floor, by the Probus Bridge?'

'Find one who can swim in the spring floods . . .'

We worked through all the dreary dumps he must have had on the stocks for ages, but eventually Cossus acknowledged he would have to shift those onto some raw provincial visitor. 'Now this is just the thing for you – a short lease in the Piscina Publica. Someone else has expressed an interest, but seeing as it's you, Falco – '

'Don't make a drama. Tell me what it offers?'

'Four good rooms arranged conveniently on the third floor – '

'Over the courtyard?'

'The street – but it's a quiet street. The neighbourhood is most attractive, well away from the Aventine warehouses, and favoured by a genteel clientele.' What comedian writes their speeches? He meant that it was too far from the markets and peopled with snobbish hydraulic engineers. 'The premises are being offered on a six-monthly basis; the landlord is uncertain of his plans for the block.' That suited me, since I was uncertain of my plans for staying solvent enough to pay him.

'How much?'

'Five thousand.'

'Annually?'

59

'A *half-year!*' Cossus gave me a frosty stare. 'This is the market for men of means, Falco.'

'It's a market for fools, then.'

'Take it or leave it. That's the going rate.' I gave him a look to say in that case I was going. 'Well, I could probably come down to three thou for a friend.' Half the price was his commission, if I read him right – which made him no friend of mine. 'Because of the short lease,' he explained unconvincingly.

I sat frowning in silence, hoping this would beat him down: nothing doing. The Twelfth *is* a tolerable district. It lies east of the Aventine on the far side of the Via Ostiensis – nearly home to me. The public fishponds which supplied its name dried up years ago, so I knew the mosquitoes had decamped . . . I made an appointment to troop along with Cossus tomorrow and inspect the let.

By the time I approached Fountain Court that evening I was determined to take the Piscina Publica apartment whatever it was like. I felt tired of bursting blood vessels climbing up stairs. I was sick of dirt, and noise, and other people's sordid troubles intruding into my life. Tonight I came back into the tangled mass of those Aventine lanes which feed into each other like the underground filaments of some disgusting fungus, and I told myself that four rooms, conveniently arranged, anywhere else must be better than this.

Still dreaming, I turned the corner within sight of Lenia's laundry. Tomorrow I would sign the lease that enabled me to stop feeling ashamed whenever I had to tell a stranger my address . . .

A pair of feet stopped my happy plans.

The feet, which were enormous, were kicking at each other in the portico of the basketweaver's lock-up about ten strides away from me. Apart from their size, I noticed them because that was where I always parked myself if ever I had some reason to squint at my apartment discreetly before I showed myself.

Those feet were definitely loafing. The person they were attached to was taking no notice of the weaver's artefacts, even though he had lolled up against a gigantic pile of general purpose wicker carrying-hods which would be a boon to any household, while at his feet lay an excellent picnic basket which any genuine bargain-hunter would have snapped up fast . . . I squeezed behind a pilaster for a closer scrutiny. I knew he was not a burglar; burglars like to have something to steal. Even the incompetent ones steer clear of Fountain Court.

A client or a creditor would go in and chat to Lenia. These outsize platters must have been sent here by Anacrites, the Chief Spy.

I eased myself backwards, and nipped through a side alley to the back lane. The area behind the laundry appeared its normal self. On this muggy summer evening the open cess trench was polluting the nostrils vibrantly. Two starved black dogs lay asleep on their sides in the shade. From behind a cracked shutter above my head I could hear the spiteful daily conversation of a husband and wife. A pair of female chicken-pluckers were arguing, or just gossiping, by a pen of off-colour capons. And a man I had never seen before was sitting on a barrel, doing nothing much.

He had to be another spy. He was in full sun. It was the last place you would choose to sweat, if your only motive in planting your posterior on a barrel was to rest your legs. But it was the only place to sit if you wanted to survey comings and goings from Lenia's drying-yard. Unless he was in love with one of the teazle girls, he must be up to no good.

I opted for a strategic retreat.

A large family can be useful. I had numerous relations, all of whom assumed they owned me. Most would condescend to give me a bed in return for the chance to complain about my habits. My sisters would want to rant about our mother having to arrange my jailbreak, so I went to mother's instead. I knew that meant being obsequious about her standing sponsor but I thought I could put on a polite show. I did manage to play at being grateful for as long as it took to devour a bowl of her prawn dumplings, but when the strain of remembering to look humble became too oppressive I went home after all.

The watcher in the back lane must have been the well-organised one; he had fixed up a relief for himself. His replacement was now perched on the barrel trying to look inconspicuous; not a success, since he was a bald-headed, hook-nosed midget with a drooping left eye.

Around the front the monstrous feet were still outside the basket shop – all the more unconvincing since the weaver had taken in his produce, dragged across his sliding screen and bolted up. I slid into the local barber's, and paid one of his offspring to tell the feet that a homunculus wanted to speak to them in the lane. While footsie plodded round there for a fruitless chat with the midget, I planned to be pouring myself a goodnight drink six floors up on my balcony.

And so I was. Some days, some things actually go right.

XI

Next morning I was up early. Before Anacrites' scruffy assortment were back watching my warren, I had hopped out of my hole and off to an outdoor cookshop table two districts away. I was enjoying a slow breakfast (bread and dates, with honey and hot wine – nothing too lively for a man on surveillance), while *I* watched the home of the professional bride.

Severina Zotica lived in the Second Sector, the Caelimontium. Her street lay some way beyond the Porticus Claudia (at that time in ruins, but earmarked for restoration in Vespasian's public building programme); the gold-digger inhabited the sedate triangle which lies between the Aqueducts and the two major roads which come together at the Asinaria city gate. Cossus must have realised the Caelian Hill region was too select for me. For one thing, the streets had names. I expect he thought this might have worried me; I expect the beggar thought I couldn't read.

Severina had established herself in Abacus Street. It was a tasteful thoroughfare, a single cart's width. The junction at one end had a well-kept public fountain; the other had a small street market, mainly kitchen pottery and vegetable stalls. In between, the shopkeepers washed and swept their own frontages; they were doing this at the hour I arrived, in a way I found pleasantly businesslike. Both sides of the street were lined with artisans' booths: cutlers, cheese shops, picklesellers, cloth merchants, and locksmiths. Between each pair ran an entry with stairs to the apartments above, and a passage to the ground-floor accommodation which lay behind the shops. The buildings were about three storeys high, brick-faced without balconies, though many had neat window boxes supported on brackets, while in other places rugs and counterpanes were already being given their daily airing over windowsills.

Residents came and went. A straight-backed old lady, quiet businessmen, a slave walking a lapdog, children with writing slates. People rarely spoke, yet they exchanged nods. The atmosphere suggested most of them had lived there a long time. They were acquainted, though they kept to themselves.

There was a brothel four doors down from me. It was unmarked, but evident if you sat for any time. Patrons slipped in (looking strained) then strode out half an hour later (looking pleased with themselves).

I stuck with my breakfast. Though it made me remember mornings when I had woken warm from a night in companionable sleep, and enjoyed an extra hour in bed with some young lady I had lured home the evening before . . . Soon I was missing one in particular. I told myself there was no one in a brothel who could compensate for her.

Certainly, no one who would pay my rent.

It was still quite early when a slightly battered carrying chair emerged from the passage between the cheesemaker's booth and a tablecloth shop, which was where I had been told Severina Zotica lived. Curtains hid the occupant. The bearers were a couple of short sturdy slaves, chosen for the breadth of their shoulders rather than for cutting a dash on the Sacred Way; they had large hands and ugly chins, and looked as if they did everything from carrying water to mending boots.

I had paid for my food already. I stood up, brushing off crumbs. They marched past me and away towards the city. I followed, casually.

When we arrived at the first aqueduct they branched left, cut through some backstreets, came out on the Via Appia, then followed the road round the Circus Maximus towards the Aventine. I felt a shock: the gold-digger was apparently having herself ferried straight towards the Falco residence . . .

In fact she went somewhere more civilised. The chairmen dropped her at the Atrium of Liberty. A woman of medium height emerged, swathed so modestly in a russet-coloured stole it was impossible to see more of her than a slight figure, an upright carriage and a graceful walk. She entered the Library of Asinius Pollio, where she handed in some scrolls, exchanged pleasantries with the library clerk, then booked out another selection which he had already prepared. Whatever I had expected, it was not that the woman had set off from home purely to change her reading matter at the public library.

As she left, she passed quite close. I pretended to be browsing among the pigeonholes of philosophy, but managed to glimpse a white hand, clasping her new volumes, with a ring on her third finger with some red stone. Her gown was a subdued shade of umber, though its folds gleamed with an expensive lustre. The hem of the stole which still hid her face was embroidered and set with seed pearls.

Had I lingered to quiz the librarian, I should have lost the chair. Instead I tailed her to the Emporium where she purchased a Baetican ham and some Syrian pears. Next stop was the Theatre of Marcellus; she had sent one of the chairmen to the ticket office for a single in the women's gallery that night.

After that the lady in brown had herself lugged back to the Caelimontium. She bought a cabbage (which I thought looked on the tough side), entered a female bathhouse for an hour, then minced out and went home. I had lunch at the cookshop (rissoles), then sat on there all afternoon. One of her slaves trotted out to get a knife sharpened, but Severina did not re-emerge. In the early evening she was taken straight back to the theatre. I excused myself from attending. It was a *pantomimus* performing a farce about adulterers pushing cuckolded husbands into conveniently open blanket chests; I had seen it; the dancing was terrible. In any case, observing a female subject at the theatre has its tricky side. If a good-looking specimen like me stares up at the women's seats too often, hussies from the cheap end of society start sending him shameless notes.

I went to see Helena. She had gone out with her mother to visit an aunt.

I met Cossus in a Piscina Publica wineshop, bought him a drink (a small one), then was taken to view the apartment.

To my surprise it was not bad: up a rather narrow lane, but a plain tenement block where the stairs were dusty but free of other detritus. Metal lamps stood in one or two corners on the way upstairs, though they were dry of oil.

'You could fill them if you wanted to light the way up,' Cossus said.

'The lessor could light them.'

'True!' he grinned. 'I'll mention it . . .'

I suspected there had been a recent change of ownership: I glimpsed builders' props in a passageway, the shops at ground level were vacant, and although the principal tenant (who would be my landlord) reserved the large apartment behind them for his own use it was empty at present. Cossus told me I need not expect to see this main tenant; all the subletting was arranged through himself. I was used to spending so much time and trouble avoiding Smaractus, the new landlord's arrangements seemed sweet as a dream.

The apartment on offer was as good as any in the block, since they were all identical units piled on top of one another. In each the door opened into a corridor with two rooms on either hand. These were not much bigger than those I had at Fountain Court, but with four I could plan a more refined existence: a separate living room, bedroom, reading room and office . . . There were sound wooden floors and an encouraging smell of new plasterwork. If the roof leaked there were upper tenants whom the rain would soak before it dripped on me. I found no signs of pest infestation. The neighbours (if alive) sounded quiet.

Cossus and I smacked hands on the bargain.

'How many weeks' rent would you want at a time?'

'The full half year!' he exclaimed, looking shocked.

'If the term starts in July, I've lost two months!'

'Oh well – the next four months' then.' I promised to cash in my betting tokens right away and bring him the money as soon as I could. 'And the deposit against lawsuits,' he added.

'*Lawsuits*?' He meant I might drop a flowerpot out of a window and brain some passer-by; the main leaseholder could be held liable, if I was just a subtenant. My current landlord Smaractus had never thought of demanding such indemnities – but most people on the Aventine find ways to right their grievances without becoming litigants. (They run up the stairs and punch your head.) 'Is this premium normal at your end of the market?'

'On new tenancies a deposit is traditional, Falco.' Since I wished to appear a man of the world, I gave way gracefully.

With Anacrites watching my old place, the sooner I moved into an address he didn't know the easier life would be. In any case I could hardly wait for the pleasure of telling Smaractus he could hire a slow mule to Lusitania and take the lease for his filthy sixth-floor dosshouse with him when he went. Before I could move however, I would have to arrange some furniture.

At home the spies were still watching. I marched straight up to the one with the feet. 'Excuse me, is this where Didius Falco lives?' He nodded before he could help himself. 'Is he in at the moment?' The spy looked vague, now trying to disguise his interest.

Still playing the stranger, I went up to see whether Falco was in. Which he was, once I got there.

Anyone watching a building should record who goes in and make sure they come out again. I rigged up a trip rope attached to an iron griddle pan which would wake the whole tenement if it was kicked down the stairs in the dark, but no one followed me upstairs. Cheap expertise is all the Palace pays for. I knew that; I had once worked there myself.

XII

On the second day of my surveillance Severina Zotica must have stayed in to read her library scrolls. There were household deliveries – amphorae of olive oil and fish pickle – followed by a woman trundling a rackety handcart full of hanks of wool. It had badly set wheels, so I strolled over and lifted the base with the toe of my boot as she struggled to lever the thing up a kerb.

'Someone's going to be busy!' I commented nosily.

'She always buys a quantity.' The wool distributor backed her ample rear down the entry to Severina's house, huffing as she towed the load. 'She weaves it herself,' she told me, boasting on her customer's behalf. A likely tale.

It was a poor day if I was hoping to publish my diary to literary acclaim: breakfast; Lucanian sausage for lunch (with indigestion afterwards); hot weather; a dogfight in the afternoon (no interesting bites) . . .

The chair finally veered out of the passage in the early evening, followed by a thin maid with a cosmetics box in one hand and a strigil and oil flask dangling from her other wrist. Severina vanished into the same bathhouse as before, dragging the maid. An hour later she flounced back out down the steps. Her sandals were gilded, a lacing of gold threads embroidered every hem on her get-up, and what looked like a diadem came to a point beneath the inevitable stole. The maid who had tricked her out in this finery set off home on foot with her cast-offs and the cosmetics, while the chairmen hauled Severina north to the Pincian: a social call at the Hortensius house.

She stopped at Minnius' cake stall, where she acquired one of his leaf-lined baskets. I pursued her as far as the Hortensius gatehouse and winked at the porter, who confirmed for me that madam was dining with her fancy man. There seemed nothing to gain by waiting outside all evening while they gorged themselves and exchanged pretty nothings. I went back to see Minnius.

'Does Severina call here often?'

'Every time she goes to see Novus. He's a glutton for sweet stuff; they have a regular order up at the house, but she usually takes him a titbit.'

I bought another piece of must cake for my sister, but I ate it on my way to visit Helena.

'Marcus! How are you getting on with your enquiry?'

'All the evidence suggests the gold-digger is just a home-loving girl, improving her mind, who wants a classic tombstone. Apart from *She lived with one husband*, which we can assume she has abandoned, it's to be *Chaste, virtuous, and well-deserving . . . She spun and worked in wool* – '

'Perhaps she really *is* well-deserving!'

'And perhaps there will be a snowstorm in Tripolitania! It's time I took a closer look at her – '

'In her women-only bathhouse?' Helena pretended to be shocked.

'My darling, I'll consider most disguises – but I can't pass for a female once I'm in the nude . . .' Wondering whether I could somehow manage to infiltrate myself as a sweeper, I gave Helena a salacious grin.

'Don't flash your teeth at me, Didius Falco! And don't forget you're already on bail from the Lautumiae . . .' After a moment she added apropos of nothing, 'I missed seeing you yesterday.' Her voice was low; there was a true note of yearning in it for a man who wanted to be persuaded.

'Not my fault. You were out when I came.'

She stared at the toes of her shoes (which were leather in a discreet shade, but with dashing purple laces). I mentioned, also apropos of nothing, that I had taken a new lease. I was wondering how she would take it. She looked up. 'Can I come and see?'

'Once I've acquired some furniture.' No self-respecting bachelor invites a good-looking girl to his apartment until he can provide a mirror and anything else they might need. Such as a bed. 'Don't worry – as soon as word of my move gets round among my family, I expect to be showered with everything they've been longing to get rid of – especially my brothers-in-law's bodged efforts at carpentry . . .'

'My father has a battered reading couch he intended to offer you, but perhaps you won't want it now you're going up in the world?'

'I'll take it!' I assured her. Her gaze faltered. Helena Justina could always interpret my motives too easily.

Reading is not the only thing you can do on a couch.

I left early. We had run out of things to talk about.

One way and another I had hardly given my darling so much as a kiss. By the time we said goodbye she seemed rather standoffish, so I kept aloof too and strode away with just a nod.

Before I fetched up at the end of her father's street I felt a serious pang of misery, and wished I had been more affectionate. I nearly went back. But I had no intention of letting a senator's daughter see me behave like a dithering idiot.

XIII

I spent the rest of that evening turning my betting tags into cash. I found Cossus, clinched the deal, and received my key. I had a few drinks with the agent – business courtesy – then a few more later with my best friend Petronius Longus (in fact a few more than we meant to have, but we revelled in having something proper to celebrate). I ended up feeling far too happy to dupe the spies at Fountain Court so I stumbled to the new apartment, crashed inside, stretched out on the floor and sang myself to sleep.

Someone banged on the door and I heard a voice demanding whether everything was all right. Nice to know my new neighbours were such concerned types.

I woke early. The best-laid floorboards tend to have that effect.

Feeling pleased with life despite my headache, I went out to hunt for a snack. All-night cookshops in the Piscina Publica seemed a rarity, which could prove an inconvenience for my erratic way of life. But eventually I found a bar full of bad-tempered flies where a bleary-eyed waiter served me a slab of ancient bread with a pickled cucumber in it and told me I had to take it off the premises to eat.

It was too early for watching Severina's house. Even so, that rapacious little lady was firmly in mind. Clients have the unreasonable habit of expecting rapid progress, so I would soon need to report.

My feet took me east. They brought me up below the Esquiline, in the old part of town which people still call the Subura, though it had been variously retitled after Augustus enlarged the city and redrew the administrative sectors. Some folks grumble that was when Rome lost all its character; still, I dare say while Romulus was ploughing up the first boundary furrow there were hidebound old peasants

71

standing about the Seven Hills and muttering into their frowsty beards that life would never be worth living in this wolf-man's newfangled settlement . . .

The Subura still kept its republican character. Much of it had been wiped out under Nero in the Great Fire. He had grabbed a large swathe of the blackened ground for his Golden House and its enormous parks and pleasure grounds. He then ordered Rome to be rebuilt on a classic grid pattern, with really strict fire regulations. (Even Nero had recognised that the Golden House was big enough for a petty prince, so there was no need to plan on any more Imperial land clearance.) In fact many streets had been rebuilt ignoring his proclamations, higgledy-piggledy on top of the old ones. I liked it. The Empire has far too many pious four-square towns all looking exactly the same.

This area had once been the most sordid in the city. There were plenty of rivals for that honour now. The Subura seemed like an elderly whore; it still had a tawdry reputation, though it was past living up to it. Yet you could still be robbed. Like everywhere else, the footpads in these tense one-man lanes were far from slack. They were set in their ways: an arm round the throat, a dagger in the ribs, lifting your purse and finger-rings, then kneeing you face-down in the mud while they hopped it.

I kept my wits about me. I knew the Subura, but not well enough to recognise the faces and not well enough for its villains to steer clear of me.

Coming this way was deliberate: to dig deeper into Severina's past. The Praetor's clerk Lusius had mentioned that her first husband, the bead-threader Moscus, used to own a shop which still existed somewhere here. I started looking for jewellers. They usually know where their rivals hang out. Sure enough, on the third try I was given directions and reached the right booth just as it was opening.

The new incumbent was probably another ex-slave from the Severus Moscus household, now free and self-employed. He sold every kind of gemstone work, from intaglios, where he cut into the jewel's surface, to cameos, where the design stood proud. He used all the semi-precious stones, but agates in particular – pale blues laced with milky striations; stone whites which blossomed with green or red ochre threads like lichen; translucent-streaked charcoals; handsome mixtures of matt buff and bronze. He was already at his bench, sorting tiny gold spacing beads. Apparently he did all the work himself.

'Hello!' I cried. 'Is this where Severus Moscus lives? I've been told to look him up; my mother knew his mother – '

He gave me a thoughtful glance. 'Would that have been in Tusculum?' He had a curiously high-pitched voice for one whose manner was so completely confident.

Thinking it might be a trap I shrugged offhandedly. 'Could be. My ma has lived all over the place. She did tell me; I didn't bother to listen, I confess – '

'Moscus is dead.'

'No!' I whistled. 'I've had a wasted journey then. Look – my old biddy's bound to ask; can you tell me how it happened?' He leaned on the counter and told me the tale about the heart attack in the hot amphitheatre. 'That's bad luck. Was he very old?'

'Sixties.'

'No age!' No response. 'Did he have any family? Ma would want me to pay her condolences – '

I thought the man's face closed. 'No,' he said. That was odd; also inaccurate.

'What about you?' I pressed him cheerfully, like a crass stranger. 'You've got his business – were you involved with him?'

'I worked with him. He gave me a good apprenticeship; I ran the business when he started feeling his years, then I took over after he passed away.'

I admired his stuff. There was everything from strings of cheap coral to fabulous sardonyx pendants half the size of my fist. 'Beautiful! I know a lady who would happily accept anything I took her from your stock . . .' Not that I intended to, with a houseful of furniture to buy. Helena possessed enough jewellery. Most of it was better than I could afford; no point trying to compete. 'Look, don't get me wrong, but I'm sure my mother told me Moscus had a wife.'

'She remarried.' He sounded brief, although not particularly grim. 'I rent the shop from her. Anything else you

73

want to know about Moscus, sonny? The position of his birthmarks, or the size of his feet?'

At his increasingly aggressive tone I backed off with a look of shamefaced innocence. 'Jupiter; I didn't mean to pry – my ma never has enough to do; she'll expect to hear a proper tale.'

'That's it. You've heard it,' stated the cameo-cutter tersely.

'Right! Thanks!' I risked a final impertinence: 'Don't you find it a bit galling to have kept the business afloat for old Moscus yet end up still a tenant, while his widow gaily flits off with somebody new?'

'No.' The lapidary gave me a level stare. He was daring me to put it even more plainly – though giving notice that he would cut up rough if I did. 'Why should I?' he continued in his squeaky voice, apparently unperturbed by my badgering. 'She charges a fair rent; she has a decent business sense. Moscus is dead. It's up to the girl what she does with her life.'

If I wanted scandal, I stood no chance here. I grinned foolishly, and ambled off.

Back to watching the gold-digger's house in Abacus Street. The diary took its usual course. Breakfast. Hot weather. Wine delivery. Dog chasing a cat. Gold-digger to bathhouse . . .

This was reaching the point where I could describe Severina's day before she yawned and decided her plans. It was easy work, though so unproductive it made me depressed. Then, just when I was wondering how to initiate some action I acquired several new pieces of information in rapid succession.

The chair emerged just after lunch. I followed for five streets and watched it carried down an entry through a pottery shop. I stayed in the outer street. After over an hour, doubt set in. I walked through the shop, expecting to see Severina's chair waiting at the far end of the dark passageway.

The chair had vanished. While I was outside like a fool, being buffeted by piemen's trays and having mules stamp on my feet, the gold-digger had been carried indoors – then probably out afterwards through the garden gate. Clever work, Falco!

I walked up to the house. The ground-floor apartment was pretty unobtrusive. No windows; no potted creepers; no kittens on the step; just a dark painted door with a secretive grille. Beside it a small ceramic tile had been fixed to the wall. The plaque was midnight blue, with black lettering and a decorative border of tiny gold stars. It bore a single name in Greek script:

I knew what sort of place this was. I knew just what sort of mad, withered hag this Tyche must be.

I braced myself. Then I raised my fist, and banged firmly on the door.

'Any chance of an appointment?'

'Do you want to see her now?'

'If there's nobody else with her – '

'It should be all right. Her last visitor left some time ago . . .'

I swallowed. Then in I went, for an immediate appointment with a female astrologer.

XIV

I dread these places.

I prepared myself for a filthy Babylonian, muttering gibberish. To my relief, the smoky caboose for predictions must be elsewhere in the house; the neat slaveboy led me instead to a disturbingly handsome reception room. It had a gleaming black and white mosaic floor. The walls were painted black above a simply patterned dado; their panels were divided by stylised candelabra and featured tiny gold medallions – scallop shells and flower sprays. There were two long-backed chairs such as women use, either side of a low white marble table that must have weighed half a ton. Positioned on the table (rather obviously, I thought) were an astrolabe at one end and at the other an open scroll of planetary records. Opposite the door stood a set of shelves holding a score of very old Greek vases which an auctioneer I knew would have drooled over – all perfect, all a substantial size, all in the ancient geometric style whose repetitive rows of whorls, circles and stylised antelopes must be the specialised choice of a collector with cool taste.

The antiques impressed me more than the atmosphere. Apart from a lingering scent of women's perfume, as though the room had been recently vacated, there were no wafts of incense or drugs to lull the unwary visitor. No tinkling bells. No subtle intoxicating music. No deformed dwarves leaping out of hidden cabinets . . .

'Welcome. How can I help you?' The woman who had slipped in through the door curtain was perfectly clean, calm, and possessed a pleasant, cultured voice. She spoke her Latin with a better accent than me.

She looked about sixty. Her straight dark gown hung from two small silver niello shoulder-brooches, so her arms were bare, though hidden in spare folds of the material. Her hair was rather thin, mostly black yet with broad silver streaks. Her face lacked professional mystique, except for

76

severely hooded eyes. The eyes were no special colour. It was the face of any businesswoman in the male world of Rome: accommodating, yet with an underlying stubborn strength and a trace, faint as snail tracks, of personal bitterness.

'You the astrologer?'

Her mouth was tight, as if she disapproved of me. 'I am Tyche.'

'Greek for *Fortune* – very nice!'

'That sounds insulting.'

'I have several less nice names for people who pointlessly raise the hopes of those in despair.'

'Then I must remember,' Tyche commented, 'not to raise yours!'

I was expecting to find myself the subject of some shrewd scrutiny. So I stared back openly. 'I can see you are not a customer,' she commented, though I had said nothing. Of course pretending to read minds would be part of her trade apparatus.

'The name's Falco – '

'I have no need to know your name.'

'Spare me the patter. Enigmatic piffle makes me grind my teeth.'

'Oh I see!' Her face relaxed into ruefulness. 'The régime here disappoints you. You wanted to be frightened to death. You expected a cackling harridan casting dried entrails backwards into a bright green fire? – I stopped doing spells. The smoke ruins the decor . . . You had better tell me when you were born.'

'Why?'

'Everyone who comes on other business expects a free prophecy.'

'I don't! March, if you must know.'

'Pisces or Aries?'

'Never quite sure. "On the cusp".'

'You would be!'

'I was right; you do disapprove of me,' I growled.

'Don't most people? Your eyes have witnessed too much you may not speak of among friends.'

'My feet have tramped too many uneven pavements on

the trail of too many grasping girls who are conniving at death! *Her* name is Severina, by the way.'

'I know that,' said Tyche quietly.

'Oh?'

'Severina was a customer,' the astrologer explained, with mild reproof. 'I needed her name and address to send my bill.'

That did surprise me. 'What happened to crossing the palm with a silver denarius? I thought you people only did business on a strict cash basis?'

'Certainly not! I never handle money. I have three perfectly adequate accountants who look after my financial affairs.' This must be one fortune-teller who had moved up a long way from telling half-truths to shepherds' girlfriends in hot little canvas booths. Tyche serviced the gilded-litter trade; I bet she charged for it too. 'What do you want, Falco?'

'A seer ought to know! What did Severina Zotica want?' The woman gave me a long stare that was meant to start a shiver between my shoulder blades. It did. But my work was as much based on bluff as her own. 'Was she buying horoscopes?' She assented in silence. 'I need to know what you told her?'

'Professional secret!'

'Naturally I'll pay the going rate for it –'

'The information is not for sale.'

'*Everything* is for sale! Tell me whose future she was putting a marker on.'

'I can't possibly do that.'

'All right; let me tell you! Her story goes, she is about to be married and wants to reassure herself about her prospects afterwards. One horoscope was her own; that was to make it look good. And the other subject was –'

'Her future husband.'

Tyche smiled wryly, as if she realised the news was bound to be misinterpreted: some people believe that to possess another person's horoscope gives you power over their soul.

XV

The first positive signal about Severina's motives: I felt my toes curling inside my boots, while my heels tried to press themselves through the unyielding tessellations of the mosaic floor. The coarse fibres of my worn woollen tunic prickled against my collarbones. Into this oddly civilised room with its austere occupant, horror had stalked.

Before I could comment, the astrologer took the initiative. 'I presume you are not a superstitious man?'

'The point,' I exclaimed, 'is whether *Severina* believes this gives her a hold over her fiancé!' Rome accepts anyone who takes a keen interest in their own destiny – but to peek at someone else's must be a sign of bad intentions. Indeed, in political life, to acquire an opponent's horoscope is a deeply hostile act. 'Future husband or not, Severina has broken a serious taboo of privacy. Tyche, you could be heading for indictment as an accessory to an unnatural death: if the freedman dies *I'd* be prepared to cite you for encouraging his murderer – unless you co-operate. What did you tell her?'

'I told her the truth, Falco.'

'Stop fencing! If Novus is supposed to die in the next few weeks, better warn me now – '

'If the man is *supposed* to die, then he will!'

'Next you'll tell me that we *all* die – '

'My gifts are passive; I can interpret fate. It is not my role to change it.'

'Ha! Don't you ever try?'

'Do you?' she chipped back.

'I was brought up by a good mother; compassion has a habit of intruding into my working life – '

'You must get very despondent!'

'I should be even more despondent if people with evil intentions were allowed to proceed unchecked – '

'Any force has its opposite,' Tyche assured me. 'Malign

influences must be balanced by kindly ones.' Still standing quite motionless, she suddenly gave me a smile of such intensity it was impossible to meet head-on. 'Perhaps *you* are an agent of the stars?'

'Forget it!' I growled, fighting back a grin. 'No ethereal committee of management owns me; I am an independent spirit.'

'Not quite, I think!' For a moment she seemed to hesitate over whether to laugh. She let the desire pass and stood aside from the doorway.

I prognosticated (privately) that a handsome dark-haired man with intelligent eyes was about to make a brisk exit from her house. 'Tyche, if you refuse to tell me whether Novus is secure, at least say this: will Severina Zotica be executed for her crimes?'

'Oh no. She may never be happy, but she will live long and die in her bed.'

'You told her that?'

The wry look returned to the fortune-teller's face. 'We spoke only of her hopes for happiness.'

'Ah well, I imagine very few people ask you, *am I likely to be fed to the lions as a common criminal*?'

'True!'

'And what did you tell her about her marriage?'

'You will not believe it.'

'Try me.'

'Severina's next husband will outlive her in old age.'

I said that was good news for the husband!

Time to leave. I saluted the seer thoughtfully, with the respect I give anyone who can keep three accountants busy. They never let you get away that easily: 'Would you like a prediction, Falco?'

'Can I prevent it?'

'Someone who loves you may have a higher destiny.'

'Anyone who loves me could do better in life!' As we mentioned Helena I could not prevent the fortune-teller seeing the change in my face. 'The someone in question would not be in love with me now, if she had the sense to opt for a less cranky fate.'

'Your heart knows whether that is true.'

There was no damned reason why I should justify Helena to a postulating, nit-picking, Babylonian mountebank. 'My heart is at her feet,' I snapped. 'I shall not blame her if she gives it a nudge with her toe then kicks it around the floor a bit! But don't underestimate her loyalty! You have seen me, and made a few accurate deductions, but you cannot judge my lady – '

'I can judge anyone,' the woman answered flatly, 'by seeing the person they love.'

Which, like all astrological pronouncements, could mean anything you wanted – or nothing at all.

XVI

I retraced my steps to Abacus Street. Almost immediately
Severina's chair appeared from the house. I had not even
reached my usual place at the cookshop table, but was
pausing at the opposite end of the street to buy an apple
from an old man who kept a fruit stall there. He was telling
me about his orchard, which was out on the Campagna and
only a few miles from the market garden my mother's family
ran. We were so deep in conversation about Campagna
landmarks and characters that I could not easily disengage
myself to pursue the sedan.

Then, while I was still trying to deflect the old chap's
offers of complimentary fruit, who should slyly put her head
out of the passage beside the cheese shop, but a heavily
veiled woman who looked just Severina's shape and size?
The maid at her elbow was definitely the gold-digger's . . .

My surveillance had been fairly casual. This gave every
suggestion that my presence had been noted; that giving
me the slip at Tyche's had been deliberate; and that sending
out the chair was a decoy.

Both women were now looking towards the cookshop. I
waited by the fruit stall until they seemed satisfied by my
empty bench. Eventually they set off on foot, this time with
me adopting my strictest procedures for tailing a suspect
invisibly.

If the visit to the fortune-teller had been indicative, that
was nothing to what happened next: Severina Zotica took
herself to a marble yard.

She was ordering a tombstone.

I could guess who it was for.

After selecting her square of marble, I watched her depart.
As soon as I felt sure she was heading homewards, I nipped
back to see the stonemason myself.

His name was Scaurus. I found him deep in a narrow

corridor amongst his stock. On one hand were room-high stacks of rough-cut travertine for general building purposes; on the other, pallets protecting smaller slabs of finer marble which would be made into self-congratulatory epitaphs for second-rate officials, monuments for old soldiers, and poignant plaques to commemorate sweet lost children.

Scaurus was a short, strong, dust-covered character with a bald dome, a broad face, and small ears which stuck out like wheelbosses each side of his head. Naturally his dealings with clients were confidential. And naturally the size of bribe my clients could afford soon got us over that.

'I'm interested in Severina Zotica. She must be the kind of regular client you love – so much domestic tragedy!'

'I've done one or two jobs for her,' Scaurus admitted, not quarrelling with my jocular approach.

'Three husbands down – and the next looming! Am I right that she's just ordered a new memorial stone?' He nodded. 'Can I see the text of the inscription?'

'Severina only came in for an estimate, and to put down a deposit on the slab.'

'She give you the deceased's name?'

'No.'

'So what was the story?'

'Other people are involved – a subscription effort. She has to consult them about the words to use.'

'I bet! The fact is, this poor fellow's relations may have the good manners to want him dead first, before they commit themselves!' I was starting to feel angry. 'Does she normally have the tombstone cut in advance?'

Scaurus was becoming more cautious. A thriving trade was one thing, but he did not want to be identified as an accessory before the fact. I warned him I would be back for a sight of the finished carving, then I left it at that.

He had given me what I needed. The horoscope and the memorial stone spoke for themselves. If nobody weighed in to stop Severina, Hortensius Novus was a dead man.

XVII

Some informers with a telling piece of information rush straight off to report. I like to mull things over. Since I met Helena Justina most of my best mulling had been done in company; she had a sharp brain, with the advantage of a dispassionate view of my work. Her approval always reassured me – and sometimes she contributed a thought that I could hone up into a clever ploy for solving the case.

(Sometimes Helena told me I was a patronising ferret, which just proves my point about her perceptiveness.)

I arrived at the Senator's door at about nine, just before dinner. The porter on duty was an old antagonist. He eagerly told me Helena was out.

I asked where she had gone. The bathhouse. Which? He didn't know. I didn't believe him anyway. A senator's daughter rarely leaves home without mentioning where she is going. It need not be true. Just some tale to delude her noble father that his petal is respectable, and give her mother (who knows better) something new to worry about.

I shared a few choice witticisms with Janus, though frankly his intellect had never been up to my standard. I was turning away when their lost pigeon decided to wing in home.

'Where were you?' I demanded, more hotly than I meant.

She looked startled. 'Bathing . . .'

She was clean all right. She looked delicious. Her hair shone; her skin was soft, and perfumed all over with some distinctive flowery oil that made me want to move very much closer to investigate . . . I was working up a froth again. I knew she could tell, and I knew she would laugh, so I retreated into banter. 'I just encountered a fortune-teller who promised I was doomed in love. So naturally I dashed straight here – '

'For a dose of doom?'

'Works wonders on the bowels. *You're* due for "a higher destiny", by the way.'

'That sounds like hard work! Is it like a legacy? Can I pass it on hastily to somebody else?'

'No, madam, your stars are fixed – though luckily the prophetess has decided I am the constellations' agent. For a small backhander I can undertake to unfix fortune and unravel destiny . . .'

'Remind me never to let you near when I'm spinning wool . . . Are you coming in to make me laugh, or is this just a tantalising glimpse to make me pine for you?'

Since the porter had opened the door for her, I was already inside.

'Do you?' I asked nonchalantly.

'What?'

'Pine for me?'

Helena Justina gave me an unfathomable smile.

She whisked me further indoors and seated me under a pergola in a secluded colonnade. Helena slid onto a seat next to me and fastened a rose in my shoulder-brooch while she kept the houseslaves running about bringing me wine, warming it, fetching dishes of almonds, then cushions, then a new cup because mine had a minute chip in the glaze . . . I lay back in her own reclining chair and enjoyed the attention (gnawing my thumb). She seemed extraordinarily loving. Something was up. I decided some burnished bugger with a senatorial pedigree must have asked her home to see his collection of blackfigure jars.

'Marcus, tell me about your day.' I told her, gloomily. 'Cheer up. You need more excitement. Why not let some floosies flaunt themselves at you? Go and see your clients. The lapidary sounds a complete waste of time, but tell them about the astrologer and the mason, then see how they react.'

'You're sending me into a witches' lair!'

'Two overfed spenders, with no taste and even fewer scruples, both falling out of their frocks . . . I think you can handle them.'

'How do you know all this?'

'I've been to have a look at them.' Her face grew warmer, but she faced me out as I screwed round in the chair, full of alarm.

'Helena Justina! *How?*'

'I called on them this afternoon. I said I was trying to start a school for female foundlings, and – as women of feeling, and in one case a mother – could I persuade them to contribute?'

'Mars Ultor! Did they?'

'Only Atilia at first. That Pollia is an unyielding little bodkin – but I shamed her in the end. Then of course she gave me a *huge* donation, trying to impress on me what plutocrats they are.'

'I hope you never told them who you were?'

'I certainly did. There was no reason for them to connect me with you.' Cruel, but true. I was having a hard time connecting us myself. 'People who live on the Pincian are terrible snobs. They were delighted to have a senator's daughter sip mulled wine amid their outrageous artwork, while she entreated them to involve themselves in her modest civic works.'

'Did they get you drunk?'

'Not quite. Trust them to believe they were immaculate hostesses for giving a visitor monstrous goblets of boiling hot liquor, totally unsuited for the time of day; what I really needed was a nice fingerglass of herbal tea. Did they get *you* drunk?'

'No.'

'Bad luck! They wanted me to admire their solid silver goblets – too heavy to lift and too ornate to clean. Mine had the biggest topaz I have ever seen.' She looked thoughtful, then commented, 'They judge the world by what it costs. Unless the price is vulgar, nothing counts . . . Your rates are too reasonable; I'm surprised they employed you.'

'Thanks!' I barked, though I had the uneasy feeling my darling might be right. I buried my face in my hands for a moment then laughed. 'What will you do with the money?'

'Found a school. I'm not a hypocrite, Marcus.'

She was amazing. It seemed best to keep my admiration to myself. Helena needed no encouragement. I had witnessed her in public as endearingly shy – yet she forgot all about that whenever some daft idea like this invaded her head. 'I worry when you career off uncontrollably. Why ever did you go?' She would not answer me. 'Curiosity!' I slid my nearest arm round her and pulled her over against my chest, looking into her great dark eyes with their perplexing mixture of love and dismissiveness. 'So what did you think of my clients?'

'Rather too obvious – if I go again I must take them a present of some dress pins . . .' Her old sense of mischief was dancing there, I was glad to see. 'Sabina Pollia clawed her way up from nothing – and may still have dirt under her fingernails. The maternal one looks like the kind of tremulous sweetheart who begs for protection – while she savagely manipulates everyone around her . . . Did you meet her little boy, by the way? I suspect that tot has the full measure of his mama. Atilia has big plans for him. Her life's work will be putting him up for the Senate the minute he's old enough – '

I could think of bigger ambitions for a family who had the energy and funds to promote a child; tactless to say so to the daughter of a senator. 'But a wonderful mother!' I teased, without thinking: equally tactless, in fact.

'*Lots of us might be wonderful mothers!*'

Even before the violence flared I had enveloped her fiercely with both arms. 'You will!' We had never discussed this; no opportunity. I had assumed I was glad to avoid it; yet now I found myself launching into an urgent, prepared speech: 'My love, neither of us was ready; losing that baby may have been the best fate for the poor mite – ' Helena squirmed angrily. I glimpsed some dark mood I didn't care for, but I was not prepared to dump the girl and run just because she expected it. 'No, listen; I need to talk about this – Helena, I never rely on anything, but so far as I'm concerned we now have to find some way of being together; we'll enjoy that – and when it really seems a good idea we will start a new generation of quaint curiosities like us – '

'Perhaps I don't want to – '

'I'll win you round – '

'Marcus, I don't want to think about it; I need to live with what has happened first!'

'I know that – ' I suspected I would lose her altogether if she crashed the bolts home on me now. Besides, I was annoyed. 'Don't block me out of it – and don't suppose it had no effect on me!'

'Oh you and your old republican code!' Helena murmured with one of her sudden changes of mood, kissing my face. 'Stop being so reasonable – ' I said nothing. 'Didius Falco, somebody ought to explain to you, informers are tough; informers are hard men who lead mean lives, and whenever they have a lucky escape, informers speed off back to their own low world – '

'Wrong. Informers are soft slugs. Any woman in decent shoes can stamp on us.' That reminded me of something: 'Though I have no intention of letting the Hortensius females squash me on a garden path. There was no need for you to reconnoitre the terrain; my darling, I can look after myself . . .' I could certainly do that. My problem was looking after Helena. 'Don't get involved.'

'No Marcus,' she promised, with a meek air I knew was false.

'Well don't tell me afterwards!' She was still watching me. 'There's no need to worry about me. Those two women at the Hortensius house are trash. There's no one to compete with you. Besides, I have a rule: never sleep with a client.'

'Ever broken it.'

'Once.'

I gave her a sheepish grin. She gave me a twitchy smile. I tugged her head down onto my shoulder and held her close.

The colonnade where we were lurking was a completely private area. I stayed as I was, holding Helena. I felt relaxed, and more affectionate than I usually allowed myself to be. She still looked troubled; I stroked her hair, which soothed the look away. This encouraged me to range more widely, in case there were any other little tension spots that needed attention . . .

'Marcus!' I decided to carry on. Her sleek, soft skin seemed to have been oiled at the baths especially to attract an appreciative hand. 'Marcus, you're making things impossible for both of us . . .' I decided to prove I was as tough as she had said earlier; so I stopped.

Not long afterwards I chose to make my excuses; the various chinks of silverware which announced that her parents were at dinner were becoming an embarrassment. Helena invited me to dine, but I did not want Helena or her parents (especially her mother) to get the idea I was the sort of parasitic hanger-on who kept turning up at mealtimes in the hope of being fed.

On leaving the house I walked north, thoughtfully. Some informers give the impression that wherever they go ravishing women shed their scanty clothing without the slightest encouragement and want to fall into bed. I told myself it so rarely happened to me because I appealed to a more selective type of girl.

Well; I had appealed to her once.

XVIII

The ladies were at home. Their men were elsewhere. The ladies were bored. I turned up like a treat from the gods, to fill the vacant after-dinner entertainment spot. If I had brought along a flute and a couple of Phrygian sword dancers I might have been better use to them.

In all my visits to the Hortensius house, I would never be received for an interview in the same room twice. Tonight I was shown into a dramatic azure leisure suite, with heavy boudoir overtones. All the couches had expensive coverlets flung over them with suggestive abandon. Bulbous cushions with shiny covers were piled on top, with fringing and fat tassels much in evidence. The room was stuffed with furniture: bronze side tables held up by priapic satyrs; silver daybeds with lions' feet; tortoiseshell cabinets. The cabinets were displaying a job lot of spiralled Syrian glassware (including at least one vase which had been recycled in Campania recently), some ivory, a collection of quite pretty Etruscan hand mirrors, and an extremely large solid gold vessel of doubtful purpose which they probably called 'a votive bowl', though it looked to me like the personal chamberpot of a particularly gross Macedonian king.

With their burnished skin and antimonied eyes the women looked as plush as the drapery. Sabina Pollia occupied her couch with the thrusting sprawl of a sage bush taking possession of a herb garden. Hortensia Atilia lolled with a neater habit, though she held one foot up behind in a way which made it impossible not to notice the nakedness of her exposed leg. In fact, as they faced one another over a huge platter of grape bunches I could not forget Helena's disparaging comments (her intention, presumably). They both wore their gowns in luxuriant folds that were designed more for sliding off than draping the shapely forms beneath. I kept wondering whether Pollia's left or right shoulder-brooch would be the first to slither down a lovely arm further than decency permitted. Pollia was in emeralds; Atilia dripping with Indian pearls.

Atilia's son, an ordinary child, was with them, kneeling on the marble with a terracotta model donkey. He was about eight. I winked at him, and he stared back with the stark hostility of any little boy facing a strange beak in his nest.

'Well, Falco, what have you brought us?' Pollia demanded.

'Only news,' I apologised.

The left shoulder of Pollia's crimson dinner gown descended so far it was annoying her. So she twitched it up. This gave the right side more free play to droop appealingly over her breast.

'Do tell!' urged Hortensia Atilia, wriggling her raised toes. Atilia preferred to keep her brooches properly centred on her fine shoulders. This meant that as she lay on a couch the front of her gown (which was marine blue, verging on good taste but not quite making it) draped itself in a low parabola so anyone who was standing up at the time had a clear view straight down to the big brown mole two inches below her cleavage line: an abundant mother goddess, making good use of the area which mother goddesses love to display. (Naturally it left me unmoved; I was not the religious type.)

Without further preamble, I gave my two clients details of my findings so far. 'Regarding the astrologer, I don't want to dwell on the superstitious aspects, but better not to mention this if Hortensius Novus is likely to become anxious; nervous men tend to have accidents – '

'It proves nothing,' Pollia decided crushingly. She had wined well with her dinner. Now it was time to bring out the nutcrackers; I was the filbert she had her eye on, I could tell.

I kept cool. 'I'm the first to admit that. But ordering a memorial stone is rather a different matter! Severina Zotica is approaching her wedding with a practical grit which – if *I* was her intended – would send my scurrying for sanctuary.'

'Yes.'

The small boy crashed his toy donkey into the leg of a side table; his mother frowned, and signalled him to leave the room. 'To be fair to the girl,' suggested Atilia, 'perhaps we should not blame her if she wants to feel sure her previous ill luck will not recur. The horoscopes could be entirely innocent.' Of the two, Hortensia Atilia certainly had the most ample generosity. Like everything else which she possessed in abundance, the lady made it freely available to public view.

'What I want to do now,' I said, 'is tackle Severina at an interview – '

Atilia and Pollia glanced at one another. For some reason I recalled Helena's fear that something in this conundrum was not quite right.

'That sounds rather tricky.' Atilia's diffident expression implied she was a simple blossom looking for some manly type to fend off her troubles in the meadowland of life; I tried to strut like a city thug who liked to swipe the heads off marguerites for fun.

'Perhaps we should wait,' Pollia added, smiling at me brilliantly. 'You won't lose by it financially – '

My interest sharpened. 'Sabina Pollia, you and I agreed that I should discover the gold-digger's price.'

Pollia gave me a special pout which assured me there were other things we might agree. 'I was suggesting we try for more evidence first. But you are the expert, Falco. You must decide the moment; I'm sure your timing is immaculate . . .'

I eased the edge of my tunic where it sweltered against my neck. 'It's your choice; I can watch her some more. If you are willing to pay my expenses, I can watch her for as long as you like – ' I was never at my best while being treated as a plaything of the rich.

I normally prevent my clients running up unnecessary bills. With four empty rooms at home to furnish, and two females who could well afford to buy their puppet a new table, my upright morals were becoming more relaxed.

I left straightaway. The small boy was sitting on the steps of their mighty portico; his stare as he watched me skipping down the polished marble was full of dark scorn for the fact that I had obviously left too soon to have enjoyed myself.

I strode home, feeling aggressive. Everyone in Rome had just enjoyed their dinner; everyone except me. At this time of day cookshops in the Piscina Publica were more visible, though equally unpromising. I hoofed off to see my mother. I found several of my sisters there, so I ventured that if anyone had any unwanted furniture I could give it a home. Junia actually came up with a bed. Junia, who thought herself superior, had somehow entrapped a husband who was salaried, a customs clerk supervisor; they never kept anything longer than two years. Normally I avoided whatever they were turfing out since I hate feeling like some grovelling parasite, but for a decent bed I bent my pride. This bargain among the nearly-news had cost my sister's husband two hundred sesterces, I was pleased to hear. Might as well cadge quality.

It was after the wheeled-traffic curfew. My brother-in-law Mico could always lay his hands on a cart, so he and I whisked away the bed that night before Junia changed her mind, then we went round the rest of my family collecting their gifts of pans with crooked handles and stools with missing legs. As soon as I could get rid of Mico I enjoyed myself arranging and rearranging my apartment like a little girl playing with her dolls' furniture. It was late, but Ma had given me some lamps and Maia had thrown in half a jar of oil, spluttery but adequate. As I dragged stuff about, other people in the block banged on the walls from time to time. I banged back cheerfully, always glad to make new friends.

My new bed was fine, but the mattress had never seen much life at Junia's; it was like perching on a granite ledge halfway up a mountainside. Still, the nocturnal adventures I promised myself would soon create accommodating dents.

XIX

Since my clients had demanded more evidence, at first light I set off, armed with the name and address I had been given by Lusius at the Praetor's house: I was going to interview the doctor who had been called to Severina's second husband, the apothecary, after he had choked.

The quack was highly annoyed at being disturbed so early, though not so annoyed as I was when I discovered his uselessness. My frustration was nothing new to him; I gathered Lusius had been just as short with him at their previous interview.

'I told the clerk the facts, and facts don't change!' This presupposed that the self-opinionated duffer had the facts right in the first place – something I soon doubted. 'The apothecary went into convulsions – '

'Were you there then?'

'I was told! Then his servants ran away, while the wife did her best to revive him.'

'No luck?'

'She could hardly get near. The man was struggling violently – '

'You mean – '

'Don't you tell me my professional duty!' he interrupted angrily, though my unposed question had been perfectly subservient. 'I've already had all this from the Praetor's clerk! He wanted to convince me the wife may have suffocated her husband – ' So my friend Lusius had been diligent in his earlier investigation. 'It's nonsense. The poor woman was badly shaken and bruised, but she did her best. Eprius must have lashed out so hard he nearly knocked her senseless too – '

'Don't you find that suspicious, if she was helping him?'

'Certainly not. He had no idea what he was doing; he was having a fatal fit!'

'Try this scenario,' I insisted. 'Severina had tried to

poison him; it was not working properly so she held him down; Eprius understood what was going on and fought with her – '

'Unnecessary speculation. I found the medicament that choked him.'

'Did you preserve it?'

'Of course,' he replied coldly. 'I gave the item to the Praetor's clerk.'

'I believe it was a cough lozenge. An apothecary ought to have known how to suck a jujube! Had you prescribed it for him?'

'I was not his doctor. I doubt if he had a doctor; he was qualified to make up medicines for himself. They called me to the accident because I lived nearby. Eprius was already dead when I got there; there was nothing anyone could do but comfort the widow. Luckily a freedman she knew happened to call at the house, so I was able to leave her being cared for by a friend – '

'She recovered!' I assured him. 'She remarried within the month.'

The arrogant noodle still refused to make an adverse report.

The story he told me was chilling, though it took me no further forwards. I left in disgust. Yet I was still determined to prove to Pollia and Atilia that my expenses were well earned. Since I had drawn a blank with the beadseller and the apothecary, my last resort was the importer of wild beasts.

I hired a mule, and rode out to the north-east part of the city. I knew that animals for the arena were housed beyond the city boundary, the other side of the main Praetorian Camp. Before I even reached the bestiary I could hear roaring and trumpeting, strangely incongruous in the environs of Rome. The Imperial menagerie had every strange creature I had ever heard of, and plenty besides. I made my initial enquiries with crocodiles snapping in cages behind me and ostriches looking over the shoulders of everyone I approached. All around were half-dead rhinos, sad apes, and lacklustre leopards, attended by long-haired men who looked as surly and unpredictable as the animals themselves. The smell was sour and disconcerting. Between all the cages there was a thin wash of sordid-looking mud underfoot.

I had asked for Grittius Fronto's nephew. I learned that the nephew was back in Egypt, but if I was trying to arrange party entertainment of a spectacular nature I ought to speak to Thalia. Since I never know when to cut and run, I followed directions to a striped tent where I boldly pulled back the entrance flap and even more recklessly went in.

'Ooh!' shrieked a voice that would sharpen ploughshares. 'My lucky day!'

She was a big girl. By which I mean . . . nothing. She was taller than me. She was big, all over; she was young enough to be described as a girl without too much irreverence; and I was able to see that her assets were entirely in proportion to the height of her. Her attire was what the well-dressed artiste was wearing that month: a few stars, a couple of ostrich feathers (which explained why some of the birds I had seen outside looked so miffed), a skimpy drape of transparent stuff – and a necklace.

The necklace might pass for coral – until you observed that its jewelled folds sometimes shuddered with a sluggish allure. From time to time an end of it slipped from her neck and she draped it back dismissively. It was a live snake.

'Unusual, eh?' She had a peaceful expression which told its own story; in any contest with a tricky reptile I would feel sorry for the snake.

'With a gem like that decorating your windpipe, I imagine you rarely encounter trouble from men!'

'Men are always trouble, darling!'

I smiled apologetically. 'All I want is a few kind words.'

She cackled with ribald laughter. 'That's what they all say!' Then she gazed at me as if she wanted to mother me. I was terrified. 'I'm Thalia.'

'One of the Graces!' This case was tilting into lunacy.

'Oh my word; you're a cheeky one – what's your name?' Against my better judgement I told her my name. 'Well, Falco? Have you run away from home to be a lion-tamer?'

'No; my mother wouldn't let me. Are you a contortionist?'

'Anyone would turn into a contortionist if they had a python looking up their – '

'Quite!' I interjected hastily.

'I am a professional snake dancer,' she informed me coolly.

'I see! Is this the snake you dance with?'

'What this? This is just for everyday wear! The one in my act is twenty times this size!'

'Sorry. I thought you might have been rehearsing.'

The snake dancer grimaced. 'What I do at a performance is dangerous enough if you're paid for it! Who needs to rehearse?'

I grinned. 'I'd like to see the act some time!'

Thalia gave me the shrewd, still stare of people who live with venomous animals. She was used to paying attention even when she seemed to be busy elsewhere. 'What do you want, Falco?'

I told her the truth. 'I'm an informer. I'm trying to finger a murderer. I've come to ask if you ever knew a man called Grittius Fronto?'

Thalia tidied her snake again. 'I knew Fronto.'

She patted the bench beside her. Since her manner seemed not unfriendly (and the snake appeared to be sleeping) I risked the close approach. 'I've been speaking to the clerk who helped the Praetor's investigation into Fronto's death; did Lusius ever talk to you?'

'Who trusts a female who does unusual things with snakes?'

'People should!' (It seemed a moment for gallantry.)

She nodded. I could see she was depressed. 'Some men are attracted to danger – at the time Fronto died my latest disaster was an unsteady tightrope walker so short-sighted he could never see his balls!'

I tried to look sympathetic. 'Wasn't a tightrope walker mauled in the same accident?'

'He would never have been the same again – but I nursed him through.'

'Still with him?'

'No! He caught a cold and died of that – men are such bastards!'

The snake suddenly unravelled and expressed a startling interest in my face. I tried to sit tight. Thalia tucked it back in place around her neck, two loops, then head and tail neatly below her ample chin. Since I was too faint to speak, she set off unaided: 'Fronto had an import business; had it for years. In some ways he was good at it, but his nephew did the hard work, finding the animals in Africa and India, then shipping them home. The best times for arena fighting were under Nero, but even during the troubles there were sidelines like mine – and plenty of private customers who wanted strange beasts to exhibit on their estates.'

I nodded. Rome had done its bit towards eliminating vicious species from the wilder provinces. Tigers stripped from India and the Caucasus. Whole herds of destructive elephants wiped out in Mauretania. Snakes too, presumably.

'What do you want to know?' Thalia enquired, suddenly more self-conscious.

'Anything that may have a bearing. As a matter of interest, did you know Fronto's wife?'

'Never met her. Never wanted to. She was obviously trouble; you could tell Fronto thought so too. He kept her out of things. He never let on to her he had that nephew, did you know?'

'I gathered as much. So what happened? I was told a panther ran Fronto and the tightrope walker up against some lifting gear?'

Thalia exclaimed mournfully, 'Well that's a lie for a start!'

'What do you mean?'

'It happened at Nero's Circus.'

Suddenly I caught on; unlike an ampitheatre, a racing circus is simply a level course. 'No substructures? Nothing underground at all – and so no requirement to lift the cages?' Thalia nodded. I wished she wouldn't; it disturbed the snake. Every time she moved, that creature perked up and started inspecting if I was properly shaved, and whether I had nits behind the ears. 'So did some cack-handed aedile write a report about the accident without even going to look?'

'Must have.'

That was good news; it left open the possibility of discovering new evidence. 'Were *you* there?' Thalia nodded; her curious pet unroped itself; she twined it back again. 'So what's the true story?'

'It happened inside the starting gates. Fronto had provided beasts for the morning interlude before the charioteers – a mock hunt. You know! Archers on horseback scampering about after anything spotted or striped that happened to be in the menagerie at the time. If you have a very tired old lion, with no teeth, you sometimes let a few sons of aristocrats in for a go . . .'

'Was the panther tired and toothless?'

'Oh no!' Thalia rebuked me. 'That panther was the real thing. He's beautiful. You can see him if you want. Fronto's nephew kept him afterwards – act of respect; just in case any of his uncle was still inside. The funeral, you know Falco, was very difficult – '

'I don't think I need to look at him; I don't suppose the animal would talk to me but even if he did, no court would accept his evidence! So what happened?'

'Someone let him out.'

'You mean, deliberately?'

'Look, Falco; for Nero's Circus they bring the cages all across the city. They do it at night but it would cause a commotion if even a very small lion got loose!' I had seen the special cages used for transportation of wild animals – just big enough to contain them and fit on ampitheatre lifts. The top section had the hinge. 'Fronto was very particular about the animals; they cost him enough! He checked the locks himself before a journey, and he checked them again while the cages were standing on site. There was no way that panther could have escaped by accident.'

'But the cages must have been unlocked at some time?'

'Just before the scene. Fronto would always be there to supervise. In an arena, he always waited to unlock them until the cages were on the lifting hoists; then there would be just a slip catch for the slaves at the top to undo – '

'But the procedure was different at the Circus?'

'Yes. The cages for the mock hunt were being kept in

the chariot stalls; the plan was to release the animals through the starting gates. They would be lively after being cramped up overnight, so they would run well out into the Circus – which was set up with wooden trees like a forest – lovely it looked! Then the huntsmen would ride in after them . . .'

'Never mind the topiary. What happened by the gates?'

'Someone unlocked the panther early. Fronto and my tightrope walker were in one of the chariot lanes. They rushed to escape through the starting gates – but the gates were still roped up. They were trapped. I ran in the back with some of the men; we saw the panther just finishing his first course and going for dessert. The tightrope walker got in the open cage and pulled the lid down like a lover in a laundry box; that was how he escaped.'

'Oh Jupiter!'

'You can't blame the panther,' Thalia said kind-heartedly. 'He was hungry; and we reckoned that somebody had been annoying him!'

'Well this is the critical question,' I answered with more sobriety than I was feeling. 'Who upset him – and is that who let him out?'

Thalia sighed. From a girl of her size sighs tended to be considerable gusts. The snake shot out a portion of its neck and peered at her reproachfully. She tucked its head down her bosom; the ultimate sanction (or, possible, treat). 'We had a stockman,' said Thalia. 'A stockman I never liked.'

XX

I leaned forwards on my knees. Even Thalia's necklace was forgotten now. 'Will I have any chance of finding this stockman?'

'Do you think Fronto's nephew didn't try? Why do you reckon we said nothing to the lawmen? Why did Fronto's nephew drop his action?'

'You tell me.'

'The stockman's dead. An accident.'

'What was it?'

'He was walking past a derelict house. A wall fell on him.'

'Are you quite sure it was an accident?'

'Fronto's nephew was convinced. There was a local outcry about the way the building had been neglected, but since no one came forward to claim kinship with our stock-man, there was no one able to prosecute the leaseholder. Fronto's nephew was hopping mad, because it ruined his case against the widow if somebody completely unconnected had caused Fronto's death. The vigilantes identified the stockman's body, you see, from a key in his purse which had Fronto's name on it – it was the missing key to the panther's cage.'

'So what had been his grudge against Fronto?'

'No one ever knew. He had only been with us a few weeks, and he had no traceable connections. We get a lot of temporary staff like that.'

'What did you call him?'

'Gaius.'

'That's a great help!' More than fifty per cent of the population answers to Gaius. Most of the rest are called Marcus or Lucius; it makes an informer's life very trying. 'Can't you do better?'

'He may have had another name. I racked my brains, but

I simply can't remember it. Fronto was the only one who could have said.'

I asked the contortionist a few more questions, but she had nothing significant to add. She promised to go on trying to remember further details about the stockman. I left the menagerie, feeling dazed.

My early-morning's work had produced little concrete evidence, yet the pictures it had given me of Eprius and Fronto meeting their deaths were so vivid that when I made my way to the Caelimontium and took up my usual station I was abnormally subdued.

Abacus Street was baking; we were in for a scorcher. The pavements were drying almost as soon as buckets of water were sluiced over them, and the locksmith's singing finch already had a cloth tied round his cage to keep the sun off his little feathered head. When I arrived I raised my arm to the cookshop owner; he knew my order by this time so since I could see someone else at the counter I stayed outside, to bag the only table in the shade.

I was waiting for mine host to warm my wine. It was a pleasant morning (if you were the man with the shady table) and I knew Severina was unlikely to put in an appearance for a couple of hours. Happy with the prospect of being well paid for such easy labour, I linked my hands behind my head and had a good stretch.

Someone came out of the shop behind me. I thought it was the waiter but soon learned my mistake. As I dropped my arms, they were lassoed to my sides with a thick hemp rope. The rope jerked tight. And my cry of alarm was muffled by a large sack dragged swiftly over my head.

I flung myself upright, roaring. I felt the bench topple behind me but hardly knew where I was. Blinded, choked by a confusing smell within the sack, and utterly surprised, my instinctive attempts to free myself were thwarted; my attackers pushed me over violently, face down on the table. I twisted just in time – saved my nose from snapping, but took a hard knock that made one ear sing. I kicked out backwards, found a soft target, repeated the manoeuvre but kicked air. Still flattened on the table I jackknifed sideways.

Hands grabbed at me; I thrashed in the other direction heavy as a shark – too far; I fell off the edge.

There was no time to reorientate my senses. Other people had their own ideas about where I was going: on my back, towed feetfirst at high speed. I knew better than to expect passers-by to assist. I was helpless. The villains had a leg of me each – dangerous if they ran two ways round a post. Most parts of me already hurt. Quarrelling with my abductors from this position could only make the pain worse. I went limp and let it happen.

The kerb down into the road posed no great problem; anticipating the next one up I arched my spine. The sack protected me to some extent, but the base of my neck took a scrape that made me feel like a chicken being boned. I grunted. Jolting over lava blocks was no tonic for my head either.

I knew we had turned, because my side wanged against the corner of a wall, grazing skin even through the sack. We passed into a cooler space: off the street.

A threshold bumped every knob of my spine, then finally my skull. More veering; more knocks. At last my heels crashed down; I had been dumped. I lay still and enjoyed the peace while I could.

The smell was lanolin, I decided. I was trussed in a sack that had been used for unspun wool: a clue so unwelcome I rapidly discarded it.

I listened. I was indoors, not alone. I heard movement; something unidentifiable, then clicks, like big pebbles knocking together.

'Right.' A female. Displeased, but not greatly disturbed. 'Get him out. Let's have a look at him.' I thrashed angrily. 'Careful! That's a good bag he's ruining – '

I recognised the sturdy slave with the big hands who unsheathed me from the hopsack. Then I identified the clicking sounds: big round terracotta loom weights, which swung against each other as someone tugged at the warp threads on the weights. She had just moved down the heddle bar to the next pegs on the frame, and was squaring up the cloth again. I had never seen her bareheaded, but I recognised her too.

So much for my professional expertise: I had been kidnapped in broad daylight by Severina Zotica.

XXI

The red hair was the crinkled gingery type. It was red enough to call for comment, though not too vivid. It would not distract nervous cattle, for instance – and it did not frighten me. With it came pale skin, invisible eyelashes, and sluice-water eyes. The hair was drawn back in a way that emphasised her brow; it should have given her face a child-like quality, but instead her expression suggested that Severina Zotica had passed through childhood too quickly for her own good. She looked the same age as Helena, though I knew she must be younger by several years. She had a witch's *old* eyes.

'You'll get the pip,' she said sourly, 'sitting out in the shade all day.'

I tested my limbs for broken bones. 'Next time, try sending me a simple invitation to come indoors.'

'Would you accept?'

'Always glad to meet a girl who has made a success of herself.'

The professional bride wore a sleeved overtunic in a shade of silver green which combined both simplicity and good taste. An eye for colour: the work on her loom was in happy shades of amber, oatmeal and rust. Her room had matt saffron walls, against which glowed the chair cushions and door curtains worked in brighter tones, while a great floor rug stretched in front of me, thickly tufted with flame, dark brown and black. I ached in so many places I gazed at it, thinking the floor would be a nice place to lie down.

I felt the back of my head, finding blood in my hair. Inside my tunic something trickled depressingly from my last mission's unhealed wound. 'Your musclemen have knocked me about. If this chat is going to be drawn out, could one of them bring me a seat?'

'Fetch it yourself!' She motioned her slaves to absent

105

themselves. I folded my arms, braced my legs, and stayed on my feet. 'Tough, eh?' she mocked.

She started working at the loom. She was sitting sideways, pretending to give me little of her attention, but it was all there. The repetitive movements of the shuttle frayed my tender nerves. 'Lady, would you mind not doing that while you're talking to me?'

'You can do the talking.' Her mouth compressed angrily, though she kept her voice level. 'You have plenty to explain. You have been watching my house all week and following me around blatantly. One of my tenants tells me you were in the Subura asking crass questions about my private life – '

'You must be used to that!' I interrupted. 'Anyway, I don't follow you everywhere; I gave the pantomime a miss: seen it. The orchestra was flat, the plot was an insult, and the mime himself was a balding old paunch with goggle eyes, too arthritic to make a decent stab at it!'

'I enjoyed it.'

'An awkward type, eh?'

'I make my own judgements – do you have a name?'

'Didius Falco.'

'An informer?'

'Correct.'

'Yet *you* despise me!' I was not one of those pathetic worms who eavesdrop on senators in order to sell their sordid indiscretions to Anacrites at the Palace or to their own dissatisfied wives, but I let the insult pass. 'So, Falco, who is hiring you to spy on me?'

'Your fiancé's family. Don't blame them.'

'I don't!' Severina retorted crisply. 'They and I will reach an understanding in due course. They have his interests at heart. So do I, as it happens.'

'In love?' I demanded caustically.

'What do you think?'

'Not a chance! Is he?'

'I doubt it.'

'That's honest!'

'Novus and I are practical people. Romantic love can be very short-lived.'

I wondered if Hortensius Novus was more smitten than

she was. A man who has survived so many years as a bachelor usually likes to persuade himself his reason for abandoning his freedom is a special one. The girl spoke to me with a cool competence she probably restrained in his company. Poor old Novus might be deluding himself that his beloved was demure.

Reaching into a basket for a new hank of wool, Severina lifted her head; she was watching me. I meanwhile was still trying to decide why she had taken the initiative today. It could be simple impatience at me following her about. Yet I sensed that she really loved playing with fire.

She sat up, and rested her pointed chin on tapering white fingers, 'You had better bring the family's anxieties into the open,' she offered. 'I have nothing to hide.'

'My clients' anxieties are those anyone would have, young lady – your sordid past, your present motives, and your future plans.'

'I am sure you know,' Severina interpolated, still composed but with a glint I welcomed, 'my past has been investigated thoroughly.'

'By an old praetorian bombast who had not enough sense to pay attention to his extremely able clerk.' The look she gave me might be renewed respect – or increasing dislike. 'I reckon the clerk took a shine to you – and not necessarily in secret,' I added, remembering Lusius as a straightforward type who might speak out. 'What did you think?'

Severina looked amused by the question but managed to make her answer sound genteel. 'I have no idea!'

'Lies, Zotica! Well, I'm the new boy here; strictly neutral so far. Suppose you whisper into my kindly ear what really happened. Let's start with your first manoeuvre. You had been dragged from the Delos slave market in your childhood, and ended up in Rome. You married your master; how did you wangle that?'

'Without trickery, I assure you. Moscus bought me because I looked quick; he wanted someone to train as a stock-keeper – '

'An aptitude for figures must stand you in good stead as a legatee!'

I saw her take a breath, but I failed to raise the flash fire

I was hoping for. As redheads go she was pinched and secretive – the kind who broods on the ruin of empires. I could imagine her plotting revenge for imagined insults years after the event. 'Serverus Moscus never touched me, but when I was sixteen he asked me to marry him. Perhaps *because* he had never abused me – unlike others – I agreed. Why not? His shop was the best place I had ever lived in, and I felt at home. I gained my freedom. But most marriages are based on bargains; no one can sneer at me for taking my chance.' She had an interesting way of anticipating both sides of a conversation. In private she probably talked out loud to herself.

'What did he get?'

'Youth. Company.'

'*Innocence*?' I chided.

That did make her burn more fiercely. 'A faithful woman and a quiet house where he could bring his friends! How many men can boast so much? Do *you* have that – or a cheap scut who shrieks at you?' I made no reply. Severina went on in a low, angry voice, 'He was an elderly man. His strength was fading. I was a good wife while I could be, but we both knew it would probably not last long?'

'Looked after him, did you?'

Her straight look rejected my sly tone. 'None of my husbands, Didius Falco, had cause for regret.'

'Truly professional!' She took the sneer on the chin. I stared at her. With that pallid skin, an almost brittle frame and her self-contained manner it was impossible to imagine what she must be like in bed. But men in search of security might easily convince themselves she was biddable. 'Did you send Moscus to the amphitheatre that day?'

'I knew he had gone.'

'Did you realise how hot it was? Had you ever suspected that he had a weak heart? Try to stop him?'

'I am not a nag.'

'So Moscus boiled over; you just wiped the froth off the cooking bench and moved up a clean pot! Where did you find Eprius, the apothecary?'

'He found me.' She was forcing too much patience into her tone; an innocent party would have sworn at me by now. 'After Moscus collapsed at the theatre someone ran to his shop for a draught that might revive the invalid – no use. Moscus had already gone to the gods. Life can be brutal; while I was mourning my husband, Eprius called to request payment for the cordial.'

'You soon won round your creditor!' Severina had the grace to let her small mouth slide into a smile, and I was aware that she noticed my answering twitch. 'Then what – he choked, didn't he?' She nodded. Those busy hands worked at their loom while I lost any temptation to sympathise: I was imagining those same little hands struggling to hold down the apothecary during his fatal convulsion. 'Were you in the house?'

'Another room.' I watched her mentally adjust to the new line of interrogation. She had practised this story far too many times for me to unnerve her. 'He was unconscious when they called me. I did what I could to make him breathe again; most people would have panicked. The lozenge was wedged a long way back. A doctor discovered it afterwards but at the time, distraught and fairly frightened, I admit I failed. I blamed myself – but you can only call what happened an accident.'

'Had a cough, did he?' I demanded with a sneer.

'Yes.'

'Had it long?'

'We lived on the Esquiline.' Well known as an unhealthy area; she made her murder methods fit convincingly.

'Who gave him the menthol jujube?'

'I presume he had prescribed it for himself! He always kept a little soapstone box of them. I never saw him take them, but he told me they were for his cough.'

'Was it your habit to involve yourself in his business? A bright and helpful partner like you – I bet the first thing you did when he brought you home in your bridal wreath was to offer to catalogue his recipes and cross-reference his poison lists . . . What happened to Grittius Fronto?'

This time she shuddered. 'You must know that! An animal ate him. And before you ask, I had nothing to do with his business. I never went to the arena where it hap-

109

pened, nor was I there – or anywhere nearby – when Fronto died!'

I shook my head. 'I hear the scene was very bloody!'

Severina said nothing. Her face was so white normally it was impossible to decide whether she was truly upset now. But I knew what I thought.

She had too many well-prepared answers. I tried tossing in a silly question: 'Did you know the panther, by the way?'

Our eyes met. It felt an interesting clash.

I must have shaken her confidence. Severina was looking at me much more speculatively. 'You must be very brave,' I said, 'to contemplate making your flame-coloured veil stretch to yet another wedding.'

'It's good cloth; I wove it myself!' The redhead had rallied. Self-mockery stirred quite attractively behind those cold blue eyes. 'Single women without guardians,' she commented more sombrely, 'have a limited social life.'

'True – and it's miserable being a homemaker, with nobody left to welcome home . . .'

By this time, if I had not heard so many sordid details of what happened to her husbands I might well have let her win me over. I had expected some sort of dinner-party vamp. I hated the thought that Severina's quiet domestic habits were a front for calculated violence. Girls who weave and go to the library are supposed to be safe. 'You must be delighted to discover an astrologer who prophesies your next husband will outlive you?'

'Tyche told you that?'

'You knew she would. Did you warn her I would follow you in? She seemed extremely well prepared.'

'We professional women stick together,' replied Severina in a dry tone that reminded me of Tyche herself. 'Have you finished, Falco? I have things I want to do today.' I felt disappointed as she chopped off the discussion. Then I saw her stop herself. A mistake, trying to be rid of me; my grilling must have been making an impression. Rather feebly, she added: 'Unless you have anything more to ask?'

I smiled slightly, letting her know she was looking vulnerable. 'Nothing else.'

My bruises had stiffened up. The pain had become more nagging; it would take days to shift. 'Thanks for your time. If there is anything else I need to know, I'll come here and ask you directly.'

'How thoughtful!' Her eyes were back on the coloured hanks of wool she kept in a tall basket at her feet.

'Admit it,' I wheedled. 'A maid does the hard work for you after the visitors have gone!'

Severina looked up. 'Wrong, Falco.' She let a trace of sadness filter across her normally guarded face. A touching effect. 'Wrong about everything, actually.'

'Ah well; I loved your tale. I enjoy a well-turned comedy.'

Unperturbed, the gold-digger instructed me, 'Get out of my house.'

She was tough, and up to a point honest; I liked that. 'I'm going. One last question: the Hortensius mob seem a tight little clique. Don't you feel out of place?'

'I am prepared to make the effort.'

'Clever girl!'

'It is the least I can do for Novus!'

She was clever; but when I left, her eyes followed me more keenly than they should have done.

I limped into the first open bathhouse, pushed straight through the steam rooms, and eased my aches and grazes into a hot basin to soak. The sword-cut I had been nursing while I was imprisoned in the Lautumiae had cracked open partially when the gold-digger's house-slaves were slinging me about. I lay in the hot basin, letting myself sink into the next best mood to oblivion while I pulled at the loose scar the way you never should but always do.

Eventually I realised I had forgotten about trying to buy Severina. Never mind. I could still make an offer. Have to go back to negotiate a price – another day. Another day, when I was mentally prepared for the encounter and my limbs could move freely again.

She was certainly a challenge. And the idea that *I* might pose a challenge for *her* didn't bother me at all.

XXII

I had had enough excitement. I could never have found the
energy to struggle to the Pincian and report to my clients,
even if I had wanted a further brush with feminine iniquity.
I also decided not to irritate Helena by sporting around the
Capena Gate the bruises another woman had given me.
That left one attractive prospect: home to my new bed.

As I carefully scaled the three flights to my apartment,
more grateful than ever that it was not the six gruelling sets
of climbers at Fountain Court, I ran into Cossus.

'Falco! You look worse for wear –'

'Overenergetic girlfriend. What brings you here; collecting back rent?'

'Oh no; our clients all pay up prompt.' I schooled my
face not to reveal he might be in for a shock later. 'The
widow on the fourth floor has made a complaint; some idiot
keeps disturbing the peace at midnight – singing raucous
songs and crashing about. Know anything about it?'

'I've heard nothing.' I lowered my voice. 'Sometimes
these old biddies who live alone imagine things.' Naturally
Cossus was more prepared to believe the widow might be
batty than that some other tenant – one who might thump
him if criticised – had antisocial tendencies. 'I have heard
the widow banging walls,' I grumbled. 'I would have mentioned it but I'm a tolerant type . . . By the way,' I said,
changing the subject smoothly, 'Doesn't the rent in a place
like this normally include a porter to carry up water and
keep the steps swept?'

I expected him to quibble. 'Of course,' agreed the agent,
however.'A lot of the apartments are empty, as you know.
But organising a porter is the next thing on my list . . .'

He sounded so obliging I even tipped him for his trouble
as he left.

My front door was open. No need to rush in with cries of

112

outrage; familiar noises informed me of the cause. Mico, my unreliable brother-in-law, must have given away my address.

I leaned round the doorframe. A broomful of grit shot over my feet and stuck under my bootstraps. 'Good morning, madam; is this where the distinguished Marcus Didius Falco lives?'

'Judging by the dust!' She whisked the besom twigs across my toes, making me hop.

'Hello Ma. You found me then?'

'I suppose you intended to tell me where you were?'

'What do you think of my billet?'

'None of our family ever lived in Piscina Publica.'

'Time we moved up, Ma!' My mother sniffed.

I tried to walk as if I had just sprained myself slightly during a pleasant morning's exercise at the gym. It failed; Ma leaned on her broom. 'What happened to you this time?'

The enthusiastic girlfriend joke seemed a bad idea. 'Some people with rough manners caught me by surprise. It won't happen again.'

'Oh won't it?' This was not the first time she had seen me sooner than I wanted after a beating I preferred to hide. 'At least in prison you were in one piece!'

'Being gnawed by a big rat, Ma! I was lucky to be fetched out of it –' She gave me a whack with the besom that told me she saw through that as easily as all my other lies.

Once I was home my mother decamped. Having me there grinning on a stool stopped her looking for evidence of my immoral life; she preferred to upset herself in solitude so she could make more of the occasion. Before she flounced off, she made me some hot wine from ingredients she had brought to stock my larder in case anyone respectable came to call. Consoled, I went to bed.

About halfway through the afternoon I woke, thoroughly chilled, since I had never acquired a bedcover for Junia's bed. After three days I was needing clean clothes too, and missing various treasures I normally kept around me wherever I called home. So, as if today had not been lively enough already, I decided to exert myself with an expedition to Fountain Court.

The shops were still shuttered as I hopped over the Aventine. In my old street everything looked quiet. My landlord's plug-uglies Rodan and Asiacus were treating the neighbourhood to a day of peace. There was no sign of the Chief Spy's dog-eared minions. It was siesta at the laundry. I reckoned it was safe to go in.

I crept upstairs slowly, and slipped into my apartment. There I equipped myself with my favourite tunics, a useful hat, my festival toga, a pillow, two cooking pots which were more or less sound despite five years of wear, the waxed tablet where I wrote sentimental poetry, spare boots, and my favourite possessions: ten bronze spoons, a gift from Helena. I corded all these in a blanket I had brought home from the army, then set off back to ground level humping my bundle like any burglar leaving with his swag.

A burglar would have got away with it. Real thieves can strip a mansion of ten cartloads of antique marble, a score of bronze statues, all the vintage Falernian and the beautiful teenage daughter of the house – while nobody in the neighbourhood notices a thing. I emerged legitimately – only to have some gross female sausageseller whom I had never even seen before spot me and assume the worst. Even then, most robbers would have strolled on their way safely while the witness winked her eye. *I* met the only interfering citizen this side of the Aventine. The minute she spied me sauntering off, she hoiked up her coarse woollen skirts, let out a shriek they must have heard on Tiber Island, and scuttled after me.

Panic – and annoyance – lubricated my stiffened limbs. I hared off up the lane ... just as Anacrites' two spies popped out from the barber's where they were having the top half-inch scraped off their beards. Next thing I was brought up short howling, with my left boot trapped inextricably under one of the monstrous feet.

I swung my bundle at the other spy. From inside it my biggest iron skillet must have caught the brute right across the throat; he flew backwards with a croak it hurt to hear. The owner of the feet was too close for me to swipe him, but his idea of overpowering a helpless victim was simply to yell for assistance from passers-by. Most of those knew

114

me, so when they stopped guffawing at my plight they jeered at him. They were also bemused by the sight of the sausageseller – who was all of three feet high – laying into us ferociously with her salami tray. I managed to angle myself so that coracle-feet caught the worst of it, including a violent thwack with a giant smoked phallus which must have put him off peppered pork for life.

But he still had his massive flipper planted on my toes. I was hampered by the need to cling onto my bundle, for I knew if I once let go some Thirteenth Sector layabout would run off with my chattels and have them auctioned on a street corner before I could blink. So Footsie and I leaned against one another madly, like partners in some tribal wrestling match, while I tried to dance myself free.

I could see his fellow spy reviving. Just then Lenia rushed out of the laundry to investigate the racket, carrying a vast metal basin on her hip. She recognised me with a scornful look, then upended her cauldron over the man I had hit with my skillet; not his day with ironmongery. As his skull took the weight and his legs buckled, I managed to get enough purchase with my trapped foot to slew my other knee inwards; I aimed it angrily at a section of the spy which was much less developed than his feet. His girlfriend would curse me. His toes curled in agony; I hopped free. Lenia was treating the sausageseller to some irreligious language. I finished off Footsie with a wack from my luggage, and did not stay to apologise.

Home again.

After the havoc in the Aventine it seemed ridiculously quiet. I livened things up by whistling a rude Gallic ditty, until the queer widow on the floor above began banging again. She had no idea of keeping time, so I drew my recitation to a close.

Exhausted, I hid Helena's spoons in my mattress, then rolled myself up in my moth-eaten blanket and collapsed on the bed.

Snoring away whole afternoons is an enjoyable pastime; one which private informers carry out with practised ease.

XXIII

Next day I woke refreshed, though aching. I decided to go and give Severina Zotica a piece of my mind while suitable phraseology was suggesting itself fluently.

Before I left I had breakfast. My ma, who believes home cooking keeps a boy out of moral danger (especially when he is the one stuck at home stirring the cooking pot), had organised a brazier, which would heat the occasional panni-kin until I constructed a home griddle. That might have to wait. In August there was not much incentive to lug home stolen builders' bricks, only to fill my elegant new quarters with smoke, unwanted heat, and the smell of fried sardines. On the other hand, it might be easier to start at once than to keep defending myself to my mother for not getting round to it . . . Ma had never yet grasped that private informers might have more enterprising things to do than household jobs.

I drank my home-brewed honey drink, pondering the proposition that having fierce mothers may explain why most informers are furtive loners who look as if they have run away from home.

By the time I strolled into Abacus Street other people had forgotten their early-morning snacks and were musing on the possibility of lunch. I recalled my own recent breakfast with a refined belch – then joined the trend and considered acquiring further refreshments myself. (Anything I ate here could be charged up to the Hortensius mob as 'surveillance costs'.)

I was diverted from the cookshop by spotting the gold-digger. From the scrolls under her arm, this dedicated scholar had been to the library yet again. The cheese shop which fronted her apartment was having supplies delivered, forcing her to dismount from her chair in the street because her entry was blocked by handcarts carrying pails of goat's milk and made-up cheeses wrapped in cloth. As I approached, she was flaying the delivery men with sarcasm. They had made the mistake of complaining that they were only doing their job; this gave Severina Zotica a fine opportunity to describe how their job should be done properly if they had any consideration for fire regulations, local street bye-laws, the peace of the neighbourhood, other occupants of the building, or passers-by.

For Rome it was a normal scene. I stood back while she enjoyed herself. The men with the handcarts had heard it all before; eventually they edged aside a cream-encrusted bucket so if she gathered in her skirts she would be able to squeeze past.

'You again,' she threw back over her shoulder at me, in a tone some of my relations tend to use. Once again, I felt she was enjoying the sense of danger.

'Yes – excuse me . . .' Something had distracted me.

While I was waiting for Severina a lout on a donkey had ridden up to speak to the fruitseller, the one with the Campagna orchard to whom I had spoken yesterday. The old chap had come out from behind his counter and appeared to be pleading. Then, just as the lout appeared to be riding away from the lock-up, he backed his donkey savagely against the counter. Destructiveness was the creature's party trick; it swung its rump as accurately as if it were trained to entertain arena crowds between gladiatorial fights. All the careful rows of early grapes, apricots and berries spilled into the road. The rider snatched up an untouched nectarine, took one huge bite, laughed, then tossed the fruit contemptuously into the gutter.

I was already sprinting across the road. The lout prepared to back his mount a second time; I wrenched the bridle from his grasp and dug my heels in. 'Careful, friend!'

He was a seedy slab of insolence in a knitted brown cap, most of whose bulk was arranged horizontally. His calves were as broad as Baetican hams and his shoulders would have blocked the light through a triumphal arch. Despite the muscle he oozed unhealthiness; his eyes were gummy and his fingers sore with whitlows. Even in a city full of pimply necks, his was a marvel of exploding pustulence.

117

While the donkey bared its teeth against my grip on its bridle, the enforcer leaned forward and glared at me between its pointed ears. 'You'll know me again,' I said quietly. 'And I'll know you! The name's Falco; anyone in the Aventine will tell you I can't bear to see a bully damage an old man's livelihood.'

His rheumy eyes darted to the fruitseller, who had been standing cowed among his massacred pears. 'Accidents happen . . .' the old man muttered, not looking at me. Interference was probably unwelcome, but blatant intimidation makes me furious.

'Accidents can be prevented!' I snarled, addressing the bully. I hauled on the bridle to pull the donkey further from the stall. It looked as mean as a wild colt that had just been caught in a thicket in Thrace – but if it bit me I was angry enough to bite the brute straight back. 'Take off your four-hoofed wrecker to some other morning market – and don't come here again!'

Then I gave the beast a whack on the rump that set him wheezing in protest and cantering off. The rider looked back from the end of the street; I let him see me planted in the middle of the road, still watching him.

A small crowd had been standing by in silence. Most of them now remembered appointments and dispersed hurriedly. One or two helped me pick up the old man's fruit. He shoved the produce back anyhow, bundling the broken pieces into a bucket at the back of his lock-up, and trying to make the rest look as if nothing had happened.

Once the stall was more tidy he seemed to relax. 'You knew that oaf,' I said. 'What's his hold on you?'

'Landlord's runner.' I might have guessed. 'They want to increase the rent for all the frontage tenancies. Some of us with seasonal trade can't afford any more. I paid at the old rate in July but asked for time . . . That was my answer.'

'Anything I can do to help?'

He shook his head, looking frightened. We both knew I had caused him more trouble with the enforcer by defending him today.

Severina was still standing outside the entry to her house.

She made no comment, though her expression was strangely still.

'Sorry for dashing off – ' As we turned down the entry I was still boiling with indignation. 'Do you have the same landlord as the people with the lock-ups?' She shook her head. 'Who owns the title to the shops?'

'It's a consortium. There has been a lot of trouble recently.'

'Violence?'

'I believe so . . .'

I had done the fruitseller no favour. It was preying on my mind. At least if I was hanging about this area while I tracked Severina I would be able to keep an eye on him.

XXIV

After her morning ride out of doors Severina had called for
a recuperative beverage; I was invited to join her. While it
was served she sat frowning; like me, preoccupied with the
attack on the fruitseller.

'Falco, did you know that old man was in trouble with
his landlord?'

'Once I saw him being bullied it was the obvious thing
to suspect.'

She was wearing blue today, a deep sulphur-glass shade
with a duller girdle into which she had woven strands of
the vivid orange she favoured to add flecks of contrast. The
blue brought unexpected colour to her eyes. Even that wiry
red hair seemed a more luxuriant shade.

'So your better nature triumphed!' She seemed to admire
me for doing my bit. I stirred the spoon round my drink.
'How long have you hated landlords, Falco?'

'Ever since the first one started dunning me.' Severina
watched me over the rim of her cup, which was a ceramic
redware beaker, inexpensive yet comfortable in the hand.
'Leaseholding is a foul infection. A great-uncle of mine – '
I stopped. She knew how to listen; I had already let myself
be drawn in. 'My uncle, who was a market gardener, used
to let his neighbour keep a pig in a shack on his land. For
twenty years they shared it harmoniously, until the neighbour prospered and offered an annual fee. My great-uncle
accepted – then found his immediate thought was whether
he could insist that his old friend ought to pay for reroofing
the shack! He was so horrified he returned the rent money.
Great-uncle Scaro told me this when I was about seven, as
if it was just a story; but he was warning me.'

'Against becoming a man of property?' Severina flicked
a glance over me. I wore my normal patched tunic, workaday
belt and uncombed hair. 'Not much danger of that, is there?'

'Fortune-hunters don't hold a monopoly in ambition!'

She took it with good temper. 'I had better confess, the reason I do not share a landlord with the shops – '

I had guessed. 'Your apartment is freehold?'

'I happen to control all the domestic leases in the block; but the shops are separate – nothing to do with me.' She spoke meekly, since this admission took us straight back to the issue of her swiftly acquired legacies. I had learned from the Subura lapidary that at least some of Severina's tenants were content. But I was more interested in the way she first acquired her loot than how she had invested it.

I stood up. We were in a bright, yellow-ochre room which had folding doors. I pushed them back further, hoping for greenery, but only found a paved and treeless yard.

'You have a garden here?' Severina shook her head. I tutted, turning back from the sad little patch of outdoor shade. 'Of course you always move on too quickly; planting is for people who stay put! . . . Never mind, with Novus you are acquiring half the Pincian – '

'Yes; plenty of scope to amuse myself with topiary . . . What sort of home do you have?'

'Just four rooms – one an office. It's a new lease I've taken out.'

'Pleased?'

'Not sure; the neighbours are behaving snootily and I miss having a balcony. But I like the space.'

'Are you married?'

'No.'

'Girlfriends?' She spotted me hesitating. 'Oh let me guess – just one? Is she giving you trouble?'

'Why should you think that?'

'You seem like a man who might overreach himself!' I scoffed but with five sisters, I had learned to ignore nosiness. Severina, who was brighter than my sisters, changed the subject. 'When you are being an informer do you have an accomplice?'

'No. I work alone.' At that she laughed; for some reason I still felt as if she was baiting me. A long time afterwards I discovered why.

121

'You look uneasy, Falco. Do you object to discussing your private life?'

'I'm human.'

'Oh yes. Under the firm-jawed cliché lurks a fascinating man.'

It was a line: straight professional flattery. I felt my spine stiffen. 'Cut it, Zotica! If you're practising winsome dialogue, I shall have to excuse myself.'

'Relax, Falco!'

I was still fighting back: 'Flattery's not what I go for. *That*'s big brown eyes and smart repartee – '

'Sophisticated!'

'Besides, I hate redheads.'

She flashed me a sharp look. 'What have redheads done to you?'

I smiled faintly. A redhead ran off with my father once. But I could hardly blame the whole flame-haired tribe for that; I knew my father, and I knew it was his fault. My opinion was purely a matter of taste: redheads never appealed to me.

'Perhaps we should talk about business,' I suggested, without letting her question get to me.

Severina leaned across to a side table and refilled her beaker, then took mine and topped that up. Since I believed she was responsible for killing her three husbands and that one of them, the apothecary, might well have been poisoned, I experienced a qualm. Knowing Severina's history, a sensible man ought to have turned down hospitality from those graceful white hands. Yet in her comfortable house, lulled by the skilful turn of her conversation, when offered polite refreshments it seemed bad manners to refuse. Was I being disarmed by the same trickery with which new victims were lined up to be despatched?

'So what can I do for you, Falco?'

I put down my cup, then linked my hands, with my chin touching my thumbs. 'I'll pay you the compliment of being perfectly straight.' We were speaking in a soft, open tone, though the thrum of serious business heightened the tension. Her eyes were on mine, their calculation softened by

122

the pleasure she obviously took in bargaining. 'My clients, the Hortensius women, have asked me to find out how much it will take to persuade you to leave Novus alone.'

Severina was silent for so long I began to run over the words in my head, in case I had made some mistake in phrasing them. But it must have been what she expected. 'That's certainly straight, Falco. You're well practised in offering women sums of cash!'

'My elder brother was a man of the world. He made sure I knew how to tuck half a denarius down a whore's bodice.'

'That's harsh!'

'This is not so different.'

I settled the Falco features into what she had called the firm-jawed cliché, while Severina drew herself up slightly. 'Well, this *is* flattering! How much are the dreadful Pollia and Atilia offering me?'

'Tell them what you want. If your claim is too exorbitant I'll advise them to reject it. On the other hand, we *are* talking about the price of a life –'

'I wonder what that is!' Severina muttered angrily, almost under her breath. She sat up even straighter. 'Falco, querying the offer was simple curiosity. I have no intention of breaking my engagement to Novus. Any attempt at bribery is insulting and a complete waste of time. I promise you, it is not his money that interests me!'

The last part of the speech was so passionate I felt obliged to clap. Severina Zotica breathed hard, but she suppressed her irritation because a visitor interrupted us. There was a scratching sound. The door curtain trembled. For a moment I felt puzzled, then beneath the hem of the curtain appeared a bad-tempered beak and a sinister yellow-rimmed eye, followed by a white face and twelve inches or so of grey bird, shading from moonshine to charcoal.

I saw Severina's mood change. 'I don't suppose you want a parrot, Falco?' she sighed.

To my mind birds belong in trees. Exotic birds – with their repulsive diseases – are best left in exotic trees. I shook my head.

'*All men are bastards!*' the parrot shrieked.

XXV

I was so astonished I laughed. The parrot mimicked my laughter, tone for tone. I felt myself colouring. '*Bastards!*' the parrot repeated obsessively.

'He's very unfair! Who taught him the social commentary?' I asked Severina.

'He's a she.'

'Oh foolish me!'

The bird, which looked as nasty a clump of feathers as you could find biting a perch, eyed me suspiciously. It shrugged itself free of the door curtain in a stubby flash of scarlet tail, then stalked into the room, dragging its rump over the floor with the air of a louche peacock. It stopped, just beyond reach of my boot.

Severina surveyed her pet. 'She's called Chloe. She was like this when I got her. A love token from Fronto.' Fronto was the wildbeast importer.

'Yes; well! Anyone who gets through men as fast as you do must accumulate more than her share of misjudged presents!'

The parrot fluffed its feathers at me; stray bits of down drifted loose unhealthily. I tried not to sneeze.

At that moment the curtain was pulled aside again, this time by one of Severina's two stocky slaves. He nodded to her. She got to her feet. 'Novus is here. He normally comes for lunch.' I was ready to vanish discreetly, but she signalled me to stay put. 'I'll just go and speak to him. Then would you like to join us?' I was too startled to answer. Severina smiled. 'I have told him all about you,' she murmured, revelling in my discomfiture. 'Do stay, Falco. My fiancé is extremely keen to meet you!'

124

XXVI

She left the room.

The parrot made chobbling noises; I had no doubt it was sneering at me. 'One word out of place,' I growled menacingly, 'and I'll glue your beak together with pine resin!'

The parrot Chloe heaved a histrionic sigh. '*Oh Cerinthus!*'

I had no time to ask the bird who Cerinthus was, because Severina came back with her husband-to-be.

Hortensius Novus was corpulent and self-absorbed. He wore a tunic so glistening he must change five times a day, together with double fistfuls of heavy rings. All the weight in his face was concentrated low in a swarthy chin; his fleshy mouth turned down with broodiness. He was about fifty, not too old for Severina in a society where heiresses were betrothed from the cradle and gross senators in mid-career married patrician snippets of fifteen. The parrot chuckled at him derisively; he ignored the thing.

'Hortensius Novus . . . Didius Falco . . .' A terse nod on his side; a quite salute on mine. Severina, who had become the professional at work now, smiled at us without her usual sharpness – all milky skin and creamy good manners. 'Let's go to the dining room . . .'

Her triclinium was the first room I had seen here with wall paintings – unobtrusive trails of vine tendril and delicate urns sprouting blossom, on a formal garnet-coloured background. When Novus took his couch Severina herself removed his outdoor shoes, though I noticed the loving attention stopped there; she let one of her slaves wash his large, horny feet.

Novus swilled his hands and face too, while the slave held a bowl for him. The bowl was silver and of a good capacity; the towel from the slave's arm had a fine nap; the slave himself had been trained to high standards of

125

competence. It all gave an impression that Severina Zotica could, with minimal fuss and extravagance, run a good home.

Even the meal was an affair whose subtleties disturbed me: the most simple kind of Roman lunch – bread, cheese, salad, diluted wine and fruit. Yet there were flattering touches of luxury: even for three people a complete range of cheeses made from goat's, sheep's, cow's and buffalo's milk; tiny quails' eggs; refined white rolls. Even the humble radishes were cut into sprays and fantails, decorating a fabulous composition salad moulded in aspic – evidently made at home for it was turned out in front of us (with deliberate panache). Then to finish, a whole orchard of fruits.

This was plain fare all right: plain fare as afforded by the very rich.

Novus and Zotica seemed completely at ease together. They had a short conversation about arrangements for their wedding, the sort of short-tempered debate over avoiding unlucky dates which preoccupies most engaged couples for weeks (until they opt for some gouty aunt's birthday – only to find the old groucher is off on a cruise with a handsome young masseur to whom, without question, she will leave all her loot).

With so much to eat there were plenty of silences. Novus in any case was a full-blooded businessman fired only by finance and totally preoccupied with work. He made no reference to being the subject of my investigation; that suited me, yet left me awkwardly deprived of a social reason for my presence. In fact Novus contributed little; mainly a few remarks from which I gathered Severina had his full confidence.

'That shipment of mine from Sidon has arrived at last.'
'That will be a relief to you. What held it up?'
'Bad winds off Cyprus . . .'
She passed him the potted salad. He was the sort of lump who sweated freely and frowned a lot as he ate fast and greedily. He might be thought coarse – but a woman who yearned for comforts would overlook that if his presents

were generous. Severina treated him with a kind of formal respect; if she married him, her attitude would certainly work – provided she could keep up the deference (and he could keep alive).

He *was* generous. He had brought his betrothed a necklace of twenty violet amethysts. He handed it over almost as a routine exercise; she received the gift with quiet pleasure; I kept my cynical thoughts to myself.

'Falco here had a run-in this morning with a representative of Priscillus,' Severina remarked eventually.

Novus showed his first signs of interest in me. While I chewed on an olive modestly, she described me rescuing the old fruitseller from his landlord's enforcing agent. Novus barked with laughter. 'You want to watch that! Offending Priscillus can be hazardous to health!'

'What is he? Property tycoon?'

'Businessman.'

'Dirty business?'

'Normal business.' Novus was not interested in my views on men who peddle real estate.

Severina tackled her fiancé in a thoughtful voice: 'Is Appius Priscillus getting above himself?'

'He's collecting his rents.'

'It seemed – '

Novus brushed her murmur aside: 'The tenant must have been owing – you cannot be sentimental about debt.' He behaved like a man who was used to being stubborn, though he did give her an indulgent look on the word 'sentimental'. I knew this type: hard as a Noricum knife – yet pleased to own a fluffy kitten who would act as a conscience for him. Fair enough – provided he listened when his conscience spoke.

Severina looked unconvinced, yet she fell silent without quarrelling. Just the sort of women to have at the lunch table: intelligent in conversation – but intelligent enough to show restraint . . . I began thinking about Helena Justina. When Helena had something on her mind she reckoned to make her point.

I found Severina quietly watching me; for some reason I revived the conversation Novus had crushed. 'Is this character Priscillus making you nervous, harrying the neighbourhood?'

The reassuring smile of a tactful hostess lit Severina's pale face. 'I take my advice from Hortensius Novus on business affairs!'

I should have known not to waste my breath.

As a final gesture to the Novus appetite we had cakes: just three (for it *was* lunch, not a banquet), but perfect gems of the pastry cook's art and elegantly displayed on a costly silver platter which Severina then presented to Novus. A gift from her to him looked as regular as her acquisition of the amethysts. It also gave him the indisputable right to lick the plate; his fat, sloppy tongue flickered over it, while I watched jealously.

He left shortly afterwards, with his platter under his elbow but still without any acknowledgement of why I was there. Severina went out with him, which gave an impression they were exchanging kisses in private. I heard a squawk of mockery from the parrot, anyway.

When the hostess came back I had swung myself upright on the dining couch and was giving the amethyst necklace a frank valuation, comparing its cost with her silver plate. 'I reckon Novus came out ahead financially today. That looks good, Zotica – nicely done!'

'You're so cynical it's pitiful.'

I stood up, and dangled the jewels from the fingers of one hand. 'Pretty – but one or two flaws which you'll soon spot. If it wasn't my job to drive a wedge between the two of you, I might warn the good Novus not to give gemstones to a girlie who has been through a lapidary's training . . .' She tried to take the necklace from me; I insisted on fastening it round her slender neck. 'Not quite right with blue.'

'No; amethysts are always difficult.' She remained impervious to my attempts to rile her.

'Time I was going.' I took both her hands in my own and bent over them gallantly. They were scented with a flowery fragrance which reminded me of the oil from the baths which Helena had taken to frequenting recently. Camomile must be the universal fragrance this month.

128

On her left hand Severina wore a massive gold betrothal ring with a red jasper stone. The false symbol of fidelity: one of those travesties where two hands, very badly drawn, are clasping each other. Novus had worn an identical ring. On the matching finger of her other hand was an elderly band of copper, its front flattened into a coin-shaped boss which was scratched with a simple picture of Venus. A cheap trinket. A memento, I guessed. Not many girls wear copper rings, because of the verdigris.

'That's pretty. From one of your husbands?'

'No; just a friend.'

'A man?'

'A man,' she agreed, as I pulled down my mouth to show what I thought of women who lived without a male protector yet had followers they called 'just friends'.

She took back her hands. 'What did you think of Novus?'

'He's too set in his ways, and you are far too bright for him – '

'Normal criteria for marriage!' she quipped defensively.

'Cobnuts! How long do you intend to waste your life coddling mediocre businessmen?'

'Better to do it while I have all my energy than later, when I may need coddling myself!'

'Ah, but meanwhile are you really the deferential type? . . .' She gave me an evasive smile. 'You implied Novus wanted to discuss something. He never told me.'

'He wanted to see if he liked you.'

'So did I impress the man?'

'I can tell you what he wanted, anyway. If you are going to be hanging round on hire to Pollia, there is something you could do for Novus too.'

'Sorry,' I replied at once, suspecting some plot of her own. 'I can only work for one client at a time. But I'd be interested in hearing what he wants.'

'Protection.'

'Ouch! I've still got bruises; don't make me laugh, Zotica!'

For once she lost patience. 'Must you always wield my slave-name like a Herculean club?'

'People should acknowledge their origins – '

129

'Hypocrisy!' she chipped back. 'You are a free citizen; you always were, you cannot know.'

'Wrong, Zotica. I know poverty, hard work, and hunger. I live with disillusionment. I face sneers from both the rich and rich men's slaves. My ambitions are as far beyond my reach as they would be for any chained wretch in a filthy hutch who builds the fires in bathhouses – '

'What ambitions?' she demanded, but things were already far too friendly for me.

We were still positioned in the dining room with me about to leave, but Severina seemed to want to delay me.

'I find I enjoy talking to you,' she grumbled. 'Is this your method of wearing people down?'

'Letting suspects enjoy themselves never achieves much.'

'It worries me when you're frank!'

'Lady, it worries me!'

Suddenly she smiled. It was a smile I had seen before in my life: the dangerous weapon of a woman who had decided we two were special friends. 'Now I shall tell you,' Severina promised, 'the real reason why I went to the astrologer. I hope it will show you why I worry about Novus.' I tipped my head on one side, preserving my neutrality. 'He has enemies, Falco. Novus has been the victim of threats – threats followed by inexplicable accidents. It started before he and I were introduced, and it has happened again recently. I consulted Tyche about the risk, with his full knowledge – in fact, on his behalf.'

I hid a grin. She did not know I had also watched her ordering a tombstone for the hapless man. 'Who are these enemies? And what exactly have they done to him?'

'Will you help us?'

'I told you; I cannot divide my interests in a case.'

'Then Novus would not want me to say any more.'

'Your choice.'

'What can he do?' she cried, putting on a good show of anxiety.

'The best way to treat enemies is to make friends with them.' Severina's eyes met mine, mocking my pious advice. For an instant we shared a dangerous sense of affinity. 'All right; I admit it: the best way is to nobble them.'

'Falco, if you won't help us, at least don't joke!'

If she was lying she was an impressive actress.

But I did not rule out the possibility that Severina was a liar.

XXVII

I spent the afternoon at the Forum, listening to the tired old rumours which the Rostrum lags were handing round as news; then I went on to my gymnasium for exercise, a bath, a shave, and to hear some *real* gossip. Next I devoted some attention to my private affairs: my mother and my banker. Both were trying events for the usual reasons, and also because I discovered that both people had been plagued with visits from Anacrites, the Chief Spy. His attentions were becoming a serious problem. Anacrites had made it official that Didius Falco was a jail-breaker. And when my mother had protested that she paid my surety, Anacrites snapped back that that made me a bail-jumper too.

Ma was very upset. What annoyed me was being portrayed as unreliable to my banker. Limiting my future credit was a really dirty trick.

By the time I had calmed my mother I felt in need of comfort myself, so I trailed along to the Capena Gate. Bad luck again: Helena was at home, but so were half her well-heeled Camillus relations; the Senator was giving an entertainment to mark the birthday of some aged aunt. The porter, who could tell from my informal get-up that I had not been favoured with an invitation, let me in solely for the pleasure of seeing me kicked out again by the people of the house.

Helena emerged from a reception room; sedate flute music trilled behind her before she closed the door.

'Sorry if this is an awkward time – '

'It's something of an event,' remarked Helena coolly, 'to see you at all!'

Things were not going well. A morning at Severina's had spoiled me for banter. I was tired; I wanted to be soothed and fussed over. Instead Helena reproached me that I might have been invited to the party if I had been on hand the night before, when her father had been arranging it. Apart

132

from a nice impression that Camillus Verus must have forgotten his auntie's birthday until the last minute, I also glimpsed how Helena had been embarrassed by not knowing when (*if ever*) she might see her vague hanger-on again . . .

'Helena, my heart,' I apologised obsequiously, 'wherever I am, you are there – '

'Cheap philosophy!'

'Cheap, therefore simple, simple therefore true!'

Cheap meant simply unconvincing. She folded her arms. 'Falco, I am a woman, so I expect my loyalty to be taken for granted. I know my place is to wait until you roll home drunk or hurt or both – '

I folded my own arms the way one does, unconsciously imitating her. A lurid bruise just below one elbow must have become visible. 'Helena, I am not drunk.'

'You've taken some knocks!'

'I'm all right. Look, don't fight. I'm deeply involved in my case now; I have all the trouble I can handle – '

'Oh I forgot – ' she scoffed. '*You* are a *man*! The mildest criticism brings out the worst in you – '

Sometimes I did wonder what I thought I had been doing letting myself be smitten by an outspoken termagant with no sense of timing. Since I was off duty, and probably off guard, I allowed myself to mention this, then added a highly rhetorical description of her ladyship's hasty tongue, hot temper – and complete lack of faith in me.

There was a small silence. 'Marcus, tell me where you have been.'

'Nose to nose with the Hortensius gold-digger.'

'Yes,' Helena answered sadly. 'I thought that must be it.'

Her tone implied she had been moping. I took a critical look at her: Helena's idea of moping was to throw on a vivid carmine dress, adorn her hair with a rope of glass beads like a crown of hyacinths, then courageously enjoy herself in company. I was about to respond with some crabby badinage, when a young man stepped out from the party room.

In honour of the Senator's aunt's birthday he wore a toga

133

whose luxurious nap rebuked the worn shine of my own workaday tunic. His haircut was crisp; a shiny wreath was parked on it. He had the sort of clean-cut aristocratic looks most women call attractive, even though the effect was simply due to phenomenal arrogance.

He expected Helena to introduce us. I knew better; she was too annoyed at his interruption. I beamed at him tolerantly. 'Evening. One of the family?'

'A friend of my brothers,' Helena interposed, recovering rapidly. The aristo looked quizzical at my plebian presence, but she gave him his orders with her usual forcefulness. 'Falco and I were discussing business, if you don't mind.'

Quelled, he returned to the reception room.

I winked at Helena. 'Friend of your brothers, eh?'

'It's an elderly gathering; my parents provided him to talk to me. *You* were inaccessible.

'Just as well, sweetheart. They would not have wanted me.'

'Falco, *I* might have wanted you.'

'You seem to be making do.'

'I have to!' she accused me hotly. 'Anyway, father would have asked you, but who knows where you are living now?'

I told her my new address. She returned graciously that now her father would be able to send the cast-off couch they had promised me. 'Father was trying to contact you urgently yesterday. He had been approached by Anacrites.'

I swore. 'The man's a complete pest!'

'You will have to do something about it, Marcus. With him hounding you, how can you do your work?'

'I'll deal with it.'

'Promise?'

'Yes. Life's becoming impossible.'

I returned to the issue of my new address: 'I'm living in two rooms and another will be the office; that leaves one which could quite easily become yours. You know what I want – '

'A tolerant housekeeper, a free bedmate – and someone brave to catch the crawlies who scuttle out of the floorboards! – No; that's wrong,' Helena corrected herself.

'Someone timid who will let *you* batter the insects and look tough!'

'Well the offer stays open, but I don't intend to remind you again.' She knew it; pleading for her attention was not my style. 'Your noble pa will want you at his party; I'd better go.'

Helena reacted with her customary snootiness: 'So you had.' She relented: 'Are you coming again?'

'When I can,' I answered, accepting the weaker note in her voice as the nearest I would get to an apology. 'I just have a lot to think about. But now I've met the woman, it ought not to be beyond me to sort it all out pretty smartly.'

'Do you mean you won't come until the case is over?'

'That sounds like a brush-off.'

Helena stuck out her chin. '*I'm* getting the brush-off. It was a sensible suggestion.'

My teeth set. 'Gods, I hate sensible women! You decide. I'll come if you ask me. Whenever you want me you know where to find me.'

I waited for her to dissuade me, but Helena Justina was as obstinate as me. It was not the first time we had driven ourselves into some pointless deadlock.

I was leaving. She was letting me. '*Io*, my darling! What I *really* need is a girl to stay at home and take messages!'

'You can't afford to pay her,' Helena said.

XXVIII

Boasting that I would settle the case quickly had been rash. The case was nowhere near its end yet. In fact it was only just beginning, as I would soon find out.

As I sloped off home I was thinking less about work than about women. A normal preoccupation – though weighing on me more heavily tonight. My clients, Severina, my lady-love, my mother, all had designs on my peace of mind. Even my sister Maia, whom I had still not seen since Ma sprung me out of prison, loomed as a subject of guilt because I had not yet made any attempt to thank her for rescuing the betting tags which financed my new apartment . . . It was all getting beyond me. I needed to take action; the best kind of action, which is nothing at all: I had to stand back, give myself a breather, and let the ladies gently mull.

I planned to spend the next three days devoting myself to my own pleasure and profit. I even managed it for two of the days: not a bad success rate for a plan of mine.

First I spent a morning in bed, thinking.

Then, as I still officially worked for the Emperor (since I had never bothered to inform him otherwise) I went to the Palatine and applied to see Vespasian. I hung around the labyrinth of Palace offices for a whole afternoon before a flunkey deigned to tell me that Vespasian was away, enjoying a summer holiday in the Sabine hills. Now that he wore the purple, the old man liked to remind himself of his humble roots by kicking off the Imperial sandals and wriggling his toes in the dust of his old family estates.

Afraid I might run into Anacrites if I stayed too long, I left the Palace and put the Falco personality at the disposal of my private friends. That night I dined with Petronius Longus at his house. He had a wife and three young children, so it was a quiet occasion which ended early (and, by our standards, fairly soberly).

In the morning I redirected my request for an audience

to Vaspasian's elder son, Titus Caesar. Titus was governing the Empire in virtual partnership with Vespasian so he held ample authority to overrule Anacrites in my little bit of bother. He was also known as a soft touch. This meant my appeal had to take its place in a mountain of other scrolls full of hard-luck stories from ambiguous characters. Titus worked hard, but in August lavishing clemency on down-and-outs was bound to proceed at a slower pace than normal.

While I was waiting for my own screed to grab his Caesarship's jaded attention I went to a horse sale with my brother-in-law Famia. I hated to part with Little Sweetheart, but the chariot stables where Famia worked as a vet for the Greens could not be expected to house a horse of mine for ever – well, not for nothing, which was the present arrangement (unbeknown to the Greens). So Famia and I auctioned poor old Little Sweetheart, before the cost of keeping him in hay outstripped his winnings. With money in my pocket I made a trek to the Saepta Julia where I let myself be tempted by a dirty, candelabrum which looked as if it might clean up (wrong, as usual) and an Egyptian cartouche ring (which fitted when I tried it on but felt too big when I got it home). Then I browsed in a couple of literary dealers and came away with an armful of Greek plays (don't ask me why; I hate Greek plays). I took some cash to my mother for her day-to-day expenses, and finally stowed what was left of the proceeds in my bankbox in the Forum.

Next day there was still no invitation to climb up to the Palace and make Titus laugh with my tale of woe, so I did go to see my sister Maia. She let me hang around her house for most of the morning, which led to lunch, followed by an afternoon asleep on her sun terrace. I promised her some of the Pincian cakes but Maia knew how to handle me; she managed to upgrade this to the offer of a house-warming in my spacious new abode. Like a speculator promising to square things with his banker I made a rapid escape: forgetting to agree a date.

Petronius and I spent that evening touring various wine-shops to see if they were as good as we remembered from our youth. What with the free cups we were offered to encourage us to come more often, the flagons I bought him, and the drinks Petronius (who was a fair man) stood me in return, *this* occasion ended neither early nor soberly. I saw him home, since a watch captain risks all sorts of vindictiveness if villains he may have arrested in the past spot him stumbling about the city.

His wife Silvia had locked us out. Still, law officers know how to pick most locks and informers can force the ones that defeat them, so we got ourselves indoors without too many of his neighbours flinging open their shutters to bawl at our noise. We broke a bolt, but the door itself remained in one piece. Petro offered me a bed, but Silvia had come downstairs cursing us; she was trying to repair the door lock with a pair of eyebrow tweezers while Petro manhandled her affectionately with a view to a peace treaty (unlikely, I thought). Then their children woke up frightened, and Petro's youngest daughter started crying that her kitten had been sick in a sandal – so I left.

Like most decisions made after trying five or six amphorae of mediocre vintages in cheap commercial drinking rooms, this was not a good idea.

An important occasion: the first time I tried to find my new apartment when crazily drunk. I got lost. A big dog with a pointed snout nearly bit me and several prostitutes shouted uncalled-for abuse. Then, when I finally located the Piscina Publica, and found my own street, I failed to notice that a low-rank five-days-in-uniform Praetorian Guardlet was waiting to greet me – with a warrant from Anacrites, a painful set of leg irons, and three other baby-faced recruits in shiny breastplates who were all as keen as Baetican mustard to carry out their first official mission by arresting a dangerous renegade who apparently shared my name.

After they fastened the irons on me, I just lay down in the road and told them I would go wherever they wanted – but they would have to carry me.

XXIX

I spent the next two days recovering from my hangover, back in the Lautumiae jail.

XXX

By the second evening I was reacquainted with my old cellmate the rat. I tried keeping to one corner so as not to inconvenience him, but he was starting to look at me hungrily. I had to disappoint him. I was called away; someone very influential made enquiries about my case.

Two of the schoolboy Praetorians turned up to fetch me. At first I resisted. My hangover had been replaced by light-headedness. I was in no state to endure a confrontation with Anacrites and the bullies he used to encourage frank confessions. No fear of that! Anacrites had planned to imprison me until I was incontinent and toothless. With a kick to my kneecap the jailor let slip that a High-Up wanted a look at me. My petition to Titus must have surfaced on the pile . . .

The young troopers were bursting with excitement at the prospect of a royal audience. In the past the Imperial bodyguard had shown itself prone to replacing the Caesar who was entrusted to their care with anyone who caught their eye after a good night's carousing (Claudius, for heaven's sake, and that primped liability Otho). Not any longer. On his father's accession Titus had shrewdly taken direct charge of the Praetorians; so long as he gave them a good bounty on his birthday, they would stick by their own commander like burs on a shepherdess's skirt. Now Proculus and Justus (if you happen to get arrested, always find out the names of your guards) were about to come face to face with their famous new Prefect in their first week, thanks to me.

They were so wrapped up in their own glory they tactlessly escorted me across the open Forum, still in chains. But they were too new in uniform to have lost all their charity; they let me scoop up a drink from a public fountain to cure my dehydration before dragging me into the cool of the Cryptoporticus, that long galleried entrance which leads up to the various palaces that hog the crest of the Palatine. Outside the guardroom their centurion, a hardened regular, made them take the leg irons off me. He knew what was proper. We exchanged the imperceptible scowl of old soldiers as he inspected his inexperienced rankers for sloppy belts and smears on their armour. He came with us to the throne room, fretting in case his babes put a step wrong.

At the first waiting room an usher who claimed to know nothing about me showed us into a side cubicle on our own. Proculus and Justus were starting to look rosy; the centurion and I had been through this stupid quarantine on other occasions so we saved our sweat.

Half an hour later we were moved to a corridor, which was full of tired people in limp togas hanging about. Proculus and Justus exchanged glances, thinking they would be stuck in this endless trail of ceremonial long after their watch was supposed to end. But immediately my name was called; minor flunkeys bustled us past the crowd; then we reached a cavernous antechamber where an elegantly spoken secretary inspected us like vermine while he crossed us off a list.

'This man was summoned an hour ago! What kept you so long?'

A major-domo produced Anacrites, looking sleek in a grey tunic; like a conjuror's tame dove – but not so cute. In contrast to me he was well bathed and barbered, with his straight hair slicked back in a way I disliked intensely. It made him look like the trickster he was. At the sight of him I felt crumpled and crusty-tempered, with a mouth like the bottom of a cementmaker's hod. He narrowed his pale, suspicious eyes at me, but at this stage I forwent the chance of insulting him. Next minute Proculus and Justus had been ordered to march me in.

When we first entered through the grand travertine entrance pillars, Anacrites was the trusted official and I the seedy hangdog, under guard and in disgrace. But no protocol that I knew said I had to go along with it. Two days in bruising leg irons made it easy to adopt a brave expression and a limp. Which meant the first thing Titus Caesar asked me was, 'Something wrong with your leg, Falco?'

'Just an old fracture, sir. I broke a leg last winter, on that job for your father in Britain; it bothers me when I'm cramped up without exercise . . .'

'Cut the pathos, Falco!' Anacrites growled.

Titus shot a sharp glance at the spy. 'Britain; I remember!' His tone was clipped. The work I did for his father in Britain was too confidential to be mentioned in detail, but Anacrites would know of it. I heard him mutter with annoyance. I also noticed the secretary, whose job was to take shorthand notes, hold his stylus discreetly at rest as confidential subject matter came up. His exotic oriental eye caught mine momentarily; finely tuned to atmosphere, he anticipated fun.

Then Titus gestured to a slaveboy. 'Didius Falco needs looking after. Will you bring him a seat?'

Even at that stage Anacrites had no real need to worry. I had never made any secret of my rampant republican views. Dealing with the Imperial family always caused me difficulty. The Chief Spy knew as well as I did what to expect. M Didius Falco was about to be rude, ungracious, and a fool to himself as usual.

XXXI

So there we were. Titus relaxed on a throne, with one ankle crossed on the opposite knee, crushing the braid-encrusted pleats of his purple overtunic. To the slaveboy it seemed natural to place my cushioned footstool near the only other person who was seated, so he carried it right up onto the plinth at the base of His Caesarship's throne. He helped me hitch myself up. Anacrites took a step forward, then suppressed the protest as he was forced to accept his Imperial master's courtesy to me. I refrained from smirking; Anacrites was far too dangerous. I perched on my footstool, occasionally rubbing my leg unconsciously, as if it was a habit when my poor cracked bones were distressing me . . .

Titus was thirty. Too happy to be called handsome and too approachable for his rank, though a grave sense of public duty had recently sobered him. Even those forced to endure existence in the provinces knew from the coinage that he had a less craggy version of his father's bourgeois face, and curly hair. While he was a boy that mop probably caused his mother to pass the same remarks as mine did, but had Flavia Domitilla still been alive she could have relaxed now: a circus of hairdressers kept her eldest trim, so he would not let the Empire down in front of foreign ambassadors.

Titus and I made a nice friendly group, up on his plinth. My letter was in his hand; he tossed the roll back at me. There was a glint in his eye. Titus was always so gracious I suspected a joke – yet the charm was genuine. 'This is a moving narrative!'

'Sorry, Caesar. I'm a spare-time poet; my style tends to lyrical excess.' Titus grinned. He was a patron of the arts. I was on safe ground.

It was the wrong moment to force the Chief Spy to watch us enjoying ourselves. Infected by my own wariness, Titus gave Anacrites the nod to approach and state his case.

Anacrites took the floor without bluster. I had seen him in action on other occasions so was prepared for the worst. He possessed the true bureaucrat's knack of sounding reasonable whatever lies he told.

In some ways I felt sorry for the unprincipled carbuncle. His was a classic case of career blight. He must have studied his craft under Nero, those crazy years of suspicion and terror, when prospects for intelligence agents had never looked more golden. Then as he reached his prime he found himself stuck with the new Emperor Vespasian, a man so irredeemably provincial that he did not really believe in palace spies. So instead of enjoying himself at the centre of some crawling network of undercover termites, Anacrites now had to devote every day to proving that his place on the payroll was justified.

No joke. Vespasian was tight with the salaries bill. One slip, one mistake in diplomacy, one door opening too suddenly to reveal him napping in his office when he had said he would be out on surveillance, and the Chief Spy would find himself selling catfish on some Tiber wharf. He knew it. I knew it. He realised I knew. Perhaps that explained some things.

I made no attempt to interrupt his speech. I wanted him to shoot all the dice from his cup. Out it poured, a subtle slime of misinterpreted facts, at the end of which *he* sounded like the honest professional whose superiors had lumbered him with a bungling outsider to work with. *I* emerged as a straightforward thief.

The facts were straightforward too: some ingots of lead from the Imperial mines had been stored in a warehouse. I knew they were there, forgotten by the Treasury. When I was sent to Campania I took the ingots with me, and sold the lead for waterpipes. I had never paid back the proceeds.

Titus listened with his hands linked behind his head. He himself was not a great speechmaker but he had served his time as a barrister before he came into higher things. Despite his impatient energy he knew how to listen. Only when he was sure Anacrites had finished complaining did he turn to me.

144

'The case against you was well put. The lead ingots belonged to the State; you took them without leave.'

'Anacrites is a good speaker; it was a good exercise in rhetoric. But Caesar, there's no case.' Titus shifted position. I had his full attention; he was leaning forwards now with both elbows on his knees. 'Caesar, I had a particular reason to respect those bars of lead; I probably hacked some of the ore from the seam myself!' I paused, to give those present time to absorb another reference to my mission in Britain, where I had been forced to disguise myself as a lead-mine slave. 'Harsh, Caesar – but necessary, for your father's sake. And when I used up the ingots, I was in disguise again. We were seeking a fugitive. Anacrites can confirm it was a frustrating task, one on which he himself had spent several fruitless weeks – ' His jaw stiffened pleasingly. 'I was asked to try my own ingenuity. Unorthodox methods were, after all, why your father was augmenting his regular staff with me – '

'True,' said Titus to Anacrites pointedly.

' – acting as a black-market plumber helped me find the missing man. So the disguise worked, Caesar, as you know.'

In a silky voice Anacrites reminded Titus that the ingots I borrowed might have been needed as evidence in a conspiracy case.

'What prosecutor was going to produce multiple tonnage of metal in open court?' I asked. 'We all knew the ingots existed. There were documents to prove it: the Praetorian Guards had stacked them, and the victor of Jerusalem won't need me to tell him that the first thing military conscripts are taught is to *count* everything they handle . . .'

Titus smiled tolerantly. He was willing me to explain the charge away. I was not naïve. I knew why it probably suited the Empire to set me loose: Titus and his father must have some real pig of a problem they wanted me to solve for them.

'I suppose,' Anacrites suggested heavily, 'you intended to repay the money from selling the ingots? Or have you blown away your profits on women and drink?'

I looked shocked. Just *one* woman (Helena Justina); though on holiday in Campania she and I, and a nephew of mine, and Petronius Longus, and Petro's wife and family, had freely eaten and drunk the Treasury's cash, using my imperial mission as our excuse. 'Don't blame me for the delay, Anacrites! Being thrust into the Lautumiae hampered me unfairly – though I did make use of my few days of freedom to see my banker on the very subject of transferring funds to the Privy purse . . .'

'Good news!' Titus sounded relieved. Having to write off the money was his main stumbling block to releasing me.

'I must warn you though, Caesar,' I apologised swiftly, 'since I was selling the metal on back-door terms, the sum involved is not as great as it would have been using official franchises . . .'

'He's lying!' snarled Anacrites. 'I have a complete list of his assets – ' A short list! 'This windbag hasn't a bean!'

So much for my banker keeping his client's confidence . . . Yet I knew that Anacrites had pried open my private money chest the day before I sold my racehorse; I now possessed funds he must have overlooked. Now there was no escape. Even if it ruined me I was not prepared to let a pernicious undercover agent do me down. Sighing, I kissed goodbye to Little Sweetheart (or what was left of the poor nag after my Saepta Julia spending spree).

'There is a liar in this throne room, but it's not me!' I pulled off my signet ring. 'Caesar, if you will send someone to my banker we can settle this tonight – ' Suddenly suspicious, Anacrites chewed his lip.

'Spoken like an upright citizen!' Titus, embarrassed, aimed a frown at the spy while a minion took my ring away as a sanction to my financier to bankrupt me. 'That does seem to cover your charges, Anacrites!'

'True, Caesar – if the cash comes!'

'You can trust me! Mind you,' I grumbled touchily, 'I don't want to be cleared on false pretences. If this is just a gag in order to make me available for some filthy undercover mission which none of your regular Palace employees will handle, frankly I prefer jail – '

Titus soothed me, too eagerly for honesty: 'Didius Falco, there are no complications; I pronounce you a free man!'

'And a free agent?' I haggled.

'As usual!' he chipped – but then, overcome by his keen-
ness he jumped straight in: 'So, are you free to do something
for my father?'

Excellent: one bound from prison, straight back in favour.
Anacrites glowered. He need not have worried. 'Love to,
sir – but prison didn't suit me; I need to recuperate.' Back
in favour – then straight back out in one more bound.

Titus Caesar had known me for the past four months;
long enough. He became his most agreeable, always a civilised sight. 'What can I do to persuade you back, Falco?'

'Well,' I mused. 'First you could try paying me for the
last mission I carried out for Vespasian . . .'

'And then?'

'It might help, sir, to pay me for the mission before that!'

He drew a sharp breath. '*Britain?* Have you never been
paid for Britain?' I looked humble. Titus barked something
at a secretary standing in the shadow of his throne, then
assured me that immediate arrangements would be made.

'Thank you, Caesar,' I said, letting him know I thought
'immediate' was a Palace codeword for 'indefinitely
deferred'.

'Once you receive the money perhaps you will feel able
to resume your official career?'

'Once I receive it!' I challenged him. 'By the way – ' I
leaned sideways to include Anacrites in this comment ' – if
today's verdict is that I should not have been in prison in
the first place, can I assume you will be repaying to my
elderly mother the money which she lodged with the jailor
as my bail?'

The bastard was stuck; do it, or expose the fact that the
jailor had accepted Mama's savings as a bribe. At present
the Lautumiae staff were in the Spy's pocket and gave
Anacrites the run of the cells. Naturally Anacrites wanted
to preserve the status quo . . .

Titus told him to see to it. (Titus came from an odd
family: the women respected their menfolk and the men
respected their mothers.) Anacrites cast one furious glance
at me, promising revenge later, and slunk off. *His* mother
probably took one look at him when he was born, then

147

let out a screech and abandoned him over a drain in an alleyway.

After him Proculus and Justus, with their centurion, were also dismissed. I sensed the attendants relaxing as Titus yawned and stretched; he must have saved interviewing me, like the olive in the middle of an omelette, as his last treat of the day. Then, since I was a free man and a free agent, Titus asked if I was also free to stay on at the Palatine and dine with him.

'Thanks, Caesar. This reminds me that there are *some* pleasant reasons why I let myself be coerced into political work!'

The chief jewel of the Empire gave me a sweet grin. 'Maybe I am keeping you on hand – in case your banker fails to send a certain sum . . .'

I had been right in the first place. Getting involved with politicians is complete stupidity.

XXXII

Like everyone else, I had heard that the parties Titus gave tended to be riotous, late-night affairs. People like to believe in scandal; I like to believe in scandal myself. After my second stint in prison I was ready to handle a riot at the Empire's expense, but that night on the Palatine we only enjoyed a pleasant meal with unobtrusive music and easy talk. Perhaps Titus was just a good-looking, unmarried lad who had seen in the dawn with his cronies (once or twice, when he was younger), and now he had a reputation for loose living which would be held over him whatever else he did. I sympathised. I was a goodlooking, unmarried lad myself. My own wicked reputation was so hard to shift, I didn't even try.

Before we ate I had made myself respectable in the Imperial baths, so once I was fed and comfortably wined my energy renewed and I excused myself, with the plea of work. Might as well air my new haircut around the city while the Palace barber's lotions were still exuding interesting whiffs. When he saw a slave strapping my sandals back, Titus called out, 'Falco – I have not forgotten your present, you know!'

'What present was that, Caesar?' I asked cautiously, thinking he meant the promise of work.

'To thank you for my luck at the races!' Thundering Jupiter; something else I really did not want.

That horse, Little Sweetheart, had been a mixed blessing. Titus had backed him, and I knew he was eager to demonstrate his pleasure at winning. I remembered now what my reward was to be – and I would need my most devious resources to deal with it.

'An honour and a treat, Caesar – ' I lied diplomatically, adding (with less good sense) that Titus might like to drop into the Falco residence to sample a sliver . . . He promised he would remember (while I prayed he would forget).

My present, in case you wondered, was a fabulous fish.

I left the Palatine feeling thoughtful. Titus intended to send me a turbot.

Turbot was strange meat to me – me and most of Rome. I had seen one once in a fishing boat; it was half a yard across. That one fish would have cost five or six times my annual income – though in fact they rarely hit the markets since most fishermen who catch a turbot present it smartly to the Emperor.

Now I was in a dilemma. I could cook. I quite enjoyed it. After five years of living solo in squalor I was the king of one-man cuisine; I could grill or poach or fry most edibles, in cramped spaces, with no decent utensils and only a basic range of condiments. My best efforts were delectable, and my worst blunders had gone into the scrap bucket before they made me ill. But it was obvious not even I could barbecue a *turbot* in a dribble of olive oil on a household skewer over a few burning twigs. The marvel Titus promised me would call for a monumental fishpan and a massive serving platter, the high arts of a first-rate sauce chef who had access to a sophisticated cooking range, a train of uniformed bearers to present the royal creature handsomely to my slavering guests, an orchestra, and an announcement in the *Daily Gazette*.

My only real alternative was to give the fish away.

I knew that. And I knew what I would probably do instead.

Wandering into the Forum, I paused by the Temple of Vesta. To my left, at the Rostrum end, some magnate was being taken home from a banquet in a canopied litter flanked by eight marching bodyguards whose torches bobbed like well-drilled fireflies as they negotiated the steep curve of the Vicus Argentarii.

At the Palace I had lost all track of time. It was a hot August night, with serene violet light tinting open skies. Cookshops were still doing heavy business, and although some booths were shuttered and bolted I passed a cabinet-maker, a mirror-seller and a goldsmith who had all kept their folding doors open and lights burning in the interior; dogs and toddlers and companionable women could be glimpsed inside. Folk still hogged pavement tables, reluctant to abandon their wine beakers and gaming-boards. The dangerous men who took control of Rome during darkness were probably about by now, but the citizenry had not yet surrendered the streets to them.

There was plenty of action. I stopped to gape at a house fire. It was a four-storey block, smouldering from the ground up. The lesser tenants had come rushing out with their possessions in bundles; the main householder was struggling to drag his tortoiseshell bedstead out of the doorway, hampering the municipal firefighters as they and their buckets waited to go in. Eventually he and they were all driven away as the whole building flared ablaze. The man sat on the pavement with his head in his hands sobbing, until some passing tycoon jumped out of a greasy brown sedan chair and offered to buy up the ground lease. I could hardly believe it. The oldest fiddle in the world – but the fool with the burning bed just clutched a pillow to his heart and accepted on the spot.

I thought everyone had heard how Crassus came by his legendary millions – touring Rome looking for fires then preying on people while they were still in shock. And I thought everybody nowadays knew to reject any helpful shark who popped up offering a pittance for a smoking building site – aiming to redevelop at a profit as soon as the ashes cooled. Evidently there were still idiots who would succumb to the lure of cash in hand . . . For a second I considered intervening, but the acceptance of terms was too far advanced; thwarted property developers are notoriously vindictive and I could not risk involving myself in a breach of contract case.

Halfway along the next dark alley I kicked something which turned out to be a tinderbox; it was lying near a tangle of rags which someone in a hurry had dropped in the street.

Apparently speculators no longer relied on luck when looking for their next site. It would be hard to prove now

151

the building was burnt to a cinder, but that fire had been arson without any doubt.

Stars winked above the Capitol. Small slaveboys slept on their lanterns as they waited in doorways for masters who were still being entertained. The air was full of rumbling wheels as the carters plied their evening trade; then above the chinks of cheap metal on harnesswork came the sweet shiver of silver bells on the slim ankles of the dancing girls in some overpriced saloon. Passing along the gloomy lanes I knocked into empty amphorae which careless tavernkeepers had put out in piles; among the dried mud and mule droppings on broader streets I trod upon loose flower petals which had flittered from dinner garlands as their wearers came and went. It was a vibrant night. I was a free man in my own city – and not yet ready for bed.

It was too late to call at a senator's house. I also failed to drum up any desire to visit my own relations. Instead my feet took me northwards. The Hortensius crowd always gave the impression theirs was a home which kept long social hours. I would be fully justified if I apologised to Sabina Polia and Hortensia Atilia for having been out of action for the past few days. Besides, I did need to ask the ladies if they had noticed any developments after my meeting with Hortensius Novus at Severina's lunch party.

The whole Pincian area was lively at this hour. By day these private palaces seemed sedate enough. By night houses and grounds throbbed with activity. Contracts for business and pleasure of every kind (legitimate or otherwise) were being worked out on this elegant mount. Some were already sealed and concluded. One of those affected me.

From the Forum to the Pincian, avoiding dossers, drabs and happy drunks, takes half an hour. By the time I turned off the Via Flaminia a subtle change had transformed Rome. The violet had drained from the skies, leaving greyness and a more wary atmosphere. Now the good would go home while the bad came out to play. Even my own mood was different. I slipped along, keeping to the centre of each street. My concentration stayed on the alert. I wished I had a knife.

There was no one at the Hortensius gatehouse. I walked through the gardens, staring twice at every darkened bush. Near the house torches lined the driveway, some still lit, a few atilt and smoking, but most burned out.

Clearly the family had been entertaining. The main door still stood open, with lamps aglow throughout the reception halls. I could smell the kind of perfume which is used to drench dinner guests – that light but cloying odour of rose petals, which to me always seems too close to the tang of decay. But there was no music, and nobody about. Then a gaggle of servants emerged through a curtain, with a relaxed air that betrayed the fact they were unsupervised.

One of them was fooling about with a tambourine; another was swigging wine, spilling it down his tunic as he took it straight from the lip of a golden ewer. They noticed me just as I recognised the runabout Hyacinthus, the thin slave who had first commissioned me. Like the others he was wearing a tunic with more ornament than cloth, a bawdy concoction of glittering guilloche which must be the Hortensius party livery – on a night like this, unbearably heavy and hot. 'Looks like you've been having fun here tonight!' I said.

'Welcome, stranger! Rumour had it you were in prison.'

'Malicious gossip! What was the party – special occasion?'

'Just dinner with an old acquaintance.'

'Business or pleasure?'

'Business.' I should have known. Everything was business in this house. 'Did you have an appointment? Pollia and Atilia have both gone up to bed – '

I grinned. 'I'm not brave enough to disturb either of them in the bedroom!' One of the slaves giggled.

'The men should still be available,' Hyacinthus added.

I had had no dealings with Crepito or Felix. It might be useful to speak to Novus, but if I wanted to improve on our minimal chat over lunch I would need to see him on his own. 'Is Severina here tonight Hyacinthus?'

'She's been here since the afternoon but I haven't seen her lately.'

153

Someone else said, 'Her chairmen have gone; she must have left.'

'Can I see Novus then?' A young lad volunteered to ask.

The slaves were still joshing among themselves, and they wanted to be rid of me. Luckily the delay was short; the lad returned to say Novus was not in his own bedroom, nor with Crepito and Felix though they were expecting him to join them for a late-night glass of wine.

The houseslaves lost interest but after I had walked so far, heading back with nothing to show for my blisters was too dispiriting. 'Novus must be up and around somewhere!'

The man with the golden wine flagon laughed. 'Last I saw he was up all right – doubled up and running!'

'Something he ate disagreed with him?' It was a sultry night. My tunic stuck to my neck and chest unpleasantly as I asked.

'Probably the amount!' sneered the drinker. I remembered the ill-mannered gusto with which Novus licked his plate.

'How long ago did you see him on the trot?'

'About an hour.'

I glanced at Hyacinthus. 'Any chance he's stuck in a lavatory – flaked out, or still chucking up?' The slaves exchanged bored glances. 'Would he call for an attendant if he had a bad attack of the gyp?'

'Only to bawl at us to leave him on his own – he likes privacy when his gorging upsets him. Anyway – ' the man with the flagon was a caustic social satirist ' – there's not much help you can offer; shitting is one thing the rich have to do for themselves . . .'

Hyacinthus, who had been standing silent, finally returned my thoughtful stare. 'No harm in looking,' he said. The others refused to make the effort, so the search was left to Hyacinthus and me.

As in most houses which possess their own facilities, the Hortensius lavatories were situated alongside the kitchen so any water which was sluiced out of pots and sinks could be utilised to swill the channels clean. The freedmen's house boasted a triple-seater, but we only found one occupant.

Hortensius Novus must have burst in and let the heavy

154

door swing behind him; the clatter from the kitchen where the remains of the dinner party were being cleared would have suddenly stilled: after that he was alone, in this dark, quiet place. If he was sober enough to understand what was happening, he must have been terrified. If he had called out, before the ghastly purge became paralysis, no one would have heard.

It would have been painful and degrading. But the speed of it had some mercy. And it was a private death.

155

XXXIII

'I-o!' exclaimed Hyacinthus. He instinctively turned away towards the kitchen, but I clapped my hand over his mouth and held him still.

'Don't raise the alarm yet!'

Hortensius Novus was lying on the floor. He had been felled in mid-stride; halfway between the door and the latrine seats. Cut down by death, the last embarrassment of all. If he was lucky, he was gone before he crashed face first onto the slabs.

Stepping carefully I bent to feel his neck, though I knew it was a formality. Then I saw his wild grimace. Something far worse than the violent purge had overwhelmed him. Perhaps the horrific certainty of approaching death.

He was warm, though not warm enough to be revived. I was no doctor; but I knew it was more than the strain of digesting too much dinner which had stopped the freedman's heart.

'Somebody got to him after all, Falco!'

The slave became hysterical; I felt a rush of panic myself, but I had been in this situation often enough to control it. 'Steady. Don't let's overreact.'

'He's been murdered!'

'Could be. But people often pass away during a fit of diarrhoea ... and gluttons do die from overeating occasionally Hyacinthus – '

The speech, too, was a formality. I was filling in time while I looked around.

Novus had clutched his light banqueting gown up around his waist. I steeled myself then tugged away his left hand, with its jasper betrothal ring, and dragged the garment down. The dead deserve some decency.

I stood up quickly. Then I gripped Hyacinthus by one elbow and wheeled him outside the door. There might still be time to find some evidence before it was destroyed –

156

either accidentally or by someone with a vested interest. 'Hyacinthus, stand there and don't let anyone go in.'

One glance in the kitchen confirmed my fears. The house was slackly run. Flies circled over the work surfaces with a languidly possessive air. But the used utensils from the banquet, which might have furnished clues, were already lost to me. The tousled skivvy who washed the platters knew she would have to do it some time so she had already made a start at scraping away, before the food on the dishes and serving tureens had caked too hard. When I strode round the door she was on her knees beside a cauldron of greasy water, surrounded by finished piles of gold plate. I saw her squint at a huge silver dish, which I recognised as the one Severina gave Novus the day we had lunch; the tired drudge tried to persuade herself the comport was clean, but found a sticky smear and listlessly dunked it into her tub.

Only the skivvy was working. (Any skivvy will tell you that is a perfectly normal event.)

Some of the cooks and carvers were lolling around now the toffs had dispersed. They were picking at the leftovers with the sluggish air of kitchen workers who knew some of the meat had looked slimy when it came from the butchers, which of the sauces had not wanted to thicken, and how many times the vegetables had fallen on the floor among the mice droppings in the course of being prepared.

'Who's in charge here?' I demanded. I guessed it was the kind of slapdash servery where no one would be in charge. I guessed right. I warned them that one of the guests had been taken ill, and none of the underlings looked surprised. I then said that the illness was fatal, at which they did suddenly lose their appetites. 'If you can find a dog that no one likes, start feeding him these leftover titbits one at a time . . .'

I strode back to Hyacinthus. 'We'll put a bar across this door – ' That would serve my purpose; people would think the lavatory had flooded: common enough. 'Now before some busybody tidies it up, I want you to show me the dining room – '

A house where nobody empties the rubbish pails and the kitchen boards are never scrubbed may nonetheless feed its visitors amid breathtaking opulence.

The blazing candelabra were beginning to die down now, but not enough to dim entirely the gilding on the pedestals and finely fluted pillarwork, or the shimmer from the brocaded swags of curtaining, cushioning and valencing which made the room and its three gigantic couches suitably luxurious for a set of jumped-up lamp-boys and the female trash who married them. I could not be bothered to take in all the details, but I remember there were huge paintings of battle scenes and highly polished onyx urns. Grilles overhead in the vaulted ceiling remained open after raining down a sickly perfume which made my throat clench.

A pageboy was curled up with his thumb in his mouth and a peach in his hand. He was so fast asleep he looked as if all breath had left him. Hyacinthus kicked at him anxiously, but the child started awake and stumbled away.

I gazed around, searching for clues. Here the worst signs of domestic upset were the wine-stained napery which would pose problems for the Hortensius linenkeeper, and a sea of spilt lamp oil on one of the couch coverlets. I kicked a hardened bread roll out of my path. 'Who was here tonight, Hyacinthus? How many of the family?'

'All three, with both women.'

'The guests?'

'Just one. A business associate.'

'And Severina.' Seven. Plenty of elbow room on the couches. 'What was the table plan?'

'Mealtimes are not my province, Falco. You want the chamberlain.' The chamberlain would be full of himself, a wearying talker (I had met them before). He could wait.

I walked all around the triclinium, but nothing caught my eye. Wine flagons and water jugs had been left on several side tables after the meal, with a litter of spice bowls and straining equipment. The only relic of the food was a complicated structure on a low central table. It was a tree, sculpted from golden wire, which must have arrived festooned with the fruit for dessert. Bunches of grapes and apricots still hung from its twisting arms and loaded its plinth.

I was still lost in thought, and Hyacinthus was hunched miserably on a dining couch, when the stillness was interrupted by a man arriving explosively.

'Someone has died – yes?'

'Someone may have done,' I answered sombrely, giving the wild apparition a once-over. He had a bald forehead, a wide mouth, a nose two sizes bigger than his other features and darting mid-brown eyes. His stature was unexceptional but he filled extra space by exuding the operational energy of a well-oiled Cretan windmill left with its brake off in a steady gale. 'Who gave you the information?'

'A skivvy ran and told me!'

'Why? What is it to do with you?'

Hyacinthus looked up. 'If you are blaming the food for poisoning Novus,' he told me, with a faint trace of amusement, 'he thinks you're after him – he's the chef, Falco!'

XXXIV

'*Novus!*" The wild-eyed chef grew still. He was visibly upset.

'Steady! What's your name?'

'People here call me Viridovix,' he informed me stiffly. 'And if my master has been poisoned – then you want to talk to me!'

'If you're the chef,' I commented, 'most of the people who ate here tonight will want to do that!'

If I needed confirmation that the Hortensius crowd were a clutch of social amateurs, I would have found it in the fact that they had a Gallic cook.

It was a hundred years since Rome decided to civilise the Gauls; since then we had moved on from genocide at Julius Caesar's hand to taming the tribes with commodities which came cheaper for the Treasury: ceramic bowls, Italian wine, and the finer points of democratic local government. Gaul's response was to fill Rome's artists' studios with life models who specialised in posing as Dying Barbarians, then later to inflict on us a rash of heavy-going middle-class bureaucrats in the mode of Agricola. Many prominent Gauls come from Forum Julii, which was graced by what passed for a university – plus a port, so they could easily ship themselves out to Rome.

I am prepared to concede that one day the three cold Gallic provinces will come up with a contribution to the civilised arts – but nobody is going to convince me that it will be mastery of cuisine. Even so, I never imagined that Hortensius Novus died because his cook came from Gaul. His dinner almost certainly killed him – but that was nothing to do with the cook.

Calming Viridovix was my first priority; he might become less agitated without an audience. I winked at Hyacinthus, who obligingly disappeared.

'I'm Didius Falco. I'm investigating this tragedy – and frankly, after finding your master's body I need a drink!

Considering that he was poisoned, I imagine you'd like to join me – let's try and find something we can assume has not been tampered with . . .'

I sat him down to simmer off boiling point. I found one wine flask, an elegant sky-blue fluted glass affair with a silvery, lustrous finish, which stood with its bung out, breathing, like a special vintage set aside for the after-dinner toasts. The amber wine was brimming well up the neck of the vessel; the diners had plainly overlooked their treat. I took a risk that anything that was meant to be partaken of by the company in common was probably safe. It was a big risk; but Viridovix was obviously badly shaken, and I was desperate.

'This should do us – ' The contents were thick as nectar and probably of great age. Although I took my own cup neat Viridovix asked for spices; I found a little bowl in matching blue glass standing handy beside the flask and, thinking a cook would appreciate flavour, I emptied the entire contents – myrrh and cassia, by the sniff of it – into his cup.

One gulp convinced me the person who should be enjoying this was my expert friend Petronius. It was fifteen-year-old Falernian, if I was any judge. I recognised the way it slid down my throat like molten glass, and the warm burn of the aftertaste. I knew it because Petro used to treat me on his birthday; he always said it was a waste pouring this noble grape juice into a cluck like me, but Falernian should not be drunk alone (a philosophy I encouraged).

We quaffed. The cook immediately looked less pale. 'Better? Viridovix, the fact is Novus has died, but no one is likely to blame you – unless you had a grudge against him.' I wanted to remind the cook that when a free citizen died by violent means the first suspects were his slaves, but to offer a hope of my protection if he was innocent. 'The best thing you can do to help clear yourself – '

'I have done nothing wrong.'

'I realise that.'

'Yet others may not agree with you?' I liked his wry attitude.

'They will if I identify the real killer.' Viridovix looked

uncertain. 'I was hired to prevent this,' I grumbled. 'So yours is not the only reputation under threat, my friend.'

My glum mood had convinced him. We took another swig, then I persuaded him to go through the dinner menu. Obviously a worrier, he had been carrying it around, written on a scrap of parchment which was still in a pouch at his waist:

DINNER FOR SEVEN; HOSTED BY HORTENSIUS NOVUS

Appetisers:

Salad of Lettuce and Mallow Leaves
Peacocks' Eggs
Sausage in a Ring
Baian Oysters Hortensius
Artichoke Hearts
Olives

Main Dishes:

Hare in Rich Wine Sauce
Lobster in Saffron
Pot Roast Pork Crowned with Laurel
Wild Crane
Halibut Pancakes
Fennel; Potted Peas; Stewed Leeks and Onions: Mushrooms

Dessert:

White Cheeses
Fruits Presented on a Hesperides Tree
Purchased Pastries

Wines:

With the Appetiser, *Mulsum (first pressing), warmed with Honey and malabathron flavouring*
With the Main Dishes, *a choice of Red or White Chian Served to Individual Taste*
For the Toasts after Dinner, *Setinum*

'And who devised this elegant collation?' I asked.

'I myself,' boasted Viridovix, then added, 'with some suggestions from Severina Zotica . . .'

I was not ready to think of Zotica. 'Was the evening a success, Viridovix?'

'Certainly.'

'Your creations were well received?'

'Good ingredients,' he shrugged. 'You cannot go wrong. I am free to buy the best.' He was evidently conscientious. I discarded my private joke earlier about shiny meat – and with it any lingering doubt that his master might have been poisoned by accident, simply through eating unsafe food.

Rereading the list, I put some further queries to the cook, not all of them for professional reasons. 'What are Oysters Hortensius?'

'Poached in a light bouillon of white wine, laurel leaves, juniper berries and lovage – '

'Invented by one of the family?'

'Invented by *me*!' I was corrected. Of course. No one as pretentious as these freedmen would allow visitors to be served up with a recipe named after a Celtic slave. Viridovix provided the creative skill; they took the credit.

'Mushrooms make people think twice nowadays . . .' I was referring to the infamous murder of the Emperor Claudius by his wife. Viridovix, who was well down his winecup, merely sniffed. 'Did the pastries come from Minnius along the road?'

'As usual. His work is not bad, and he gives us special rates.

'Because one of the freedmen leases him the stall?'

'I don't know why, I am a cook.'

'How did that come about?'

'Prisoner of war. Novus acquired me,' Viridovix murmured rather sweetly, 'because the slavemaster declared I was a tribal leader.'

'Snobbery!'

'He likes having his porridge stirred by a ruined prince.' The cook was not a bitter man. I enjoyed the light way he mocked his master's vulgarity.

'Were you one?' He smiled in silence. 'Still, perhaps you

were once something better than a cook . . . Was it hard, coming here?'

'This is how I have to live,' Viridovix said quietly.

'So you knuckle down?'

'This is my work – I choose to do it well,' he added, with the dignity of the mildly drunk.

'An individual's privilege!' I must have been drunk too. I noticed he wore the same overdone uniform as Hyacinthus, laden with gaudy braid. The cook also sported a twisted silver torque. 'Did that necklet come with you when you were a prisoner?'

'Hardly! I have been supplied with it.'

'Extra colour? Do I gather from the full fancy dress that you supervised the servers personally?'

'Bad carving can ruin my best work.'

'I intended to ask the chamberlain who ate what.'

'He will not know,' said Viridovix dismissively.

'But *you* noticed?' I hazarded. 'You know what they all took – and what they all left on their plates!'

He glanced at me, pleased by the compliment, then graciously answered my query. 'I should say everyone sampled almost everything. Pollia left every scrap which she could call gristle; Felix looked for fat to peel off; the guest pushed his food around all night –'

'Any reason?'

'A man who does not know how to eat.'

'Or how to live!' I cried, glancing enthusiastically at his menu.

Viridovix accepted the compliment. 'As you say! Novus as usual devoured a large plateful, then called for a further helping. But none of them really noticed what they ate.'

'Disappointing?'

'Normal, Falco. In this house.'

'Does that rankle with you?'

'Not enough,' responded Viridovix shrewdly, 'to make me want to murder them!'

'It's my theory cooks commit their murders when they overheat in the glare of the ovens – then their method is to run amuck with meat cleavers.'

'Poison would be highly unprofessional!' he smiled.

'Tell me – as an observant man – were any of those present nervous?' I carefully avoided naming Severina Zotica.

'All of them,' he replied at once.

'Even Novus?'

'Especially him.' Somehow that was a surprise.

'What accounted for this edginess?' He gave me a wide-mouthed Gallic smile again, full of intelligent charm. I laughed. 'Oh sorry; you will not know details; you are just the cook!'

'Ah, cooks are all ears while people eat their food!'

'Going to tell me?'

'It was because of the business they had gathered to discuss.' I waited. He timed it nicely for effect: 'I think, forming a new partnership.' This time he actually grinned at me.

'In what field?'

'City property.'

'Did you learn any details?'

'No, Falco. When they were ready to talk, all of us serving were dismissed. I expect you want to ask me,' Viridovix suggested quietly, 'if I saw Hortensius Norvus eat or drink anything that nobody else touched?'

'I would probably have worked around to it!'

'Nothing,' the cook disappointed me. 'Most of them dipped into most of the dishes and all of the wines. If poison was in the food, they are all dead. The servers were being attentive – but it was also a party where people made much of passing delicacies to their neighbours – '

'Best behaviour night?'

'Much graciousness. *Too* much.'

'So the general mood was amicable?'

'It seemed so, but the tension was high. I was afraid it would infect the servers; something would be dropped. A harpist had been engaged, but he was paid off without playing. They finished fairly early – '

'Did you see what happened then?'

'Of course; we were waiting to clear . . . After they came out, Crepito and Felix stood in the portico for some time, with their guest – '

'Still discussing?'

'Low voices – something Novus had done seemed to be causing controversy. Then I overheard talk of them going on drinking, but nothing came of it; the guest said he had something else to do. When he left, Felix and Crepito disappeared, heads together.'

'Happy?'

'No; I would say.'

'Where was Novus?'

'Novus had stomped off somewhere.'

'With Severina Zotica?'

'No,' said the cook. 'I should have told you earlier – Severina Zotica was never there!'

At that point a shoe scratched on marble. Viridovix dropped a warning hand on my arm. I turned on my seat. Standing in the doorway in a waft of garlic and frankincense was a man who could only be another of the Hortensius triumvirate.

XXXV

He looked older than Novus, though similar: the same skin tones and well-fed solidity. A fleshy body with a heavy head, and a bushy black moustache which hid the movements of his mouth.

He exhibited a strange lack of curiosity about who I was or what I might be talking about here in their family dining room, with the family cook. Instead, he crossed in front of us and seized the fluted blue flagon from which Viridovix and I had helped ourselves. Luckily I had previously put down my cup on the floor where it was hidden behind my feet. Viridovix somehow let *his* winecup burrow invisibly into the folds of our couch's coverlet. The freedman glanced at the flask, spotting that some of the liquor was missing.

'Novus couldn't wait!' he grumbled.

I detached myself from Viridovix. 'Excuse me, sir. Are you Crepito?'

'Felix.' The one married to Pollia. He was still scowling at the flask as if accusing Hortensius Novus of starting it. Neither Viridovix nor I disillusioned him.

'I'm Marcus Didius Falco. Here on an assignment for your wife . . .' Impossible to tell if he knew anything about it. 'If Hortensius Crepito is anywhere around can I request an urgent interview?'

He lifted the flask. 'Special vintage! Crepito and Novus are both about to join me – '

'Not Novus, sir. Something has happened. May we talk – with Crepito as well, if possible?'

Still more concerned with the flask than this mystery, Hortensius Felix shrugged and led me out.

The three freedmen had meant to marshal and sample their Falernian in a small room on the other side of their main hall. Another which was new to me. It was exuberantly foreign – Nilotic paintings, fans, statuettes of ibis-headed

167

gods, vibrantly striped cushions and ivory couches with sphinxes for arms.

'Our Egyptian salon.' Felix noticed me step back a pace. 'Like it?'

'Every home should have one!' Like a wasps' nest, or a door that will never stay closed.

Another gust of garlic billowed in after us: Crepito – who must have been searching for Novus. 'I can't find the fool; what's he playing at?'

Although Pollia had assured me these freedmen had no direct blood relationship, now that I had seen all three they definitely sprang from the same eastern tribe. Crepito had a smaller moustache than Felix, less flesh than Novus, and a louder, bluffer voice than either, yet the same jowls, swarthiness, and irritable temperament. Novus must have been the youngest of the three.

I introduced myself a second time. 'Hortensius Crepito? I'm Didius Falco, on hire to your wives.' Crepito grunted, so I proceeded on the assumption that I was a known quantity. 'I'm sorry to be the one who breaks this; Hortensius Novus has had a sudden accident – a fatal one.'

Both showed proper evidence of surprise. 'Impossible! We were with him no time ago – ' That came from Crepito.

'I found him myself,' I declared quietly. 'He must have had some kind of seizure, immediately after your meal tonight.'

The two freedmen exchanged glances. 'You mean – '

'Yes; it looks like deliberate poisoning.'

'How?' demanded Felix, with the urgency of a man who realised all too keenly that he had just eaten the same meal as the murdered man.

I reassured them sympathetically. 'What happened to Hortensius Novus seems to have struck with great rapidity. If anyone else was affected, I'm sure they would know by now.'

Despite this, Felix put down the fluted blue flask on a side table, and stepped away hastily.

I was wishing I had met Crepito and Felix earlier. Breaking news to strangers is always unsatisfactory. It's harder to judge which of their reactions are due to shock – and how much of the shock is genuine.

Hortensius Felix had grown sombre and uncommunicative. Crepito requested details, so I described how I had found Novus dead on the floor of the lavatory, which was where he remained. 'You may feel,' I suggested, 'you ought to call in a magistrate before you have him moved.'

'Is that normal?' demanded Felix abruptly. 'Normal to call in the authorities?' Under stress he had revealed for the first time signs that the freedmen had come to Rome from some different culture.

'Best to act responsibly, sir. Most householders report a suspected murder to the Praetor of their own accord, rather than have him sending his aedile round after tip-offs from their neighbours.'

'People don't – '

'People do,' I said grimly. 'Don't expect solidarity from the folks you used to dine with, once the nasty rumours start to fly.' Once again the two of them exchanged glances. 'I know Hortensius Novus was like a brother to you both,' I said, more gently. They received this with a distinct air of reserve. My sense of dealing with foreigners increased. I thought I needed to reassure them again: 'I'm trying to advise you. If the murderer were fleeing from the scene, you should send for the vigilantes to dash in pursuit. But poisoners normally hope they will remain undetected; so they stay put, looking innocent. You can rely on the magistrate's office to investigate tomorrow. Then the matter will be handled with greater sensitivity – ' I meant, polite incompetence.

'Where do you fit in?' Felix asked brusquely.

'I can continue to act for you privately. I'm so angry about this, I may beat the Praetor to the truth.' As businessmen I hoped Crepito and Felix might contribute the local Praetor's name; no luck. 'There was no way I could prevent this,' I told them levelly. 'But I shall not rest until I have exposed the poisoner. Severina has to be the prime suspect. My next move is to interrogate her. I'm intrigued to hear she was an absent guest tonight?'

'She gave some excuse to Novus,' Felix said.

'But she was here earlier?' Both Felix and Crepito shrugged. 'Well, if she thinks being off the scene is enough to clear her, I'll have news for that young lady!' Once again the two freedmen made eye contact.

A silence fell, which warned me to disappear. 'I'll be on my way . . . Ought I to see Sabina Pollia and Hortensia Atilia first?' I hoped to witness the ladies' first reactions to the tragedy.

'Not necessary,' Felix replied, with a curtness which just fell short of hostility. He rang a bell to reinforce the message.

'Fine! Well, I will call again tomorrow of course. I want to pay my condolences in person . . . By the way,' I asked in a neutral tone, just as I was leaving. 'Were relations between you and Novus fairly friendly this evening?'

For once, they avoided looking at each other; in fact the rigidity with which they kept their eyes fixed ahead was suspicious in itself. Both solemnly assured me the party had been relaxed and harmonious.

Thanks to Viridovix I knew they were lying. Which raised an interesting question: why?

I guessed there would be some vivid debate later that night in the Hortensius house. I wished I could overhear it. I wondered what part the two women who employed me would play.

But in the meantime I was speculating on something else: how I would face Severina with news of this crime.

It was only then, as I walked south through the streets full of delivery wagons, trying to avoid having my toes crushed under a cartwheel, that a thought I had been too busy to frame consciously finally found space to present itself: *what was the point of it?*

Hortensius Novus had died too soon. Severina had no hope of inheriting his fortune, except as his wife. At this stage in their affairs she would be lucky to get a sack of apples and his kind regards. Whatever was the woman playing at?

170

XXXVI

Most of Abacus Street lay in darkness. A few dim lights showed, but the passage to Severina's accommodation was pitch-dark; I stubbed my toe on a bucket left outside the cheesemakers. Her house itself looked dead.

It took a quarter of an hour to rouse one of her slaves. I tried to attract attention discreetly, but I could only batter the metal knocker continually. The noise must have carried all over the Caelimontium, though no one threw open their shutters to investigate or protest. How unlike the intolerant types I knew on the Aventine!

The slave recognised me; he made no comment on the time. Perhaps Severina knew other men who called on her during the silent hours. As he admitted me I noticed the house seemed muffled, with few lamps lit, all apparently at rest.

I was left to wait in the room where the girl and I first met. The work on the loom had been changed to a new pattern. I glanced at a library scroll lying on a couch: something about Mauretania. I lost interest. I was listening for movements elsewhere in the house.

The slave put his head round the door curtain. 'She'll come down,' he muttered grudgingly.

'Thanks. Tell me,' I asked, 'have Novus and Severina fixed a date for their wedding yet?'

'Ten days' time.'

'When was that agreed?'

'Earlier this week.'

'So Novus may have announced it to the world at large tonight?'

'She'll be down!' the slave reiterated, giving me a caustic look. He could tell that I was just firing off ballista bolts in the dark.

I never heard her coming.

171

She was tricked out as if the slave really had roused her from her bed: unshod feet; bare-armed in a short white undershift; face slightly puffy; the drift of that coppery hair all spread loose down her back. She probably *had* been in bed: lying awake, waiting for a messenger to bring the news.

'You've got some talking to do, Zotica!' She met my bald scrutiny and held my gaze. I expected that. There would be no faltering from this one. 'Novus is dead.'

'Novus?' She said it, quickly, then frowned as if confused. 'Did you know?'

'*Dead?*' she repeated.

'Keep it up, Zotica! I teased insultingly.

Severina drew an indignant breath. 'Do you need to be so brutal?' She came into the room, putting both hands to her face. 'What has happened? Tell me properly.'

'I found your intended tonight, face down in a lavatory. Poisoned, Severina. Don't tell me this is unexpected news.'

She bit her lip when I mentioned the details, but she was angry now. Excellent. She walked over to a couch and sat, apparently shivering. 'What time is it, Falco?' I had no idea. 'The question people always ask,' she murmured abstract-edly, 'when time no longer matters anyway . . .'

The stricken look failed to convince me. 'Cut the pathos! What kept you from the dinner party?'

Her face clouded. 'I was feeling unwell, Falco. Women's problems.' Her chin came up defiantly as she hugged her stomach. 'You know what I mean!'

'Or I'm supposed to be too embarrassed to ask? Forget it! I grew up with five sisters, Zotica. Victorina was the prize artist – she could make "a bad time of the month" last three weeks, especially if there was some boring religious festival she wanted to miss.'

'I did go up to the house this afternoon,' Severina said shortly. 'But in the end I could not face a long evening of strained formality among people who make no secret of their dislike for me –'

'Yes; you would need courage – to recline alongside your victim while he sampled the poisoned sauce!'

'That's slander, Falco!' she fought back. 'I went to reassure the cook. Novus has been fussing ever since he

172

sent out the invitations – ' I noticed she used the present tense, the way people continue to do after a genuine bereavement: a delicate touch! 'It was a big responsibility for Viridovix – '

'Whatever possessed Novus to buy himself a Gallic cook? If a man must have a chef from the ends of the Empire, surely he turns to Alexandria?'

'You know how they are in that house – their captive "prince" is a novelty.'

'He's certainly a rarity: he makes the best of things.' I could see this temporary diversion was making no impression, so I abandoned it. 'Tell me about tonight's party. Why the grand performance? Who were the guests?'

'Appius Priscillus.'

For a moment I was at a loss. 'Oh the property tycoon! The beater-up of fruitsellers. What is his link with the Hortensius crew?'

'Same interests. Leasing; property; land use. Relations between their two empires had deteriorated badly. They were all acting against their own interests by prolonging the rivalry, so the dinner party was suggested to resolve their differences.'

'*Who* suggested it?' I asked, frowning. I already knew.

'I did. But, Falco, bringing them together was your idea originally ... Excuse me a moment.' Severina murmured abruptly. She looked as if she was going to be sick.

She slipped from the room. I gave her a few minutes, then set off to look for her.

Intuition led me into an anteroom alongside the gracious triclinium where Novus and I had been given lunch. Severina stood motionless in the darkness. I held up a lamp I had carried in with me. 'Are you all right?'

'So much to think about.'

I stepped closer carefully. 'Zotica?' Her intense quiet and fixed gaze were signs of true shock. For a moment she stood with one hand to her forehead. Then she started to cry.

Restraining my annoyance, I said, 'The first rule of an informer is: women who burst into tears are up to no good.'

173

'Keep out of their way then!' Severina snapped. I put two fingers under her elbow and moved her to a couch. She sat down, without arguing, then turned away and sobbed. I perched alongside and let her get on with it. 'Sorry about that,' she murmured finally, bending forwards to mop her face on the skirt of her shift. I had a glimpse of knee, which I found oddly distracting.

She breathed slowly, as if coming to terms with some unexpected trouble. She was obviously acting. She had to be. I remembered the Praetor's clerk Lusius saying that Severina was naturally undemonstrative under stress, and friend Lusius had seemed observant enough. Yet I still felt that the need to release all this emotion had been partly genuine.

'I hope you've got your story composed for the enquiring magistrate.' She stared ahead, still in a kind of trance. 'Better still,' I suggested, 'why not tell your nice Uncle Marcus exactly what happened, and let him take charge?'

Severina sighed, stretching her minute feet in front of her. Her feet, and what I could see of her legs (more than usual), were freckled; so were her bare arms. 'Oh leave it alone, Falco!'

'You are not going to talk to me?'

'If I did poison Novus, certainly not!'

'Did you?'

'No. Juno and Minerva – if all I wanted was his money, what would be the point?'

'I had thought of that.'

'Brilliant! So what twisted explanation have you come up with instead?'

'I feel certain that you killed him – but I have no idea why.'

She had jumped to her feet. 'Didius Falco, you have no reason to be here! Either arrest me, or go away – '

'What are you doing, Zotica?'

'I'm fetching a wine jug from the dining room – then I intend getting drunk!'

My heart was pounding out a warning – but I told myself this might be the only chance I ever had of persuading Severina to say something indiscreet. 'Oh sit down, woman!

I'll get the jug. Take some advice from an expert: getting drunk is quicker, as well as much more cheerful, if you have a friend to help!'

XXXVII

Why do I do these things? (Why does anyone?)

I found cups on a sideboard, and a half-filled amphora of something which tasted brash enough for the kind of deliberate drinking which is bound to make you ill. Severina fetched a ewer of cold water. We did not bother with flavourings. Our mutual suspicion would provide a bitter spice if we needed it.

We ended up sitting on the floor, leaning our heads against a couch behind us. At first we drank in silence.

Even after five years as an informer, finding a corpse always unsettled me. I let the memory come surging in as it was trying to do: Novus, bare-buttocked in that undignified spasm. Novus, pressed face-down against the floor slabs, with that expression of stark terror . . .

'Are you all right, Falco?' Severina asked quietly.

'Murder offends me. Like me to describe the death scene?'

I noticed that her knuckles whitened as she gripped the stem of her ceramic cup. 'I can probably endure it!'

I had told her the worst of it. I spared myself dwelling on any more details.

Severina topped up her winecup. We had been serving ourselves – not letting formal manners interfere. It was like drinking with a man.

'Do you do this often?' I asked.

'No!' she conceded. 'What about you?'

'Only when the memory of the headache I had the last time has faded . . .'

'If we are going to do this, shall I call you by your first name?'

'No.'

She chewed the side of her thumb for a moment. 'I thought you were my nice Uncle Marcus?'

'I'm Falco – and I'm not nice.'

'I see! Drunk but distant!' She laughed. Whenever Severina laughed she sounded arrogant – and that irritated me. 'I think you and I have more in common than you admit, Falco.'

'We have nothing in common!' I splashed more liquor into my cup. 'Novus is dead. What next, Zotica?'

'Nothing.'

'*What* was the wrong word. I should have asked, *Who?*'

'Don't be so offensive!' she told me – but she said it with a half-smile and a glint behind these pale eyelashes. She was daring me to ask fiercer questions. Interrogation was a thrill.

I knew better than to fight a suspect who so loved to be the centre of attention. Instead, I stretched lazily. 'Never again, eh? Sounds like what I always used to say, when some flighty piece took my cash and broke my heart.'

'Past tense?' Severina immediately wormed at me, unable to resist prying.

'Too old. Flighty bits want boys, who go like fire in bed and let themselves be bossed about – '

'You're romancing, Falco,' she scolded, as if something had suddenly made her more wary. 'Why can you never hold a straight-forward conversation?'

'I get bored,' I admitted. 'That straightforward enough?' We both fizzled with tipsy laughter.

Severina was sitting cross-legged, with her back very straight. She was on my left. So I had lolled with my right knee bent, supporting my winecup hand. It enabled me to turn inwards, and watch her unobtrusively.

She filled her cup again. 'I'm drinking more than you!'

'I had noticed.'

'You intend to stay sober, so you can winkle out my secrets . . .'

'I like a woman with secrets – '

'You don't like me! Stop inventing . . . I should have asked,' she murmured, with what she probably thought was a sly approach, 'if anyone is waiting up for you at home?'

'No.' I drained my cup. The action was more drastic than I intended; I nearly choked.

'You surprise me!' she taunted in a soft voice.

When I stopped coughing I said, 'You were right the other day; I overreached myself.'

'Tell me!'

'Not much to tell. One of us is yearning to settle down and start a family; the other wants to stay footloose.' Severina looked uncertain, as if she missed the joke. 'Women are so feckless!' I complained. 'They can't take the responsibility – '

'So how will you entrap her?' Severina now joined in the game, though with a scornful expression.

'I have my methods.'

'You men are so devious!'

'Once she discovers my wonderful cooking and my sweet devoted nature, I'll tie her down . . .'

'Does she help you in your work?'

'You asked me that before. I keep her out of my work.'

'I wondered if you sent her to spy on people in places you can't go?'

'I'd never let her go anywhere I couldn't go myself.'

'How considerate!' Severina said.

We had both stopped drinking and were staring ahead like crass philosophers. The effect of a harsh young grape-pressing on top of the subtle Falernian I had quaffed earlier, not to mention the smooth dinner wines Titus had served up at the Palace, was beginning to make me wonder if it would be possible to stand upright when I wanted to. Even Severina was now breathing drowsily.

'A night of revelations!'

I grunted, feeling bilious. 'Bit one-sided so far! The plan was that I would open up, then lure you into a confession . . .'

'Plan, Falco? You won't wheedle confessions out of *me* by such a transparent trick as getting me drunk!'

'You got yourself drunk.'

'I hate you when you're logical.'

'And I hate you – Oh forget it,' I sighed. 'I'm too tired to rise to the challenge of cheap dialogue.'

'You're falling asleep!' Severina chortled next. Perhaps I was. Perhaps I just wanted her to think so. (Perhaps I could no longer help myself.)

When I made no answer she tipped back her head, groaning. Then she pulled from her finger the red jasper ring with the two hands clasped; she tossed it wryly in the air, caught it, then set it down beside her on the floor. A spark seemed to leap from the gemstone to glint in her hair. Her action was not irreverent, yet obviously marked a formal end of her betrothal to the dead man. 'Nothing left to do . . . no one who needs me . . . no one to turn to . . . What is it all for, Falco?'

The jewel she had removed looked almost as heavy as the one Novus himself had worn: far too massive for Severina's fingers, which were tiny as a child's. 'For profit, lady! That ring at least was a decent piece of gold!'

Severina moved the jasper ring dismissively on the mosaic. 'Gold wears thin. Like the love it pretends to represent.'

'Some lasts.'

'Do you really believe that?' she demanded. 'Does your famous ladyfriend?'

I laughed. 'She's a realist. She keeps me on a short rope, just in case.'

After a moment Severina lifted her right hand, showing the cheap ring with a crudely etched Venus and a small blob that was meant to be the Cupid nestling her knee. 'Now copper – ' she declared obscurely, '*that*'s for eternity!'

'Eternity comes cheap! Did you know, copper is named for the mountains of Cyprus, where the oxhide ingots come from?' I collect obscure facts. 'And Cyprus is the birthplace of Venus, so that's why copper is the metal of Love – '

'It gives you verdigris in the soul, Falco!' she murmured.

'You ought to see a doctor about that.' I refused to ask her what she meant. There is nothing you can do with a woman when she wants to be mysterious. 'So who gave you the copper ring?'

'Someone who was a slave with me.'

'He have a name?'

'Only among the Shades in the Underworld.'

179

I smiled wryly. 'Like so many of your friends!'

Severina leaned to collect the flagon. I raised my palm in protest but she shared the last of the wine between us.

She sat back, slightly closer. We drank, slowly, both deep in the glum privacy that passes for thought when drunk.

'I ought to be leaving.'

'We can give you a bed.'

What I desperately needed was untroubled sleep. In this house I would lie awake expecting a mechanical ceiling to lower itself and crush me . . . I shook my head.

'Thank you for staying anyway.' Severina compressed her lips, like a girl who was all alone but trying to be brave. 'I needed somebody tonight – '

I turned my head. She turned hers. I was two digits away from kissing her. She knew it, and made no attempt to move away. If I did, I knew what would happen: I would start to feel responsible.

Leaning on the couch behind me, I hoisted myself to my feet.

Severina scrambled upright too, holding out her hand for me to steady her. The wine, and the sudden motion, made us both sway. For a moment we lurched together, still clutching hands.

Had it been Helena, I would have found my arms were round her. Severina was smaller; I would have to stoop. She was not the birdlike bony type who gave me goose-pimples; under her loose shift I could see inviting flesh on her. Her skin always looked clean and smooth; it was poignantly perfumed with some familiar oil. In the lamp-light, and so close to me, the wintery grey of her eyes was suddenly a deeper, more interesting, blue. We both knew what I was thinking. I was relaxed, and susceptible. I was missing my lady; I too needed company.

She made no attempt to stand on tiptoe; she wanted the decision – and the blame – to be all mine.

Too tired out and tipsy to think fast, I searched for a way to escape with some tact. 'Bad idea, Zotica!'

'Not tempted?'

180

'Too far gone,' I pretended gallantly. At that moment I felt so overcome with weariness I could easily have agreed to any procedure which allowed me to lie down. 'Another time,' I promised.

'I doubt it!' she answered – pretty vindictively.

I managed to stagger home.

I had not been back to my Piscina Publica apartment since Anacrites arrested me. I would have been relieved to find a message from Helena Justina: some signal that she missed me, some reward for my own good faith. There was nothing.

Still, I could hardly blame a senator's daughter if she was too proud to make overtures. And, having said I would wait to hear from her, there was no way on earth that *I* was going to approach her first . . .

I went to bed, cursing women.

Severina didn't want me; she wanted me to want her; not the same thing.

Nor, I thought angrily (for the drink was now making me belligerent), was there any way that a pair of cool blue eyes would make me forget the girl who really made me furious; the girl I wanted to think about; the girl whose brown eyes once said so frankly that *she* wanted *me* . . .

Frustrated beyond endurance, I crashed my clenched fist as hard as I could against the bedroom wall. Somewhere close by, within the building fabric, a shower of falling material rattled disturbingly as if I had shifted a joist. The debris trickled for a long time.

In the darkness I moved my hand over the wall surface. Unable to find any damage to the plasterwork, I lay rigid with guilt and foreboding, listening for noises.

Pretty soon I forgot to listen and fell asleep.

XXXVIII

I woke earlier than I might have done, due to my dreams.
Dreams which disturbed me so badly I won't bother you by
revealing what they were.

To avoid further nightmares I sat up and dressed – a
drawn-out procedure, given that it only consisted of pulling
on a clean tunic over the crumpled one I had slept in, then
finding my favourite boots where Ma had hidden them.
During this struggle, I could hear some sort of racket going
on. The old woman upstairs was bawling away at some poor
soul as if he had thieved her only daughter's virginity.

'You can only regret it!' a man's voice raged. Pleased that
for once *I* was an innocent party in her delusions, I stuck
my head out just as Cossus the letting agent tumbled downstairs past my door. He looked flustered.

'Trouble?' I asked.

'She's a mad old bag – ' he mumbled, glancing back over
one shoulder as if he feared the woman would call down a
witch's curse on him. 'Some people never know what's good
for them – '

He seemed disinclined to dispel my curiosity so I con-
tented myself with chivvying, 'What's happening about that
water-carrier you promised me?'

'Give us a chance . . .'

This time I let him depart without a tip.

I left home without any breakfast. Nursing a sore head, I
set off to see the women on the Pincian. It took me some
time to get there. My feet had apparently taken a vow
against walking anywhere today. I fooled them by hiring a
mule.

Novus was being honoured in a brave style on his departure across the Styx. Throughout the house there was a
dark smell of embalming oils and incense. Instead of a few
indicative cyprus boughs, each doorway was guarded by a

182

pair of whole trees. They must have uprooted a small forest. Trust this lot to create a spectacle even out of a funeral.

The slaves were in strict black. The cloth looked brand-new. The freedwomen must have had sempstresses working all night.

When I managed to get in to see them (for they were putting on a show of being too overwrought for visitors), Pollia and Atilia were veiled in elaborate swathes of exquis-ite white: the upper-class colour for mourning wear (more flattering).

I muttered condolences then squared up to the situation: 'You may ask me how I dare to show my face . . .'

Sabina Pollia cackled briefly. Grief can affect some people with irritability. As usual her face was beautifully presented, yet today it was apparent that her voice was ten years older than the face.

I braced myself. 'Look; I did my best – which is all I ever promised you.' Hortensia Atilia's huge dark eyes, which looked more frightened than sorrowful, fastened on me anxiously. Sabina Pollia glared. 'You were right about Sev-erina – though her timing seems inexplicable . . . There was no way to prevent what happened. But she won't escape justice this time – '

'How can you be so confident?' Pollia asked me cuttingly.

'Experience.'

'You were confident before!'

'No; I was cautious before. Now I'm angry – '

'The matter has been reported to the Praetor,' Pollia broke in.

'Yes; I suggested that myself – ' I already guessed what was coming.

'Then *I* suggest we leave the Praetor to deal with it!'

After the whiplash of scorn from Pollia subsided, I started again cautiously: 'You commissioned me because I worked for the Palace, which happens to be where I was detained last evening – '

'Our husbands have instructed us to discontinue your services.' This was Atilia, who had always appeared the more timid of the pair. Neither of these women would care a bent hairpin for what their husbands said; Felix and

Crepito were mere ciphers. But one excuse was as good as another when clients were set on dismissing me.

'Of course,' I said, 'you must respect your husband's wishes!'

'You failed, Falco!' Pollia insisted.

'Apparently!'

Even with a raging hangover I knew how to be professional. They were both tense, expecting an angry outburst; I could relieve my feelings later so I disappointed them. 'Ladies, I never stick around if I have lost my clients' confidence.'

I saluted them politely (since I wanted them to pay me). Then I left.

The end of the case. Ah well; if I failed to recruit any other business I could always go back to working for the Palace.

Signed off.

Signed off *again*! It was always happening to me. Somehow the only clients who ever commissioned me were vacillating types. Hardly had I drummed up interest in their tawdry lives, than they changed their fretful little minds about needing me.

I could have solved this one. I would have enjoyed doing so. Never mind; for a few weeks' surveillance I could now charge the two women extortionate expenses, then nip off out of it before the messy part. It was the best way to do business, for a philosophical man. Let the local law and order people give themselves headaches puzzling how Severina managed it this time. Let the Pincian magistrate try to bring her to court where the Praetor Corvinus on the Esquiline had failed. I was laughing. I could send a bill for my expenses, spend some time at the baths, enjoy myself, then read about official bungling in the *Daily Gazette* . . .

But that was not the end of the case.

I was about to stride haughtily past the ornate lodge where the Hortensius porter lurked, when I spotted somebody waiting nearby in the shade: thin arms and a black wire moustache bisecting his face.

'Hyacinthus!'

He was waiting for me. 'Falco – can we talk?'

'Certainly – '

'I have to be quick. We have all been ordered not to speak to you.'

'Why's that?' He glanced nervously up towards the house. I drew him off the main path and we squatted on our haunches beneath an elderly pine tree. 'Never mind why then – what's up?'

'You were talking to Viridovix – '

'Yes; I intended to have another word today – '

Hyacinthus laughed briefly, then picked up a pine cone and hurled it among the trees. 'Did they pay you off?' he demanded.

'Well I'm sent off – it remains to be seen whether I get paid!'

'Just present your bill. They don't want trouble.'

'Trouble? What trouble?'

He was silent for a moment, then out it came: 'You won't be able to talk to the cook, again. Viridovix is dead!'

XXXIX

As soon as he said it I felt a cold sweat. 'What happened?'

'He died last night. In his sleep.'

'The same way as Novus?'

'Don't think so. He looked quite peaceful. It appeared to be natural – '

'Hah!'

'He was healthy,' frowned Hyacinthus.

'Cooks can always scavenge nourishment.' Viridovix was no age either; thirty, I reckoned. Like me; a boy. 'Is anyone looking into it?'

'No chance! Someone suggested foul play to Felix – but he retorted that maybe Viridovix was so ashamed Hortensius Novus died after one of his meals, he committed suicide – '

'Is that likely?'

'You met him!' Hyacinthus scoffed.

'Yes! Are the rest of you going to do anything about it?'

'If the freedmen say no, how can we? He was,' pointed out my companion dourly, 'just a slave!' So were his friends.

I chewed a fingernail. 'The Praetor who is investigating what happened to Novus ought to hear of this!'

Hyacinthus scuffled to his feet in the loose earth. 'Forget that, Falco! The Praetor has a large loan underwritten by Crepito; he is bound to co-operate. The family want Novus buried quietly – and no other distractions.'

'I thought they wanted to protect his interests? I thought that was why they hired me!'

Hyacinthus looked shamefaced. 'I could never understand why they chose you,' he let slip. 'You had a reputation for bungling . . .'

'Oh thanks!' I bit back an oath. Then I spat it out after all. It was one of my brother's: particularly colourful: the slave looked impressed. 'If they believed that, why commission me?'

'Perhaps they thought you would be cheap.'

186

'Then perhaps that was just one of their mistakes!'

I remembered Helena saying that what impressed these ghastly people was expense.

Even without seeing the body I shared the runabout's doubts about the cook's death. 'Viridovix was poisoned too,' I said. 'Though not with the same violent paralytic that dispatched Novus. 'You saw both corpses afterwards: do you agree?' The runabout nodded. I made up my mind. 'I needed to talk to Viridovix in more detail about yesterday afternoon. Now he's gone, can you possibly find me someone observant who would have been in the kitchens while the food for the dinner party was being prepared?'

He looked uncertain. I reminded him that no one else would lift a finger to avenge the cook's death. Fellow feelings made him promise to find someone who would help. I told him my new address. Then, since he was growing anxious about being seen here with me, I let him scamper back to the house.

I sat on under the tree, thinking about the man from Gaul. I had liked him. He accepted his fate but kept his own style. He had integrity. He was dignified.

I thought about him for a long time. I owed him that.

He had definitely been murdered. It must have been a slower poison than the one which struck down Novus, a less vicious kind. Presumably this too was intended for Novus – though I could not rule out the possibility he was not the only victim hoped for.

Nor could I yet be certain that the same person had prepared both poisons. Or why at least two different attempts had been made; insurance, possibly. But I did know how the second drug was administered; that would haunt me for a long time. The poison must have been among the bitter-smelling spices which the cook took in his cup of Falernian.

I still remembered how I mixed the wine for him: I had killed Viridovix myself.

As I rode the hired mule south again, part of me was now saying this case would not be over until I had solved it, even if I had to work without a fee. That was the brave and noble part. Another part (thinking of Viridovix) merely felt sordid and tired.

I went home. There was no point going anywhere else. In particular, there was no point tangling with Severina Zotica until I had some unbreakable hold over that freckled female snake.

Half an hour later she knocked on my door. I was thinking. To help, I was doing something practical.

'Holiday, Falco?'

'Mending a chair.' I was in a pedantic, bad-tempered mood.

She stared at the battered wicker article, which had a semicircular back curving into boudoir arms. 'That's a woman's chair.'

'Maybe when I've mended the chair I'll get a woman to go with it.'

The redhead smiled nervously.

She was wearing not black exactly, but some dark purple berry-juice shade; in her unconventional way this managed to imply greater respect for the dead than Pollia and Atilia had shown with all their yardage of dramatic white.

I continued my work. The job had turned into one of those treasures where you start off intending to wind back a few strands of loose material, but end up dismantling half the piece of furniture and rebuilding it from scratch. I had already spent two hours on it.

To fend off Severina's annoying curiosity I snapped, 'The chair comes from my sister Galla. My mother produced some new cane. It's a pig of a job. And all the time I'm doing it I know that once Galla sees the thing serviceable, she will coo "*Ooh, Marcus, you are clever!*" – and ask to have her chair back again.'

'You have the cane too dry,' Severina informed me. 'You ought to dampen it with a sponge – '

'I can manage without advice.' The cane I was weaving snapped, halfway along a row. I fetched a wet sponge.

Severina found herself a stool. 'You go to a lot of trouble.'

'Thoroughness pays.'

She sat quiet, waiting for me to calm down. I had no intention of obliging. 'An aedile came to see me today, on behalf of the Pincian Hill magistrate.'

I negotiated a tough end change, tugging at the cane to keep the work taut. 'No doubt you bamboozled him.' I repositioned the chair between my knees.

'I answered his questions.'

'And he blithely went away?'

Severina looked prim. 'Perhaps *some* people can see that without a motive, accusing me is illogical.'

'Perhaps the Praetor likes a holiday in August.' I soothed my aching fingers on the wet sponge. 'Anyway, here's another bonus: so long as you can fend off this aedile of his, no one else will bother you.'

'What?'

I got up from my knees, righted the chair, and sat in it. That put me higher than her slight, neat, shawl-wrapped figure as she still hugged her knees on my stool. 'I'm off the case, Zotica. Pollia and Atilia have dispensed with my services.'

'Stupid of them!' Severina said. 'Anyone who cared about Novus would have let you carry on.'

'They always did seem strangely half-hearted.'

'I'm not surprised.' I suppressed any reaction. Whatever was to follow could only mean trouble. Still, with Severina that was nothing new. 'The fact they have dismissed you,' she continued, 'proves everything I say.'

'How's that?'

'Pollia and Atilia hired you to throw suspicion on me.'

'Why?'

'To disguise their own ambitions.'

189

'What ambitions would those be?'

Severina took a deep breath. 'There was serious friction between the three freedmen. Crepito and Felix disagreed with the way Novus handled their business affairs. Novus hated trouble, and wanted to end the partnership.'

Much as I distrusted her, this reminded me what Viridovix had said about sensing disagreement among the freedman following their dinner. 'The other two would lose badly if he broke with them?'

'Novus had always been the leader; he had all the initiative and ideas.'

'So he would take a large sector of their business away with him?'

'Exactly. Meeting me had not improved matters; if he married — especially if we had children — his present heirs would suffer.'

'Felix and Crepito?'

'Felix and Crepito's son. Atilia is obsessive about the boy; she was relying on an inheritance to found the child's career.'

'What about Pollia?'

'Pollia wants to plunder her husband's share of the cash.'

What she said was making sense. I hated that: having established in my own mind that Severina was a villainess, I could not bring myself to readjust. 'Are you claiming that the freedmen, or their wives, would go so far as to kill Novus?'

'Maybe they were all in it together.'

'Don't judge other people by your own perverted standards! But I have to agree, the timing of the murder — when you and Novus had just announced the date of your wedding — does look significant.'

Severina clapped her small white hands triumphantly. 'But it's worse than that: I told you Novus had enemies.' She had told me a number of things that were probably lies. I laughed. 'Listen to me, Falco!' I made a small gesture of apology, yet she kept me in suspense for a moment, sulkily.

'What enemies?'

'Apart from Crepito and Felix, he had also antagonised Appius Priscillus.

'Do I gather *he* runs a rival organisation with overlapping interests? Tell me about that, Severina. What was the form at last night's dinner?'

'A reconciliation; I've already told you. It was Priscillus I tried to warn you about before.'

'He was threatening Novus?'

'Novus, and the other two as well. That was why Atilia hardly lets her son out of her sight – one of the threats was to abduct him.' I knew Atilia took the child to school herself, which was highly unusual.

'So which of these multiple suspects are you fingering?' I asked sarcastically.

'That's the problem – I just don't know. Falco, what would you say if I asked to hire you myself?'

I'd call for help, probably. 'Frankly the last thing I want is a commission from a professional bride – especially when she's midway between husbands, and tends to react unpredictably – '

'You mean what nearly happened last night?' Severina coloured.

'We can both forget last night.' My voice sounded lower than I had intended. I noticed that she started slightly, so her shawl slipped back, revealing her flame-coloured hair. 'We were drunk.' Severina gave me a straighter look that I liked.

'Will you work for me?' she insisted.

'I'll think about it.'

'That means no.'

'It means I'll think about it!'

At that moment I was ready to throw the gold-digger downstairs. (In fact I was in two minds whether to give up my career altogether, hire a booth and take up chair mending . . .)

There was a knock; Severina must have left my outer door ajar, and before I could answer it was pushed open. A man staggered in, gasping. His predicament was clear.

He had just struggled up two flights of stairs – to deliver the biggest fish I ever saw.

XLI

I stood up. Very slowly.

'Where do you want him, legate?' He was a small man. As he lurched in from the corridor he was holding my present up by its mouth because he could not get his arms round it: the fish looked almost as long as its deliverer was tall. It was wider than he was.

'Slap him down here . . .'

The man groaned, leaned back, then launched the fish sideways so it landed across the small table I used to lean my elbows on sometimes. Then, being a game trier, he jumped up and down, each time hauling my slippery present further on. Severina bobbed upright, daunted by a tailfin the size of an ostrich feather fan, which stuck over the edge of the table a foot from her nose.

There was no smell. He was in beautiful condition.

The delivery man seemed to take sufficient pleasure from the drama his arrival had caused – but I decided for once to squeeze out the half-aureus I kept in my tunic for really serious gratuities.

'Thanks, legate! Enjoy your party . . .' He left, with a much lighter step than when he came.

'Party?' hinted Severina, looking coy. 'Are you going to invite me?'

I felt so weak I might have let her persuade me. It would have created a Mount Olympus of complications for myself.

Then the door swung open a second time, to admit someone who never reckoned to knock if there was half a chance of interrupting something scandalous. 'Hello Mother!' I cried valiantly.

Ma raked Severina Zotica with the look she reserved for unpleasant squashy things found at the back of dark kitchen shelves. Then she glanced at my extravagant present. 'That fishmonger of yours needs a talking-to! When did you start buying by the yard?'

'Must be a mix-up: all I ordered was a cuttlefish.'

'That's you all over. Palace ideas on pigsty money . . . You'll want a big plate!'

I sighed. 'I can't keep this, Ma. I'd better send him as a gift to Camillus Verus; do myself some good that way – '

'It's one way to show your respect for the Senator . . . Pity. I could have made a good stock from the bones.' My mother was still blocking Severina out of the conversation, but letting her know that I had influential friends. Redheads always upset my mother. And she generally disapproved of my female clients.

Ma made herself scarce so I could rid us of this inconvenience. 'Severina, I'll have to think about your offer.'

'Will you have to ask your mother?' she sniped.

'No; I have to consult my barber, look up the "black days" on my calendar, sacrifice a beautiful virgin, and peruse the internal organs of a sheep with twisted horns . . . I know where I can get the sheep, but virgins are harder to come by and my barber's out of town. Give me twenty-four hours.' She wanted to argue, but I gestured at the turbot so she could see that I was serious about having things to organise.

My mother promptly reappeared, stepping out of Severina's way with insulting delicacy. Severina retaliated by giving me a much sweeter smile than usual before she closed the door behind her.

'Watch that one!' muttered Ma.

Ma and I gazed sadly at the giant fish.

'I'm bound to regret giving him away.'

'You'll never get another!'

'I'm itching to keep him – but how could I cook him?'

'Oh I dare say we can improvise . . .'

'Camillus Verus is never going to approve of me, anyway – '

'No,' agreed Ma, obliquely. 'You could invite him to eat some of it.'

'Not here!'

'Invite Helena then.'

'Helena won't come.'

'She never will if nobody asks her? Have you upset her?'

'Why do you assume it's my fault? We had a few words.'

'You never change! . . . So that's settled,' decided my mother. 'Just a family party. Mind you,' she added, in case this news had somehow cheered me up, 'I always reckon turbot is a tasteless fish.'

XLII

Sometimes I feared my mother must have led a double life. I resisted the thought, because that is not what a decent Roman boy wants to suspect about the woman who gave him birth.

'Where on earth have you eaten turbot?'

'Your Uncle Fabius caught one once.' That made sense. No one in our family had the nous to present a turbot to the Emperor; anything my relations got their hands on went straight in the pot. 'It was a baby. Nowhere near as big as this.'

'If Fabius caught it, that was predictable!' Everything about Uncle Fabius was small: a family joke.

'You don't want him bitter. I'll take out the gills for you,' volunteered mother.

I let her. She liked to delude herself I still needed looking after. Besides, I enjoyed the thought of my tiny, elderly mother laying into something quite that big.

Ideally I would bake him in an oven. That called for a clay pot (no time to have one made), then entrusting him to the dopey rakemen at some public bakery. I could have built my own oven, but apart from having to lug the bricks home I was frightened of the fire risk and strongly suspected that any structure big enough to contain this turbot might cause my floor to cave in.

I decided to poach him. Flatfish only need gentle simmering. I would have to find a huge pan, but for that I had had an idea. In the roof space at my mother's house, where members of the family stored unattractive New Year gifts, was a huge oval shield which my late brother Festus brought home. It was made of some bronzed alloy, and Festus maintained it was a pricey Peloponnesian antique. I upset him by swearing it had to be Celtic – which meant it was just another cheap souvenir my daft brother had won in a

195

bet or picked up on the quay at Ostia. Festus would have been even more annoyed at me turning his dusty prize into a monstrous fishkettle.

I nipped off to mother's. When I clambered up to get the shield I found a nest of mice in one end, but I tipped them out and said nothing. The handle inside had already lost one securing bolt when Festus was larking about; the other was rusted fast with verdigris but I managed to shear it off (cutting open a few knuckles). The pointed boss on the front might cause problems. I reckoned I could suspend the shield on two or three steaming pans of water over braziers and just keep the fish going if I heated his liquor first. I spent an hour burnishing the metal, washed it at a public fountain, then carried it home. It was indeed big enough for the turbot – but too shallow. I put him in, filled up with water, and found it reached the rim of the shield before it fully covered the fish. The scalding stock would swoosh about. And turning the turbot over half-way through cooking time might be difficult . . .

As usual my mother let me devise my own solution, then sat at home brooding how my brilliant plan would fail. While I was still staring at the half covered fish in the shield she rattled into my apartment, almost invisible under a huge copper washtub from Lenia's laundry yard. We tried not to think what might have been trampled clean in it. 'I gave it a good scrub . . .' The tub was shorter than the Celtic shield, but the turbot could be crammed in diagonally if I turned up his great triangular head and his tail. Ma had also brought some cabbage nets to lift him out after he turned gelatinous.

Now I was ready.

I invited my mother, my best friend Petronius and Petro's wife Silvia, with a couple of my relatives. At least my family was so large that nobody could expect me to entertain the entire tribe at once. I chose Maia, to thank her for the betting-token feat, and Junia, to repay her for the bed. I did not invite my brothers-in-law, but they came anyway.

I told the guests they could arrive early, since watching the fish cooked would be part of the fun. None of them needed encouragement. They all turned up before I had

196

time to look out a clean tunic or go for a bathe. I let them wander about criticising my new quarters and rearranging my personal property, while I worried over the fish.

I was planning for us to eat in the room I had earmarked as my office, but they all brought their stools and crowded into the living room, where they could get in my way and clammer advice.

'What stock are you using, Marcus?'

'Just water with wine and bay leaves; I don't want to destroy the natural flavour; it's supposed to be delicate – '

'You ought to add a dash of fish pickle – Maia, shouldn't he add fish pickle?'

'I reckon he ought to cook it in the sauce – '

'No; the sauce will be handled separately – '

'You're going to regret that, Marcus! Is it Saffron or Onion?'

'Caraway.'

'Caraway? Ooh! Marcus is making Caraway Sauce – '

In the midst of this babble, I was pestling the herbs for my sauce (should have been lovage but Maia had thought I asked her to bring parsley; should have included thyme but I had left my pot at Fountain Court). Someone knocked; Petronius answered the door for me. 'Camillus Verus has sent you a reading couch – where do you want it?' Petro bawled. I wanted the couch in my office, but that was where I had laid out everything for our meal (everything that had not yet been removed again by my visitors). 'Shall we stick it in your bedroom?'

'Not enough space; try the empty one opposite – ' One of my braziers flared up dangerously, so I had to leave him to it.

My mother and Junia had chosen this moment to hang up door curtains for me, so I could not see out into the corridor for their arms waving amongst folds of striped material. Both my brothers-in-law had involved themselves in banging up nails to carry the lintel string; the simple task of putting up a straight line had developed into a major surveying project. Whatever was happening in the rest of the house I could hear distressing indications of damage to both my doorframes and Petronius' good temper, but the liquor for my fish was beginning to sizzle on the sides of the washtub so I had to ignore the raised voices outside. I was red-faced from stabilising a brazier beneath the weight of the hot washcopper; I had just heaved up the turbot into my arms to introduce him to the pan when I heard Maia shriek, 'Sorry; this is a private family party; Didius Falco is not on call to clients – '

There was an uneasy lull. I turned round, fish and all. For one horrid moment I expected Severina, but it was far worse. Petronius, with desperate eyes, was shepherding someone in the doorway, someone who was a stranger to most of my family, but certainly not to me ... Helena Justina.

For a moment she failed to grasp the situation. 'Marcus! I thought you must have been developing other interests, but I never expected to find you with your arms locked round a *fish* – '

Then the lull sank to a silence. And all the sparkle died in her eyes, as Helena absorbed the houseful of merrymaking visitors, the fabulous gift I was cooking – and the fact that I had not invited her.

XLIII

After five years in the Aventine watch Petronius had a keen eye for trouble. 'Someone take hold of the man's fish for him!'

My sister Maia leapt to her feet and grappled with me for the turbot, but with the stubbornness of someone in shock I refused to let it go. 'This is Helena,' Petronius announced to everybody helpfully. He had planted himself behind her to stop her backing out. She and I were both helpless. I did not want to talk to her in front of other people. With people watching, Helena would not speak to me.

I gripped the fish like a drowning sailor clutching a spar. It was all my fault as usual, but it was Helena who looked horrified. She struggled against the avuncular arm which Petronius had slung round her. 'Marcus, Helena came to supervise the delivery of your reading couch – Helena,' Petronius battled on, 'Marcus has been presented with a wonderful treat from Titus – are you going to stay and dine with us?'

'Not where I am not invited!'

'You are always invited,' I spoke up at last unconvincingly.

'It's considered convenient to tell people!'

'Then I'm telling you now – '

'That's gracious of you, Marcus!'

With the strength of the tipsy, Maia dragged the turbot away from me. Before I could stop her she placed him on the edge of the copper, over which he slipped as gracefully as a state barge on its maiden trip. A tide of scented water surged over the opposite edge making all the braziers crackle; members of my family cheered.

Maia sat down looking proud of her efforts. My brothers-in-law started passing round the wine I intended for later. The turbot was safe temporarily but he had started to cook, before I had time to count the spoons, thicken the sauce, change my tunic – or reconcile the girl I had insulted so appallingly. Petronius Longus was fussing over her, trying to apologise for me, but with a final effort Helena forced herself free. 'Marcus will see you out – ' he got in hopefully.

'Marcus has to cook his fish!'

Helena disappeared.

The water in the fish copper boiled.

'*Leave it!*' squealed Maia, fighting me over the braziers.

My mother, who had been sitting in silence, pushed us both aside with a mutinous growl. 'We can look after it – *go on!*'

I rushed out into the corridor: empty.

I threw open the outer door: no one on the stairs.

With my heart bumping angrily I ran back inside, and glanced in the other rooms. Alongside the Senator's reading couch in the cubicle I never used stood a trunk I had seen Helena travel with . . . *Oh Jupiter*. I guessed what *that* meant.

Petronius had cornered her in my bedroom. Helena was normally so resilient he seemed more upset than she was. I strode in, to his immense relief. 'Would you like us all to leave?' I shook my head vigorously (thinking of the fish). Petronius slunk away.

I placed myself between Helena and the door. She stood shaking with anger, or possibly distress. 'Why didn't you invite me?'

'I thought you wouldn't come!' Her face was white, and tense, and miserable. I hated myself for making her hate me. 'I was still waiting for you to contact me. You obviously didn't want to. Helena, I could not face staring at the door all evening, waiting for you – '

'Well, I came anyway!' she retorted crisply. 'And now I suppose I'm expected to say "Oh that's just Marcus!" the way your family do!' I let her rant. It did her good, and gave me time. I could see that she had completely despaired. That trunk of hers had told me why. Not only had I slapped her in the face; I did it on the very day she had decided to come and live with me . . . 'Don't try anything!' she warned me, as I started walking towards her. 'I cannot deal with this any longer, Marcus – '

200

I put both hands on her shoulders; she braced herself against the weight. 'My darling, I do know – ' I pulled her towards me. She resisted, but not hard enough.

'Marcus, I cannot bear seeing you go away and never knowing if I shall ever see you come back – '

I gathered her closer. 'I'm here – '

'Let me go, Marcus.' Helena was leaning away from me; I must have stunk of uncooked fish.

'No; let me make things right – '

'I don't want you to!' she answered, in that same thin, despondent voice. 'Marcus, I don't want to be bamboozled by some clever piece of oratory. I don't want to co-operate in cheating myself. I don't want to hear you squirming, *'Helena Justina, I didn't invite you because I knew you were coming anyway; Helena, I'm letting you blame me because I deserve it'* – '

'I am sorry. Don't tell me I'm a bastard; I'll say it myself – ' Helena nodded rapidly. 'I won't insult you by saying I love you, but I do, and you know it – '

'Oh stop pretending to be so strong and comforting!'

Grateful for the hint, I wrapped myself around her. 'Forget I've been cuddling a turbot; come here . . .'

Her face crumpled as she leaned against my fishy chest.

Maia poked her head in through the new door curtain, saw us and blushed. 'Shall we lay another bowl?'

'Yes,' I said without consulting Helena. Maia disappeared.

'No Marcus,' said Helena. 'I'll be friends; I cannot help it – but you will never make me stay!'

She had no time to finish. Before she could demolish me utterly, someone else started banging at my door. Petro would go. I could imagine his dread in case he found another girlfriend smirking on the threshold . . . I grimaced at Helena and started off to assist. Before I reached the doorway he burst in.

'There's a panic on, Marcus; can you come?' My quiet friend looked highly excited. 'It's a posse of damned Praetorians! Only Mars knows what they are after – but apparently you asked Titus to bring his dinner napkin, to sample your fish . . .'

This had all the makings of a social disaster.

I winked at Helena. 'Well! Are you just going to stand there looking beautiful – or are you going to rally round?'

XLIV

She saved me. She had to. She was a girl with a conscience. She would not risk exposing Titus Caesar to embarrassment from a clutch of raucous plebians. Helena ground her teeth, I grinned at her – and for one night at least I had a senator's daughter to act as my social hostess. I did not expect her to be able to cook, but she knew how to supervise.

The members of my family saw no reason to alter the habits of a lifetime just because I had produced an Imperial guest. Titus had already edged in, looking startled, before Helena and I could emerge with the kind of refined welcome he had learned to expect. My relations immediately grabbed him and sat him on a stool with a bowl of olives on one knee, to watch his turbot cooking. Next thing I knew, everyone seemed to have introduced themselves without waiting for me, Helena was testing the fish with a knife-point, Petronius shoved a full winecup under my elbow, and the chaos redoubled while I stood there like a drowned vole in a thunderstorm.

After five minutes and a cup of inferior Campanian wine, Titus had grasped the house rules and joined in with the rabble shouting advice. None of my family was snobbish; they accepted him as one of us. Most of them were much more curious about the superior young lady whose sweet-scented head was bent close to mine over my makeshift cooking pot.

The Praetorians had to wait outside. Luckily, when the Didius women bring bread rolls for a party they supply enough to send out several basketfuls if any high-ranking visitor happens to bring his bodyguard.

'What kind of sauce?' Helena murmured, dipping in her finger.

'Caraway.'

'It hardly tastes.' I was looking up the recipe – one I once stole from Helena herself. She peered over my shoulder

203

and spotted her own handwriting. 'You ruffian! . . . It says a scruple; I'll put more – did you squash them?'

'Have you tried grinding caraway seeds? They sit there and laugh at you.'

She tipped in more from the bag. 'Don't crowd me; I'm doing this!'

'You're the staff; I'm the chef – I'll get the blame.' I sampled it myself. 'Rasps a bit!'

'That's the mustardseed and peppercorns.'

'Stir in a spoonful of honey while I make the thickening – '

'This man is good!' cried Titus; the kind of guest I like.

'My younger brother is extremely self-sufficient,' Junia boasted complacently. (Junia had always cursed me as an incompetent clown.) I caught Helena's eye. My sister Junia took great pride in her civilised behaviour and good taste; somehow at any family gathering she seemed stiff and out of place. I was pleased to detect it was Maia the madcap whom Helena already liked best.

It took four of us to transfer the fish from his bath. I hooked up the cabbage nets on the end of a spoon; the cooked turbot proved firm enough for us to ease him out whole, then swing the cradle onto my brother's Celtic shield which Petronius was holding. As we fiddled about removing the nets, the heat of the fish, conducted through the metal shield with amazing rapidity, was burning his arms. When he complained we told him it was a test of character.

'Be careful of the prong on the underside!'

'Gods, Marcus; have I got to hold up the fish tray all evening? How can I put this thing down with a spike underneath?'

My brother-in-law Gaius Baebius, the customs clerk, stepped forward. Gaius Baebius (who would not dream of being mentioned in somebody's memoirs by less than two of his names) silently swung an iron cauldron onto the table top. Petro dropped the boss into the pot, which supported the shield quite steadily; Gaius Baebius had created a two-piece comport of some style.

My brother-in-law must have been secretly planning this coup since he got here. What a creep.

The turbot looked wonderful.

'Oh Marcus, well done!' Helena cried – almost letting some affection show.

Now the company had expanded, there were the usual party problems: not enough dishes and not enough seats. Titus pretended he did not mind squatting on the floor with his dinner served up on a lettuce leaf, but with my mother present better standards were required. While Mama took a carving knife to the turbot I sent Maia, who had no inhibitions after wine on an empty stomach, rushing off to knock up my neighbours and demand a loan of extra stools and bowls. 'Most of the other apartments are empty, Marcus; your block is a sanctuary for ghosts! I cadged these for you off an old lady upstairs – do you know who I mean?'

I knew.

Remembering what the pretentious Hortensius family served up to Priscillus at *their* dinner party, you may like to know the menu I produced at *mine*:

FISH SUPPER AT THE HOUSE OF M DIDIUS FALCO

```
Salad
The Turbot
More Salad
Fruit
```

Plain – but none of it was poisoned, I could guarantee.

We did have an exquisite wine which Petronius had brought (he told me what it was, but I forgot). And perhaps I exaggerate. My mother's brothers were all market gardeners so our family's idea of a salad had never been just a sliced hard-boiled egg on a bunch of endive leaves. Even my three uninvited sisters sent contributions to make me feel guilty; we had a large tray of white cheeses, plus cold sausage and a bucket of oysters to gobble with the basic greenery. There was food flowing out of the doors – literally, since Junia enjoyed herself more than once taking dishes down to our guest of honour's loitering Praetorians.

Everyone told me the turbot was delicious. As the cook, I was too busy worrying to taste it myself. The Caraway Sauce must have been an effective side dish, since when I looked round for it the serving jug had been scraped bare. By the time I sat down to eat, the only space was in the corridor. There was so much noise my head ached. Nobody bothered to talk to me since I was merely a tired scullion. I could see my mother squashed in a corner with Petro and his wife, discussing their offspring, probably. My brothers-in-law just ate and drank, or farted surreptitiously. Maia had the hiccups, which was hardly surprising. Junia was taking pains to look after His Caesarship, which he tolerated pleasantly – though he appeared much more taken with Helena Justina.

Helena's dark eyes constantly watched over my guests; she and Maia were doing good work for me, nudging along the conversation and passing round the food. Helena was beyond my reach. If I called out she would never hear me. I wanted to thank her. I wanted to go across and fetch her, then take her to one of my empty rooms and make passionate love until neither of us could move . . .

'Where did you find *her?*' squealed Maia's voice behind my right ear, as she lurched up to spoon more of the glutinous turbot onto my plate.

'She found me, I think . . .'

'Poor girl, she adores you!'

I felt like a man stumbling out of the desert. 'Why's that?'

206

'The way she looks at you!' giggled Maia, the only one of my sisters who was actually fond of me.

I toyed with my second helping. Then across the hubbub of eight people talking at once Helena raised her head, and noticed me watching her. Her face had always contained a mixture of intelligence and character which jolted me. She smiled slightly. A private signal between us, to tell me everybody was enjoying my party; then a shared moment of stillness after that.

Titus Caesar bent sideways to say something to Helena; she was answering him in the quiet way she conversed with people publicly – nothing like the tyrant who trampled over me. Titus seemed to admire her as much as I did. Somebody should tell him that when an Emperor's son indulges himself with a visitation to a poor man's house, he could eat the fish and swig the wine and leave his guards outside to amaze the neighbours – but he should draw the line at flirting with the poor man's girl . . . He had effortlessly impressed all my relations. I hated him for his happy Flavian skill at mucking in.

'Cheer up!' someone chaffed me, the way people do.

Helena Justina appeared to be lecturing Titus; she glanced at me, so I realised I was the subject. Helena must be attacking him over the way the Palace treated me. I winked at him; he smiled back sheepishly.

My sister Junia squeezed past me on her way somewhere. She tossed a glance at Helena. 'Idiot! You must be heading for a tumble there!' she chortled, not bothering to wait and see if I was upset.

Once again I was the typical host: tired and left out. My fish had gone cold while I brooded. I noticed glumly that where my landlord had has a wall replastered it must have dried out and now there was a crack the whole length of the corridor, wide enough to insert my thumb. So here I was, presiding over an ideal Roman evening: a tasteful dinner for my family, friends, and a patron I respected. Here I was feeling depressed and with a dry mouth; insulted by my sister; watching a handsome Caesar attempt to capture my girlfriend; and knowing that when everyone else

207

reeled off cheerfully, the debris they left behind would take me hours to tidy up.

One good feature of my family was that once they had eaten and drunk everything they could get their hands on, they vanished speedily. My mother, with the excuse of her age, was leaving first, though not before Petro's wife Silvia had shrieked to prevent Titus from helpfully throwing away the turbot remains. Of course Ma had fixed on carrying off the skeleton and the jelly from the serving tray for stock. Petronius and Silvia were taking my mother home (with her bucket of bones). Titus remembered to say something complimentary to her about Festus (who had served under Titus in Judea). Still reeling from his near disaster with the fish tray his honour decided it would be tactful if he left too. He had already thanked me and was taking Helena lightly by the hand.

'Camillus Verus' daughter has been defending your interests, Falco!' I wondered if he had heard that my relationship with Helena was more than professional and if he knew how intensely I was trying to keep her here. He appeared unaware of it. A smooth operator, this one.

I shook my head at her gently. 'I thought we agreed: your role here tonight was to pass round the olives nicely and to count up the winecups before anybody left!'

Titus was offering Helena transport home.

'Thank you, sir,' she responded in her firm style. 'Didius Falco has a commission to look after me –' (I used to be her bodyguard.) Titus tried to insist. 'He needs the money!' she hissed, quite openly.

Titus laughed. 'Oh, I'll give him the money –'

'No use, sir,' Helena quipped. 'Without the work he won't take any payment – you know how touchy Falco is!'

But she was a senator's daughter. I had no public claim on her. It was impossible to cause the Emperor's son offence by quarrelling on the doorstep over a matter of simple etiquette, so finally I lost Helena among the noisy throng which was escorting Titus downstairs to the street.

It was rude of me, but I felt so depressed I stayed upstairs. Once my relatives had trampled down three flights to the thoroughfare and waved my Imperial visitor back to the Palantine, they saw no reason to march back up again, merely to say goodbye to me. They went home. The respectable citizens of the Piscina Publica must have winced at the racket as they left.

The apartment was dismally quiet. I braced myself for a long night clearing up. I flipped some strands of watercress into a rubbish pail, straightened a couple of cups lethargically, then collapsed on a bench in the traditional manner of a weary host, as I stared at the mess.

A door closed behind me. Someone with gentle fingers and a delicate sense of timing tickled my neck. I bent forwards to give her more scope. 'Is that you?'

'It's me.' A girl with a conscience. Naturally she had stayed behind to help me wash the plates.

XLV

I should have expected it. The real question was, whether I could persuade her to stay with me afterwards.

I decided to do the housework first, and the hard stuff when I was too tired to feel any pain.

Helena and I made a useful team. I could square up to hard work. She was fastidious, but shrank from nothing that needed to be done. 'Which end of the street is the midden?' Grasping two disagreeable slop buckets she paused in the outer doorway.

'Stand them out on the landing tonight. The neighbourhood seems peaceful, but never take the risk in the dark.' Helena was sensible, but there were a lot of things I needed to teach her about plebian domestic life.

Still from the corridor she called, 'Marcus, have you seen this crack in your wall? Is it structural?'

'Probably!'

We finished in the end. The smell of fish still pervaded the house but everything was clean except the floor, which I could wash down tomorrow. 'Thanks; you're a gem.'

'I quite enjoyed it.'

'I enjoy knowing it's finished! There's a difference, my love, between doing the work of twenty servants once for fun – and doing it every day.' I sat for some minutes, polishing my good bronze spoons; taking my time. 'Something you're not telling me?' Helena said nothing. 'You might as well spill it; you've run away from home.' Even when we were on the best of terms she grew restless if I seemed to understand her private motives too well. In fact with Helena, nudging her into opening up had always been part of the challenge. She scowled. I scowled back at her. 'I am a professional informer, Helena – I can decipher clues! As well as your father's reading couch, there's a box here with your second-best dress and your life savings – '

'I'm wearing my second-best dress,' she contradicted me.

'The box is for the title deeds from my Aunt Valeria's legacy – '

When I fall in love as heavily as I had done with Helena Justina, I soon enquire what I have let myself in for. I knew her aunt's Sabine farm was a fraction of Helena's portfolio. I knew Helena too; it sounded as if she was deliberately turning her back on any income which her father had allowed her.

'Fallen out with your family?'

'If I'm disgracing myself I cannot take family property.'

'That bad, is it?' I frowned. Helena was not the usual spoiled society kitten, stamping her foot and demanding the freedom to be scandalous. She loved her family. She would hate upsetting them. I was none too keen on having persuaded her to do it – then letting her down.

She surprised me by trying to explain: 'I'm twenty-three; I have been married and divorced; but it *is* a disgrace to leave my parents' house – I simply cannot settle down at home any more.' There was a difference between running away from the conventional life of a dutiful daughter and running to me. Which was this?

'They trying to make you marry again? Some stiff-backed senatorial stripe?'

'Now you live here,' she suggested (ignoring the question), '*I* could take over your old apartment – '

'Not on your own.'

'I'm not afraid!'

'Then you ought to be. Fountain Court frightened me.'

'I'm sorry,' Helena said glumly. 'I should have let Titus take me home – '

'To Hades with Titus.' We had an unfinished quarrel, which was impeding a sensible decision here. If we started fighting at this time of night, the results might be disastrous. 'If you want to go, *I'll* take you home. But tell me first what you were coming here to say.' She closed her eyes wearily, blocking me out. 'Helena, you owe me that!'

'I wanted to ask if there was still a vacancy for a girl to take messages.'

'For the right applicant.' She said nothing, but she looked at me again. 'Stay here tonight and think about it,' I said

211

quietly. 'I'll give you a good home. I'd hate to find you sleeping rough in temple doorways and begging coppers from passers-by at the Probus Bridge!' Helena was still uncertain. 'We have a bed and a couch; you can choose; I'm not asking you to share with me.'

'You have the bed,' Helena said.

'All right. Don't worry; I can keep my hands off you.' Luckily I was exhausted, or that might not have been true. I heaved myself upright. 'In my bedroom there's a wicker chair begging for an owner. Here's a lamp; here's some warm water you can take to wash. Is that enough?'

She nodded and left me.

We had achieved something. I was not certain what. But Helena Justina had taken a huge step – and I would have to see it through with her.

Restless, I tried to scrub the fishiness off myself, then pottered about like a regular householder: fixing shutters; dousing braziers; feeling big. Now that I had Helena to look after, I locked the outer door. I was not sure whether this was to keep out cat burglars, or keep Helena in.

I whistled as a warning, then went in, carrying two beakers of warm honey drink. Lamplight flickered in the draught I caused. Helena was curled up on her father's couch, plaiting her hair. With Galla's chair and Helena's box and other things, the little room looked cosy; it felt right. 'I brought you a drink. Anything else you need?' *Me, for instance?* She shook her head apprehensively.

I put her beaker where she could reach it, then shuffled towards the door. 'I usually add cloves, but tell me if you don't like it and I'll leave them out next time.'

'Marcus, you look unhappy. Is it my fault?'

'I think it's the case.'

'What's wrong?'

'That freedman was murdered despite my pitiful efforts. His cook is dead too – and it's partly my fault. I have to decide tomorrow what I want to do.'

'Will you tell me about it?'

'Tonight?'

Helena Justina smiled at me. Taking an interest would

212

be part of her new role. She intended to ask constant questions, vet my clients, interfere . . . I could handle that. Fighting over my work with Helena would be glorious. Her smile grew; she had seen my grin. I sat in Galla's chair, balanced my hot drink on my knee, and finally told Helena everything that had happened since we last had a chance to talk.

Almost everything. Being nearly seduced by Severina seemed not worth mentioning. 'Is that all?' Helena asked.

'First the Hortensius women hired me to entrap Severina. Now they've dumped me, and *she* wants me to indict *them* . . .'

Helena considered my options while I gazed fondly at her. 'Pollia and Atilia have excluded you from the Hortensius house, which is a blow. I think you should accept Severina as a client. If she is innocent, what's to lose? And if she's guilty it gives you more chance to prove it and do right by your late friend the cook. Besides,' Helena concluded, 'Severina has to pay you if you work for her.'

'Can't object to that!' I did not mention my fear that the gold-digger might be expecting to pay me in kind.

'Feel better?'

'Mmm. Thanks. I'll go and see Severina tomorrow.' Time for bed. 'Also, daughter of Camillus Verus, I must call on your noble papa to explain how I have dishonoured you – '

'No case to answer! I dishonoured myself.'

'Your father may quibble. A scruff who lures off a senator's daughter is held to have injured her father's good name.'

Helena dismissed it: 'Any father should be proud to discover his daughter dines on turbot with the elder son of the Emperor as her fellow guest.'

'Sweetheart, sometimes in the Falco house, we do not dine at all!' She was looking tired. I picked up the lamp. Our eyes met. I walked to the doorway. 'I won't kiss you goodnight. But that's only because if I did, I could not trust myself to stop.'

'Marcus, at the moment I cannot tell what I want – '

'No. But it's plain what you *don't* want – ' She started to speak but I hushed her. 'The first rule of this household is, don't argue with the master; however I expect you to break that.' I quenched the lamp. Under cover of darkness I added, 'The second rule is, be kind to him because he loves you.'

'I can do that. What else?'

'Nothing. That's all. Except, Helena Justina – welcome to my house!'

XLVI

Severina spotted the change in me immediately. 'What happened to you?'

'A good dinner last night.' Since relations with Helena were on such a tentative basis, I had decided to keep news of my lodger to myself. Anyway, vetting clients might be Helena's business but Helena Justina's position was no concern of my clients.

'Is that all?' Severina demanded jealously. The words sounded familiar.

I told her I was accepting her commission. I would investigate two avenues: relations between the Hortensius and Priscillus empires, and the exact details of the dinner the night Novus died. She asked if she could assist, and looked surprised when I said no. 'You were a suspect, Zotica. Best stand back.'

'Well, if I think of anything helpful I can call in at your apartment – '

'No, don't do that. I let one of my rooms to a subtenant, whom I don't trust alone with female visitors. I'll come to you.'

'I want to know what you are doing though – '

'You will!' I already had to explain my every move to Helena. One overseer was enough.

Severina's light eyes flickered. 'What made up your mind to help me?'

'I hate unfinished business.'

I was on my way out. 'Going so soon?' She followed me. 'You are my only hope now, Falco,' she said clingingly. 'Everyone distrusts me – '

I fixed her with a playful finger, squashing the tip of her small freckled nose. 'Not when I've proved your innocence.' Now she was paying for the privilege, I let myself sound protective. In fact the pose was so convincing I startled myself. Even half a commitment from Helena had made me feel light-hearted. 'By the way; are you still trying to find your parrot a new home? I know someone who might like a pet for company.'

'Who's that?'

'Distant relative of mine.' Well, someone who might *become* a relative in some distant aeon. But actually I had reasons of my own for wanting the bird. 'I can't promise to make it permanent, but if you like I'll take Chloe on a month's trial . . .'

After I left I made a long detour riverwards, to drop in on Petronius Longus at the booth which the Aventine watch used as its lock-up and chophouse. It was full of his men, dicing and complaining about the government, so we sat outside watching the bumboats scull up the Tiber.

Petronius was my best friend, so telling *him* about Helena was obligatory. To forestall awkward jokes, I also had to mention that arrangements were slightly precarious. He shook his head, smiling into his hands. 'You two! You never do anything the easy way . . .'

'*Is* there an easy way for a plebian to entice away the daughter of a senator?'

'No one but you would try!'

He started to thank me for last evening but I cut him short. 'My pleasure; I owed you and Silvia hospitality – Petro, tell me, what's the word these days about the world of high-finance property?'

'Nothing unusual – all swindles, scams and harassment. You working on something?'

'Could be. Ever come across a shoal of real-estate predators by the name of Hortensius?' Petro shook his head. 'What about Appius Priscillus?'

'Oh I've heard of him! If you intend to go and see Priscillus, wear a peg on your nose.' I lifted an eyebrow quizzically. 'Everything he does stinks!'

'Any stink in particular?'

'I've never run across him myself, but I do know half the shopkeepers on the Via Ostiensis hide their heads in a cauldron at the mention of his name. Do you want some background? I can ask around.'

'Appreciated . . .'

'You're trying to net a big one, Falco!' Petro told me in a warning voice. Size as such – or even size as a measure of social status – never worried Petronius; he meant the man was dangerous.

Back home I found an immaculate factotum, with her nose in a scroll of poetry. She had been to the baths; the disturbing undernotes of some perfume I half disliked were filling the house. She gave me a swift sneer as if I had six legs and mandibles, then carried on brazenly skiving in office time.

I adopted a furtive whine. 'Falco live here?'

'On and off.' She refused to raise her well-groomed head from the scroll.

'Can you give him a message?'

'If I feel like it.'

'It's just that I might have a job for him – if he's not too particular.'

'Falco's not fussy.' She laughed bitterly.

'So what are his prices?' She looked up from her reading at last. 'No; don't tell them, fruit. The answer is *more than you can afford by the look of you!*'

'Why? I can tell them. I know what you charged me – '

'You were a beautiful woman and I wanted to impress you. I gave you special rates.'

'Specially dear, you mean!' Beneath the surface of this bonhomie I had been throwing out hard messages of domineering lust. Helena was starting to flounder. 'Am I doing this right?' she asked.

'Cut down on the friendliness! Clients only mean trouble. Why encourage them?'

'What's that fighting in the bag?'

I untied the string and Chloe hopped out angrily. *'Don't just stand there, woman,'* she cackled, *'give me a drink!'*

Helena was furious. 'Didius Falco, if you want to bring home presents, I draw the line at pets who answer back!'

'I wouldn't insult you! Job for you, my darling. I reckon this flying ferdango may give us a clue. It's female; name of Chloe; eats seeds, I'm told. As witnesses go she's the tricky kind, and thoroughly unreliable. Better keep her in a room with the shutter closed in case she tries to do a flit before she's squawked. I'll find you a slate – just write down anything she says.'

'What sort of clue am I listening for?' The parrot obliged with three words which are mostly seen on the walls of tavern latrines. 'It will be a pleasure!' Helena muttered rebelliously.

'Thanks, beloved! If you see the letting agent – name of Cossus – will you ask him to look at that crack for me?'

'I can tell him it's interfering with your plans for a thousand sesterces' wall painting of *Bellerophon and Pegasus*.'

'That should do the trick. Any questions, fruit?'

'Staying in for lunch?'

'Sorry; no time.'

'Where are you going?'

'Knocking on doors.'

'Who does the dinner?' She was a single-minded girl.

I dropped some money in a bowl. 'You buy it; I cook it; we eat it together while we talk about my day.'

I gave her a swift, chaste, parting kiss which left her unmoved but had a troublesome effect on me.

XLVII

The address I had for Appius Priscillus turned out to be a gloomy fortress on the Esquiline. This made him a close neighbour of the Praetor Corvinus, inhabiting the area which had once been notorious for fevers but was now host to pestilence of a different kind: the rich.

The house reeked of money, though the owner displayed his wealth in a different way from the Hortensii with their flash parade of interior design and art treasures. Priscillus emphasised how much *he* possessed by the pains he took protecting it. His property had been stripped of any balconies or pergolas which could offer cover to a thief's approach; its few upstairs windows were permanently barred. Private guards playing board games sat in a pillbox on one corner of the street, all of which was taken up with the sombre mansion where this grandmaster of real estate was supposed to live. His outer walls were painted black: a subtle hint of character.

Two white eyeballs, belonging to a big black African, squinted at me through a grille in a particularly solid black front door. The eyes let me in, but raced through the formalities with a speed designed to prevent anyone becoming too familiar with the layout. The entrance hall contained a brace of British hunting dogs (on chains), who were just fractionally friendlier t'an the leather-clad bodyguards; I counted at least five of those, patrolling the precincts with glittery daggers prominent in their handspan belts.

I was shunted into a side room where, before I could get bored and start writing my name on the wallplaster, a secretary stepped in with the clear intention of despatching me whence I came.

'May I see Appius Priscillus?'

'No. Priscillus greets his followers in the morning, but we keep a list. If you're not on the list, there is no chance of dole. If you are a tenant, see the rent clerk. If you are seeking a loan see the loans clerk – '

'Where do I find the personal information clerk?'

He paused. His eyes said information was at a premium. 'That's possibly me.'

'The information I'm after is extremely sensitive. Priscillus may prefer to give it to me himself.'

'He's not the sensitive type,' said his man.

Clearly Priscillus had not lashed out much on his secretarial services; this was no high-flown Greek who could speak and write five languages. He had an uninspiring north European face. The only indication that he acted as a scribe was the fact he had a split-nibbed reed pen stuck in the swag of brown cloth that he used as a belt, and ink all over him.

'My name is Didius Falco,' I said. He hadn't thought it polite to ask me, but I thought it polite to say. 'I would like you to inform Appius Priscillus that I have certain questions regarding events at the Hortensius house two nights ago. Clearing up these questions will be in his interests as much as mine.'

'What questions?'

'Confidential.'

'You can tell me.'

'Maybe – but I'm not going to!'

The secretary disappeared grumpily, without telling me I could sit down. In fact there were no stools or benches. The room contained only heavy coffers which were probably stuffed with money. Anyone who sat on the strongboxes would imprint himself with a vicious pattern of studs, bands, and bolts. I decided to keep my delicate posterior unmarked.

If I had been a barrister the court usher would barely have had time to set the waterclock to time my speech before my messenger returned. 'He will not see you!' he informed me triumphantly.

I sighed. 'So what's to be done?'

'Nothing. You're not wanted. Now you leave.'

'Let's go through this again,' I said patiently. 'My name is Marcus Didius Falco. I am investigating the poisoning

220

of the freedman Hortensius Novus; also, incidentally, the murder of his cook – '

'So what?' jeered the secretary.

'So somebody has suggested to me that Appius Priscillus may be implicated in these deaths.' This accusation raised not a flicker. 'It did seem to me,' I suggested, 'in view of the serious charges, Priscillus might like a chance to vindicate himself – '

'If he did anything, you'd never prove it! If you could prove something, you would not be here!'

'That sounds persuasive – but it's the rhetoric of a thug. Now tell Priscillus this: if he did it I will prove it. When I prove it I'll be back.'

'I doubt it, Falco. Now I suggest you leave quickly of your own accord because if I ask the Phrygians to convey you outside, you may land rather heavily.'

'Give Priscillus the message,' I repeated, making my own way to the door. As I reached the smirking stylus-pusher I did a quick twirl and yanked his arm up his back at the very moment his vigilance relaxed. 'Let's give the message to him now, shall we? We can deliver the second part together – and try him out with the first, because I think he may not have heard it yet . . .' The fool started to bluster. 'Stop fidgeting, or taking shorthand notes will be painful for a week or two – ' I gave his arm a jerk to emphasise the point. 'Don't take me for an idiot – you never saw Priscillus. You were only gone long enough to scratch your lice.'

'He's not here!' gasped the inkblot.

'Where is he then?'

'This is his business address. He has a house on the Quirinal and two others opposite the Salarian Gate; or he may be over the river at his new place on the Janiculan. But he only sees his private friends in his private homes.'

'So when do you expect him here again?'

'No way of telling – ' Suddenly he squirmed free and let out a shout which attracted the attention of one of the bodyguards.

'Keep cool. I'm going – but give your master my message just as soon as he turns up!'

'Don't worry! And when I do, Falco, you can expect to be hearing from him!'

I smiled. Some threats do lead to inconvenience. But mainly they evaporate.

As I crossed the hall, keeping half an eye on the Phrygian muscle, I noticed a sedan chair. Whatever Priscillus spent his takings on, it was not this conveyance: this was a stained brown leather veteran, so crumpled and grimy it was conspicuous. I had seen it before: at that housefire, the night Hortensius Novus died. Which meant that I had seen Priscillus too: leaping out of it.

Tough life, being a businessman. Hardly time to take a well-earned break after murdering your rival, before you had to be back out on the streets, greeting sobbing arson victims with a contract in your hand . . .

The presence of the chair probably meant Priscillus *was* here. But I left without further argument. I had hurt the scribe's arm enough to ensure he would rush to his master to complain. My message would get there now.

I recognised something else unpleasant outside the street door: descending from his mule was the pustulent piece of aggravation I last saw attacking the old fruitseller in Abacus Street. I braced myself for a fight, but the bleary bug failed to remember me.

I amused myself that afternoon at the Temple of Saturn, going through the Censor's register of citizens and their property, which was kept for safety at the Treasury. Appius Priscillus was a freedman of long-standing, attached to the Galerian voting tribe. We were long overdue for a full Roman census, but he should have featured somewhere in official documents. He had managed to hide his existence. I was not surprised.

I found myself more eager than usual to wander off home. This had less to do with the sour taste left by Priscillus than a certain smile I might encounter in my own den.

She was out. That was just about acceptable. I would have to let her stroll around loose occasionally. Sceptical types might think that I was holding her to ransom otherwise.

222

At home there was evidence that the morning had been lively. Severina had assured me her parrot was house-trained, but apparently this only meant that Chloe was trained to eat household effects. There were beakmarks scarring several doorframes, and a broken dish in the rubbish pail. Something, presumably not Helena, had attacked my office stool ferociously and bitten halfway through its leg. Now the parrot was missing too.

Helena had left me a list of the bird's sayings, brightly annotated by herself:

> *Chloe's a clever girl. (Doubtful. H.)*
> *Manicure set.*
> *Where's my dinner?*
> *Let's go out to a party!*
> *Eggs in a basket. (Is this rude? H.)*
> *Three obscenities. (I refuse to write them. H.)*
> *Chloe, Chloe, Chloe. Chloe's a good girl.*
> *Gone to Maia's; taking your stupid bird.*

The last line confused me until I realised it was a joke addressed to me in my sister's spiked handwriting.

I dashed off to Maia's in a state of annoyance; I had intended to censor news of Helena's arrival. I should have known that after the fish supper my family would come poking round, on the lookout for scandal and leftovers.

Helena and my sister had settled themselves on Maia's sun terrace. A wide variety of empty plates, bowls and mint-tea glasses littered the edge of the stone parapet and the rims of Maia's great flowerpots. Neither Maia nor Helena roused themselves to suggest feeding me. They must have been nibbling most of the afternoon and were too well stuffed to budge.

Helena put up her cheek which I brushed with a kiss. Maia looked away. Our formality seemed to embarrass her more than a passionate clinch.

'Where's the parrot?'

'Hiding,' said Maia. 'It thought it was going to terrorise

223

my children but they fought back. We had to cover it with a stewpot for its own protection.'

'I saw what that pest did at home,' I complained, still pecking round for crumbs like a forlorn sparrow. 'I'll get a cage.'

I managed to find a few lacklustre almonds at the bottom of a bowl. They tasted off. I should have known no titbit which had already been rejected by my lass and my youngest sister would provide much sustenance.

'I believe "two eggs in a basket" is a reference to testicles,' I informed them, using clinical neutrality to indicate I saw them both as women of the world. 'Though if "manicure set" is a soldiering term its translation escapes me.' Maia pretended she knew, and she would tell Helena afterwards.

They let me sit down, threw me a few cushions, then condescended to hear about my day. I soon deduced Helena had told Maia all about my case. 'I never managed to see Priscillus. But he seems what I thought – high rents and low motives. It's beginning to look as if Severina may have a point.'

'Don't you dare start feeling sorry for her!' my sister instructed. It seemed to me she and Helena had exchanged a knowing glance.

Their set reaction immediately made my own attitude to the fortune-hunter more sympathetic. 'Why not? What if everyone has misjudged her? What if she really is just a home-loving girl, acting from the best of motives with regard to Hortensius Novus, and has simply had bad luck with everything she touches?' This fair-minded attitude surprised even me. I must be going soft.

My sister and my lady bestirred themselves to jangle their bracelets at me, then I was ordered to report on Severina Zotica in detail so they could systematically destroy her character. Maia, who had been a professional weaver, was particularly interested in her domestic handicrafts. 'Does she really do it herself? How fast can she work? Was she using a pattern? When she changed colours did she have to think, or could she choose the next hank of wool automatically?'

224

'Oh I can't remember.'

'Marcus, you're useless!'

'I reckon she's genuine. Isn't this dutiful Penelope act more likely to mean she's innocent? Sitting at a loom seems a nice quiet occupation – '

'Sitting at a loom quietly,' Maia rebuked me, 'gives her plenty of time to scheme and plot!'

'Traditional life of a decent Roman matron. Augustus always insisted that the women of his household wove all his clothes at home.'

Helena laughed. 'And his female relations all ended up a byword for debauchery!' She gazed at me, considering. 'Are scratchy homespun tunics what *you* want?'

'Wouldn't dream of it.' I wouldn't dare!

'Good! Tell us about all these trips to the library. What is she studying?'

'Geography.'

'That's harmless – apparently,' Helena agreed, though she and Maia exchanged another silly glance. 'Perhaps she is searching for a pleasant province where she can go into voluntary exile with her ill-gotten loot!'

'Doubt it. The only scroll I noticed had some references to Mauretania. Who wants to retire to a desert, overrun by plagues of elephants?'

'If she had taken out three volumes on taming parrots,' Maia giggled, 'there might be some point. Are you attracted to this female?'

Helena was scrutinising me out of the corner of one eye, so to cause trouble I said, 'She's not bad, if you like redheads!'

Maia told me I was disgusting; then she instructed Helena Justina to take me (and my parrot) home.

Not long after we reached the apartment I discovered that my sister had taught the parrot to squawk, '*Ooh! Marcus has been a naughty boy!*'

XLVIII

Next morning, while I was making fruitless attempts to track down Appius Priscillus at one or other of his fancy bivouacs, Helena Justina bought a parrot cage and later took two messages.

'You had a visit from a slave, who refused to leave his name – though he must be the runabout from the Hortensius house.'

'They owe me a packet.'

'He brought that. I counted and wrote a receipt for it. Am I going to keep your accounts for you?'

A cold sweat struck me, faced by aspects of togetherness I had never allowed for. 'Certainly not! My brains and my body are at your disposal, but a man needs some privacy . . .'

'We'll see!' Helena look unimpressed. 'The runabout has found someone who can help you; he will bring her tomorrow morning. Can you be here? She works in the kitchen so it has to be early. Also the cook's funeral will be on Thursday, if you want to go.'

'Yes; I owe Viridovix a respectful gesture.'

'I said I thought you would. The other message was from Petronius Longus; he wants to see you urgently.'

Petronius was working, so I found him on the Aventine. He took time out from policing the Emporium to snatch a glass of wine with me. I told him about my morning chasing around the Priscillus properties and being shown the door at all of them. 'Apparently he was out shopping for Alban holiday retreats. If he can't decide which location he wants, he'll just buy them all . . .'

'Priscillus was why I wanted to see you.' Petro gave me one of his sombre looks. He swilled the wine round his gums, as a sign that it tasted like toothpowder. 'Falco, what muleshit are you stepping in? Everyone I asked about this mogul reckons he's about as safe to deal with as a bucket

226

of snakes. And come to that,' added Petro, with relish, 'your Hortensius brothers – or whatever they are – have little more to recommend them!'

'What's the dirt?'

'Start with Priscillus. The story is pretty sordid. He first surfaced on a big scale during the clearances after the Great Fire. He was "doing the public a service" preying on the dispossessed tenants Nero had kicked out to make space for the Golden House. Priscillus moved in on them, with his greedy eyes fixed on compensation claims –'

'I thought "compensation" was a bad joke?'

'Is this Rome? What actually happened was that Nero removed the corpses and the rubble free of charge – though that was a ploy so he could pick over the debris and grab anything left to loot. The Fire Relief Fund, to which we citizens all contributed so graciously –' Petro meant, it was screwed out of us by the taxfarmers, '– went no further than the Emperor's own coffers. Thousands were left homeless and absolutely desperate. So firstly there were good pickings for contractors providing temporary shelters outside the city. Then racketeers were able to make their piles building cheap slums for the refugees who had salvaged anything, and even cheaper billets for the ones who had nothing left. They cleaned up: as soon as the refugees were settled in, the rents soared. Once the costs bit, cynical Priscillus moved in again – this time as a loan shark.'

Most of Rome lives on credit. Everyone from temple-cleaner to consul tends to be in debt for most of their lives. People at the upper end of society can juggle their mortgages; the less fortunate spiral down under the burden of five per cent interest into selling their sons as gladiators and their daughters as cheap brothel fare.

'What about the Hortensius triumvirate, Petro? Is their operation similar?'

'Yes, though slightly cleaner. Their interest appear more diversified –'

I mentioned what the cakeman had told me about Pollia's venture into fitting out corn ships. 'Looks as if Novus believed in a well-balanced portfolio: mercantile fiddles nicely balanced against landlease fraud!'

227

'Their business style is less brutal than the one Priscillus adopts. As landlords they seem to be merely bad managers. Why should they care if their tenants can see daylight through the walls?'

'Almost as friendly as Smaractus!' I joked.

'Not funny. Three children died recently at an apartment in the Third Sector when a floor fell in. The Hortensii average a lawsuit a month from pedestrians who have narrowly escaped falling roof tiles or pieces breaking off balcony balustrades. A whole wall gave way and killed a man not long ago, somewhere on the Esquiline. Neglecting a dangerous structure is second nature; their collateral stays solid, even though their property is always collapsing – '

'And rebuilt at a profit?'

'Oh yes!' Petro confirmed with a delicate lift of both wrists. 'But their main method of raising finance is the multiple-pledge fiddle.'

'What's that?'

'You still in the cradle, Falco?' Petronius seemed unable to believe I was serious. He was more alert to fraud than me; as a salaried officer he sometimes had cash to invest. Sometimes he lost it – but not as often as most people; he had a canny business sense. 'The legal term is a "hypothec". Are you with me?'

'I'm not stupid . . . So what does it mean?'

'It means a fiddle, Falco!'

'I have heard the word, or read it somewhere; isn't it just the term lawyers use for a pledge, when the pledge is on property? How can a fiddle operate?'

'What happens is: the Hortensii own a piece of property, and raise a loan secured on it. Then they repeat the process – same property but a new lender; and again, as many times as possible. They pick simple-minded investors who don't know – or don't enquire – that there are previous secured debts.'

'So they mortgage the building, to its full value, as often as they can?'

'Insight is penetrating that drunken little brain! Next, as you'll guess, the Hortensii default. Of course they lose the original property, but they don't mind that! They have raised its value several times over in loans.'

'But what about their creditors, Petro? Can't they sue?'

'Paid off in strict order of precedence; earliest contract date first. One or two will recoup when the building is sold; but once its selling price is covered, the rest have no claim.'

'What? No protection at all?'

'They should protect themselves by checking first! If not; hard luck. It's fraud which relies on punters' laziness.' Petro sounded unsympathetic. Like me, he was a man who took trouble over things. 'I had all this from a Syrian financier. Normally he just shakes his greasy ringlets and I can't get a word out of him, but this Priscillus is so notorious everyone in the Forum would like to see his operations limited. My contact told me about the Hortensii out of sheer spite at their success with the duplicate loans charade. None of the professional moneylenders touch it – but there are always fools in the private market who can be intrigued by clever talk of quick percentages. The regular dealers are grousing that the Hortensii are pinching all the spare collateral, while Priscillus, with his brutal methods, is making everybody nervous on the fringe.'

'What,' I suggested, 'if the two groups joined forces?'

Petro winced. 'That's the big fear.'

I sat and thought. Now that I had an inkling how the Hortensius and Priscillus empires worked there seemed plenty of scope for them all to make a profit – but that also encouraged endless jealousy about making even more. The poor get used to making do; people with real money never feel it is enough.

'Thanks, Petro. Anything else I ought to be aware of?'

'Only that my informant says if you're going to upset Appius Priscillus I ought to ask where you deposited your will.'

'Ma knows,' I said tersely.

His quiet brown eyes surveyed me. 'Wear a body belt under your tunic and keep a dagger in your boot! If you get in trouble, let me know.'

I nodded. He went back to work; I lingered over my drink.

I won't say I felt apprehensive – but the little hairs were standing to attention all over my skin.

To give myself something else alarming to think about, I went to see Severina.

'As promised: come to report.'

'How is my parrot?'

'I hear she's been making herself at home . . .' I described Chloe's trail of destruction, being careful to omit the fact that the aviary she was destroying was my own.

'What do you expect?' rebuked the gold-digger crossly. 'She's a sensitive female. You have to introduce her to a new habitat gradually!' I smiled, thinking not of Chloe, but Helena Justina so warily agreeing to unfurl her tent at my water hole. 'Falco, what are you grinning at?'

'I may have to chain the birdie to a perch.'

'No; don't do that. If she tries to fly she may fall and just dangle there!'

'Thought you were anxious to get rid of her?'

'I am. Chloe,' declared Severina, 'was a gift from Grittius Fronto, whose unpleasantness I want to forget as soon as possible.'

'Relax! I gave your feather duster to a person of humane tendencies; a proper cage has been purchased . . . I want to talk to you about more rapacious birds. Sit down, keep a clear head, and don't give me the "I'm just an ignorant little woman" tale again.' Before she could argue I told her what I had found out so far about Priscillus. 'It does fit with your story – but *proves* none of it. Tell me what you know about relationships between Priscillus and your group on the Pincian. You mentioned a quarrel, which the dinner was supposed to reconcile. What caused the initial rift? Would I be correct if I guessed that the Hortensii had somehow double-crossed the other organisation with their duplicate hypothecs scam?'

'That's sharp of you!' Severina admitted. 'Hortensius Novus always claimed it had happened accidentally, but he *had* tricked Appius Priscillus into underwriting one of those dubious schemes of his. That was why Priscillus started threatening the family, and why Felix and Crepito, who had less nerve than Novus, wanted to end the feud by accepting an offer from him to co-operate in future.'

'I get the impression they were shaking hands on more than just compensation for rooking him! *I* think Felix and Crepito desired a full business merger – Mars Ultor, they could still do it, and stitch up the whole of residential Rome! Was your Novus resisting it?'

'You could be right,' she suggested doubtfully. I recognised the simple woman act again, so left the conversation there. The trick with Severina, I had discovered, was to move one line ahead in the board game, then force her to follow your move.

'Will you stay to lunch with me, Falco? I need some decent conversation; my girlfriend at the baths was too busy to stop, and I'm missing my fiancé – '

For a moment I forgot Severina was my client now. 'Don't worry,' I smiled sweetly. 'You'll soon find another to fill the void.'

Her parrot's wilful damage in my apartment must have eroded my natural tolerance.

I wanted to see Helena; I was anxious to mend relations by helping her cope with the truculent bird.

Walking home, I did feel I was advancing on the case. Not that it cleared any undergrowth: I still had three sets of suspects and there were more motives than fleas on a cat. The only thing they had in common was that none could yet be proved.

I was enjoying myself though. This was much more satisfying than some dead-end mission for Vespasian. It offered a livelier challenge, and if I managed to solve it I should not just be removing some tired political grub whose disappearance would hardly be noticed by the man in the street; here there were real social undesirables to unearth and convict.

I had flushed one of them out already, apparently. Waiting on the bottom step to my apartment was a messenger. A pasty youth with a stye and a stammer told me Appius Priscillus had received my messages. If I wanted to meet him I was to be in the Forum of Julius in half an hour.

There was no time even to pop up and mention it to Helena. I thanked the youth (who looked surprised anyone should be grateful for an introduction to Priscillus) then I set off hot-foot.

I knew Petronius would have warned me against going solo, but I had my knife and my self-reliance, which had seen me through plenty. Besides, the Forum of Julius Caesar is an open public place.

I approached by what I thought was the subtle way, walking through the Curia and letting myself out of the great double doors at the back. It *would* have been a discreet approach – but Priscillus was not yet there so I had been wasting my time.

Everywhere seemed quiet. I had the big public lavatory on one hand and the shops on the other: ready for anything! Caesar had built his overspill Forum with a gracious surrounding colonnade; I moved out into the open, just in case.

The brown sedan turned up five minutes later. It entered from the eastern end and parked there, just inside the arch.

I had a good look round for ambushers: none in sight. In the end I ambled over. The carriers were standing motionless, staring ahead, ignoring me. They could be mute or stupid or foreign – or all three. I glanced back over both shoulders, then approached. When I whipped aside the lank leather curtain I had already convinced myself that Appius Priscillus would not be there. But I was wrong.

'*Get in!*' he said.

XLIX

It was like coming face to face with another rat: he was all teeth and piercing eyes. I got in, but I would rather have been tangling knees with my cellmate in the Lautumiae.

No one could accuse Priscillus of indulging in luxury. He had the skinny frame of a man who was too preoccupied to enjoy eating. He wore a dull old tunic, which had nothing actually wrong with it but was so depressing even I would have tossed it out for a tramp (though most tramps I knew had more sartorial style). A barber had made a few practice feints over his narrow chin fairly recently, but that was probably only because businessmen believe the barber's chair is a place to pick up tips. (I don't know why; all *I* ever pick up is a rash.) Attending to the Priscillus toilette had stopped short of the expensive frills. His thin hair was too long; his talons needed cleaning and clipping. And I could not imagine his razorman ever bothered offering any little flasks of cedar gum for contraceptive purposes . . .

Priscillus was unmarried; now I knew why. Not because a woman would be too fastidious to have him (most would tolerate grimy fingernails in return for all those strong-boxes), but this mean runt who barely kept himself alive would begrudge paying board and lodging for anything so inessential as a wife.

Even with two passengers the chairmen set off at a cracking pace. 'Where are we going?' I demanded in some alarm, before I even introduced myself.

'Business on the Campus Martius.' Well, I realised it had to be business; he would never spare time to visit a temple or indulge in exercise! 'So, you're Falco. What do you want with me?' His voice had a wheeze in it, as if he hugged in his breath as grudgingly as everything else he did.

'A few answers, please. I'm working on the Novus case – '

'Who are you working for?'

233

'I'm being *paid* by Severina Zotica,' I answered pedantically.

'More fool you! You want to look at your own client, Falco!'

'Oh I treat her very warily – but I'm looking at you first!' It was difficult to concentrate, for the bearers were still running and the chair jogged every syllable we tried to speak. 'Severina's a professional bride; she had no motive to kill Novus before she was in line to inherit his loot. You and the Hortensii must be much more viable suspects – ' The rat's eyes flashed a threat which made me shiver. 'Sorry, but I'm judging by the facts: it looks black for you if you are planning to merge operations with Felix and Crepito – when all Rome knows their dead partner was so strongly set against it. Why was that, by the way?' Priscillus only glared at me; I answered it myself. 'He saw it not as a merger but a takeover – by you. He was used to being top cockerel on his own dungheap; he refused to take second place to anyone . . . different for the other two, since they had always been subordinate to Novus anyway – '

The chair had stopped.

'You annoy me, Falco.' Priscillus spoke with the tired slur thugs always use for threats. He could have been any overstuffed off-duty guardsman who had crossed the street for the simple pleasure of shoving me aside.

'Then help me.'

'Help yourself!' he snarled insultingly. 'This is where we get out.'

I could tell we were well out on the Campus, on open ground. I experienced a sudden yearning to stay safe inside this chair of his, even joggling along and trying to keep from being bruised by his bony knees. He pulled back the curtain and climbed out himself. This almost had the foolish effect of reassuring me.

I got out. My foreboding had been correct. If I had clung on, the waiting Phrygians would simply have rolled the sedan chair onto its side and tackled the problem like poking a limpet to death inside its shell. Being out of it was no better. We had stopped in the middle of an exercise ground, and they all held javelins. The heads of the javelins were

234

not weighted with practice dummies, but sharp Noricum steel – *really* sharp. When I climbed out and straightened up I was pinned between them so that a move in any direction would slit my hide.

I said nothing. One spearhead was nuzzling my windpipe. Speech would have cut my own throat.

Nowadays the Plain of Mars is well built up with monuments but some parts are still desolate. We were in one of those. A dry wind off the river lifted my curls but barely brushed my sweating arms. A few cantering horseriders were visible, too far away to notice what was happening even if they were willing to interfere.

None of the Phrygians spoke to me. There were eight of them: taking no chances. They were slight, but all sinew. They had high-cheekboned features, distinguished one from another only by old scars. Aliens, from the mountainous interior of Asia; probably straight descendants of the Hittites – whose fame was based on cruelty.

They tired me out first. Playing, they nudged me this way and that. Some lifted away their spearheads; others shoved me towards them; I would lurch on my toes as the first javelins engaged again, then be pushed off another way. Too little interest on my part was corrected by a warning nick. Too much effort would spit me. All the time we all knew I was looking for a chance to break away and make a run for it – but it would be a long sprint. Even if I could ever put distance between us, the javelins would come winging after me . . .

The signal to act must have come from the man behind me. He grabbed me. The Phrygians all flung down their weapons. Then they played a new game – throwing me from one to another while they battered any parts of me they could reach. Not too hard: they wanted the fun to last.

I did manage to jackknife and land vindictive punches of my own, but that only made the jeers louder and the returns harder while my own anger burned more vilely in my mouth.

I knew by then Priscillus did not want me dead. He would have had them slash my throat at once and leave my corpse for the early-morning riders to stumble across next day, damp and stiff in the river mist. He wanted me to be

235

able to warn anyone else who looked at him too closely what crossing the mighty Appius Priscillus would entail.

At the end of all this I would still be alive.

Just so long as the Phrygians knew how to follow orders and were sufficiently well trained. Otherwise, there seemed a fair chance they might finish me off by accident.

L

For thugs, they were neat. They put me back where they first found me – in the Forum of Julius. When sensation returned, I could recognise the dictator's equestrian statue as his honour stared loftily at the world he had conquered (though he omitted to notice me).

I started to crawl. I had no idea where, since my eyes blurred. When I found the steps, I told myself carefully it must be the Temple of Venus Genetrix.

I passed out on them.

Next time I came round, I looked up and confirmed my impressive knowledge of topography. Here was the high platform, with me sprawled upon it, and up there were the gorgeous Corinthian columns. If any foreign visitors had stooped to ask me about the temple I could have informed them that inside they would find fine statues of Venus, Caesar, the youthful Cleopatra, and two ravishing pictures (by Timomachus) of Ajax and Medea. Meanwhile, they could make a note in their tour diary that *outside* they had seen the slightly less glorious informer M Didius Falco, calling for help so croakily no passers-by thought it safe to hear.

Nice work, Falco. If you have to be immobilised it may as well be on the steps of a world-famous temple in the most beautiful forum in Rome.

A priest came out. He gave me a kick and passed on quickly, thinking I was one of the usual beggars who loiter on temple steps.

Hours later he came back from his errand. I was ready for him now. 'Aid me, sir, in the name of the Divine Julius!'

I was right: most priests can be swayed by a plea in the name of the patron who provided their livelihood. Perhaps they are afraid you maybe one of the cult's auditors, testing them in disguise.

Once I managed to stop him, the priest condescended to clear my leaking carcass off his previously pristine marble steps, and load me into a litter which would be paid for by Petronius.

I missed the sensation my bloody arrival must have caused, by dint of being unconscious. A good trick if you can do it. Avoids fuss.

It was not the first time I had had myself delivered to Petronius like a package of overripe provisions which had been left steaming too long in the midday heat. But I had never before been tortured to a jelly quite so efficiently.

He was at home, luckily. I became aware I was in Petro and Silvia's house. Silvia was braising meat. Her small daughters were thundering about like a legion on rapid drill somewhere directly above us in the upstairs rooms. One of the children had a squeaky flute, adding to the agony.

I felt Petro cutting away my tunic; I heard him curse; I heard my boots thud into a bucket; I smelt the familiar potpourri of Petro's unlocked medicine chest. I let him force cold water into me to counter the shock. I swallowed some of a burning draught, though most seemed to trickle down my chest on the outside. After that it did not really matter if I passed out while he worked on me; so on the whole I did.

He had the sense to soak off the dirt and the loose blood, before he allowed his wife to leave the house to run for Helena.

LI

It was impossible to speak to her.

She said nothing either. Only the light pressure of her hand on mine altered fractionally. My swollen eyes could hardly open, but she must have detected the moment when I woke. I could see her against the dazzle: the familiar outline of her body; the shape of her hair, turned up the way she sometimes wore it, with boxwood combs above her ears. Her hair was too soft; the left-hand comb always ended up lower than the right.

Her thumb was moving faintly, caressing the back of my hand; she was probably unaware of doing it. By aiming through the left side of my mouth I managed to make some unintelligible sound. She bent forwards. Somehow she found the only square inch of my face which did not hurt for her gentle kiss.

She went away. Unreasonable panic swept over me, until I heard her voice. 'He's awake. Thank you for looking after him; I can manage now. Could you possibly find someone with a litter to carry him?' Petro's bulk filled the doorway, protesting that it was best to keep me here. (He thought Helena was too refined to deal with the nursing I would need.) I closed my eyes, waiting for it; the convincing voice of ownership: 'Petronius Longus, I am perfectly capable! I am not a schoolgirl, *playing* at house with pots and pans in miniature!'

'You're in serious trouble, Falco!' Petro said laconically. He meant, all this pain from Priscillus, and now another tyrant taking me over and shouting at my friends.

I could only lie there and let Helena fight it out. She certainly intended to get her own way. Could she cope? Petro thought not. What did I think? Helena Justina knew that too. 'Lucius Petronius – *Marcus wants me to take him home!*'

239

Petro muttered some swearwords; then he did as he was told.

The journey passed quickly but the men with the litter refused to attempt the stairs. I walked it. The whole three flights. There was no alternative.

When I swam fully back to consciousness I was propped upright against my own bedroom wall. Helena glanced across at me, then continued preparing my bed; Silvia had provided her with an old sheet in case I bled on my own decent one. Women are so practical.

I watched Helena's figure as she worked, with rapid movements and an economy of effort that would soon have things ready. Not soon enough.

'I'm going to fall over – '

'I'll catch you . . .'

I could trust Helena's promises. She reached me in one stride. Thank heavens for small rooms.

Without knowing how I got there, I found myself on the bed. I could smell that floral perfume all the women's bathhouses seemed to be using nowadays. What had brought me round was the sensation of being unwrapped from the cloak Petro rolled me in for travelling. Underneath all I had on were bandages.

Helena caught her breath. 'Well! This is going to take more than a bowl of hot soup inside you and a bean-meal mash outside . . . I've seen your manly attributes before, but I can throw a cover over you if you're shy.'

'Not with you.' In my own home I had recovered enough to slur a few words. 'You know everything about me; I know everything about you – '

'That's what you think!' she muttered, but delirium was taking hold and I was laughing too much to be sensible.

When she leaned over to square me up neatly on the pillow, I got my arms round her. Helena snorted. She struggled, on principle, but she was trying too hard not to hurt me as she landed; she missed her chance to escape. There was nothing else I could manage, but I held on tight. She gave in; after some mild squirming of a different kind I heard her sandals drop on the floor, then she unhooked

240

her earrings and laid them aside. I kept my arms locked round her as I drifted off into oblivion. She was lying quiet; she would still be there waiting when I awoke. If I had known this was all it would take to get her back in bed with me, I would have run out and had myself beaten up by some bully long before.

LII

She was there. Sitting at my bedside in a clean grey gown with newly pinned hair. Sipping something from a beaker, thoughtfully.

The changed light told me it was the next morning. Every part of me that had been swollen yesterday had now become stiff as well. Helena did not ask if I felt better; she could see I was worse.

She looked after me, in her sensible way. Petronius had supplied her with painkilling cordial, ointments and wads of lambswool; she had already mastered the medical régime. Anyone who had ever had charge of a baby understood my other needs.

When I was lying still, recovering from being cleansed and dosed, she sat on the bed and held my hand again. Our eyes met. I felt very close to her.

'What have you got to smile at?'

'Oh, any man feels a special attachment for the girl who washes his ears and empties his chamber pot.'

'I see this hasn't stopped you talking nonsense,' Helena said.

I was woken next by the parrot having one of its shrieking fits. A good scream several times a day seemed its way of taking exercise. Chloe's throat must have had the best toned-up set of muscles in Rome.

When the antisocial mobster finally shut up, Helena came in to see me.

'I'll suffocate that voice box!' I had never had to endure the full performance before. I was horrified. 'The old lady upstairs will be complaining –'

'She already has!' Helena informed me. 'I met her when I took back the bowls your sister borrowed for the fish supper. I was getting on with her quite nicely, but the bird stopped that. I feel sorry for the pathetic old thing; she has a running feud with the landlord; he keeps trying to winkle her out. Ranting at you is her only joy in life – I suppose I'll be like that one day . . .'

It must have been a couple of hours since I was last awake. Helena now had a different beaker; hot honey, which she shared with me. While I was still recovering from the effort of sitting up to drink it, someone knocked.

It was Hyacinthus. He had brought with him the scullion I remembered from the Hortensius kitchen. I glanced at Helena in desperation; I could never cope with this.

Nothing disturbed Helena Justina, once she deemed herself in charge. She patted my bandages. 'Didius Falco has had a slight upset as you can see.' The gods only know what I looked like. The visitors were crowding against the doorframe, completely quelled. 'There's no need for you to have a wasted journey; we'll fetch some stools into the bedroom and you can talk to me instead. Marcus will just lie still and listen in.'

'What happened to him?' Hyacinthus whispered.

Helena replied briskly, 'He tripped over a step!'

The washtub princess was called Anthea. She was three-foot high, and looked about twelve, though Helena and I agreed afterwards that we reckoned her secondary function had been warming the chef's bed. Her miserable life had given her a bad complexion, a sad face underneath it, a depressed outlook, chapped hands, and probably sore feet. Her threadbare scrap of a tunic barely reached down to her reddened knees.

I lay there and listened dreamily while Helena Justina tried to tease information out of this poor little mite: 'I want you to tell me everything about the day of the dinner party. Were you in the kitchen all the time? I expect there were plenty of pans and ladles to wash, even while Viridovix was just preparing the food?' Anthea nodded, proud to have her importance recognised. 'Did anything happen that *you* thought seemed peculiar?' This time the girl shook her head. Her dry, colourless hair had an annoying way of constantly falling over her eyes.

Helena had apparently remembered the entire party menu, because she mentioned most of the dishes. She

243

wanted to know who stirred the saffron sauce for the lobsters, who jointed the hare, who folded over the halibut pancakes, even who tied the damned dessert fruit onto the golden tree. Hearing it made me so queasy I only just held out. 'And was the lady they call Severina in the kitchen at any time?'

'From about halfway through.'

'Talking to Viridovix?'

'Yes.'

'Did she help him at all?'

'Mostly she sat up on the edge of a table. Viridovix used to get very excited when he was working and hot; she was keeping him calm. I think she tasted some gravies.'

'Was it a busy period? So you could not pay much attention?'

'Yes, but I did see her whisking the egg whites.'

The pot-scourer had a sniff sometimes, caused by neither grief nor a nasal infection; wrinkling her snitch merely added variety to her empty life. 'Sometimes eggs take ages don't they?' Helena chirped; she was more patient than I would have been. 'It's a good idea to pass the bowl around – what were they being used for?'

'A glaze.'

'A glaze?'

'It was her idea.'

'Severina's?'

'Yes. He was too polite to argue, but Viridovix thought it wouldn't work.'

'Why? Was the glaze spread on something the people were going to eat?' Helena asked, her dark eyes narrowing.

'No; just a plate.'

'A plate?'

'No one ate it. It was to decorate a plate.'

Under pressure the scullion was starting to look angry and confused. I was about to issue a signal, but Helena moved on anyway. 'Anthea, can you tell me how long Severina stayed with you, and what happened when she left?'

'She stayed all the time.'

'What – during the dinner?'

'Oh no; not that long. Until the party had started. Just

244

started,' she repeated, shoving that hair out of her eyes again while I gripped my bedcover.

'Then what?' Helena queried pleasantly. I think she knew I was getting annoyed.

'Severina sighed a bit and said she was feeling poorly so she would go home.'

'By then all she had done was taste some things, talk to Viridovix, and decorate a plate?'

'She inspected the dishes before she went.'

'What happened about that?'

'Nothing. She said it all looked lovely, and Viridovix should be proud of himself.'

If Helena was feeling the strain of this interview, no one would have known. 'So Severina left, then Viridovix went up to the triclinium to oversee the carvers. Did anyone except your own household servants come into the kitchen after that?'

'No.'

'Did you ever see any of the dinner guests?'

'They might have gone past to the lavatory. But I was busy by then.'

'None of them came in, for instance to say thank you for the splendid food?' I choked with mirth, echoed by Hyacinthus. Helena ignored us. 'Anthea, in your house where are the prepared dishes kept while they wait for the bearers to take them upstairs?'

'On a table by the kitchen door.'

'Inside the room?'

'Yes.'

'Could anyone have tampered with them without being seen?'

'No. A boy has to stand by the table to keep off the flies.'

'Ah! I expect there are quite a lot of flies in your house,' Helena allowed herself to jibe sarcastically. She had run out of questions for a moment.

'There was one thing,' Anthea broke in, almost accusingly. 'Severina and Viridovix were giggling about the cakes.'

Helena stayed calm. 'These were the bought pastries

which had come up to the house from the cakeseller Minnius?'

'One was a very big one.'

'A special one!' Helena exclaimed.

'Yes, but it can't have been the one that poisoned the master – ' For the first time Anthea was carried away by what she had to impart. 'I know about that cake; no one else does! Severina said it was going to cause a quarrel, because everyone would fight to snatch it off the plate. She *said* she would take it away, and keep it for Hortensius Novus to have afterwards in his own room by himself – '

Helena's head spun in my direction. We were both holding our breath, and even the runabout tensed, realising what this tale implied. But the scullion, having built up her big moment, deflated us. 'He never ate it though.'

She sat, enjoying the anticlimax she had caused. Helena murmured 'How do you know that?'

'I found it! After the dinner was over, when I was scraping scraps from the big gold plates so I could wash them. I saw that in one of the slop buckets. I remember, because at first I was going to pick it out again and eat it, only it was all covered with wet onion peel. I don't like onions,' Anthea added, as if she would have eaten the cake regardless, but for that.

'I wonder,' pondered Helena, 'who can have thrown the cake away?'

'Nobody knew. I was mad; I called out, what miserable rat dumped this good cake in here? I would have belted them – but no one knew.'

I roused myself. 'Anthea, had all the other cakes been eaten when the serving dish came back?'

'I'll say. We never see pastries sent back to the kitchen in our house!'

'How were they served – on the vine leaves Minnius sends them wrapped in?'

'No; just on a platter. I washed it,' she added bitterly. 'Not a crumb left; not a crumb! I nearly didn't bother to wash it at all.'

I fell back on my pillow. The cakes had to be a false

lead. Most people present must have eaten one, and none of the other diners had suffered ill effects.

Helena said quietly, 'Falco's tired. I think you must leave now – but you have been of immense help. Viridovix will be avenged, I promise you.'

She was shepherding them out, but that brain of hers was still reasoning rapidly for as they went I heard her ask Anthea whether the platter the cakes had been served on was the one with the egg white glaze.

Hyacinthus called out that he would see me on Thursday if I was able to attend the funeral, then he led off the little washer-upper. (Another thing Helena and I agreed afterwards, was that if we were right about Anthea's relationship with Viridovix, Hyacinthus had probably taken her over now.)

At the outside door I heard the runabout mention to Helena that downstairs in the street there were two men prominently watching our block. Rough types, he said.

Helena went into the living room alone. She would be thinking about what Hyacinthus had just said, not wanting to worry me. I heard her battering something in a bowl to take her mind off it.

Eventually she reappeared. 'Omelette for dinner.'

'What's that?' She was holding a dish covered in a thin layer of wet white froth.

'Egg white. I think if it's left it will set on the dish. It doesn't look much. But I suppose if it was Severina's own idea she could have convinced herself it resembled a decorative bed of snow.'

'Especially on silver.'

Helena was surprised. 'The dishes were gold!'

'Not all. Anthea said she nearly didn't wash up the cake plate; I saw that. It was a giant silver comport Severina had given to Novus.'

'I still think she was wasting eggs,' Helena muttered, inspecting our own crock doubtfully.

'All right. Tell me instead what the runabout said about men watching the house.' She concentrated on the egg white; Helena did not believe in sharing her troubles with an invalid. 'I think we're safe,' I told her, because I knew who the watchers would be.

'Marcus – ' she began indignantly.

'When you go out, march straight up and ask who sent them here.'

'You know?'

'Petronius. He has equipped us with a highly visible vigilante guard.'

'If Petronius thinks that necessary, it frightens me even more!' We stared at each other. Helena must have decided there was no point creating a fuss. 'Did I ask the right questions?'

'You always ask the right questions!'

'The cakes are important, Marcus; I *know* they are. You could poison cakes individually. But ensuring the right victim took the right cake . . . I thought it must be the extra large one.'

'I know you did,' I smiled at her.

'That would have been perfect, Marcus! Hortensius Novus was the host. In such a vulgar house I bet they offer platters to the host first; Novus could be guaranteed to grab the best!'

I smiled again. 'Yet Severina took it off the plate!'

'This is a complete puzzle.'

'Perhaps not. It could be that Severina is innocent. Maybe she went to the house, even though she was feeling off colour, because she had realised the banquet could be dangerous for her beloved. Maybe she really wanted to check for anything suspicious in the food.'

'Is that what she says?' Actually, that was one line she had not inflicted on me yet. 'It could be,' Helena retorted bleakly, 'this is just what Severina *wants* you to think. Do you believe Viridovix knew she was checking for people trying to get at his food?'

'Viridovix was no fool.'

Helena growled. 'Perhaps you were meant to discover the business with the giant pastry; it could be a clever double bluff, while the poison was really somewhere else – '

'Oh it was somewhere else!' We both fell silent. 'If he was poisoned at the dinner,' I said, 'it may rule out any connection with Priscillus. His business rival could not easily snuff him out in his own house.'

'Could not Priscillus have bribed one of the Hortensius slaves?'

'Risky. Slaves fall under suspicion so easily. It would take a large bribe – and then there is a risk that a slave with too much money becomes conspicuous.'

'Not if the slave was Viridovix; and if Viridovix is now dead!'

'I won't believe it was the cook.'

'All right. You met him!' She noticed I was really too tired to go on. 'Are we any further forwards?' she asked, smoothing my bedcover.

I lifted a scratched finger tenderly to her cheek. 'Oh I think so!' I leered at her cheekily.

Helena put my arm back under the cover. 'It's time I fed the parrot; go to sleep!'

'The parrot is old enough to feed itself.'

She was still sitting quietly with me. 'You sound better; it's a good sign when you can talk.'

'I can talk; I just can't move.' Something was on her mind. 'What is it, fruit?'

'Nothing.'

'I know my girl!'

'Marcus, how do you bear the pain?'

'At the time you're being beaten up, you tend to be too busy to notice it. Afterwards, you just have to be brave . . .' I was watching her. Sometimes Helena's dogged way of tackling life made her close in on herself. It was hard for anyone to reach her then, though sometimes she would turn to me. 'Sweetheart . . . when you lost the baby did it hurt?'

'Mmm.' Despite the brief answer, she was prepared to communicate. There might never be another opportunity like this.

'Is that why having another frightens you?'

'I'm frightened of everything, Marcus. Not knowing what will happen. Not being able to do anything about it. The *helplessness* . . . Incompetent midwives, crass physicians with terrifying instruments – I'm frightened I'll die. I'm terrified that after all that effort the *baby* will die, and how will I

249

bear it? . . . I love you very much!' she said suddenly. It did not seem irrelevant.

'I would be there,' I promised her.

She smiled sadly. 'You would find some urgent job to do!'

'No,' I said.

Helena wiped away her tears while I lay trying to look reliable. 'Now I'll go and feed the parrot,' she said.

She made the mistake of looking back from the door.

I grumbled plaintively, 'You're only using that parrot as a handy alibi!'

'Look at the state of you!' Helena scoffed. 'Who needs an alibi?'

Then before I could reach out and grab her she had to run, because a grinding noise announced that the damned parrot was learning to bend open the bars of its cage.

'Oh stop being so wicked and tell me who did it!' Helena roared.

But Chloe only shrieked back, *'Marcus has been a naughty boy!'*

Untrue, unfortunately.

250

LIII

Helena decided *she* would visit her parents before the Senator (with a large cudgel) came to visit *me*.

I was half dozing when I thought I heard her returning; I lay low until someone came into the bedroom, when I shouted out, 'Is that you?'

'*Oh Juno!*' Wrong voice! 'Yes; it's me – you frightened me!'

Severina Zotica.

I sat up abruptly. She had the parrot on her forearm, so she must have been into the office where we kept its cage. I wondered if the prying cat's little feet had also invaded Helena's room. Her nose would have brought her tripping in here, for Helena was a determined believer in fenugreek poultices, continually applied (unlike Petronius, who cleaned wounds once with his balsam resins, then tended to lose interest).

My mashed features stopped the gold-digger short. 'Oh no! Oh, Falco, whatever happened to you?'

'Appius Priscillus.'

She was at the bedside, fluttering with concern. 'But you need looking after – '

'Someone takes care of me.'

Her eyes darted round quickly. She had already absorbed the fact that despite half a week's dissolute growth of beard, I was well sponged down, combed, and fitted out like an eastern potentate with cushions and bowls of figs. My abrasions and swellings had finished growing worse, though they had not yet begun to improve; the bandages were off to air them, but I had been covered up with a clean tunic – not for modesty, but to stop me prodding the bumps and scabs to check progress every five minutes.

'Your mother?' Severina queried sharply.

'Girlfriend,' I stated, for some reason not wanting her to know.

251

Severina's white face seemed to become taut. At that moment the parrot crooned softly in its throat, so she stroked the feathers on its grey neck. 'You lied to me, Falco – about this bird – and about your woman friend too.'

'Not at all.'

'You said – '

'I know what I said. It was true at the time. It's my girlfriend who needs Chloe for company. They both have tricky tempers; I think they're taming one another . . .' These jolly jests were making little headway. 'I'm sorry I couldn't keep in touch; I've not left the house since this. What can I do for you?'

'One of my slaves heard a rumour Priscillus had had you worked over, so I rushed round here of course – I never imagined it would be so bad!'

'It's getting better. No need to get fluffed up.'

Helena's wicker chair was by my bed, so I motioned Severina to sit down. 'Nice to have a visitor.' The atmosphere seemed tense and I wanted to loosen the screw.

She scowled. 'So where is your attendant?'

'Helena?' The girl's insistency was irritating me, but stretched out on my own bed in comfort, I could not be bothered to fight. The redhead seemed to have an envious urge for possession, like a child snatching at other infants' toys before it has been taught self-control. 'Helena Justina has gone to explain to her father, who happens to be a senator, why *I* have yet to put in an appearance to apologise for pinching his noble child. If a man rushes in with red crescents on his boots – ' (the traditional patrician uniform) ' – bearing a sharp sword and a furious expression, just step aside and let him get to me!'

'You unspeakable hypocrite – you're after her money!'

'Oh she's after mine. I have great difficulty keeping her away from my accounts!'

People never believe the truth.

There was a silence. I was still too sick to concern myself with other people's touchiness.

'What's this, Falco?'

I had a slate on the bed. 'Today's diagnosis was boredom;

252

I was left here with orders to write a poem. Thought I might scribble a satire on why I hate parrots.'

'What a rude man!' crooned Severina to the parrot.

'*What a rude man!*' Chloe instantly answered her.

'Quick learner!' I observed.

Unabashed Severina turned back to me. 'Does this mean the investigation has ground to a halt?'

'Ah! The investigation . . .' I joked, teasing her with flippancy. There were several queries I could have put to her: concerning egg-white glazes for instance, or thrownaway patisserie. But I had decided to complete my enquiries before I let Severina Zotica confuse the issue with more easy answers. I adopted my brave professional voice: 'I need a week at home in bed – but I shall have to make do with three days. Tomorrow morning is the funeral of the Hortensius chef, which I want to attend.'

Severina looked troubled. 'What happened to Viridovix, Falco? I heard he had died, very suddenly. Is it something to do with what happened to Novus?'

I smiled reassuringly. 'Viridovix died peacefully in his sleep.'

'Then why are you going to his funeral?'

'Firstly, I liked him. Also, it gets me near the house.'

'Looking for clues?'

'Could be.'

'Falco, I don't understand you sometimes! I am your client, Falco. Why is it necessary to be so secretive?'

'No complicated motive. All right: I think it might be useful to show the Hortensius family – and probably through them to warn that bastard Priscillus – that contrary to rumour I am still able to get about.' She looked down at me, as if she was afraid I might not manage it. 'Tell me, have you ever encountered this Priscillus?'

She frowned suspiciously, though in fact the question was mere curiosity. 'When I was married to the apothecary, we lived near that house of his up on the Esquiline. Then when things between him and Novus were at their worst recently, I went to see Priscillus myself. I acted as go-between and took his invitation to the dinner – '

'Novus agreed to that?'

'Of course! I would never have gone otherwise.' I nodded gravely, amused by this shocked protest; of course no respectable female visits men. But then who is respectable? 'If it was Priscillus who killed my fiancé, I helped bring it about!' She had a quaint way of overlooking ironies.

'Calm down,' I clucked. 'A property war was about to erupt well before you took a hand in it. And now I've been on the receiving end of Priscillus when he felt disgruntled, I reckon Hortensius Novus was destined for Hades whatever you did.'

'Do you think it *was* Priscillus? Did he attack you because you had some evidence?'

'Priscillus would probably have killed Novus if he could get away with it. I am not sure yet. My money is on Pollia and Atilia at the moment – ' She looked satisfied with that alternative, as any woman would.

I was starting to worry why Helena had been gone so long; I missed her if she left the house. I suggested Severina could stay and meet her. 'No; I was on my way to the baths – ' So much for making a special journey to see me! She persuaded the parrot to hop on to the post at the end of my bed. 'Now: you are going to the cook's funeral; I still don't really know why – ' She paused, as if she did not entirely trust me. I scowled, which may not have given the reassurance she required. 'Will you come and see me afterwards?'

'If madam requires.'

Before she left she told me to take care of myself (though I thought we had established someone else was doing that), then at the last moment she leaned over and kissed my cheek.

I swear she expected me to grapple her onto the bed. Some people show no respect for an invalid.

'Alone at last!' I sighed at the parrot.

'More front than the beach at Baiae!' the parrot returned colloquially.

I started my poem.

Afterwards I did some thinking.

254

Anyone else who had been battered to cow-heel glue by Appius Priscillus might decide that alone convicted him of any unsolved deaths that month. I was not so sure. The sequence of events seemed illogical. Hortensius Novus had invited Priscillus to dinner, promising a pact; there was no way Priscillus could have known until the night was over that Novus would reject a merger after all. When things were looking hopeful, why come armed to murder him?

The over-ostentatious cake rang with the women's resonance. Obvious and vulgar. Too obvious, it seemed to me – but crimes are often committed with ludicrously poor judgement. Criminals are supposed to be cunning and clever. Sometimes fools get away with a crackpot scheme because no one can believe they would have behaved so stupidly. Not me though. After five years as an informer, I was prepared to believe anything.

I had been thoughtful too long.

'*So tell me who did it!*' Chloe screamed.

I threw my boot at her, just as Helena came in. She rushed out again, giggling helplessly.

'How was your father?' I shouted after her.

'He wants to talk to you.'

'I thought he might!'

She poked her head back round the door curtain and gave me a smile which ought to have warned me there was worse to come. 'Actually, my mother does as well . . .'

Helena Justina reckoned Falco's *Satire* I.1 ('*Let me tell you, Lucius, a hundred reasons why I hate this parrot . . .*') was the best work I had ever done.

Just my luck.

255

LIV

I make it a rule never to go to the funerals of people I have killed myself. But it seemed fair to make an exception for someone I had killed by accident.

Helena was still sleeping on the reading couch in the other room, on the poor excuse that she would not disturb my convalescing frame. Something would have to be done about that. I was already enjoying myself, planning schemes for changing things.

I got up quietly on my own. The day before I had dressed and mooched about the house to test my strength, but there was a subtle difference now I knew I was going outside. For the first time since I was hurt I made my own morning drink; watered the sleepy parrot; and looked about like a proprietor again (noticed that the crack in the wall seemed to be growing steadily). I took a beaker in to Helena. Hiding her anxiety, she pretended to be half asleep though an inch of warm cheek emerged from the coverlet to be kissed goodbye.

'Take care . . .'

'And you.'

On legs which felt like cotton floss I walked downstairs, then I noticed a carrier staring at my bruises so I walked all the way back to find a hat. In case Helena had heard me and was frightened, I popped in to reassure her it was me.

She had gone.

Puzzled, I turned back into the corridor. The apartment was silent; even the parrot had hunched up and gone back to sleep.

I pushed aside the curtain to my bedroom. Her beaker of hot honey now stood among my own pillowside litter of pens, coins and combs; Helena was in my bed. As soon as I left she must have scampered out and curled up here, where I had been.

Her brown eyes stared at me like some defiant dog, left alone, which had jumped up on its master's couch the moment he left the house.

She did not move. I waved the hat in explanation, hesitated, then crossed the room to kiss her goodbye again. I found the same cheek – then as I moved away she followed; her arms came round my neck, and our lips met. My stomach tensed. Then a brief moment of questioning dissolved into certainty: this was the old, sure welcome only Helena could give – the girl I so badly wanted, saying that she wanted me . . .

I made myself stop. '*Work!*' I groaned. No one would hold up the cook's funeral if I stayed to play.

Helena smiled, still hanging round my neck as I feebly tried to free myself while my hands began to travel over and round her more deliberately. Those eyes of hers were so full of love and promise I was ready to forget everything. 'Work, Marcus . . .' she echoed. I kissed her again.

'I think it's time,' I murmured, against Helena's mouth, 'I started coming home for lunch like a good Roman householder . . .'

Helena kissed me.

'Stay there!' I said. 'Don't stir – stay there and wait for me!'

LV

This time as I reached ground level some contractor's men were unloading their tools from a hand-drawn cart. A helpful sign. If the landlord was bringing in the finishing trades at last, maybe we should soon have new tenants too. Make the place less like living in a mausoleum. And some time – though probably not today! – I might persuade those fellows to stuff some hair and plaster in our crack.

I felt good. Even though I was going to someone else's funeral, *my* life was cheering up.

It was the Kalends of September. In Rome, still hot well into the evening, though in the northern parts of the Empire – Britain, for instance, where I had served in the army and later met Helena – there would be a damp chill now in the mornings and the long winter dark would already be making its approach felt on the late afternoons. Even here, time had taken a new turn round the spindle. I felt like a stranger. I had that uneasy mood which besets the emerging invalid, as if the city had lived through centuries in the few days I was confined to my sickroom.

I had come out too soon. The air felt troublesome on my fragile skin. The bustle disconcerted me. Noise and colour shouted alarm signals to my brain. But the first real shock of my working day was that when my hired donkey blundered up the slope of the Pincian, the stall where Minnius used to sell his cakes had gone.

There was nothing left. The stall, the awning, the delectable produce had all vanished. Even the oven had been dismantled. Someone had completely levelled the cakeman's pitch.

Within the extensive Hortensius grounds, smoke from a portable altar led me to the scene of the funeral. Members of the household were still winding out in convoy from the mansion; I stood back while they assembled in a space

258

among the pine trees. Viridovix would be in famous company. Pincian Hill boasts the Emperor Nero's surprisingly tasteful monument.

There were no shocks at the funeral. Revelations at the bierside are a cheap device employed by epic poets. I was a satirist now, so I knew better than to expect surprises; we satirists are realists.

In my Greek brimmed hat, and the black cloak I wear on these occasions, I tiptoed discreetly among the mourners. I may not have passed entirely unnoticed, since the normal rule at funerals is that half the people present spend most of their time peering about for family celebrities; the keen-eyed, looking for long-lost half-brothers to complain about, would have worked out that I was an unknown quantity who might be good for a few hours of speculative gossip later on.

Crepito, Felix, and their two wives made a cursory appearance as their loyal servant was bundled into the Underworld with the minimum of fuss. The sweet oils were pleasant though not overpowering. A plaque had been commissioned; it would be set in the high boundary wall. I noticed it had been purchased and dedicated not by the masters of the house, but by his fellow slaves.

Once the Hortensii had paid their brief respects while the fire was lit, they went about their business; probably racing off to the slave market to acquire a new cook.

I pushed back the hat and made myself known to Hyacinthus, who was standing with the household chamberlain. As the flames burned up, we talked.

'Falco! You still look ready to step up on the pyre there with him!'

'After four days on nothing but grape jelly in milk, don't sneeze, or you'll blow me over. I was hoping to cheer myself up with some tipsy cake – what happened to Minnius?'

'Some trouble about his lease for the stall. Felix cancelled it and kicked him out.'

'So where has Minnius gone?'

'Who knows?'

Now the owners had departed I could sense undercurrents of bad feeling here among the slaves. The cook's

259

death had caused rumours, however much the Hortensii convinced themselves it had been hushed up.

'It hasn't helped,' grumbled Hyacinthus, 'that they buried Novus in high old style – whereas poor old Viridovix had to wait around at the embalmers for the best part of a week, and now his send-off is as brisk as possible. He was a slave – but so were they once!'

'So much,' I said, 'for the concept of family!'

Hyacinthus introduced the chamberlain, an uneasy type with pointed ears who had been glancing at me curiously. 'Hello! I'm Falco. Viridovix and I shared a drink and some good conversation the night he died, that's why I'm here. Do you mind if I ask you something?' He looked shy, but let me proceed. 'I was talking to Viridovix about that dinner party; he told me how smoothly it passed off – ' Without a remit from the family I had to be quick and careful. 'Do you know what happened after the diners settled down in private?'

The chamberlain had remained within call after the servants were shooed out. He was classy enough to know he ought to keep things confidential, and human enough to want to spill his tale. 'There was a bust-up,' he let out.

'What was the problem?'

He laughed. 'The problem was Novus!'

'What – he let the rest of the party know there would be no joint stock confederation as they hoped?'

'That's right. He refused to play; they could all put their knucklebones back in the drawstring bag . . .'

So that was it; I sucked air through my teeth. 'When Novus stomped off afterwards, leaving Felix and Crepito with Priscillus, did those three get their heads together? Wasn't it hugs all round on the doorstep when Priscillus left?'

'If you ask me – ' he lowered his voice ' – Crepito and Felix have been hooked up with Priscillus for a long time.'

'Unknown to Novus,' I commented. Then I realised. 'No . . . no, that's wrong – of course! *Novus* had found out!'

That explained everything – his partners and Priscillus believed he had invited them to dinner to reconcile their differences – but in fact, Novus was planning a spiteful scene: once the doors were closed and the conversation became sub rosa, he confronted them with his knowledge of their previous canoodling – to which his solution was: marry Severina Zotica, abnegate the time-honoured partnership, probably move house when he got married, set up solo – and take the business off with him. That would horrify Felix and Crepito – because not only would they lose their share of the Hortensius business empire, they would also forfeit any passing interest they had held for Appius Priscillus. He was no man to take on dud partners. They were dumped off both sides of the boat!

'Felix and Crepito must have been shitting Nile delta mud – how did Priscillus take it?'

'Surprisingly well,' said the chamberlain.

Up until then I had been surviving, but I suddenly felt too much aware that it was my first day out of doors. Excitement and the heat from the pyre were threatening to keel me over. I stopped talking. I had to concentrate on fighting this sudden sweat.

The chamberlain had done enough that day for truth and justice; I could feel him closing up.

A small group of us watched the last spurt of the sweet-scented flames as Viridovix went in the Roman fashion to his own remote gods.

'He was a prince!' I murmured. 'Though a dedicated cook. A classic. He and I saw out his last night in the way any cook would have wanted – with a good drink, pilfered from the higher-ups . . . in fact,' I sighed, 'I wouldn't mind knowing what the vintage was, so I can buy myself an amphora and drink it in his memory – '

'Here's your man then – ' The chamberlain stopped a youngster, with the swollen eyelids of a late-riser up before his natural time, who was on his way forward to pour a libation on the pyre. 'Galenus keeps our cellar – '

'Thanks! Galenus, can you tell me what variety of Falernian Crepito and Felix drink – would it be Faustianum?'

'Falernian?' He pulled up. 'Not here! You must mean the Setinum – they reckon it's superior – one of their fads.'

261

Setinum was what Viridovix had listed on his menu, certainly.

'Are you sure you hadn't made an exception for a special occasion? There was a nice wine here the night your master died. It was in a blue glass flask with silver lustre on the shoulders . . .'

The lad became even more definite. 'Not one I ever put out that night.'

'We were on orders to impress,' confirmed the chamberlain. 'Nothing less than the gold jugs and anything set with gemstones.'

'Your flask isn't one of mine,' Galenus assured me. 'I don't recall even seeing one like that.'

'It never came back to you in the buttery?'

'No; I'm sure. I keep my eye open for fancy glass, for when the ladies want a tipple served up daintily in the afternoons.'

'That's very interesting!' I said. 'I wonder if it could have been a present someone brought?'

'Priscillus,' inserted another lad, a round and red-faced little apple who had been listening to us avidly. 'I was on shoe duty,' he explained. In the thick of it, removing people's sandals as they arrived. 'Priscillus brought the sparkling blue flask.'

I smiled at the russet. 'And was there a little bowl in matching glass?'

He did not hesitate. 'Oh Priscillus had that in a satchel put aside with his cloak. When he was leaving he suddenly remembered, and rushed to put the bowl on the sideboard with the flask. He had even brought some myrrh in a little bag, which he tipped in to make the present all complete . . .'

What a touching thought. I could hardly contain my admiration: a model guest!

LVI

I looked around for the skivvy Anthea, but the burning pyre
seemed to have brought the cook's death fully home to her;
the wheyfaced scullion was sobbing in the arms of two
weepy cronies the way teenage girls do. I had a couple of
questions ready, but I abandoned them.

Not long before the smoke died down, I recognised a
figure approaching from the gatehouse. It was one of Severina's slaves.

'She wants you to come for lunch.' It was typical of this
solid doorstopper that he grunted it without preliminaries.

'Thanks, but I won't be able to manage it.'

'She won't like that!' he said.

I was tired of his mistress trying to make demands on
me when I had busy plans of my own, but to get rid of him
I said I would break my previous appointment if I could
(not meaning to try). Then I slung one end of my black
cloak over my shoulder and studied the pyre like a mourner
who was lost in melancholy thought: the transience of life,
inevitable death, how to avoid the Furies, how to placate
the Fates (and how soon can one politely make an escape
from this funeral . . .).

When the slave had gone I cast my garland and poured
my oil, said a few words in private to the cook's soul, then
collected my hired donkey and left the scene.

At the site where the cake stall once stood I reined in
thoughtfully.

I had to be clear what I intended doing now. I had been
working for Severina simply to stay close enough to study
her as a suspect. It must be nearly time to choose where I
really stood.

Yet it was beginning to look as if Severina's theories
about who killed Hortensius Novus might be accurate. Priscillus for one had attempted it, after Novus took his stub-

263

born business stand. And apparently either Pollia or Atilia was responsible for another try, with a poisoned cake.

I considered the one line of events which I could now trace satisfactorily: Priscillus planting the poisoned spices which killed Viridovix. A murder which did remove a key witness to what had happened that day in the kitchen – yet a murder brought about by chance. If I had not gone into the dining room for professional reasons that evening, Viridovix would never have rushed in there too. No one could have planned that. Poor Viridovix was an accident.

For obvious and very strong reasons I wanted to avenge the cook. For equally strong social reasons, there was no future in doing it.

True, I had enough evidence to ask a magistrate to indict Appius Priscillus. But face facts: Viridovix was a slave. If I showed that Priscillus had killed him – especially without intending to – what would probably happen if it ever reached a court would be not a murder trial, but a civil suit by the Hortensii for the loss of their slave. The worst charge levelled against Appius Priscillus would be a compensation claim for lost property. No court would put much value on a Gallic prisoner of war; a cook, and not even Alexandrian! Two hundred sestercii, at the outside.

That left my only hope of exacting retribution for Viridovix in the indirect approach: through proving what had happened to his dead master and bringing *that* culprit to book. All I knew was what had *not* happened. I could name suspects with motives, but possessing a motive to kill someone was not, in these enlightened days, enough to have them denounced publically. They had made attempts; yet as far as I knew the attempts had failed. Again, probably no charge.

Lastly, there was Severina Zotica. Severina, who had established a wonderful motive for herself when Novus agreed to marry her – and lost it, the moment he died before their wedding contracts were exchanged.

Perhaps she had *another* motive. But if so, I could not fathom what it was.

Why do funerals always arouse such a tearing appetite? I

264

had to stop thinking about life, death, and retribution. All I could apply my mind to was the now futile memory of delectable cakes.

What ineptitude makes a landlord destroy such a boon to the community? Minnius would have been an asset to the neighbourhood whatever rent he paid. By clearing him out, Hortensius Felix must have made his name a byword for pointless destructiveness all over the Pincian. Well, landlords are used to that. Who knows what labyrinthine form of reasoning churns in a lessor's perverted mind? Though in this case the answer was unfortunately obvious: Minnius knew too much.

What could he have known? Simple: Minnius knew who bought the dinner-party cakes.

It was dangerous knowledge. For a moment I even wondered if the cakeman might be dead. Perhaps one dark night after Hortensius Novus was poisoned, sinister shapes had come flitting down the hill from the freedmen's mansion, battered the unlucky pastry king while he was sleeping, and buried the corpse in a shallow grave on the site of his flattened oven and stall . . . No. I was still sick and rambling. One glance round the area convinced me that no soil had been disturbed. (I was a market gardener's grandson – but more than that, I had been in the army; the army teaches you all there is to know about digging hostile ground.) After a long hot Roman August it would be obvious if anyone had attempted to scrape at this hard-baked hillside. Only the sun had forced open these giant cracks where furiously aimless ants ferried themselves to and fro with specks of chaff while the more sensible lizards basked. Only wheels and hooves had ever packed down the surface of this road.

Minnius might be dead, but if so he wasn't here. And if he wasn't here, in the absence of other evidence I might as well hope he was alive.

So where would he go? Thinking back to my previous conversations with him, it was possible he had told me the answer himself: ' . . . *in those days I was still selling pistachio nuts off a tray in the Emporium . . .* '

I turned the donkey down the hill, and set off across Rome.

It took me an hour to find him, but I managed eventually. So it was an hour well spent.

The Emporium sits on the city side of the Tiber bank, under the shadow of the Aventine. It is the main exchange in Italy for produce imported by sea, quite simply the greatest, most fascinating commodity market in the Empire – the hub of world trade. You can buy anything there, from Phoenician glass to Gallic venison; Indian rubies; British leather; Arabian peppercorns; Chinese silk; papyrus, fish pickle, porphyry, olives, amber, ingots of tin and copper or bales of honey-coloured wool; and from Italy itself all the building bricks, roof tiles, ceramic dinner services, oil, fruit and wine you could ever want – provided you are prepared to buy it in wholesale quantities. No point asking the man politely if he will pick you out just one nice nutmeg; it must be twenty caskfulls, or you'd better be on your way before he reinforces his raucous sarcasm with the sole of his boot. There are stalls outside for timewasters who only want something tasty for the family lunch.

I had known the cavernous interior of the Emporium building, the wharves where the Tiber wherries jostled in queues before they landed, and the unloading bays for the creaking wagons that rumbled overland from Ostia, since I was knee-high to a Macedonian. I knew more people in the Emporium than my brother-in-law Gaius Baebius did, and he worked there (mind you, unless he landed you with the calamity of his marrying your sister, who would want to know Gaius Baebius?) I even knew that although the place appeared to be stuffed with produce, there were good days at the Emporium; but when the right ships had just landed there could be even better ones. Mind you, the normal rules of human life applied here as well: if you dropped in for that special rose-tinted marble your architect had recommended to face your reconditioned atrium, the odds were that the very last sheets in stock would have gone out yesterday to some baker who was building himself an atrocious mausoleum, and as to when another consignment could be expected, legate – it would depend on the quarry, and the shipper, and the winds, and frankly, *who could say?* Odds on, you would buy yourself a Syrian perfume jar to save being altogether disappointed by the trip – then drop it on the doorstep when you reached home.

Leave that aside. *My* trip was a success.

The main building was the usual throng of porters and patter. Pushing my way round this noisy bazaar was not the wisest occupation for a recent invalid. But I did find him. He had gone down from a stall but was still one up from his old tray; he was now selling from a stone-faced counter, though he told me he had to take his wares to be cooked first at a public bakery.

'So why did Felix chuck you out?'

'Novus was the sweet tooth in that house,' Minnius mentioned warily.

'Oh I know that! I'm working on a theory that his sweet tooth was what finished Novus – ' I stopped short. Best to avoid too much stress on the possibility that Minnius sold cakes that caused poisonings – even if it was somebody else who put the poison into them. 'So how are you managing?'

'Oh it's home from home. I should have come back years ago. I kept telling myself I ought not to leave there because I had built up a good passing trade, but you just as soon create your regulars in a place like this.'

'You like the bustle. On Pincian Hill even the fleas are snobs.' Minnius served a porter with a giant-sized slab of tipsy cake. 'So – three questions, my friend, and then I'll leave you to get on!' He nodded. People like to know there will be set limits to the invasion of their time. 'One: tell me about the batch of confectionery you sent up the hill the night Hortensius Novus died. Were there any special instructions, or was the choice left to you?'

His face set slightly. My guess was, somebody had warned him to keep his mouth shut, but he decided to tell me anyway. 'The original request was for seven luxury pastries. The runabout ambled down the day before and placed the order – a mixture, my choice; but on the afternoon somebody came by and picked another out.'

'Much bigger than the ones you sent,' I said quietly. 'It was to go in the centre of the platter for effect. It would have caused an effect all right!' I commented, leaving Minnius to

267

work out why. 'Question number two, therefore: who picked the extra cake, Minnius?'

I had money on two of them, mentally. I would have lost. Minnius, with his eyes steady, answered, 'Hortensia Atilia.'

The meek one! *That* was an unexpected treat. I thought about it. 'Thanks.'

'And your third question?' he nagged. Behind me a queue was waiting to be served.

I grinned at him. 'The third is; how much to buy two of your raisin-stuffed pastry doves, for me and my special lady?'

'How special?'

'Very.'

'Better do you a special price.' He wrapped two of the biggest in vine leaves, and gave them to me for nothing.

I put the cakes in my hat, which I carried. Then I set off for home and the special lady who was waiting for me there.

I left the donkey in the hiring stables since I expected to be indoors some while; there was no need to deprive him of shade, hay and companionship. Besides, I hate paying standing time.

The stables were just around the corner from where we lived. From this corner, you could see the entire block. I was like a lad with his first sweetheart, staring round in wonder at everything. I looked up, which you normally never do at your own house since you are thinking about wherever you have just come from, and trying to find your latch-lifter.

The sun was above me, hitting my left eye. I started to squint, looking away from the apartment. Then I had to look back.

Something produced an odd effect. I shaded my eyes. The building seemed to shimmer for a second, though not with light. I was about fifty yards away. The street was busy; no one else noticed anything at first.

The entire frontage of my apartment block crumpled, quite quickly, like a human face dissolving into tears. The building swayed, then visibly hung in the air. All the natural forces which keep a structure upright had lost their effect;

for an instant every component was suspended in space individually. Something maintained the shape of the building – then nothing did. The block neatly folded, with a strangely compact motion, falling in upon itself.

Then the noise overwhelmed the street.

Immediately afterwards we were swamped by a great cloud of masonry dust which enveloped everyone in its stinging, suffocating filth.

LVII

First the incredible silence. Then people start to scream.

You have to clear the dust from your eyes first. Shaking yourself makes it worse. You cannot move until you can see. Your senses are fighting to catch up with what is happening.

The first screams are the people in the street, startled and shocked, but grateful that they at least still have breath to scream. After that there may be others, from underneath the rubble, but it is difficult to tell until the panic quietens down and someone starts to organise. Someone always will.

There is a procedure to follow. In Rome, buildings often come falling down.

Word goes round the neighbourhood quickly; the noise assures that. In no time men run up with shovels and props. Others will follow with carts, grapplers, barrows from building sites, makeshift stretchers and perhaps even a hoist. But not soon enough. If the building was known to be occupied, those of you on the spot don't wait. Before the men come with shovels you start in with bare hands. It achieves little. But how can you just stand?

All I had in the world to worry about was two pastries in a hatful of dust. I put the hat down on a doorstep and laid my cloak over it. A gesture really; while I tried to cope.

Stay there . . . Don't stir – stay there and wait for me!

The walk to what had been our apartment seemed to take a year. Others were moving forwards with me. Even if you are a stranger you do what you can.

I wanted to shout; I wanted to roar. I could not bear to speak her name. Someone did shout: a cry, just a noise to say we were there. So next we stood, listening to the debris settling. That is the procedure; you shout or you knock on something; then listen; then dig. With luck, you are digging for someone. But you dig anyway. You wrench away whole

270

beams as if they were cordwood, turn over doors which are still attached to frames, bend jagged spars, and scrabble among tons of anonymous rubble which somehow no longer bears any resemblance to the materials which originally went into the block. All around the air is cloudy. Shapes move. The mass beneath your boots sinks suddenly, with a lurch that makes your heart race, amid more sick clouds of filth. A four-inch nail, still as bright as the day it was first hammered home, gouges your bare knee. The backs of your hands are in shreds from scraping against bricks and concrete. Your sweat can hardly manage to trickle through the thick coating of pale dust that dries your skin. Your clothes are stiff with it. Your boots will never be worth pulling on again. Through their thongs your toes and ankles bleed. That dust clogs your lungs.

Every now and then people stop again and call for silence; then somebody who has the heart for it shouts. And you listen to the slow trickle of loose mortar among the broken bricks and tiles and papery lathes that were once your home.

If it was a large building, you know before you listen that there is very little chance of anybody ever answering.

While we are working I hardly spoke to anyone. Even strangers must have realised the place was known to me. When the first spades came I snatched one at once; I had proprietary rights. At one point there was a sudden rattle of subsidence so we all jumped back. I took the lead then, to supervise the forcing of props into place. I had been in the army. I was trained to take command of civilians when they were running round like chickens. Even in a catastrophe, you have to be businesslike. Even if I had lost her, she would expect that. The girl would expect me to do what I could, in case I could save someone else. If she was here, at least I was close to her. I would stay here, day and night if necessary, until I knew for certain where she was.

What I felt would have to come later. The later the better. I was not sure I could ever endure what my brain already said I felt.

When they found the woman's body, everything went quiet.

271

I never knew who said my name. A space cleared. I forced myself to stumble over there and look; they all waited and watched. Hands touched my back.

She was grey. Grey dress, grey skin, grey matted hair full of plaster dust and fragments of building material. A complete corpse, made of dust. So covered with filth that it could be anyone.

No ear-rings. The wrong curve to the lobe, and no gold there – in fact no tiny hole to take the hook.

I shook my head. 'Mine was tall.'

Besides, once I was certain it was safe to look properly, I could tell that under the grey dust this woman's hair would still be grey. The hair was thin – just a sad trail in a braid no broader than my little finger, which petered out to a few strands after a foot or so. Mine had a thick plait, hardly varying in width, down to her waist.

Someone dropped a neck scarf over the face. A voice said, 'Must be the old woman on the upper floor.' The mad old bag who had so often cursed me.

I went back to work.

It had upset me. I was beginning to imagine now what I was going to find.

I paused, wiping the sweat from my filthy brow. Someone who knew he had more will than me at that moment took the shovel from my hand. I moved aside, as he attacked the swamp of masonry where I stood. Standing idle for a moment, something caught my eye.

It was the handle of a basket. I recognised the shiny black raffia wound round it by my mother when the original canework started to unwind. I dragged it to the surface. Something of mine. It used to hang beside the doorway in our living room.

I walked aside. Bystanders were quietly handing drinks to slake the rescuers' throats. I found a beaker shoved into my hand. There was nowhere to sit. I squatted down on my heels, swallowed the liquid, put down the cup, shook the dirt off the basket and looked inside. Not much. All I had left. The pride of our household: ten bronze spoons Helena once gave me; she had refused to let me hide them

272

in my mattress now they were needed for daily use. A dish that belonged to my mother, put aside for her. My best boots; hidden from the parrot . . . And a cheese grater.

I had no idea why the grater had been singled out. I would never be able to ask. So much unfinished business: the worst result of sudden death.

I replaced everything in the basket, shoving my arm through the handles right up to the shoulder. Then my bravery ended; no longer any point to it. I buried my head in my arm and tried to shut out everything.

Somebody was shaking my shoulder. Someone who must have known me, or known her, or both of us. I looked up, full of rage. Then I saw him point.

A woman had turned round a corner, just as I did half an hour ago. She had a big circular loaf in her arms. She must have been out to buy something for lunch; now she was coming home.

Home was no longer there. She had stopped, as if she thought she had turned into the wrong street in a daydream. Then the truth of the collapsed building struck.

She was going to run. I spotted her before she started moving, but her intention was clear. She thought I might have been in the apartment; now she thought I was dead underneath. There was only one way to let her know.

I whistled. *My* whistle. She stopped.

I was on my feet. She had heard me. At first I could see she could not find me. Then she did. There was no need any longer, but I was already shouting. At last I could say it. '*Helena!*'

'My lass, my love – I'm here!' The loaf crushed to a thousand fragments between us. Then she was in my arms. Soft – warm – living – Helena. I gripped her skull between my two open palms as if I was holding treasure. 'Helena, Helena, Helena . . .' Her hair caught on my roughened fingers where I had been dragging beams aside in search of her. She was clean, and untouched, and crying her heart out helplessly because for one fraction of a second she had believed she had lost me. 'Helena, Helena! When I saw the house fall down, I thought – '

'I know what you thought.'
'I said you were to wait for me – '
'Oh Didius Falco,' Helena sobbed, *'I never take any notice of what you say!'*

LVIII

People were slapping us on the back; women kissed Helena.
I would have returned to the digging, but the crowd voted
otherwise. We were jostled into a tavern where a flask,
which I needed, appeared in front of us followed by hot
pies, which I could have done without. My hat and cloak
were brought in to me. Then, with that gentle tact which
strangers discover for one another at the scene of a catastrophe, we were left alone.

Helena and I sat close, heads together. We hardly spoke.
There was nothing to say. Just one of those times of deeply
shared emotion when you know that nothing can ever be
the same again.

A voice I knew cut through my concentration when almost
nothing else would have broken it. I turned. A sleepy-eyed
gawper in a brown and green striped tunic was buying
himself a drink while he stood unobtrusively in the shade
of the awning and peered outside. He was surveying the
extent of the damage. It was the letting agent: Cossus.

I got to him before he received his order. I must have
sprung out, still covered all over with dust, like a spirit from
the Underworld. He was so amazed he had no time to
dodge away.

'Just the man I want to see!' I gave him the elbow treatment, and fetched him indoors. 'If you want a drink, Cossus,
come and have one with us – '

Helena was sitting on the nearest bench so I made Cossus
take the other. There was a table in the way of it, but I
lifted him, slewed him sideways, and threw him across there
anyway. I leapt the table myself with a one-handed vault,
landing astride his bench. Cossus gasped. 'Helena, this is
Cossus; Cossus is the wonderful chap who controlled our
lease! Sit down, Cossus – ' He had been trying to struggle
upright but sank down immediately. 'Have a drink,

Cossus – ' I gripped him by the hair, screwed his head against my side, seized the flagon and poured all that was left of it over his head.

Helena did not move. She must have realised it was a pretty awful draught of wine.

'That's your drink. Next,' I said, still in the same convivial tone, 'I'm going to kill you, Cossus!'

Helena reached across the table. 'Marcus – ' Cossus looked up at her sideways with what must have been (for a letting agent) gratitude. 'If this is the man who controlled our apartment,' said Helena Justina at her most refined, 'I should like to be the person who kills him myself!'

Cossus squeaked. Her measured, aristocratic tones were more chilling than any grit of mine. I let him go. He straightened up, rubbing his neck. He flashed a glance round the tavern in search of support. All he saw were turned backs. They knew his pedigree. If I killed him no one would help him; people were hoping that I would. Helena had made herself popular in the neighbourhood. If *she* killed him, people would probably help.

I walked back round the table and sat with my lass.

'You chose the wrong day, Cossus,' I said grimly. 'The Kalends of September is a white day in the calendar; it's tomorrow people mark with the sign of bad luck. No style, Cossus! How can your tenants plan ahead?' He started to mutter. I cut him short. I turned to Helena and asked her quietly, 'I noticed this morning the landlord's contractors had turned up to do some work on the ground floor. Were they still there when you went out?'

'They were just finishing,' Helena returned. 'They were taking away all that scaffolding that used to be in the entrance.'

'Bit of a mix-up,' Cossus mumbled, still too crass to know when to stop the bluff. 'Must have disturbed something – '

'Me, for instance!'

'Sorry, Falco,' Cossus reluctantly answered, knowing his skull was in danger of being shattered by my fist.

'So am I, Cossus.'

'The landlord will offer compensation – '

'He will, Cossus! That would be very sensible!'

'How,' Helena enquired levelly, 'can he compensate the old lady from the fourth floor, who is dead?'

'Unforeseeable miscalculation by our civil engineer,' he hedged, trying out the excuse they must keep rehearsed for appearances in court.

'Rather drastic solution to your problem with her lease!' I weighed in. Cossus sighed. At last he appreciated that my grasp of the situation made resistance irrelevant. He was lazy; he hated trouble. My interference made him too depressed to answer, so I elaborated myself: 'The landlord was trying to terminate the old woman's tenancy so he could pull down the building and replace it with a more prestigious block. When she refused to leave, this charitable man saved her lawyers the trouble of fleecing her by demolishing the building anyway!'

'But why not simply give her notice?' demanded Helena.

'We did. Well,' the agent admitted, 'we should have done. The old biddy had been living up there for so long, I forgot she was there. We have a huge number of clients. I can't remember everyone. In June she tripped into the office and paid up, grumbling into her chin like they all do, so I just got rid of her as quickly as possible and only noticed her address after she had scuttled off cursing me. The owner had never really given me firm instructions about the place so I just let it lie. Come July, he suddenly made up his mind to redevelop, but we were stuck with the old mother for another year.'

'Why exactly,' Helena enquired, 'did you then grant a new tenancy to us?'

He forced his aggravating features to appear ashamed. I would not trust him as far as I could see up a camel's backside at midnight; Helena might have put it more elegantly, but she felt the same.

'Make it look good,' I stated. 'When the place crashes down, it is easier to justify if the landlord pretends he was filling the empty apartments; then it's not deliberate demolition, but an accident during refurbishment. Tough luck, tenants (if you happen to have survived the shock): here's some of your rent back, so make sure you look grateful; now go away!'

277

'I told you the lease was temporary,' Cossus grumbled self-righteously.

'Excuse me! I must have misread my contract. I never realised it ran "*for six months – or until your house falls down*." '

'We can give you a pro rata rebate – ' Cossus began. His mouth was like the doors on the Temple of Janus: never shut.

'Wrong!' snapped Helena. 'You will give Didius Falco a *full* refund, plus compensation for the loss of his effects and furniture!'

'Yes, madam.'

The concept of men making eager promises then changing their minds later was familiar to my love. 'You will write out a banker's draft for us here and now,' Helena decreed decisively.

'Yes, madam. If you want to put a new roof over your heads urgently, I may be able to find something – ' He was a true landlord's agent; a complete fool.

'Another of your temporary specials?' I sneered. Helena took my hand. We stared at him.

Helena Justina stormed off up the road to the local stationer's while Cossus and I agreed a price for my lost furniture. I enjoyed myself, and the agreed price was better than the furniture.

When she came back, Helena dictated the draft. 'Make it out to the lady,' I instructed. 'Her name is Helena Justina; she keeps all my accounts.' Cossus looked surprised. I cannot say how Helena looked, since I avoided her eyes.

We had reached the point where we either had to let the agent leave or have him arrested. It was Helena who said quietly, 'I should like to know our careless landlord's name.'

Cossus looked uneasy; I confirmed his fears: 'Getting our money back is just the start.'

'He has to be brought to justice,' Helena said.

Cossus started to bluster but I cut him short. 'Your principals have made a slight error. This lady who was nearly killed today by your so-called accident is the daughter of a senator. When her father hears what happened to his treasure he is bound to raise the issue of landlords'

278

derelictions in the Curia – and that won't be the end of it!'
The last thing Helena wanted was to let her father know
how dangerous life with me could be. But he was bound to
find out, and Camillus Verus was one of the few in the
Senate who would be prepared to tackle the issue. 'I want
to know anyway,' I continued. 'Just tell me, Cossus. So I
can sleep tonight with a clear conscience – tell me I did
not entrust myself and this precious lady to that calamity
Priscillus!'

He looked relieved. 'Oh no, Falco!'

'Well then?'

Edging away, his voice withered to a croak as he tried to
confess: 'I work for the Hortensii. Novus controlled your
lease.'

LIX

I gripped the front of his baggy tunic in my two blackened claws and gave him a shake that would loosen his teeth.

'Don't blame me,' pleaded Cossus. 'I would have thought it was obvious!' He was waiting for me to let go of him, but I kept hold.

'Novus is dead! Novus died last week!'

'So what's the panic?'

'On whose instruction did the demolition go ahead?'

'Novus told me to put in the order weeks ago – '

'And when Novus died, did you never think of checking with his heirs?'

'I did check.' Something in the bluff way he said it rang untrue.

'With Felix or with Crepito?' I stopped shaking him, but screwed the tunic tighter round my fists. I felt certain he had been too idle to go up to the house and ask.

'She was in the office,' he muttered. 'She often gave me messages from Novus before, so I asked her. She said not to bother the others during the period of mourning, but to proceed as Novus planned . . .'

'Who, Cossus?'

'Severina Zotica.'

'The woman had no jurisdiction,' I replied immediately. I said it without passion, though I meant the words to go home. 'Cossus, she's made you an accessory to murder – '

I lost interest in the agent, as the full meaning of what he had told me sank in: Severina, ordering the destruction of my apartment; trying to lure me away this morning; making no attempt to warn me that Helena was in danger . . .

Disgusted, I gave Cossus a shove. People who were standing at the bar helped push him along. As he reached the street he stumbled. Someone outside must have recognised him. I heard a shout and he started off running. By the

280

time I reached the door he was past saving even if I had
wanted to help.

Angered by unearthing bodies, the crowd cornered the
agent, and battered him with the tools they had been using
to dig. Then they strung together a cross, using beams from
the rubble, and hoisted him up on that. But I reckon he
was gone before they lashed him to the spar.

I sat down again, and put my arm round Helena. She put
both hers around me.

I spent some time talking very quietly, not to Helena in
particular but to the world at large. I was raging against
landlords – the whole disgusting class of them. The mean;
the shoddy; the grasping; those who acted with violent
malice like Priscillus; and those like Novus who relied on
slack, incompetent agents so they could distance themselves
from the filthy conduct of their crimes.

Helena let me finish, then quietly kissed my grimy face.
The pain eased slightly.

I leaned back far enough to look at her. 'I love you.'

'I love you too.'

'Should we get married?'

'Now? With no money?' I nodded. 'Why?' she asked. 'I'm
happy as we are. Who needs ceremonies, and contracts,
and idiots throwing nuts? If we live together in trust and
love – '

'Is that enough for you?'

'Yes,' she replied simply. My strong, sarcastic lady had a
strangely romantic streak. Besides, she had experienced the
ceremony once and knew it guaranteed nothing. 'Is it not
enough for you?'

'No,' I said. I wanted to make the full public statement.

Helena Justina laughed softly, as if she thought *I* was the
romantic one.

We left the tavern. I had things to do. Bad things. I was
not sure how I could tell Helena I would have to leave her
now.

We walked slowly to the ruin of the building that had so
briefly been our home. Now I understood why the crowd

281

who caught Cossus had felt so violent: there were other bodies laid in a sorry line – a whole family, including three children and a baby. More 'temporary' occupants; we had never even known this sad group shared the tenement with us.

The diggers were still working. Only a few bystanders remained. Overnight the looters would descend. Tomorrow morning the Hortensii, looking diligent, would send the carts which they must already have on order to clear the site.

'At least we are together,' Helena whispered.

'We will be. Helena, I have to – '

'I know.'

She was wonderful. I held her tight and told her so. 'Do you still want to live with me?'

'We belong.'

'Oh my darling, we belong somewhere better than this!' As usual she calmed me down. 'We can find somewhere else, but I shall look into it more carefully than this place! Helena, I may not be able to rehouse us today – better go to your father's, and I'll meet you there later – '

'Slinking home with my tail between my legs?' Helena sniffed. 'I don't care for that!'

'I want you to be comfortable – '

'I want to be with you.'

'And I want you! Believe me, I don't want to leave you alone now; all I do want is to lock us away and hold you tight until *you* feel safe, and *I* feel better – '

'Oh Marcus, look!' Helena interrupted. 'There's the parrot!'

It was perching on a pile of rubble. Totally bedraggled, but not in the least cowed. Helena called, 'Chloe! Chloe, come here – '

Perhaps the cage had saved it. Somehow the creature had emerged alive and was now staring around at the wreckage with its normal air of dissolute superiority.

Small boys (whose mother would not thank them) were approaching with the aim of catching it. Chloe never liked men. She let them come within arm's reach, then fluffed

282

up her feathers, hopped a yard in the other direction, and took off. Her tail flashed scarlet as she lifted. I joked, 'Better warn the local starlings they are likely to be mobbed!'

Helena was straining up to watch the parrot's flight. Chloe swooped in a defiant circle near her head.

'Marcus, can she live, if she's loose?'

'Oh that bird leads a charmed life.'

Chloe landed briefly. 'Chloe! Chloe!' Helena cried.

More desperate to catch her now someone else was interested too, the small boys lunged. Chloe slipped away from them, and fluttered to a rooftree far out of reach.

'Come down here and tell me who did it!' Helena screamed with frustration.

'*Oh Cerinthus! Cerinthus! Cerinthus!*' squawked Chloe obligingly.

Then we watched the parrot soar in ever-diminishing parabolas away into the hot blue Roman sky.

LX

There was nothing to gain by delaying any longer.

'Sweetheart! This job I do is stupid. You get knocked about; your house falls down; the most gorgeous woman you ever went to bed with is telling you she needs you; and yet off you go to round up villains – when you've just found out that the man the villains murdered is someone you would only have kept alive so you could murder him yourself!'

Shivering, I flung my black cloak round me. That reminded me; in my hat there were still my two cakes from Minnius, wrapped in his vine leaves so more or less free from dust. 'Take these; we'll eat them together at your father's house tonight,' I said, trying not to acknowledge Helena's painful need to stay close. 'Promise!'

She sighed. 'Father wants to see you anyway, now you're up and about.'

'It should cheer him up if I have to give you back to him!'

'We can talk about that,' Helena said; implying that there was nothing to discuss.

I banged my hat to shift some of the mortar dust, and rammed it on.

'You look like a messenger of vengeance! Anyone who sees you outlined in an archway will want to turn and run . . .'

'Good!' I said.

The dirt on my skin and in my hair was obsessing me; I sluiced off quickly at a bathouse while I laid my plans.

It was midafternoon. Enough of this mosaic now existed for me to feel confident that once I started to manipulate the tesserae, I could fill in the gaps by guesswork and good luck. I had to see Priscillus, the Hortensius women, and Severina Zotica. Cerinthus could be a false lead. But if I could discover where this Cerinthus hung out, I had to see him too.

I chose Appius Priscillus first, and at his house on the Janiculan. Fired by my new incentive, I chose well.

Tension cramped my guts at the thought of meeting the Phrygian bodyguards, but the Priscillus organisation had been stood down – off watch during the siesta. I knew from the disgusting brown sedan in the hall that Priscillus himself was there.

The first mistake his porter made was letting me in. The second was going off to tell his master a visitor had called, without noticing that the visitor was padding behind.

'Thanks!' I smiled at the porter, steering him out of the way as I went in. 'No need to introduce us – Appius Priscillus and I are old friends.'

I had a grudge against Priscillus, which was embellished with bitter envy once I entered the room.

It was a spacious study, with large pannelled doors folded back to give an amazing view across the Tiber towards Rome. In the hands of any competent designer, the effect would have been spectacular. Priscillus probably bought the house for its position, but then he completely wasted it. It was full of natural light – and nothing else but heavily sealed strongboxes. Priscillus begrudged the most basic sticks of furniture. He had confined himself to such dingy paint and fixtures that he managed to ruin everything; there should be a law against spoiling the potential of such a perfect spot.

I felt my nose wrinkling. Its glorious position made the house much more palatable than his business address on the Esquiline; but there was a sordid smell of neglect.

'The game's up, Priscillus. Time for you to leave Rome!'

Priscillus, the same rat-faced runt in what looked like exactly the same frowsty tunic, found his voice with a venomous wheeze. 'Don't waste my time, Falco!'

'Or you mine! I'm calling you to account for the murder of Novus.'

'You've nothing on me, Falco!'

'Oh no? What about your party gift – the excellent Falernian!'

'There was nothing wrong with the Falernian,' Priscillus assured me a little too smugly.

'I'll go along with that!' I grinned. 'I tried a drop. A connoisseur might have said it overheated while it was standing in the dining room – but it was as smooth as I have ever drunk. On the whole best taken neat, however! The spices that came with it were a rather queer selection . . .' He shot me a glance. 'Myself,' I said, 'I never take myrrh and cassia in a wine of real character. Too bitter. Though it's true that in an inferior vintage, myrrh will disguise a multitude of sins . . .'

Enough said. I walked further into the room.

Priscillus started to run round under his fingernails with the pointed end of a stylus. 'What do you want, Falco?'

'Revenge, actually.'

'You'll be disappointed!'

'I don't think so.' My confidence was baffling him. He was too amazed even to send for reinforcements. I liked that. He was afraid I might have something on him so all I had to do was let him know I had. 'Priscillus, I know how Hortensius Novus was murdered. If it ever comes to court I'll be subpoenaed as a witness – '

'It won't.' He carried on digging out grime. Some of that silt probably found its way under his talons when he still had his milk teeth.

'Wrong. What I know is far too incriminating for Crepito and Felix to buy off the investigating praetor, however deeply he's in hock to Crepito.'

'How come you know so much?' Priscillus sneered.

'I found out while I was being hired to fend off the little gold-digger – '

'The girl did it!' he tried; a half-hearted attempt. 'She sat in this room, when she brought the invitation, and actually admitted that if she ever felt like disposing of an unwanted husband, she would poison him!'

'Novus was never her husband,' I responded logically. 'Useful though! Severina's presence must have seemed an ideal cover for the rest of you who wanted Novus dead. Don't think she didn't realise! I reckon her involvement was to come here and give you the idea. She set you up!

286

You were supposed to do it after they were married – but unluckily for her you couldn't wait.'

'What's your evidence?' Priscillus mooned morosely.

'I went up to the house on business that evening. I witnessed your spice being stirred into the winecup; I saw the poison drunk. Well!' I exclaimed, as if I were still startled by the memory, 'I don't know what you were expecting, but poor old Novus certainly doubled up with surprise! Next minute he was stretched out on the latrine floor!'

This quaint mixture of detail and informed bluff started to have the desired effect. 'How much?' asked Priscillus wearily.

'Oh I'm not looking for a bribe!'

'*How much?*' he repeated. Evidently he had dealt with coy extortionists before.

I shook my head. 'You can't buy me. Things have gone too far. For one thing, I was pretty upset when you had me knocked about the other day – so anything I said to the Hortensius mob while under the stress of injury is your own fault!'

'Cut the pretty talk, Falco,' Priscillus growled, but I could see him wondering what I had said.

I straightened up. 'Here's my theory: Crepito and Felix had discussed with you the possibility of getting rid of Novus if he kicked up rough. He did, so you left him the extra present. When he died, those two went along with it at first.' Priscillus agreed none of this; though he failed to deny it either. 'It came as rather a shock when I pointed out to them that by poisoning the Falernian – which you rushed off without sharing – you must have been hoping to polish off not just Novus, but the entire Hortensius clan.'

He was good. He was so good it was dangerous. 'Why,' Appius Priscillus asked me serenely, 'would Felix and Crepito imagine I wanted to do that?'

I smiled. 'Did you warn them not to take any spice?' He said nothing. That was a mistake; it dropped him into my hands. 'Felix and Crepito are not the brightest boys on the Via Flaminia, but even they finally realised: you wanted a clear field. They only escaped by accident. Novus could never wait; it was just like him to start into the wine on his

287

own. Before he knew Novus was dead, Felix had carried the flask to another room – their Egyptian salon – ' I added, for extra conviction. 'He left the spice bowl behind. At first Felix and Crepito thought you had accomplished the Novus killing by some brilliant and undetectable method – '

'But you told them otherwise!' Priscillus threatened coldly.

'That's right,' I said. 'And now Pollia and Atilia also know you tried to poison their husbands. They have sent Felix and Crepito running to the law.'

Priscillus scowled. His narrow, secretive mentality would fight me all the way. 'You're stupid coming here today – I'm going to wipe you out, Falco!'

'No point. This is out of my hands. You'll be convicted by the Hortensii. Their servants saw you hand over the flask. They saw you run back with the spice bowl after quarrelling with Novus. Felix and Crepito may even corroborate that there was a prior conspiracy.'

'They're stupid enough to do that! What are you up to?' Priscillus demanded with contempt in the wheeze.

I let my hands drop. 'I hate the lot of you. I hated Novus; I was a tenant of his. The apartment he leased me was overpriced and undermanned, and today it fell down. Nearly killed my girlfriend; nearly killed me – '

Priscillus had such a spiteful spirit he could understand this kind of anger. 'You're fingering them for it?'

'What else?' I snarled. 'If I could implicate those bastards in the poisoning too I would! And now while they are spilling the dirt to their own pocket magistrate, denouncing you and preening themselves, I've run up here. I wanted to see your face when I told you I've already watched the law officers making enquiries at your house on the Esquiline, and their next stop must be here – ' I could tell from his rat's face that Priscillus was already working out that this place was outside the city boundary, so the vigilantes might not arrive immediately.

'Time to move if you want to pack a sponge and a few moneybags!' I insisted. 'Rome's too small to hide in now, Priscillus. Your only hope of survival is to nip off and see the high spots of the Empire for a few years – '

'Get out!' he said. He was too preoccupied with his urgent need for escape even to shout for the Phrygian bodyguards to make their mark on me.

I scowled, as if I didn't like the order. Then I tipped my hat back on its string, flung my cloak around me bitterly, and left.

The grimy brown sedan chair scurried off a few minutes later.

Lying among the garden bushes, I watched some ponderously heavy trunks departing with him, supported on their shoulders by the sweating Phrygians. I could hear Priscillus bawling at them to hurry, as he was carried down the Janiculan towards the Via Aurelia and the Sublician Bridge.

There were more than thirty mileposts between here and the port at Ostia. I hoped he would make those Phrygians run all the way.

LXI

Easy really.

Just a handful of pathetic suggestions and a few lies. Bullies are so sensitive. You can bamboozle them with any soft tale which threatens their way of life.

What next?

Before I could tackle his rivals, those sly females on the Pincian, frankly I needed a rest. I found it – and possibly more than I bargained for – by taking a quiet stroll along the Transtiberina bank.

I walked north. I had to go north anyway. There was nothing to lose by trekking up past the farthermost spur of the Janiculan, and looking in at the scene of an old crime.

The Circus of Caligula and Nero – as lurid a pair of characters as you could meet at the back of a bathhouse – lies opposite the great right-hand bend of the river which encloses the Plain of Mars. As luck would have it, there were no races that week but there *was* a small exhibition of caged wild animals, surrounded by the usual nervous schoolboys wondering if they dared throw things, a little girl who wanted to pat a tiger, and a desultory trainer who rushed out from time to time to warn people away from the bars. On show were a hippopotamus, the inevitable elephant, two ostriches, and a Gallic lynx. There were a few bales of wet, dirty straw and a sad smell.

The showfolk owned some canvas booths in the shadow of the starting gates; as I went past to enter the Circus, I overheard a familiar female voice relating some tawdry tale. '. . . I thought he had just gone for a tinkle with his winkle, but he was *hours*; anyway I forgot all about him – why bother? – but when I went to feed the python, there he was; he must have stripped for action before he saw the snake – I found him cowering up against the awning, too scared to

290

shout – all knobby knees and his poor little set of equipment dangling there like a three-piece manicure set . . .'

I pulled back a battered curtain and beamed. 'I shall never be able to look at an earscoop again! Thalia! How's the performing snake business?'

'Falco! You still trying to run away from home to do something adventurous? How did you know it was me?'

'Oh – I think I've met a parrot you must have known at one time . . .'

'That terrible bird!' she said.

Her companion – a thin specimen who must be the woman who fed the man who watered the hippopotamus – gave me a prim smile, and slipped out of the booth.

Thalia became more serious. 'You're dressed up like a messenger with bad news for somebody.'

'For villains, I hope. That talk we had the other day helped me a lot. Have you got a moment?'

'Let's get some air,' she suggested, perhaps afraid of being overheard.

She led me outside, and into the Circus. We paused slightly at the starting gates, where once the panther must have made its meal of Severina's husband Fronto. In silence Thalia and I climbed up a few rows and sat on the marble seats.

'I'm developing a theory about Fronto's death. Thalia, you said you never met his wife. So I suppose you wouldn't know whether Severina had a fancy man?'

'Couldn't say. But Fronto thought she did.'

'Did he suspect who?'

'I never heard a name. But Fronto seemed to believe there was someone she had known for a long time who could be hovering offstage.'

'That fits,' I said. 'She's mentioned a fellow slave from her original master's; she wears a ring he gave her. And a doctor who attended another of her husbands told me a "friend" came to comfort her afterwards. But there's no sign of this fellow anywhere now.' In fact when we were getting drunk together she had said he was in the Under-world. 'Tell me, Fronto and Severina were only together a few weeks. She seems to think badly of him. Did he knock her about?'

'Probably.'

'A rough type? All sweetness until they were married, then he cut up sour?'

'You know men!' she grinned. But then she added, 'Fronto didn't like to be made a fool of.'

'And he reckoned Severina had pulled a fast one on him?'

'Didn't she?' We sat brooding for a moment. 'Have I got to go to court, Falco?'

'Not sure.'

'Who would take care of my snake?'

'I'll try to keep you out of it . . . But I know a girl who's kind to animals, if it comes to anything.'

'I've been thinking about that stockman,' Thalia said, explaining why she was so worried about matters going further. 'I'm sure he came to work for us about the time Fronto got married – I can't be sure, but I had an idea that *she* persuaded Fronto to take him on.'

I smiled. 'That's the theory I've devised.'

'The thing is,' she told me slowly. 'I reckon I can remember the stockman's name now – '

'The mysterious Gaius?' I sat up straight. 'The one who let the panther out, who was then crushed by a falling wall?' Something else had clicked into place while we sat here quietly; details I had heard from Petronius: "Three children died when a floor fell in . . . The Hortensii average a lawsuit a month . . . *A wall gave way and killed a man, somewhere on the Esquiline . . .*" 'The name wouldn't be Cerinthus, I suppose?'

'You rotten bug – ' Thalia accused me laughingly. 'You knew all along!'

I knew something else too. I now understand the real reason why Hortensius Novus died.

292

LXII

Time had gone by. It was dusk when I reached the Hortensius mansion, but its owners were so fond of displaying their lucre that they had already set up rows of resin torches and dozens of flickering lamps. As usual I ended up in a reception room which was completely new to me, alone.

The freedmen had bravely set aside their grief for Novus and were entertaining friends. There was a faint lick of perfumed garlands, and from time to time when a door opened I caught a distant swell of laughing voices with the shiver of a tambourine. The message which I sent in was framed to intrigue, with a warning beneath. A slave came back from Sabina Pollia asking me to wait. To while away the time while the company gorged she had me provided with a few titbits of my own: a feast, nicely presented on three silver trays, accompanied by a flagon of their well-aged Setinum wine. I discovered it was good quality because I was in no mood for tasting titbits so imbibing at least their Setinum seemed only polite.

On the wine tray were a matched pair of jugs with hot water and cold, a small charcoal burner, bowls of herbs, a pointed strainer, and fine twisted winecups of green Syrian glass: I amused myself for half an hour with these, then sat back on a couch decorated with silver lions and gazed thoughtfully about the vividly furnished room. It was too splendid to be comfortable but I had reached the stage where reclining amid tastelessness, despising it, suited my bitter mood.

Before long Sabina Pollia did appear. She was swaying slightly, and offering to serve me more wine with her own fair hands. I told her mine was a large one, leaving out the herbs and the water. She laughed, poured two, sat beside me, and then we both dashed off daring quaffs of Setinum, neat.

After days on an invalid diet, it tasted richer than I could

293

handle. But I polished it off, swung to my feet and poured myself some more. I came back to sit beside Pollia. She laid one elbow on the back of the couch just behind my head, leaning on her hand as I gazed into her exquisite face. She smelt of some drowsy perfume squeezed from the glands of animals. She was slightly flushed and she watched me through experienced half-closed eyes.

'Have you something to tell me, Falco?'

I smiled lazily, admiring her at close quarters while her hand idly tickled my ear. The excellence of the wine burned comfortably into my windpipe. 'There are many things I could tell you, Sabina Pollia – most of them not relevant to the reason why I've come!' I drew my finger along the perfect line of her cheek. She gave no sign of awareness; I asked quietly, 'Do you and Atilia realise there are witnesses to what you tried to do with the poisoned cake?'

She grew very still. 'Perhaps Atilia should be here?' She spoke with neither embarrassment nor any other kind of feeling that I could recognise.

'As you wish.' She made no move to send for her crony, so I went on, 'Hortensia Atilia at least had the excuse that she thought she was providing for her young child. What about you?' Pollia merely shrugged. 'No children yourself?'

'No.' I wondered if that was a conscious choice to preserve her figure. Then she asked, 'Falco, have you come to threaten us?'

'In theory I am on my way to see the Praetor and report what I know. I realise,' I broke in as she tried to interrupt, 'the Pincian Praetor is heavily in debt to your family. But I shall remind him that under Vespasian's new administration, if he wants to win a consulship it will be in his interest to demonstrate how impartial he can be. I'm sorry; impartiality tends to be tough on a Praetor's private friends!'

'Why should he listen to you?'

'I have influence at the Palace, as you know.'

Pollia moved. 'Atilia will want to hear this. Atilia is involved in this, Falco; Atilia bought the cake – ' She tailed off. I guessed she had been drinking steadily all night.

I had kept them separate long enough to disturb their composure; I nodded. She clapped her hands for a slave and not long afterwards Hortensia Atilia hurried in. Pollia spoke to her in a low tone on the far side of the room, while I played with the stuff on the wine tray.

'So what have you come to tell us?' Atilia asked, advancing towards me and taking the brisk role.

'Actually, I thought you would like to know that Appius Priscillus has just left town.' Atilia frowned immediately; Pollia, who was the more drunk, followed her lead. 'It was my suggestion. I informed him,' I said, sounding helpful, 'that Crepito and Felix had found out how Novus was poisoned by the flask of wine Priscillus left here, and that they had realised he also meant to kill them. Priscillus saw ⚉ that this news might rouse them to some heat! He thinks they are denouncing him.' I sat down on the couch with the lions, threw my head back, and smiled at them. 'May I ask you, ladies, what you did with the flask?'

Pollia giggled. 'We poured the wine as a libation on the pyre – ' At the funeral of Novus, this must be; not when we buried the cook. 'And then,' she explained with a mild explosion of silliness, 'we added the flask to the fire too!'

'Destroying the evidence? Never mind; it wasn't relevant.'

'Not relevant?' Atilia queried. For the mother of a future senator, she was unfashionably sharp.

'The Falernian was harmless. Priscillus had poisoned the spices which he left to be mixed with it. It was Viridovix who took the spices, poor fellow. So you see, Priscillus only killed your cook.'

'Then what happened to Novus?' Atilia demanded.

'Hortensius Novus was poisoned by something he ate.' They were at full attention. 'I expect you noticed,' I told them, 'that when the cake platter came to the table, your special item had been removed?' Atilia went rigid; Pollia would have done, but she was too drunk. They must have geared themselves up to do the poisoning, then relaxed when they thought someone had thwarted their efforts. Now I was telling them they were murderers, when they were no longer prepared to deal with it. 'Unfortunately, the cake had been removed by Severina Zotica, who thought Novus would enjoy it as a treat after dinner on his own ... I presume you realise,' I said gravely, 'that if this comes to court, the penalty for murder is to be fed to the arena lions?'

Guilt blinded my listeners to any holes in this tale. They came to sit either side of me. 'What are you saying?' Pollia murmured. '*If* it comes to court?'

'Well; I've had to deposit details in a place where I keep my records – in case anything ever happens to me, you know . . . But at present, apart from Zotica, I'm the only one who knows.'

'Are you and she intending to do anything about it?' Atilia asked.

I scratched my chin. 'I've been thinking about that on my way up here.' They were cheering up. 'The redhead won't bother you. Zotica will have to cut her losses; I hold evidence about her past husbands' deaths which she can't risk having exposed.'

'And what about you?' Atilia cooed sweetly.

'This could bring me a good bonus.'

'Who from?' snapped Atilia, changing tone.

'Any prosecuting barrister who wants a juicy case; several of them buy my information to provide lustre for their careers. Your story is guaranteed to pack the courts and make lawyers' names overnight. I could earn a lot of money if I turned you in.'

Pollia said bluntly, 'Then you can earn a lot of money if you don't!'

She deserved the Novus empire: a really snappy business-woman, full of practical ideas! I gazed at each of them in turn. With the evil reputation some informers have, I knew I could convince them of anything. The blacker the better. 'I'm open to offers. There is a scheme which I run with my girlfriend for simplifying movements of large sums of cash.' Deplorable suggestions were what they understood. 'You've met her actually; I sent her up here to get a second opinion when you were hiring me – Helena Justina.'

'The senator's daughter?'

I laughed. 'Is that what she told you? She's with me! That school she pretended to be founding – well, that's

296

how we operate. If you want to, you can donate an endowment for Helena's school.'

'How much?' rapped Atilia. I plucked a huge figure from the air. 'Falco, that's enough for a Greek university!'

'Got to make it right,' I assured her. 'We shall need to build a real school or the cover's no good. Luckily I know where there's a piece of land you can give us – one of your own apartments fell down this lunchtime in the Piscina Publica – *My* apartment!' I growled, as Pollia started to protest.

There was a small silence. I turned genuinely serious. 'People were killed. Too many people. Questions will be asked in the Senate. Better warn Felix and Crepito that that lackadaisical agent of theirs has already been strung up on a street crucifix, and they are facing intense public interest in their affairs. Face facts, ladies; you need to clean up the business methods Novus used – and you need to do it fast. I suggest a rapid programme of civic works: start paying for public fountains. Erect a few statues. Get yourselves a better name, because at present your standing couldn't be worse. For instance,' I suggested, 'we might name the new school after the Hortensius family. That's a decent and respectable project, to impress the community!'

No one laughed, though one of us was trying to.

Pollia swayed to her feet. She was feeling ill. I raised my winecup as she fled the room. Silence fell, as I drained the cup and made ready to leave.

Atilia had turned her head; she came so close her breath tickled my cheek. I began to sweat. Then there was nothing to do but wait while Hortensia Atilia lifted her beautiful face into position for my kiss.

'Sorry,' I said gruffly. 'The night is too young, I have too much to do – and besides, I'm a good boy!'

LXIII

On Pincian Hill the scent of the stone pines wafted cleanly to my jaded brain. Rome lay clothed in blackness ahead, its geography distinguished only by faint lights on the Seven Hills; I could make out the Capitol and the twin peaks of the Aventine; in the other direction what must be the Caelimontium. A cake would have been nice, to speed my steps. But I had to do without, as I turned down through the lively early-evening streets, to face my last ordeal.

On the way to tackle Severina, I completed one further piece of outstanding business; I called at the marble yard. It was open, but lit with only a taper or two. The mason approached through the eery lines of rough-cut stone; his unforgettable ears stuck out like roundels either side of his bald dome. He peered at me anxiously as I stood waiting at the end of an alley among the travertine, still shrouded in my shapeless black cloak and shadowed by the wide brim of my hat.

'Scaurus! Has Severina been in about her commission? You told me she had to consult other people.'

'Her other friends backed out. Severina paid for the monument.'

'She can afford the occasional tribute to the dead! Scaurus, I never forget a promise; I told you I would be back when she'd made up her mind . . .'

Scaurus grunted. 'The stone's already gone.'

'Where to?'

'Tomb on the Via Appia.'

'Not in the family name of Hortensius?'

'Name of Moscus, I believe.'

The mason was mistaken if he thought that would be good enough; I was in a mood for perfecting things. 'I'm not traipsing out there among the ghosts at this time of night.' I smiled at him. 'Don't try it on, Scaurus. I can

298

always go another day, but I know that I won't need to . . .
All I want is the wording. Just show me your pocket
scribble-board . . .'

He knew I could see the waxed tablets which he used to
take notes, hanging from his belt. So he turned back a
couple containing more recent orders, and there it was.

Not what I had assumed the first time I made enquiries.
But exactly what I was expecting now:

> D + M
> C+CERINTHO
> LIB+C+SEVER+
> MOSC+VIXIT+
> XXVI+ANN+SEV
> ERINA+ZOTICA
> +LIB+SEVERI+
> FECIT

I read it aloud, slowly deciphering the monumental shorthand: ' *"To the spirit of the departed, Gaius Cerinthus, freedman
of Gaius Severus Moscus, lived twenty-six years: Severina Zotica,
freedwoman of Severus set up this"* . . . Very subdued. There's
spare space on your diagram. What have you deleted at the
end?'

'Oh . . . she couldn't make up her mind whether to add,
"well deserving of him". In the end she left it out for some
reason.'

An innocent enough phrase – much used on tombstones
set up by wives, or their informal equivalent. Sometimes,
no doubt, the tribute was ironical. But anybody reading it
would infer a close relationship.

So I could tell the mason the reason why Severina made
herself omit those words: however much she wanted to
speak well of her fellow freedman, the girl was too professional to leave the slightest clue.

LXIV

It seemed an age since I had visited the house in Abacus Street. It was night now, but the house was flooded with light; she had three hefty legacies to pay for oil in her candelabra. In most homes work would have stopped. But Severina was doing the only thing left to a home-loving girl who had no prospective husband this week; sitting at her loom, planning how to catch another one.

I watched her, remembering what my sister Maia had told me about noticing whether the weaving was genuine. I reckoned it was. Even if nothing else about her could be trusted, she worked with a sure touch. When I came in she was able to keep the shuttle moving even though she glanced up angrily.

'Lunch has been cleared, Falco!'

'And dinner too! Sorry.' I walked to the couch, so she had to skew round from her work. I buried my face in my hands wearily. 'Oh Zotica! Today's been one trial after another; gods, I'm tired . . .'

'Anything we can get you?' she felt compelled to ask.

'No. All I want is honest company and conversation with a friend!' I breathed in heavily, then expelled the air hard to clear my lungs. When I looked up, she had dropped her wool altogether and was watching me nervously. 'I just left the Hortensius place. Before that, Priscillus.'

'What happened?' By now she was prickling with delight at facing a grand occasion. She knew I had come to finish things. Excitement was her medium; I would have to trip her over unexpectedly, or I would never succeed.

'Bad acting and lies mostly! Anyway, I've wrapped it all up for you . . . afraid the women filled me up with wine; I'm not myself – ' I forced a grin, then flung up my hands. 'I feel soiled, Zotica! I resent being toyed with. I particularly resent the none-to-subtle implication that I am just another attractive artwork any freedwoman with more cash than discrimination can buy!' I had set off rambling pleasantly. 'I like to be a genuine find. The years have given me one or two knocks that will never be hammered out again, but my personality has been burnished into a choice investment for a connoisseur . . .'

'What's the matter, Falco?' Severina giggled.

'Nothing. Actually, I think it's all right. I think that without a shred of proper evidence I put the frighteners on all of them!'

'Tell me then!'

I ticked them off on my fingers. '*Crepito and Felix* know Priscillus would happily have poisoned them – so the dangerous idea of a joint partnership is scuppered. Now Novus is gone, their grip on the Hortensius empire has slipped a bit – especially since I've said that they are liable to a senatorial enquiry. They should be hastily cleaning up their business habits and devoting their lives to public works . . . *Priscillus* believes the other two are turning him in to the law. He's rushed off on a long sea cruise. That should be good news for his tenants. With any luck, he'll drown before he dares return to Rome.'

'How did you achieve all this?'

'It was nothing! Persuasiveness and charm. Meanwhile *Pollia and Atilia* are terrified that if they put a foot wrong I'll send them to the arena for their attempts to poison Novus. In return for my silence they are taking up noble deeds – in their own lavish style of course. I persuaded them to apply their energy to an establishment for orphaned girls. You're an orphan, aren't you; I could get you a place if you want – '

'How much liquor have they given you?'

'Not enough; it was a highly acceptable vintage!'

Severina laughed at me. I beamed at her. Suddenly she realised the merriment was a ploy and I was sober after all.

'My house fell down today,' I said. I let the smile go out of my eyes. 'But of course, you know all about that.'

LXV

I watched Severina's uncertainty gnawing.

'How ironic it would be, Zotica, if I brought you to court not for any of your husbands – or even for killing Novus – but charged with murdering the people who died today! An old lady I only heard banging on walls, and a family I had never even realised were living there.'

We both sat motionless.

'Why don't you ask?' I sneered.

She forced out the words: 'Is your friend all right?'

'What is it to you?' The danger of her situation had long informed those still blue eyes, but whatever she thought lay too deep to penetrate. 'You knew her didn't you?' I asked. There was enough steel in my voice for her to think Helena *might* be dead. 'She used the same baths as you.'

'I thought you sent her –'

'Yes, I realise that. You were wrong. It was her own idea. She must have wanted to know what I was dealing with. She never told me, or I would have forbidden it – tried to, anyway. Helena's resistance to domineering was one of the things I first fell for.'

'What happened to her?' Severina managed to ask.

'The apartment collapsed. Everyone who was inside was killed.' I paused. 'Oh there's no need to sit there wondering whether you should confess, Zotica! I know who to blame. Cossus told me. You knew. You gave the order, in effect. Then the nearest you came to warning me was a pathetic attempt to lure me here today – never mind anyone else who might be there!'

There was a change in Severina's face, but so imperceptible I could not define it. Not that I wanted to. Even if she felt regret I was hardened against her.

'I hold out no hopes of indicting you. I've lost my witness; Cossus is dead. He let himself be recognised, and the

302

locals dealt with him. In any case, the Hortensii were the landlords. Their agent should never have taken instructions from you. Why did you do it? To dispose of me, because I became a threat to you? What made you change your mind? A hope of using me after all?'

She spoke at last. 'You should be grateful I tried to keep you away!'

'While you eliminated Helena?' She was sharp; she realised I would not have been able to discuss it at all if that were true. 'Helena was out of the building, or you'd be dead. You had a reason for what you did today. Don't pretend you wanted me. Even if you did, do you really believe I would have turned to you – or any woman – if I lost her in that way? But your motive was much more complicated. I knew you were jealous – yet you were jealous of us both. You hated the thought of other people possessing what you had lost . . .' I leaned forwards so I came closer, down to her level as she crouched on her stool. 'Tell me about Gaius Cerinthus, Zotica.'

It was the first time I was ever certain I surprised her. Even now she refused to give anything away: 'You obviously know!'

'I know you and he both came from the Moscus household. I know Cerinthus killed Grittius Fronto. I could prove it; there was a witness. But the Fates decided for me that Cerinthus would not come to trial. I know Cerinthus was then crushed by a falling wall. I know Hortensius Novus owned the wall.'

She closed her eyes, a bare acknowledgement.

I could guess the rest: 'Cerinthus was a slave with you. What happened – you grew fond of him? After you were married to Severus Moscus, or before?'

'Afterwards,' she said calmly.

'Once Moscus died, you were a free woman with a handy legacy. You and Cerinthus could have been married and led pleasant lives. Why so much greed? Was amassing a huge dowry his idea or yours?'

'Both.'

'Very businesslike! How long were you intending to carry on?'

'Not after Fronto.'

'So first there was Moscus – was it Cerinthus who chose his master's seat in the hot amphitheatre?'

'Cerinthus bought the ticket; you cannot blame him for the sun!'

'I can blame him for not keeping old man Moscus out of it! Then the apothecary, Eprius; you managed that yourself somehow. And finally the wild-beast man. Two mistakes there – Fronto never told you he had a nephew who was expecting to inherit, and he also battered you. Cerinthus must have been able to cope with you going to bed with other men, but he took against brutality. His solution was as vicious as he could make it. But Cerinthus soon walked under some typically unstable Novus masonry. You ended up with a sticky reputation, a dead lover, money you had probably lost the taste for – and nothing to occupy you but revenge.'

Her skin had a yellowy papyrus look, yet her spirit was unchanged. 'You can say what you like, Falco.'

'And you won't budge? I'm not so sure. You must have worked your way close to Novus with real passion in your heart, but the night I told you he was dead it shook you, Zotica. Don't pretend otherwise! I think you realised the truth: hate was an empty motive. Novus was dead, but so was your lover. Cerinthus would never know you had avenged him. This time there was no one to share your triumph. This time you were alone. What, as you said to me, was the purpose of it all? Killing Novus was nothing like the joy of planning a future with someone you loved, was it, Zotica?'

Severina was shaking her head, refusing to accept my arguments. 'I know, Zotica! I know just how you felt when you lost him, and I know how you still feel now. Once you have shared yourself like that, the other person becomes part of you for ever.' This time she let out a small exclamation of protest. It was too late; forcing her to admit the kind of emotion I felt for Helena only sickened me. 'What I cannot understand is how a person who had experienced real loss herself could deliberately inflict the same on anybody else!

At least, dear gods, when Cerinthus died you did not have to stand in the street and watch the falling wall!' There was a tremor in her face; I no longer wanted to see it. 'I know you killed Novus.'

'You don't know how.'

'I have some pointers.'

'Not enough, Falco.'

'I know you nudged Priscillus into thinking of poison, and probably the Hortensius women too – '

'They never needed pushing!'

'I know you prevented the women's feeble effort, and would probably have stopped Priscillus, but you had left the house before the meal. Nerve failed, did it – without Cerinthus to support you? But why set the others up as suspects, then keep them all out of it? Why risk destroying your alibis by hiring me? Oh you do love flirting with danger, but you did chance it, Zotica. I'm not completely useless; I've cleared them, even if I can't convict you. And why not let them take things to their conclusion, and carry out the deed for you?' She said nothing. I realised the answer; it lay in her obsessiveness. 'You hated Novus so deeply, you had to finish him yourself!'

'No proof, Falco!'

'No proof,' I agreed gently. No point pretending otherwise. 'Not yet. But evidence is bound to exist, and I'll find it. You condemned yourself by what you tried to do to Helena today. She's safe – but I'll never forgive you. I can be just as patient as you were with Novus, and equally devious. You may never rest now, Zotica. One false move, and I'll be on to you – '

She stood up. She was fighting back. 'Helena will never stay with you, Falco! She was brought up in too much comfort and she knows she can do better. Besides, she's too intelligent!'

I gazed up at her benignly. 'Oh she'll stay.'

'Stick with your own kind, Falco.'

'I'm doing that!' I swung myself upright. 'I'm leaving now.'

'I'll thank you and pay you then.'

'I want neither from you.'

Severina laughed ruefully. 'You're a fool then! If you want to live with a senator's daughter, you need money even more than Cerinthus and I did.'

Her jibe failed to rouse me. 'I need money all right. I need four hundred thousand sesterces; let's be precise.'

'To qualify as a middle ranker? You'll never manage it!'

'I will. And I'll keep my integrity.'

My ludicrous social position seemed to fire her with a desperate hope of suborning me after all. 'You should stay with me, Falco. You and I could do good work in this city. We think alike; we both have ambitions; we never give up. You and I could make a useful partnership in any area we chose — '

'We have nothing in common; I told you before.'

She gave me her hand, with a strange, grave formality. I knew I must have nearly broken her. I knew I never would achieve it now.

I pressed my thumb against the copper ring, her love token from Cerinthus. 'So all this was a clever vengeance campaign, eh? All for Venus? All for love?'

Sudden laughter lit her face. 'You never stop trying, do you?'

'No.'

'Or failing, Falco!'

It was her familiar vindictive farewell.

As I left the house, someone else was just arriving. A figure as smart as a bookmaker's uncle: bright tunic, bronzed skin, buffed boots, plenty of hair tonic — but not all swank. He was as sharp as pepper. Although it was a long time since I had seen him, I recognised him immediately: 'Lusius!'

It was the Esquiline Praetor's clerk.

LXVI

As soon as I realised who it was, my heart bumped: I guessed that there had been a new development.

We danced round one another on the doorstep. 'I'm just leaving,' I smiled.

'Corvinus heard there was another case to answer – ' We carried on dodging, and squinting like rivals. 'How have you got on?' Lusius asked.

'She's clear again. I did manage to work out who arranged to do in the animal importer – but the perpetrator's dead. He was her lover, but without him there's not enough to take her to court alone. I made her admit she had a partner until recently, but that's all.'

'No other evidence?' asked Lusius.

'Zilch.' I gained the impression he was holding something back. I gripped his elbow and drew him into the pool of light from a bronze lantern which hung on Severina's porch. He made no resistance. 'What's the idea, Lusius? You look pretty pleased with yourself!'

The clerk grinned. 'This is mine, Falco!'

I raised both hands, backing off. 'If you found something . . . It's a bargain, Lusius.'

He told me in a quiet voice, 'I've got her on the apothecary.'

I had thought we had both run the apothecary angle into the ground. 'How? Will that doctor who examined him make a report at last?'

'No. But did he tell you that he never attended Eprius normally?'

I nodded. 'Apparently he was called in after the choking because he lived across the street.'

'And probably because Severina knew he was a fool . . . What I've found out,' Lusius continued, 'is that Eprius *did* have a physician of his own.'

'For the famous cough that killed him?'

'Eprius never had a cough.'

'I gather you spoke to his regular quack?'

'I did. And I discovered that for years his own doctor had been treating him for piles. The medicine man reckoned Eprius was very vain – and so embarrassed about his problem that Severina may not have known.'

'Does this have a bearing on our enquiry?'

'Ah well!' Lusius was really enjoying himself. 'I showed the normal doctor the remnants of the cough lozenge that allegedly choked Eprius – though I didn't tell him what it was supposed to be. It was rather mutilated, and partly dissolved, but he was fairly sure the thing was his own handiwork.'

'Then what?'

'When I did tell him which end of his patient the lozenge had been recovered from, he was extremely surprised!' I was beginning to guess. 'That's right,' said Lusius cheerfully. 'She must have known Eprius possessed a little box of magic gumdrops – but he lied to her about their purpose. The "cough lozenge" which Severina says choked him was actually one of his suppositories for piles!'

I said, trying not to laugh too hard, 'This will make a sensation in court!'

A narrow expression crossed the clerk's face. 'I told you this was mine, Falco.'

'So what?' He said nothing. I remembered he liked redheads. 'You're mad, Lusius!'

'I haven't made up my mind yet.'

'If you go in there to see her, she will make your mind up for you . . . Whatever do you see in her?'

'Apart from quiet habits, interesting looks – and the fact I would be living on the verge of danger every minute I was with her?' the clerk asked, with a rueful lack of delusion.

'Well you know exactly what you're in for – which is more than most people do! She says she has no intention of remarrying – which means she's actively looking for her next husband. Step right up, my boy – but don't fool yourself you'll be the one who can control her – '

'Don't worry. What's left of the lozenge will do that.'

'Where is the disgusting evidence?'

'It's safe.'

'*Where*, Lusius?'

'I'm not an idiot. Nobody can get at it.'

'If you ever tell her where it is, you're a dead man!'

Lusius patted my shoulder. He had a quiet confidence that almost frightened me. 'I've arranged perfect protection, Falco: If I'm a dead man before I'm ready to go, my executors will find the evidence together with the doctor's sworn statement, and an explanatory note.'

A true lawyer's clerk!

'Now I'm going in,' he said. 'Wish me luck!'

'I don't believe in luck.'

'Neither do I really,' admitted Lusius.

'Then I'll tell you this: I met a fortune-teller, who told me the next husband Severina fastens on will live to a ripe old age . . . it depends if you believe in fortune-tellers, I suppose. Have you got a nest egg?'

'I might have,' answered Lusius warily.

'Don't tell her.'

Lusius laughed. 'I was not intending to!'

I stepped away from the porch; he lined up to bang the bell.

'I still think you ought to tell me where you have put the fatal jujube.'

He decided it might be useful for someone else to know: 'Corvinus deposited his will in the House of the Vestals recently.' Standard procedure for a senator. 'He let me put mine in with it. If anything happens to me, Falco, my executors will find that my testament has a rather intriguing seal . . .'

He was right: he was no idiot. No one, not even the Emperor, could get hold of a will without proper sanction, once it had been given for safekeeping into the Vestal Virgins' charge.

'Satisfied?' he asked me, smiling.

It was brilliant. I loved it. If he hadn't had such a ghastly taste in women, Lusius and I could have been real friends.

I even thought, with just the slightest tinge of jealousy,

that it was possible Severina Zotica might at last have met her match.

XLVII

The Senator was sitting in his courtyard garden, talking to his wife. In fact they looked as if they had been wandering round and round some subject until they were both tired of it: probably me. But Camillus Verus had a cluster of grapes in his hand and continued pulling off the fruit in an easy manner even after he saw me, while Julia Justa – whose dark hair in the dusk made her startlingly like Helena – made no move to breach the peace.

'Good evening, sir – Julia Justa! I hoped I might find your daughter here.'

'She comes,' grumbled her father. 'Borrows my books; uses up the hot water; raids the wine cellar! Her mother usually manages some snatch of conversation; I count myself lucky if I glimpse her heel disappearing round a doorframe.' I started to grin. He was a man, sitting in his garden among the moths and flower scents, allowing himself the privilege of sounding off against his young. '. . . I brought her up; I blame myself – she's mine . . .'

'True!' said his wife.

'She has been here tonight?' I butted in to ask her mother, with a smile.

'Oh yes!' her father burst out rowdily. 'I hear your house fell down?'

'One of those things, sir! Lucky we were out . . .'

He waved me to a stone bench with a flourish. 'Your house fell down; so Helena Justina had to ask me how to replace the deeds for her Aunt Valeria's legacy; Helena came to raid her old room for dresses; Helena wanted me to tell *you* that she would see you later –'

'Is she all right?' I managed to squeeze in, turning again to her mama in hope of sense.

'Oh, she seemed her usual self,' Julia Justa commented.

The Senator had run out of jokes; a silence fell.

I braced myself. 'I should have come before.'

311

Helena's parents exchanged a glance. 'Why bother?' shrugged Camillus. 'It's pretty clear what's going on –'

'I should have explained.'

'Is that an apology?'

'I love her. I won't apologise for that.' Julia Justa must have moved abruptly for I heard her ear-rings shivering and the flounce on her stole swished against the stonework with a scratch of embroidery.

The silence stretched again. I stood up. 'I'd better go and find her.'

Camillus laughed. 'Can I assume you know where to look, or should we get up a search party?'

'I think I know where she is.'

Tired as I was, I walked. I approached my old lair over the high crest of the Aventine; I came to it with dragging feet, thinking about the handsome houses rich people own, and the awful holes where they then expect the poor to live.

I entered the Twelfth district. Home smells assaulted my nose. A wolf whistle, without violence, followed me in the darkness as I took the lane.

Fountain Court.

Of all the groaning tenements in all the sordid city alleyways, the most degrading must be Fountain Court . . .

Outside the barber's, Rodan and Asiacus lifted their gladiatorial frames from a bench where they were chatting; then they sank down again. They could find another day to batter me. At the laundry I heard convivial strains from where Lenia must be entertaining her sordid betrothed. Rome was full of women planning how to fleece their men; grinning, I wondered if she had managed to persuade him yet to name a day.

A door opened. Outlined against the light behind I glimpsed a disorderly lump, topped by a few scrags of hair; Smaractus!

I was all paid up until November; no point stopping to insult him. It would keep. I could exercise my rhetoric some other day. Pretending not to notice him, I tightened my cloak and pulled down my hat so I could pass by like some sinister wraith, enveloped in black. He knew it was me; but he stepped back.

I steeled my legs, then warmed by nostalgia for familiar aggravation, I broached the first of those depressing six flights of stairs.

LXVIII

The place was a dump.

An amphora, nobbled from the Senator's mansion, stood leaning against what passed for a table. The bung was out. So this was what went on here when I was off elsewhere, struggling with a case . . . Two pastry doves, oozing with raisin juice, were standing in an old chipped dish, beak to beak like battered lovebirds. One still managed to look sleek enough, but the other had a tired droop to his tail – like me.

The glamorous piece who pretended to take in messages was sitting on the balcony with a beaker of wine, reading one of my private waxed tablets. Probably the one I would have ordered her not to read. The poetry.

She had left a spare cup on the table in case anyone happened along who liked decent wine. I poured myself a drink. Then I leaned against the folding door and rapped with my signet ring. She appeared to take no notice, but her eyelashes ruffled slightly so I reckoned that my manly presence had registered.

'Falco live here?'

'When he feels like it.'

'I've got a message.'

'Better give it to me.'

'You're beautiful.'

Her eyes lifted. 'Hello, Marcus.'

I gave her my masterful grin. 'Hello, fruit! It's all over. Gone as far as I could.'

'Will you convict her?'

'No.'

Helena laid aside my poetry. Alongside her on the bench was a small pyramid of published works. She was wearing one of my more disreputable tunics and her feet were pushed into a pair of crumpled old slippers, also mine. I

314

said, 'Trust me to pick a girl who pinches my clothes and raids my library!'

'These came from Uncle Publius – ' She gestured to the scrolls. I knew the Senator had a brother who died earlier that year, *lost at sea* (made a bad mistake in politics). 'His house had jumble going back to the province where he served as a young man – '

'You read all those this evening?' I asked, afraid it would be an expensive business keeping this quick reader stoked.

'Just skipping.'

'Skipped anything good?'

'I've been reading about King Juba. He married Cleopatra Silene, the daughter of Mark Antony. He seems quite an interesting person – for a king. One of those eccentric private scholars who write detailed notes on curious subjects – a treatise on Spurge, for example.'

'Good old Juba!'

'Are you familiar with Spurge?'

'Naturally.' I sounded as if I were thinking *What in Hades is Spurge?* I grinned. 'Spurge is that green plant, all the same sickly colour: spear-shaped leaves and bitty flowers – '

Helena Justina brought her two strong eyebrows together, then went quiet in a way that meant *How does this idiot know about Spurge?* I heard a warm gurgle: the laugh, full of delight, which she reserved for teasing me. 'Oh you're a market gardener's grandson!'

'And full of surprises!' I said defensively.

'You're clever,' Helena replied, giving me a soft look.

'I like to show an interest. I can read. I read everything I can lay my hands on. If you leave those scrolls around the house, I'll be an expert on King Juba by the end of the week.' I was feeling sore; due to failing in the case maybe. 'I'm not an Aventine lout. Wherever I go I notice things. I pay attention to the Forum news. When people talk I listen properly – ' Helena's patient silence stopped my bitter, boisterous flow. 'I know, for instance, that you, my darling, have something particular to say to me about Spurge.'

She smiled. I loved Helena's smile. 'It can be used in medicine. King Juba named one kind Euphorbia, after his physician. Euphorbus employed it as a purgative. Mind you,'

315

declared my darling caustically, 'I wouldn't allow Euphorbus to spoon a dollop into me!'

'Why not?'

'The dose has to be exactly right. Spurge has another use.'

'Tell me,' I murmured, leaning forwards expectantly at the glint in her bonny eyes.

'In King Juba's province archers use it to paint on arrowheads. Spurge is also highly poisonous.'

'Poisoned arrows usually work by causing rapid paralysis . . . so where,' I asked, to give her the pleasure of telling me even though I already knew, 'is this province your uncle once served in, which had the famous and scholarly king?'

'Mauretania,' said Helena.

I closed my eyes.

Helena stood up and wrapped her arms round me. She spoke in the quiet, reasoned way she used when we were unravelling a case. 'Of course, this proves nothing. A jurist might deny it was even evidence. But if a prosecution lawyer read out an excerpt from King Juba's treatise, then you told the court about the scroll you saw in Severina's house, then – if the barrister was persuasive and you managed to look more sensible than usual – this is the kind of colourful detail which might condemn.'

I opened my eyes. 'The plants have a milky sap; I remember from weeding. Probably tastes bitter. She may have mixed the juice with honey so Novus would lap it up greedily . . .'

Helena found a way to hold me even closer; I coloured but met her, as they say, halfway. 'Have you worked out how she applied it?' she asked.

'We both knew that some time ago – ' Helena nodded. 'She spread the poison on that silver dish, the one used at the dinner party for the cakes. Then she fixed it with her egg-white glaze, so none of the poison touched the cakes. Minnius sent seven; so when Severina failed to attend the dinner, if everybody was polite – as I was told they were – one last cake must have stayed on the dish. All through the

316

business conference Hortensius Novus must have had his eye on it. When the party broke up and he disappeared, he had dashed back into the dining room. He gobbled up the remaining pastry. Then – '

I stopped.

'Then,' Helena completed for me, 'Hortensius Novus licked the plate!'

Would it convict? Only circumstantially. But all evidence is circumstantial in some way. A defence lawyer would be keen to point that out.

Was there any point going on? The gold-digger had made her fortune. She might reform now; she might be reformed by Lusius. I had a personal reason for denouncing Severina, but an even stronger motive for attacking my ex-landlord Novus. If Severina had not murdered Novus for me, I would be a murderer tonight myself.

'Marcus, you're exhausted. I wish I had never told you. You did enough; now let go!'

'No client,' I said. 'No reason to do anything . . . No justice!' I exclaimed.

Justice was for people who could afford it. I was a poor man, with myself and a decent woman to support, on an income that would hardly stretch to let me breathe, let alone save.

Justice never paid a poor man's bills.

I freed myself and walked out to the edge of my balcony, looking over towards the dark shadow of the Janiculan. That was a place to live; good homes with delightful hillside gardens and wonderful views. Close to the Tiber, yet set apart by the river from the jostling of the city, and its noise, dirt and intensity. Some day, when I had money, the Janiculan might be somewhere to look for a home.

Helena came up behind me, nuzzling against my back.

'I saw a house today that I'll buy for you, if ever we're rich,' I said.

'What was it like?'

'Worth waiting for . . .'

We went to bed. The bed there was as horrible as I

remembered it, but felt better once Helena was in my arms. It was still the Kalends of September; only this morning I had promised to pay my lady some attention. I was falling asleep. She would wait for me. Tomorrow morning we would wake up together with nothing to do but enjoy ourselves. Now the case was over, I could stay in bed for a week.

I lay there, still thinking about what had happened today. When Helena thought I had fallen asleep, she stroked my hair. Pretending that I *was* asleep, I began caressing her.

Then both of us decided not to wait until tomorrow after all.

THE IRON HAND
OF MARS

ROME; ROMAN GERMANY; GERMANIA LIBERA
September–November AD 71

'The story upon which I embark is one full of incident, marked by bitter fighting, rent by treason, and even in peace sinister . . .'

Tacitus, *The Histories*

PRINCIPAL CHARACTERS
(Not all of whom are free to appear)

The Emperor Vespasian who needs an agent he can trust, eg:

M. Didius Falco an informer in need of work, who wants:

Helena Justina who wants the impossible, but not:

Titus Caesar who wants Falco off the scene

Plus in Rome, or thereabouts:

A widow in Veii a mere distraction (honestly!)

Canidius an unwashed clerk of censored archives

Balbillus a one-legged free-speaking ex-legionary

Xanthus a sharp barber who wants to see the world

Silvia wife to Petronius (who keeps out of the way)

Decimus Helena's father, an apologetic man, also parent to:

Camillus Aelianus (in Spain); a high-minded youth

And in History:

P. Quinctilius Varus a disastrous general (long dead)

Petilius Cerialis a renowned general (not as disastrous as Varus)

Claudia Sacrata a woman of intrigue (preferably with generals)

Munius Lupercus a missing officer (probably dead)

Julius Civilis a rebel chief in need of a haircut

| *Veleda* | a priestess who lives alone with her thoughts and: |
| *Some relatives of hers* | who live there too |

In Gaul:

| *A Gallic potter* | who will soon be a long way from Lugdunum |
| *Two German potters* | who may never go home |

In Germany:

Dubnus	a pedlar who sells more than he should
Julius Mordanticus	a potter who knows a few things
Regina	barmaid at the Medusa; an angry girl
Augustinilla	Falco's niece, laid low by love and the toothache
Arminia	her little flaxen friend

Belonging to the famous Fourteenth Legion:

Florius Gracilis	their legate; another missing officer
Maenia Priscilla	his wife, who is not missing him
Julia Fortunata	his mistress, who says she is
Rusticus	his slave, who is just missing
The Primipilus	the Fourteenth's sneering chief centurion
The Cornicularius	their snooty commissariat clerk
A. Macrinus	their arrogant senior tribune
S. Juvenalis	their truculent camp prefect

In the much-less famous First Legion:

| *Q. Camillus Justinus Helveticus* | Helena's other brother; an *ingénu* tribune |

Dama	a centurion with a problem, which includes:
Twenty rather dim recruits	his servant, who yearns for Moesia, and including:
Lentullus	the one who can't do *anything*

Also featuring:

The aurochs	a legendary beast famous for ferociousness, and:
Tigris	a dog who finds an interesting bone

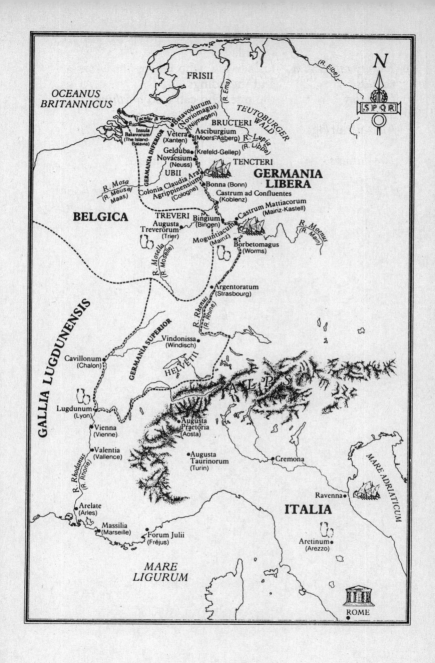

N
SPQR

OCEANUS
BRITANNICUS

FRISII

(R. Elbe)

(R. Ems)

TEUTOBURGER
WALD

Vacalus (R. Waal)
Balavodurum
(Noviomagus)
(Nijmegen)
BRUCTERI
Insula
Batavorum
(The Island-
Batavia)
Asciburgium
(Moers-Asberg)
Vetera
(Xanten)
R. Lupia
(R. Lippe)
Gelduba
(Krefeld-Gellep)
Novaesium
(Neuss)
TENCTERI
GERMANIA
LIBERA
UBII
Colonia Claudia Ara
Agrippinensium
(Cologne)
Bonna (Bonn)
Castrum ad Confluentes
(Koblenz)
R. Mosa
(R. Meuse/
Maas)
Castrum Mattiacorum
(Mainz-Kastell)
BELGICA
TREVERI
Augusta
Treverorum
(Trier)
Bingium
(Bingen)
Moguntiacum
(Mainz)
R. Moenus
(R. Main)
Borbetomagus
(Worms)
R. Mosella
(R. Moselle)
Argentoratum
(Strasbourg)
GERMANIA SUPERIOR
R. Rhenus
(R. Rhine)
Vindonissa
(Windisch)
Cavillonum
(Chalon)
HELVETII
GALLIA LUGDUNENSIS
A L P S
Lugdunum
(Lyon)
Augusta
Praetoria
(Aosta)
Vienna
(Vienne)
Valentia
(Valence)
Augusta
Taurinorum
(Turin)
Cremona
MARE
ADRIATICUM
R. Rhodanus
(R. Rhône)
Ravenna
Arelate
(Arles)
ITALIA
Massilia
(Marseille)
Forum Julii
(Fréjus)
Aretinum
(Arezzo)
MARE
LIGURUM
ROME

PART ONE:
REFUSING TO GO

ROME
September, AD 71

'My official career owed its beginning to Vespasian, its progress to Titus . . . I have no wish to deny this.'

Tacitus, *Histories*

I

'One thing is definite,' I told Helena Justina; 'I am *not* going
to Germany!'

Immediately I could see her planning what to pack for
the trip.

We were in bed at my apartment, high up on the Aventine.
A real sixth-floor bughole – only most bugs grew tired of
walking upstairs before they ever got this far. I passed them
sometimes, flaked out on halfway landings, with droopy
antennae and tired little feet . . .

It was a place you could only laugh about, or the squalor
would break your heart. Even the bed was rocky. And that
was *after* I had pieced in a new leg and tightened the
mattress webs.

I was trying out a new way of making love to Helena,
which I had devised in the interests of not letting our
relationship go stale. I had known her a year, let her seduce
me after six months of thinking about it, and had finally
managed to persuade her to live with me about two weeks
ago. According to my previous experience of women, I must
be right on target to be told I drank too much and slept too
much, and that her mother needed her urgently back at
home.

My athletic efforts at holding her interest had not gone
unnoticed. 'Didius Falco . . . wherever did you . . . learn
this trick?'

'Invented it myself . . .'

Helena was a senator's daughter. Expecting her to put
up with my filthy lifestyle for more than a fortnight had to
be pushing my luck. Only a fool would view her fling with
me as anything more than a bit of local excitement before
she married some pot-bellied pullet in patrician stripes who

could offer her emerald pendants and a summer villa at Surrentum.

As for me, I worshipped her. But then I was the fool who kept hoping the fling could be made to last.

'You're not enjoying yourself.' As a private informer, my powers of deduction were just about adequate.

'I don't think . . .' Helena gasped, 'this is going to work!'

'Why not?' I could see several reasons. I had cramp in my left calf, a sharp pain under one kidney, and my enthusiasm was flagging like a slave kept indoors on a festival holiday.

'One of us,' suggested Helena, 'is bound to laugh.'

'It looked all right as a rough sketch on the back of an old rooftile.'

'Like pickling eggs. The recipe seems easy, but the results are disappointing . . .'

I replied that we were not in the kitchen, so Helena asked demurely whether I thought it would help if we were. Since my Aventine doss lacked that amenity altogether, I treated her question as rhetorical.

We *both* laughed, if it's of interest.

Then I unwound us, and made love to Helena the way both of us liked best.

'Anyway, Marcus, how do you know the Emperor wants to send you to Germany?'

'Nasty rumour flitting round the Palatine.'

We were still in bed. After my last case had staggered to what passed for its conclusion, I had promised myself a week of domestic relaxation – due to a dearth of new commissions, there were plenty of gaps in the schedule of my working life. In fact, I had no cases at all. I could stay in bed all day if I wanted to. Most days I did.

'So . . .' Helena was a persistent type. '. . . You have been making enquiries then?'

'Enough to know some other mug can take on the Emperor's mission.'

Since I did sometimes undertake shady activity for Vespasian, I had been up to the Palace to investigate my chances of earning a corrupt denarius from him. Before presenting myself in the throne room, I had taken the precaution of sniffing round the back corridors first. A wise move: a well-timed exchange with an old crony called Momus had sent me scurrying home.

'Much work on, Momus?' I had asked.

'Chicken-feed. I hear your name is down for the German trip?' was the reply (with a mocking laugh that told me it was something to dodge).

'What trip is that?'

'Just your sort of disaster,' Momus had grinned. 'Something about investigating the Fourteenth Gemina . . .'

That was when I had pulled my cloak round my ears and scarpered – before anyone could inform me officially. I knew enough about the Fourteenth Legion to put quite a lot of effort into avoiding closer contact, and without going into painful history, there was no reason why those swaggering braggarts should welcome a visit from me.

'Has the Emperor actually spoken to you?' insisted my beloved.

'Helena, I won't let him. I'd hate to cause offence by turning down his wonderful offer . . .'

'Life would be much more straightforward if you just let him ask you, and then simply said no!'

I gave her a smirk that said women (even clever, well-educated daughters of senators) could never understand the subtleties of politics – to which she replied with a two-handed shove that sent me sprawling out of bed. 'We need to eat, Marcus. Go and find some work!'

'What are you going to do?'

'Paint my face for a couple of hours, in case my lover calls.'

'Oh, right! I'll go, and leave him a clear field . . .'

We were joking about the lover. Well, I hoped we were.

II

In the Forum, life was proceeding much as normal. It was panic season for lawyers. The last day of August is also the last day to bring new cases before the winter recess, so the Basilica Julia was humming. We had reached the Nones of September and most barristers – still rosy from their holidays at Baiae – were scurrying to settle a few hasty cases to justify their social standing before the courts closed. They had the usual noisy touts out all round the Rostrum, offering bribes for cheerleaders to rush into the Basilica and barrack the opposition. I shouldered them aside.

In the shadow of the Palatine, a sedate procession of functionaries from one of the priestly colleges was following an elderly white-robed Virgin into the Vestals' House. She glanced about with the truculence of a loopy old lady who has men who should know better being respectful to her all day. Meanwhile, on the steps of the Temples of Saturn and Castor lounged throngs of sex-crazed idlers, eyeing up anything (not only female) that looked worth whistling at. An extremely angry aedile was ordering his heavy mob to move on a drunk who had had the bad judgement to pass out on the pavement sundial at the base of the Golden Milestone. It was still summer weather. There was a strong smell of hot donkey droppings everywhere.

Just lately I had been sizing up a piece of wall on the Tabularium. Having come armed with a sponge, a few deft strokes soon washed off the electioneering puff that was besmirching the antique stonework, (*Supported by the Manicure Girls at the Agrippan Baths* . . . the usual sophisticated candidate). Deleting his offensive rubbish from our architectural heritage left a good space, just at eye-level, for me to chalk up graffiti of my own:

Didius Falco

334

For All Discreet
Enquiries + Legal
Or Domestic
Good Refs + Cheap
Rates
At Eagle Laundry
Fountain Court

Seductive, eh?

I knew what it was likely to bring in: shifty import clerks who wanted financial health checks on rich widows they were cultivating, or corner-shop barmen who were worried about missing girls.

The clerks never pay up, but barmen can be useful. A private informer can spend weeks looking for lost women, then, when he gets tired of putting his feet in wineshops (if ever), he only has to point out to the client that missing waitresses are generally found with their heads bashed in, hidden under their boyfriends' floorboards at home. This generally gets the bills for surveillance paid ultra-promptly, and sometimes the barmen even leave town for a long period afterwards – a bonus for Rome. I like to feel my work has community value.

Of course a barman *can* be disastrous. The girlfriend may be genuinely missing, having run off with a gladiator, so you still spend weeks searching, only to end up feeling so sorry for the dumb cluck who has lost his tawdry turtle-dove that you can't bring yourself to ask him for your fee . . .

I went to the baths for a spot of exercise with my trainer, just in case I did manage to land myself a case which required putting myself out. Then I looked for my friend Petronius Longus. He was captain of the Aventine Watch, which involved dealing with all types, many of them the unscrupulous variety who might need my services. Petro often sent work my way, if only to avoid having to deal with tiresome characters himself.

He was not in any of his usual haunts, so I went to his

house. All I found there was his wife – an unwelcome treat. Arria Silvia was a slightly built, pretty woman; she had small hands and a neat nose, with soft skin and fine eyebrows like a child's. But there was nothing soft about Silvia's character, one aspect of which was a searing opinion of me.

'How's Helena, Falco? Has she left you yet?'

'Not yet.'

'She will!' promised Silvia.

This was banter, though fairly caustic, and I treated it warily. I left a message to tell Petro I was light in the occupation stakes, then hotfooted out of it.

While I was in the area I dropped in at my mother's; Ma was out visiting. I was not in the mood for hearing my sisters bemoaning their husbands, so I gave up on my relations (not a hard decision) and went home.

A worrying scene greeted me. I had crossed the stinking alley towards Lenia's laundry, the cut-price, clothes-stealing wash-shop which occupied the ground floor of our building, when I noticed a set of tough tykes bristling with buckles who were standing about the stairwell trying to act inconspicuous. A hard task to set themselves: the battle scenes on their breastplates were polished to a dazzle that would stop a water-clock, let alone a passer-by, and ten determined children had stationed themselves in a circle to gape at their scarlet helmet plumes and dare one another to try and poke sticks between the mighty mens' bootstraps. It was the Praetorian Guard. The whole Aventine must know that they were here.

I could not remember having done anything lately that the military might object to, so I assumed an innocent saunter and kept going. These heroes were out of their own refined environment and looking pretty jumpy. I was not surprised to be stopped at the steps by two spears slamming together across my chest.

'Steady, lads, don't snag my outfit – this tunic still has a few decades of life in it . . .'

A laundry girl barged out of the steam with a sneer on her face and a basket of particularly disgusting unwashed goods. The sneer was for me.

'Friends of yours?' she scoffed.

'Don't insult me! They must have been going to arrest some troublemaker and lost their way . . .'

They were obviously not here to apprehend anybody. Some lucky citizen in this sordid part of society was no doubt being visited by a member of the imperial family, incognito apart from the vivid presence of his bodyguard.

'What's going on?' I asked the centurion in charge.

'Confidential – move along!'

By now I had guessed who the victim was (me) and the reason for the visitation (cajoling me into the mission in Germany Momus had warned me about). I felt full of foreboding. If the mission was so special or so urgent it demanded such personal treatment, it must involve the kind of effort I would really hate. I paused, wondering which of the Flavians was venturing his princely toes in our alley's pungent mud.

The Emperor himself, Vespasian, was too senior and too sensitive about status to make free with the populace. Besides, he was over sixty. At my house he would never manage the stairs.

I had crossed paths with his younger son, Domitian. I once exposed a piece of dirty work by the junior Caesar, which now meant that Domitian would like to see me wiped off the earth, and I felt the same about him. However, we ignored each other socially.

It must be Titus.

'Titus Caesar come to see Falco?' He was impetuous enough to do it. Letting the officer know that I despised official secrecy, I lifted apart the impressively polished spear tips with one delicate finger. 'I'm Marcus Didius. Better pass me in so I can hear what joys the bureaucracy are planning for me now . . .'

They let me through, though with a sarcastic look. Perhaps they had been assuming their heroic commander had lowered himself for an off-colour intrigue with some Aventine wench.

Making no attempt to hurry, since I was a fervent republican, I took myself upstairs.

When I went in, Titus was talking to Helena. I stopped short abruptly. The look I had seen the Praetorians exchange began to make more sense. I began to think I had been a fool.

Helena was sitting out on the balcony, a small affair which clung perilously to the side of our building, its old stone supports held on mainly by twenty years of grime. Although there was room for an informal type like me to share the bench with her, Titus had remained politely standing beside the folding door. Ahead of him lay a spectacular view of the great city which his father ruled, but Titus was ignoring it. In my opinion, with Helena to look at, anybody would. Titus shared my opinion pretty openly.

He was the same age as me, a curly-haired optimistic type who would never be soured by life. In my unmajestic billet here, the crusted gold palm leaves embroidering his tunic made an incongruous show, yet Titus managed not to seem out of place. He had an attractive personality and was at home wherever he went. He was pleasant, and for a top-ranker, cultured to his sandalstraps. He was an all-round political achiever: a senator, a general, Commander of the Praetorians, a benefactor of civic buildings, a patron of the arts. On top of that, he was good-looking. I had the girl (though we did not declare it in public); Titus Caesar had everything else.

When I first saw him talking to Helena, his face had a pleased, boyish expression which made my teeth set. He was leaning on the door with his arms folded, unaware that the hinges were quite likely to give way. I hoped they would. I wished they would dump Titus in his splendid purple tunic flat on his back on my ramshackle floor. In fact the moment I saw him there, in deep conversation with my girlfriend, I sank into a mood where almost any sort of treason seemed a bright idea.

'Hello, Marcus,' said Helena – paying far too much attention to putting on a neutral face.

III

'Afternoon,' I forced out.

'Marcus Didius!' The young Caesar was effortlessly agreeable. Refusing to let it fluster me, I stayed glum. 'I came to commiserate about the loss of your apartment!' Titus was referring to one I had been renting just recently which had had every advantage – except that where this repulsive den somehow stayed upright in defiance of all engineering principles, the other had collapsed in a cloud of dust.

'Nice shack. Built to last,' I said. 'That is, to last about a week!'

Helena giggled. Which gave Titus an excuse to say, 'I found Camillus Verus's daughter waiting here; I've been keeping her occupied . . .' He must have known I was trying to lay claim to Helena Justina, but it suited him to pretend she was a model of modest propriety just waiting for an idle prince to pass the time of day with.

'Oh thanks!' I retorted bitterly.

Titus glanced at Helena Justina in an appreciative way that left me feeling out of things. He had always admired her, and I had always hated it. I was relieved to see that despite what she had told me, she had *not* painted her eyes as if she was expecting a visitor. She did look delicious, in a red dress I liked, with agates on slim gold hoops swinging from her ears and her dark hair simply twisted up in combs. She had a strong, quick-witted face, rather too self-controlled in public, though in private she would melt like honey in the warm sun. I loved it, so long as I was the only one she melted for.

'I tend to forget you two know one another!' Titus commented.

Helena stayed silent, waiting for me to tell His Caesarship just how well. I held back stubbornly. Titus was my patron;

if he gave me a commission, I would do it for him properly – but no Palace playboy would ever own my private life.

'What can I do for you, sir?' With anyone else my tone would have been dangerous, but no one who enjoys existence makes threats to the Emperor's son.

'My father would like a talk, Falco.'

'Are the Palace clowns on strike then? If Vespasian is short of laughs, I'll see what I can do.' Two yards away, Helena's brown eyes had assumed an unforgiving steadiness.

'Thanks,' Titus acknowledged easily. His suave manner always made me feel he had spotted yesterday's fish sauce spilt down my tunic. It was a feeling I deeply resented in my own house. 'We have a proposition to put to you . . .'

'Oh good!' I answered darkly, with a moody scowl to let him know I had been warned the proposition was dire.

He eased himself off the folding door, which lurched sickeningly but stayed upright. He made Helena a slight gesture, implying that he thought she was here to discuss business so he would not intrude. She rose politely as he strode to the door, but she left me to see him out as if I were the sole proprietor.

I came in and started fiddling with the rickety door. 'Someone should tell His Honour not to lean his august person against plebeians' furniture . . .' Helena remained silent. 'You have on your pompous look, my darling. Was I rude?'

'I expect Titus is used to it,' Helena replied levelly. I had omitted to kiss her; I knew she had noticed. I wanted to, but it was too late now. 'The fact Titus is so approachable must make people forget they are talking to the Emperor's partner, a future Emperor himself.'

'Titus Vespasianus never forgets exactly who he is!'

'Don't be unfair, Marcus.'

I ground my teeth. 'What did he want?'

She looked surprised. 'To ask you to see the Emperor – to talk about Germany, presumably.'

'He could have sent a messenger to ask me that.' Helena was starting to look annoyed with me, so naturally I became even more stubborn: 'Alternatively, he could quite well have talked about Germany himself while he was here. And in greater privacy, if the mission is sensitive.'

Helena folded her hands at her waist and closed her eyes, refusing to quarrel. Since normally she fought me at the slightest opportunity, that was bad news in itself.

I left her out on the balcony and slouched indoors. There was a letter on the table. 'Is this scroll for me?'

'Mine,' she called out. 'It's from Aelianus in Spain.' She meant the elder of her two brothers. I had received the impression Camillus Aelianus was a prick-eared young bastard I wouldn't be seen drinking with; but since I had yet to encounter him in person, I kept quiet. 'You can read it,' she offered.

'It's your letter!' I rejected her unbendingly.

I went into the inner room and sat on my bed. I knew exactly why Titus had visited us. It had nothing to do with any mission he was offering me. It had nothing to do with *me* at all.

Sooner than I expected, Helena came in and sat beside me quietly. 'Don't fight!' She looked equally gloomy as she dragged my fingers apart, forcing me to hold her hand. 'Oh Marcus! Why can't life be simple?'

I was not in the mood for philosophy, but I changed my grip to something slightly more affectionate. 'So what did your regal admirer have to say for himself?'

'We were just talking about my family.'

'Oh were you!' In my head I ran over Helena's ancestral pedigree, as Titus must have done: senators for generations (which was more than he could say himself, with his middle-class, tax-farming Sabine origins); her father a stalwart supporter of Vespasian; her mother a woman of unblemished reputation. Her two young brothers both abroad doing their civic duty, with at least one of them bound for the Senate eventually. I had been assured by everyone that great things were expected of the noble Aelianus. And Justinus, whom I had met, seemed a decent lad.

'Titus seemed to be enjoying the discussion. Did he

341

talk about you?' Helena Justina: liberal education; lively character; attractive in a fierce, unfashionable way; no scandals (except me). She had been married once, but divorced by consent and anyway the man was dead now. Titus himself had been married twice – once widowed, once divorced. *I* had never been married, though I was less innocent than both of them.

'He's a man – he talked about himself,' she scoffed. I growled. She was a girl people talked to. I liked to talk to her myself. She was the one person I could talk to about pretty well anything, which I felt made it my prerogative.

'You know he's in love with Queen Berenice of Judaea?'

Helena gave a little smile. 'Then he has my sympathy!' The smile was not particularly sweet, and hardly aimed at me. After a moment she added more gently, 'What are you worried about?'

'Nothing,' I said.

Titus Caesar would never marry Berenice. The Jewish queen came with a vividly exotic history. Rome would never accept an alien empress – or tolerate an emperor who tried to suggest importing one.

Titus was romantic, but realistic. His attachment to Berenice was supposed to be genuine, yet a man in his position might well marry someone else. He was the heir to the Roman Empire. His brother Domitian possessed some of the family talents, but not all. Titus himself had fathered a young daughter, but no son. Since the Flavian claim to the purple had been principally based on offering the Empire stability, people would probably say he *ought* to look actively for a decent Roman wife. Plenty of women, both decent and otherwise, must be hoping that he would.

So what was I supposed to think if I found this prestigious character talking to my girl? Helena Justina made a thoughtful, graceful, sweet-natured companion (when she wanted to); she always had sense, tact, and a high concept of duty. If she had not fallen for me, Helena was exactly the sort that Titus should be looking for.

'Marcus Didius, I chose to live with you.'

'Why suddenly come out with that?'

'You look as if you might have forgotten it,' Helena said. Even if she left me tomorrow, I would never forget. But that did not mean I could view our future together with any confidence.

343

IV

The next week was a strange one. I felt oppressed by the thought of the ghastly trip to Germany that was being held over me. It was work – something I could not afford to refuse – but touring the wild tribal frontiers of Europe was high on my list of entertainments to avoid.

Then I found myself checking the apartment for signs that Titus had been hanging around. There were none; but Helena noticed me looking, so that caused more strain.

My advertisement in the Forum first produced a slave who would obviously never be able to pay me. Besides, he was searching for his long-lost twin brother, which a second-rate playwright might view as good research but it looked dreary work to me. Next I was approached by two clerks, fortune-hunting; a mad woman who had convinced herself that Nero was her father (the fact that she wanted me to prove it was what warned me she was barmy); and a rat-catcher. The rat-catcher was the most interesting character, but he needed a diploma of citizenship. It would be an easy day's work at the Censor's office, but even for intriguing personalities I don't involve myself in forgery.

Petronius Longus sent me a woman who wanted to know if her husband, who had been married before, had any children he was keeping quiet about. I was able to tell her there were none registered. While I was at it I turned up an extra wife, never formally divorced. This woman was now happily married to a poultry chef (I use 'happily' in the conventional sense; I expect she was as angry with life as everyone else). I decided not to advise my client. A good informer answers what he has been asked – then retreats from the scene.

Petro's case brought in enough silver to have red mullet for dinner. I spent the change on roses for Helena, hoping to look like a man with prospects. It would have been a happy evening, only that was when she informed me she seemed to have prospects of her own: Titus had invited her to the Palace with her parents, but without me.

'Let me guess – a discreet dinner that will not appear on the public fixtures list? When is it?'

I noticed her hesitate. 'Thursday.'

'Are you planning to go?'

'I really don't want to.'

Her face was strained. If her respectable upper-crust family ever got wind of a possible liaison with the star of the imperial court, the pressure on Helena would become unbearable. It was one thing for her to leave home while her parents had no other plans. Given one unhappy marriage, her papa had told me frankly he felt diffident about ushering her into another. Camillus Verus was unusual: a conscientious father. Still, there must have been trouble after she ran off. Helena had shielded me from most of the barrage, but I can count the knots in a plank of wood. They wanted her back, before all Rome heard she was playing around with a hangdog informer, and satirical poets started putting the scandal into salacious odes.

'Marcus, oh Marcus, I particularly want to spend that evening with you – ' Helena seemed upset. She was thinking I ought to intervene, but there was nothing I could do about this ominous venture; rebuffing Titus could only come from her.

'Don't look at me, sweetheart. I never go where I am not invited.'

'That's news!' I hate ironic women. 'Marcus, I'm going to tell Papa I have a prior engagement which I cannot break, with you – '

She was avoiding the issue, it seemed to me. 'Sorry,' I said tersely. 'I have a trip to Veii on Thursday. I need to check out a widow for one of my fortune-hunting clients.'

'Can't you travel another day?'

'We need the fee. You take your chance!' I sneered. 'Go to the Palace and enjoy yourself. Titus Caesar is a soft piece of lard from a dull country family; you can handle him, my darling – assuming, of course, that you're wanting to!'

Helena went even whiter. 'Marcus, I am asking you to stay here with me!' Something in her tone disturbed me. But by then I was feeling so sorry for myself I refused to alter my arrangements. 'This means a lot to me,' Helena warned in a dangerous tone. 'I'll never forgive you . . .'

That settled it. Threats from women bring out the worst in me. I went to Veii.

Veii was a dead end. Somehow I expected it.

I found the widow easily enough; everyone in Veii had heard of her. She may or may not have possessed a fortune, but she was a pert brunette with sparkling eyes who freely admitted to me that she was stringing along four or five abject suitors – gents who had called themselves friends of her late husband and now thought they could be even better friends to her. One of them was a wine exporter, selling multiple consignments of foul Etruscan rot-gut to the Gauls – an obvious front runner if the wench remarried anyone. I doubted if she would bother; she was enjoying herself too much.

I myself received certain hints from the widow that I might have profited from a stay in Veii, but on the journey there I had been plagued by the memory of Helena's pleading expression. So, cursing, and by now fairly penitent, I rushed back to Rome.

Helena was not at the apartment. She must have already left for the Palace. I went out and got drunk with Petronius. He was a family man, so had strains of his own, and was always glad to make himself available for a night out cheering me up.

I came home late, deliberately. It failed to annoy Helena because she never came home at all.

I assumed she had stayed the night with her parents. That was bad enough. When she failed to show up at Fountain Court the next morning, I was horrified.

V

Now I was a real sprat drowning in fish pickle.

I ruled out any thought that Titus had abducted her. He was too straight. Besides, Helena was a strong-minded girl; she would never stand for it.

There was no way I could bring myself to turn up at the Senator's house, begging to be informed what was going on. For one thing, whatever it was, her high and mighty family would blame me.

Finding missing women was my trade. Finding my own should be as easy as picking peas. At least I knew that if she had been murdered and nailed under the floorboards, the floorboards were not mine. It was not particularly comforting.

I started where you always start: searching the apartment to see what she had left behind. Once I had tidied away my own detritus, the answer was not much. She hadn't brought many clothes or pieces of jewellery; most had now disappeared. I came across one of her tunics, mixed up with a rag-bag of mine; a jet hairpin under the pillow on my side of the bed; a soapstone pot of her favourite face-cream which had tumbled behind the storage chest . . . Nothing else. Reluctantly I came to the conclusion that Helena Justina had stripped my apartment of her own possessions and left in a huff.

It seemed drastic – until I noticed a clue. The letter from her brother Aelianus still lay on the table where it had been when she said I could see it. I read it now. At first I wished I hadn't. Then I was glad I knew.

Aelianus was the casual, idle one who usually never bothered to correspond with his family, though Helena regularly wrote to him. She was the eldest of the three Camillus children, and treated her younger brothers to the kind of old-fashioned affection that in other families had gone out of the window at the end of the Republic. I had already gathered that Justinus was her favourite; her letters to Spain were more of a duty. It seemed typical that when Camillus Aelianus heard that she had attached herself to a plebeian in a grubby profession, he did write — and a letter filled with such vitriolic ranting that I dropped it in disgust. Aelianus was livid at the damage Helena had done to their noble family name. He said so with all the crass insensitivity of a youth in his twenties.

Helena, being such a family girl, would have been deeply hurt. She must have been brooding over this without me noticing. And then Titus had loomed, with his threat of disaster . . . It was like her to say nothing much. And like me, when she did finally appeal for help, to turn my back on her.

The moment I read that letter I wanted to wrap her in my arms. Too late, Falco. Too late to comfort her. Too late to shelter her. Too late for everything, apparently.

I was not surprised when a short, bitter message came for me, saying that Helena could not tolerate Rome any longer and had gone abroad.

VI

So that was how I let myself be sent to Germany.

Without Helena, there was nothing for me in Rome. It was pointless to try catching up with her; she had timed her message so that the trail was cold. I soon grew tired of members of my family making it plain they had always expected her to dump me. I could produce no defence; I had always expected it myself. Helena's father often used the same baths as me, so avoiding him became tricky too. Eventually, he spotted me trying to hide behind a pillar; he shook off the slave who was scraping his back with a strigil, and rushed over in a cloud of scented oil.

'I am relying on you, Marcus, to tell me where that daughter of mine is – '

I swallowed. 'Well, you know Helena Justina, sir – '

'No idea either!' her father exclaimed. Next thing, he was apologising for Helena as if I was the one who ought to be offended by her extravagant behaviour.

'Calm down, senator!' I tucked a towel around him soothingly. 'I've made my business out of tailing other people's treasures when they disappear. I'll track her down.' I tried not to look too worried at my lies. So did he.

My friend Petronius did his best to jolly me along, but even he was fairly amazed.

'*Abroad!* Falco, you have the brain of an inadequate catfish. Why couldn't you have fallen for a normal girl? The kind who rushes home to mother whenever you upset her, but then slinks back the next week with a new necklace you'll have to pay for?'

'Because only a girl who likes pointless dramatic gestures would fall for me.'

He let out an impatient growl. 'Are you looking for her?'

'How can I? She could be anywhere from Lusitania to

349

the Nabataean desert. Leave off, Petro; I've had enough stupidity!'

'Well, women never travel far alone . . .' Petronius himself had always favoured simple, timid fluff-balls – or at least women who convinced him that was what they were.

'Women are not *supposed* to travel. That simple rule won't deter Helena!'

'Why did she flit?'

'I can't answer that.'

'Oh I see: *Titus*!' The Praetorian Guard must have been spotted by one of his troopers when they were squatting outside my house. 'That's you finished, Falco, anyway!'

I told him I was tired of other people's optimism, then I slouched off by myself.

The next time a summons came from the Palace, ostensibly from Vespasian, I knew it must really be Titus who was plotting to remove me from the scene. I suppressed my annoyance, and made a vow to extract the largest fee I could.

For my interview with the purple I made a sartorial effort, as Helena would have wanted me to. I wore a toga. I had a haircut. I kept my lips pressed close together to hide my republican snarl. That was the most any palace could ever hope for from me.

Vespasian and his elder son were governing the Empire in effectual partnership. I asked for the old man, but the receiving official had gum in his ears. Even with a written invitation from his father, apparently it was Titus on that night's duty rosta to handle pleas, pardons and wine-bar rejects like myself.

'Wrong throne room!' I apologised, when the limp flunkey passed me in to him. 'Sir, I gather the good of the Empire will be best served by despatching me elsewhere! Rumour says your noble father has a horrible proposition I'm just dying to hear.'

Titus recognised my jibe at his personal motives. On hearing the news I might be leaving, he gave a short laugh, which I did not join. He signalled a slave, presumably to lead me to the Emperor, but then held us back. 'I've been trying to get wind of a certain female client of yours,' he admitted – too offhandedly.

'So she gave us both the slip! What did she tell you?' He made no answer; at least Helena favoured *me* with angry messages. Feeling braver, I risked sneering. 'She's travelling. Fraternal visit, apparently. She received a letter from the noble Aelianus recently, in high dudgeon over some imagined slight.' I saw no need to confuse Titus by saying it was over me.

Titus frowned warily. 'Surely if her brother was annoyed, avoiding him would be more logical?'

'Helena Justina's reaction would be to rush straight there.' Titus was still looking quizzical. I believe he had had a sister himself, an impeccable girl who had married a cousin and then died young in childbirth, as Roman women from good families are supposed to do. 'Helena likes to face up to things, sir.'

'Does she!' he commented, perhaps with irony. Then he asked more thoughtfully, 'Camillus Aelianus is in Baetican Spain? But surely he's too young for a quaestorship?' Would-be senators normally serve as provincial finance officials just before their formal election to the Curia at twenty-five. Helena's brother had two or three years to go before that.

'Aelianus is the son his family all think a lot of.' If Titus wanted Helena, he would need to bone up on her relatives. I described the situation for him with a familiar ease: 'The Senator persuaded a friend in Corduba to find the boy a staff position ahead of time, to give him the early benefit of experience abroad.' Judging by the way he had written to his sister, this plan to teach Aelianus diplomacy was a waste of time and cash.

'Does he demonstrate special qualities?'

I replied gravely, 'Camillus Aelianus seems well equipped for a spectacular public career.'

Titus Caesar glanced at me, as if he suspected I might be suggesting that the normal criterion for rapid advancement in the Senate was a touch of the dungheap. 'You seem well briefed!' He eyed me shrewdly, then called up an outdoor messenger. 'Falco, when did Helena Justina leave?'

'No idea.'

He muttered something to his mercury; I caught a mention of Ostia. Titus realised I had overheard. 'The lady is a member of a senatorial family; I can forbid her leaving Italy,' he told me defensively as the messenger left.

I shrugged. 'So she's taken an unauthorised holiday. Why not? She's not a vestal, or a priestess of the imperial cult. Your predecessors in office might have had her exiled to an island for displaying such independence, but Rome expected better from the Flavians!' Still, if he could find her – and I had myself already spent a day fruitlessly searching the Ostia quays – I was quite prepared to let Titus have my lady escorted back to Rome. I knew she would be handled respectfully because of her status. I also knew that Titus Flavius Vespasianus was in for a Charybdis of trouble if he ordered it. 'Helena Justina will object forcibly to being hooked off her ship. I'll stay if you like,' I offered. 'Her ladyship in a temper may be more than your Praetorian Guard can handle without help!'

Titus made no attempt to call back his messenger. 'I'm sure I can mollify Helena Justina . . .' No woman he ever seriously wanted would be able to turn her back on him. He smoothed down the ample folds of his purple tunic, looking grand. I planted my feet apart and just looked tough. Then he demanded abruptly, 'You and Camillus Verus's daughter seem unusually close?'

'Do you think so?'

'Are you in love with her?'

I gave him a simple smile. 'Caesar, how could I presume?'

'She's a senator's daughter, Falco!'

'So people keep telling me.'

Both of us were heavily aware of his father's power and of how much authority had already devolved on Titus in his own right. He was too polite to draw comparisons between us, but I did.

'Does Verus approve of this?'

'How could he, sir?'

'Does he *allow* it?'

I said quietly, 'Helena Justina is a sweetly eccentric girl.' I could tell from his face Titus had already learned that. I wondered what he had said to her; then I wondered more painfully what she had said to him.

He moved in his seat, closing our interview. He could dismiss me from his throne room; he could order me out of Rome; but both of us were a good deal less certain whether he could exclude me from Helena's life. 'Marcus Didius, my father needs you to take a journey. I feel that would be best for everyone.'

'Any chance of Baetica?' I ventured cheekily.

'Wrong direction, Falco!' he whipped back with more relish than he should. Recovering, he murmured, 'I was hoping to entertain the lady here last Thursday. I was sorry that she would not come – still, most people like to celebrate their private feasts amongst those who are closest to them . . .' This was some kind of test. I stared at him, giving nothing away. '*Helena Justina's birthday!*' he explained, like a man throwing a double six with weighted dice.

It was news to me. He could see that.

With difficulty I restrained my instinctive reaction, which was to punch his superbly barbered chin straight through his handsome teeth to the back of his Caesarly skull.

'Enjoy Germany!'

Titus subdued his air of triumph. But that was when I forced myself to accept the plight Helena and I were in. If this situation had become awkward for her, it was positively dangerous for me. And whatever scabby mission I was to be despatched on this time, it would suit Titus Caesar most of all if I failed to finish it.

He was the Emperor's son. There were plenty of things he could do to make sure that once he sent me out of Rome, I would not be coming back.

VII

I was passed through the perfumed offices of three chamberlains, lost in my own moody thoughts.

I am not completely deficient. After ten years of what I called a successful love life, a new girlfriend's birthday was something I reckoned to find out fast. I asked Helena; she laughed off the question. I tackled her father, but without his secretary's list of family feasts, he dodged the issue shiftily. Her mother could have told me, but Julia Justa had better ways of upsetting herself than by discussing her daughter with me. I even spent hours in the Censor's office searching for Helena's birth certificate. No luck. Either the Senator had panicked on the arrival of his first-born (understandably) and had failed to register her properly, or else he had found her under a laurel bush and could not call her a Roman citizen.

One thing was certain. I had committed domestic sacrilege. Helena Justina might overlook many insults, but my bumming off to Veii on her birthday was not one of them. The fact I didn't *know* it was her birthday was irrelevant. I should have done.

'Didius Falco, Caesar . . .' Before I was ready to concentrate on political matters, a major-domo who reeked of long-standing vanity and recently braised onions announced my name to the Emperor.

'That's a long face. What's up, Falco?'

'Woman trouble,' I admitted.

Vespasian enjoyed a laugh. He threw back his great head and guffawed. 'Want my advice?'

'Thanks, Caesar.' I grinned. 'At least this heartthrob didn't run off with my armpurse or elope with my best friend . . .'

We hit a small moment of stillness, as if the Emperor

354

had remembered with disapproval who my latest heartthrob was.

Vespasian Augustus was a beefy bourgeois with a down-to-earth manner who had risen to power on the tail of a vicious civil war and then set out to prove that men who lacked flash ancestors could still own a talent to rule. He and his elder son Titus were succeeding – which guaranteed that the snobs in the Senate would *never* accept them. Still, Vespasian had been struggling for sixty years – too long to expect easy recognition, even when he wore a purple robe.

'You're in no hurry to know about your mission, Falco.'

'I know I don't want it.'

'That's normal.' Vespasian humphed mildly, then told a slave, 'Let's see Canidius now.' I didn't bother wondering who Canidius was. If he worked here, I didn't like him enough to care. The Emperor beckoned me closer. 'What do you know about Germany?'

I opened my mouth to say, '*Chaos!*', then closed it again, since the chaos had been stirred up by Vespasian's own supporters.

Geographically, what Rome calls Germany is the eastern flank of Gaul. Sixty years ago, Augustus had decided not to advance across the natural boundary of the great River Rhenus – a decision dragged out of him by the Quinctilius Varus disaster, when three Roman legions were ambushed and wiped out by the German tribes. Augustus never recovered. It was probably this throne room which he used to pace, groaning, '*Varus, Varus, give me back my legions . . .*' Even so long after the massacre I myself felt extreme reluctance to spend time where it had occurred.

'Well, Falco?'

I managed to sound impartial. 'Sir, I know Gaul and our Rhine provinces played a rich part in the civil war.'

It was the recent Vindex revolt in Gaul which had sparked everything by causing Nero's downfall. The governor of Upper Germany crushed the revolt, but on his recall to Rome after Galba claimed the throne, his troops refused to take the New Year's oath to Galba. When Galba died, Otho took over in Rome, but the Rhine legions rejected him and decided to elect their own emperor.

They chose Vitellius, then governor of Lower Germany. His reputation was as a brutal, loose-living drunk – obvious imperial material by the standards of the time. From Judaea, Vespasian challenged him. Seeking to pin down the legions in Germany who were his rival's main supporters, Vespasian contacted a local chieftain who might raise a diversion. It worked – too well. Vespasian grabbed the imperial wreath, but the rebellion in Germany ran completely out of control.

'A part which culminated dramatically in the Civilis revolt, Caesar.'

The old man smiled at my careful neutrality. 'You are familiar with events?'

'I read the *Daily Gazette*.' I matched his sombre tone. It was a bleak moment in Roman history.

The fiasco in Germany had had everything. At the time, Rome itself was a city torn apart, but the shocking scenes on the Rhine outdid even our own problems of panic, fire and plague. The leading rebel – a Batavian hothead called Civilis – had attempted to unite all the European tribes in some impossible vision of an independent Gaul. During the mayhem he managed to cause, a string of Roman forts were overrun and burnt. Our Rhenus fleet, which had native rowers, rowed itself over to the enemy. Vetera, the only garrison which held out with any credit, was starved into submission after a grim siege; then the troops who surrendered were set upon and slaughtered as they marched out unarmed.

While the native revolt raged up and down Europe, the mood of our own troops also deteriorated. Mutinies occurred everywhere. Officers who showed any spirit were assaulted by their men. There were wild tales of legionary commanders being stoned, making a run for it, and hiding in tents disguised as slaves. One was murdered by a deserter. Two were executed by Civilis. The governor of Upper Germany was dragged from his sickbed and assassinated. In a particularly horrific incident, the legate from the surrendering fort at Vetera was sent off in chains by Civilis as a present to an influential priestess in the barbarian part of Germany; even today his fate remained unknown. Finally, at the height of the upheavals, four of our Rhineland legions actually sold their services and we had to endure the ultimate horror of Roman soldiers swearing allegiance to the barbarians.

It sounds fantastic. At any other period it would have been impossible. Yet in the Year of the Four Emperors, when the whole Empire blazed in ruins while the imperial contenders slogged it out, this was just one especially colourful sideshow amongst the wide-scale lunacy.

I wondered glumly how the colourful Rhenus frontier was about to impinge on my drab life.

'We have Germany in hand,' Vespasian declared. From most politicians this would have been self-deception. Not him. He was a good general himself, and he attracted strong subordinates. 'Annius Gallus and Petilius Cerialis have achieved a dramatic turnaround.' Gallus and Cerialis had been sent to subdue Germany with *nine* legions. It was probably the largest task force ever sent out by Rome so success was a foregone conclusion, but as a loyal citizen I knew when to look impressed. 'I'm giving Cerialis the governorship of Britain as a reward.' Some reward! Cerialis had served in Britain during the Boudiccan Revolt, so he would know what dismal privilege he had just won.

A lucky fluke reminded me that the esteemed Petilius Cerialis was related to Vespasian. I swallowed a witty rejoinder and asked meekly, 'Caesar, if you can spare Cerialis for higher duties, the frontier must be under control?'

'Some unfinished items – I'll come to those.' Whatever was said in public, the whole region must still be highly sensitive. Not the time for a quiet cruise downstream on a wineship. 'Petilius Cerialis held a meeting with Civilis – '

'I heard about that!' Dramatic stuff: the two opposing commanders had confronted each other in the middle of a river, both bawling across the void from the ends of a severed bridge. It sounded like some incident from the mists of Rome's heroic history that schoolboys learn about.

'Civilis has fallen unnaturally quiet since then ...'

Speaking of the rebel chief, Vespasian paused, in a way that ought to have worried me. 'We were hoping he would settle down peacefully in the Batavian homeland, but he's missing.' That did arouse my interest; I read in it a bad prophecy for me. 'Rumour says he may have travelled south. On that subject, I'd like to say to you – '

Whatever he had intended to tell me – or warn me – about the rebel Civilis never happened, because just then a curtain swung open and the official who must be the one he had called Canidius arrived.

VIII

When he shambled in, the sharp lads in glittering white uniforms who waited on the Emperor all stepped back and glared at him bitterly.

He was a real papyrus beetle. Even before he opened his mouth, I guessed he must be one of those odd cases who hang around secretariats doing jobs no one else will. No well-kept palace would tolerate him unless his contribution was unique. He wore a dingy damson tunic, shoes with one lace tied up crookedly, and a belt so poorly tanned it looked as if the cow it came from was still alive. His hair was lank, and his skin had a grey pallor that might have washed off when he was younger, but was now ingrained. Even if he did not actually smell, he looked musty.

'Didius Falco, this is Canidius,' Vespasian himself introduced us in his brisk way. 'Canidius keeps the legionary archive.'

I was right then. Canidius was a clerk with unpromising prospects who had found an offbeat job he could invent for himself. I grunted noncommittally.

Vespasian shot me a suspicious glance. 'Your next assignment, Falco, is as my personal emissary to the Fourteenth Gemina in Germany.' This time I saved myself the hypocrisy of politeness and openly grimaced. The Emperor ignored it. 'I hear the Fourteenth are in a truculent mood. Brief us, Canidius.'

The eccentric-looking clerk recited nervously, without notes. 'The legio Fourteenth Gemina were an Augustan creation, originally raised at Moguntiacum on the River Rhenus.' He had a thin whine of a voice that tired a listener rapidly. 'They were among the four legions chosen by the Divine Claudius for the invasion of Britain, acquitting themselves bravely at the Battle of the Medway, much assisted by their native auxiliaries, who were Batavians.' North

359

Europeans from the Rhenus delta, Batavians are rowers, swimmers and river pilots to a man. All Roman legions are supported by such units of foreigners, in particular native cavalry.

'Falco doesn't need your Claudian anecdotes,' muttered Vespasian. 'And I was there!'

The clerk blushed; forgetting the Emperor's history was a bad mistake. Vespasian had commanded the Second Augusta at the Battle of the Medway, and he and the Second had played a celebrated part in the conquest of Britain.

'Caesar!' Canidius writhed in misery. 'The Fourteenth's roll of honour includes defeating Queen Boudicca, for which – along with the Twentieth Valeria – they were awarded the honorific title of "Martia Victrix".'

You may wonder why the Second Augusta did not win that prestigious handle too. The answer is that due to the kind of mix-up which we like to pretend never happens, the wonderful Second (my own legion as well as Vespasian's) failed to show up at the battlefield. The legions which did face the Iceni were lucky to survive. That was why any member of the Second needed to avoid the Fourteenth Gemina, honorific titles and all.

Canidius went on: 'In the recent wars, the Fourteenth's Batavian auxiliaries featured crucially. They had been separated from their parent legion and summoned to Germany under Vitellius. The Fourteenth themselves were devoted first to Nero – since after the Boudiccan Revolt he had called them his best legion – and then supported Otho. Otho brought them to Italy. This placed the legion and its native cohorts on opposing sides, and at the first battle of Bedriacum . . .' Canidius tailed off unhappily.

He was intending to fudge the issue, so I barged in: 'Whether the Fourteenth Gemina actually took part at Bedriacum is a moot point. Rather than admit they had been beaten in battle, they claimed they had not been there!'

Vespasian grumbled under his breath. He must think they were simply covering up.

Canidius rushed on again. 'After Otho's suicide, the

legion and its auxiliaries were reunited by Vitellius. There was some rivalry,' the archive clerk said, with quaint discretion. He had no real grasp of what the Emperor required.

'You're leaving out the picturesque details!' I interrupted. 'Be frank! The Fourteenth's subsequent history involved squabbling and public scuffles with their Batavians, during which they burned down Augusta Taurinorum . . .' This episode at Turin placed the main question mark over their discipline.

Wary of handling a sensitive issue, Canidius raced to finish. 'Vitellius ordered the Fourteenth itself back to Britain, attaching the eight Batavian cohorts to his personal train until he redeployed them in Germany.' More politics. Canidius was looking unhappy again.

'In Germany, the Batavian cohorts promptly attached themselves to Civilis. It gave the rebellion a tremendous boost.' I was still angry about it. 'Since Civilis is their chief, the Batavians' defection should have been foreseen!'

'Enough, Falco,' rasped Vespasian, refusing to criticise another Emperor – even the one he had deposed.

He nodded encouragement to Canidius, who squeezed out: 'The Fourteenth returned from Britain again to assist Petilius Cerialis. They now occupy Moguntiacum.' He finished his tale with relief.

'Only the Upper German forts survived,' Vespasian told me crisply, 'so Moguntiacum is at present policing both parts of the territory.' Clearly while the fort where they were stationed had such a vital role, he needed to feel absolute confidence in the Fourteenth. 'My priority is to tighten up discipline and dissipate old sympathies.'

'What happens to the troops who swore allegiance to the Gallic federation?' I asked curiously. 'Which were they, Canidius?'

'The First Germanica from Bonna, the Fifteenth Primigenia from Vetera and the Sixteenth Gallica from Novaesium – plus the Fourth Macedonia from . . .' He had forgotten; it was his first sign of humanity.

'Moguntiacum,' said the Emperor. It emphasised why he wanted loyal legions there now.

'Thank you, Caesar. When Petilius Cerialis received the culprits,' the clerk informed me, 'his words to the mutineers were . . .' Canidius for the first time referred to a note tablet in order to thrill us with the exact historical detail: ' *"Now the soldiers who revolted are once more soldiers of their country. From this day you are enlisted in the service and bound by your oath to the Senate and People of Rome. The Emperor has forgotten all that has happened, and your commander will remember nothing!"* '

I tried not to sound too shocked at this enlightenment. 'We call the circumstances exceptional, and give out lenient treatment, Caesar?'

'We cannot lose four legions of crack troops,' Vespasian growled. 'They will be disbanded, stiffened up and reformed in different units.'

'These new legions will be shifted from the Rhenus?'

'No sensible alternative. The forces which Cerialis and Gallus commanded will guard the frontier.'

'It won't take all nine legions.' I could now see the options that were facing the Emperor. 'So the Fourteenth Gemina could either be sent back to Britain or stationed at Moguntiacum permanently. I believe Canidius told us it was their original home base. What's your plan, sir?'

'I have not yet decided,' the Emperor demurred.

'Is that my mission?' I like to be frank.

He looked annoyed. 'Don't pre-empt my instructions!'

'Caesar, it's obvious. They served you well under Cerialis, but were highly restless beforehand. Ever since they defeated the Iceni, the Fourteenth have become a byword for wilfulness – '

'Don't decry a good legion!' Vespasian was an old-fashioned general. He hated to believe any unit with a fine reputation could deteriorate. But if they did, he would be ruthless. 'Moguntiacum is a two-legion fort, but they are doubled up with some inexperienced troops. I need them – if I can trust them.'

'The legion was raised there,' I mused. 'There's nothing like their own interested grannies living locally to keep soldiers meek . . . Also, it's nearer than Britain, which makes supervision easier.'

'So, Falco, how do you feel about making a discreet inspection?'

'What do you think?' I scoffed. 'I was serving in the Second Augusta during the Icenean thrash. The Fourteenth will well remember how we abandoned them.' I can handle myself in a street fight, but I shied away from taking on six thousand vengeful professionals who had good reason to thumb me out of existence like a woodlouse on a bathhouse wall. 'Caesar, they are liable to bury me in quicklime and stand around grinning while I frizzle!'

'Avoiding that should test your talents,' the Emperor sneered.

'What exactly,' I queried, letting him see I felt nervous, 'are you asking me to do, Caesar?'

'Not much! I want to send the Fourteenth a new standard, to mark their recent good conduct in Germany. You will be transporting it.'

'Sounds straightforward,' I muttered gratefully, waiting to discover the catch. 'So while I'm handing over this token of your high esteem, I size up their mood and decide whether your esteem ought to last?' Vespasian assented. 'With respect, Caesar, if you are planning to sponge the Fourteenth off the army list, why don't you ask their commanding legate to report in suitable terms?'

'Not convenient.'

I sighed. 'That suggests there is a problem with the legate too, sir?'

'Certainly not,' replied Vespasian decisively. He would say that in public, unless he had firm grounds to cashier the fellow. I guessed I was supposed to produce grounds.

I moderated my tone. 'Can you tell me something about him?'

'I don't know the man personally. Name's Florius Gracilis. He was suggested for a commander's post by the Senate, and I knew no reason to object.' There was a myth that all public posts were awarded by the Senate, although the Emperor's veto was absolute. In practice, Vespasian would normally suggest his own candidates, but he might sometimes flatter the Curia by allowing them to nominate some dumb cluck of their own. He seemed suspicious of this man – but did he fear blatant corruption, or everyday inefficiency?

I let it lie. I had my own resources for boning up on senators. Gracilis was probably the usual upper-class fool doing his stint with the legion because a military command when he was thirty formed a fixed step in the *cursus publicus*. He was bound to have been posted to one of the frontiers. Getting a legion in Germany was just his bad luck.

'I'm sure His Honour is well up to the demands of his post,' I commented, letting the Emperor know that while I was squinting at the legion he could rely on me to cast my usual sceptical eye over Florius Gracilis as well. 'This sounds like my usual complex mission, sir!'

'Simplicity!' the Emperor declared. 'While you are out there,' he added inconsequentially, 'you can apply yourself to some loose ends that Petilius Cerialis was forced to leave behind.'

I took a deep breath. This was more like it. The Fourteenth's loyalty could be assessed by any competent centurion on the spot. M. Didius Falco was being sent racing in circles after some other escaped goose.

'Oh?' I said.

Vespasian appeared not to notice my sour face. 'Your written orders will cover what's required . . .'

Vespasian rarely skimped discussing business. I knew from the airy way he ducked out of giving details that these 'loose ends' which I was inheriting from the fabled Petilius Cerialis had to be really filthy tasks. Vespasian must be hoping that by the time I read my instructions I would be safely en route and unable to quibble.

He made them sound unimportant. But these unspecified items tossed after me like party gifts were the real reason why he was sending me to Germany.

IX

It grieved me to be seen in public with a wraith like Canidius. He looked as if he had lost himself going to the bathhouse and three weeks later was still too shy to ask the way.

Still, I needed to pick his well-informed noddle. Stationing myself to windward, I led this sallow fellow to a wineshop. I chose one I rarely frequented, forgetting that the outrageous prices were why it had lost my patronage. I installed him on a bench among the desultory dice players, where he let himself be introduced to the warmth of an expensive Latian red.

'You've slung me the official spiel on the Fourteenth, Canidius; now let's hear the truth!'

The archive clerk looked uneasy. His orbit involved only the manicured version of public events. But with a beakerful inside him, he ought to give me all the grubby, hangnail stories that are never written down.

His eyes wandered slightly at the muffled sounds of commercial pleasure from the barmaids' overhead bedroom. He must have been forty, but he behaved like an adolescent who had never been let out before. 'I don't involve myself in politics.'

'Oh neither do I!' I retorted dismally.

I chewed my winecup, pondering the mess I was in. Ordered to a province on the harsh rim of the Empire, at a moment when its prospects for a civilised future were bleak. A mission so vague it was like trying to pick burs off a rumbustuous sheep. No girlfriend to comfort me. Every chance I would find a hit man lurking in some way station, with orders from Titus Caesar to make sure that that was the limit of my trip. Every chance, too, that if I ever did reach Moguntiacum, the Fourteenth Gemina would roll me into a trench like a foundation log and build their next rampart over my corpse.

I tackled the archive clerk again. 'Is there anything else I ought to know about Nero's favourite legion?' Canidius shook his head. 'No scandal or gossip?' No luck. 'Canidius, have you any idea what special tasks the Emperor wants me to do out in Germany?' Ideas were not his strong point. 'All right, try this one: what was the Emperor going to tell me about the rebel chief Civilis? He was interrupted in mid-flow when you arrived.' Hopeless.

I had wasted both patience and money. There were plenty of facts I still needed; once on location, I would have to discover the gaps – and the answers – myself.

Cursing myself for being gracious to this dim-wit, I left him with the flagon. Canidius let me pay, of course. He was a clerk.

Returning home, I brought in a loaf and some cooked sausage. Night was falling beyond my open window. The apartment block reverberated with distant knocks and cries as its occupants beat all Hades out of each other in various happy ways. The street below my balcony was full of oddly muttering voices which I preferred not to investigate. The night air brought a city cacophony of grumbling wheels, off-tune flutes, squalling cats and dolorous drunks. But I had never before noticed how intense the silence was indoors when Helena was not there.

Intense, until footsteps approached.

They were light, but reluctant – tired out by the long haul upstairs. Not boots. Not slipshod sandals either. Too long a stride for a woman, unless it was a woman I would not welcome. Too casual to be any man I needed to fear.

The feet stopped outside my door. There was a lengthy pause. Someone knocked. I leaned back on my stool saying nothing. Someone opened the door gingerly. The high-class odour of an extremely subtle unguent sneaked in and shimmied curiously around the room.

A head followed. It had sharply layered dark locks, held in place by a fillet of braid. It was a haircut you were meant to notice. It looked clean, neat, well attended, and as out of place in the Aventine as bees in a feather bed. 'You Falco?'

My own scalp began to feel dandruffy and hot. 'Who's asking?'

'I'm Xanthus. I was told you would be expecting me.'

'I'm not expecting anyone. But you can come in now you're here.'

He came in. He was sneering at the place; that made two of us. He left the door open. I told him to close it. He did so as if he was afraid he would be grappled to the floor by a pair of wild centaurs and robbed of his manhood amid much whinnying.

I gave him a rapid scan. He was a daisy. Not the usual Palace messenger, with a brain as thick as his bootsoles. This one had class – in his queer way.

While I stared, the inappropriate shaving-lotion continued to make itself at home. The chin that was sporting the magic Eastern mixture had been bristling gently for about ten years. The messenger wore a white Palace uniform with gold on the hem, but the shoes I had heard on the apartment stairs were his gesture to personality: round-toed vermilion calfskin jobs that must have cost a lot of money, though they were in questionable taste. The sort of supple footgear a low-grade actor might accept in return for paying attention to a female devotee.

'Letter for you.' He held it out: the papyrus I had come to dread, solid as piecrust, and weighed down with an ounce of sombrely embossed wax. I knew it contained orders for my German trip.

'Thanks.' I sounded thoughtful. This odd bod in the lurid shoes already had me wondering. He was not all he seemed. Although that applies to most of Rome, with Titus Caesar jealously concerned about my private life I felt more nervous than usual about social frauds. I took the letter. 'Hang yourself up on a cloak-peg, in case I want to send a rude reply.'

'That's right!' he ranted bitterly. 'Give me your orders! My sole purpose is to dally on doorsteps while people read their correspondence.'

Something was wrong here. I needed to probe. 'You seem a restless sort of messenger. Are your corns worse than usual?'

'I'm a barber,' said he.

'Stick with it, Xanthus. There are fortunes to be made out of bristle for a man with a deft hand.' And other fortunes, too, for hired hacks who deftly applied sharp weapons to people's throats. I checked him over discreetly; if he was carrying a blade it was well hidden. 'Whose barber are you anyway?'

He looked thoroughly depressed. 'I used to shave Nero. He killed himself with a razor, I heard; probably one of mine. Since then they've all passed through my hands. I shaved Galba; I shaved Otho – I laundered his toupee as well, in fact!' For the first time it sounded like the truth: only a genuine barber would make so much of name-dropping eminent clients. 'After that, when he remembered to let somebody attack his fortnight's undergrowth, I even shaved Vitellius . . .'

Distrust had struck again. I rasped bleakly. 'You ever scraped Vespasian?'

'No.'

'What about Titus?' He shook his head. I was too old to believe it. 'Know a man called Anacrites?'

'No.'

Anacrites was the official chief spy at the Palace, and no crony of mine. If anyone at the Palace was commissioning a private extermination, Anacrites was bound to be involved. Especially if they were exterminating me. Anacrites would enjoy that.

I bit my lip. 'So how come, when a clean shave is as rare as an emerald in a goose's gizzard, an imperial razorman has been reduced to footslogging round the Aventine in his natty scarlet lace-ups?'

'Demoted,' he said (unhappily).

'To the seedier end of a delivery round? It's hardly apt. I think you're lying.'

'Think what you like. I did my best to satisfy whoever turned up under the towel, but I'm told there's no further call for my skills and since Vespasian hates waste, I'm reallocated to the secretariat.'

'Tough!'

'It is, Falco! The Flavians have a set of strong chins. I had been assigned to Titus Caesar – '

'Nice mop of curls!'

'Yes. I could have done decent work on Titus . . .'

'But the victor of Jerusalem declines to trust his handsome epiglottis to a sharp Spanish blade in the hands of a man who has previously scratched Nero and Vitellius? Who can blame him, friend?'

'Politics!' he spat. 'Anyway, I'm now shoved off to tramp through the dung in stinking alleys and struggle up endless smelly stairs bringing so-called urgent despatches to unfriendly types who don't even bother to read them when I arrive.'

The complaints did not deflect me. 'Sorry, I'm not convinced. Did Titus send you here?' The barber shook his head impatiently, but by now I knew better. 'Stop jiggling like a whore on a busy night after the races.'

'Why the heavy suspicion? I'm just a runt they have no other use for.'

They had a use for him all right.

I broke open the scroll Xanthus had delivered, only to reveal more bad news.

My orders from Vespasian had been written by a secretary whose pretty Greek lettering would make a good vase decoration, though it was torture to read. While I struggled to decipher the rambling-rose script, the barber clung against one wall of the apartment. He seemed frightened of something. Possibly me.

When I had finished, I sat in silence. I was feeling bilious from the wine I had drunk with Canidius and from eating my sausage too fast. I would have been squeamish anyway. What I had to do in Germany was:

Deliver the Emperor's gift to the Fourteenth Gemina – and make a report to the Emperor.

Any fool could do that. I might even manage it myself.

Ascertain the fate of the most noble Munius Lupercus.

Who was he? I'll tell you: only the commanding legate of the legion at Vetera, the fort which had held out against the rebels to the verge of starvation before its surrendering troops were all butchered. All except Lupercus. The freedom fighters had sent *him* over the Rhine as a present to their thoroughly nasty priestess.

Attempt to curtail the activities of Veleda.

You guessed: Veleda was the priestess.

Ascertain the whereabouts of Julius Civilis —

'Oh gods!' Even with my long history of resistible commissions, this final task was unbelievable.

Ascertain the whereabouts of Julius Civilis, chieftain of the Batavians, and ensure his future co-operation within a pacified Gaul and Germany.

Vespasian had already sent two commanders-in-chief in full purple panoply plus nine trusted legions to undertake the reclamation of Civilis. Whatever the *Daily Gazette* trustingly reported from its pillar in the Forum, they must have failed. Now Vespasian was sending me.

'Bad news?' quavered Xanthus nervously.

'A disaster!'

'You're going to Germany, aren't you?' So I had intended, until I read this catalogue of impossible treats. Now the obvious thing was to head the other way. 'I really envy you,' the barber enthused, with the true tactlessness of his trade. 'I've always wanted to see something of the Empire outside Rome.'

'There are cheaper ways to be uncomfortable here. Try a hot afternoon in the Circus Maximus. Try a bad play at Pompey's Theatre. Try buying a drink near the Forum. Try shellfish. Try women. Go for a swim in the Tiber in August if you want to catch some exotic complaint ... Xanthus, I badly need to think. Shut up. Get out. And try not to walk your horrible scarlet footwear in my direction again.'

'Oh I have to,' he assured me smugly. 'I'm coming back tomorrow to bring the package that you have to take to Germany.'

I thanked him for the warning, so I could make sure I was out.

X

I ought to have refused this mission. I wanted to.

I desperately needed the money. It would be good – if I survived to apply for it. I was also keen to remove myself from Rome before the glances which Titus Caesar was casting in my direction led to something worse. Most of all, now that I had grown used to her lively presence in my billet, I could not bear it here without Helena.

I could have coped with poverty. I might even have faced up to Titus. Missing Helena was different. Helena was why I went on sitting sadly, in the squalor of my room at Fountain Court, unable to bestir myself even to rush to the Palatine and complain. Helena provided one pressing reason why I did want to go to Germany. I wanted to be there even if it meant enduring a European winter in a province stripped of all pretence of luxury by a barely quelled rebellion, where my own tasks ranged from the risky to the ludicrously impossible.

I had told Titus that Helena Justina was visiting her brother. I had said it because I believed it was the truth.

But I might have misled Titus slightly. Helena had one brother called Aelianus, who was studying diplomacy in Baetica. She had another called Justinus. I had met Camillus Justinus. It had been at the fort where he was serving as a military tribune, at a place called Argentoratum. Argentoratum is in Upper Germany.

Next day I made preparations. A secretary whom I cultivated at the Palace promised me copies of despatches relating to the Civilis revolt. I made my request for a travel pass and a set of official maps. Then I strolled out to the Forum, positioned myself against a pillar on the Temple of Saturn, and waited. I was looking for someone: a one-legged man. I wasn't particular which single-limbed person hopped into my orbit, so long as he met a condition: he had to have been on active service in the civil war, preferably with Vitellius.

I tried four. One was home from the East, which was no use, and three were fakes who ran off on normal sets of legs when asked questions. Then I found one who fitted. I took him to a cookshop, let him order a full bowl, paid for it – then held up the order while I made him talk to me.

He was an ex-legionary, pensioned off after his amputation, which was recent, for the red-raw stump had barely healed. I use the term 'pensioned off' somewhat lightly, since Rome has never provided well for troops who become unavailable for further action without having the consideration to be actually dead. This poor fellow failed to qualify for either a tombstone or his veteran's retirement landgrant; he had limped back to Rome, where only the corn dole and his fellow-citizens' consciences stood between him and starvation. Mine seemed to be the only active conscience this week, and it seemed a normal week.

'Tell me your name and legion?'

'Balbillus. I was in the Thirteenth.'

'Did that include the battles at Cremona?'

'Bedriacum? Only the first.'

Vitellius had fought both his important battles – against Otho, whom he defeated, and Vespasian, who defeated him – in the same place: a village called Bedriacum, near Cremona. Don't find this confusing. Once he had selected a decent spot with a river view and interesting features, why should he change?

'Bedriacum will do. I want to hear about the conduct of the Fourteenth.'

Balbillus laughed. The Fourteenth Gemina tended to produce a derisive reaction. 'My lot drank with them sometimes . . .' I took the hint and procured him liquid encouragement. 'So what do you want?' He was out of the army, on the worst possible terms; he had nothing to lose from democratic free speech.

'I need background. Only recent stuff. You can omit the Fourteenth's glorious feat against Queen Boudicca.'

We both laughed that time.

373

'They always were a stroppy lot,' Balbillus commented.

'Oh yes. If you care to study history, the reason the Divine Claudius chose them to conquer Britain was that he needed to keep them occupied. Even thirty years ago they were disruptive. Something about serving in Germany apparently leads to mutiny!' *Everything* about it, if I was any judge. 'So, Balbillus, tell me the florid details. First, how did they react to Vespasian?'

This was a risky question, but he half answered me: 'There were plenty of mixed feelings around.'

'Oh I know. In the Year of the Four Emperors, people had to readjust their positions every time a new man took the stage.' I could not recall adjusting mine. That was because I had, as usual, despised the entire list of candidates. 'I'm assuming all the British legions viewed Vespasian as one of their own?'

Balbillus disagreed. 'A lot of officers and men in the British legions had been promoted by Vitellius.'

No wonder Vespasian was now so keen to send Britain a new governor he could trust. Petilius Cerialis must be sailing across the Gallic Strait with a brief to weed out dissent.

Balbillus tore at a piece of bread. 'There were some very strange scenes in Britain.'

I shoved an olive bowl his way. 'What happened? The scandalous version, if possible!'

'The Fourteenth told us the British governor had upset his troops even more than governors normally do.' This burst of cynical wit endeared the ex-soldier to me even more than his pathetic wound. 'He had a running feud with the legate of the Twentieth Valeria.' I had run across them in my service days. Dull, though competent. 'The war inflamed the row, the troops sided with the legate, and the governor actually had to flee the province.'

'Jupiter! Whatever happened to Britain?'

'The legionary commanders formed a committee to run things. The Fourteenth seemed rather sorry to be missing it.'

I whistled. 'Nothing of this jolly scandal got out!'

'I expect in a wild bog like Britain,' Balbillus confided sarcastically, 'unusual arrangements seem perfectly natural!'

I was thinking about my own problem. 'Anyway, this means when the Fourteenth crossed to Europe, they already had a habit of inventing their own orders? Not to mention infighting.'

'You mean the Batavians?'

'Yes, especially their escapade at Augusta Taurinorum. They were fighting under Vitellius and met up with their legion at Bedriacum, am I right?'

He savaged the bread again. 'You can imagine how before the battle we were all on tenterhooks because the renowned Fourteenth Gemina were supposed to be approaching.'

'It was a crucial engagement, and the Fourteenth could swing it?'

'Well, they thought so!' Balbillus grinned. 'They never showed. The Batavian cohorts did fight on the winning side – they took on a group of gladiators in a clever skirmish on an island in the River Po. Afterwards, of course, they made the most of it. They paraded before the rest of us, jeering that they had put the famous Fourteenth in its place, and that Vitellius owed his entire victory to *them*.'

'So the Fourteenth felt obliged to squabble with them as publicly as possible?'

'You picture the scene, Falco. They were one set of hooligans paired with another, but at Augusta Taurinorum Vitellius quartered them together – even though relations had broken down.'

'That led to the rumpus? Did you see it?'

'Couldn't miss it! A Batavian accused a workman of cheating, then a legionary who had been billeted on the workman threw a punch at the Batavian. Running street battles broke out. The whole legion joined the scrap. When we forced them apart and mopped up the blood – '

'Corpses?'

'Just a few! The Fourteenth were ordered back to Britain. As they marched out of the city they left fires alight everywhere – quite deliberate – so Augusta Taurinorum burned to the ground.'

Inexcusable – in ordinary circumstances. However, even though the Fourteenth behaved like delinquents, they had never mutinied, whereas the Batavian cohorts they hated had defected to Civilis. The Fourteenth themselves served whoever happened to be Emperor that month. Vespasian could well decide that all these buoyant heroes needed now was a commander who could rein them in.

'He'll need a fierce grip!' snorted Balbillus, when I suggested it. 'On their way home to Britain, after Vitellius got rid of them, they had specific orders to avoid Vienna because of local sensitivities. Half of the idiots wanted to march straight there. Did you know that? They would have done it too, but for others who were thinking about their careers . . .'

I noted, in the Fourteenth's favour, that wiser council had prevailed. But it all confirmed that they were not in a mood to have me turning up to say they should reconcile themselves to a future of sitting in barracks fiddling their ration allowances, instead of boasting and burning towns . . .

I gave Balbillus the price of a shave and another wine flask, then left the one-legged soldier tucking into his hot food while I went home like a respectable citizen.

I should have stayed out drinking. I had forgotten about the Palace barber. He was waiting in my room with a chirpy smile, foul cherry-coloured shoes and a large wicker basket.

'I promised!'

'Yes, you warned me.'

Cursing, I grabbed a handle and attempted to drag the basket nearer. It stuck. I braced myself against a bench and heaved. The dead weight scraped a floorboard with an ear-splitting screech of cane. I unbuckled some heavy-duty straps and we peered in at the Fourteenth's new standard.

Xanthus was startled. 'Whatever is that?'

I prefer to travel light (if I have to go at all). The Emperor had selected just the kind of trinket anyone on a long journey hates to have tossing about in his backpack. I was being sent to Germany in charge of a two-foot-high, strongly sculpted human hand. It was gilded – but under the pretentious ornamentation the object which I had to carry across Europe was made of solid iron.

I groaned at the barber. 'Depending whether the expert you ask is an optimist or a realist, this represents an open-palmed gesture of international friendship – or a symbol of ruthless military power.'

'What do you think?'

'I think lugging it across Europe will ruin my back.'

I slumped on the bench. I wondered who had helped this frail blossom carry his basket upstairs. 'Well, you've brought it. What are you waiting for?'

The dubious Palace messenger looked coy. 'Something I wanted to ask you.'

'Cough up.'

'Can I come with you to Germany?'

This fitted my conviction that Titus had him lined up to do me some mischief. I wasn't even surprised. 'I don't think I heard that correctly.'

He was absolutely brazen. 'I have my savings – I've already applied to buy my freedom. I'd love to travel before I settle down –'

'Jupiter!' I growled into the neck of my tunic. 'It's bad enough having your chin snicked while some inane fellow demands whether sir intends visiting his Campanian villa this summer, without having one of the bastards wanting to join you on holiday!'

Xanthus said nothing.

'Xanthus, I'm an imperial agent visiting the barbarians. So what, my friend, is supposed to be the point of a *barber* sharing my misery?'

Xanthus replied morosely, 'Somebody in Germany might need a decent shave!'

'Don't look at me!' I rubbed my palm across my chin; the stubble was fierce.

'No,' he agreed, insultingly. Nothing stopped him once he got an idea beneath that well-trimmed thatch. 'No one will miss me here. Titus wants to be rid of me.' I could believe that. Titus wanted his private knife-man firmly attached to me. All the better if I took Xanthus somewhere remote before he pulled his blade.

'Titus can spread your travel pass with fish pickle and eat it under water – I journey alone. If Titus wants to retire you from official duties, let him give you a bounty so you can set up in a booth at some bathhouse – '

'I won't be a nuisance!'

'The qualification for a career in scissors must be being born with your ears missing!'

I closed my eyes to close him out, though I knew he was still there.

I was reaching a decision. I was now convinced that Titus had decided this piece of scented buffoonery could usefully strop his razor on my throat. If I went along with it – or appeared to – at least I knew whose dagger hand to watch. Turn down this chance, and I would be forced to make myself suspicious of everyone.

I looked up. The barber must have been stretching his mental capacity too, because he suddenly asked, 'People hire you, I gather?'

'Foolish ones do.'

'How much does it cost?'

'Depends how much I dislike what they commission me to do.'

'Give me a clue, Falco!' I obliged, with a show of distaste. 'I can find that sort of money,' he snivelled. I was not surprised. Any imperial slave is well placed to garner heavy tips. Besides, I reckoned Xanthus had a banker standing him his European tour. 'I'll hire you to escort me on the same trip as you.'

'The lure of adventure!' I scoffed. 'So do I get a bonus every time I can arrange for you to be cudgelled and robbed? Double rates if you catch a nasty rash from a cheap continental prostitute? Triple if you drown at sea?'

He said stiffly, 'You will be there to advise me how to avoid the perils of the road.'

'Well my first advice is, don't take this road at all.'

My world-weariness appeared to strike him as a romantic pose. Nothing was going to put him off; he must have been

378

ordered to come with me by persons whose orders are obeyed. 'Falco, I like your attitude. I reckon we could rub along together successfully.'

'All right.' I pretended I was too tired to argue. 'I was always a soft option for clients who enjoy being insulted twenty times an hour. I'll be taking two more days to finish my background enquiries and put my own affairs in order. Meet me at the Golden Milestone – on a journey this long, I always start from Zero. Be there at dawn with all your savings, wear more sensible footgear than those ghastly pink things, and bring your valid diploma of freedom from slavery, because I do *not* want to be arrested for stealing imperial property!'

'Thanks, Falco!'

I looked annoyed at his gratitude. 'What's another encumbrance? The Emperor's present to the army weighs a bit. You can help me transport the iron hand.'

'Oh no!' exclaimed the barber. 'I can't do that, Falco; I'll be carrying all my shaving kit!'

I told him he had a lot to learn. Though in agreeing to be lumbered with this Xanthus, I must have been suffering from brain failure myself.

PART TWO:
GETTING THERE

GAUL AND UPPER GERMANY
OCTOBER, AD 71

' *"Lukewarm! We'll be in hot water soon, though . . ."* '

Tacitus, *Histories*

XI

We made a pretty picture travelling, the barber, his trunk of emollients, the Hand in its basket, and I.

There were two ways to tackle getting there: over the Alps via Augusta Praetoria, or by sea to southern Gaul. In October both were best avoided. Between September and March, anybody sensible stays safe in Rome.

I hate ocean travel even more than I hate mountaineering, but I chose to go via Gaul. It's the route the army uses most – someone must once have worked out that it was the least dangerous logistically. Also, I had been that way with Helena once (though in the opposite direction), and I convinced myself that if she *was* going to Germany instead of Spain, she might want to revisit places which held fond memories . . .

Apparently not. I spent the whole trip scanning round for a tall, dark-haired woman throwing insults at customs officers, but there was no sign. I tried not to think of her being buried alive in an avalanche, or attacked by the hostile tribes who lurk in the high passes above Helvetica.

We landed at Forum Julii, which was comparatively pleasant. Things deteriorated when we reached Massilia, where we had to pass a night. So much for a well-planned trip. Massilia is, in my opinion, a rotten gumboil on the Empire's most sensitive tooth.

'Gods, Falco! This is a bit rough . . .' complained Xanthus, as we struggled against the tide of Spanish oil-sellers, Jewish entrepreneurs and wine merchants from all countries who were competing for a bed in one of the least disreputable inns.

'Massilia has been a Greek colony for six hundred years, Xanthus. It still thinks itself the best thing west of Athens, but six hundred years of civilisation have a depressing effect. They possess olives and vines, a brilliant harbour

surrounded by sea on three sides, and a fascinating heritage
– but you can't move for stallholders trying to interest you
in trashy metal pots and statuettes of plump deities with
funny round eyes.'

'You've been here before!'

'I've been *cheated* here! If you want dinner, you'll have to
entertain yourself. There's a long road ahead of us, and I'm
not going to sap my strength getting gut-rot from a bowl of
Massilia shrimps. Don't start talking to any locals – or any
tourists, come to that.'

The barber unhappily slunk off for a bite by himself.

I settled down with a very sick oil-lamp to study my maps.
One benefit of this trip was that the Palace had equipped
me with a first-rate set of military itineraries for all the
major highways – the full legacy of seventy years of Roman
activity in central Europe. These were not merely mileage
lists between the towns and forts, but decent, detailed travel
guides with notes and diagrams. Even so, I would have to
rely on my wits in some places. There were huge, worrying
blank spaces east of the River Rhenus: *Germania Libera* . . .
Endless tracts of territory where 'free' meant not only free
from Roman commercial influence, but with a complete
absence of Roman law and order too. That was where the
priestess Veleda lurked, and where Civilis might be hiding
up.

The frontier was uncertain enough. Europe was full of
restless tribes constantly trying to migrate to other districts,
sometimes in great numbers. Since Julius Caesar's time,
Rome had been attempting to settle friendly groups of them
in ways that created buffer zones. Our Upper and Lower
German provinces formed a military corridor along the
River Rhenus between the pacified lands in Gaul and the
great unknown. That was the policy at any rate, until the
civil war.

I studied my map thoughtfully. In the far north, alongside
Belgica, around the Rhenus Estuary, lay the Batavian homeland, with the stronghold they called The Island. All along
the river stood the Roman forts, guard posts, watch-towers

and signal stations which had been built to control Germany; most of them were now neatly lined through by the scribe who had brought the maps up to date for me. Furthest north was Noviomagus, where Vespasian was planning a new fort to watch over the Batavians, but which was currently just a cross on the map; next came Vetera, scene of the grim siege. Then there was Novaesium, whose pathetic legion had defected to the rebels; Bonna, which had been overrun by the Fourteenth's Batavian cohorts amid horrible slaughter; and Colonia Agrippinensium, which the rebels had captured but spared from the flames for strategic reasons (also I think Civilis had relations living there). On the River Mosella stood Augusta Treverorum, tribal capital of the Treveri, where Petilius Cerialis had roundly defeated the rebels. Where the River Moenus joined the Rhenus, lay my initial destination: Moguntiacum, capital of Upper Germany. I could reach it on a direct highway from the great Gallic crossroads at Lugdunum.

Alternatively, I could branch off the highway at a junction town called Cavillonum, and approach Upper Germany from further south. It was a good excuse to acclimatise myself to the province. I could travel to Moguntiacum and my rendezvous with the Fourteenth by water. This alternative route was no greater distance (I convinced myself) and I would hit the Rhenus most conveniently at Argentoratum, home station of a certain party whose sister I doted on.

While I was still frowning at the immense distance that lay ahead of us, the barber scuttled in looking green.

'Xanthus! Which hazard of travel has blighted your life now? Garlic, constipation, or just being fleeced?'

'I made the mistake of ordering a drink!'

'Ah! Happens to everyone.'

'It cost –'

'Don't tell me. I'm already depressed. The Gauls have a crazy standard of values. They are wine-mad, and spend like lunatics in the quest for liquor. No one who believes that a sound-bodied slave is fair exchange for one amphora of mediocre imported wine is reliable. And the vintner won't

385

charge you less than he paid for it just because *you* were brought up to expect a flagon on the tavern table for half an as.'

'What are people supposed to do, Falco?'

'I believe seasoned travellers carry their own.'

He stared at me. I gave him the peaceful smile of a man who had probably been drinking a private supply while his companion was out being rooked.

'You want a shave, Falco?' He sounded hurt.

'No.'

'You look like a savage.'

'Then I'll merge in nicely where we have to go.'

'I heard you were a ladies' man.'

'The lady whose man I happen to be happens to be somewhere else. Get to sleep, Xanthus. I warned you that having your pretty sandals on foreign soil would involve pain and stress.'

'I hired you to protect me!' he grumbled, winding himself into the thin blanket on his narrow bed. We were in a small dormitory. Massilia believes in packing in the customers neck to neck, like pickle jars on a cargo boat.

I grinned. 'That's the spirit! Adventures were what you wanted. They always involve suffering.'

Just before the lamp died of exhaustion, I let him see me testing my dagger and placing it under what passed for a pillow. I think he understood the message. I was a highly trained professional. Danger was my way of life. If so much as a mouse scratched a floorboard, knifing the barber would be my instant response. Given the amount of shaving-lotion he splashed on, I would smell him coming even in the pitch-dark. And I knew where to sink my weapon for the best effect. Whatever the Palace had told him, or not told him, he must be aware of that.

His first day in Gaul had made him too miserable to try anything that night.

There would be plenty of other chances. But whenever he decided to do the dirty work for Titus Caesar, I would be on the alert.

386

XII

We reached Lugdunum. I won't say without incident. We had fought off a gang of village urchins who thought my basket of symbolic ironwork contained something they could sell, then I hitched a lift on a wineship and nearly dropped the Hand overboard. In fact, every time we rode away from the previous night's mansio, I ran the risk of leaving Vespasian's present for the Fourteenth behind on a shelf.

The drinking-water started to affect us at Arelate; Gallic cooking oil knocked us sideways as we were rowed past Valentia; some tricky pork laid us low for a day at Vienna; and by the time we slunk into the civic capital, the wine we had gulped down to try and forget the pork had given us splitting heads. All along the route we were playing patball with the normal autumnal quota of fleas stocking up before the winter, bedbugs, wasps, and invasive little black things whose favourite lodging was up a luckless traveller's nose. Xanthus, whose pampered skin had rarely been outside the Palace, broke out in a rash whose progress he described for me at tedious length.

So, Lugdunum. As we disembarked, I favoured Xanthus with an informative travelogue: 'Lugdunum – capital of the Three Gauls. That's as in *"Caesar divided Gaul into three parts . . ."*, which every schoolboy is compelled to know, though you barbers may escape such low points of education . . . A handsome city, established by Marcus Agrippa as a focus for communication and trade. Notice the interesting aqueduct system, which uses sealed pipes constructed as inverted syphons to cross the river valleys. It's extremely expensive, from which we can deduce that in provincial terms the people of Lugdunum are *extremely* rich! There is a temple to the imperial cult, which we shall not be visiting – '

'I'd like a chance to sightsee!'

'Stick with me, Xanthus. This city also boasts an out-station of the mighty Arretinum pottery. We'll go there for our treat. You and I will be following the grand tourist tradition of trying to take home some dinnerware – at twice the cost and three times the trouble of shelling out for it in Italy.'

'Why do it then, Falco?'

'Don't ask.'

Because my mother told me to.

The samian tableware factory offered a fabulous chance to make our feet hurt tramping about all morning staring at thousands of pots, not to mention the opportunity of lashing out on presents that would make our bankers wince. The Lugdunum potters were bidding to supply the whole Empire. Theirs was the big commercial success story of our time. They were cornering the market, and their compound had that atmosphere of tenacious greed which passes for business enterprise.

Kilns and stalls stretched around the town like a besieging army, dominating normal life. Wagons blocked all the exit roads, hardly able to creak forwards under towering crates of the famous red dishes packed in straw for transit all over the Empire and probably beyond. Even in the depression that had followed the violence of the civil war, this place thrived. If ever the ceramics market slumped, Lugdunum would see widespread grief.

There were acres of workshops. Each one contained a local craftsman, most of whom were freeborn, unlike at the main factory in northern Italy, which I knew was run by slaves. My mother (who always made helpful suggestions for a present I could bring her) had informed me that Arretinum was in decline, whereas its outstation here at Lugdunum was known by discerning housewives as a source of more refined goods. They were certainly expensive, but as I gazed at the tottering stacks of dishes, jugs and comports, I acknowledged I was chasing quality. The moulds used here had crisply defined patterns or delicately sculpted classical scenes, and the finished clay was fired with great

388

assurance to a warm, deep red gloss. I could see why these ceramics were sought after as eagerly as bronze or glass.

My mother, who had brought up seven children mainly without my father's assistance, deserved an item of decent redware, and I would have liked to buy a handsome platter to mollify Helena. I owed them both some attention. But I resented being set up. Every time I risked asking a price, I moved on again hastily.

There were no bargains. The loss-leader principle was unknown in Lugdunum. These artisans believed that if people were stupid enough to come two hundred miles upriver to inspect their fancy goods, they might as well pay the going rate. The going rate was just about as high as the potters thought they could push it, after weighing up the gemstones in your finger-rings and the nap on your travelling cloak. In my case that meant not very high – but still more than I was prepared to pay.

I burrowed around, but they all thought the public existed to be squeezed. I ended up under a trestle-table, rooting through a basket of cut-price chipped pieces.

'Those look a waste of time,' Xanthus muttered.

'I'm an auctioneer's son. I was taught that alongside the junk in the discard box sometimes nestles a treasure . . .'

'Oh you're full of homespun lore!' he grinned.

'I can spot a sound turnip – see?'

I had found a hidden serving dish that was relatively free from cracks and firing blemishes. The barber acknowledged graciously that persistence had paid; then we went to find someone to sell it to us.

Not so easy. The potters at Lugdunum certainly had their own ways of obstructing cheapskates. The lads shifting the sacks of wet clay pleaded ignorance of prices; the man carving a new mould was too artistic to barter; the stokers at the kiln were too hot to be bothered; and the craftsman's wife, who normally took the money, had stayed at home with a headache.

'Probably got it worrying how they can possibly spend all their profits!' I muttered to Xanthus.

The craftsman himself was temporarily unavailable. He

and most of his neighbours had formed a surly crowd on the cart-track outside. When we came looking for him a dispute was in progress, and there was pushing and shoving. I made Xanthus hang back.

A small, angry group of potters, with wet clay on their aprons and forearms, had gathered round a spokesman who was giving rough answers to two men who appeared to be trying to force a debate. There were more beards and side-whiskers in evidence than you would find in a male gathering in Rome, but not much to choose between any of them otherwise. The two men arguing most heatedly wore the same Gallic tunics as the locals, with high collars of folded material at the throat for warmth, but over these they had European felt capes, with vertically slashed necks, wide sleeves and pointed hoods thrown back. They were both shouting fiercely, with the air of men losing a struggle. The others made loud retorts from time to time, but tended to stand back contemptuously, as if they had less need to haggle because they were in control.

Things grew distinctly ugly. A tall chap with a cleft chin and vivid sneer appeared to be the local leader. He made a sudden obscene gesture at the two men. The stouter party swung a fist, but was restrained by his comrade, a younger man with reddish hair and warts.

I had been hoping the heat would simmer down so I could buy my pot. Now it looked as if any bargains today would be sealed with bloody noses. I handed Ma's present to a local, grabbed Xanthus and made a fast exit.

'What was that about, Falco?'

'No idea. When you're travelling, never get drawn into feuds. You don't know the history, you're bound to pick the wrong side, and all that can happen is both parties will turn on you.'

'You've left your dish!'

'That's right.' It was lopsided anyway.

XIII

On the next leg of our journey things started to happen.

I was fast losing heart. Visiting the ceramics factory had served as a diversion, though one which produced its own anxieties since I had bought nothing and would be due for a drubbing back at home. Still, I gave no more thought to potters and their problems; I had troubles of my own. My real mission loomed. By Lugdunum we had put a third of the distance across Europe behind us, with the tiring sea trip from Ostia before that. Now we were on the final push, and the nearer we drew to the great Rhenus river, and to the ludicrous tasks Vespasian had set me, the more depressed I felt.

Not for the first time, I had become horrified by how far we had to journey in order to cross Europe, and by how long it was taking.

'More bad news, Xanthus! River travel's too slow. At this rate I'll hit winter before I finish my mission. I'm transferring to horseback, courtesy of my imperial travel pass, so you'll have to hire yourself a mule if you want to keep up.'

Don't imagine that Vespasian had kitted me out with the wherewithal to commandeer a horse from the state despatch stations because he wanted me to travel in comfort; he probably thought it more convenient for the Iron Hand.

The terrain looked decidedly foreign now. Instead of huge Italian villas with absentee landlords and hundreds of slaves, we were riding past modest tenant farms. Pigs instead of sheep. Fewer olive groves and thinner vineyards with every milestone. We were being held up at bridges by army supply convoys; it was definitely the approach to a military zone. Towns became a novelty. Everywhere was colder, wetter and darker than when we had left home.

As a traveller Xanthus was becoming more confident, which meant that as the idiot's nursemaid I had to be even more on guard. Explaining trivial regional habits every time we stopped to change horses was maddening. In addition, it had started to rain.

'I've been slipped some duff coins, Falco – cut in quarters and halves!'

'Sorry, I ought to have warned you: there's a long-term small-coin shortage. No need to show your ignorance by causing a fuss. Cut halves are accepted locally, but don't take any home. Assuming we ever go home.' I was so gloomy I doubted it. 'You'll adapt. Just try not to waste an as or a quadrans if you can pay with one of your larger coins, and pick up change for when we're desperate. If they run out of coppers altogether the barmaids use kisses, and when they run out of *those* . . .' I shuddered pointedly.

'Seems daft!' Xanthus moaned. A true barber. Jokes were lost on him.

Sighing inwardly, I supplied the sensible explanation: 'The army has always been paid in silver. Sesterces are easier to transport in bulk, so the Treasury never thinks of sending out a few chests of coppers for the lads to use as pocket money. There is a mint at Lugdunum, but civic pride seems to make them prefer turning out the big shiny ones.'

'I wish they'd cut their prices in half too, Falco.'

'And I wish a lot of things!'

I spoke with restraint, though I was near breaking-point. I wished it would stop raining. I wished I could find Helena. I wished I was safe in my own city, commissioned for a risk-free job. Most of all, as the barber prattled on relentlessly, I wished I could lose him.

We stayed the night in a village typical of that highway: a long skein of ribbon development with one main street devoted mostly to entertaining travellers. There were plenty of rest-houses, and once we found a clean one to dump our baggage at, there were plenty of taverns we could walk to for a change of scene. I chose one of the porticoed bars that was throwing light across the street, and we fumbled our way down into a back basement where other travellers were seated at circular tables enjoying cold meat or cheese with beakers of the local fermented beer. The scent of damp woollen cloaks and sodden boots hung everywhere as we all steamed after the day's wet ride. The bar was warm, dry and lit with reed tapers. It had a we-are-here-to-please-you atmosphere which eased the strain of travelling even in those of us who were reluctant to be eased by anything too much in case Fate made us pay a sour penalty.

We drank. We ate. Xanthus perked up; I said nothing. He called for a drink again; I jingled my purse morosely. I would be paying as usual. Xanthus found plenty of ways to squander his holiday cash, but possessed a knack of digging deep only when I let him out by himself. He had cluttered us up with souvenirs – rattling lanterns, statuettes of muscular local deities, and chariot-wheel talismans – yet somehow funding our supper always seemed to be my responsibility.

This bar was casual about payment: you settled up at the end. It was a good way to part people from more money than they had intended, though in fact when I heaved myself over to sort out the reckoning, the extortion was not too painful, considering how much the barber had eaten and drunk.

A good evening – for a man who could feel free to enjoy it.

I told Xanthus to press on ahead while I waited for the usual scramble among the staff to find coins for my change. When I emerged on the main street my tame pest had already vanished. I was in no hurry to catch up. It was a dry night, with crazy stars dotting a black sky among a few fast, high clouds. Tomorrow we would probably have teeming showers again, but I stood for a while enjoying this fierce, dry wind on my face. The street was empty at that moment. I was suffering a pang of traveller's melancholia.

I turned back into the bar, where I ordered a dish of raisins and another drink.

The room had thinned out. Feeling independent, I changed seats. This allowed me to survey my drinking companions. Men were talking together in small parties; some were

393

dining alone. Two caught my eye because they seemed to be together yet never spoke. There was no impression of a quarrel; they simply looked even more depressed than I had been before I shook off Xanthus.

A barmaid lit a new taper on their table. As it flared, I recognised the pair; they wore high-necked tunics under blackberry-coloured Gallic wraps with pointed hoods. One was overweight and middle-aged; the other had reddish hair and a particularly florid crop of warts on his cheeks and hands. They were the two I had seen at the ceramics factory, arguing.

Had they looked more communicative I might have gone over and mentioned the coincidence. As it was, they were sunk in their thoughts and I was sleepy, enjoying my snatched period of privacy. I finished my raisins. The next time I looked up they were on their way out. Just as well, probably. I doubted if they had noticed me at Lugdunum, and in any case, they had been so angry there that they might not welcome a reminder of the scene. Tomorrow we would all continue our journeys to different destinations. It was highly unlikely another chance meeting would occur.

But it did. Well, *I* saw *them*.

Next morning, half an hour out of the village, while the barber was still maundering on about where I had disappeared to for so long the previous evening, and I was ignoring the flow of complaint with my usual tight-lipped tact, we came across two tent parties of army recruits. There were no legions stationed in Gaul itself. These goslings must have been waddling towards the frontier. Now they had stopped. They were standing about the highway like spilled carrots, twenty seventeen- and eighteen-year-olds still unused to the weight of their helmets and only just discovering the drear boredom of a long march. Even the centurion in charge of them, who must have been around a bit, was inadequate for the crisis they had stumbled across. He knew he represented law and order, so he knew he had to do something. But he would rather have kept going with his eyes fixed straight ahead. Frankly, so would I.

The problem was that the recruits had spotted the bodies of two travellers lying in the drainage ditch. They had called out eagerly to the centurion, so he had had to stop. When we arrived he was not a happy man. As he had clambered down to investigate, his boot had skidded on the wet, slippery turf. He had twisted his back, soaked his cloak, and smeared mud all down one leg. He was cursing repetitiously as he tried to clean his leg with a bunch of grass. Xanthus and I reining in to watch made him even more upset. Now, whatever he decided to do about the problem would have critical witnesses.

We had ridden out north from Lugdunum, following the River Sâone on the consular highway constructed by the army as a fast route towards the two Germanies. Maintained by commissioners at public expense, it was a top-quality piece of engineering: rammed earth, then a layer of pebbles, another of rubble, a bed of fine concrete, then squared paving with a camber that would shed water like a tortoise shell. The highway rode a little above the surrounding countryside. On either side were steep ditches to provide both drainage and security from ambushers. Looking down from the road, I had a perfect view.

The keenest young lads had slithered down after their centurion. This was the best thing that had happened to them since they had left Italy. They were rolling the fat corpse onto his back. I think I was ready for what was to follow even before I had a look at his face. It was puffed up from lying in rainwater, but I knew this was one of the two men from Lugdunum. I knew his stiffening companion, too, though he was still face down; I could see the warts on his hands. They were visible because before depositing him in the ditch-water, someone had bound his arms behind his back.

Whatever had made these two so angry, fortune had found a decisive way of helping them get over it.

XIV

The centurion tucked up the swinging, bronze-weighted ends of his groin-protector into his belt, then handed his helmet to a soldier, who held it gingerly by the carrying loop. The rain had stopped temporarily, but the officer's scarlet cloak twisted awkwardly against his silvered sword baldric, the cloak's woollen folds clinging to him with the dampness you never seem to lose when travelling. As his head lifted, I spotted weary resignation because our arrival had dispelled any plan he might have had for dragging brushwood over the bodies and hurrying off out of it.

Leaning on my horse's neck, I gave him a slight nod.

'Move the crowd on, soldier!' he called up. The recruits were so new to army life that instead of each stubbornly assuming the order was for the next man along, they all squared up to us. I stayed where I was.

'Show them your pass!' Xanthus hissed at me loudly, assuming we were in trouble – which, once he had spoken, we immediately were. I ignored him, but the centurion stiffened. Now he would want to make quite sure who we were, and if he was as thorough as he looked, where we were going, who had sent us, what we were up to out here in this wilderness, and whether anything in *our* business was likely to produce repercussions affecting him.

This seemed good for holding us all up for at least a couple of weeks. My dangerous stillness communicated itself to the barber, who subsided unhappily. The centurion glared at us.

By now I was more or less resigned to people concluding that Xanthus and I were two fancy boys out on a spree. Xanthus was unmistakably a barber – and I was just as obviously too poor to afford a personal attendant. Our horse and mules were drawn from the local stables who supplied the imperial despatch-riders, but there was nothing about

396

the beasts to give that away. The basket with Vespasian's gift to the Fourteenth had a well-buckled, military air. My own luggage looked businesslike. Yet any hint of officialdom I managed to carry clashed heavily with the barber's daintiness. Like everyone else, the centurion assessed his Greek-looking cloak and violet tunic with saffron embroidery (it was probably a cast-off from Nero, but I had refused to enquire and give Xanthus the pleasure of telling me). The officer considered the brighter-than-life complexion, the fastidiously trimmed hair and today's shoes (hole-punched, purple-tasselled jobs). He took in the simpering, insufferable expression. Then he turned to me.

I stared back, uncombed and unperturbed. I allowed him three seconds of failing to explain me. Then I suggested quietly, 'One for the municipal police at the next town with a magistrate?' I was consulting my itinerary; I let him see it was army issue. 'We're three days past Lugdunum; Cavillonum should be only a cricket's jump ahead. That's a substantial town . . .'

People are never grateful. Offering him a let-out only made him take an interest. He turned back to the corpses. I should have ridden on, but our previous contact with the dead men gave me some sort of fellow-feeling. I dismounted and half jumped, half slid down into the *fossa* too.

I felt no sense of surprise at finding them here, dead. They had carried the marks of men in the midst of crisis. Maybe it was hindsight, but what I had seen of them had seemed to forebode tragedy.

Signs of what had done the actual damage were minimal, but it looked as if both men had been beaten to subdue them, then finished off by pressure to the neck. Their bound arms proved pretty conclusively that the killings were deliberate.

The centurion searched them without emotion while his young soldiers stood back more shyly. He glanced at me. 'Name's Falco,' I said, to show I had nothing to hide.

'Official?'

'Don't ask!' That told him I was official enough. 'What do you think?'

397

He had accepted me as an equal. 'Looks like robbery. Horses missing. This stout party has had a pouch cut from his belt.'

'If that's it, report their positions as you pass through Cavillonum. Let the civilians deal with it.'

I touched one of the dead men with the back of my hand. He was cold. The centurion saw me do it, but neither of us commented. The clothing of the one they had turned over was wringing wet where the brackish bog at the base of the ditch had soaked right through the material. The centurion saw me looking at that, too.

'Nothing to show who they are or where they were going! I still put it down to thieves.' He met my gaze, daring me to disagree; I smiled faintly. In his position I would have taken the same line. We both stood. He shouted up to the road, 'One of you run back to the milestone and take a note of it.'

'Yes, Helvetius!'

He and I took a run at the bank and regained the road together. The recruits below had a last poke at the bodies for bravado, then followed us; most of them floundered and fell back a few times. 'Stop fooling!' Helvetius growled, but he was patient with them.

I grinned. 'They seem up to the usual dim standard of nowadays!' He hated them, as recruiting officers do, but he let it pass. 'What's your legion?'

'First Adiutrix.' Brought over the Alps by Cerialis as part of the task force that quelled the rebellion. I had forgotten where they were based presently. I was just happy not to hear he belonged to the Fourteenth.

Xanthus was asking one of the soldiers what fort they were heading for; the lad was unable to tell him. The centurion must have known, but he didn't say; nor did I ask.

We parted company from the soldiers and rode on towards the Cavillonum junction, where I was planning to fork south. After a while Xanthus informed me, with obvious pride, that he had recognised the dead men from Lugdunum.

'So did I.'

He was disappointed. 'You never said!'

'No point.'

'What will happen now?'

'The centurion will instruct a town magistrate to collect the corpses and organise a posse to search for the thieves.'

'Do you think they'll be apprehended?'

'Probably not.'

'How do you know he was a centurion?'

'He wore his sword on the left.'

'Do ordinary soldiers carry them differently?'

'Correct.'

'Why?'

'Keeps the scabbard out of the way of the shield.' To a foot-soldier unimpeded freedom of movement could mean life or death, but such details failed to interest Xanthus.

'You know, it could have been us!' he trilled enthusiastically. 'If you and I, Falco, had set out earlier than they did this morning, *we* could have had that chance meeting with the thieves.'

I said nothing. He assumed I was unnerved by the suggestion, so he rode on looking superior. It was another of his irritating habits; he could reason himself halfway through a problem, then his brain stuck.

Even if he and I had ridden out at dawn with clinking saddlebags marked 'Help yourselves' in three European languages, I did not believe that whoever killed the pair would have touched us. This was no straightforward highway robbery. There were oddities here which both Helvetius and I had spotted. For one thing, the two men from Lugdunum had *not* died that morning. The bodies were cold, and the condition of their clothing showed that they had been lying in the ditch all night. Who travels by night? Not even imperial despatch-riders, unless an emperor has died or they have details of a *very* lurid scandal involving people at the top. In any case, I had seen the victims at their supper. They had looked unhappy, but had given no impression of needing to dash on with lanterns. They had been resting as leisurely as the rest of us at the tavern that night.

No. Somebody had killed those two men, probably at the village not long after I saw them, then transported the bodies a fair distance in the dark. Perhaps if I had not lingered over my drink, I would have run into the fracas. Perhaps I might even have prevented it. At any rate, after I watched them leave the tavern they must have been sought out, beaten and throttled, then the murders disguised as a natural hazard of travelling so that no questions would be asked.

'All a bit of a coincidence, eh Falco?'

'Possibly.'

Possibly not. But I had no time to stop and investigate. The only question I could ponder as I rode through Cavillonum was, did their sad fate derive entirely from their personal business in Lugdunum – or did it have some bearing on my own task?

I told myself I would never know.

It didn't help.

400

XV

Argentoratum had forgotten how to welcome strangers – assuming it had ever possessed the knack. The town had hosted a huge army base for as long as Rome had taken an interest in Germany, and its good manners had suffered. This was the original home station of my own legion, the Second Augusta. By the time I had been sent out to them in Britain there had been only a few grumpy veterans with any recollection of life on the Rhine, but Rome's foothold in Britain had always seemed perilous, and in any case, we had always hoped to be posted somewhere better, so Argentoratum had always been a place whose name the men of my legion spoke with a proprietary twang.

That did not mean I could call up old favours when I made the mistake of going there.

I had passed through this hard-faced habitation before, en route to even worse places. At least the last time I had met young Camillus Justinus, who had treated me to a dinner I still remembered plus a tour of the high spots and the low life – which were neither as high as Argentoratum liked to think, nor as low as I was hoping for at the time. I had been depressed – a man in love, though one who had not yet noticed it. I wondered now if Camillus had been able to see that his stately sister (whom I was supposed to be escorting, though as usual Helena had placed herself in charge) had been busy caging me like some little pet singing finch. I looked forward to asking him, and sharing the joke. But I would have to find him first.

Big military centres have their drawbacks. At the fort you can never encounter any sentry you recognise. No friendly official from your last visit has ever stayed in post. The town is equally unpromising. The locals are too busy making money out of the soldiery to bother with casual visitors.

The men are brusque and the women contemptuous. The dogs bark and the donkeys bite.

Eventually I dragged Xanthus to the front of a complaining queue at the main guardhouse. I could have registered as an imperial envoy and been poked into a billet inside the fort, but I spared myself a night of being polite to the commissariat. One of the men on guard told me all the bad news I needed to winkle out: they had no listing for the arrival here of any noble tribune's noble sister, and his honour Camillus Justinus had left Argentoratum anyway.

'His replacement came two weeks ago. Justinus had completed his tour.'

'What – gone home to Rome?'

'Hah! This is the Rhine; no one gets to escape that easily! Posted on.'

'Where's he stationed now?'

'No idea. All I know is we get the password for the night watch from some beardless little idiot fresh out of philosophy school. Last night's little gem was *xenophobia*. Today there are three sentinels in the cells for forgetting it, and a centurion's optio is striding round like a bear who just sat on a thorn-bush because he has to do disciplinary reports on his best tent party.'

No legion in Germany at present could risk mistakes by the guard. The province was under strict martial law – for very good reasons – and there was no room for idiotic tribunes who wanted to show off.

'I imagine your clever new boy is listening to a rich lecture from the legate!' I fought back my worries about Helena, concentrating on her brother. 'Maybe Camillus Justinus was deputed to one of the task-force legions?'

'Want me to make enquiries?' The gateman gave every impression he was prepared to help a tribune's friend, but we both knew he did not intend to leave his stool.

'Don't trouble yourself,' I answered with a courteous sneer. It was time to go. I was all too aware that the barber, who had been peering over my shoulder in a haze of exotic skin lotion, was starting to make a poor impression on this hard-nosed front-line legionary.

I made one last play for information. 'What's the word on the Fourteenth Gemina?'

'Bastards!' retorted the guard.

This unsophisticated parley was all I could expect. In a legionary gatehouse on a dark, wet October night, there was not much scope for light salon conversation. Behind me, two exhausted despatch-riders were waiting to register, Xanthus was looking even more indiscreet, and a very drunk venison-supplier who wanted to dispute a bill with the centurions' dining club was jostling me so closely that I left, not wanting a fight right then, yet feeling as bruised and indignant as a barmaid at a Saturnalia feast.

I booked us into a civilian lodging-house between the fort and the river, so we could make a quick departure at first light. We went to the baths but were already too late for the hot water. Dazed by the way foreign towns draw their shutters so early, we ate a grim supper, forcing it down with acidic white wine, and were then kept awake most of the night by tramping boots. I had settled us in a street full of brothels. Xanthus became intrigued, but I told him the disturbance was just troops on a night exercise.

'Listen, Xanthus. When I go up to Moguntiacum, you can stay here if you like. I'll pick you up for the trip home when I've done what I have to for the Emperor.'

'Oh no. I've come this far, I'll stick with you!'

He spoke as if he was doing me a gigantic favour. I closed my eyes wearily and made no reply.

Next morning I tried to hitch us a ride for nothing, but no luck. The trip down the Rhenus is a highly picturesque one, so the owners of the river barges were charging equally highly for the privilege of surveying a hundred miles of its scenery.

Ours was a wineship; most of them are. We shared the slowly passing vistas with two old fellows and a pedlar. The grandads had bent backs, bald heads, and a series of mouth-watering picnics which they had no intention of sharing round. They sat opposite each other for the whole journey, talking hard, like people who have known one another for a very long time.

The pedlar, who came aboard at a small settlement called Borbetomagus was bent too, but under the trappings of a fold-up stall and the ghastly stuff he sold. Xanthus and I were a captive audience so he soon unknotted the corners of his cloth bundles and spread his offerings on the deck. I ignored him. Xanthus immediately throbbed with crass excitement.

'Look at this, Falco!'

Since I did sometimes make a feeble attempt to save him from his stupidity, I glanced at the trash he was about to invest in now. Then I groaned. This time it was militaria. You may suppose our footslogging heroes would have had enough of kit and harness without spending their pay on more, but never believe it; this canny pedlar was doing a fine trade flogging the legionaries his sad souvenirs of ancient wars. I had seen it in Britain. I had seen it in the cartload of junk my elder brother, who had no sense of proportion, had dragged home from the exotic souks of Caesaria. Here, with nine legions along the Rhenus, most of them bored and all of them flush with imperial silver, there must be a vast scope for trading in quaint tribal buckles, worn-out weaponry and odd jags of iron that could have come off any farm implement.

The man was a native Ubian, all top lip and small talk. The lip was stretched over big buck teeth; the chat was his softening-up technique. It worked on Xanthus. Most things did. I let the two of them get on with it.

The pedlar's name was Dubnus. He was selling the usual native helmets with spikes over the ears, several bowls of 'old' arrowheads and speartips (which he had obviously gathered up last Thursday from a rubbish tip at a previous fort), a dirty drinking-cup which he swore to Xanthus was an aurochs' horn, some links of 'Sarmatian armour', half a set of 'Icenean horse-trappings', and just by the way, a collection of Baltic amber.

None of it contained fossilised insect life, but the amber was the only stuff worth considering. Naturally Xanthus passed straight on without a second glance. I said I would have bought some beads for my girlfriend if they had been matched and threaded properly. Not entirely to my surprise, Dubnus immediately produced from his unsavoury pocket three or four decent necklace strands – at three or four times the price.

We spent a tolerable half-hour haggling over the string with the smallest beads. I beat him down to about a quarter of the asking price just for the vocal exercise, then snapped up one of the better necklaces as I had intended all along. The pedlar had weighed me up cannily, but Xanthus looked startled. He did not know I had spent my childhood burrowing around the Saepta Julia second-hand stalls. I also thought it might be wise to buy a present for Helena's birthday in case I ran into her. I was missing her. It made me an easy mark for anyone hawking trinkets that showed slight vestiges of taste.

Judging that my purse was now firmly closed, Dubnus turned his whining charm on Xanthus again. He was an artist. As an auctioneer's son, I almost enjoyed watching it. Luckily, we were not sailing all the way down to the delta, or the barber would have bought up the pedlar's entire stock. He did fall for the aurochs' horn, supposedly hacked by Dubnus himself from one of the wild Gallic oxen whose savage temper is legendary . . .

'I'd really like to see one of those, Falco!'

'Just be thankful it's unlikely!'

'You ever spied one on your travels?'

'No. I'm sensible, Xanthus – I never wanted to.'

His acquisition was a fairly useful drinking-cup, which didn't spill too much down his tunic neck when he attempted to use it. He managed to polish it up to a handsome shine. I never told him that aurochs don't have twisted horns.

As the wineship floated on to our destination, Dubnus slowly rewrapped his treasures. Xanthus began to handle a helmet. Partly to rescue him before he was bankrupt (because that would mean I'd have to pay for *everything*), I took the item away from him.

405

It looked like army issue at first, but with differences. The modern helmet incorporates a deeper guard around the back, protecting the neck and shoulders; it also has cheekpieces and extra protection over the ears. I suspect the revised design was developed to counter damage from Celtic broadsword swipes. The original pattern had been superseded long before my time, but I was staring at one now.

'This must be quite an antique, Dubnus.'

'I call that a relic of the Varus disaster!' he confessed amiably, as if owning to a fake; then his eyes met mine and he had second thoughts. I managed to stop myself shivering.

'Where did you get it?'

'Oh . . . somewhere in the woods.' His voice faded evasively.

'*Where?*' I asked again.

'Oh . . . up in the north.'

'Somewhere like the Teutoburger forest?'

He was reluctant to clarify. I dropped to one knee, surveying his stock more attentively. He had marked me up as trouble, so he didn't like me doing it. I ignored his agitation. That worried him even more.

Now I noticed a piece of old bronze that could have come from a Roman sword pommel; clasps that resembled a set I had seen at my grandfather's house; a holder for a helmet plume – another discontinued line, now altered to a carrying loop.

'Sell a lot of these "Varus relics", do you?'

'People believe what they want to.'

There was also a blackened object I refused to handle because I guessed it was a human skull.

I stood up again.

Augustus's stepgrandson, the heroic Germanicus, was supposed to have found where the massacre had taken place, collected the scattered remains of the dead, and given the lost army of Varus some kind of decent funeral – but who believes that out in the hostile forest Germanicus and his nervous troops spent too much time offering themselves

406

as another target? They did their best. They brought the lost standards back to Rome. After that we could all sleep with clear consciences. It was best not to think that somewhere deep in the dark woods of unconquered Germany broken weapons and other booty might still lie among unburied Roman bones.

The troops of today would buy this mouldy paraphernalia. Army lads love souvenirs that smack of manly deeds in dangerous venues. The grislier the better. If Dubnus really had discovered the old battle site, he must be coining it.

I avoided the issue by probing for my own purposes. 'So you go across the river, do you? In the north?' He shrugged. Commerce breeds daring. In any case, free Germany had never been a no-go area for the purposes of trade. 'How far do your travels take you? Ever come across the famous prophetess?'

'Which prophetess would that be?'

He was teasing. I tried not to look particularly interested, in case word of my mission ran ahead of me. 'Is there more than one sinister spinster wielding influence over the tribes? I mean the bloodthirsty priestess of the Bructeri.'

'Oh, Veleda!' sneered Dubnus.

'Ever met her?'

'No one meets her.'

'Why's that?'

'She lives at the top of a high tower in a lonely place in the forest. She never sees anyone.'

'Since when have prophets been so shy?' Just my luck. A really weird one. 'I never imagined she kept a marble office, with an appointments secretary serving peppermint tea for visitors, but how does she communicate?'

'Her male relations carry messages.' Judging by the effect Veleda had had on international events, her uncles and brothers must have busily trampled a wide swathe through the woods. It rather took the shine off her elusiveness.

The barber was wearing his excitable look. 'Is Veleda part of your mission?' he hissed. His wide-eyed simplicity was beginning to afflict me like a stitch in the side when you're running away from a mad bull.

'Women I can handle. But I don't do Druids!' It was a line. Two of us knew it, yet poor old Xanthus looked impressed.

I had to act fast. Our barge was approaching the great bridge at Moguntiacum; we would soon berth at the quay. I gave the pedlar a thoughtful glance. 'If somebody wanted to contact Veleda, would it be possible to get a message to this tower of hers?'

'Could be.'

Dubnus looked disturbed by the suggestion. I made it plain I was speaking with some authority, and told him not to leave town.

The pedlar assumed the air of a man who would leave town exactly when he wanted to, and without telling me first.

PART THREE:
LEGIO XIV GEMINA MARTIA VICTRIX

MOGUNTIACUM, UPPER GERMANY
October, AD 71

'. . . above all the Fourteenth, whose men had covered themselves in glory by quelling the rebellion in Britain.'

Tacitus *Histories*

XVI

Moguntiacum.

A bridge. A tollbooth. A column. A huddle of civilian huts, with a few handsome homes owned by the local wool and wine merchants. All dominated by one of the Empire's biggest forts.

The settlement stood just below the confluence of the Rhenus and the Moenus waterways. The bridge, which joined the Roman side of the Rhenus to huts and wharfs on the opposite bank, had triangular piers thrust out to break the current, and a wooden rail. The tollbooth was a temporary affair, about to be superseded by a massive new customs-post at Colonia Agrippinensium. (Vespasian was a tax-collector's son; as Emperor it coloured his approach.) The column, erected in the time of Nero, was a grand effort celebrating Jupiter. The huge fort declared that Rome meant business here, though whether we were trying to bluff the tribes or convince ourselves was open to debate.

My first disappointment was immediately thrust on me. I had been telling Xanthus he could busy himself setting up shop with his razors among the *canabae*. Most military establishments grow a thicket of booths, a shanty-town fringe that hogs the outer walls, offering the troops off-duty entertainment of the usual sordid kinds. It springs up when the baths are constructed outside the fortress as a fire precaution, after which breadshops, brothels, barbers and bijouteries rapidly collect – with or without licences. Then the inevitable camp-followers and the soldiers' unofficial families arrive, and soon the extramural clutter swells into a civilian town.

At Moguntiacum there were no booths.

It was a shock. We could see where they had all been cleared. The operation must have been swift and thorough. A mound of bashed-in shutters and splintered awning poles

411

still stood nearby. Now bare ground surrounded the fort, forming a wide defensible berm from which the turf walls rose a clean eighteen feet to the watch-towers and patrol-track. Among the visible defenses I counted one more Punic ditch than usual, and in the midfield a fatigue party was planting what the legions call a lily garden; deep pits dug in a quincunx pattern, set with sharpened stakes, then covered with brushwood to disguise their whereabouts – a savage deterrent during an attack.

The civilians had been deposited way back beyond the outer ditch, and even a year after the Civilis Revolt no re-encroachment was allowed. The impression was stark. It was meant to be.

At the fort itself, instead of the usual organised but easy-going atmosphere of an army in peacetime, we soon grasped that this army sketched in its civic role with a light hand. Its gestures to the local community were mostly obscene.

The barber and I counted as locals until we proved otherwise. When we presented our persons at the Praetorian entrance, even Xanthus stopped twittering. We had to leave our horses. There was no making ourselves agreeable to bored sentries inside the guardroom; we were detained in the square chamber between the double sets of gates, and it was plain that if our story and our documents failed to match, we would be pinned up against a wall by a nine-inch javelin-tip and vigorously body-searched.

The atmosphere upset me. The jolt reminded me of Britain after the Boudiccan affair. That was something I had intended to forget.

We were passed in, however. My docket from the Emperor aroused suspicion but worked the trick. We were eyed up, listed, given order to go directly to the Principia, then allowed through the inner gates.

I myself was ready for the size and scope of the immense interior, but even being born and bred in the labyrinthine corridors of Rome's imperial court had failed to prepare Xanthus for this. Moguntiacum was a permanent fort, and a double one at that. With two legions stationed there, almost everything was in duplicate. It was a military city.

412

Twelve thousand men were packed inside, with enough stores, smithies and granaries to withstand months under siege – not that that had worked for the poor devils attacked by the rebels at Vetera. Within the base, the two commanding legates would occupy minor palaces designed to reflect their grandeur and diplomatic standing; the housing stock for the twelve young military tribunes who supported them would make the best villas in most Italian towns look mean; and even the commissariat buildings, where Xanthus and I were heading, were dramatic in their blunt, military way.

We came out from the cold shadow of the rampart walkway. With the guard-towers of the gatehouse looming overhead, we had first to cross the perimeter road. It was eighty feet wide. The perimeter track, which was designed to give protection from missiles as well as provide ready access to all parts of the fort, was kept well clear of obstruction. I made a mental note that the Fourteenth Gemina must take half the credit for the immaculate housekeeping, though they probably made their lesser colleagues empty the rubbish skips and sweep the roads. Stacks of spare javelins were stored handy for the ramparts, along with piles of heavy shot and field ballista bolts, but there were none of the roaming beasts or the litter of wagons that you often see. If the sacred chickens were allowed free range, it was not on this side of the fort.

I towed the barber past the endless barrack blocks: nearly fifty pairs (though I can't say I counted), each housing a hundred and sixty men in groups of ten, with a double set of centurions' quarters at one end of every block. Adequate space for the legionaries, plus more cramped quarters for their native auxiliaries – not that that applied to the Fourteenth at present, since their eight famous cohorts of Batavians had defected to the rebels . . . Vespasian would not be replacing them until I made my report.

Xanthus was already awed by the atmosphere; I merely felt a throb at re-encountering the familiar. To me the fort had a daytime, half-empty feel. Many of the troops would be in training or sweating on fatigues, others on their monthly ten-mile route march in full kit. Most of the rest would be on local patrol, and it would be no mere exercise.

'Impressed, Xanthus? Wait until the camp's full this evening! Then you will have the unique experience of being among twelve thousand men who all know exactly what they are doing!' He said nothing. 'Are you thinking of the potential in twelve thousand stubbly chins?'

'Twelve thousand flavours of halitosis!' he responded valiantly. 'Twelve thousand variations on "the girl I stuffed last Thursday". And being warned not to nick twelve thousand different wens!'

We reached the main thoroughfare. 'Xanthus, in case you get lost, try to remember the most important street is this one. It's called the Via Principalis. It's a hundred feet wide; even you can't miss the thing. Take your bearing now. The Principalis bisects the camp crossways between the Sinister and Dexter Gates, and the Via Praetoria meets it at right angles at the HQ. The headquarters always face the enemy, so as long as you can see which way the sling-stones are flying in, you can orientate yourself in any fortress in the world . . .'

'Where's the enemy?' He was dazed.

'Across the river.'

'Where's the river?'

'*That* way!' I was losing my temper and wasting my breath. 'The way we came in,' I reminded him, but he was already too confused.

'So where are we going?'

'To introduce ourselves to the nice fellows of the Fourteenth Gemina.'

It was not a success. Still, I had come prepared for that.

For one thing, no job I ever undertook concluded itself that easily, and for another the XIV Gemina had *never* been nice.

XVII

The fortress headquarters were designed to overawe any wild tribesman who dared put his nose round the Praetorian Gate. They formed the main vista as we stared ahead, and tramping closer certainly awed us.

There was one administration block in the fort. The two legions currently in post took up their quarters on either side, but they shared this edifice, which represented the fort's permanence. It was massively constructed. The façade comprised heavily colonnaded stonework on either side of a magisterial triple gate that looked straight at us down the Via Praetoria. Dwarfed, we crept in through the left-hand arch to find ourselves facing a well-tramped parade-ground that occupied more land than the forum in most provincial towns. Luckily no one was parading at the time. My timid companion would have expired from shock.

'We can't go in here!'

'If anyone issues a challenge, keep your pearly teeth clamped together and let me talk. As a general rule, while we're inside the fort don't argue with anybody wearing a sword. And, Xanthus, do try not to look so much like a lost understudy from one of Nero's theatricals . . .'

Three sides of the square were taken up by storerooms and the quartermaster's offices. Opposite, stood the basilican hall, which provided a focus for the formalities of both legions. It was where we were going, so I set off straight across the parade-ground. By halfway, even I felt slightly exposed. It seemed to take us half an hour to reach the other side and I could sense enraged centurions breathing fire from all the overlooking offices. I realised how the lobster feels when the water in the cooking pot slowly starts heating up.

The Principia was enormous. It stretched the full width of the complex. Decoration was minimal; it achieved its

415

effect through size. The central nave was forty feet wide, separated by gigantic columns from sombre aisles each half its width again. The columns supported an almighty roof whose weight it was best not to contemplate while standing underneath. On a rainy day a whole legion could be crushed in there like anchovy bones in fish pickle. The rest of the time this formidable hall stood empty and silent, guarding secrets and forming a bold tribute to the skill of the army's engineers.

Through the gloom we could see the commander's tribunal at one end. The main feature, directly opposite the entrance, was the legionary shrine.

I walked across. My boots rang on the paving. There was a lurking scent of ceremonial oil, recent not rancid. Behind a border of stone screens lay a fireproof vaulted chamber; it guarded that other religious sanctum, the underground strongbox room. Up here, in the unlocked part, they kept the portable altar for taking auguries. Around it the standards were spikily arranged.

The Fourteenth had grabbed the most prominent position for their display, their companion legion obligingly tucking itself up on one side. In the place of honour gleamed the Fourteenth's eagle and a portrait of the Emperor wreathed in purple cloth. By the dim light from remote clerestory windows high in the main hall, I could see on the centuries' standards more medals for acts of valour than I had ever seen assembled together. Predominantly honours from the Emperors Claudius and Nero, they must have been awarded for outstanding service in Britain. Naturally they also had bronze statues of their titular patrons, Mars and Victory. The other legion's standards were by contrast unadorned.

We had not come to make obeisance. I winked at the eagle who was guarding the naked set of standards. Then I wheeled Xanthus into the nearby offices. The secretariat occupied the most significant place, alongside the shrine. Since no one else wants to bother with accommodation problems, the clerks always control the fortress plan. They naturally allocate the most desirable roost to themselves.

A bald will clerk nodded us towards the lavish suite which

the Fourteenth had commandeered. Things were peaceful. That could mean either the legion were a dozy, inefficient outfit, or that the day's business had already been stamped up and cleared away. Perhaps their legate was taking a siesta at his own house, and the camp prefect had a cold. Perhaps the tribunes had all snatched a day's hunting leave. I reserved judgement. So long as they were keeping full granaries, a careful weapons count and an up-to-date log of what went into the savings bank, Vespasian was not a man who would quibble at the Fourteenth maintaining an unrushed commissariat. His interest was in results.

In the biggest room, we found two of the legion's senior men.

One, who was a non-combatant, wore a red tunic but no body armour. On a nail hung his helmet, adorned with the two horns that gave him his title of Cornicularius: head of the commissariat. In my opinion, the little horns are the legions' joke to make their chief clerks look ridiculous. His companion was a different species. A centurion in full kit, including a complete set of nine *phalerae*, the chest medallions awarded for dedicated service. He was over sixty, and his air of ingrained contempt told me this was the Primipilus, the First Spear, leading centurion. This sought-after rank is held for three years, after which lies a gratuity equivalent to middle-class status, and a passport into plum civilian jobs. Some, and I guessed this was one of them, opt to repeat their first spear posting, thereby making themselves public menaces in the way they know best. Dying in harness in some godforsaken province is a first spear's idea of a good life.

This primipilus had a short, thick neck and looked as if his party trick was killing flies with a head-butt. He had broad shoulders and his torso hardly narrowed on the way to his belt, but none of what went on below the chest was paunch. His feet were small. He hardly moved while he was talking to us, but I guessed he would be nippy when he wanted to exert himself. I didn't like him. That was irrelevant. He didn't care for me, either; that was what would count.

417

The cornicularius was much less impressive physically. He had a turned-up nose and a small, bitter mouth. What he lacked in presence he made up in personal venom and his ability to express himself.

When we entered, these two were tearing shreds off a soldier who had committed some misdemeanour, like asking an innocent question. They were enjoying themselves, and were ready to humiliate their victim all afternoon unless someone who disgusted them even more turned up. Someone did: Xanthus and I.

They told the soldier to sheath himself in his own scabbard, or words to that effect. He slunk out past us gratefully.

The primipilus and cornicularius looked at us, glanced at each other, then stared back at us derisively while they waited for the fun to start.

'I don't believe this!' the primipilus marvelled.

'Who let this rabble in? Someone must have bopped the gate security on their heads!'

'Those slack bastards in the First!'

'Good afternoon,' I ventured from the doorway.

'Shove off, curly!' snarled the primipilus. 'And take your garland girl.'

In my business insults are the normal convention, so I rode out the squall. I could feel Xanthus throbbing indignantly, but if he expected me to defend him in this company he could think again. I moved further in, and dumped the basket containing the Emperor's gift. 'Name's Didius Falco.' It seemed wise to be formal. I flipped my imperial passport at the cornicularius, who lifted it between one finger and thumb as if it had been found in a sewer. He let a sneer play around his tight little mouth, then shoved my tag across his table for the primipilus to laugh at too.

'And what do you do, Falco?' asked the mouth. It squeezed out his words like stuffing from a badly sewn mattress case.

'I deliver awkward packages.'

'Hah!' commented the primipilus.

'So what's in the picnic basket?' jeered his more talkative pal.

'Five bread rolls, a sheep's-gut sausage – and a new standard to mark the Emperor's personal favour to the Fourteenth. Want to take a look?'

The primipilus was the man of action around here, so while the cornicularius attended to a snag in his manicure with the stump-end of a stylus, he forced himself to approach as I unbuckled the basket straps. The Iron Hand weighed as much as a chunk of aqueduct supply pipe, but he lifted it by its thumb as lightly as an amulet.

'Oh very nice!' No one could fault the words. Only the tone was treasonous.

I kept my own voice level. 'I am to deliver Vespasian's gift to your legate in person. I also have a sealed despatch for him, which I believe contains the programme for a suitable investiture ceremony. Any chance of a word with Florius Gracilis at once?'

'No,' said the cornicularius.

'I can wait.'

'You can measure yourself for a funeral urn and pour yourself into it.'

I remarked to Xanthus pleasantly, 'This is the Fourteenth legion's famous helpfulness and charm.'

'Who's the flower with the disgusting reek?' demanded the primipilus suddenly.

I gave both sections of the military a narrow look. 'Special envoy from Titus Caesar.' I drew one finger across my neck in the time-honoured gesture. 'I haven't worked out yet whether he's a well-disguised assassin looking for someone to dispose of, or just an auditor with a fancy dress sense. Now we've got here we should soon know. Either there'll be a body count, or you'll find him peering at your daily accounts . . .'

Xanthus was so startled that for once he kept his trap shut.

The two wits consulted each other wearily. 'As we thought!' sighed the cornicularius. 'Things must be rough in Rome. Now they're sending us rejects from musical parties and bogus scum like this – '

'Steady on!' I grinned, attempting to go along with them.

419

'Whatever I am, it's genuine! Let's get back to the point. If Gracilis is too busy now, make me an appointment when his schedule has more space.'

Sometimes ingratiation works. Not here. '*Genuine* scum!' commented the primipilus to his crony. 'Disappear up your own arse, curly!'

'Leave my orifices out of the orders of the day! Listen, centurion. I've just lugged an Iron Hand halfway across Europe and I'm intending to deliver it. I know the Fourteenth are a blasphemous, uncultured mob, but if your legate wants his consulship he's not going to let a drill-swank and an ink-swab reject an award from the Emperor –'

'Don't get clever,' the cornicularius warned. 'You can leave the trophy, and you can leave the sealed despatch. Maybe,' he speculated with his most cheerful expression yet, 'the despatch says "*Execute the messenger*" . . .'

I ignored that. 'I'll happily ground the ironwork, but I'm going to hand the confidential orders to Gracilis himself. Do I get quarters at the fort? Your accommodation must be flush now you're light of the loyal Batavians!'

'If that's a jibe at the Fourteenth's expense,' the primipilus snorted, 'make the most of it; you won't manage another!'

I said I wouldn't dream of insulting the victors of Bedriacum, and that I'd find my own roost.

As I shoved him down the corridor outside, Xanthus whined, 'What's Bedriacum?'

'A battle where the Fourteenth escaped being called losers by the simple trick of claiming they had never arrived for the fight.'

'I thought it would be something like that. You've upset them, Falco!'

'Suits me.'

'And they know you are working for the Emperor –'

'No, Xanthus; they think *you* are!'

'What's the point of that?'

'They appreciate they have a tricky record. They know the Emperor will send someone to look them over, but they reckon I'm the dregs. So long as I behave stupidly, they'll never believe I'm the spy.'

Fortunately, Xanthus didn't ask why I was so anxious to identify someone else as the Emperor's agent.

Or what I thought the Fourteenth Gemina might try and do to whoever they thought it was.

As we reached the exit, two tribunes came from another office, arguing in a gentlemanly way.

'Macrinus, I don't want to be a nuisance, but – '

'He's incommunicado; planning one of his forays against imagined troublemakers. Remind me tomorrow and I'll get you in to see him when he has some breathing-space.'

At first I listened because I guessed they were referring to the legate Gracilis. The young man speaking was the assured and stocky type that had never impressed me, with an athletic build, square head and a burnished tint to his tight curls. The one who seemed to be protesting struck me as familiar.

He must have been twenty, but looked younger. An ordinary, boyish face. A tall, slim frame. A quiet manner but a ready smile from a wide mouth.

'Camillus Justinus!' At my cry of recognition for his companion, the first tribune reacted deftly. Coming from a senatorial family, he had had a good education: he knew Latin, Greek, mathematics and geography, how much to tip a prostitute, where the best oysters come from – and the old forum art of escaping from someone he wanted to avoid. 'Sorry, Justinus. Were you in conference?'

Helena's brother growled after the gleamingly armoured and fast-retreating back. 'Never mind. He wasn't going to oblige me. It's Falco, isn't it?'

'Yes. Marcus Didius. I heard you were posted – not to the Fourteenth I hope?'

'Oh, I don't meet their high standards! No, I was persuaded to "volunteer" for an extra tour with the First Adiutrix – they're a new outfit.'

'Glad to hear it. The Fourteenth are an impolite mob. I

just brought them a trophy and they refused me a billet,' I hinted without shame.

Justinus laughed. 'Then you'd better stay at my house! Come on. After trying to wrestle sense out of this crew I need to go home and lie down in the dark.' We started to walk. 'What are you doing here, Marcus Didius?'

'Oh, nothing very exciting. Business for Vespasian. Mostly routine. One or two extra tasks to toy with in my free time – coercing rebels, that sort of stuff,' I joked. 'There's a missing legate to find, for instance.'

Justinus stopped in his tracks. He seemed amazed.

I pulled up too. 'What's up, tribune?'

'Does the Emperor have access to new kinds of Etruscan augury?'

'Something not right?'

'You flabbergast me, Falco! That was what I was trying to get straight with my oppo just now. I don't see,' he grumbled, 'how Vespasian could have known there was something fishy out in Germany in time for you to turn up here before my commander has even made up his mind that he needs to signal Rome!'

As he ran out of breath, I simply said, 'Explain?'

Camillus Justinus glanced over his shoulder then lowered his voice, even though we were crossing the empty parade-ground. 'Florius Gracilis has not been seen for several days. The Fourteenth won't admit it even to my own chief, but we in the First reckon that *their* legate has disappeared!'

XVIII

I set a warning hand on the tribune's arm. Then I told Xanthus to walk ahead and wait for us at the main gate opposite. He sulked, but had no choice. We watched him set off, scuffing his feet in the dust at first as a gesture, but soon preferring to save the turquoise leather of his nattily bethonged shoes.

'Who exactly is that?' queried Justinus in a wary tone.

'Not sure.' I gave him a stiff look, in case he thought it was a companion of my choice. 'If you want a boring couple of hours, get him to tell you why Spanish razors are the best, and the secrets of German goosefat pomade. He's a barber by trade – that's genuine. He forced himself on me as a tourist. I suspect there's a more sinister reason behind his trip.'

'He may simply have a yearning for travel.' I remembered that Helena's youngest brother had a touching faith in humanity.

'Or he may not! Anyway, I'm passing him off as Vespasian's nark.' Justinus, who must have known about my own undercover duties, or my past history anyway, smiled faintly.

As we waited for Xanthus to trot out of earshot, a slight breeze lifted our cloaks. It carried the characteristic aromas of cavalry stables, oiled leather and mass-produced stewed pork. Dust bowled across the parade-ground, stinging our bare shins. The hum of the fort reached us, like the low undernotes of a water-organ as it grinds into life: metallic hammering; rumbling carts; the clack of wooden staves as troops practised sparring against an upright stump; and the sharp cry of a centurion giving orders, raven-harsh.

'We won't find anywhere more private than here. Now Justinus, what's all this about? Tell me about Gracilis.'

'Not much to tell. He hasn't been seen.'

'Is he ill, or taking leave?'

'If so, it's highly impolite of him not to inform his senior colleague in the same fort.'

'Bad manners would be nothing new!'

'Agreed. What alerted the First to something peculiar was that even his wife, who is with him here, seems unsure where he is. She asked *my* legate's wife if there was a secret exercise going on.'

'Is there?'

'Joke, Falco! We have quite enough operational tasks without playing board-games or throwing up practice camps.'

I paused for a moment, considering him. He had spoken with a flash of authority. Last time we met he had been holding down a junior tribune's place, but now he was wearing the broad purple stripes of a senior – his legate's right-hand man. Those posts were mainly earmarked for senators designate; promotion to them while in service was highly unusual. Justinus qualified socially – he was a senator's son – but his elder brother was using up all the embalming oil. The family had long ago decided this one was destined merely for middle-rank bureaucracy. Still, he would not be the first young man to discover that the army lacks preconceptions, or to find that once away from home he could surprise himself.

'So how are the Fourteenth reacting? What do the men say?'

'Well, Gracilis is a new appointment.'

'So I heard. Is he unpopular?'

'The Fourteenth have been having a few problems . . .' Justinus was a tactful lad. The Fourteenth *were* a problem, but he glossed over that. 'Gracilis has a rather abrasive attitude. It goes down badly when a legion are in a touchy state.'

'Gracilis was the Senate's choice,' I confided, based on what Vespasian had told me. 'You know, "*Step up, most excellent Florius. Your grandpa was a friend of ours; it's your turn next . . .*" What's he like?'

'All virile sports, and shouts a lot.' We both winced.

'So let's be clear what you are suggesting, tribune. I

already know the Emperor has doubts about this character, and now you say he's vanished. Has the First Adiutrix convinced itself that he has been bumped off – and by his own men?'

'Olympus!' Justinus flushed. 'That's an alarming suggestion!'

'Sounds like one you have grounds for.'

'The First is in a tricky position, Falco. We have no remit to interfere. You know how it is – the governor is away reviewing deployments at Vindonissa, so if Gracilis is playing truant, "honour among commanders" comes into play. Besides, my legate is reluctant to march in directly and demand to see his opposite, in case we're wrong.'

'He would certainly look foolish if Gracilis strolled out to greet him, wiping his breakfast porridge off his chin!' I agreed. Then, influenced by too long in a barber's company, I suggested, 'Gracilis may have had a haircut he's ashamed of and is hiding until it grows out!'

'Or he's developed an *extremely* embarrassing rash . . .' He sounded like Helena and their father, his serious air covered a highly attractive humorous streak. 'It's no joke though.'

'No.' I quashed the pang of misery his familiar laugh had roused. 'Gracilis had better be exposed, whatever crab he's caught.' I hoped it was nothing worse. Mutiny in the legions just when things were looking settled would be disastrous for Vespasian. And there were grim political implications if yet another Roman legate should disappear in Germany. 'I can see good reasons for keeping this news stitched up. Vespasian will want to plan how it is to be presented publicly . . . Camillus Justinus, you don't think the Fourteenth have reported the facts, and are waiting for special orders back from Rome?'

'My legate would have been informed.'

'Oh, that's what he thinks! Bureaucracy thrives on secrecy.'

'No, Falco. Despatch-riders are still bringing "Your eyes only" messages for Gracilis. I know because my own man keeps getting asked to sign for them. Neither Vespasian nor the governor would send confidential flags unless they believed Gracilis was available.'

My sour welcome from the primipilus and cornicularius was beginning to make sense. If they had simply lost their man, things looked bad for them; if he had been throttled in a hastily hushed-up mutiny, that was desperate. 'Their senior trib brushed you off pretty shamelessly; my reception was much the same. Is that what always happens?'

'Yes. All the officers seem to be covering up.' This couldn't happen on the march, where Gracilis would have to be seen in the column, but here in the fort they could run things themselves. It reminded me of Balbillus's story of the legionary commanders coolly running Britain after having driven out their governor. But the era of anarchy was supposed to be over.

'Until the next festival occasion, there's no need to pro-duce anyone in a commander's cloak,' I grinned. 'But if there *is* a conspiracy, I've just upset the tray of drinks! I brought an Iron Hand, plus orders for its investiture with a full colour ceremony. They'll need to parade their legate then.'

'Ha! The governor will make a point of being back for that!' Camillus Justinus had a streak of tenacity I liked. He showed real pleasure that the Fourteenth's attempts to thwart him were about to be wrecked. 'When must they hold the ceremony?'

'The Emperor's birthday.' He looked uncertain. Vespasian was too new in power to be thoroughly enshrined in the calendar. I knew (a scribe who thought informers were ignorant had noted it in my orders). 'Fourteen days before December.' We were still in October. 'Which gives you and me the rest of this month plus the first sixteen days of November to sort out the puzzle discreetly and make names for ourselves.'

We grinned. Then we set off towards the main gate. Justinus had enough character to see the possibilities. It would do him good if he could untangle this conundrum before Rome had to be involved.

I felt obligations looming. I was his sister's lover – almost one of the family. It was my duty to assist him to good fortune. Even though Justinus probably hated the thought of what his sister and I had been up to. And even though I would be landing myself with most of the work.

As we walked, falling into companionable silence, I was thinking hard. This had the smell of serious trouble. I had been chasing enough of that already. I had only been at Moguntiacum a bare hour and now there was a second senior officer missing – just one more complication to add to the *official* missing legate, the mutinous troops, the maniacal rebel chieftain and the loopy prophetess.

XIX

We picked up Xanthus and braced ourselves for the hike to the First's sector of the fort. To cover the journey with neutral conversation, I asked Justinus about his unusual promotion.

'I remembered your last command was at Argentoratum – in fact I went looking for you there. You weren't a senior then?'

'No, and I never expected to be. That was the lure that made me accept an extension to my tour. Obviously, in the long-term it's good to be able to say I held a broad-stripe position . . .'

'I hope your ambitions run to more than that on your tombstone! You must have impressed someone?'

'Well . . .' He still seemed a boy in a man's world. Big words like ambition startled him. 'My father is a friend of Vespasian; perhaps that was it.'

I thought the lad was doing himself down. People must have thought he had something to offer. Germany was not a province where they could carry dead wood. 'What's your new unit like? I don't know the First.'

'It's a legion Nero formed – with men drawn from the Misenum fleet, actually. Both the First and Second Adiutrix were put together using marines. That explains some of the tension here.' Justinus smiled. 'I'm afraid the illustrious Fourteenth Gemina Martia Victrix regard *our* outfit as a useless gang of wharfingers and matelots.'

Regular troops have always regarded marines as web-footed hangers-on – a view I rather shared. Shoving an untried unit out on this volatile frontier seemed like madness, too. 'So you're here to stiffen them up with your experience?' He shrugged in his self-deprecating way. 'Don't be so shy,' I said. 'It will all look good on your manifesto when you stand as a town councillor.'

Ten or twelve years ago, Titus Caesar had led the replacements that filled the gaps in the British legions after the Boudiccan Revolt. And now every town in the misty bogs was erecting his statue and remarking how thoroughly well liked he had been in his days as a young tribune.

It made me wonder uncomfortably if Justinus, like Titus, would one day find himself related to a reigning emperor – by marriage, for instance . . .

I wanted to ask if he had any news of his sister. Luckily we had reached his house, so I could spare myself the embarrassment.

XX

The senior tribune's house lacked its own bathhouse, but for one lad barely into his twenties who only needed space for his parade armour and the stuffed heads of any wild animals he speared in his spare time, it was an extravagant hutch. Tribunes are not famous for taking home bulky documents from the commissariat to work on, and their schedule of domestic entertainment tends to be thin. They are invariably bachelors, and not many invite their loving relatives to stay. Still, providing single officers with mansions that would house three generations is the kind of extravagance the army loves.

Justinus had enlivened the place with a pet dog. It was a scruff, not much more than a pup, which he had rescued from some soldiers who had been having fun torturing it. The dog now lorded it here, rampaging through the long corridors and sleeping on as many couches as possible. Justinus had no control over the creature, but one yap from it could make *him* sit up and beg.

'Your puppy's found a lavish kennel! I can see why so many tribunes rush to get married the minute their service ends. After so much independence, who wants the restrained parental home again?'

Marriage was another concept that made Justinus nervous. I could understand that.

Helena's brother definitely needed a crony to liven up his life. Well, I was here now. (Though Helena herself would probably disapprove of me doing it.)

Justinus decided after all that he ought to advise his legate of the lack of progress against the Fourteenth's wall of silence. While he jogged off to report, someone was sent to the fortress gate for our luggage. One of the tribune's private slaves stowed the barber somewhere appropriate, while I at last regained the luxury of a room to myself. Almost immediately I sauntered out of it, intent on a quiet look round. I noticed I had been given a good bedroom, though not the best. From that I could gauge my position: a friendly guest, but not a family friend.

My mother would have been shocked by the dust on the side-tables; my standards were not so immaculate, and I felt I could settle here. Justinus came from a family of thinkers and talkers, but the Camilli liked to talk and think with fruit bowls at their elbows and cushions at their backs. Their treasure had been sent abroad well equipped to fend off homesickness. His house was comfortable. His attendants were only so slovenly because they were unsupervised. I wrote 'Falco was here' with one finger in the bloom on a vase plinth, as a gentle hint.

It could have been worse. There were too many mice droppings and no one bothered to replenish the lamp oil, but the servants were polite enough, even to me. They wanted to avoid forcing their young lord into any stressful show of discipline. That seemed wise. If he was anything like his sister, he could summon an exotic temper and a vivid way with words.

If he *was* anything like Helena, Justinus also had a soft heart and might commiserate as I roamed about his quarters gloomily wondering wherever in the Empire his temperamental sister had hidden herself. Mind you, if he was as touchy as Aelianus on family matters, my connection with Helena was more likely to get me rolled up in a sack and flung from a heavy catapult halfway across the Rhine. So, even though I was frantic over her whereabouts and safety, I decided to keep that to myself.

I went out to the legionary baths, which were hot, efficient, cleanly run and free.

Justinus and I returned to his house at the same time. In my room someone had unpacked my togs, taking away my dirty clothes. My wardrobe was so frugal that to lose three garments for laundering had emptied my saddlebag, but I managed to find a tunic which would just pass at the dinner

431

table here, given the dim lamps. Afterwards we stuck our noses out into the courtyard garden, but it was too cold, so we settled indoors. I felt conscious of the difference in our ranks, but Justinus seemed glad to play the good host and chat. 'Eventful journey?'

'Nothing too fraught. Gaul and Germany still seem pretty lawless.' I told him about the two bodies we had seen in the Gallic ditch.

He looked alarmed. 'Should I do something about it?'

'Relax, tribune!' I brushed aside his insecurity. 'It happened in another province and the civilian magistrate ought to deal with highway robbery . . . Mind you, the centurion I mentioned – Helvetius – must be one of yours. He told me he was assigned to the First, though I failed to make any connection as I thought you were still in your old post.'

'The name's unfamiliar. I've not been here long enough to know them all. I'll look him out.' Expecting to recognise all sixty centurions in his legion was stretching it. I was amazed this lad had ever been promoted. He worked with all the dedication and thoroughness that are traditionally overlooked in personal character reports.

I thought he might be amused by what I had heard at Argentoratum about his successor's progress. 'Would *you* give out a password like "Xenophobia"?'

'Afraid mine are always more mundane. "Mars the Avenger", or "Pickled fish", or "The camp surgeon's middle name".'

'Very wise.'

We had a flagon. 'The wine's rather basic here . . .' Justinus was either too timid or too lazy to be rude to his wine merchant. It tasted like goat's pee (from a goat with bladder stones), but a glass in the hand helped pass the time. 'So Marcus Didius, why did you come through my old base?'

He must have known I was looking for Helena. 'Looking for you.'

'Oh that was kind!' He managed to sound as if he meant it.

'I thought you might like news of your family. They all seem well. Your father wants to buy a yacht but your mother won't hear of it... Have you heard from your sister recently?'

I posed the question before I could stop myself; too late to make my interest sound merely banal. Justinus whipped back, 'No, she seems unusually quiet these days! Is there something I ought to know?'

He must have heard about her choosing to eat the gritty bread at my table. Explaining our relationship was beyond me. I said briefly, 'She's taken herself off from Rome.'

'When?'

'Just before I came away.'

Justinus, who was reclining on an army-issue reading-couch, stretched slightly to ease the pressure on his arm. 'That seems rather sudden!' He was laughing, though I could see solemnity looming. 'Did someone upset her?'

'Probably me. Helena has high standards and I have low habits ... I hoped she might have invited herself to stay with you.'

'No.' The reason for my keen interest still hovered unhealthily, but remained unsaid. We both felt shy of turning that boulder. 'Should people be worried?' Justinus asked.

'She's sensible.' Justinus thought a lot of his sister and was prepared to accept that. I cared about her too, and I was not. 'Tribune, as far as I know your sister made no arrangements with her banker, and took no bodyguard. She never said goodbye to your father; she completely bamboozled your mother; she surprised mine, who is very fond of her; and she left no forwarding address. That,' I said, 'worries me.'

We were both silent.

'What do you suggest, Falco?'

'Nothing. There's nothing we can do.' That worried me as well.

We changed the subject.

'I still don't know,' Justinus broached, 'how you came to be here seeking a missing legate the minute we had a problem with Gracilis?'

433

'Coincidence. The one I'm chasing is Munius Lupercus.'

'Olympus! That's a forlorn hope!'

I grinned unhappily.

Several of his relatives were close to the Emperor, and I felt satisfied that Justinus had inherited their discretion. I spoke freely about my mission, though I shied off mentioning the XIV Gemina. This courtesy to them was probably pointless, but I do have some standards. 'One or two challenges!' he commented.

'Yes. I've already discovered that the prophetess Veleda lives at the top of a tower, and can only be approached through her male friends. This must be to endow her with a sinister aura. Going across the Rhenus river unnerves me enough, without any theatricals!' Justinus laughed. He could. He didn't have to go. 'You seem the type who keeps up to date, Justinus. Can you tell me anything about the rebel chief?'

'Civilis has disappeared – though there are plenty of stories about his horrible habits!'

'Thrill me!' I growled.

'Oh, the most lurid anecdote has him handing over Roman prisoners to his small son as targets for arrow practice.'

'True?'

'It could be.'

Wonderful. Just the sort I enjoy taking out to a wine bar so I can have a quiet word in his ear. 'Before I try to buy a drink for this civilised parent, is there anything less colourful that I ought to know?'

I knew the general background. Before the revolt the Batavians had always had a special relationship with Rome: their lands were exempt from colonisation – and therefore from taxes – in return for them supplying us with auxiliary troops. It was not a bad bargain. They got excellent pay and conditions – a vast improvement on what they could achieve by the rough-and-ready Celtic tradition of raiding their neighbours when the grain pits ran low. We acquired their nautical skills (pilotage, rowing and swimming). They were

434

famous for being able to cross rivers in full kit, paddling alongside their horses.

Justinus plunged straight in, cogently and without floundering: 'You know Julius Civilis is a member of the Batavian royal family. He spent twenty years in Roman military camps, leading auxiliaries for us. When the recent upsets started, his brother Paulus was executed as a troublemaker by the then governor of Lower Germany, Fonteius Capito. Capito sent Civilis himself in chains to Nero.'

'*Were* they troublemakers at that stage?'

'The evidence suggests it was a trumped-up charge,' Justinus declared in his measured way. 'Fonteius Capito was a highly dubious governor. You know he was court-martialled and killed by his own officers? He had a reputation for governing greedily, but I can't tell you whether that was justified. Galba omitted to investigate his execution, so perhaps it was.' Or perhaps Galba was a geriatric incompetent. 'Anyway, Galba acquitted Civilis of treachery, but only lasted eight months as emperor, so then Civilis became vulnerable again.'

'How come?' I asked.

'When Vitellius seized power his armies called for various officers to be put to death, ostensibly for loyalty to Galba.' I remembered that nasty episode now. Quite blatantly, it had been about settling old grudges. Unpopular centurions were the main target, but I knew the troops had also clamoured for the Batavian leader's head. Vitellius ignored them and confirmed Galba's 'pardon', but it must all have left Civilis with a great bitterness against his so-called Roman allies. 'Also in that period,' Justinus went on, 'the Batavians were being sorely treated.'

'Example?'

'Well, for instance, during conscription for Vitellius, imperial agents were calling up the infirm and the old in order to extract bribes for their release from the levy. And young lads and lasses were dragged behind the tents for unpleasant purposes.'

Batavian children tend to be tall and good-looking. All Germanic tribes have a strong sense of family, so this treatment must have festered sordidly. That was why the next imperial claimant, Vespasian, had felt he could call on Civilis to help him oppose Vitellius. But far away in Judaea, Vespasian had misread the situation. Civilis co-operated at first, in alliance with a tribe called the Cannenefates. They made a joint attack on the Rhenus fleet, thereby capturing all the arms and ships they needed and cutting Roman supply lines. Vespasian was then proclaimed Emperor.

'That forced Civilis to come out in his true colours,' Justinus explained. 'He summoned all the chiefs of the Gallic and German tribes to a meeting in a sacred grove in the forest, let the wine flow freely, then fired them with powerful speeches about shaking off the Roman yoke and establishing a free Gallic empire.'

'Stirring stuff!'

'Oh, highly dramatic! Civilis himself even dyed his hair and beard bright red, then swore never to cut them until he had driven out every Roman.'

This colourful detail gave my own mission a picturesque quality I hated. 'Just the sort of ethnic madman I love trying to outwit! Did he ever shave?'

'After Vetera.'

We were silent for a moment, thinking of the siege.

'A fort like that should have held out.'

Justinus shook his head. 'I haven't been there, Falco, but by all accounts Vetera was neglected and understaffed.'

We buried ourselves in the tribune's gruesome wine, while I reflected sourly on what I had heard about Vetera.

It had been a double fort, though nowhere up to strength after Vitellius had drawn off large vexillations for his march on Rome. The remnant of the garrison put up the best show they could. Plenty of initiative. But Civilis was Roman-trained in siege warfare. He made his prisoners build batter-ing-rams and catapults. Not that the defending legions lacked invention: they had devised an articulated grab that could scoop up attackers and toss them into the fort. But by the time they surrendered, they really had eaten all the mules and rats and were down to chewing roots and grass torn from the rampart walls. Besides, with the civil war raging in Italy, they must have felt completely cut off. Vetera was one of the most northerly forts in Europe, and Rome had other preoccupations.

A relief force *was* sent, under Dillius Vocula, but he bungled it. Civilis stopped him fairly decisively, then paraded the Roman standards he had captured around the fort at Vetera, just to add to the occupants' despair. Later Vocula did break through and raise the siege, but he found the garrison sullen. His own men mutinied, and he himself was murdered at Vetera by the troops.

The fort surrendered. The soldiers, having despatched their commander, swore allegiance to the Gallic Empire. They were disarmed by the rebels, ordered to march out of camp – and were then ambushed and cut down.

'Justinus, did Civilis have a reputation that should have led our men to expect to be betrayed?'

'I think not,' replied Justinus slowly, not wanting to prejudge the Batavian. 'I believe they assumed that an ex-Roman auxiliary commander would honour their parole. It's said that Civilis did protest to his allies about it.'

We were silent again for a moment.

'What kind of man is he?' I asked.

'Highly intelligent. Massive charisma. Intensely dangerous! At one time most of Gaul plus several tribes from Germania Libera were supporting him, and he achieved a completely free run of Lower Germany. He regards himself as a second Hannibal – or Hasdrubal, in fact, since he too has only one eye.'

I groaned. 'So I'm searching for a tall, one-eyed prince with flowing bright red hair, who hates Rome bitterly. At least he ought to stand out in the market-place . . . Did he also,' I wondered, 'make an objection when Munius Lupercus was captured in the ambush and bundled off as Veleda's gift?'

'I doubt that. Civilis encouraged her prophetic authority. They were regarded as partners. When Civilis seized the flagship of Petilius Cerialis, he sent that to her too.'

'I'm too far gone to ask you how that disaster came about!' I had heard that our general Cerialis had his faults.

He was impetuous and kept poor discipline, which led to losses he could have avoided. 'So Veleda received her personal state barge – in addition to a high-ranking Roman trussed up and delivered to her tower to use as a sex slave, or whatever! What do *you* think she did with Lupercus?'

Camillus Justinus shuddered, and would not try to guess.

My head was spinning. This seemed a good point to yawn a lot like a tired traveller and depart for bed.

The notes of the twisted trumpet sounding out the night watch upset me, and I dreamed I was a young recruit again.

XXI

Next day I pondered fitfully on the brain-teasers Vespasian had commissioned me to pursue. It was hard to raise any enthusiasm for this crazy selection, so I looked instead into the one problem where no one had asked me to interfere: I went to see the missing legate's wife. As I crossed to the XIV's side of the fort, I must say I felt fairly confident that the eminent Florius Gracilis would turn out not to be missing at all.

The legate's house was everything you would expect. Given that Julius Caesar, even when campaigning in hostile territory with all his resources stretched to the limit, carted panels of floor mosaic to lay in his tent in order to demonstrate Roman splendour to the tribes, there was no chance that a full-scale diplomatic residence inside a permanent fort would lack any convenience. It was as large as possible, and decorated in spectacular materials. Why not? Each succeeding occupant, his noble wife full of design ideas, would call for improvements. Every three years the house would be stripped out and refurbished to a different taste. And every extravagance they ordered came at State expense.

The residence was based around a series of courtyard gardens with long pools and exquisite fountains that filled the air with a fine, luxurious mist. In summer there must have been strident flowers; in October the impeccable topiary assumed a lonelier grandeur. But there were peacocks. There were turtles. In the morning, when I turned up with my hopeful grin, leaf-sweepers and twig-pruners were crawling over the scenery like aphids. Real aphids stood no chance. Neither did I, probably.

Indoors was a parade of frescoed reception rooms. The brilliant-white stuccoed ceilings were astounding. The floors comprised geometric mosaics with fascinating three-dimensional effects. The lamps were gilded (and screwed to the walls). The urns were immense (too heavy to run off with). Discreet wardens patrolled the colonnades, or were stationed unobtrusively among the Hellenic statuary. The salon furniture would have made my auctioneer father gnaw his nails and ask for a quiet word behind a pillar with the household steward.

The steward knew his stuff. Florius Gracilis had long ago made a smooth transition from the casual bachelor disorder in which Camillus Justinus lived to a world of constant public entertainment on the grandest scale. His residence was organised by troops of purposeful flunkeys, many of whom would have been with him for nearly two decades of hectic senatorial social life. Since high officials travel out to their provinces all expenses paid, the legate had not only brought his tortoiseshell bedheads and gold Cupid lampstands, but while he was packing he also made space for the wife. But I knew even before I met her that adding a young bride to this slick regime had almost certainly been superfluous.

My research in Rome had told me Gracilis was the normal age for a legionary commander. He was in his late thirties − still free of arthritis, but mature enough to strut impressively in the circular purple cloak. His wife was twenty years younger. In patrician circles they tend to marry schoolgirls. When alliances are being made for blunt political reasons there is a premium on the untouched and biddable. Not for men of this status the haphazard attractions that mess up life for the rest of us. Florius Gracilis had first married in his twenties, when he was aiming for the Senate. He had shed the woman as soon as it seemed convenient, then equipped himself adroitly with a new wife − this time from an even older, even richer family − about eighteen months ago. That must have been when he started looking for his legionary command and wanted to appear a man of public probity.

Maenia Priscilla interviewed me in a gold and black salon, the kind of highly lacquered room that always makes me notice where a flea bit me the previous day. Half a dozen maids escorted her, broad-browed, slightly hirsute wenches who looked as though they had been bought at the slave market as a matched set. They seemed remote from their mistress, sitting quietly in two groups and getting on with rather dull embroidery.

Priscilla ignored them. She was small. A sweeter nature might have given her a dainty air. Time and money had been spent on her, though without disguising her inbuilt surliness. She favoured a languid, catlike expression, which grew harder when she forgot to cultivate it. She was probably the daughter of some offhand praetor who only perked up when his female offspring were old enough for flashy dynastic marriages. Now she was married to Gracilis. Not much fun either, probably.

She took several minutes settling herself in a shimmer of violet flounces. She wore pearl ear-drops, amethyst-studded bracelets and at least three plaited gold necklaces, though more may have lurked in the lustrous folds that swathed her. This was her Thursday-morning set, completed by the usual battery of finger-rings. Somewhere among the tinsel was a half-inch wedding band; it failed to make its presence felt.

'Didius Falco, madam.'

'Oh really?' Sustaining a conversation was just too wearisome. My mother would have put this limp little creature on a red meat diet and had her digging turnips for a week.

'I am an imperial representative.' Interviewing an imperial envoy ought to have brightened her morning. Indeed, life in the most dangerous part of the Empire would have fascinated some girls, but I could tell Maenia Priscilla's interests rarely stretched to current affairs. A bird who had managed to avoid learning. She despised the arts. I could not envisage her busy with charitable works. Altogether, as the partner of one of the Empire's most prominently placed diplomats, she failed to impress.

'How nice for you!' No wonder the Empire had been creaking at its seams lately. I refused to react, but it was ill-judged and inexcusable. The girl possessed a mixture of schoolgirl arrogance and ignorance that was likely to cause trouble. If Gracilis didn't watch her, I gave him six months before there was a scandal with a centurion or an incident in a barrack block that had people being sent home hurriedly.

'Excuse me for invading your privacy. I need to see your husband, but he was not at the Principia – '

'He's not here either!' This time she spoke out quickly, with the triumphant edge some people use instead of wit. Her brown eyes gave me the once-over, which was fair enough since I had done the same to her. Yet she was seeing nothing, trying only to insult me.

I twitched up an eyebrow. 'You must be very concerned. Does Gracilis make a habit of vanishing?'

'The legate's habits are his own affair.'

'Not quite, madam.'

Annoyance yanked her mouth into an uglier twist. Men in shapeless sorrel-coloured tunics with woolly linings in their battered boots did not usually answer her back. (I would have liked to be kitted out more excitingly, but my banker had counselled against overstretching my budget that year. Bankers are so predictable. My budget, too.)

'Your ladyship, there seems to be a problem here! A man of your husband's standing ought not to become invisible. It worries the lower orders. In fact, the Emperor might consider it politically inept . . . If Gracilis is dodging his creditors – ' I had been joking, but she let out a bitter laugh. A wild guess had struck lucky. 'Oh, is that it?'

'Possibly.'

'Can you give me a list of his debts?'

She shrugged. Gracilis had probably brought her to Germany to avoid the risk that back in Rome she might suborn his numerous stewards into letting her spend cash. Men like that keep their wives securely cut off from the household abacus. I prodded, but she seemed genuinely uninformed. I was not surprised.

'So you cannot tell me where to start looking? You have no idea where your husband may be?'

'Oh I know that!' she exclaimed archly. I bit back my irritation.

'Madam, this is important. I have a message from Vespasian for Florius Gracilis. When the Emperor sends despatches, he expects me to deliver them. Will you say where your husband is?'

'With his mistress, presumably.' She was so vapid, she did not even watch me to see the effect it had.

'Look,' I said, still trying to keep my temper, 'your domestic life is private, but however modern your views on marriage, I assume you and Gracilis follow *some* rules. The conventions are clear enough.' I stated them anyway: 'He fritters away your dowry; you eat into his inheritance. He can beat you; you can slander him. He supplies you with moral guidance and an extravagant dress allowance; you, madam, at all times protect his reputation in public life. Now try to grasp this: if I don't find him quickly, there is going to be a scandal. Whatever else, he will want you to avoid that!'

She jumped up in a jangle of atonal jewellery. 'How dare you!'

'How dares a public man have the front to disappear right under the nose of the provincial governor?'

'I couldn't care less!' cried Maenia Priscilla with her first real sign of liveliness. 'Get out of here, and don't come back again!'

She swept from the room. A gust of unlikeable balsamic perfume swirled round after her. She bounced off so angrily that an ivory hairpin shot itself from the torsion of a castellated braid in her elaborate hair, and landed at my feet.

I picked it up, then silently handed the missile to one of the waiting-women. The maids looked resigned, then gathered their trappings and followed her out.

I was not alarmed. Somewhere in the residence there would be a wizened accountant who would take a more realistic attitude to my enquiry than the petulant wife had. He was bound to know exactly which creditors he was fobbing off on a daily basis, and if I took an interest in his work, he would probably tell me.

As for the name of the legate's mistress, that would be common coin anywhere in the barracks.

XXII

During my search for information, I at one point bumbled into the legate's private gymnasium. I saw what Justinus meant about Gracilis being a sporty type: his den was packed with weights, dumb-bells, beanbags for throwing-games, and all the other paraphernalia that normally suggest a man who is afraid of seeming puny – probably because it's true. At one end of the room his spears and hunting trophies were hung on hooks. A sad Egyptian who would have been better employed mummifying kings for their meeting with Osiris sat cross-legged, engaged in taxidermy on a rather small deer. I never waste time talking to Egyptians. He could stuff a roebuck, but hearing his views on life as a timeless river of sorrows would not help me find his master. I nodded and passed on.

I finally tracked down the accountant, who supplied me with a lengthy list of disappointed wine merchants, furriers, bookmakers, stationers and importers of fine-scented oils.

'Jupiter, this man certainly does not believe in paying bills!'

'He's a little unbusinesslike,' the scribe agreed mildly. The fellow had swollen eyes and a restrained manner. He looked tired.

'Is there no income from His Honour's estates in Italy?'

'They're flourishing, but mostly mortgaged up.'

'So he's in trouble?'

'Oh, I doubt that!'

He was right. Gracilis was a senator. In the first place, teetering on the brink of financial disaster was probably second nature, so unlikely to worry him. Marrying Maenia Priscilla must have given his collateral a fillip. In any case, he came equipped with massive clout. To the small trades-men of a remote provincial town, his lordship must be

444

untouchable. A few adroit business fiddles would soon get him out of any temporary squeeze.

'Can I take it you have no idea then why your master might have disappeared?'

'I was unaware of any mystery.'

'He left you no instructions?'

'He's not renowned for forethought. I thought he was off on business for a few days. His bedchamber slave is absent too.'

'How do you know that?'

'Heard the man's girlfriend bemoaning the fact.'

'She works in the house?'

'She's a barmaid at the Medusa, near the Principia Dexter Gate.'

I took away the names of both the creditors and the slave's girlfriend scratched on my pocket memo tablet. Its wax had hardened up through lack of use, a sure hint that it was time to do some work.

'Tell me something else: is your master a ladies' man?'

'I couldn't possibly comment.'

'Oh, stretch a point!'

'My sphere is purely financial.'

'That needn't be unrelated to what I asked! His funds could be tight as a result of expensive mistresses . . .'

I let him stare me out. We both knew I would find other sources eager to supply me with the sordid facts.

I left the residence with a light step. Having clues always gives my optimistic side a boost.

I then made the mistake of pushing my luck again with the high-handed XIV Gemina.

Prefect of the camp was never a post in the traditional republican legion. As with so much else, I reckon the old republicans got it right. Nowadays these prefects wield an undue influence. Each legion appoints one, and they have a wide range of responsibilities for organisation, training and kit. In the absence of the legate and senior tribune they take command, which is when things 'become dangerous. They are drawn from the pool of first spears who are resisting retirement, which makes them too old, too pedantic, and too slow. I don't like them on principle. The principle being that it was a camp prefect whose obtuse behaviour destroyed the Second Augusta's reputation in the British Revolt.

At Moguntiacum there was just one, responsible for the whole fort. Since the Fourteenth were the only experienced legion stationed there, he had been supplied by them.

The camp prefect occupied an office whose oversized proportions must have appealed to his underdeveloped personality. I found him in it. He was reading scrolls and writing busily. He had made his nook deliberately spare. He used a folding stool with a rusted iron frame and a campaign table that looked as if it had served at Actium. It was supposed to give the impression that he would have preferred to be on active duty in the field. In my view, if Rome was to sustain any military reputation, men like this had to be kept in camp – gagged, bound and bolted to the floor.

'Sextus Juvenalis? I'm Didius Falco. The envoy from Vespasian.'

'Oh I heard some worm had poked its head out of a hole on the Palatine!' He wrote with a quill. He would.

Setting down the quill, meticulously balanced on the inkpot in a way that prevented drips, he bounced at me: 'What's your background?'

I assumed he didn't want to hear about my aunties in the Campagna. 'National service in the usual stinking province, then five years as a scout.'

'Still in uniform?' Army life was his only social yardstick. I could imagine him boring everyone rigid with his stubborn theories that traditional values, antique equipment and dreadful old commanders whose names no one had heard of were unsurpassed by their modern equivalents.

'Self-employed now.'

'I don't approve of men who leave the legions before time.'

'I never supposed you would.'

'National service lost its glint?'

'I copped a tricky spearhead wound.' Not as tricky as all that, but it got me out.

'Out of *where?*' he persisted. He should have been an informer.

'Out of Britain,' I admitted.

'Oh we know Britain!' He was eyeing me narrowly.

I braced myself. There was no escape. If I dodged any more he would guess anyway. 'You know the Second Augusta then.'

Sextus Juvenalis barely moved, but contempt seemed to flood his features like new colour in a chameleon. 'Well! You were unlucky!' he sneered.

'The whole Second were unlucky – in a certain camp prefect called Poenius Postumus!' Poenius Postumus was the imbecile who had ignored orders to join battle against the Iceni. Even we never really knew what his motives were. 'He betrayed the Second just as much as the rest of you.'

'I heard he paid for it.' Juvenalis lowered his voice a semitone, overcome by horrified curiosity. 'The word was, Postumus fell on his sword afterwards. Did he *fall* – or was he dropped?'

'What do you think?'

'Do you know?'

'I know.' I was present. We all were. But what happened on that angry night is the Second Augusta's secret.

Juvenalis stared at me as if I were a guardian at the gates of Hades with a downturned torch. He rallied soon enough, however. 'If you were with the Second, you'll need to tread carefully here. Especially,' he added heavily, 'if you are Vespasian's private agent!' I put up no attempt to quibble. 'Or is it your fancy companion?'

'So people have noticed Xanthus?' I smiled quietly. 'I honestly don't know his role. I prefer not to.'

'Where did you acquire him?'

'An unsolicited gift from Titus Caesar.'

'Reward for past services?' the prefect sneered.

'I suppose it could be for future ones.' I was ready to tighten the ligature: 'You're the best man to make excuses for the Fourteenth. Let's talk about Gracilis.'

447

'What's to say?' Juvenalis queried in a light tone. He appeared to be taking the reasonable line. I was not fooled.

'I need to see him.'

'It can be arranged.'

'When?'

'Soon.'

'Now?'

'Not immediately.'

I shifted restlessly. 'October in Upper Germany is hardly the time or place for legates to be snatching unofficial holidays.'

'He doesn't ask advice from me.'

'Perhaps he should!' Blatant flattery was also a failure. Camp prefect is an immodest rank; he thought it was his due. 'Maybe taking advice is not your legate's strong point. I hear he's been making himself unpopular.'

'Gracilis has his methods.' He defended his commander loyally. Nevertheless, I saw the flicker behind the prefect's eyes – annoyance at the legate's abrasive attitude.

'So is he off with a woman, or moonlighting from the bailiffs?'

'Official business.'

'Tell me. I'm official too.'

'It's officially secret,' he jeered. He knew I had no come-back. Men like that can judge your status from the way you lace your boot-thongs. Mine must have been twisted the wrong way.

'I have my orders, Prefect. If I can't carry them out, I may have to send a query back to Rome.'

Juvenalis let a thin smile play on his lips. 'Your messenger won't leave the fort.' I was wondering how much I could remember of the smoke-and-bonfire semaphore code when he forestalled me contemptuously: 'You'll find the signal station out of bounds.'

'And I don't suppose Moguntiacum keeps carrier pigeons?' I gave way with an air of grace I didn't feel. But I preferred not to find myself in the tiny cells beside the main gate, rationed to one bowl of barley gruel a day. I changed tack. 'I was sent here to take political soundings. If I can't get a briefing from Gracilis, I'll have to pick your brains instead. What's the mood among the local tribes?'

'The Treveri were roundly beaten by Petilius Cerialis.' Juvenalis ground it out in a tone which implied he was too long in the tooth to be openly obstructive, though he could easily spoil my mission if he decided to.

'At Rigodulum? The Twenty-first Rapax did well for Cerialis there!' I replied, jibing at the Fourteenth's less notable contribution.

Juvenalis ignored it. 'The tribes have gone back to earning their living and keeping their nasty heads down.' This was unexpectedly helpful. No doubt he was hoping I would go out into the local community and offend someone there, to save him the trouble of smacking me senseless.

'What are the staple industries hereabouts?'

'Wool, shipping on the river – and ceramics,' Juvenalis informed me, striking a chord with that last one.

'Cloaks, boats and pots! Didn't the rebel leader Civilis have family contacts in this area?' I asked. 'I'm told his wife and sister stayed at Colonia Agrippinensium during the revolt.'

His face set. 'The Batavians come from the north coast.'

'Spare me the geography lesson, Prefect. I know their habitat. But Civilis has made himself scarce from The Island and that whole region. I have to find him – I wonder if he's been back south?'

'Funnily enough,' Juvenalis replied, with some sarcasm, 'we do hear of him being sighted from time to time.'

'Really?'

'It's just rumour. He had a certain mystique among his people. When men like that die or disappear, you'll always find fake versions.'

He was right, up to a point. In the early days of the Empire, impersonators of tyrants were a constant phenomenon: Caligula, for instance, was continually being reborn among crazy supporters in exotic eastern states.

'So you reckon these rumours of local sightings are all moonshine?'

'He's a fool if he comes anywhere near the Fourteenth!'

The defection of their Batavian cohorts obviously rankled sorely.

'Do you send out patrols to investigate?'

'They find nothing.'

I thought that did not necessarily mean there was nothing to find. 'What are the chances rebellion will flare again among the tribes?' Juvenalis did not regard it as a function of his appointment to give political briefings, so I let myself speculate: 'It's the old joke still. If a Greek, a Roman and a Celt are shipwrecked on a desert island, the Greek will start a philosophy school, the Roman will nail up a rota – and the Celt will start a fight.' He glared at me suspiciously; even as a joke it was too metaphysical. 'Well, thanks – ' I never finished, for the door opened.

I should have expected it.

Whether by coincidence, or, more likely, in response to a conspiratorial grapevine, several of the Fourteenth's men of influence were joining us. As I skewed round to inspect them, my heart sank. They all had a grim air of purpose. Among them I recognised Macrinus, the gilded senior tribune I had seen arguing yesterday with Justinus, my antagonist the primipilus, at least three other dour-faced centurions, and a sturdy, silent man whom I guessed was their specularius, a post I had held once myself, when I had first carried out undercover assignments and studied interrogation – along with all the unkind techniques that speed it along.

I knew what the presence of this sinister individual would have meant in my day. Still, perhaps things had changed.

XXIII

I was seated on a stool. They gathered round. The space became too cramped for me to rise. The small room grew warmer and darker. I heard a soft chink of bronzes on a groin-protector, too close for comfort behind my left ear. It was impossible for me to turn and see what movement had caused the noise. The tribune and the centurions stood with their hands resting on their sword pommels.

I could feel the power that formed within a long-established legion. Messages passed with no visible effort. Councils of war almost summoned themselves. Internal conspiracies would be unbreakable by an outsider, and the men came equipped with menace like bear cubs – murderous from birth.

Since it was his office we occupied, the prefect retained the initiative. None of the other centurions spoke.

It was the tribune who started, however. The gilded Macrinus ran his free hand through his hair in a habitual gesture that emphasised the natural glints. 'We have had a complaint from the legate's wife about an intruder.' His cultured tones expelled the syllables as distinctly as if he had been spitting out seeds. He was a handsome, lazy-eyed, conceited hunk. I could imagine Maenia Priscilla scuttling with her troubles to this one. He was her own generation, her own rank. If she wasn't already going to bed with him, I bet she wanted to.

'A most gracious lady,' I murmured. He was daring me to call their legate's wife a spoiled little cat. They all were. I could see the prefect's fingers twitching for his quill, longing to write out a charge for disrespect.

'Dogs like you call our tribune "Sir"!' Juvenalis spat.

'Sorry, *sir*! I did apologise for intruding. I had thought the noble Florius Gracilis might be at home with a cold.'

451

'The residence is out of bounds.' Camp prefects adore drawing demarcation lines. 'Use the proper sources!'

'The proper sources had proved unforthcoming, and I have duties for the Emperor.' Once again I was aware of a worrying movement behind me.

The tribune burst out irritably, 'Who is this inquisitive slob?'

'A pest called Didius Falco,' the prefect announced. 'He's an ex-ranker from the Second Augusta. We ought to pass *that* news along the lines with the watchword.' I suppressed a groan. He had ensured that not a man in the legion would talk to me – and was probably preparing for me a worse fate than that. By curfew tonight I would be a soft target for every drunken muscleman who wanted to show off to the boys. 'Now he works for Vespasian – as you would expect.' The allusion to the Emperor's former command of the Second in Britain sounded as caustic as Juvenalis could make it without disloyalty to his service oath. 'But that's all right,' he assured the gathering. 'He's not here to bother us. This idiot is going to annoy the locals searching for their rebel chief. *He thinks he's going to tame Civilis!*'

No one laughed at the joke.

I sighed quietly. 'I am, as it happens, charged to find a missing legate, but it's Munius Lupercus, so the trail's cold . . . Lads, I read your message. Members of the Second are *persona non grata* with your notable selves. I'll go.'

There was silence, but a shift in the light and colder air behind my shoulders told me the armed wall had parted. I stood up. They continued to crowd me, so I blundered against the stool as I turned. I felt surprised that no one jumped me. They meant me to be. They all enjoyed my nervousness, but they let me leave. Someone kicked the door shut. I expected to hear laughter, and when none came that was worse. I walked out on to the parade-ground, where bright autumn sunshine from low on the horizon streamed uncomfortably in my eyes.

No one had touched me. But I felt as if I had been thrashed with knotted ropes by the entire legion at a ceremonial punishment parade.

XXIV

These cheerful events had taken up enough of the morning for me to stroll back to the tribune's house, where we had agreed to meet for lunch. 'I'm taking you out – I owe you a drink. There's a tavern called the Medusa that's been recommended to me . . .'

Justinus looked alarmed. 'Nobody I know drinks there!'

I admitted that that was probably because his friends were much too cultivated types, then explained my reason for going. Justinus enjoyed being part of the investigation, so overcame his qualms. As we walked he enquired after progress.

'I just had another encounter with the Fourteenth. They claim their man is away on official business, which is hard to disprove. But something is up. They overreact preposterously.'

I warned him about the Fourteenth's ominous attitude towards me. Justinus was too young to remember detailed events of the British Rebellion, so I had to relate the whole sorry tale of how the Second Augusta had been deprived of glory. His face fell. Apart from having a marked man for a house guest, he was probably as unimpressed as most people were by my legion's contribution to history.

The Medusa was less attractive than I had hoped, though not so fusty as I had feared. It had the air of an all-night establishment that by day was only half awake. In fact, *nowhere* in Moguntiacum was open all night; the Medusa's sleepy atmosphere at lunch-time was simply the result of being slackly run. The tables lolled against peeling walls like fungi clinging to ancient trees, and the winejars were grotesque misshapes from an inefficient pottery. It was full of boorish soldiers and their shifty hangers-on. We ordered the meal of the day, on the premise that it might be prepared freshly – a vain hope.

It was just about warm enough to take a table outside in the fresh air.

'Ah, meatballs!' exclaimed Justinus politely when the food came. I could see him fast losing interest. 'Looks like rabbit . . .' In fact, the eats seemed to be the crudely minced remains of a worked-out, broken-down pack-mule that had died of grief and mange.

'No need to worry what they may have used for flavour, as there doesn't appear to be any . . .' The thought crossed my mind that my companion's noble mother, Julia Justa, who already had a low opinion of what I had done to her beautiful daughter, was unlikely to form a kinder view of me if I finished off her son in a dive like this.

'You all right, Falco?'

'Oh, I'm fine!'

Tribunes were a rarity here. The landlord had served us himself. He probably thought we were inspecting him – a task neither of us liked to face too closely. After a while he sent a barmaid to ask whether we needed anything. It was a question which had nothing to do with food or wine.

'What's *your* name?' I asked, pretending to go along with it.

'Regina.' At this Justinus twitched excitedly, though not for the reasons she thought. (He knew from me that Regina was the name of the girlfriend of the missing legate's missing slave.)

'A queen!' I exclaimed to Justinus, so archly it was unbelievable. She loved it. I ordered another half-flagon, and told her to bring an extra beaker for herself.

'She doesn't seem to mind entertaining us,' Justinus murmured while she was fetching them. He seemed anxious that we might be treading on dubious moral ground by seeming to encourage her. My scruples about the Medusa were purely practical. I was only afraid we had risked eating those sordid rissoles while following a false lead.

'Entertaining us is her job, and it doesn't rule out a pretty complicated private life off duty. I'll talk to her,' I added,

454

switching into Greek as the girl came back with our wine. 'Let me tell you some rules for living, lad: never play board-games for money with strangers; never vote for the favourite candidate; and never trust a woman who wears an ankle chain . . .'

'You're the expert on women!' he replied wryly, in Greek that was more confident than mine. He had, at any rate, enough fluency to be rude without much effort.

'I've been fended off by a fair number of barmaids, certainly . . .' Switching back to Latin, I joked with Regina; 'Men's talk! His Honour was complaining about me ruining his sister.' The dozy girl had forgotten a beaker for herself; she flashed a meaningless smile and trotted off again.

Justinus kept his eyes on his bowl of rissoles (which certainly looked as if they needed cautious reconnaissance) as he continued in that lightly inflected, challenging Greek of his. 'As a matter of fact, Falco, I would like to ask if this business of yours with my sister is serious?'

My jaw set. 'It's as serious as I can make it.'

He looked up. 'That says nothing.'

'Wrong, tribune. It says what you really want to know: no harm will ever come to Helena from me.'

Our barmaid returned again.

Regina sat down, allowing us to go on talking among our-selves. She was used to men of commerce who finished their own business before trading with her. She seemed amenable to anything, in fact.

Justinus and I both let our previous conversation drop.

I ate as much as I could tolerate of the tasteless stew, then rinsed my mouth with wine. I smiled at the girl. She was a squat, flat-chested moppet with short red hair. Her shorn bob had curls of the 'assisted' type much favoured by girls who serve up drink with less useful commodities. She wore a fairly clean white tunic and the usual glass-bead necklace and cheap serpentine rings, as well as the inevitable ankle chain I had referred to earlier. Her attitude seemed servile, but with suggestions of a defiant streak. Back in Rome I had a bunch of hard, contemptuous sisters.

Regina reminded me of them. 'Regina, do you know a bedchamber boy called Rusticus?'

'Maybe.' She was the type who avoided answering questions on principle.

'You know who I mean?'

'He works in the fort.'

'For one of the legates. Don't worry – there's no trouble!' I reassured her quickly. 'I heard you were good friends with Rusticus.'

'I may have been.' I thought I saw her confident blue eyes darken sullenly. Maybe she was frightened. Or perhaps it was something more furtive.

'Do you know where he is?'

'No.'

'Has he gone away somewhere?'

'What's it to you?' she demanded.

'I'd very much like to find him.'

'Why?' I was about to explain my search for the legate when she fetched out angrily, 'I haven't seen him for ages. I don't know where he is!' She jumped to her feet. Justinus, taken aback, pushed his stool away from the table with a screeching skid. 'What do you want?' Regina shouted. 'Why have you started pestering me?'

Other customers – mostly soldiers – glanced over in our direction, though without much interest. 'Steady on, Falco,' Justinus interrupted. The girl rushed indoors wildly. 'Yes, barmaids do seem to be your speciality!' Justinus scoffed. He glared at me reprovingly, then followed her inside the tavern.

'That's Regina!' one of the soldiers grinned.

'Scratchy?'

'Gets het up over everything.'

I left payment on the table, sauntering nearby until the tribune reappeared. 'I'm glad to see you in one piece! I gather her temper is legendary. She loves screaming and bursting into tears at innocent customers. For an encore she'll throw an amphora at your head. If you're unlucky it's

456

a full one . . . Have you been drying her tears, or just trying to dodge?'

'You're too harsh, Falco!'

'She expected it.'

'Oh really?' Justinus muttered through his teeth. 'Well, I found out what we wanted without bullying the girl. It's quite simple. She and the slave Rusticus had a lovers' tiff. She doesn't see him any more.'

'What about the legate nipping off?'

'All she knows is she heard some mention that her boyfriend's master might be planning a few days away. She wasn't told why or where.'

'That's fine, if it's true.'

'Why should it not be?'

'She's a girl in a bar, you're a stranger, and I know when I've just seen a lying little strumpet who has something to hide!'

'Well *I* believed her.'

'Good for you,' I said.

We strode back towards the gate of the fort. Justinus still pretended to be angry, but his good nature was overcoming it. I shook my head and laughed softly.

'What's so funny?'

'Oh . . . there's a traditional method of extracting information where first you send a cruel brute who upsets the suspect, then his mild and friendly partner goes in and comforts them until they open their hearts.'

'It appears to be effective,' Justinus commented, rather stiffly.

'Oh yes!'

'I still don't see the joke.'

'It's nothing.' I grinned at him. 'Only the "soft" partner is *supposed* to be a fake!'

XXV

Back at the house news awaited us. 'A woman came asking for you, Marcus Didius.'

I laughed. 'That kind of message needs a careful approach!' Justinus looked prim. If I wanted to look a reliable friend to Helena, flippancy was a bad response. We were having too much banter of barmaids and not enough of the dull bombast that prevails among senators. Still, I couldn't help it if he wasn't used to me. His sister was, and she had made her choice. 'Who is this matron?'

'Julia Fortunata, Marcus Didius.'

I saw Justinus start at that. I raised an eyebrow. 'Let me guess – is she connected with Gracilis?'

'So you've heard something?' murmured the tribune. In front of his servants he was being discreet.

They were not my servants. 'Maenia Priscilla mentioned to me this morning that Gracilis flaunts a mistress somewhere. Is this her? Coming to the fort in such a public way seems strange – I wonder what she wants so urgently? Do you know where she lives?'

'I believe so,' Justinus replied, still cautiously. 'They say Gracilis has established her in a villa not far away . . .'

I told him that if he had a free afternoon he could come with me for the entertainment. He hesitated. Then he shouted for a slave to fetch both our cloaks.

We had to ride out through the Decumana Gate and go south. Once we had turned down the incline outside the gate, peace descended. Apart from the broad curve of the waterway, the square fort behind us remained the most prominent feature of the landscape, which, unusually in this section of the river, lacked the dramatic crags and rocky narrows that occur downstream. Here it was mainly low ground, sometimes broken by natural or man-made mooring creeks, though it was obviously not marshy. There were large trees, which frequently hid the Rhenus and Moenus from view.

Justinus took me by the road that enabled me to admire the Drusus Monument – a pleasure I did not let detain us long. Memorials to long-dead establishment heroes fail to excite me. I hardly glanced at it.

A mile or so further on stood a fortlet guarding a small village which Justinus told me regarded itself as the official Moguntiacum *canabae*. Julia Fortunata was renting a place just this side of the settlement. For a woman of standing it was only just safe. The Rhenus lay within sniffing distance. However, heading upstream to Argentoratum and Vindonissa, there was a military road parallel with our bank of the river, and the guard post afforded first-instance protection if trouble ever flared.

It was a villa farm with a basically Roman look, despite the usual provincial differences of layout, and a much-reduced scope from the vast estates of Italy. We entered by a small grassy path that ran between the barn and a duck pond, passed some apple trees, took a detour by an empty byre, avoided a loose pig, then came to a colonnaded house.

Indoors there was a square, Germanic hall with a central hearth where the milder Mediterranean climate would have allowed an open atrium with a pool. Julia Fortunata had imposed deliberate Roman style: drapery in sophisticated colouring, scroll-ended couches, well-placed statuettes of Greek runners and wrestlers, a side-table with a small library of scrolls in silver canisters. There were touches of drama too: sudden swags of purple cloth and multiple bronze acanthus-leaf lamps.

When she appeared, even though we knew she had been anxious to see me, she gave me her hand calmly and formally. This one would have made a proper wife for a highly placed official, had fortune not made her background good, but not quite good enough. While the young bride Maenia Priscilla possessed money and arrogance, Julia had to settle for culture and breeding. She lacked the social benefits that in Rome were conferred by a family of famous ancestors and decades of accumulated cash. She could have married a customs officer and been queen of some small town for life, but what strong-willed woman wants to be dragged down to dull respectability?

If Gracilis was the age I thought – late thirties – then Julia Fortunata must be older by at least enough to show. Justinus had told me their arrangement was known to be of long standing: it had survived the legate's first marriage, and looked ready to outlast the present one. Julia Fortunata travelled with Gracilis on all his postings. Wherever he arrived in Italy or Europe, it was understood that the lady would turn up, settle herself within visiting range, and provide whatever she customarily provided. The set-up had long ago ceased to be scandalous. It seemed a poor life for her, particularly if, as I had deduced, Florius Gracilis was a pathetic man. But sophisticated women pay that price for a senatorial link.

She was fairly tall, and dressed in subdued greyish-mauve material. No real beauty. An angular face, a neck that showed its maturity, and the ankles she crossed as she seated herself to talk to us were hideously bony. She had style, though. Graceful hands arranged her stole. An elegant carriage. Composure when meeting men. She was that rare goose, an independent matron – determined, self-possessed and chic.

'Madam, I'm Didius Falco and this is Camillus Justinus, senior tribune of the First Adiutrix.' As he moved in her social circle, I was willing the tribune to take the lead, but he held back and stood beside me as an observer. Julia Fortunata glanced between us: Justinus in the crisply pleated white tunic and broad purple stripe, quieter and more serious than most of his rank; me ten years older in fact and a hundred in experience. She elected to deal with me.

'Thank you for returning my visit so promptly.' Her voice was refined and assured. It matched perfectly the strong taste of her muted robes and her jewellery, which was sparse but striking – a bold bracelet of Middle Eastern origin, and two huge beaten-gold discs of earrings. Even her sandals had an interesting design. She was a woman who chose

460

,things for herself, and liked a touch of the unusual. 'You are conducting some sort of enquiry?'

I made a gesture of assent but gave no details. 'You called at the fort today? I admit I was surprised.'

'It was urgent. I presume that if you are investigating something that affects my old friend Florius Gracilis, you will welcome any help.'

I attempted to unsettle her. 'Maenia Priscilla thinks he may be with you.'

'Can Maenia Priscilla *think*?' It flashed out like a bright flood of spilt wine, making us jump. 'I'm afraid he's not here.'

I smiled. I could see what might attract him. You knew exactly where you were in this establishment. 'Have you known him long?'

'Ten years.' A slight dryness in her tone acknowledged that we could regard it as more than a nodding association.

I did try to be specific. 'And what are relations between you?'

'Cordial,' she said, in a firm tone.

I let it go. No point being crude. We all knew the tally. 'Julia Fortunata, I am an envoy from Vespasian. I was sent to Upper Germany on another matter, but any odd circumstances that occur while I am here may be related, so they need investigation. You are correct: I should welcome any information about the whereabouts of Gracilis. You may speak completely frankly.'

For a moment she was silent, candidly considering me. I rode out the scrutiny. She reached a verdict and gestured us to a seat.

She had planned what to say. It came out with little prompting and in a concise form. Gracilis had definitely vanished. His friend Julia was extremely concerned. She had asked to see me because she felt that 'other elements' were either taking the matter too lightly, or knew something and were involved in a cover-up. It was inconceivable that he should go off somewhere without mentioning it to Julia in advance.

'Does he even discuss military matters?'

461

'Within the proper bounds of course.'

'Of course,' I said. At my side the upright Justinus made an effort to control his disapproval. 'Tell me, did he have any worries?'

'Gracilis is extremely conscientious. He frets over everything.' A fidget, eh? A man who harried his men and aggravated his wife no doubt, though probably his mistress of ten years had learned to ignore the agitation. Perhaps, I thought, Julia Fortunata's role in his life had always been to calm him down and boost his morale.

'What most recently? Can you give me examples?'

'Since we came to Germany? In general terms, the political situation. He feared that Petilius Cerialis may have been posted away to Britain prematurely; that subduing the rebels may still be only half complete. He sensed further trouble brewing.' She discussed politics like a man. I wondered if Gracilis was really so fluent himself, or whether he relied on his mistress to frame his thoughts. Yet now, as she described him evaluating the situation as a local commander should, I had for the first time some sense of this man acting with authority. She certainly did well by him.

'What were his relations at the fort?'

'He was very conscious that the Fourteenth legion possessed most of the experience and were to a great extent carrying their colleagues.' She made a slight gesture of apology to Justinus for disparaging the First; her sensitivity was something we had come to expect. Justinus grinned back ruefully.

'Anything else? Money worries?'

'Nothing abnormal.'

'Problems with his wife?'

'Oh, I think Gracilis can handle that one!' Once again she had permitted herself a faintly bitter and contemptuous note, though it was well controlled. Julia Fortunata knew her position was one of strength.

'*Other* women?' I suggested lightly. She said nothing, reprovingly. 'So what has he been most preoccupied with? Anything to do with the rebels, for instance?'

'He did discuss with me a theory that the chieftain Civilis

would refuse to accept defeat and might try to rally support again.'

'Any evidence?'

'Nothing firm.'

I smiled. 'Had he decided to do something about it?'

'He would like to finish the task Petilius Cerialis left behind. Gracilis is ambitious, naturally. Dealing with Civilis would enhance his status in Rome and win the Emperor's gratitude. As far as I know he had nothing to go on, however.'

To an envoy who also needed enhanced status and imperial thanks, that was reassuring news! 'Does the legate's interest extend to Veleda?'

'He never mentioned her.' It sounded like loyalty. The legate was probably as fascinated by the famous prophetess as any other man.

'So he had taken no action, and as far as you know he had no immediate plans?'

'The legate was on guard for trouble. It's all I can say. Other than that,' she said emphatically, as if she felt she had given us sufficient information for professionals to act upon, 'Florius Gracilis takes a close interest in everything that affects the fort, from the quality of the grain supply to the franchise for the bowls which his soldiers eat it from!'

I grew thoughtful. 'There must be a large number of supply contracts being renegotiated after all the commotion of the civil war?'

'Yes. As I said, Gracilis likes to involve himself closely in the details.' I bet he did!

'And how do the contractors regard him?'

'I would have thought that was obvious!' Julia Fortunata replied acerbically. 'The successful ones applaud his judgement; those who lose the work tend to grumble.'

I felt a prickle of excitement. I wondered if any contract winners ever gave the legate more material thanks than praise – or if any of the losers accused him of being less than fair . . . I had to phrase it discreetly: 'Are you aware of any recent problems with commercial deals that might have a bearing on the legate's disappearance?'

'No.' I think she knew what I meant. 'He left no clues at all.'

I felt Julia's concern for him went much deeper than her measured tones suggested, but she was too proud, both in her own right and on behalf of Gracilis, to display anything other than this cool self-control.

I allowed her to close the interview. She promised to be in touch if she thought of anything else that would help us. She was the type who would continue to ponder what had happened to her lover until she knew the answer.

I hoped it would not be the one she dreaded. I would probably despise him, but I liked her.

As we rode back to Moguntiacum, Justinus asked, 'What's your verdict?'

'A woman of strong character tied up with a man who lacks it. The usual, as your caustic sister would say!'

He passed over my reference to Helena. 'Did that get us anywhere at all?'

'It may do. My bet is something to do with Civilis.'

'Really!'

'Well, either it's that, or His Honour has embroiled himself in a cavalry-fodder fiddle or unwise scheming with the ceramic contractors. As a matter of national pride, I'd rather he's being held hostage by a dangerous rebel than just learn eventually that the fool has got himself bopped on the head with a redware porridge pot!'

Camillus Justinus grinned in his slow, appreciative way. 'I think I'll go for the pot,' he replied.

XXVI

Justinus was duty officer for the night watch, so we spurred back towards the fort as dusk drew in. Nearer to, I asked him to take my horse on while I peeled off to familiarise myself with the locale. In sight of the gate he left me to mooch about on foot.

I tramped around, exploring. The fort was set back a lengthy step from the busy wharves on the waterside, so I left those. Most civilian life sheltered behind the fort, where a competent-looking aqueduct brought water in. On the far side, some way from the military base, lay a customs post and the Jupiter Column, which paid civic lip-service to the Palatine. I made up my own version of the usual painful stuff: *Long life to Nero, companion of the Olympian Gods, say the citizens of our town (ardently hoping Nero will invest us with a theatre)*. They must have mistimed it, because there was no theatre that I could find.

From its vantage point on slightly higher ground, the fort commanded a wide view downstream as the river curved away and widened after its junction with the Moenus. I took the road to the bridge, then tramped across. Only then did I really appreciate how wide the Rhenus is. It made the Tiber seem like a minnow stream meandering through watercress beds. A guard post had been thrown up on the far side, large enough to have its own name: Castellum Mattiacorum. Now I was standing in Germania Libera.

At first it felt just the same as the Roman side. The atmosphere was less alarming than the lawless immigrants' quarter of the Transtiberina in Rome. But this was not the Transtiberina, and nor – for me – was it really safe. A Roman watch-tower this side of the river was an extreme rarity. Standing as it did at the head of the great trade route that followed the course of the Moenus into the interior, this one existed only as a gesture. I had taken my first tentative step beyond the frontiers of the Empire. Behind me the lights of Moguntiacum twinkled faintly in neat rows. Ahead lay hundreds or thousands of uncertain miles, inhabited first by tribes who openly despised Rome, then by other tribes we Romans had never yet encountered in lands whose existence and features no one in my world even knew. On this rather drear evening, with night falling early, the sense of vast-scale European geography suddenly made me feel mournful and far from home.

The guard post was surrounded by a relaxed group of civil dwellings. On the water's edge I found a tavern with fewer customers and higher standards than the Medusa, where I could sit and watch the solemn flow of the Rhenus and the last ships homing in at nightfall.

I was thinking about my mission. Although developments were slow, I was beginning to feel much more assured of my role here – and aware of new drawbacks. I had a distinct sense of having discovered a rival. If Florius Gracilis had made it *his* mission to reclaim the chieftain Civilis – and whatever Julia Fortunata believed, that could well include a similar yearning to dispose of Veleda, too – I hoped he failed. Otherwise I could end up stuck in this backwater, a thousand miles from home and who knew how far from Helena, robbed of my task for the Emperor, and with it any chance to earn some cash. Vespasian was a snob. He would much rather handsomely reward a senator than find himself forced to hand out a few grudging sesterces to me.

It certainly seemed possible that Gracilis had dashed off on a search. Maybe for once he had deemed it too secret to enlighten the forceful Julia. Maybe he had even felt a need to strike out independently. The Fourteenth must be aware of what he was up to. It followed that once I let them know why Vespasian had sent me, they would have a double reason to act innocent, then interfere with my own plans. New broom or not, they would support their commander. And Gracilis himself was bound to consider this mission more suited to his elevated status rather than flung away on me . . .

Tough luck, legate! If this was a race, then M. Didius Falco was determined to win.

I had no idea how. But mere technical details can be worked out any time. All a hero needs is grit.

Satisfied with the day's progress, I enjoyed my drink. The night was calm. The atmosphere along the waterfront was pleasant and businesslike. Now I was thinking about women: barmaids, officers' wives, mistresses . . . and finally a woman it was a more creative pleasure to dream about: Helena.

That led me again into wondering where she was. Despondent, I made the dark trek home.

On the home side of the river, the provincial tradesfolk were promptly closing up, which reminded me that in four or five hours I might feel sleepy myself. If Argentoratum had been quick to draw its shutters, Moguntiacum made them look like degenerate owls. When the first man yawned in Moguntiacum, the whole town disappeared to bed. By the time a cosmopolitan Roman was just starting to feel hungry and ready for his evening's entertainment, the eating-spots here had up-ended benches on all the tables and the besoms were sweeping out lingerers. Anyone who left too slowly risked having his tunic pinched in the folding door as it slammed shut.

I crept through the sober streets hoping no one would notice me roaming about. I didn't want them to be shocked.

At the fort I hit a snag.

'Password?'

'How should I know? I'm just a visitor.' In Germany a year after the rebellion rules were rules. It was sound practice – and a thorough menace to free-and-easy types like me.

Luckily the guard party belonged to the First and wanted to help. If they had been assigned from the Fourteenth I would have had to camp out all night.

I remembered my discussion with Justinus. ' "Mars the Avenger"?'

'Try another.'

' "Pickled fish"?'

'Yesterday's.'

'Oh Hades – what about "The camp surgeon's middle name"?'

'Spot on,' said the sentry, though he failed to readjust his speartip from its dangerous aiming point, dead centre on my throat.

'So what's the problem, soldier?' I croaked wearily.

'What is it?'

'What's what?'

'What,' he enunciated clearly, 'is the camp surgeon's middle name?'

The Fourteenth were right: the First Adiutrix were a gang of crass deck hands and rigging monkeys, with brains as dense as cork.

I got in eventually. Anyone who has bluffed his way into a brothel on the Via Triumphalis while attempting to rescue a fake virgin from Cyrenaïca – and got out again without losing his sense of humour or something worse – can deal with the simple-minded gateman of a frontier fort.

Fuming, but fighting it back in case anyone embarrassed me by asking what the matter was, I stepped out briskly for my billet. There was a good chance that if I failed to turn up by dinner-time, Camillus Justinus would go out to eat with his fellow-officers, leaving me to make the best of yesterday's bread rolls. I lengthened my stride, oblivious to everything but my traditional obligation as a guest to eat my host out of house and home.

The ambush was lying in wait for me four strides from the tribune's door.

XXVII

Three of them. A trio of soldiers wandering down the Via Principalis in a sweet reek of recent barley beer, sufficiently affected by the drink to become dangerous, but not drunk enough for me to handle on my own.

At first I thought they were just clumsy. They had lurched in my path, causing me to pull up short, like lads who were just too bad-mannered to notice my presence. Then they stumbled apart and regrouped: one either side of me, one behind.

Experience gave me an instant's warning that saved my life. I missed sight of the personal dagger, but registered the arm movement. I swung away sharply, crashing aside another assailant, but grabbing him to me like a bolster. For a moment he provided a human shield as I spun on the spot. His bristles scraped my cheek; his sour breath was disgusting. The moment of safety passed – he posed a greater threat if he went for me at close quarters. Loosening my grip would be fatal, but holding on was so bad I nearly opted for a one-way ferry ticket across the Styx.

He jerked free. Somehow I sensed what was in his mind and seized the chance to scramble half backwards. There was a house wall fairly close behind me, which offered slight protection. Instinct said to huddle close, but then I would be lost if they all rushed me at once. I managed a shout – not loud enough. After that I was too busy. There were plenty of personnel in the vicinity, but this incident was being nicely choreographed to look like nothing in particular. Who expects to see a mugging outside the officers' quarters? Come to that, who expects to be mugged?

Me, was the answer. Anywhere and everywhere I prepared myself for the worst. Thank the gods, these thugs had assumed I was whistling homewards in a trance. They

469

had planned to catch me out completely, but found themselves surprised.

Quickly, I tried to take stock. I could see – there was a broad bar of light from an unshuttered first-floor window in the tribune's house. Right at the start a shadow had wavered across that light from someone moving in the room behind. I glanced up, hoping to attract attention, but now there was no sign of life.

My own knife was safely in my hand. Letting me get it had been a bad mistake. I was breathing hard with the shock of the first assault, but I was upright and mobile. Even so, the prospects looked gloomy. Every time I made a dagger feint, I tried to edge closer to the tribune's portico. I stood little chance of reaching it. Every time one of *them* made a feint, I was at risk from the others while I parried. At least they stuck with their daggers – drawn swords would arouse too much public interest. As we sidestepped in all directions they were still laughing and nudging one another so that it would look like good-humoured jostling. I had no time to rouse help.

I had made it one stride nearer the door, but was trapping myself in a tighter wedge between two of them and the wall, while the third soldier guarded against flight the other way. It was time for some fast talking, but my mouth dried so that I couldn't speak.

Almost without planning it, I lunged at the single man, then changed direction and tackled the other two ferociously. Blades clashed with a screech that hurt my eye-teeth; sparks flew. I was working so hard I hardly noticed that in the remote depths of the tribune's house a woman's voice cried out. I barged an arm skywards, and heard steel skidding on masonry behind me. Light from above increased. I glimpsed faces more clearly. Another shadow came and went, but I was too preoccupied to shout.

My own dagger went home somewhere, but awkwardly. I wrenched my shoulder retrieving it as one of my two men cursed and hopped on the spot. Events were becoming too public; the second mugger was all for scarpering. The third had more guts – or less wits. He sprang at me. I roared with annoyance. Then, just as I had enough to do dealing with all three at once, the tribune's door burst open. Someone stepped out, framed in black by the light behind. Wrong build for Justinus; too slight for his guards. Whoever he was, a trimly sinister shadow came gliding out of doors.

Defending myself against my attackers as they put up a last furious struggle, I could hardly take in what happened. The shadow stepped straight past me, met one of the soldiers and pulled his head back with a disturbing action. The soldier folded noiselessly, and-dropped to the ground in a manner that was unmistakable. There was a moment of stillness. The two survivors ran for it with the speed of troops who knew what they had witnessed. I knew too, though it was difficult to comprehend.

No time for pursuit. I was too winded, anyway. The tribune's guards now rushed out with torches, followed by Justinus. Chaos and commotion raged, then sank in a sickly diminuendo as light revealed the dead man.

It was a horrific killing. The amount of blood was unbelievable. The soldier's head had been nearly severed from his body by a blade sharper even than military steel.

I turned to the man who had done it. He stood motionless, the weapon still held in a workaday grip. One of the tribune's guards made a feeble attempt to remove it, without achieving much – his nerve failed. Another raised a flare slowly, as if afraid of revealing something supernatural.

No such luck. All we saw were the glazed and manic eyes of a tourist whose latest adventure had left him startled at his own bravado and ingenuity.

'Xanthus!'

Oh dear. Now someone was going to have difficult questions to answer before the hapless world-traveller was given back his passport and allowed to go home.

XXVIII

He still saw me as his protector, and turned to me with a worried bleat. I left him with the razor – he seemed to know how to handle it. 'I won't ask how many times you've done that before!'

'No, better not.' His voice sounded matter-of-fact, but I could see he was in shock.

'I always thought you'd been sent to assassinate me. Turns out I'm in more danger from my own past history . . .'

'I think I want to go home, Falco.'

'You're all right.'

'No, I wish I was in Rome.'

Justinus was taking charge. He had examined the scratched identity marks on the dead man's sword scabbard. 'One of the Fourteenth's hooligans . . .' He told one of his guards to fetch their senior tribune. 'Be discreet. Try to bring Aulus Macrinus by himself. I don't want their whole bloody legion turning up in high dudgeon.' He came to help me deal with the barber. 'Don't worry, Xanthus. You'll have to be interviewed by my commander, but that should be the end of it.'

'You sound confident!' I muttered in an undertone. 'Are you happy about explaining to your notoriously sensitive colleagues how one of their number came to be wiped out like this on the First's side of the fort?'

'I'll find something to tell them.' He responded well in a crisis. His eyes were bright with intense excitement, but he was planning coolly. His self-control calmed others in the vicinity too. 'Marcus, be prepared. *Some* things are worse than you think!' After teasing me with this mystery, kindness filled his voice. 'Let's move this poor fellow away from here . . .'

Xanthus had started trembling slightly. He stood transfixed by the corpse; nudging him indoors would need tact. In fact we all found it hard to avoid staring at the scene.

While we were still in the street, the guard returned with Macrinus. Even his aristocratic sneer paled slightly when we stepped back and let him see why he had been summoned.

'Is that one of ours? Dear gods, Camillus!'

'Aulus, hear the explanation –'

'It had better be good!'

'Don't threaten us!' snapped Justinus, with surprising force. 'There's no argument. I have a reputable witness. Three of your rankers set on Falco –'

'A drunken prank.'

'No! It was unprovoked *and* planned. They had been dawdling outside my house for half an hour – my witness noticed them. And much more than a prank, Aulus! The night could have ended nastily –'

'I'd say it did!'

'The alternative was for my guest to be fatally stabbed.'

In the face of this, the Fourteenth's man pulled himself up. 'If what you say is true, the culprits will be found and disciplined. But I'm protesting about the secretive way this has all been handled. I don't care for the way you had me brought across here alone. I want my own observers present, I want one of my centurions to take notes at the scene of the crime –'

As he soared off into complaint, I broke in: 'There will be no cover-up. But no one wants another riot like your legion's public rumpus at Augusta Taurinorum!'

Macrinus ignored me. 'Who did it?'

'The barber.'

That set him back. We could see him remembering how Xanthus had been called the Emperor's hit man. We all stared at Xanthus. As a hit man he looked pretty meek.

'Some of us are going to feel uneasy the next time we need a shave,' I said. A fine spray of the dead soldier's blood disfigured the crisp white linen of the barber's tunic. As usual, he was turned out so smartly that away from the court his brilliant presence became embarrassing. The

473

stains were doubly disconcerting, as if he had been careless during a routine shave.

'In my job,' he answered quietly, 'a man can become a target for abuse quite easily. I've had to learn how to defend myself.'

'That's no excuse for murdering a soldier!' Macrinus barked. He had no finesse.

'The soldier,' I pointed out rationally, 'had no excuse for trying to murder me!'

At this stylish rebuke he condescended to subside. It was apparent that Justinus intended to take control of any necessary enquiry, which, since the crime had occurred within the First's jurisdiction, was his entitlement. Macrinus grumpily fell back on one last jibe: 'You mentioned a witness. I hope it's one we can rely on!'

'Perfectly,' Justinus answered, with a faint impression of gritting his teeth.

'I think I must insist on knowing who.' Macrinus had sensed a joke, but was too crass to withdraw.

'My sister,' Justinus told him placidly.

I winced. He had been right earlier when he had teased me. Things certainly were worse than I had realised: Helena Justina was here.

We glanced up at the window above us. She was still standing there, as she must have been during some of my fight. Her face lay in darkness. Her unmistakable figure, the outline of her smoothly upswept hair and even the elegant pendant drops of her earrings sent down a perfect, elongated shadow that reached the corpse, hiding its ghastly wound in decent shade.

The tribune Macrinus straightened up, smoothed back his crisp, curly locks, and produced a salute suitably emphatic for a tribune who thought a lot of himself greeting the only unmarried senator's daughter this side of the Alps.

I was wearing the wrong boots for heel-clicking. I waved at her, grinned at her brother, and strode indoors.

XXIX

'Fighting again, Falco?' Mild medicine from her.

She was in long-sleeved wool, with rather sombre jet earrings. Her dark, silky hair had been caught up in combs either side of her head, perhaps with more care than usual, and I could detect her perfume from two strides away. But after travelling, or possibly after seeing me attacked, she looked washed out and tense.

I was not in the mood for pleasantries. 'I gather it tickled you to watch me suffering?'

'I sent people to help.'

'You sent me a barber!'

'He seems capable.'

'You weren't to know that — I don't think he knew himself.'

'Don't quibble. He was the first person I found . . . You kept us waiting for dinner!' she grumbled, as if that settled it.

I threw back my head and commented to the gods, 'Well, things seem to be normal again!'

We always sparked like this after spending time apart. Especially when we met again with strangers watching us. For me, it held off the moment when I had to admit to missing her. For Helena, who knows? At least now she had spoken to me there was a spark in her eyes that I didn't object to seeing there.

Her brother had brought Xanthus indoors and was shepherding us all into a reception room. He had refrained from suggesting that his tribunal colleague come and be introduced to the noble newcomer, so watching Macrinus showing off was one horror we were spared. Xanthus was kept with us to be applauded and cosseted after his ordeal.

We found ourselves in the dining-room. A meal lay ready,

which had obviously been set for some time. At this point I felt prepared for formalities. I would have marched over and kissed Helena's cheek, but she plonked herself decisively on her brother's dining-couch. Unless I offended Justinus by invading the host's eating space, she was out of reach. It annoyed me. Failing to greet her made it look as if I didn't care.

I excused myself to clean up – some blood, but mostly dirt. When I returned I had missed the hors-d'oeuvres (my favourite course) and Helena was regaling the company with outrageous stories of her journey. I ate in silence, trying not to listen. When she reached the part about the wheel coming off her carriage and the chief of the mountain bandits kidnapping her for ransom, I yawned and went to my room.

An hour or so later, I re-emerged. The house had fallen quiet. I searched its bowels until I found Xanthus, lying on his bed and writing up his diary. I knew from travelling out with him that he was keeping a richly boring travelogue.

'At least "the day I killed the soldier" should keep your grandchildren enthralled! And here's another excitement: this is going to be the night when you give me a proper shave.'

'You going out?'

'No. Staying in.'

He had rolled to his feet and was unpacking his gear, though mildly unimpressed by the bonanza I was offering. Wine at dinner had calmed him down to the point of utter silliness. 'Has a brush with death made you vow to dedicate your stubble to the gods in an alabaster pyx, Falco? I'm not sure they make vases big enough!' I let him sit me down and envelop me in a fine cambric wrap, but I ignored the joshing. 'What does sir prefer – depilatory liniment? I use a nice white vine paste. I never recommend my gentlemen to try the weird stuff like bat's blood – ' He was enjoying himself more than I reckoned to tolerate.

'A razor will do.' Superstition made me hope he would change to a different blade from the one that he had used earlier.

'Sure? I can do you ground pumice or individual tweezing just as easily. My word, you've been neglecting yourself. It's probably best to try and burn this off with bitumen!' I *think* the last one was a joke.

'Whatever will have the smoothest result. And I want a haircut as well – but leave some curl. Just trim off the worst shagginess . . .' Xanthus put an engraved copper mirror into my hand, like somebody keeping a baby quiet with a rattle. I carried on describing what I wanted, even though I knew barbers never listen. A private informer needs to possess some stubbornness.

'Jupiter, Falco! Who are you trying to impress?'

'Mind your own business.'

'Oh!' Xanthus spat on his whetstone. '*Oh, I see!*' Even he caught on eventually. His normal eagerness to please turned into the ribaldry I met everywhere on this subject: 'You'll have your work cut out there!' Quite often that was Helena Justina's line too, I remembered pessimistically. 'This calls for my Norican steel . . .'

I wanted the best, so was unable to quibble. But I felt pretty sure that the Norican steel was what he had used to cut my attacker's throat.

To his credit, he made the best of the unpromising material I had placed at his disposal. I had never been shaved so closely, nor with so little discomfort, and even the haircut just about fitted the style of subdued dishevelment with which I felt most at home. After years of delicately gauging the wishes of emperors, Xanthus could judge his client as nicely as you'd expect in a barber who would be sent to the public strangler if he snipped a wrong curl.

As it turned out, he might have spared himself the trouble. Still, I dare say it was not the first time he had spent hours preparing someone for an assignation that flopped.

With a stinging chin and in a fug of disconcerting unguents, I quietly admitted myself to what I knew was the best guest-bedroom. I kept telling myself that everything would be all right once I had cornered Helena on her own and treated her to my adoring attentions. I could hardly wait to see her. I had a fairly pressing need to re-establish normal relationships.

No such luck. There was a taper, but the large room lay half in darkness. I stood for a moment, adjusting to the dim light and trying to think up a suave line of conversation if my beloved was reclining on swansdown and reading a light ode or two while she waited impatiently for me ... No point: there was no Helena. The high bed with its tortoise-shell frame, fringed coverlet and engagingly carved footstool stood empty. Instead, a small hunched figure lay snoring on a lower couch – presumably a slavegirl she had brought to look after her.

So much for me! No chance of a passionate reunion with a servant looking on! I could remember when she *never* let a slave stay in her room at night if I was in the vicinity.

I stepped back. Closing the door, my pent-up emotion gripped me. She must have known I would come. She must be keeping out of the way deliberately. Chatting with Justinus. Frightening that simple soul with her tales of broken wheels and brigands. Chewing over family business. Putting his career to rights. Anything that would avoid having to face me, angry at the way she had disappeared from Rome, yet badly wanting to go to bed with her.

I decided to take my outrageously barbered person out on the town and get as drunk as possible.

Indignation carried me as far as the front door. Then I remembered that Moguntiacum had small-town, small-minded habits. There was nowhere open for entertainment, except for the usual places too sordid to contemplate. Besides, the prospect of trying to work tomorrow with a head like a sack of oatmeal after a night gossiping inanely with some drab in a tavern when I had hoped to spend it with Helena, became too hard to bear. I sat in the tribune's garden for a while, feeling miserable, but Justinus was no devotee of landscape and it was a poor spot to sulk in. His dog found me and climbed alongside on the seat to chew at my tunic hem, but even the bench had damp moss on it and he soon jumped down and snuffled off into the dark-ness. I too slunk away to my room.

I had my back to the door. I had just pulled off my tunic (a clean one; too good for sleeping in) when someone came in.

'As nice a view of a nude wood sprite's back as I ever had the privilege to glimpse!'

Helena.

Having been attacked once that day, I spun round jumpily. Helena's warm appraising eyes were smiling as I lowered my handful of tunic in an attempt at decency. Her smile always had an irresistible effect on me.

'This is a private room, lady.'

'Good!' she said. I could feel my face colouring, but applied a scornful expression; it only encouraged her. 'Hello, Marcus.' I said nothing. 'I thought you wanted to see me?'

'What gave you that idea?'

'A strong scent of lotions in my room.' She sniffed. I cursed Xanthus. He had doused me in pomade until a bloodhound could have tracked me all the way from the Gallic Strait to Cappadocia.

Helena tipped her head to one side, watching me. She was leaning on the door behind her, as if to stop me escaping. My jaw set. 'How's Titus?'

'How should I know?'

'So what brings a stylish young lady to this wilderness?'

'Someone I follow about.' Helena had the knack of making her most illogical action sound like a rational response to some crazy slight from me.

'You left me!' I accused her, in a low tone.

'And how was Veii?' Her well-bred voice had a sarcastic note that dried my mouth like grape skins.

'Veii's a dump.' Suddenly, for no obvious reason, I felt tired.

'Are the widows attractive?' As I expected, it sounded like fighting talk. Now I knew why I felt defeated.

'Some of them think so.'

'I was talking to one,' Helena said crisply. 'She implied that your trip to Veii was a wild success.'

479

'The widow's a liar.'

Helena looked at me. She and I were friends for a good reason: we knew one another well enough to be able to pick a resounding fight, yet we both knew how to appeal for a truce. 'That's what I tell myself,' she answered quietly. 'But why, Marcus?'

'Jealous that I refused her and went home to you. What were *you* doing in Veii?'

'Trying to find you.'

Somewhere between us the quarrel died. 'You've found me now,' I said.

Helena Justina came across the room. She had a purposeful air I was not quite ready for, though I would be. 'What's on your mind, lady?'

'Nothing you won't like . . .' She tugged the tunic from my hand.

For pride's sake I tried to bluff it out: 'I warn you, I hate forward women – '

'Wrong. You like a girl who looks as if she knows exactly what you're thinking, and doesn't care . . .'

All the same, uncertainty flickered. She stepped back. I stepped after her.

I could feel her physical warmth even before her bare arms came through mine. She must have changed from the woollen dress I had seen earlier to a lighter one. If I undid two brooches, the flimsy material would drift to the floor, leaving all of her available. They looked like brooches with easy clasps. I put my hands on her shoulders, as if undecided whether to hold her off or hold her closer. My thumbs found the clasps automatically.

Helena started to pull away from me. It brought us effortlessly to the bed. 'Don't look so nervous, lady!'

'I don't frighten that easily.'

'You should do . . .'

'Oh stop pretending to be tough!' Helena knew most things about me, and what she didn't know she guessed. 'You're not a thug; you know how to be affectionate . . .' I felt affectionate all right. I felt so affectionate I could think of nothing else.

We landed on the bed. I let her take charge. She always liked organising. Tonight I liked whatever she liked. Today had posed enough problems. Now I had Helena Justina in my arms, in the friendliest of moods; I had everything I wanted, and was prepared for anything.

She was making herself comfortable, arranging the bed-clothes, taking off her earrings, unfastening her hair, killing the lamp . . . 'Relax, Marcus!'

I relaxed. I relaxed utterly. All the anxieties in my hectic brain grew calmer. I hauled Helena closer still and sighed heavily while my hands travelled slowly over the familiar shape of her, reacquainting themselves with her secrets. I held her, and closed my eyes in gratitude. Then I did the only thing a man could be expected to do in the circumstances.

I went to sleep.

XXX

Most of the night had passed. I woke in a sweat, realising what I must have done.

'Pleasant nap?' She was still there anyway.

'You told me to relax . . . I'm awake now,' I said, trying to make it sound meaningful.

Helena merely laughed at me, and snuggled against my shoulder. 'Sometimes when I'm trying to make friends with you, I feel like Sisyphus pushing his rock up the mountain.'

I laughed too. 'Just when he's shoved the thing up farther than ever before, he gets a terrible itch on the shoulder that he's compelled to scratch . . . I know.'

'Not you,' she disagreed. 'You'd find some clever way to poke a wedge under the rock.'

I loved her eccentric faith in me.

I rolled over suddenly, seizing her in a domineering hold. Then, as she stiffened, expecting something fierce, I kissed her so gently she was overcome. 'Sweetheart, you are the one person who will never need to worry about making friends with me.'

I smiled into her eyes. She closed them. Sometimes she hated me to see how deeply she felt. I kissed her once more, making a deliberately thorough job of it.

When she looked at me again her eyes were richly brown, and full of love. 'Why did you run away from the dinner table, Marcus?'

'I hate stories where dangerous bandits are grabbing women I care about as hostages.'

'Ah, the bandit was a sweetie!' she teased softly.

'I bet you handled him.'

'I have some practice with curmudgeons who think they know all about women!' she mocked, but she was stretching beneath my weight so invitingly I could hardly concentrate. Helena grew still. '*Do* you care about me?'

482

'I do.'

'Did you miss me?'

'Yes, my darling . . .'

As I set about the pleasant task of showing her how much, she murmured restively, 'It's starting to get light, Marcus. I ought to go.'

'I don't think I can allow that . . .'

For a moment longer I could tell she was unhappy. I pressed on, letting her know it would have to be all her decision if she wanted us to stop. Then she forgot about the proprieties of living in her brother's house, and was all mine again.

XXXI

Light had worked round a stout northern European shutter to reach my comfortably untidy bed. We had not been asleep long this time, since we were still locked close in a way that made sleep fairly difficult.

'Thank you, lady. I needed that.'

'So did I.' For a modest girl, she could be very direct. Having grown up among women whose shameless behaviour was rarely matched by honesty in bed, it always startled me.

I kissed her. 'What am I supposed to say to your brother?'

'Nothing. Why should you?' That was more like what I expected in a girl: totally unhelpful. She smiled. 'I love you, Marcus.'

'Thank you – but are you going to forgive me for not celebrating your birthday?' It now seemed safe to broach the issue.

Good timing, Falco: she wanted a fight about it, but her sense of fairness won. 'You didn't know it was my birthday.' She paused. 'Did you?'

'No! You should know that . . .' I leaned across, then, after a slight delay caused by her sweetness and nearness, I fetched out the amber necklace I had bought on the wineship from Dubnus the pedlar.

That reminded me – I had to do something about Dubnus. Why do crucial thoughts always interrupt at such inconvenient moments? I had been happily forgetting the Ubian scavenger, not to mention my plan to use him in my search for Veleda. With Helena Justina here in my arms, going into the barbarian forest was a prospect I now found unbearable.

I let Helena inspect the glimmering skein of beads, then fastened it around her neck. 'Suits you – especially with nothing else on.'

'That should cause a sensation when I'm next asked to a dinner party! It's lovely . . .' The sight of Helena wearing nothing but her birthday present encouraged me to further reconciliation, especially as I had managed to keep our physical union intact even when stretching sideways to my bedside table. 'Marcus, you ought to be exhausted – '

'I had a good night's sleep.'

'Are you afraid you might have forgotten how to do it?' she taunted wickedly, but accepting my attentions. Helena knew how to be gracious after she had received a well-chosen necklace of daunting cost. 'Or had you just forgotten how good it is?'

'Forgotten? Sweetheart, when you leave me pining, the problem is that I remember all too well.'

For some reason this manly reassurance worked on Helena so well she responded with what might have been a sob, though it was well muffled. 'Oh hold me – touch me – '

'Where?'

'There – anywhere – *everywhere*.'

Nearby in the house something fell over with a loud crash.

Something large. A statue of museum proportions, or an immense vase.

No one squealed. But after a second, we heard small desperate feet scampering.

'That's a child!' I was amazed.

'Oh Juno, I forgot – ' Helena reached the door first. The child was fleeing down the long corridor, leaving the giant shards behind. Unluckily for her, she had fled towards us.

What she had pushed over was a dramatic, two-handled vessel that was trying to pass for a middle-period Hellenic black-figure wine crater. It almost succeeded, but I had been trained by experts and I knew a fake, even when it was the kind of high-class fake that has better workmanship than the original (and costs more). It had been displayed on the plinth where I had once written *Falco was here* in the dust to annoy the tribune's servants. The crater had been big enough for a Treasury clerk to bury his savings in, and was probably the most expensive item Camillus Justinus possessed. The first piece in his lifetime collection, possibly.

'Stop! Stand still at once!'

Helena Justina could fix me in my tracks when she wanted to; she had no trouble with an eight-year-old. It was, however, the culprit who demanded: 'What are you doing there?' The rude defiance seemed familiar.

'Escaping from you!' I growled, for this must be the unwelcome soul I had observed snoring in Helena's bedroom earlier. I strode to the remains and picked up a curved fragment. Odysseus with a jutting spade beard was enjoying being tempted by some female; she had a tantalising ankle, but the rest of her was broken off.

I turned back angrily and surveyed the infant. She had a plain face and a petulant expression, with five or six thin little plaits tied together with a skinny rag on top of her head. My brain struggled to pin down which pot-bellied little disaster this was, and what relationship she bore to me. For it was one of ours all right. The gods only knew how she came to be in Upper Germany, but I could spot a member of the rampant Didius clan even before the wail of, 'I was only playing – it fell over on its own!'

She was hip-high, wearing a tunic that ought to have been decent, though she managed to have it hitched up so her bottom showed. That settled it; I knew her parentage all right. Augustinilla. An elaborate name, but a very straightforward personality – dumb insolence. She was my most hated sister Victorina's most objectionable child.

Victorina was the eldest in our family, the bane of my childhood and my worst social embarrassment since then. As a child she had been a tough little tyke with a constant runny nose and her loincloth at half-mast around her scabby knees. All the local mothers had warned their children not to play with us because Victorina was so violent; Victorina made them play with her anyway. When she grew up she played only with the boys. There were plenty. I could never understand why.

Of all the naughty children who could have walked in on my tender reunion with Helena, it had to be one of hers . . .

'Uncle Marcus has got nothing on!' The reason was that the tunic Helena had plunged into as she rushed to the door was mine. With a good amber necklace it looked highly incongruous, increasing the impression that a Bacchanalia had been occurring in my room. The child's accusing eyes went to Helena too, but there she had better sense than to comment. Presumably Augustinilla had witnessed at close quarters how Helena Justina had dealt with the wild bandit chief.

I took up an athletic pose; a mistake. Flashing the oiled muscles of a handsome physique may succeed in a sunlit stadium within sniff of the Mediterranean, but in a dim domestic corridor halfway across Europe being unclad only makes you feel cold. In a dark mood, I waited for Helena to utter the traditional imperative: 'She's your niece; you deal with her.'

She said it, and I issued the traditional rude reply.

Helena tried not to let the child see she was annoyed. 'You are the head of the Didius family, Marcus!'

'Purely notional.'

Being head of our family was so punishing that the real claimant to the title, my father, had abandoned his ancestors and completely changed his identity to avoid the ghastly task. Now the role fell to me. This explains why I was no longer on speaking terms with my papa the auctioneer. It may even explain why I myself had felt no qualms about entering a profession which most of Rome despises. I was used to being cursed and treated with contempt; my family had been doing that for years. And being a private informer had the great advantage of taking me undercover or right away from home.

Perhaps all families are the same. Perhaps the idea that paternal power holds sway was put about by a few hopeful lawmakers who had no sisters or daughters of their own.

'You brought her; you can have the joy of beating her,' I said coolly to Helena. I knew she would never strike a child.

I strode back inside my room. I felt depressed. Since we were not married there was no reason for Helena to take notice of my relatives; if she did, it boded the kind of serious pressure I had come to dread.

Sure enough, after a few rapid words, followed by a surprisingly meek reply from Augustinilla, Helena came in and began to explain: 'Your sister is in trouble – '

'When was Victorina ever out of it?'

'Hush, Marcus. *Women's* trouble.'

'That's a change; her trouble is usually men.'

I sighed and told her to spare me the details. Victorina had always been a moaner about her insides. Her wild life must have strained her system intolerably, most of all after her marriage to an inane plasterer who in his ability to father horrid children in rapid succession outshone every rodent in Rome. I would never wish surgery on anyone, however. Let alone those painful, rarely successful businesses with forceps and dilators that I vaguely knew were inflicted on women.

'Marcus, the children were being parcelled out to give your sister a chance of recovery, and in the lottery you won Augustinilla . . .' Some lottery – a blatant fix. 'No one knew where you were.' That had been deliberate.

'So they asked you! Augustinilla is the worst of the bunch. Couldn't Maia take her in?' Maia was my one half-likeable sister, which worked against her whenever problems were being handed out by the rest. Her amiable nature meant she was frequently leeched on even by me.

'Maia had no more room. And why should Maia always have to be the obliging one?'

'That sounds like Maia talking! I still don't understand. Why ever did you have to bring the nipper here?'

'What else could I do with her?' she snapped crossly. I had a few suggestions, but sense prevailed. Helena scowled. 'As a matter of fact, I didn't want to admit to other people that I was running around Europe after you.' She meant that she had refused to say she was storming off after we had had a fight.

I grinned at her. 'I love you when you're embarrassed!'

'Oh shut up. I'll take care of Augustinilla,' she assured me. 'You have enough to do. Justinus told me about your mission.'

I sat on the bed, cursing morosely. With one of Victorina's badly brought-up brats on hand, I would certainly not be staying around the house. Helena, of course, would be at home, like a decent Roman matron. Even my lady's wild flights of freedom would have to be constricted inside a military fort.

Helena squashed in beside me while she swapped my tunic for her own. As she pulled her gown over her head, I fondled her in a desultory way.

'Talking to you is like interviewing a centipede for a job as a masseur . . .' Her head popped out. 'How's your mission?' she enquired, checking up on me.

'I've made some progress.' It was my turn to start dressing and Helena's to make overtures, but she failed to take up the opportunity, even though I was repossessing my tunic as languidly as possible. Evidently I had had my fun. The passion which Augustinilla had interrupted would not be resumed today.

'How much progress, Marcus? Solved anything?'

'No. Just acquired new tasks – tracing a missing commander no one even knew about . . .'

'This ought to be an ideal location for tracking down suspects – a fort, I mean. You have a closed community.'

I laughed bitterly. 'Oh yes! Only an enclosed community of twelve thousand men! He's offended his whole legion, not to mention having a hostile wife, an interfering mistress, numerous creditors, people in the local community – '

'What people?' Helena demanded.

'He's been trying to trace the rebel I'm pursuing myself, for one thing.' She didn't ask for details about Civilis; Justinus must have filled her in last night. 'And he was apparently involved in wrangles over some military franchises.'

'That sounds like something that could easily have gone wrong if he mishandled it. Which franchises?' she asked curiously.

'Not sure. Well, pottery, for one thing.'

'Pottery?'

'Red tableware presumably.'

'For the army? Is there a lot at stake?'

'Think about it. In every legion six thousand rankers all needing cereal bowls and beakers, as well as cooking pots and serving platters for each ten-man tent. On top of that, full formal dinner services for the centurions and officers, plus the gods know what for the provincial governor's regal establishment. The legions reckon to do themselves nicely. Nothing will suffice for the army but the best-quality gloss. Samianware is strong, but it does break with rough handling, so there will always be repeat orders.'

'Does it have to be brought all the way from Italy or Gaul?'

'No. I hear there is a local industry.'

She seemed to change tack. 'Did you find your mother's comport?'

'Was it a comport she wanted?' I asked, innocently.

'You didn't buy one!'

'You guessed.'

'I bet you never even looked!'

'I looked all right. They were too expensive. Ma would never have wanted me to spend so much.'

'Marcus, you're dreadful! If there's a local factory,' Helena decided, 'you'd better take me to buy one for her. Then while I'm choosing your present, you can look around for clues.'

Helena Justina never wasted time. Left to my own devices I could have frittered away half a week helping her brother with his formal enquiry into the soldier's death. Instead, Justinus was on his own. I did manage to speak to him briefly on another subject, though, asking him to have the pedlar found and put in a holding cell.

'What has he done?'

'Leave that blank in the warrant. I just need ready access. It's for what he's *going* to do.'

By then Helena had enquired where the best ceramics

490

in Moguntiacum were to be had, and almost before I had managed to snatch breakfast I found myself escorting her sedan chair out of the fort. I did not entirely object. I still had to mention to Justinus that my niece had destroyed his wine crater, and ways of explaining the disaster were slow to suggest themselves.

Helena and I left the fort in the late morning. Autumn was making its presence felt: a chill still freshened the air several hours after dawn, and moisture clung to the sere grasses along the roadside. Spiders' webs were everywhere, making me blink whenever my horse passed under low branches. Helena looked out of her sedan chair laughing, only to brush away filaments that caught in her own eyelashes. Well, it was an excuse to stop, so I could help.

The pottery quarter at Moguntiacum was a lesser affair than the vast compound Xanthus and I had visited at Lugdunum. There were clear signs that the German enterprise was struggling to compete against its rivals in Gaul, who had backup from the original factory at Arretinum to lend them extra clout. Here the craftsmen were unsupported by the parent industry. Their goods on display were just as fine quality, yet the potters seemed surprised to see customers. The biggest workshop was actually boarded up.

We found one nearby that was open. It was owned by a certain Julius Mordanticus. Many provincial Celts adopt aristocratic names like Julius or Claudius. After all, if you are trying to advance yourself, who chooses to sound like a cheap artisan? Hardly a second-generation Romanised tribesman anywhere in the whole Empire answers to *Didius*, apart from one or two youngsters with extremely pretty mothers who live in towns which my elder brother Festus once passed through.

Helena had soon bought an impressive dish for Mother – at a price which made me wince only slightly, moreover. She then made friends with the potter, explained that she was visiting her brother the tribune, and soon led the conversation round to the legions in general. She was refined, gracious – and deeply interested in his livelihood. The

491

potter thought she was wonderful. So did I, but I fought it back. Once I had paid for his dish, I leaned against a wall, feeling surplus.

'I expect you do a lot of trade with the fort,' Helena said.

'Not as much as we'd like these days!' The potter was short, with a wide, pale face. When he talked he hardly moved the muscles of his mouth, which gave him a wooden appearance, but his eyes were intelligent. His remark to Helena had been forced out by strong feelings – his normal nature seemed more cautious. He wanted to let the military subject drop.

I hauled myself away from the wall as Helena chatted on. 'I confess I didn't know samian ceramics were made in Germany. Is your speciality confined to Moguntiacum, or does it go further afield, among the Treveri?'

'The whole area from Augusta Treverorum to the river produces samianware.'

'I should think you do well?' she suggested.

'A bit of a slump lately.'

'Yes, we were looking at your colleague's stall – the one that's boarded up, belonging to Julius Bruccius. Is that due to the depression, or is he off on an autumn holiday?'

'Bruccius? A business trip.' A shadow crossed his face.

I had a nasty premonition as I interposed: 'Would that have been to Lugdunum by any chance?'

Helena Justina immediately retired from the debate and seated herself quietly. The potter, too, had noticed my tone. 'I came through Lugdunum on my way out to Germany,' I explained to him levelly. I breathed slowly, screwing my mouth. 'Would Bruccius be a thickset man in his forties, travelling with a younger fellow who has red hair and a fine crop of warts?'

'His nephew. Sounds as if you saw them somewhere along the way.'

Julius Mordanticus already looked worried. His friends' overdue return must have prepared him for bad tidings, but possibly not as bad as this. I kept it brief. When I told him about the quarrel I had witnessed at Lugdunum, then how

I had later found the two bodies, he cried out in protest and covered his face.

Helena brought him a wicker chair. We sat him in it and I stood with one hand on his shoulder while he struggled to accept my news.

XXXII

'*Tiw!*' He spat out the Celtic name for Mars. 'Bruccius and his nephew murdered in Gaul . . .'

'I'm sorry,' I said. 'It's not much help, but there was a centurion at the fort who was going into Cavillonum to report the bodies to a local magistrate – he could tell you who is in charge and what transpired. The magistrate ought to have arranged funerals, for one thing. When Helena and I go back I'll find the centurion and send him here to speak to you. His name is Helvetius.' Julius Mordanticus nodded dully. I had been talking in order to give him time to compose himself. Now that he seemed calmer I asked carefully, 'Have you any idea who might be behind the deaths?'

He answered at once. 'Those self-seeking bastards at Lugdunum!'

I was not surprised; I had seen that Lugdunum had a great deal at stake in this industry. I felt obliged to warn him: 'Your accusation may be hard to prove.'

'If they show their faces here, we won't need proof!'

'I didn't hear that! Would you tell me what it's all about?'

Mordanticus had decided we were sympathetic; the whole story flooded out: 'Things are not easy nowadays. Trade has been bad. We rely on the military to keep us in business, but with all the recent troubles . . .' He tailed off for a moment. Helena and I avoided prying into local sympathies, but he sensed us holding back politely. 'Oh we were on the side of Rome, I can assure you. There is a close relationship between our town and the fort.' He spoke didactically, like a local leader who has to justify some peculiar festival by a neat reference to history. 'Keeping the legions here on the Rhenus is entirely in our interest. The Roman general Petilius Cerialis put it correctly when he arrived: Rome occupied this region at our forefathers' invitation when they were being harried by other tribes looking for new territory.

494

If Rome leaves, the tribes from east of the Rhenus will sweep in and take everything.' All the more so, presumably, because these tribes on the west bank were now regarded as collaborators.

'There is no love lost between you?' Helena prompted.

'No. Civilis and his sort may have sounded off in the name of liberty, but they care no more for us than their ancestors cared for our fathers and grandfathers. Civilis wants to be king over the richest nations in Europe. His people would like to leave the Batavian marshland and move into lusher pastures here. The only German independence they believe in is their own freedom to push in wherever they fancy.'

I thought this was one-sided. For one thing, my research in Rome among despatches about the rebellion had told me that Augusta Treverorum, the nearest tribal capital, had produced Julius Tutor and Julius Classicus, two of the most hotheaded rebel leaders after Civilis, so feelings ran higher here than our friend wanted to admit. But I didn't blame Mordanticus for taking the convenient view.

I changed the subject. 'What I saw happening at Lugdunum smacked of commerce rather than politics. I gather there is a strong professional rivalry between you and the Gauls. Is it all to do with your military trade?'

He nodded, albeit reluctantly. 'A big question mark hangs over who will win the contract for the new legions at the fort. Lugdunum itself is under threat from a big consortium in southern Gaul. Bruccius and I had been trying to persuade the new legate to re-award the franchise locally.'

'That legate was Florius Gracilis?'

'The same. The other man takes a much less prominent role.'

'Yes, his troops were recruited from the navy, and are rather diffident. So, your people held the franchise previously, when the Fourth and the Twenty-second were the legions based at the fort?'

'With reason! Our produce matches the quality of Italy or Gaul, and obviously distribution is easier.'

If there was suitable clay here, Rome would naturally

have encouraged a local industry, setting it up with official finance, no doubt, during the old campaigns under Drusus and Germanicus. Having established local production and persuaded people to make working for the legions their livelihood, it would then be hard to turn elsewhere. But Rome had never had much love of sentiment.

'How do your prices compete?' I asked.

He looked reproving. 'For a tender with the legions, our prices are set right! Anyway, we have no transportation costs. I refuse to believe Lugdunum can undercut our bid.'

'Unless they cheat! Was Gracilis sympathetic?'

'He never answered us directly. I felt our pleas were making no impression on the man.'

I frowned. 'Had he been got at?' Mordanticus shrugged. He was the kind of ultra-cautious businessman who never commits himself to speaking ill of those he may be forced to deal with at a later date. It looked to me as if he would have to take a more robust line. 'Let's face it, Mordanticus,' I insisted. 'Florius Gracilis would have come out through Gaul this spring by the same route that I took. He has a young wife who probably wanted new dinner-party dishes and would have dragged him to the factory site at Lugdunum. He could easily have been nobbled by your rivals before he even arrived here. You know it, don't you? The big boys at Lugdunum had stitched the legate up.'

Without directly answering, Mordanticus said, 'The potters here decided to make a last effort to sort things out, and Bruccius was elected spokesman for all of us. We sent him over to Lugdunum to try and reach a compromise. There's business for everyone. Those bullies in Lugdunum are just greedy. They already have a roaring trade in Gaul, all the legionary orders for Britain, plus Spain. They export from their southern ports all round the Ligurian Gulf and the Balearic Coast.' He spoke like a man who had eyed up the commercial possibilities carefully himself. 'They were always bitter that we were right here on the spot. After the rebellion, they saw their chance to muscle in.'

'So, it seems likely that Bruccius and his nephew did what they could there, but received no help. Things looked to me on the verge of violence, but your friends showed no physical damage when I saw them having supper the night they were killed. They must have given up on the Lugdunum mob, and were coming home with the bad news. Mind you,' I said thoughtfully, 'it means the question of who gets the franchise cannot be settled yet.'

'Why do you say that?' enquired Helena.

'No point murdering two people if Lugdunum felt confident the future trade was theirs. It's my belief the potters from Gaul felt Bruccius could be far too persuasive. With the Rhine legions right on his doorstep and the relevant legate within daily reach, he and his colleagues could pose a serious threat. That was why Lugdunum wiped him out. Somebody tracked him and the nephew far enough to deter any magistrates from making a connection, and then killed them in a spot where they might never be identified at all.'

'But why?' asked the potter. 'It still leaves plenty of us here.'

'Mordanticus, for the oldest motive in the world! Killing two of your number – or better still, having them totally disappear – will intimidate the rest.'

'No chance!' Mordanticus declared with a set face. 'We shall never give up, or let them get away with it!'

'You're a strong-willed man, but I warn you, some people will soon quaver at bullying. Don't forget there are potters with wives who don't want to be widows. Potters worried about the fate of large families if their breadwinner vanishes. Potters who just feel life has more to offer than a long-drawn-out feud which they may never win.'

'It's criminal!' raged Helena. 'Rome shouldn't even appear to sanction business methods of this type. The legate ought to show his disapproval by barring Lugdunum completely, then awarding to Moguntiacum every franchise that's available!'

I smiled at her for becoming so passionate. 'From what I've heard about Florius Gracilis, we can't rely on him for a high moral tone. I know he's desperately short of cash.'

'You mean he's taking bribes?' Helena's parents' attempts to give her a sheltered life had been partially successful.

But since meeting me she had learned enough not to be surprised at any suggestion. 'Is Gracilis *corrupt*, Falco?'

'That would be a grave charge. I'm not making it.' Not at this stage, anyway. I turned to the potter. 'Julius Mordanticus, I work for the Emperor. Your problems ought not to be my business, but they may overlap with what I came to do.'

'Which is what?' he asked curiously.

I saw no reason to hide the truth. 'Principally, to liaise with Civilis. His current whereabouts are unknown, but I believe the legate may be searching for him. On the other hand, Gracilis could have gone after Veleda, the Bructian prophetess.'

'If he has crossed the river, he's a fool!' Mordanticus looked at me as if I was mad merely for suggesting it.

'Don't say that. I may soon have to cross the river myself.'

'You're in for a wild time, then. And I should say it's death for Gracilis.'

'He may be travelling incognito.'

'A Roman official is pleading to be spotted. Is this something to do with the franchises?' Mordanticus demanded, single-mindedly.

'No, it's all about political glory for Florius Gracilis. But it means you and I have a shared interest. I don't like to make promises, but if I ever run across him I may well find an opportunity to discuss your franchise problem, and I may just make him believe that I am speaking for Vespasian.' For some reason, the Emperor's name carried weight. In a town that could compliment Nero on a civic column I should have expected it. Mordanticus looked as grateful as if I was signing his precious pots contract myself. 'Can you help me to arrange a meeting, Mordanticus? Do you know anything about the legate's recent movements, or even where I might find Julius Civilis himself?'

The potter shook his head, but promised to make enquiries. He still looked dazed. We left him to break the news of what had happened to his two colleagues. I did not envy him. He had told me there were young families involved.

XXXIII

I took Helena Justina to see the Jupiter Column so that I could talk to her in privacy. At least, that was my excuse.

We walked solemnly round, pretending to admire the four-sided obelisk which had been set up by two ingratiating financiers on behalf of the local community. It was a decent enough monument, if you like salutations to Nero. It pictured the usual plaques of Olympian deities: Romulus and Remus showing that having a peculiar mother need not hold a man back; Hercules doing his demigodly stuff with his usual hairy panache; and Castor and Pollux watering their horses, one each side of the column as if they were not on speaking terms. Up aloft stood a huge bronze of Jupiter Best and Greatest, all beard and big sandals, and wielding an extremely snappy thunderbolt that would be a hit at any fashionable soirée. The location of this edifice was too public for me to grab Helena in a clinch, though she knew that had been in my mind. I thought she looked disappointed. Since it was at least three hours since I had last touched her, I was too.

'I'll have to row you down the river with a picnic,' I murmured.

'Juno! Is that safe?'

'All right, I admit Germany isn't the place to come to at the moment if you fancy a quiet autumn cruise.'

'But *you* are going downriver, aren't you?' She asked it in an intensely level voice, which I recognised as anxiety.

'Looks as if I shall have to, my love.' She was upset. I hated that.

I had put Helena in a quandary. She never tried to dissuade me from work. For one thing, she was keen for me to earn enough money to buy myself into the middle rank so that we could be married without a scandal. To achieve that I needed four hundred thousand sesterces –

an outrageous sum for a dusty lad from the Aventine. The kind of cash I could earn only by doing something illegal (which, of course, I could *never* contemplate) or something dangerous.

'Anyway,' she said brightly, 'you came out here on political business, but you seem to have stumbled into a straightforward ceramics war.'

'It looks like that.'

Helena laughed. 'When you agree so meekly I usually discover you mean the opposite.'

'True. I think the ceramics troubles are an incidental problem.' However, if I could help out the potters while achieving my own ends, I would. 'These potters have found themselves facing the usual administrative mess. The tendering process has been bungled by an idiot who is paid enough by the state to know better. It goes on everywhere. To have Florius Gracilis involved in that, and also poking his nose into what Vespasian sent me out here to negotiate with Civilis, is just my hard luck.'

But the last thing I wanted if I was going into a danger area was some senatorial buffoon who had shown himself unfit to handle even a routine kitchenware contract travelling the same route. Especially if, as now seemed likely, he reached the trouble spot ahead of me and started blundering about, making tribal sensitivities far worse.

'Do you ever have good luck, Marcus?'

'Only the day I met you.'

She ignored that. 'You were talking about Civilis. How do you intend to find him?'

'Something will turn up.'

'And what about the priestess?'

'Veleda?' I grinned. 'Justinus told you that one too, eh?'

'Sounds like another widow in Veii story,' Helena grumbled sarcastically.

'That's all right, then; I can handle her.'

Helena Justina called me a philandering gigolo; I told her she was a cynical witch with no concept of trust or loyalty; she thwacked me with the heavy end of her beaded stole; I trapped her against the column's plinth and kissed her until I had her more or less subdued and myself highly excited.

'I will not ask,' she said when I sadly released her before our sophisticated Roman behaviour caused a public outcry, 'what your plans are for discovering the fate of the legate from Vetera. I know he disappeared somewhere on the far side of the river.'

'He was being forwarded to Veleda as a goodwill gift.'

Helena shuddered. 'So that definitely means you have to journey into Germania Libera?'

'I won't go if you don't want me to.'

Her serious expression became even more intense. 'Don't say that – don't ever say it – unless you really mean it, Marcus.'

I always had to be straight with Helena. 'All right, I'll promise I won't go if I can solve the puzzle in any other way.'

'Oh you'll go,' she answered. 'You'll go, and you'll solve it and that ought to provide some comfort for the poor man's family at least. It's impossible, therefore, for me even to try to veto your trip.'

I could not have cared less for the feelings of the family of Munius Lupercus, who had been a rich senator in a career posting and who was probably as objectionable as the rest of that type. But when Helena spoke with such certainty I could never dispute the issue, so I kissed her again and took her home instead.

At the fort we found my niece Augustinilla terrorising the sentries at the Praetorian Gate. Luckily, they were so relieved to be rescued that they let me carry her off under one arm while she screamed abuse at all of us.

XXXIV

The rest of the day passed quietly. Justinus had found out about his broken urn, and his reaction was to disappear from the house. He was deeply annoyed, but too polite to say so.

'That brother of yours is going to spend his life being put upon.'

'I thought he was making his feelings clearly felt!' Helena was the same type, another vanisher when upset.

Before dinner I made Augustinilla go up to the tribune and apologise. Since no one had ever made her apologise for anything before, she went through it with a fresh pathos that worked on him in the same way as the distressed puppy he had rescued. While she gazed at him with adoring eyes, his protective urge rose. It was Augustinilla's first experience of a rich young man in an impressive uniform; I could already see her mother coming out in her.

Schoolgirl passions apart, I reckoned Camillus Justinus, with his quiet looks and reserved manner, could wreak more havoc than he knew. Women like someone deep. Someone sensitive. (Someone who looks as if he will pay large bills without arguing.) Justinus gave the impression he needed a nice girl with a generous attitude to bring him out of himself. Back in Rome, if we were to put those thoughtful brown eyes around a few dinner parties, he might find nice girls – and equally helpful older women – bringing him out of himself three times every week.

At Moguntiacum he only had to avoid an eight-year-old who had convinced herself he looked like a young Apollo. So far, Augustinilla was too much in awe of his status to start writing his name on walls. By the time she plucked up courage to leave lovelorn notes beside his breakfast bowl, the European winter would have frozen all the ink and spared him that.

The next day began with two messages: the legate's mistress said her servants thought Gracilis had been frequenting the company of potters. And the potter was telling me there was a mistress in the case.

'This is all pleasingly circular!' I murmured to myself.

I assumed the mistress was telling me about the potters at Moguntiacum. The potter, however, meant a *different* mistress – his message stated that. I sent Julia Fortunata a politely grateful letter to say I would follow up her information when I could. Mordanticus seemed the best bet for a visit.

Before I went I looked out the centurion Helvetius, whom I had last seen near Cavillonum. He was easy to locate, bawling orders wearily as he tried to drill the ham-fisted, bandy-legged, splay-footed, pigeon-brained band of ugly-mushed recruits whom I had seen him marching through Gaul. (His own descriptions.) It was his task to teach these ideal specimens how to run, ride, swim, vault, wrestle, fence, throw javelins, cut turves, build walls, plant palisades, aim catapults, form a testudo, love Rome, hate dishonour, and recognise the enemy: 'Blue skin, red hair, checked trousers, lots of noise, and they're the ones hurling missiles at your heads!' He had to weed out the lads who had cheated on the eye test and relocate them as hospital orderlies. He had to discover who couldn't count, or write, or understand Latin, then either teach them or send them home. He had to nurse them all through crying for their girlfriends, or their mothers, or their ship (the First Adiutrix was still taking navy cast-offs) or their favourite goat (second sons from farms had always formed the backbone of the legions). He had to keep them sober and keep them from deserting; he had to teach them table manners and help them write their wills. So far he had just managed to harry them into forming straight lines in three ranks.

Helvetius gladly abandoned this depressing schedule and took time to talk to me.

'Didius Falco.'

'I remember you.'

'Thanks! I like to believe I have an impressive personality.'

It could only have been our first meeting at the side of the ditch that he recalled so piquantly. We spent a few moments recollecting it. 'That's why I want to see you.'

'I guessed as much!'

He was one of the impassive breed. Long years of service had taught him to expect the worst, and that nothing was ever worth getting excited about. He had very dark brown eyes, as if his origin was southern, and a face like an ostler's old rubbing-down cloth: deeply creased, stiff with use, and worn to a shine. His air of disillusionment was as weathered as his features. He looked a sound, utterly reliable officer.

I told him that the tribune Camillus had agreed he could be excused normal duties for a spot of goodwill effort in the local community. Helvetius was happy to visit the potter, so I took him out to the factory area with me.

It was another chilly morning, though a pallid sun was trying to burn away the mist. The changing season added to my sense of urgency. I explained to Helvetius that I would probably need to go across the river soon, and that I wanted to get the journey over before winter set in. The last thing I needed to face was being stuck in barbarian territory when the European snows came down.

'Bad enough at any time,' he said grimly.

'Have you done it?'

He didn't answer immediately. 'Only when some daft tribune fancied a boar-hunt in a more exciting locality.' Not Camillus Justinus, presumably. No one would call *him* daft.

'Naturally a young gent in senatorial stripes doesn't want to risk the *real* excitement of leaving his escort behind . . . Did you meet any trouble over there?'

'No, but you have the distinct feeling that you're lucky to reach home again without running into some liveliness.'

'Some of us have a suspicion the Fourteenth's legate may have gone across.'

'Gracilis? Whatever for?'

'Searching for Civilis – or Veleda, possibly.'

Again there was a slight silence. 'Didn't think he was the type.'

'What type would you call him, then?' I asked.

Helvetius, who was a true centurion, only chuckled into his beard, which was a richly curling military one. 'He's a legate, Falco. The same horrible type as them all.'

Just before we reached the potteries our conversation returned warily to the two dead men. Helvetius asked my particular interest. I described how I had been drawn in by seeing the quarrel at Lugdunum. He smiled slightly.

I wondered why he was curious. His face set, with a stillness that implied his mind was somewhere else – somewhere else by a long way. After yet another pause, however, just when I thought he had no comment, he suddenly spoke: 'I said nothing when we came across the bodies, because I didn't know you, Falco. But I had seen the men before, alive, myself.'

'Where was that?'

'Same as you: Lugdunum.'

'Were you there on official business?'

'Should have been. The army can be efficient! Our commander had a brainstorm and made my one journey serve two – well, three – purposes: home leave, recruiting manpower, and then a site visit to check out the ceramics tenderers. That was the plan, anyway.'

'So what happened?' I could guess.

'I turned up, but taking notes about suppliers was a waste of time. His Excellency Gracilis had been there before me and had swept up the whole business himself on behalf of all the legions in Upper and Lower Germany.'

'Fancy!' I marvelled. 'Some responsibility!'

'Some haul, if he was on the take!' Helvetius must have drawn his own conclusions.

'Careful, centurion! And the two local potters?'

'Like you, I saw them there having a right barney.'

'In a crowd?'

'No, just with a sneering beanpole and a couple of hangers-on. I spotted Lanky later as well.'

'Oh?'

'On the road. The day before we found the stiffs in the ditch.'

Now that was a detail I found most interesting. I remembered the sneering Gaul, but I must have missed him while travelling. Things looked black for Florius Gracilis. I told Helvetius we would keep this to ourselves for the time being. He looked at me askance. 'Were you sent out here to compile a dossier on graft?'

It was beginning to look that way.

At the pottery I made the introductions, then left Helvetius to discuss how he had reported the deaths at Cavillonum. There hadn't been much interest from the magistrate, needless to say. Helvetius was sufficiently discreet to disguise that while speaking to the dead men's friend, but I could tell what must have happened – and not happened – from his tone.

I left them together, still talking over Bruccius and his nephew, while I roamed around yearningly looking at samianware. When Mordanticus came out he asked whether anything particular had caught my eye.

'All of it! You create a stylish platter.' This was not mere ingratiation: his pottery was fired with a satisfying colour; it had tasteful patterns, a pleasing gloss, and a good balance in the hand. 'I'd set myself up with a decent dinner service, but the problem is a distinct lack of collateral.'

'How's that? I assumed you had a rich girlfriend!' The way he spoke made the joke acceptable even to a touchy swine like me.

For once I went along with it. 'Ah, it's her father who owns the lush estates on the Alban hills. If you were him, would you let the fruits of your vintage pass into the grip of a lout like me?' Besides, I had my pride.

It was not simply the hope of possessing Helena that drove me into these mad missions for the Emperor. I had a dream of one day living without squalor. Living in my own quiet house – a house surrounded by vine-covered walkways, luxurious in space, and full of light to read by. A house where I could age an amphora of decent wine at the right temperature, then drink it philosophising with my friend Petronius Longus beside a maplewood table laid with Spanish linen — and, maybe, samian winecups, if we were tired of my chased bronzes with the hunting scenes and my gold-flecked Phoenician glass . . .

I dragged the conversation to more useful gossip. 'Thanks for your message. What's this about a woman? Julia Fortunata is going to be put out if Gracilis has been two-timing her — not to mention the rumpus he can expect from the tight-buttocked little wife!'

'Well, I don't know anything definite . . .' Mordanticus looked embarrassed. It was pleasant to witness how respectfully the provinces regarded Rome: he was almost ashamed to confess that one of our high-ranking officials had let down the Roman moral code. 'I hate to destroy the man's character — '

'No need for you to end up in court on a slander charge,' I prompted. 'Just tell me what you've found out, and I'll draw the defamatory conclusions for myself.'

'Well, one of my colleagues was once asked how Florius Gracilis could contact a woman called Claudia Sacrata.'

'Is that significant? Should I have heard of her?'

Again he looked decidedly awkward. 'She is a Ubian, from Colonia Agrippinensium.' He studied a beaker as if he had just noticed that its handle was affixed crookedly. 'Your general Petilius Cerialis was supposed to have had an intrigue with her.'

'Ah!'

I had an impression of Cerialis; so far women did not come into it. In Britain he had commanded the Ninth Hispana legion. When the Boudiccan Revolt flared, he had made a desperate dash to help but was ambushed by the tribes in a forest — meaning he must have been rushing along without proper scouts ahead of him. Petilius lost a large contingent of his men and only just escaped with a few dregs of cavalry. The remnants of the Ninth took part in the final battle against the Queen, though unlike the Fourteenth and the Twentieth they were not honoured by Nero afterwards. By all accounts, the general's more recent

507

campaign to recapture Germany from Civilis had featured similar ill-considered incidents, from which the general himself had somehow escaped – always in time to take part in the winning engagements, and always keeping his good reputation intact.

I said with a deadpan expression, 'A Ubian temptress was not widely featured in the official accounts of his victories.' Perhaps because Petilius Cerialis wrote the accounts himself.

Mordanticus realised I was teasing, but did not quite know how to react. 'There was probably nothing in it . . .'

'I'm disappointed! But why should our own Florius Gracilis be visiting this beauty? Consoling her loneliness, now that Cerialis has popped off to Britain? I suppose he couldn't have taken her. Installing his Ubian bundle in the provincial governor's palace in Londinium would soon get back to Rome and cause a stir.' Having won his province, Petilius Cerialis would now be looking forward to a consulship. He was related to the Emperor – through *marriage* – and the Emperor was widely known to hold strictly old-fashioned views. Vespasian himself kept a long-term mistress now that he was a widower, but people seeking appointments from him dared not risk such a luxury. 'Do the Ubians have close links with the Batavians?'

Julius Mordanticus was writhing with unhappiness. 'That's difficult to answer. Some allies of Civilis punished the Ubians very heavily for their pro-Roman sympathies, but by the end some of them were battling against the Romans with him . . .'

'A right tangle! Did Claudia Sacrata know Civilis?'

'Possibly. He has relations who were living in Colonia Agrippinensium.'

'Which could explain why Gracilis has gone to see her. He knows this woman has had connections with high political circles on both sides, so she might know where Civilis can be found?'

'Perhaps.'

'Alternatively,' I suggested more facetiously, 'not content with the official mistress he brought from Rome, our trusty legate Florius Gracilis is looking for an *unofficial* one – and Claudia Sacrata fits. Perhaps a liaison with Claudia Sacrata is the traditional perk for men in purple cloaks on tours of duty in Germany? Perhaps her address is handed on with their initial briefing reports. Which only leaves one question. Mordanticus: since I'm just a low weevil, who will give Claudia Sacrata's address to *me*?'

The potter was not prepared to comment on her status; but he told me where to find the woman.

That only left one other question: how could I explain to Helena Justina that I was disappearing to visit a general's courtesan?

PART FOUR:
A TRIP DOWN THE RHENUS

FROM UPPER GERMANY TO VETERA
October-November, AD 71

'Their commander . . . was saved by a mistake on the part
of the enemy, who made haste to tow away the flagship,
thinking that the commander was aboard. Cerialis in fact
spent the night elsewhere (according to general belief at the
time, because of an intrigue with a Ubian woman called
Claudia Sacrata).'

Tacitus, *Histories*

XXXV

It caused less strain than I feared. That was because Helena decreed Colonia Agrippinensium to be a place she was dying to see. I went along with it, for reasons of my own.

My hope of some peace with Helena was thwarted. First her brother insisted that we take Augustinilla. Apparently he was reluctant to be left on his own at the fort with a lovesick little maid.

Then Xanthus eagerly joined the excursion. He was still suffering a serious reaction from having killed the soldier. He said it had made him think seriously about life. He liked Germany, and wanted to settle there – he could see plenty of scope for his hairdressing skills. Moguntiacum was too military, however, so he wanted to look for another town which might offer a more refined welcome to an ambitious former imperial slave. I told him flatly he could not come with me beyond Colonia, but he said that suited him.

We had the tribune's dog, too. It had bitten an armourer, so had to be removed from the fort fast.

So much for a gentle river cruise alone with my girl.

Despite the entourage, shipping north on an official fleet vessel was a joy: past jutting crags and green pastures, small quays and local moorings, outcrops of rocks and rapids, and slanting upland terraces where the new wine industry was establishing its vineyards for light, pleasant wines, some of which we tasted as we went. We dreamed on deck, watching the ducks floating downstream among occasional spars of driftwood, then heaving themselves out of the water to fly back and start again. Low barges, laden with every conceivable item, sailed down in twos or threes, then were rowed or dragged back the other way. It seemed a satisfying life. What was more, the merchants who plied their trade along this waterway were visibly affluent. With Helena beside me,

513

I could have stayed for ever, becoming a happy river bum and never going home.

'What's in your mighty baggage pack?' Helena demanded.

'Scrolls to read.'

'Poetry?'

'History.'

'As in Thucydides?'

'As in Great Cock-ups of Modern Times.'

Helena glanced round to see if Augustinilla was in earshot of this irreverence, but saw my niece was too busy trying to find ways of falling off the boat. She laughed. 'Why the interest?'

'Research for my various projects here. An archivist in Rome copied out some despatches about the rebellion for me.'

Now that Helena knew what I was carrying downriver, there was no point in hiding it. I excavated the basket, and was soon absorbed in Rome's sorry exploits while trying to dislodge Civilis. The more I read about the campaign, the more I cringed.

All too soon we had surged past the conjunction with the River Mosella at Castrum ad Confluentes, experienced Bingium and Bonna (both still heavily scarred and burnt, but with new ridge-poles rising), and reached our goal.

Colonia Claudia Ara Agrippinensium tried hard to live up to its overpowering titles. Founded by Agrippa (as Ara Ubiorum), it was renamed after herself by his daughter, the forceful wife of Germanicus whose domineering reputation still had the power to make brave men feel queasy. It was the officially sanctioned shrine of the Ubii and the provincial capital of Lower Germany. It also boasted the main Roman tollpost on the river and the headquarters of Rome's Rhenus fleet, guarded by a small fort.

A well-laid out, opulent provincial city served by a military-built aqueduct and home to a large colony of retired veteran soldiers, Colonia's close links with Rome had ensured there were difficult decisions during the rebellion. At first the citizens had stayed loyal to the Empire, refusing to join Civilis and placing his son under arrest – though in 'honourable' custody, in case matters swung. Only when the situation became desperate were these cautious worthies forced to heed the call from their fellow-tribesmen to acknowledge their German heritage, and even then their alliance with the freedom fighters had its equivocal aspects. They managed to negotiate their own terms with Civilis and Veleda, since by then they were holding more of the Batavian's relations under house arrest, and they were wealthy enough to send the forest priestess the kind of gifts that pacify. Careful juggling helped the town to survive without being sacked by either side. Then, as soon as Petilius Cerialis began to make headway, the good folk hereabouts appealed to him for rescue and allied themselves with Rome again.

They knew how to run their municipal affairs with grace. I felt that it was a safe place to bring Helena.

We arrived fairly early in the day. I dumped my party in a lodging-house near the prefecture, telling Xanthus he was the man in charge. Helena would soon disabuse him.

Refreshed by the river trip, I went out to make enquiries about Claudia Sacrata. I had promised Helena not to dally, but the door I chose to knock on turned out to belong to the general's ladyfriend. For her servant, a male Roman face was enough of a credential, so although I merely asked for an appointment, he whisked me in to see her straight away.

This was a modest town house. Its provincial decorator had tried hard, but had been stuck with painting frescos of what he knew. Jason discovered the Golden Fleece beneath a holly-bush in a thunderstorm. Battle scenes rolled darkly below a frieze that only came to life when crossed by a skein of Rhineland wild geese. Venus, in the local Ubian costume of high-necked dress and wimple, was wooed by Mars in a Celtic felt coat. She looked like a market-trader, and he seemed a shy, rather paunchy chap.

The servant took me to a reception room. I was met by bright colours and gigantic couches with hugely padded cushions where a tired man could flop and forget his troubles. The reds were too earthy, the stripes too broad, the tassels far too fat. The total effect was reassuringly vulgar. The men who came here relied on strong-minded wives for taste, and they probably never noticed interior-design effects. They required somewhere clean and comfortable pervaded by scents of beeswax polish and gently stewing broth, somewhere which held basic recollections of their childhoods, in Italy. It was the kind of house where the bread would be served in roughly chopped hunks that tasted like ambrosia infused with hazelnuts. The music would be dreadful, but people would be laughing and talking so loudly they would not care . . .

I found Claudia Sacrata seated in a long chair, as if she was expecting visitors. She was no ravishing seductress, but a dumpy, middle-aged woman whose bosom was trussed so firmly it might have acted as a serving tray. Her grooming was careful. She wore a Roman dress in oatmeal and ochre, with fastidiously folded pleats on her shoulders where her stole was pinned with a large Indian ruby brooch that blazed *Present from a Man!* In appearance she reminded me of a slightly old-fashioned, good-hearted aunt tricked out to make a show in front of the neighbours at a Floralia parade.

'Come in, dear. What can I do for you?' The question could have been simple politeness . . . or a commercial bid.

I played everything straight. 'My name is Marcus Didius Falco; I am a government agent. I should be grateful if you would answer a few questions.'

'Certainly.' Of course, it didn't guarantee she would answer them truthfully.

'Thank you. I hope you don't mind if I start with you? You are Claudia Sacrata, and you keep a welcoming house. Do you live with your mother?' We both understood this euphemistic phrase.

'My sister,' she corrected. It was the same flimsy veil of respectability, though I noticed no chaperone ever appeared at our interview.

I plunged straight in: 'I believe you once shared the confidence of His Excellency Cerialis?'

'That's right, dear.' She was the type who liked to catch

516

people out by admitting the unthinkable. Her shrewd eyes watched me while she tried to deduce what I wanted.

'I need to acquire some sensitive information, and it's difficult finding people I can trust.'

'Did my general send you?'

'No. This is nothing to do with him.'

The atmosphere changed. She knew I was investigating someone; if it had been His Excellency, she had intended to slap me down. Now she saw her most notable client was in the clear; her tone became proprietary. 'I don't mind talking about Cerialis.' She gestured me to a couch. 'Make yourself more at home . . .' Home was never like this.

She rang a bell for a servant, a nippy lad who seemed to have answered quite a few bells in his time. After surveying me coyly, she gushed, 'A hot-spiced-wine man, I should say!' Outside my own home I hate the stuff. To encourage good relations, I agreed to be a man who drank hot spiced wine.

It was a rich liquor, served in magnificent cups, with the spices rather overdone. A consoling warmth flooded my stomach, then seeped into my nervous system making me feel happy and safe, even when Claudia Sacrata cooed 'Tell me all about it!', which was supposed to be my line.

'No, you tell me,' I smiled, implying that women who knew what they were doing had tried to undermine me before. 'We were discussing Petilius Cerialis.'

'A very pleasant gentleman.'

'Bit of a reputation as a hothead?'

'In what way?' she simpered.

'The military way, for instance.'

'Why do you think that?'

This was a silly dance. However, I deduced that if I wanted information, talking about her precious Cerialis was the price I had to pay. 'I've been reading about his battle at Augusta Treverorum, for one thing.' I was sipping my hefty winecup as demurely as I could. If Cerialis wore his epaulettes in the usual style, he had bored everybody silly with the story of his big fight.

Claudia Sacrata posed and considered. 'People did say at the time that he made mistakes.'

'Well, you can look at it two ways,' I conceded, playing the friendly type. There was, in fact, only one way *I* could look at it. Petilius Cerialis had stupidly allowed his opponents to concentrate in large numbers while he had been awaiting reinforcements. That had been dangerous enough. His famous engagement was a shambles, too. Cerialis had built his camp on the opposite bank of the river from the town. The enemy arrived very early in the morning, crept up from several directions, and burst into the camp, throwing all into confusion.

'I understood,' Claudia defended him with solid loyalty, 'that it was only the general's brave action that saved the situation.' So that was his story.

'Undoubtedly.' My work demands a shameless ability to lie. 'Cerialis rushed from his bed without body armour, to discover that his camp was in turmoil, his cavalry were fleeing, and the bridgehead had been taken. He grabbed the fugitives, turned them round, retook the bridge with great personal courage, then forced his way into the Roman camp and rallied his men. He salvaged everything and finished the day by destroying the enemy's headquarters instead of losing his own.'

Claudia Sacrata wagged her finger. 'So why are you sceptical?'

Because the other assessment was that our troops had been led pathetically; the enemy should never have been able to get so close undetected, the camp had been inadequately guarded, the sentries were asleep, and their commander had absented himself. Only the fact that the tribesmen had been intent on grabbing plunder had averted complete disaster from our dashing general.

I restrained my bitterness. 'Why was the general not sleeping in the camp that night?'

The lady responded calmly. 'That I can't say.'

'Did you know him at that point?'

'I met him later.' So even before their intrigue started, he had preferred the comforts of a private house.

'May I ask how your friendship came about?'

'Oh, he visited Colonia Agrippinensium.'

'Romantic story?' I grinned.

'Real life, dear.' I guessed she regarded selling sexual activity as no different from selling eggs.

'Tell me?'

'Why not? The general came to thank me for my part in undermining the enemy.'

'What had you done?' I imagined some brothel intrigue.

'Our city was looking for a way to re-establish its ties with Rome. The town councillors offered to hand over the wife and sister of Civilis, plus the daughter of one of the other chiefs, who had been kept here as securities. Then we tried something more useful. Civilis, still confident, was placing his hopes in his best forces, warriors from among the Chauci and Frisii, encamped not far from here. The men of our town invited them to a feast and plied them with lavish food and drink. Once they were all completely stupefied, they locked the doors and set fire to the hall.'

I tried not to display too much shock. 'A friendly Germanic custom?'

'It's not unknown.' The most chilling part was her matter-of-fact tone.

'So when Civilis learned that his crack troops had been burned alive, he fled north, and Petilius Cerialis rode gratefully into Colonia . . . But what was your part, Claudia?'

'I provided the food and drink for the feast.'

I put down my winecup.

'Claudia Sacrata, far be it from me to pry, but can you tell me something – ' This oddly comfortable yet insensitive woman was upsetting me. I studiously changed the subject. 'What's the true story about losing the general's flagship?'

She smiled and said nothing.

It had been another stupid incident. I told her what I already knew from my research. After an unsuccessful period of campaigning in northern Europe, where Civilis and the Batavians had engaged him in guerilla warfare around the marshes of their homeland and had seemed set to fend off Rome indefinitely, Petilius Cerialis had taken a breather (his favourite kind of action) and gone to inspect some new winter quarters at Novaesium and Bonna, intending to return north with a much-needed naval flotilla. Yet again discipline was poor; yet again his pickets were careless. One dark night, the Germans crept in, slashed the guy ropes, and wreaked havoc while our men were fumbling under their collapsed tents and running about the camp half dressed and terrified. They had no one to rally them, because, of course, yet again Cerialis had slipped off elsewhere.

'Then the enemy towed off the flagship, Julius Civilis believing the general to be aboard.'

'His mistake!' Claudia agreed purringly.

'Sleeping out of camp again?' I tried not to sound critical.

'Evidently.'

'With you, as people said?' I was having great trouble imagining this.

'You really can't expect me to answer that.'

'I see.' With her.

'You said your enquiries had nothing to do with Petilius, so why all these questions about past events?' I was pushing matters further than she liked now.

'I'm a sucker for lively background.' I was hoping my interest in Petilius might appear to threaten him, so that she would try to deflect me with the information I really wanted. But she was tougher than she seemed. Any impression of foolishness hid a shrewd business sense. 'What happened to the flagship in the end?'

'At daybreak the rebels all sailed away in the Roman ships. They towed the flagship into their own territory as a present for their priestess.'

'Veleda!' I let out a low whistle. 'So if Cerialis was with you that night, you saved his life.'

'Yes,' she agreed proudly.

'If he had been aboard –' As he should have been. ' – his fate would have been gruesome. The last Roman officer the rebels sent to Veleda has never been heard of since.'

'Terrible!' she agreed, with conventional sympathy.

'That's my mission,' I told her. 'He was a legionary legate.

520

I have to find out for the Emperor and his family what unkind fate befell him. I doubt you would ever have met this one; he was stationed at Vetera, a long distance from here – '

'Munius Lupercus?' She sounded surprised. 'Oh you're wrong there, dear,' declared the imperturbable Claudia. 'I knew Munius *very* well.'

XXXVI

I sighed inwardly, I tried to shift position on the cushions beneath me, but they gripped me with embarrassing suction. When Claudia Sacrata told a man to make himself comfortable, she didn't intend him to prise himself free without the aid of a building-yard fulcrum.

I had brought myself to the home of a woman who knew everyone. Names were dropped here like water drips around a fountain. Gossip was the common language. I was sitting, on an aching bottom, at the centre of a social spider's web which might be anchored to any point in Europe.

'You knew Lupercus?' I croaked. I hate to be repetitive, but I was in no condition for more sinuous oratory.

'Such a nice man. Very genuine. Very generous.'

'I'm sure! You have a wide circle of acquaintances.'

'Oh yes. Most of the boys from Rome pass through here at some time. I am famous,' stated Claudia complacently, 'for my hospitality.'

That was one word for it.

'A woman of influence!' I threw my next dice with a casual air. 'How are you on the incumbent of the legio Fourteenth Gemina?'

She seemed equal to anything. 'Would that be Priscus? Or the new one, Gracilis?' Apparently both had hung up their armour on her cloak-peg.

'The new man.'

'I've met him once or twice.'

'Nice man?' I hazarded before I could stop myself.

'Oh very!' She took it at face value, luckily. Her sense of humour – assuming she had one – would be jolly and obvious, rather than my twisted kind.

'Has Gracilis visited you recently?'

Whatever else he indulged in here – and it was best not to speculate – Gracilis must have been asking the same

522

questions as me. She answered with a knowing wink I could hardly tolerate: 'I believe he did!'

'I expect he had a good explanation for turning up here?'

She laughed. It sounded unattractive and I noticed she had several teeth missing. 'Something about a hunting trip . . .'

'That old line!'

'Oh he must have meant it, dear – a group of Gauls were taking him.'

Gauls? I already had my hands full with the German interest. This new complication was more than I liked while my brain was infused with aromatic wine.

'What was he after?' Apart from pipping me in the search for Civilis and Veleda.

'Wild boar, I believe.'

I tried a different tack. 'People at Moguntiacum are worried about what's happened to his bedchamber slave. Has Rusticus gone along on this Gallic safari to keep his master well groomed behind the spear?'

'There was no one like that with him.'

I decided not to ask any more about the Fourteenth's infernal legate. I would only find myself trying to track down some pitiful runaway slave who might simply have seen his master's absence from home as a chance to make a break for it.

I gave in, smiling. Claudia was pleased to see she had defeated me. So pleased that she condescended to add, 'The Gauls were paying for *everything*.'

I had to know. 'I hate to be pedantic, but you do mean they were treating Florius Gracilis to his visit here to you?'

She assented without speaking.

I had him now. If the Fourteenth Gemina's legate was being trailed around on an extended sweetener of this kind, Vespasian would swipe his name off the list of officials before anyone could blink.

'What sort of Gauls were they?'

'Potters,' said Claudia.

I wondered why she had chosen to inform on this client in particular. Germanic rivalry with Gaul? Annoyance at the blatant way her services had been offered for bribery? I decided it was the commercial dishonesty. Claudia being a businesswoman herself, she would naturally hate fraud.

'I won't embarrass you by prying further. Look, we were talking about Munius Lupercus. The war was a long time ago, and I'm struggling to find leads. I'm even faced with the prospect of going across the Rhenus to follow his route as a captive. Does your useful network of contacts extend to the other riverbank? You won't have met the prophetess – '

I should have known better. 'Veleda?' cried Claudia Sacrata. 'Oh I know her!'

A faint mood of exasperation coloured my tone: 'I thought she was incommunicado? I heard she lived above the tree-tops, and that even the ambassadors who went from Colonia to negotiate terms with her had to send messages via the men in her family.'

'That's right, dear.'

A dreadful thought struck me. 'Did you take part in the Colonia embassy?'

'Of course,' murmured Claudia. 'This is not Rome, Marcus Didius.' That was certainly true. German women obviously liked to be at the front of things. It was a terrifying concept to a traditional Roman boy. My upbringing was outraged – yet fascinated too. 'I have standing in Colonia, Marcus Didius. I am well known here.'

I could guess what ensured her prominence – the universal status badge: 'You are a wealthy woman?'

'My friends have been kind to me.' So she had creamed the tops off some handsome Forum bank accounts. 'I helped choose the presents for Veleda; I provided some of them. Then I fancied seeing foreign parts, so I travelled with the ambassadors.' She was as bad as Xanthus. The world must be full of intrepid idiots trying to catch some fatal strain of alien marsh fever.

'Let me guess . . .' I was grinning despite myself. 'The men might have had to follow the rules that preserve Veleda's sanctity; *you*, however, somehow wangled a woman-to-woman chat? I suppose the venerated wench has to pop down from the tower some time – to wash her face, let's say?' This arch description seemed to fit the discreet atmosphere of Claudia's house, where Jupiter, the guardian of strangers, must have his work cut out protecting people desperate to find a polite phrase for asking their way to the latrine.

'I did my best for her.' Claudia Sacrata looked sad. 'You can imagine the life the poor girl leads. No conversation; no society. The menfolk who guard her are a feeble lot. She was badly in need of a chin-wag, I can tell you. And before you say anything dear, I made a point of asking about Lupercus. I never forget my boys if I find a chance to do one of them a good turn.'

That angered me. 'A man's death in foreign territory is no subject for gossip! Was Lupercus someone you giggled over in the Bructian groves? Did she tell you what she'd done with him?'

'No,' replied Claudia crisply, as if I had impugned all womanhood.

'Not fit for civilised ears? What did she do – hang his head up for a lantern, sprinkle his blood on her private altar and stick his balls among the mistletoe?' Rome, horrified for once by practices even more barbaric than we could devise ourselves, had outlawed those rites in Gaul and Britain. But that gave no protection to anyone trapped outside our frontiers.

'She had not seen the man,' replied Claudia.

'He never reached the tower?'

'Something happened on the way.' *Something worse than what would have happened had he arrived?*

'What was it?'

'Veleda couldn't say.'

'She must have been lying.'

'Veleda had no reason to do that, dear.'

'Evidently a nice girl!' This time I allowed my irony to grate ferociously.

Claudia was looking at me with her mouth turned down.

When she spoke again, there was a hint of complaint: 'I've given you a great deal of my time, Marcus Didius.'

'I appreciate that. I'm finishing now. Just answer this: have you ever been in contact with Julius Civilis?'

'We met socially in the old days.'

'Where is he now?'

'Sorry, dear. I thought he went back to The Island?'

For the first time, her answer sounded disingenuous. I decided she knew something. I also realised that squeezing Claudia Sacrata once she had clammed up was too daunting for me. She looked like a loose ball of duck down, but her will was formidable. I had also run up against an unshakeable tribal clannishness.

It was hopeless, but I flogged on anyway. 'Civilis has disappeared from The Island. He could well have made his way south again, hoping to re-establish his old power base. I heard he was back among the Ubii and Treveri,' I started factually, 'and I feel it may be true. His family lived in Colonia.'

'That was when Civilis was attached to the Roman forts.'

'Maybe, but he knows this area. Any suggestions where I can make enquiries?'

'Sorry,' she repeated. I was one Roman who must have ceased to be a nice boy.

We were closing the interview. Claudia's good nature reasserted itself as she asked again if there was anything she could do for me. I told her I had a girlfriend waiting who believed I had just stepped out of doors for a basket of bread rolls.

'She'll be anxious!' Claudia reproved me prudishly. She provided comfort for married men away from home, but wrecking relationships on her doorstep was a proposition that deeply offended her. 'You must hurry back at once.' She led me to the door herself – a formal courtesy of the house. No doubt when she was letting out a general, she liked her neighbours to spot the purple. They would be less impressed by today's cheap visitor.

'So how do I find Veleda?' I asked. 'All I know is she lives among the Bructeri. They're a far-flung tribe.'

'I'm hopeless at geography. When I went we travelled by river.' She meant the River Lupia.

'And she lived in the forest?' I already knew, but facing it made me freeze. Veleda lived in the area all Rome hated to contemplate, where Roman hopes of controlling the eastern tribes had been obliterated so hideously. 'The Teutoburger forest? I wish it was anywhere but there!'

'You're thinking of Varus?' For a mad moment I thought she was about to tell me that Quinctilius Varus and all his three lost legions had been her boys. She was mature, but not *that* cheesy. 'The free Germans still boast about Arminius.' They would be doing that for a long time. Arminius was the chieftain who had destroyed Varus; who had liberated Germany from Roman control; and whom Civilis was now openly trying to emulate. 'Be careful, Marcus Didius.'

Claudia Sacrata spoke as if I needed a trepanning operation – a hole drilled in my head to relieve the pressure on my brain.

527

XXXVII

'You were out a long time,' grumbled Helena. I told her why. It seemed best, in case one of Claudia Sacrata's wide circle in Colonia later let slip the information. Helena decided I had vanished intentionally. 'And have you been drinking?'

'Had to be sociable. I declined the nibbles she usually serves to her Roman boys.'

'How restrained! You're not the salon type – did being sociable work?'

'I heard some lurid gossip. She confirmed that Florius Gracilis is running one step ahead of me in searching for the rebel leaders. He's also deep into selling favours, and disguising it as an autumn hunting trip. The only useful fact I suspect she knows – where I could look for Civilis – was the one thing she deliberately held back.'

'What happened to your persuasiveness?'

'Sweetheart, I have nothing to offer a woman who is used to being coerced by men with top-level public salaries.'

'You're slipping then!' said Helena, more sharply than usual. 'By the way, I fetched the bread myself. I realised you'd gone off somewhere working, and I thought you might forget.' She gave me a consoling wholegrain roll. I ate it gloomily. The effect on Claudia Sacrata's spiced wine was negligible. I still felt drunk, in the dire way that afflicts you when you are also in disgrace. 'Marcus, I've hired a Ubian waiting-woman to help me when you have to go away. She's a widow – the troubles, you know. She has a daughter the same age as Augustinilla. I'm hoping a little friend who has been brought up more strictly might be a good influence.'

I was not ready to think about going away. 'Good idea. I'll pay.'

'Can you afford it?'

'Yes.' She gave me one of her looks. She knew I meant no.

As if to confirm her information two small heads came round the door just then and stared at me. They were as plain-faced as each other, a well-browned bun with eyes like burnt raisins, and a round dollop of pale unleavened dough. They both looked like trouble. The one with the flaxen pigtails demanded of the dark one with the topknot, 'Is that him?' She had a faint lisp, a German accent, and about six times the intelligence of my niece.

'Either get out,' I growled, 'or come in properly.'

They came in, and stood half a stride away, jostling shoulders and giggling. I felt like a hippopotamus in a seedy menagerie – the one with the reputation for making unpredictable rushes at the bars.

'Are you the uncle who is an enquirer?'

'No, I'm the ogre who eats children. Who are you?'

'My name is Arminia.' I was not in the mood for infants who had been named after heroic enemies of Rome. Arminia and Augustinilla were still egging one another on to see if they could make me charge out of my cage. 'What are you enquiring about in Colonia, please?'

'State secret.' They both went off into shrieks.

'Don't listen to him,' decreed Augustinilla. 'My mother says he couldn't find his own belly button. Everyone in Rome knows Uncle Marcus is a *complete* fake.'

Looking highly superior they stalked off hand in hand.

'I see they've palled up well,' I commented to Helena. 'Clearly there are no ethnic barriers between horrid little girls. So, we now have not one uncontrollable schoolgirl underfoot, but two.'

'Oh Marcus, don't be such a pessimist.'

Things continued to deteriorate. Helena's brother Justinus arrived at our lodging-house. He would have been a welcome visitor, but he came about a week too soon. He was greeted madly by his little dog, who then ran in and peed on my boot.

Before leaving Justinus at the fort, we had arranged for him to follow us to Colonia, bringing with him the pedlar

Dubnus, whom I wanted to use as a guide among the Bructeri. He was only supposed to follow after trying to persuade his legate to release some troops to come across the river with me. Arranging the escort had been expected to delay him. I was startled, therefore, when he burst in on our first evening.

'What's this? Your ship must have rowed the whole distance at double stroke to bring you here so soon! Tribune, I hate surprises. They rarely mean good news.'

Justinus looked sheepish. 'A letter came for Helena. I thought I ought to bring it here as soon as possible.' He handed it over. Both she and I recognised the Palace parchment and seal. Justinus evidently expected her to break the wax eagerly, but she held it on her knee and looked morose. A similar expression was probably afflicting me. 'It caused quite a stir at the fort,' he protested, when he saw her ignoring it.

'Really?' enquired Helena, with her own brand of chilling disdain. 'I keep my correspondence private normally.'

'It's from Titus Caesar!'

'I can see that.'

She was putting on her stubborn face. In kindness to her brother I said, 'Helena has been advising him about a problem with his aged aunt.' She shot me a look that would have skinned a weasel.

'Ah . . .' Justinus could detect an atmosphere. He had the tact to believe my bitter joke. 'I'd better be off now, Marcus Didius. I need a bathe. We can talk properly another time. I'm staying at the Rhenus fleet fort.'

'Did you manage to get me an escort?'

'You've been assigned a centurion and twenty men. Rather inexperienced, I'm afraid, but it was the best I could do. I told my legate you were official, in fact I invited him to meet you, but if you're undercover for the Palace he prefers to stand aloof and let you get on with it.'

I preferred to stand aloof from this mission myself. 'Old-fashioned, eh?'

'Forays across into the east are not encouraged now-

adays.' He meant Rome was in enough trouble in the territory it held, without stirring up the eastern tribes.

'Suits me. I hate formalities. Thank him. I'm grateful for
any support. Did you bring the pedlar too?'

'Yes. I warn you, though, he's protesting volubly.'

'Don't worry. I came across Gaul with a chattering
barber. I can manage anything after that.'

Justinus kissed his sister and disappeared with alacrity.

We sat apart in silence. In the circumstances I thought it
was her turn to speak. Helena generally ignored whatever
I thought.

After a moment I muttered, 'I'd kiss you too, but it seems
inappropriate with a letter from the Emperor's son lying in
your lap.' She made no answer. I wished she would jump
up and burn the thing. I remonstrated steadily: 'Helena,
you had better open that document.' Refusing would make
the tension far worse, so she slowly broke the seal. 'Shall I
go out while you read it?'

'No.'

She was a fast reader. Besides, for a love letter it was
foolishly brief. She read with an expressionless face, then
rerolled it tightly, gripping the scroll in her clenched fist.

'That was quick.'

'More like an order for new boots,' she agreed.

'He's known as a poor public speaker, but a man in his
position ought to be able to prime a jobbing poet to scribble
a few hexameters to salute a lady . . . I would.'

'You,' murmured Helena, so quietly it scared me witless,
'would write the hexameters yourself.'

'For you I would.'

She was very still. There was nothing I could do for her.

'It would take me a few thousand lines,' I warbled on
miserably. 'You might have to wait a month or two while I
polished them properly. If *I* was asking you to come home
to me, I'd want to tell you everything . . .' I stopped talking.
If Titus had offered her the Empire, Helena Justina would
be needing to think. She was a cautious girl.

I was trying to convince myself that whatever Titus had to say, it must so far be unofficial. If he was making any serious proposition, their two fathers would be negotiating. Even among emperors – *especially* among emperors – there are ways these things have to be done.

'Don't worry.' Helena looked up abruptly. It was always the same. Whenever I had reason to be worried about her, she tried to quash it by worrying over me. 'Nothing is going to happen, I promise you.'

'Has the great man asked his question?'

'Marcus, as soon as I reply – '

'Don't,' I said.

'What?'

'Don't reply yet.'

At least if any disaster happened to me, Titus Caesar would look after her. She would never lack anything. And the Empire's gain would be immense. A Caesar who reigned in partnership with Helena Justina might work incomparable deeds. Titus knew that. So did I.

I ought to set her free. Some people might say that once I reached Germania Libera I had a real duty to vanish in the woods. In the whimsical moments when I cared about Rome, I even thought that myself.

She was strange. Instead of demanding what I meant, she rose, came across to me, and then sat in silence beside me, holding my hand. Her eyes brimmed with tears she was too stubborn to shed.

She knew, of course. I wanted her myself. Even while I was crossing the Styx in Hades, I would be squabbling with the ferryman and trying to fight my way back off the boat to return to Helena. I only wanted to safeguard her future in case I would not be there.

She knew the rest, too. Going across the river would be stupidly dangerous. History was against me. The free tribes were implacable enemies of everything Roman. And I knew from Britain how the Celts treated their enemies. If I was captured I could expect to be denied diplomatic immunity. My skull would be speared up in a niche outside a temple.

What happened to the rest of me before they swiped my head off was likely to be more degrading and more painful than I could bear to contemplate. I did not ask how much Helena knew of all this, but she was well read.

When I fell for Helena Justina, I had vowed I would never expose myself to serious risk again. There had been plenty of tricky exploits in my past, most of which I would never even hint at to her. But a man grows older. He learns that other things matter. She could guess I had a horrific career behind me, but she believed that telling her I loved her meant my daredevil days were over. Nobody could blame the girl; I had made the same assumption myself.

Now I looked like one of those madmen for whom danger is an addiction. Helena's plight seemed as bleak as if she had shackled herself to a drunkard or a fornicator. She must have told herself everything would change under her influence, but now she saw it never could . . . Still, I knew I was different. This was just one last attempt to acquire a decent bounty from the Emperor, all so that I could win her.

One last throw . . . I suppose all madmen tell themselves that.

'Cheer up,' she said. Her manner was brisk. 'Come along, Marcus. Let's give Claudia Sacrata another scandal for her portfolio. How about introducing your pet senator's daughter to the general's lady-love?'

XXXVIII

There was a scarlet cloak on the hall peg. Helena and I exchanged a glance, trying not to giggle. Claudia Sacrata came out to us. Tonight she had on a crooked garland and a dress in tones of melon seed and grape skin. A heavy hand with the mercuric paint had produced the bright-eyed effect which women think men regard as youthfulness (as many men do). Pan-pipes whootled behind her, cut off abruptly by a closing door – closed by someone else. Claudia led us to a different room. When she left us again for a moment, Helena muttered, 'Looks as if we may have caught a senior officer with his breastplate hooks undone.'

'Make the most of the occasion. I reckon we won't be staying long.'

'Where's she gone? Has she nipped back to give him a Greek novel to read while she deals with us?'

'He may be skittering out through the garden gate with only one greave on his shins . . . Have I ever told you my friend Petronius says every time he raids a brothel he discovers the aedile who issues brothel licences hiding in a blanket chest? Big-name prigs are incorrigible.'

'I expect,' said Helena Justina soberly, 'the strains of office necessitate the therapy.'

She had been married to an aedile once. I hoped he had spent all his free time in blanket boxes, and not with her.

Claudia Sacrata returned.

'I've brought someone who's dying to meet you . . .' I introduced my aristocratic escort. Whatever masculine ranks Claudia had entertained, it must be the first and perhaps the only time a senator's daughter would sit in her house. For this trophy she would have let us interrupt even her general.

Helena had dressed carefully, bearing in mind that her

white dress with its little flowerbud sprigs, the shading of her cheeks, the fringe of her stole, her hooped seed-pearl earrings and the amber necklace I had given her would be all the rage in Ubian society for the next ten years.

'What a lovely girl, Marcus Didius!' cried Claudia, mentally making fashion notes. Helena smiled graciously. That smile was also going to feature in scores of Colonia dining-rooms.

'I'm glad you approve of her.' This glib retort earned me a bruising from the lovely girl's attractive beaded shoe. 'She has her wild side, but I'm slowly taming her . . . Don't judge the manners in Rome by this one's impetuous behaviour. The girls there are all mumbling violets who have to ask mother's permission for *everything*.'

'You have your hands full!' Claudia confided to her lady-ship, with a meaningful look at me.

'We all make mistakes,' agreed Helena. They both studied the object of their scorn. For escorting Helena into Colonia I too had dressed carefully: tunic, belt, boots, boot linings, cloak, saucy grin – the same scruffy rig as usual.

Our hostess was obviously wondering how a smart young woman like Helena could have let herself fall down so badly. Anyone could see she was highly refined (a prime candidate for disgracing herself on a portico), yet strongly sensible (and therefore more likely to give me a sturdy kick through the nearest victory arch). 'Are you married, Helena?' Claudia explored. She entertained no possibility that Helena Justina might be married to me.

'I was.'

'Dare one ask . . . ?'

'We divorced. It's a popular hobby in Rome,' Helena said in a light tone. Then she changed her mind and added frankly, 'My husband's dead.'

'Oh dear. How did that happen?'

'I never heard the full details. Marcus knows.'

I was angry at the interrogation. Helena handled it calmly and proudly, in her usual public style, but privately the subject always upset her. I told Claudia Sacrata in a cold voice, 'There was a political scandal. He committed suicide.'

My tone must have clearly stated that I wanted the matter dropped. Claudia's gaze sharpened thrillingly, as if she was going to demand, '*Sword or poison?*', but then she turned to Helena. 'He looks after you anyway.' Helena lifted her eyebrows, which were fined to an elegant crescent and almost certainly coloured, though their enhancement was delicate. Claudia Sacrata hissed, 'He means to spear me to the ceiling if I probe!'.

Helena gave a demonstration of how a well-bred woman should simply ignore unpleasantness. 'Claudia Sacrata, I understand you are a pillar of Ubian society? Marcus Didius tells me you are his one hope of tracing Civilis.'

'Afraid I couldn't help him, dear.' In front of Helena, Claudia Sacrata now regretted that. She wanted to be seen as a public benefactor. 'The person who would have known was his sister's son, Julius Briganticus. He loathed his uncle and always stayed loyal to Rome, but through family information he could always be relied on to know where Civilis was.'

'Can Falco get in touch with him?'

'He was killed, campaigning with Cerialis in the north.'

'What about the rest of the family?' Helena persisted.

Claudia Sacrata had obviously taken to her. Details that had been denied to me gushed out. 'Oh, Civilis had a mob of relations – his wife, several sisters, a daughter, a son, a whole clutch of nephews . . .' I was starting to feel this Civilis must be a sympathetic character. The Batavian's family sounded as terrible as mine: too many women, and the men at each other's throats. 'They won't talk to you,' Claudia continued. That sounded like my relations too. 'Most were fierce proponents of the free Gallic Empire. Civilis actually had his wife and sisters with him behind the lines on occasions, and all his officers' families – the way warriors did in the old days.'

'With a picnic?' I pondered facetiously.

'To encourage them in battle, dear.'

'And discourage slacking!' snapped Helena. I could imagine her parked on a wagon at the rear of the army, shouting harangues that would terrify the enemy and egg on her own incompetent menfolk. 'When they aren't being spear fodder, Claudia, don't they live around here?'

'They did. Civilis and other leaders even met in their houses to plot. That was way back though, when Colonia wanted nothing to do with his revolt. None of his clan show their faces now. There's too much bitterness. Civilis had the Ubians raided by neighbouring tribes; his friends from the Treveri besieged Colonia; and he was known to be in a strong mind to sack and plunder us.'

'So where would he go?' Helena pondered. 'If he wanted to hide up in this area which he knows so well, but avoid the Ubii, who would turn him straight over to Rome?'

'I don't know . . . Maybe among the Lingones, or more likely the Treveri. The Lingon leader – ' Claudia chortled suddenly. 'That's a funny story. His name is Julius Sabinus, and he was a great boaster, though completely bogus. He used to claim that his great-grandmother had been a beauty who seduced Julius Caesar.'

I muttered, 'Nothing to boast about!'

'Pardon, dear?'

'It was easily done.'

'Ooh Marcus Didius! Anyway, Sabinus was full of pretentions, but Helena, as soon as Cerialis came, he panicked. He set fire to his farmhouse to make it look as if he had committed suicide, and then slithered out. His wife Eponnina is hiding him. Everyone knows, but we don't mention it. No one can believe he won't come crawling out with a red face and straw in his trousers. Still, the way things are going, he could be battened up for years.' It was a good story – and it gave me an interesting clue to the anxieties that might also be besetting my quarry, Civilis. 'Anyway, dears, Civilis won't have any truck with such a coward. He's more likely to break bread with Classicus.'

'Who's that?' asked Helena.

'A leader of the Treveri. The one who made Colonia join the rebels temporarily. He executed some of the Roman tribunes at Moguntiacum, too, for refusing to swear allegiance to the German alliance.'

'Young men you knew?'

'One or two.' As always Claudia said it impassively, but perhaps she did care. She looked older tonight, and tired of gaiety.

'I'm sorry – I interrupted you.'

'Well, I mentioned Classicus. After my general defeated the Treveri, their chief went home and brazened it out. He lives in retirement. The Romans allow him to remain on his estate.'

'We promised there'd be no reprisals,' I confirmed. 'We know where he is. One wrong step and he's outlawed. Would he risk breaking his parole by sheltering Civilis, though?'

'Not openly. But he might make a hideaway discreetly available. Yes,' Claudia decided, convincing herself. 'Augusta Treverorum is your best hunting-ground, Marcus Didius.'

That may have been so, but it was no use to me, now I was braced to investigate Veleda. The capital of the Treveri lay over a hundred miles to the south-west – well into the province of Belgica – whereas my route lay a long way north and east. Even Vetera, where I planned to make a start searching, lay nearer. If Civilis was lurking in Augusta Treverorum, he would have to wait to have his hiding-place disturbed by me.

We had extracted more information from her, but I felt it was drying up. 'It was good of you to see us, but we'd best be on our way. Past experience tells me Helena's hot-rodded ringlets are about to droop . . .' Her new waiting-woman had helped her create a circlet of curls that fringed her face; I had been worried by the smell of singeing while it was going on.

'Yes,' she agreed sweetly. 'If that happens, panic will ensue.'

As we rose, Claudia asked, 'Where to next, then, Marcus Didius?'

'Nothing for it but a foray on to the eastern bank.'

'Germany – where the warriors have always been regarded as the fiercest in the world,' Helena said.

I smiled gently. 'I expect they have a sentimental side.'

'And the women are worse,' she tossed back.

'I'm used to furious women, love.'

She turned to Claudia. 'Is Veleda young or old?'

'Young enough.'

'Is she beautiful?'

'Men probably think so,' snapped this courtesan of legates and generals, as if mere beauty was no compliment.

She led us out. I saw her silvered eyes gleam when she found that Helena had been brought in a cedarwood sedan. She made a great fuss of putting Helena inside it, arranging her silk stole artistically and lighting our lanterns with a taper so that the neighbours would be treated to the full effect. Then she patted Helena's shoulder. 'Don't worry about Veleda. You can run rings round her.'

'I won't be there!' Helena Justina answered miserably.

539

XXXIX

As we approached our lodging-house, two small figures dashed away in the gloom. They must have been lying in wait for our return, but lost their nerve and scarpered. It was my niece and her small friend. I called after them angrily, but they ignored my shout.

Justinus was back. He was still hoping to hear what was in the letter from Titus. Helena still refused to refer to it. He then told us he had volunteered to come with me as far as Vetera. I wondered if he was really booked for the whole adventure, but neither he nor I discussed it in front of Helena. As it was, she took me aside for a few strong words about protecting him, and then dragged him off for more about looking after me.

The children had slunk back.

'Listen, you two, I want this understood: the women of my household do *not* leave home after dark!' It had the usual effect of peals of laughter, and was forgotten immediately.

The Ubian widow, a silent type who seemed capable enough, was trying to put the pair to bed. Augustinilla started snivelling. Arminia was in the same tired state, but took the opportunity to stare at the fuss her friend was making as if amazed to see someone be such a bad girl. I fought back my annoyance as Helena said crossly, 'Marcus, stop shouting. There isn't any point. She's just an exhausted child, dumped with strangers and taken far away from home. Her tooth hurts, and her doll's broken.' My niece's face was flushed and swollen unattractively, and the doll she always clung to had an arm missing.

I had been trying to avoid knowing about this, since I would rather be asked to pull out one of my own teeth than a child's. Luckily Augustinilla refused to open her mouth for me to look. 'That saves me a bite! Right. We'd better hold a dolly's funeral and burn her tastefully!'

'Shut up, Marcus. Augustinilla, Uncle Marcus is going to mend her. Give him the pieces, or he can't do it for you.'

'He won't be able to do it; he's no use . . .'

I groaned quietly. I'm not completely heartless. I felt sorry for the doll at least. But I had already spied out that the droopy object had jointed terracotta limbs of a kind I knew to be a real swine to mend. 'I'll try – but don't call me a murderer if she disintegrates. And if anyone says "*You're all heart, Marcus,*" I'm going to leave home.'

Helena muttered savagely, 'I thought you were leaving anyway!'

'No, lass. My permit's not signed yet.'

Mending the dolly took an hour and a half. I do not exaggerate.

Justinus had given up any hope of civilised conversation, let alone dinner. He left us early in suppressed bad language. The children sat wrapped in blankets, watching me. Helena and the Ubian woman ate a snack together and refrained from speaking, as if I was the type of workman who might at any moment explode irrationally. They had sausage. I had to decline, to avoid getting greasy hands.

As usual, the ball joint suddenly sank back into its socket perfectly easily. Everyone else exchanged glances as if they wondered why we had had to have so much swearing and wasting of time. Augustinilla shot me a hostile look, snatched the doll to her flushed cheek and went to sleep without a word of thanks.

I was feeling tense. 'Let's go out,' I growled at Helena.

'I thought your womenfolk were gated after curfew.'

'I need to be away from other people.'

'So why am I coming?'

I touched her neck briefly. 'You need to be with me.' I unhooked a lamp and swung out of the house, while Helena scrambled for the outer garments we had both been wearing earlier, then followed me.

'Thank you for doing that,' Helena ventured as I grabbed her hand while we walked. 'You have enough on your mind . . .'

I grunted. 'No point risking my neck unless it's for a world where children can believe magicians will always mend their broken toys.' It sounded trite. I found that comforting. No point being a hero unless you get to spout banal rhetoric.

'Her tooth really is bad, Marcus. Would you object if I took her to a healing shrine?'

I said no, provided every attempt was made there to drown Augustinilla in a sacred spring.

I took us along the river front. I managed to find a garden. It was almost the middle of October, but we could smell roses, though we couldn't see where they were. 'They must have some repeat flowerers, like the centifolia roses of Paestum . . .' I threw back my head, breathing deeply until I settled down. 'I'm thinking about another garden, Helena. A garden beside the Tiber where I once realised I was helplessly in love . . .'

'You're full of snappy talk, Falco.' With only a thin stole, she was shivering. I brought her into my arm so I could wrap my cloak round both of us. She was in a grumpy, defensive mood. 'What are we doing here?'

'You need to talk to me.'

'Oh I do,' she agreed. 'I've been trying all evening, but are you listening?'

'Give me credit. I've come here to listen.'

Defeated by my utterly reasonable attitude, she sighed. 'Thank you.' She forced an arm free and pointed across the water. The river was narrower here than at Moguntia-cum, but still so wide that in the darkness we could barely make out the other side. If there were lights, we could not see them. 'Look over there, Marcus. It's almost a different continent. Over there is the antithesis of everything Roman. Nomadic peoples. Nameless gods in wilderness places. No roads. No forts. No towns. No Forum; no public baths; no courts. Nothing organised and no authority to appeal to.'

'And no you,' I said.

I was quite certain she would ask me not to leave. Perhaps she herself had even intended to. Instead, she somehow found a rose-tree and wrenched off a flower for us. With roses it takes some force. She was a girl who had her moments of violence.

We shared the intensity of the flower's perfume. 'I'm here, lady. I'm still listening.'

She was sucking the side of her finger where a thorn had gone in. 'Claudia was right. You defend me. Ever since we met, you have been there – whether I wanted it or not. In those days you even seemed to dislike me, but you were already changing me. I had always been the first-born, the elder sister, the big cousin, the headstrong, bossy, *sensible* one. Everyone always said, *"Helena Justina looks after herself . . ."*'

I thought I could see where she was heading. 'People love you, my darling. Your family, your friends, *my* family – they all worry about you the same as I do.'

'You are the only person I accept it from.'

'Is that what you wanted to say?'

'Sometimes I'm afraid to let you know how much I need you. It seems too much to ask when you have given me so much.'

'Ask whatever you want.' I was still waiting for the big request not to go. I should have known better.

'Just make sure you come back.' Helena spoke without drama. There was no need to reply. For two barleycorns I would have ordered the Emperor to wrap up his mission in vine leaves and run his triumphal chariot over it. But Helena would have hated that.

I told her she was beautiful. I told her I loved her. Being a fair girl and well tutored in etiquette, she made corresponding remarks about me. Then I closed the shutter on the lamp so Colonia Claudia Ara Agrippinensium (Ara Ubiorum) should not have to know that on its neatly dressed quayside a plebeian with all the status of a frowsty water-rat was taking extravagant liberties with the daughter of a senator.

XL

We left the next day. I managed to shed Xanthus, but Justinus, who ought to have known better, smuggled his dreadful dog aboard.

Once again my imperial pass had obtained transport in a vessel of the official fleet. I also discovered that Justinus equipped expeditions in style. He had brought along horses, three leather tents, arms, provisions and a chest of cash. Only the quality of his manpower proved a disappointment, though since I was used to travelling solo on missions like this, I did not complain. One moment of uplift came when Justinus and I went to the dockside: the centurion supervising the loading of our ship was Helvetius.

'What's this?' I grinned. 'You commanding my escort? I thought you had too much sense for a crazy detail like that.'

Not for the first time I caught that fractional hesitation before he quipped back, 'Unluckily for you. It means your escort is two tent parties of my knock-kneed recruits.' It was bad news, but some of them were within earshot so we had to be fairly polite. 'I tried to pick out the best for you.' Helvetius had still brought me a basket of windfalls that were growing heavy mould.

'We've a hundred miles of sailing yet,' I told the centurion. 'And plenty of room on deck. I can help with extra arms practice.' It would get me in shape too. 'We should have them drilled into decent material by the time we disembark at Vetera.'

The same hint of diffidence darkened his face. 'So you're starting from Vetera?'

I thought he suspected me of being just another sightseer. 'There's nothing ghoulish in it. I'm starting where Lupercus left.'

'Wise.'

His laconic reply convinced me I had been prodding at some personal tragedy.

We were sailing out into the great plain of the lower Rhenus. The right bank between here and the River Lupia formed the territory of the Tencteri, a powerful tribe, and one of the few in Europe apart from the Gauls who made considerable use of horses. They had been firm friends of Civilis during the rebellion, eager to cross and harry our supporters – especially Colonia. They had retreated back across the water now. Still, wherever the channel allowed it, our ship clung to our own left bank.

Beyond the Tencteri lived the Bructeri. All I knew about them was their legendary hatred of Rome.

Since we had brought the pedlar Dubnus with us, we sometimes asked him questions about the east bank. His evasive answers only churned up our fears. Dubnus was producing a poor response to the lure of adventure; he seemed to regard himself more as a hostage than our fortunate scout and interpreter. He complained a lot. We were disgruntled too, mainly about him, but I laid down that we were all to coddle him. He had to believe we were sympathetic if we were going to be able to trust him as a guide.

Our days were spent exercising. We passed it off as a leisure activity; it was the easiest way to cope. But we all knew that we were hardening our bodies and preparing our minds for an adventure which could finish us.

Camillus Justinus had now confessed to me that he had his commander's permission to come the whole distance. I made no comment. His legate probably thought the lad had been working too hard; they both probably saw this excursion as a reward for enterprise.

'I wondered how we had managed to acquire the fabulous supply train! So it's down to your honoured presence . . . I take it you never told Helena?'

'No. Do you think she realised?'

'Whether she did or not, you'd better write to her from Vetera.'

'I will. She won't forgive me otherwise.'

'More to the point, Justinus, she won't forgive *me*.'

'Will she think you encouraged me?'

'Probably. And she won't like having both of us at risk.'

'She seemed very concerned about you,' he remarked. 'Visiting the witch in the woods, I mean. Was that based on past experience?'

'Your sister knows any suggestion of me succumbing to Veleda is a lie!' He looked startled by my anger. After a moment, I sighed. 'Well, you know the traditional method of dealing with a fatal beauty among your enemies.'

'That's part of the lecture on strategy I must have missed,' Justinus answered, rather coolly.

'Well, you take them to bed and give them a night of pleasure like nothing they have ever known. Next morning, thanks to your fabulous equipment and brilliant technique, they sob and tell you everything.'

'Your niece is right. You make things up, Falco.'

'It's just a myth.'

'Ever done it? In your past life, of course,' he added, in deference to Helena.

'Ha! Most women I know would cry, "Push off, chancer, and take your puny equipment with you!",' I hedged modestly.

'So why is my sister so worried?'

'The myth,' I said, 'is very deep-seated. Think of Cleopatra, Sophonisba – '

'Sophonisba?'

'Daughter of Hasdrubal and wife of the king of Numidia. She was notoriously beautiful.' I sighed again. This time it was an old man's sigh. 'How much education did they waste on you? The Punic Wars, sonny. Ever heard of Scipio?'

'I certainly never heard of the mighty Scipio bedding Carthaginian princesses!'

'Quite right. Scipio was a wise general.' And probably a good Roman prude.

'So?'

'Scipio made sure he never met her. He sent his lieutenant, Masinissa, to the beauty's tent instead.'

'Lucky old Masinissa!'

'Perhaps. Masinissa was so deeply smitten he married her.'

'What about her husband?'

'Mere detail. Masinissa was in love.'

Justinus laughed. 'So was the princess won over to our side?'

'No. Scipio reckoned she lured Masinissa the other way, so he had a few quiet words with him. Masinissa burst into tears, retreated to his tent, and then sent his bride a cup of poison. His message said he would have liked to fulfil the duties of a husband, but since his friends had advised against it here at least was the wherewithal to escape being dragged as a captive through Rome.'

'I assume that luckily for history she quaffed the poison down, and Masinissa redeemed himself . . .'

It was a boy's reply.

Helena had once read me Sophonisba's cutting answer to her bridegroom of the previous day: *I accept your wedding present. Nor is it unwelcome from a husband who can offer nothing better. However, I should have died with greater satisfaction had I not married so near to my death . . .*

Too subtle, I thought, for a tribune. Even one who, according to my horrid niece, had sensitive eyes. He would learn.

Helena Justina highly approved of Sophonisba, needless to say.

We had passed the limit of my previous experience of Germany. That ended at Colonia Agrippinensium, where the great Claudian road ran off westwards through Gaul towards the crossing-point to Britain. The large fortresses of Novaesium and Vetera had until now been only names to me. I had probably read of the minor outposts of Gelduba and Asciburgium, but you can't remember everything. Apart from Britain, these forts marked the ends of the Empire. Our hold in the north had never been tenacious, and Rome had only ever kept control by negotiating special relations with the marsh-dwelling Batavii. Re-establishing our outposts and winning back the Batavian alliance as a buffer against the savage eastern peoples would call for highly efficient diplomacy.

Now that we were past the Ides of October, the weather took a surreptitious shift, as we moved north. Nights were noticeably darker, earlier. Even during the day the golden light which had enhanced the scene at Moguntiacum was reduced to something gloomier. Once again, I felt horrified by the great distance we had to travel.

The scenery, too, was slowly changing. We lost the dramatic crags and dreamy islands. Sometimes there was attractively hilly country, where the Fourteenth's legate could have been taken on his hunting trip – if he *was* hunting. Far above us tremendous flocks of geese and other birds were migrating, adding to our anxious mood with their urgent flight and lonely cries. As the recruits became more excited, their centurion grew more silent. The pedlar scowled. Justinus was smitten by a sense of romantic melancholy. I simply felt depressed.

More and more we began to sense our approaching nearness to the other huge waterways that poured into the delta: the Mosa from Gaul, the Vaculus forming a second arm to the Rhenus, and all the tributaries, each one more powerful than the rivers we were used to in Italy. The sky assumed the lowering greyness I knew belonged to the remote Britannic Ocean – the wildest waters in the world. Sometimes we saw sea birds. The riverine vegetation of oaks, alders and willow became interspersed with sedges and marsh flowers. In those days there was no real military highway along this northern stretch. Habitation along our bank of the river dwindled to infrequent Celtic settlements, many bearing scars from the civil war, and most with sombre Roman watch-towers guarding them. On the other side, nothing was ever visible.

We stopped a night at Novaesium, where the newly rebuilt fort was full of activity. Then we sailed on past the mouth of the Lupia to our right, and finally made landfall on the left bank at Vetera.

Frankly, I did not relish disembarking there myself. And our centurion Helvetius flatly refused to leave the boat.

XLI

The ship's master had struggled to make Vetera before nightfall, not wanting to be caught out at a temporary mooring where the surrounding country must be regarded as unsafe. It was already dark when we landed, however – the worst time to arrive even at an established fort. We could all have stayed on board, but space was cramped and the lads were eager to be within walls, especially in such a famous place.

To organise billets we would have to shift ourselves. Justinus started protesting to the centurion, ready to order him down the gangplank.

'Leave it!' I said curtly.

'In Jupiter's name –'

'Just leave him, Camillus.'

Helvetius was standing to attention on the far side of the boat, staring out across the river with a set face. 'But why does he –'

'I'm sure Helvetius has his reasons.' I had realised what they were.

We marched the recruits off, made ourselves known in a dark reception building, and were allocated quarters. We knew the fort itself lay some distance away from the river, so were startled to find ourselves staying near where the ship had tied up. Our billet was just a wooden hutment, virtually on the quay. The recruits, who had expected the luxuries of a major base, were muttering about the strange set-up, and even Justinus looked mutinous. When we had stowed our kit, I made everyone gather round. The dim light of a taper gave our faces lurid shadowings, and we all spoke in low voices, as if even in this Roman enclave enemy forces might be listening.

'Well, this is a bad start . . . Lads, I know you're wondering why we haven't been allowed to march up and park in the fort. The Batavian rebels must have caused such destruction that they've had to abandon it. The troops here are living in tents and temporary barracks while they select a new site.'

'But why can't we shelter inside the old battlements?'

'You'll see in the morning what the situation is. Just use your imaginations until then. People stay outside the fort because Romans suffered and died there in great numbers. Take your cue from the troops who are stationed here: treat the place with respect.'

'Sir, I thought the legions at Vetera traded with the enemy?' They had no sense of reverence. Tomorrow would cure that.

'No, soldier.' This time Justinus answered. Quick to grasp what I was saying, his voice now was patient and informative. 'The legions at Vetera held out in desperate circumstances. Some of Vocula's relief force did sell their services to the Gallic Empire at one point, but we all have to remember that from here it looked as if the whole world had been torn apart and the Rome to which they had given their oath no longer existed.'

The recruits reacted at first with some scorn. Most of them knew nothing of recent history beyond local episodes like Vitellian soldiers killing a cow in a village three miles down the road. But as Justinus talked to them, they settled down, like listeners absorbed in a Saturnalia ghost story. He was a thorough lecturer: 'Up here, the Fifth and the Fifteenth had the worst of everything. It's true they executed a legate.' He was referring to Vocula. 'But they only surrendered when Civilis had starved them to the point of exhaustion. Then they were massacred. Some were killed as they marched out unarmed. Some fled back to the fort and died there when Civilis burned it in fury. Whatever those men did, they paid for. The Emperor has chosen to sponge the slate clean, so who are we to disagree with him? Listen to Didius Falco. None of us can judge the legions who were here, unless we can be certain what we ourselves would have done.'

The recruits were a rag-tailed lot, but they liked being

spoken to sensibly. They were quelled, though still fascinated. 'Sir, why wouldn't Helvetius come ashore?'

Justinus looked to me for help. I breathed slowly. 'You'll have to ask him.'

My guess was that the centurion had been at Vetera before. I had deduced that Helvetius probably belonged to one of the four disgraced German legions that Vespasian had reassigned elsewhere. If I was right, he must be one of the few survivors of the Fifth or the Fifteenth.

In that case, his motives in joining my expedition were ones I would have questioned had I known about them before leaving. I knew now that we were carrying a man whose mental scars could prove dangerous. It was the last thing I needed. But with an escort of only twenty untrained and untested boys, plus Camillus Justinus to look after, it was too late to act. If I shed any of our party, they would not be replaced. And we might need every man.

So I kept the centurion. In the end I was glad of him. He had volunteered to come. And even had he known what was to happen, I believe he would still have chosen to go.

XLII

Next day we unloaded our horses and rode out for the obligatory look at Vetera. The huge double fort lay empty but for the relics that confirmed all the bad reports. Siege engines which Civilis had made his prisoners build. Toppled platforms which the defenders had smashed by hurling down stones. The great Artimedorian grab which someone had managed to dream up for hooking the enemy off the ramparts. Internal faces of the turf walls gouged out from the search for roots or grubs to eat. Intense fire damage. Embedded missiles. Collapsed towers.

The fabric had been assaulted over a long period, then finished with firebrands. Reinvested by Civilis, Petilius Cerialis had battered it down again. The area had been cleared of bodies for a year now, but the dank smell of tragedy still hung everywhere.

We built a small altar. Justinus raised his hands and prayed aloud for the souls who had perished. I presume most of us added a few words for our party, too.

Coming back, chastened, we found Helvetius ashore, although I noticed that he kept his eyes averted from the road inland. He was talking to one of the regularly stationed troops. A dilemma had been offered us: despite the rumours further south, everyone here believed that Civilis was in his own territory, somewhere on The Island.

We talked it over, Justinus, Helvetius and I.

'This could be the old "He's on our patch" syndrome,' I said. 'You know, convincing themselves that a villain is hiding up locally because they want the credit for catching him. I've a friend who is a watch captain in Rome. He reckons that the minute he hears "Your man has been sighted just down the road", he starts searching at the

552

opposite end of town.' Petronius Longus had been on my mind. I was missing the old rascal. Rome, too.

'The problem is,' Justinus argued cautiously, 'if we set off east among the Bructeri without following this up, we won't relish going north again afterwards. You know what will happen if we do manage a meeting with Veleda? We'll come back down the River Lupia so relieved to be alive we'll only want to go home again.'

I wanted to go home already. 'What do you think, Helvetius?'

'I hate The Island, but I agree with the tribune – it's now or never. Now, we can somehow wind it into our itinerary. The detour will be too long later.'

'How did you acquire your local knowledge?' I queried in a bland voice.

'The way you think,' Helvetius said.

The tribune and I avoided one another's gaze. I took the plunge: 'The Fifth?'

'The Fifteenth.' His face stayed expressionless. The Fifth had just about saved their reputations, but the Fifteenth had broken their oaths pretty desperately.

Justinus followed up my question in his quiet, courteous way. 'So what was your story?'

'I'd been wounded. They shipped me out during the hiatus that followed Vocula's relief. I was in the hospital at Novaesium until Novaesium came under attack too. I ended up groaning on a stretcher in a nursing post they had managed to set up on board a barge at Gelduba. I was there throughout the last assault by Civilis on Vetera – and through its aftermath.' The result was obvious, and understandable. The survivor felt guilty that most of his comrades were dead. He even felt half guilty that he had never sworn faith to the Gallic Empire and lost his honour with the rest. 'Am I banned?'

'No,' Camillus Justinus stated. 'You're in the First Adiutrix now.'

'We need you,' I added. 'Especially if you're an expert on the territory.'

'I'm more than that.'

553

'How come?'

'I've been over in the east.'

That startled me. 'Tell us, centurion.'

'I was stationed in this hole for four years, Falco. Everyone needed a hobby; it was always a desolate post. I never cared for gambling or joining cliques of fancy boys. I did become very interested in the old Varus mystery, though. I read up the story. I used to save my leave and slip across – illegally of course, but everything was quieter then. I was curious about the battle site, fascinated by the idea of finding it.'

So this was what his talk of taking tribunes on hunting trips had meant. Soldiers love to forget their own troubles by reliving other wars. They always want to know what *really* happened to their predecessors. Had it been the enemy's treachery, or just another case of sheer stupidity from the command?

'Did you locate the site?' I asked.

'I was sure I was close. Damn sure.'

I had never liked obsessive types. 'Dubnus knows,' I told him wickedly. Helvetius whistled with annoyance. 'Forget it,' I grinned. 'That's one mystery we can leave to the exalted Germanicus. Let them lie, man. That was our grandfathers' disaster. Vespasian has given us enough to do, and so far I'm not planning to visit the Teutoburgerwald.' He was looking happier anyway, now that we had talked.

I then let myself be persuaded to search The Island. I knew as soon as we set off that the journey would be a waste of time.

I also knew that once we had travelled north, the Teutoburgerwald with its doom-laden reputation would be the sensible route back down to the haunts of the Bructeri.

We were riding. This came as a shock to the recruits. Jupiter knows why they thought we had brought thirty horses. Normally the legions march, but the distances we had to cover were too great for footwork. Besides, our boys were not exactly experienced at marching for days on end. In fact, they were generally such a shambles that most of the troops at Vetera piled out to see us off, wanting to stare at the hand-picked bunch of ninnies I was taking into the wilderness.

The recruits were like any group of adolescent boys: untidy, lazy, complaining and truculent. They spent all day discussing gladiators or their sex lives with an astonishing mixture of lies and ignorance. They were starting to have identities now. Lentullus was our problem baby. Lentullus couldn't do anything. Helvetius had only brought him because he wanted to come so badly, and he had a touching face. Then there was Sextus, who had worse sore feet than the rest of them, which meant they were virtually rotting in his boots. Probus, whom we reckoned would never learn to march with both legs at once. Ascanius, the town boy from Patavium, whose jokes were good but timed with utter tastelessness. The one whose country accent nobody could understand; the one who smelt; the one no one liked; the one with a big nose; the one with big privates; the one who had no personality. My mother would have said not a lad of them was safe to leave in charge of a cooking pot.

Mind you, she said that about me.

Leaving Vetera, we looked like a highly disreputable merchant's caravan emerging from the Nabataean desert after fifteen days of storms. Out of twenty, nineteen recruits had never ridden a horse for more than three miles before; the one left was Lentullus, who had never been on anything four-legged at all. They all seemed to have vaguely wandering eyes, their ears stuck out behind their cheek-guards like steering paddles on a ship, and their swords seemed too big for them. The horses, though Gallic, which should have been a good pedigree, were an even less attractive bunch.

Justinus and I rode first, looking as trim as possible. We were not helped by the tribune's little dog yapping round our horses' hooves. In the middle of the line we were keeping Dubnus on his bow-legged pony, which had a tuneless set of sheepbells stitched to its bridle. We made the pedlar muffle them, but the wadding fell out after the first mile. Helvetius rode last, struggling to keep a tight pack. We could hear him cursing with dreary consistency amidst the *tonk* of the pedlar's bells.

Near the pedlar rode Helvetius's servant, his treasured entitlement as a centurion. He was a mournful dot, who looked after his kit and his horse. While the rest of us kept trying to poach his services, he kept whining to Helvetius that he wanted to apply for an immediate transfer to Moesia (Moesia is a disgusting post edging the bleakest corner of the Euxine Sea). Justinus, in contrast, had brought no retinue, though his rank rated a large one. He said the dangers of our trip made it unfair. Eccentric lad. Fairness has never featured in the terms of employment for senators' slaves. Still, despite his pampered upbringing, Justinus managed to look after not only himself, but his dog too.

We were all armoured. Even me. I had found a quartermaster who sorted me out a corslet that fitted.

'We have plenty to spare, as a matter of fact!' A bald man with some sort of Gallic accent and a wry sense of humour, he was one of the army's congenital experts. Where his ghostly racks of kit came from was obvious; some of it was still marked with dead men's names. 'Are you sure you want to stand out like this? Why not all go in hunting gear and hope to meld in among the trees?'

I shook my shoulders, testing the familiar weight and the cold burn of the back hinges through my tunic as I hooked the plates together on my chest and tucked in a red neckerchief. It had been a long time. I was wriggling inside the armour like a crab in a lobster shell. 'Disguise is no use. Over there all the men are taller and heavier, with white flesh and huge moustaches you could use to sweep floors. Twenty compact and swarthy brown-eyes with naked chins will be spotted as Romans from miles away. We're in trouble the minute we cross the border. At least a breastplate and groin-protector give a nice feeling of false confidence.'

'What if you run into trouble?'

'I have a plan.'

He made no comment. 'Sword?'

'Always use my own.'

'Javelins?'

556

'We brought a load downstream with us.' Justinus had arranged that.

'Greaves, then?'

'Forget it. I'm not some flash officer.'

'Bonce pot?' I did let him kit me out with a helmet. 'Take this, too.' He pressed something into my palm. It was a small piece of soapstone engraved with a human eye speared by various mystical emblems. 'Weapons aren't going to be much use to you. Magic's the only other thing I have in store.'

Generous fellow. He had given me his personal amulet.

We spent more days than I cared for paddling in the morass. The Island must have been a dingy place even before the troubles. It was real delta country, all slime and salt flats. There were so many watercourses the land seemed a mere extension of the sea. A bad winter during the Cerialis campaign had brought down even more floods than usual. Untended by the stricken population ever since, the ground was recovering only sluggishly. Tracts that should have been farmed remained sodden. Civilis had also deliberately broken down the Germanicus weir, smashing its mole in order to devastate large areas during his last stand. We thought about Petilius Cerialis and his men, struggling to keep their horses' feet dry on the picket lines, dodging arrows and rainstorms while they splashed away looking for the shallows, constantly taunted by Batavians trying to lure them to destruction in the marshes.

The Batavian capital, Batavodurum, had been razed. Now sternly renamed Noviomagus, it was to be rebuilt and garrisoned. Vespasian had mentioned that to me but it only carried impact now that we were standing among the flattened homes, surveying the painful and desultory attempts of the population to revive their settlement while they lived under awnings with the family pig and chickens. Things must be taking a swing to the better, however, for we met Roman military engineers conducting a survey. They were on detached duty, discussing with local councillors how to bring in material and skills.

557

During the rebels' last stand, when he retreated to his homeland, Civilis had been besieged at Batavodurum, then driven deep into The Island. He had burned everything he was forced to leave behind. Any farms that escaped were destroyed by our forces – except for those belonging to Civilis himself. That was the mean old strategy of sparing the leader's estate so his suffering supporters grew jealous and angry, while he himself never reached the crucial state of having nothing left to lose. We followed his path inland. The selective scorched-earth policy meant we could see the estate where he should have been. But he had given up on his drenched fields and low dwelling-huts. None of his large family were living there, and there was no trace of him.

Perhaps the strategy had worked. The Batavians were a ruined people – temporarily at least – and their attitude to the prince who ruined them now appeared ambiguous. For the first time I began to doubt whether Civilis was still plotting. I wondered if he had simply fled in fear of the assassin's knife.

We felt no danger while on The Island. The atmosphere was sullen, but the populace had accepted peace and the old alliance. Once again they were a free people within the Roman Empire, exempt from taxes in return for armed manpower – though we all knew Batavian auxiliaries would never again serve in Germany. They let us pass among them without insult. And when we left, they were restrained in showing their relief.

By the Calends of November I was sick of searching, sick of crossing rivers on wobbly pontoons, and sick of half-submerged old roads on lurching wooden duckboards. I announced that we were moving out to seek dry toes and firmer ground.

And so we set off across the territory of the Frisii.

558

PART FIVE:
SWAMPS AND FORESTS

GERMANIA LIBERA
November, AD 71

'The legionary commander Munius Lupercus had been sent along with other presents to Veleda, an unmarried woman who enjoyed wide influence over the tribe of the Bructeri.'

Tacitus, *Histories*

PART FIVE
SWAMPS AND FORESTS

GERMANIA CERRO
November, AD 21

XLIII

It was hard to believe that Rome had once laid claim almost as far as the River Elbe. Drusus, his brother Tiberius, and his son Germanicus, had slogged away for years, trying to enclose a huge bight of Free Germany. They had used a double-ended pincer movement, invading from Moguntiacum in the south, and across the northern delta flats. Varus and his ineptitude had ended that. Some traces still remained from when Rome had fooled herself that she controlled these wild wetlands. Instead of returning to Batavodurum, we took the Drusus Canal from the mouth of the Rhenus to Lake Flevo, partly because the old canal was a wonder we might have no other chance to see.

We landed again. South of the lake there was little trace of the Roman occupation that had ended sixty years earlier. Lentullus, who was permanently impatient, asked when we would come to the first town. I explained, somewhat roughly, that there were no towns. It started raining. A horse stumbled and pulled a hamstring. We had to unpack and leave it, still within sight of the lake.

'So what do we know about the Frisii, Marcus Didius?' Justinus chaffed, as we surreptitiously made our first camp.

'Let's tell ourselves they are a placid, ranching, cereal-growing people with a yearning for the sea – and hope that their cattle are more dangerous than they are. The Frisii were conquered – no, I'll rephrase that tactfully – they were settled on Roman terms agreed by our esteemed Domitius Corbulo. That's quite recent history.' Corbulo was a real soldiers' general; one who made Petilius Cerialis look like a reject from the Roman fire brigade.

'So where were they in the rebellion?'

'Oh, keen supporters of Civilis, naturally!'

We had not yet reached the forest and were still in flat coastal country. To us it seemed a low, drear, dull land,

561

lacking features as much as it lacked warmth. But perhaps if you were born in a byre there, Batavia and Frisia were a challenge, with their endless fight against floods from rivers, lakes and seas, and their wide stirring vistas of open grey skies.

Much of this region seemed deserted. There were few of the settlements that flourished in Gaul. Even Britain was a populous, companionable place apart from its wildest parts. Germany, however, wanted to be different. All we saw were a few isolated houses, or at best crude huddles of huts and byres.

Here the people matched their reputation and lived a solitary life. If a tribesman could see his neighbour's smoke, he grew twitchy. He would want to ride over there, not for a meal and a game of dice, but to kill his neighbour, enslave his family, and plunder his goods. The presence of Romans just across the great river could only have made matters worse. Now the tribes had the decent excuse of trade to make warlike attacks on each other, seizing prisoners to meet the endless demand for slaves.

'Sir, will they try and capture us, then?'

'They know they can't sell Roman citizens back to Rome as slaves.'

'So what, sir?'

'They'll kill us, probably.'

'Is it true the barbarians are all head-hunters?' jested Ascanius.

'If it is, they'll have no trouble spotting your big noddle anyway.'

I was growing concerned about the pedlar. Dubnus appeared inexplicably restless. I had told him he could trade with the natives, yet he made no attempt to do so. When a man ignores a chance to pursue his living, I always deduce he has hopes of some bounty – and bounties are usually suspect in origin.

On one of my turns to be kind to him, I asked about trade. I knew that the great routes into the interior of northern Europe ran along the River Moenus from Moguntiacum, up the Lupia, and around the Baltic amber coast.

The Moenus and Lupia traders, along with others who came up from the Danube, tended to converge in a market among the Bructeri, where we ourselves were heading. 'I've done them all,' the pedlar said. 'All except the sea. I won't sail. I'm a loner. Sometimes I just prefer to wander on my own.' Was that why he hated being in our group?

'Is there a good trade with the tribes, Dubnus? Do they buy or sell?'

'Sell mostly. Converting their plunder.'

'Which is what?'

He was feeling uncooperative. 'Anything they may have snatched from someone else.'

'All right. So what do they snatch?'

'Oxhides and furs. Drinking-horns. Amber. Ironwork.' Dubnus must still be annoyed at being taken into custody and dragged along with us. He grinned evilly. 'In this area they still have a good stock of Roman armour and gold!'

He was trying to rile me. I knew what he was getting at. Twenty thousand men had perished with Varus – along with the field army's complete equipment, the commander's personal treasure, and boxes of soldiers' pay. Every household between the Ems and the Weser must have been living comfortably for decades off pickings from the massacre. Every time they lost a calf, all they had had to do was brave the whitening stacks of bones and gather up a breastplate to use in barter for a new animal.

I asked evenly, 'What do they like to buy? I've heard there's a fairly constant market for good Roman bronze and glass.'

'No tribal chief who takes a pride in his reputation is buried without a silver tray by his head and a full formal Roman drinking set.'

'I expect you can always find buyers for brooches or pins?'

'Trinkets. They like silver. They love coins, though only the old ones with milled edges.' Nero had devalued the currency the year before the Great Fire of Rome. I preferred the old coins too – they felt more substantial. In Rome the State guarantee held just as good for the new adulterated sesterces, but out here the weight of the metal would count.

'Do the German tribes use money?'

'Only when they barter with traders.'

'Coins are more for status and ornament? And is it true they ban imports of wine?'

Dubnus inclined his head. 'Not completely. But this isn't Gaul, where they'd give you their mother in exchange for a drink. Fighting is the serious business.'

'I thought they loved feasting. What do they drink?'

'Mead. Fermented mixes of barley and wayside fruits.'

'Pretty resistible! So, the German tribes tolerate our fancy goods, but Rome hasn't much else to offer them. They hate what we regard as civilised arts: conversation at the bathhouse, harmonious formality – a good binge on the Falernian.'

'They just hate Rome,' said Dubnus.

I gave him a sideways glance. 'You're a Ubian. Your tribe came from over the Rhenus once, so you have Germanic roots. What about you?'

'A man has to earn a living.' He let me hear an undertone of contempt.

But the conversation ended there, because we rode into our first group of Frisians. We drew to a halt like polite visitors. They approached us cautiously.

They were bare-headed – *red*-headed – blue-eyed, tunicked and cloaked in sombre wool, the way they were supposed to be. We had been telling ourselves that chroniclers exaggerated everything. Maybe it was the Germanic angry temperament they had chosen to misreport.

'Step up, Falco!' Justinus commanded cheerfully. 'Time for this famous plan of yours.'

We all breathed with more care than normal. I hauled Dubnus forwards. 'Please tell these gentlemen we are travelling to pay our respects to Veleda.' He scowled, then said something. I did catch Veleda's name.

The tribune's dog proved our best ally. He rushed up to each Frisian, barking, wagging his rump and trying to lick faces joyfully. They could see that no one who brought such a hopeless hunting hound could have hostile intentions, and that claiming our scalps would be an insult to their manhood. Fortunately, the pup forgot to nip anyone that day.

The Frisians stared at us. Since they were doing nothing more dramatic, we smiled, saluted, and passed on our way. They followed us at first, like curious cattle, then drifted off.

'Veleda seems to do the trick.'

'You mean, they looked as if they'd never heard of her!' Helvetius scoffed.

'Oh I think we can assume they had,' the tribune reproved him in his grave way. 'I believe that explains the pitying looks they all sent after us!'

He rode on, petting the dog, which peered out from a fold of his cloak looking pleased with itself. It was small, smooth, white with black patches, constantly hungry, completely untrainable, and fond of exploring dung. Justinus called him Tigris. It was inappropriate. He was as much like a tiger as my left boot.

Next day we began to encounter stretches of light woodland, and at nightfall we hit the real edge of the forest. From now on we would need all our skills to find paths and keep to the right direction. From here the tree cover continued unbroken across the whole of Europe. Frankly, as a town boy I had always felt the continental arboretum to be excessive. I like foliage – but I like it best when the greenery is leading to a pergola over a stone bench where a freelance wineseller is conveniently hanging about, and I have an appointment to meet my favourite girl under the pergola in about five minutes' time . . .

Camping for the first night on the damp, prickly forest floor, knowing we now had to endure weeks of this, our spirits flagged and tempers rapidly coarsened.

By now the recruits had worked through all the normal stages that afflict soft lads being taken out camping in rough country to harden their characters. We had run the full gamut of moans, theft of personal treasures, spoiling the evening meal, losing equipment, bedwetting and black eyes. Whatever the rough communal living was doing for them, the three of us in charge were exhausted, battered, and welded into a strong defensive team.

One evening, after a particularly sour day and a fight where we had caught them with their daggers out, Helvetius laid about him so angrily that he broke his vine stick. Then Camillus Justinus lined them up for a strong dose of tribunal rhetoric.

'Listen, you bastards!'

'Good approach!' Helvetius muttered subversively to me.

'I'm tired. I'm filthy. I'm sick of marching-biscuit and I'm sick of pissing under oak trees in the rain!' His unorthodox address had startled the group into silence. 'I hate this country just as much as you do. When you behave like this, I hate you too. I'd like to say that the next troublemaker will be sent straight home. Unhappily for all of us we have no convenient wagon going to headquarters, or I'd be first on it myself. Face facts. We all have to make the best of it, or *none* of us will be going home.' He let that sink in. 'Make up your minds. We all have to pull together – '

'Even Lentullus?' cried Probus.

Justinus scowled. 'Except for Lentullus. The rest of us will pull together – and we'll all look after him.'

They laughed. We would spend a quiet night now, and next day everyone would be wonderful.

'He'll do,' Helvetius decided.

'Infinite patience with them,' I agreed.

'Seen it before – they start off thinking he's a worthless snob, and end up dying for him.'

'Camillus won't thank them for that,' I said. 'He'll be martyred if he goes home without a single one of them.'

'Even Lentullus?'

I groaned. 'Especially bloody Lentullus! So, the tribune's all right, is he?'

'He'll probably keep us out of trouble.'

'Thanks! What about me?'

'Mithras, don't make me laugh, Falco. You'll be the one who gets us into it!'

The next morning everyone was wonderful for about half an hour. Then Lentullus in his amiable way piped up, 'Sir, sir, where's Dubnus gone?'

XLIV

I drew a heavy breath. 'What's that, Lentullus?'

'He's not here, sir. And his pony's gone.'

Justinus sprang up, on the alert. 'Anybody know when he left?' No one did.

I was on my feet too. 'First tent, come with me! Helvetius, you keep the second tent, pack the kit, then follow us . . .'

Helvetius was running at my heels as I raced for a horse. 'What's the panic? I know the terrain. I can tell roughly where we are – '

'Use your head! How are we going to converse with Veleda? Dubnus is our interpreter!'

'We'll get by.'

'It's more than that,' I gasped, bridling up frantically. 'So far we've been unobtrusive. No unfriendly groups have spotted us. But Dubnus seemed broody. He was plotting, I'm sure of it. We don't want him bringing a war party on our heads!'

'Falco, maybe he just wants to get on with his trade.'

'I told him he could do that . . .' Now, however, I was afraid the pedlar was hoping to make a packet from a new line: selling hostages. 'We can't take the risk that what he's intending to trade with may be us!'

We tracked him northwards for a long way. It was the wrong direction for us; perhaps he was using that knowledge in the belief we would give up, though it only made me stubborn. I hoped he would grow careless. I hoped he might think we were so single-minded about our mission that he was free from pursuit altogether.

My party was the slower of our two tracking groups. We were trying to pick out just one set of hooves among the litter on the forest floor, whereas Helvetius was following our great swathe. He soon caught up with us, and we all went on together, first bending east, then south again.

'What's he up to?'

'Mithras, I don't know.'

'I'm not sure I care.'

Dubnus must have left us early and travelled by night. His start was too great. I decided we would follow until the evening, and then abandon it. We lost the trail by the afternoon.

We were among taller, more thickly growing trees than ever before, in the dense silence of truly ancient woods. A huge horned insect glared at us from the curl of a dead leaf, outraged at this intrusion. There was no other sign of life.

Taking stock, we agreed that the one certainty about our present location was that we had never expected to be in this area. With good luck, no one hostile would expect us here either. Bad luck meant none of our friends would know where to bring a rescue force – but we had ruled that out, anyway. Justinus and I had left behind instructions that if anything went wrong there would be no point in a rescue attempt, so no one was to try.

Our journey from The Island had brought us across most of southern Frisia, but by now we had to be in Bructian territory. Coming this way had been unorthodox, but less exposed. We were a long way from normal trading routes. We were also a long way from both the Roman fieldworks that still survived in the delta area and the old forts that I knew had been planted along the River Lupia. We were approaching the famously hostile Bructeri not from where they were always watching for strangers – along their home river – but by surprise from the north.

During much of our trip we had been about a hundred Roman miles, give or take forty or fifty in this endless hardwood wilderness, above the Lupia's course. That offered some safety, but we had to turn south eventually. The place to change our present easterly direction would be marked by the heights of the Teutoburger ridge. We knew the famous escarpment curved down to the sources of the Lupia. All we had to do was find the northern end, then follow the hills. Helvetius had mentioned an ancient track, but none of us relished taking it. Once there, we would have another forty-mile trip before the heights petered out at the river. By now we had come far enough to be keeping our eyes peeled for the high ground whenever the forest allowed us to scan the countryside.

We began turning south.

Our detour to look for the pedlar had disorientated us slightly. This was easy country in which to lose your way. There were certainly no roads, and forest ways are notoriously aimless. Sometimes the one we took petered out altogether, so that we had to batter through brushwood, perhaps for hours, until we reached a new path. The trees crowded so thickly that though there could have been a much better track only a few strides away, we stood no chance of finding it. Helvetius, who had been near here before for his historical research, reckoned we were still some way from the topmost end of the Teutoburger escarpment, though had we not been in deep forest, the heights might have been visible in the distance. We hacked on through the dismal woods, believing him because we had no choice. Anyway, going south could never be entirely wrong. We would come to the Lupia eventually.

At dusk we stopped. While the tents were pitched, various members of the party vanished on their own for the oak-tree routine. It was cold. The light had sunk but not gone entirely. We were heating mess tins for each tent, but they were nowhere near ready. Helvetius named the night's sentries, whilst his servant groomed his horse. Justinus had a conversation going with Sextus and one of the other lads. They were teaching him some dialect words from the Adriatic coast, since he seemed interested in languages. I was just worried and miserable as usual.

I saw Lentullus creep back after his pee in the woods. He looked furtive, which was nothing unusual. He also looked frightened.

He said nothing to anyone. I decided to ignore it, then found that was impossible. I strolled across to him.

'All right?'

'Yes, sir.'

'Anything to tell me?'

'No, sir.'

'That's a relief.'

'Well, sir . . .' *Oh dear!* 'I think I saw something.'

Lentullus was the type who would spend three days wondering whether he ought to mention that a large army of warriors in wicker chariots with war horns and broadswords was heading our way. He never knew what was important. Lentullus would get us killed rather than say anything to worry the command.

'Something alive?' I asked him.

'No, sir.'

'Someone dead?'

Lentullus paused and would not answer me. All the hairs on my neck and arms rose slowly to attention.

'Come along, Lentullus. Let's you and I take the tribune's puppy for a walk.'

We hacked through the woods for about ten minutes. Lentullus was a shy soul. We had lost him twice already when attending to nature had led him so far from the camp that he couldn't find us afterwards. He stopped to take bearings. I kept quiet rather than confuse him completely. The thought struck me that we could be out here all night while Lentullus searched for his treasure again.

I hate forests. With everywhere completely motionless, it would be easy to become terrified. Among these trees bear, wolves, elk and boar all roamed. The chill air smelt damp, with an evil autumnal unhealthiness. The vegetation was a rank, flowerless kind, with no known herbal use. Fungi like lined faces hung in ancient trees. Undergrowth caught at our clothing and flesh, snagging our tunics and scratching our arms vindictively. My breastplate had become splattered with some sort of insect juice. At this spot we seemed to be the only things breathing apart from eerie watchers from the Celtic spirit world. We could sense a lot of them, both remote and close by.

Twigs snapped, too near for comfort, the way forest twigs do. Even Tigris was subdued. He stayed close to us instead of rushing off to scavenge for woodvoles and bad smells.

'I don't like it here, sir.'

'Show me what you found, then we can go.'

He led me through a few more thickets, over a giant log, past a dead fox which had been torn at by something much larger – something that was probably planning to come back for the rest of it just about now. Tigris growled worryingly. A cloud of midges was mobbing my forehead. 'This is where I was standing. I thought that it looked like a path.' Maybe. Or just a coincidental space among the crowded trees. 'I went along it for a look . . .' He was congenitally curious. And daft. Lentullus would pick up a scorpion to see if it's true they sting.

I still had no idea what he had seen, except that its effect on the recruit chilled me. 'Come on then.'

We took the supposed path. Maybe deer came this way. The air smelt even more hostile, and the light was fading fast. Dew had made our boot-leather swell, and our feet dragged with clumsiness. Leaves crunched under foot louder than I liked. Our progress must have been audible for a couple of miles.

Then the trees stopped.

I was tired. I was cold and uneasy. At first my eyes refused to focus, fighting disbelief. Then I understood why the recruit had been afraid of his discovery.

The silent clearing we had entered lay hung with mist. It was a big clearing, or had been once. Ahead of us lay a strange low sea of brambles. The brambles and brushwood sank slightly nearer to us, then rose many feet away to a regular berm of woodland. The moat-like depression stretched sideways in each direction. The canes dipped, as if the ground beneath their tangled mass had been cut away. And so it had. We knew that, even without venturing forwards – which would have been deadly dangerous. Almost at our feet the ground must fall steeply, deeper than a man's height. Below us, invisible in the brambles, fiendishly sharpened stakes no doubt snarled. At the bottom of the ditch would be a trim channel one spade wide for drainage, then the farther wall would rise diagonally into a bank, before falling back to level ground. There, woodland filled the berm. Comparatively young woodland, not the ancient trees we had been struggling through all day, which must have been standing sturdily in the old times of legend when Hercules visited Germany.

It was a different legend we had found.

Beyond the wood there was a rampart. We could glimpse only the upper part above the vegetation. But there had to be a patrol track, faced with a timber palisade and broken by the shape of familiar square towers. Further on in the gloaming we made out the formidable bulk of a standard fortress gate.

It was silent. No sentries were patrolling and no lights showed. But here, a hundred miles from the Roman provinces, stood a Roman camp.

XLV

'Sir, is anybody there?'

'Dear gods, I hope not!' I was in no mood for exchanging travellers' tales with dead men or their ghosts.

I started to move.

'Are we going in?'

'No. We're going back.' I turned him round.

'Sir, we could camp inside – '

'We'll camp where we are . . .'

Few of us slept much that night. We lay awake, listening for trumpet calls from Hades, then nodded off just before dawn. I woke early and rose while it was still dark, stiff and snuffle-headed. The rest emerged too. After a cold drink and some biscuit to brace us, we packed, brought the horses, and then set off in a close group to make a morning call on our colleagues' camp. At dawn, it managed to look even lonelier.

This was no Vetera. It was a field army's camp, and a large one. Though intended as a temporary construction, it stood in its isolation with an air of permanence. There were no signs of siege warfare. Decay, however, clung tenaciously. Apart from the rich clothing of brushwood on the outworks, some of the towers had lurched and the palisades collapsed. We could see now that further along from us the actual breastwork was broken down.

We battered a path to the gatehouse. One of the great wooden doors lay off its hinges. We edged just inside, no more. A spider the size of a duck's egg watched us entering.

The vegetation was dramatic. Everything within the ramparts was wrecked.

'Sir, was there a fight?'

'No bodies left, if there was.' Helvetius, alone of us, dismounted and wandered forwards to explore. Even he had no intention of going far. He stopped and picked up a small object. 'I don't think the place was abandoned,' he murmured in a puzzled voice.

He began to make his passage further in, and this time we followed him. It would have been a tented camp, so there were large tracts of open ground where the long leather 'butterflies' would have been pitched in rows. But wherever the legions stay for any length of time, the store-houses and the Principia are made from permanent materials. These should have been evident, in their familiar locations, as squares where only a low covering of thin weeds grew, because of their solid floors, yet rotting old timbers and mounds of other wreckage occupied their sites.

'What's your verdict, centurion?' Justinus asked. He was white-faced from the early hour, lack of sleep and anxiety.

'It was an empty camp – but not dismantled normally.'

'They had left for the winter,' I said. I spoke with some confidence. The shrine and strongroom, built of stone, still stood erect. There were of course no standards and no eagles in the shrine. I had seen the gold eagles that once flew here. I had seen them in the Temple of Mars in Rome.

Helvetius looked at me. He too knew what we had found. 'That's right. The buildings were all left here. Bad practice, but they expected to come back, of course.'

He was deeply upset. I turned to the others to explain. 'You all know the rules when you leave a marching camp.' The recruits listened attentively, looking innocent. 'You pack everything reusable in the baggage train. You take, for instance, all the staves from the palisade to use at your next stopping-point. Every soldier carries two of them.'

We all stared back. On the fortified ramparts behind us, stretches of the wooden defences lolled across the patrol track, still partly laced together, like estate fences that had suffered in a huge gale. Other pieces must have rotted; so had the stairs. Time had done this, no other force.

'You burn the rest,' Helvetius said. 'You leave nothing an enemy could use – assuming you think you have an enemy.' He was turning the remains of an old storehouse door. 'This was an empty camp!' he exclaimed, almost protesting at the breach of etiquette. 'It's been trampled pretty thoroughly, by looters, I'd guess. The camp was built by Romans, Romans who stupidly believed the area was so safe they could go out like householders, leaving their door-key under the gatehouse mat . . .' The centurion was burning with a slowly increasing wrath. 'The poor bastards hadn't the slightest inkling of how much danger they were in!'

He strode back to us, clenching his fist around the item he had taken up.

'Who were they, sir?'

'The three legions who were massacred in the forest by Arminius!' Helvetius raged. 'There was a fight – dear gods, there was – but there are no bodies because Germanicus came afterwards and buried them.'

He held up his find. It was a silver coin. It carried the special mint mark which P. Quinctilius Varus had used on his soldiers' pay.

Not many of those ever circulate in Rome.

XLVI

Somewhere in this area had to stand the burial mound. The one whose first turf Germanicus had laid with his own hands – against the rules of sanctity, since he was at the time also holding office as a priest. Here he would have been a soldier first. Standing here, we understood. We too were overwhelmed by our emotional response.

We did not search for the mound. We did not even raise an altar as we had done at Vetera. We honoured them in silence. All of them: the dead, and those who had made it a duty to find them. Gripped by the past, all of us must have wondered whether, if we were killed here in this forest, anybody who cared for us would ever even hear our fate.

We left the camp in the mist by way of its broken Praetorian Gate, on the tough old relics of its exit road. It was easier riding than any other route through the forest, and we wanted to cover distance fast. Our forebears' road did eventually become overgrown. We made the usual complaints about useless engineers, though after sixty years without maintenance some potholing and weeding-over could be excused.

We kept going. Like the army of Varus, we were moving south. Like theirs, that was where our destiny lay in wait. The only difference was: we knew.

It was impossible not to keep churning over the history. Even Justinus had now joined in: 'We know Varus was heading for winter quarters – either the forts they had built on the banks of the Lupia, or possibly right back somewhere along the Rhenus. He must have left that camp wrongly believing he had secured the territory, and all set to return there the next spring.'

'Why couldn't they stay there in winter, sir?'

'Too far from supplies to sit it out. Besides, I expect his troops were nagging for a break somewhere civilised.' The

577

tribune's own troops thought about his solemn remark, then slowly grinned.

'And this is the way they went,' Helvetius said. He was really feeling it. He loved to dramatise; he loved to speculate. 'Everyone believes they had hit the ridge when it happened, but why not here, much further north? All we really know for certain is that Germanicus found them somewhere east of the River Ems.'

'Sir, sir – ' Now they had left the lost camp the recruits felt braver and more excited. 'Will we find the famous battleground?'

'It's my belief,' Helvetius answered heavily, as if he had just worked something out, 'the battlefield is all around us. That would be why Germanicus had such trouble finding it. You don't cut down twenty thousand men – veteran campaigners, after all – in a space like a backyard.'

I agreed. 'We think it was quick, but the engagement may have lasted. No – it *must* have done. Clearly Arminius fell on them and did much damage. But after the first shock, the hardened soldiers would have made a stand.'

'Right, Falco. No choice. We know they did, anyway. Germanicus found whole heaps of bones where they had fought back in groups. He even came on the remains of some who had struggled back to their camp and been slaughtered there.'

'The camp we found?'

'Who knows. After all this time – and Germanicus clearing it as well – you'd have to spend days there to find any clues.'

'So after the initial assault,' I said, 'they faced a drawn-out agony. There were even survivors. Arminius took prisoners: some were slung up on tree branches to propitiate the Celtic gods, but some were held in gruesome pits.' We found none of those, I'm glad to say. 'Some eventually got home to Rome. A few poor sods even came back here with Germanicus.' Every war produces masochists. 'But agreeing a surrender is not the point for the tribes. It was a Celtic fight – to kill and take heads. Any legionaries who tried to make a getaway would have been hunted through the woods. Just like in Britain when the Boudiccan tribes rose.' I heard my voice growing husky with old pain. 'The chase is part of the terrible game. Blood-crazed warriors happily whooping after victims who know they are doomed . . .'

'Arminius may even have prolonged the fun deliberately,' Helvetius informed the rest. 'The upshot would have been bodies all the way from here to – '

'To the next river in any direction, centurion.'

'Tell us, Falco?'

'The warriors stop any remaining fugitives at the water's edge. Their heads and their armour are dedicated to the gods in the running stream.'

We rode on very quietly. It took us two days, even with fine weather and favourable luck, to reach the Teutoburger hills.

I know that when we rested each evening some of the recruits vanished for long periods into the undergrowth. I know they found various items. They were boys. They cared about their old colleagues, but they found relic-hunting irresistible.

The general mood of our party hardened. Meanwhile, Lentullus would sit with Justinus and me near the fire, taking no part in the secret search for souvenirs. He was withdrawn, as if somehow he thought everything was his fault.

Once I laughed, briefly. 'Here we are, stuck in the middle of nowhere with a whole basket of our own troubles, sounding off like strategists using apples on a tavern table to relive Marathon and Salamis.'

'Shut up about taverns, Falco,' murmured Camillus Justinus sleepily from the depths of his camp-bed. 'Some of us could really use a drink!'

Since I had stayed in his house and tasted his awful table wine, I knew just how desperate His Honour the tribune must be.

Next day we tackled the Teutoburger heights.

We traversed the long escarpment strangely without incident. It seemed too good to be true. It was.

On our descent, all to order, we found the headwater of the River Lupia. At sunset we camped discreetly, making no fires. I noticed that Probus and another recruit went off together and stayed absent for too long. They were no doubt scouring the terrain for antique scabbards and studs again. At first we made no comment, as usual, but we had soon finished distributing rations and still they had failed to appear. That was unheard of. Helvetius stayed in the camp whilst Justinus and I went out to search for our lost lambs. We took a recruit each. He chose one called Orosius. With my luck I got Lentullus. In case I needed more company, Tigris gambolled happily along with us.

As you might expect, it was Tigris, Lentullus and I who stumbled into the sacred grove.

It just seemed like any other clearing when we first went in. It must have been generations old. We marched boldly among the crook-armed trees, thinking the open ground between them had occurred naturally. An angry wind was rousing itself, rustling tirelessly through the dark, dry, November leaves. Tigris, who had bounded on ahead, raced back madly, bringing us a stick to throw. I bent and after the usual noisy struggle I forced him to release it.

'That looks a funny one,' said Lentullus.

Then we saw it was a human fibula.

While the dog barked in frustration, waiting for his game, Lentullus and I gazed slowly round and noticed at last that this place had a special atmosphere. There was a smell of moss and misery. The silence blocked our throats. Panic leapt. It took a few moments to recognise that empty eyes were watching us from every side.

'Stand still, Lentullus. *Stand still!*' I don't know why I said it. No one else was there ... yet there was *presence* everywhere.

'Sorry, sir,' Lentullus croaked. 'Oh great mother! I've done it again, haven't I?'

580

I tried to sound cheerful as I whispered back, 'Yes. It seems to be another of your terrifying finds . . .'

Ahead of us leaned a grotesque statue in rotting, rough-hewn wood: some god of water, wood or sky – or perhaps all of them. He loomed up like a huge gnarled oak trunk, beaded with livid orange mould and rooted in decay. He had emerged from a few strokes of a crude adze. His limbs were barely indicated caricatures. He had three primitive faces, with four staring Celtic almond-shaped eyes distributed among them. Atop him the wide antlers of some massive elk draped themselves as if trying to embrace the sky.

Before the god stood a basic turf altar where the priests of the Bructeri came to make their sacrifice. Upon it lay the head of an ox, badly decomposed. Like us, they predicted the future from the entrails of animals. Unlike us, it was their custom to hack to pieces any horses and other captured animals belonging to their vanquished enemies. They also conducted worse kinds of sacrifice. We knew that because all around the grove, nailed up in the ancient trees, were human skulls.

XLVII

Lentullus, who normally knew nothing about anything, knew about this. 'It's death to enter a druids' grove, sir, isn't it?'

'If we wait around, a druid may come along and answer that . . .' I gripped his arm, then slowly backed out the way we had come.

To our right something stood among the trees: a trophy pile. There were innumerable weapons – long, unfamiliar German swords, war axes, round shields with sturdy bosses – among other items whose Roman design we recognised with an unhappy shock.

Lentullus squeaked and tripped over a root. Only that spring I had managed to lay hands on part of Caesar's *Gallic Wars*, going cheap now that Rome had some nasty new wars to occupy its attention. According to Julius, the Suebi worshipped – in those days anyway – in a grove which people could visit for religious purposes, but if they happened to fall down there it was required practice that they should roll out of the grove horizontally. No doubt Caesar quoted other reassuring facts that might have helped us to extract ourselves from this terror, but I had never owned enough money to buy the next scroll in the set.

Here the ground was particularly rich in unpleasant flora, deer droppings, and milky-coloured fungi of the etiolated, squashy kind. I glared at the hostile wood carving and defiantly ruled out Caesar's rite. Rolling like a log to propitiate local deities was not in our recruits' training course, and this one would never have mastered it anyway. I hauled on his arm and pulled the young fool upright. Then we turned round and started to leave conventionally.

We regretted it.

We were now forced to walk past something else we didn't like.

582

The edifice at the grove exit was square-built, like another and much larger altar. It was set around a massive stake, and made from various narrow-shaped items, irregular or round-ended, and grey in colour. The construction must have been built up over many generations until now it was two strides in each direction and waist-high. Its components had been laid down in rows extremely neatly, first one way, then crosswise, like twigs in a well-ordered bonfire. But they were not twigs.

It was a giant pile of bones. Bones from human arms and legs. Hundreds of victims must have been dismembered to contribute to this ossuary – first hung in the trees as offerings, then smitten into pieces with casual savagery, like choice cuts from meat carcasses. From what I knew of Celtic rites, most of them had once been young men like us.

Before we could stop him, the tribune's dog went up to sniff this wondrous hoard of bones. We looked away, as a gesture of respect to the dead, while Tigris saluted each corner of the ossuary with his special sign of doggy reverence.

We left the grove very fast.

XLVIII

We started back to camp. That was when the next nightmare began.

Yet again I was out in a wood at dusk with Lentullus. This time it was not the silence that unnerved us. Suddenly we were surrounded by noise – something, or somebody, crashing through the trees in haste. We were already petrified. Then we heard a shout. Foreign voices filled the night. From the start it seemed like pursuit, and from the start we understood that we were their quarry. I forced Lentullus to change direction, hoping to give the rest of our party a chance.

'I'm with you, sir!' he promised.

'That's comforting . . .'

We had lost our path and were blundering over treacherous ground where branches and deceptive clumps of moss lay in wait to throw us headlong with wrenched limbs. I was trying to think as we dashed onwards through the brushwood. I felt fairly sure no one had seen us leave the grove. Perhaps we had not been seen at all. Somebody out there was looking for something, but perhaps they were hunters trying to fill the pot.

We stopped. We crouched amongst bushes while the sweat careered off us and our noses ran.

Not the pot. Whoever they were, they were making a lot of noise for men trying to lure animals into nets. They were thwacking at the bushes in order to flush out fugitives. Harsh laughter alarmed us. Then we heard dogs. Some sort of great horn boomed. Now the boisterous party was coming straight for us.

They were so close we broke cover. They would have found us anyway. Someone glimpsed us. The shouts renewed.

We set off again as best we could, unable even to glance

back to see who our pursuers were. I had lost Lentullus. He had stopped to call the tribune's dog. I kept going. They might miss him; they might miss me; we might even escape.

No chance. I was putting distance between us, but sounds broke out that could only mean one thing: they had caught Lentullus. I had no choice. Groaning, I turned back.

They had to be a band of the Bructeri. They were standing round a deep pit, laughing. Lentullus and Tigris had both fallen into it. Perhaps it was an animal trap, or even one of the pits like larders that their hero Arminius had dug for keeping prisoners fresh. The recruit must be unhurt, for I could hear him shouting with a spirit I was proud of, but the warriors were taunting him by shaking their rough wooden lances. He must have been badly shaken by the fall, and I could hear that he was terrified. One of the Bructeri raised his lance. The threat was clear. I started to yell. I was tearing into the dell when someone big, with a very hard shoulder, sprang out from behind a tree and crashed me to the ground.

Lentullus could not see me, but he must have heard my fall. For some reason my presence seemed to hearten him.

'Sir, how are we going to talk to these men without an interpreter?' *That boy was an idiot* . . .

The world stopped spinning. Since my answer might be the only friendly words he ever heard again, I had no heart for rebuking him. 'Speak slowly, and smile a lot, Lentullus . . .'

He may have had problems deciphering it. It was difficult to sound as clear-witted and self-assured as usual when lying face down on the forest floor with my nostrils pressed into the leaf-mould, while a gigantic, bare-chested warrior, who could not possibly have understood my joke, stood with his foot in the small of my back and laughed heartily at me.

XLIX

Dear gods, I hate large, simple-minded jovial types. You can never tell whether they will simply mock you, or mock you with that jolly guffaw, then swipe off your head with an axe . . .

My captor in fact hauled me to a more or less standing position, stripped off my sword and dagger, which he sneered at, but kept, then threw me further into the dell where the others were. They then encouraged Lentullus to scramble out of the pit by poking him with their lances. He brought out the dog, who immediately showed his loyalty by running away.

The happy band stood us side by side and assessed their collection like naturalists collating a set of rare beetles. These lads did not look immensely sophisticated. They probably counted creatures' legs and feelers by picking them off. I started twitching nervously in limbs I didn't even own.

They all towered over us. So did the group who soon turned up whooping triumphantly and bringing our friends from the camp. They had our missing Probus and his treasure-hunting companion. They must have discovered them first.

I anxiously looked them over for damage. Helvetius was sporting a black eye and a terminal case of bad language, and some of the recruits had been knocked about a bit. The centurion's servant appeared to have taken the worst of it, but this was not necessarily a sign of cruelty in the Bructeri; he was such a pathetic character, he was crying out to be beaten up. The lads told me afterwards they had let themselves be taken fairly quietly. After all, our journey's motives were supposed to be peaceable. The warriors had turned up suddenly at the tents. Helvetius had properly followed the rules by trying to converse. It was only when our group had started to be manhandled that he had ordered

586

them to reach for arms. By then it was too late. There had never been much we could hope to achieve by fighting, not in such small numbers and so far from home.

The warriors had then scoured the woods for stragglers. With Lentullus and me they clearly felt they had a complete set.

'Sir, what about – '

'Whoever you're about to mention – *don't*!' Justinus and Orosius were not here. They were our one hope now, though of what I dared not speculate. 'Don't speak of them – don't even think about them, in case the thought shows in your face.'

They might be dead already, as we expected to be soon.

To my intense relief we were not being taken to the grove. At least not yet.

It was now quite dark. They jostled us in a riverward direction, though we never seemed to come to the bank. That was another relief. If they chucked me off a jetty as a morsel for a river-god, I would immediately have to surrender my soul into his webby hands. I couldn't swim my way out of it. I had not much hope for the recruits either; they must have been on the same army water-skills course as me.

We stumbled along, surrounded by tribesmen. They seemed cheerful enough having somebody to jeer at. They offered us no worse harm, though we didn't push our luck by asking who their chieftain was, or when we would be stopping for a snack break.

After what seemed hours we reached a settlement. Rectangular buildings in timber and daub, with steeply pitched roofs which came down almost to the ground. A few pale faces staring at us in the light of smoky torches. A lowing ox.

Our drovers whooped us through a door in an end wall and into a long byre attached at right angles to the largest house or farm. Cattle had lived here very recently; we knew that from the smell. We had tumbled into an area which had a central aisle and stalls separated by posts and hay containers. At the other end there were no stalls, just a bare hearth. We heard a mighty bar closing the door outside. Exploring this squalid guest-suite did not take us long. We just squatted on our haunches and looked round from where we were.

'What happens now, Falco?' We had reached that point of disaster where people have no other option but to turn to me. This was when they were all likely to remind me that the trip to the River Lupia was my idea.

'Have to wait and see.' I sounded moderately confident. 'But I don't think we can expect to be asked which highly articulate defence lawyer we would like to hire from their sophisticated legal pool.'

'How did they know to look for us, sir?'

'My guess is Dubnus alerted them.'

We braced ourselves for a long wait, with not much to hope for at the end of it.

'Maybe a beautiful virgin will bring us a pail of dinner, fall in love with me and lead us to escape,' Ascanius mused. He was the skinniest and most hygienically sordid recruit we had.

'Unwise to expect dinner either, Ascanius.'

Halfway along the building was a shutter. Fascinated blond children opened it and silently peered in at us. Helvetius rapidly tired of that and went to close them out. He said the big warriors were standing about in groups debating in an aimless way. He ducked back inside in case the sight of his grizzled Roman head gave them murderous ideas.

They must have been waiting for someone. He came after an hour or so. The hum of debate increased to a livelier note. They all jabbered on in a way that reminded me of a gathering of my relatives pointlessly arguing whether Great-auntie Atia's birthday was in May or June. Even the man of note must have grown sick of it, for eventually he barged open the door and sauntered in to have a look at us.

He was about fifty. As the russet hair had thinned and faded, he must have increased its length to compensate.

Wild skeins of it ravelled behind him. Xanthus would have been horrified. He also had a long moustache, much in need of an enriching pomade, above which were a bulbous red nose and rather watery pale grey eyes. He was a big man in every way: broad shoulders, heavy bones, big head, big hands. He wore brown woollen trousers, a long-sleeved tunic, a green cloak, and a round gold brooch that not only pegged his ensemble together but rose and fell dramatically to show how far his chest expanded every time he breathed. Some of the others may have looked undernourished, but this fellow was fit.

He was followed by his bodyguard. Younger men, any one of whom would have made a handsome model for a Noble Tribesman statuette had they been fattened up and taught to exhibit a mournful Celtic gaze. Left to themselves their gaze was as vacant as village youths anywhere. Most of them did without a tunic to indicate how tough (or poor) they were. They spat a lot on principle, and glared at us whenever they remembered they were there to use objectionable behaviour towards the prisoners. They all had immensely long German swords, apparently so they had something grand to loll on while their chief was occupied. He looked the type who was always wandering off to pursue other interests, and he had an air of eccentricity that gave him character. Even in Rome that faint impression of madness sometimes works for election candidates.

We were feeling depressed and annoyed with ourselves, so when he made no attempt to communicate we stayed where we were, sitting in two rows on either side of the aisle. We let him wander up and down. None of us spoke. We were hungry and tired, and we let it show, though without appearing demoralised. A man with a proud Roman heritage to bolster him can look truculent even when squatting on two feet of compacted dung. Well, Helvetius managed it, though he had the advantage of being a centurion; it's a snooty rank.

The chief was a man who walked slowly, with a tread that consolidated ground. He paced back to his starting-point, then turned round to us again. He made a sharp noise through his teeth, as if spitting out a raspberry pip. It seemed to be his evaluation of our group, and was resonantly an expression of contempt. I was surprised that he could find two teeth to do it through, for conspicuous along his gums were large gaps.

'Somebody should tell him to watch that,' Ascanius said derisively. 'It's probably how he lost the rest.'

The chieftain's eyes fell on our joking boy. We all realised he had understood.

I stood up like a spokesperson.

'We come in friendship,' I announced. M. Didius Falco, the ever-hopeful innocent. 'We are travelling to see Veleda, your renowned prophetess.' Veleda's name produced as much effect here as trying to interest a carrion crow in lunching off a lettuce leaf.

'You come in friendship?' The chief's chin rose. He folded his arms. The pose was something of a cliché, but in the circumstances that was his prerogative. 'You are Romans in Free Germany.' His Latin accent was terrible, but good enough for snorting at a frowsty group of renegades. 'You have no choice. We are the Bructeri,' the chief informed us haughtily. '*We do!*'

He did his disgusted tooth noise again, then strode out.

'It's definite then,' Ascanius exclaimed incorrigibly. 'He's cancelling the virgin. No dinner for us tonight, lads!'

He was right, too.

L

The beautiful virgin must have been busy next morning, for she sent us her sister instead. Her sister had a figure like a tent-post, a face like the underside of a boulder and a negligible personality. That might not have depressed us, but she was the one who couldn't cook.

'Thank you, my dear,' I saluted her courteously while the others were grimacing. 'We are delighted to make your acquaintance, and that of your gracious porridge pot.' She had brought four bowls between twenty-two of us, and a lukewarm metal cauldron of some glutinous gruel.

She ignored me and stomped out. I pretended I preferred women who are not too obvious.

The breakfast was something everyone ought to experience, so whatever else he had to scoop out of a skillet in his future life he would know it could be worse.

This branch of the Bructeri were slow risers. We were in a sleepy hamlet that would have been an ideal recuperation spot, had the people liked us more. Only towards the end of the morning did we hear activity. 'Attention, men, something's happening . . .'

We looked out of our shutter and saw that runners had been back to raid our camp.

Helvetius and I shoved the others aside while we stood and counted in our baggage and horseflesh. 'I make that six beasts and one tent missing – '

'Plus the cash box, the javelins – '

'Probably some rations, and the tribune's personal kit . . .'

'Oh he'll do!' Helvetius murmured proudly. 'Mithras, he's a *good boy*!'

It looked as if Camillus Justinus would at least be able to report to Rome how the Bructeri had taken us. He had supplies, mounts, and a companion in Orosius. The tribesmen were off guard now they had captured us, and would not be watching out. He should get away. It was the best we could hope for. What else could we expect of one gently reared young officer, aided by a rather dim recruit?

Something stupid, normally. (Helvetius said that.)

The arrival of the horses signalled a change for us. Its good face was that we were saying goodbye to our smelly byre. The gloomy aspects were that they were leaving all our baggage behind, that Ascanius had lost his chance to make love to the porridge girl, and that the Bructeri were going on horseback – *our* horses. They were running us alongside them, on foot. They were rapid riders. And wherever they were taking us turned out to be several days away.

'Look on the bright side. At least we're pointing west. They could have been driving us even further into the interior . . . Every mile we trudge is a mile nearer home.'

'How far is it to Rome from here then, Falco?'

'Jupiter, don't ask!'

As soon as the Bructeri grew tired of herding us like geese, with irritating whistles and much active use of sharp thorny sticks, we settled down into a regular formation and showed them how empire-builders march. Even the recruits were now inspired to smarten up. I was worried for the centurion's servant, but it turned out that after twenty years in the army he could not only make his boots cover ground efficiently, but he could complain at the same time.

We even sang. We invented a marching-ditty that started, *Oh I love my little mess tin with my name punched in the rim* . . . and then proceeded to list numerous items of a legionary's kit (there are plenty to choose from) before reaching his girlfriend, after which the form remained constant but we introduced some obscene counterpoint. The recruits loved it. They had never made up their own song before.

'Sir, this is a really good adventure, sir!'

'How true. Swamps, forests, ghosts, glades full of skulls; filthy, frightened and famished; then all ending up as slaves . . .'

'Sir, what I think is, the people we never mention are going to rescue us. What do you think, sir?'

Helvetius gave his opinion in one word. It was anatomical.

I said that assuming the people whom we never mentioned had done what was sensible and scampered for home as fast as they could ride, I was prepared to consider suggestions for us rescuing ourselves. No one had any.

We sang another thirteen verses of the mess-tin song, to pretend to the red-headed Bructeri that they could never make Romans lose heart.

So, with blistered feet and our anxieties as well disguised as possible, we arrived in a large clearing on the riverbank, where more Bructeri were gathering near a suspiciously high tower. At the base of the tower, in some smart little daub houses, lived a group of skinny tribesmen who had managed to equip themselves with debonair quantities of gold bracelets and jewelled cloak-brooches. This seedy lot looked like the horse-thieves who live on the Pontine marshes and earn a living beating out buckled pots. They were as shifty-eyed as I had already heard, yet every man of them possessed a natty torque, a belt with good enamelled trappings, and various silver or bronze scabbards. Unlike everyone else, they wore several layers of clothing and over-sized boots. They kept some very pretty hunting dogs as pets, and the latest model of wicker-framed chariot was ostentatiously parked at their compound.

These men were a lanky, long-chinned, unimpressive selection whose power to attract rich offerings must be entirely derivative. When they whined after presents, nobody could argue. Among the Bructeri nobody wanted to. For these, without question, were Veleda's male relatives.

We were all roped together, but allowed to wander about.

We made a beeline for where the prophetess must live. I should have known all along. When did Celtic tribes ever build high towers? Veleda had ensconced herself in an old Roman signal post.

Some adaptations had been made to this now ironic edifice. It still had the platform on top for watching and for

593

making the bonfire, but that had been built up even higher with wattle walls, then provided with a snug timber roof. The near-overthrow of the Empire had definitely been supervised from one of our own buildings. We turned aside in disgust.

The headstreams of the Lupia had long since joined each other. The river here had widened enough to carry shipping. Along the banks were various native craft, including high-sided boats with leather sails, wherries and coracles. Also one much bigger, superior ship, which looked oddly out of place. The recruits were fascinated by this vessel and kept ignoring our guards' shouts to wander back and crane at it. I had forgotten that many of them came from the Adriatic seaboard.

'That's a Liburnian!'

Liburnians are light, swift, double-banked galleys derived from Mediterranean pirate ships and much used in the Roman fleet. This one had a decorative portrait of Neptune on the prow and an elaborate cabin at the stern. She was afloat, though half her oars had been robbed and her rigging looked in a fine old tangle. There was no evidence that the priestess kept her trim for floating picnics. She must have lain here deserted for many months.

I said, 'That must be the flagship which Petilius Cerialis had pinched from under his nose.'

'Cor, she's lovely, sir. How could he let that happen?'

'In bed with his fancy bit.'

'Oh sir!'

'Never mind the general's carelessness. Like his splendid Liburnian galley we must have been brought here as presents for the prophetess. So keep quiet; keep together; and keep your eyes peeled for trouble. The lady's last gift of a live Roman was never seen again. And as sure as ambrosia makes heroes belch, the poor beggar's not alive any more.'

I experienced a vague hope, nevertheless, that we would run into the missing legate, Lupercus, and discover he had gone native and was living here with Veleda like a prince. The hope was so vague that it made me feel slightly sick.

I knew only too well the more likely alternatives. And I knew they applied to us.

'Is the prophetess up in that tower now, sir?'

'I don't know.'

'Are you going to ask to see her?'

'I doubt if they would allow it. But I want to see what the situation is before I speak.'

'Ooh don't go up in the tower, sir. You might never come out.'

'I'll bear that in mind.'

The Bructian moot appeared to be a prearranged gathering.

It must have been hard work for the caterers. Celtic tribes are famous for turning up to appointments anything up to three days either side of the given date. Here a feast was in progress on rough trestle-tables. It looked fairly permanent. Presumably it was to pass the time until something like a decent quorum deigned to put in an appearance. I wondered who had issued the invitations to this casual assembly. Then I tried not to wonder how the assembly would affect us.

Our group, with its interesting string of prisoners, aroused bursts of excitement. Other chiefs' retainers felt obliged to swagger up and try to outface our chief's successful troupe. They did this by the usual offensive and threatening gestures against us, which we ignored, though plainly our captors could not allow other people to torment us when that privilege was theirs. By now we felt a proprietary interest in the party we were used to, so we cheered them on and managed to get quite a lively fight going. None of them appeared grateful for our encouragement, and eventually they all grew bored and settled down to feasting.

We were fed too, in a small way. The warriors were tucking into plain but hearty fare: loaves, fruit, hot roasted game and I think some fish. For us the cook had gone to some trouble to produce another of their speciality porridges; it was like eating a wound poultice. There was drink (some kind of fermented cranberry juice), but I warned the lads to go easy in case we needed clear heads later. The women were judged a great improvement on our brush with the virgin's sister; the girl who brought round the juice jar was definitely worth flirting with. I ordered them to lay off that too, and was firmly voted least popular man in our group.

Time went by. I leaned on a tree thinking about it. Time seemed to have no real importance. Still, what else can you expect from feckless tribes who have never invented the sundial, let alone imported an Italian water-clock for sternly governing their free hours? Dear gods, these savages seemed to believe life was about doing what you wanted, and enjoying it whenever possible. If ever the ascetic tenets of Greek philosophy filtered through these lazy forests, people were in for a bad shock. And they were so disorganised, it was no wonder the sons and step-grandson of the supremely ordered Augustus had never managed to line up enough of them together to make a decent show of surrendering to Rome. Rome had a systematic way of schooling tribal peoples – but you had to sit them down and explain the benefits first.

Here, the Bructeri made *us* sit about and wait. We took a haughty view of this breach of diplomatic etiquette.

Nothing happened. There was little sense of anybody else waiting for anything to happen. In fact to us the whole occasion made no sense at all. We sat apart, tied together in our miserable skein of rope and bursting with impatience for some formality, even if it turned out to be the formality of our trial.

Ascanius winked at the juice-jar girl. She ignored him, so he tried grabbing the hem of her rough woollen skirt. At that, with the air of a girl who had done it before, she emptied what was left in the jar all over him.

Some things are the same anywhere.

As she spun off with her pretty nose in the air, I smiled at her wearily and she gave what was really quite a nice smile back to me. My standing rose again.

Watching other people feasting is a soulless exercise.

More time passed. Evening approached. Whatever Dubnus had told me about Germanic attitudes to drink, the cranberry wine was obviously one of those country potions that have an insidious effect. My Great-auntie Phoebe made a similar linctus with myrtleberries which regularly caused a Saturnalia riot. They would have liked it here. Soon the hum of conversation rose into pricklier shouts of debate. As happens anywhere, most of the women decided that if there was going to be an argument they would take themselves off to mutter somewhere else. A few hard cases remained – obviously the ones who had been let down in life. They looked even tipsier than the men. The men, who had appeared to be able to sup their rich red jollop without losing sweat, now glistened up angrily. Opinions were being bandied, always a danger sign. Stronger opinions were offered back in slow, slurred voices that were soon emphasised by table-thumps. Then our chief swayed to his feet with drunken grace and burst into impassioned speech. Obviously a vote was being sought.

Well, naturally we would have been pleased that our own man had proved a hot debater; every prisoner likes to feel he has been captured by a worthy foe. The only problem was it became clear from fierce glances cast in our direction that the issue at stake was our fate. We also received a definite hint that the chief with the pip-spitting teeth had decided to enhance his status by offering his prisoners for use in some grove as the next human sacrifice.

It was a long speech; he enjoyed a rant. Gradually the noise changed, as the warriors began to clash their lances on their shields.

I knew what that meant.

The clashing of shields grew louder and faster. Instinctively we all scrambled into a tighter bunch. A lance, thrown with great accuracy, thrummed into the turf right at our feet.

The noise quietened. It reached the nearest to silence that can ever be achieved in a large group of people who are exhausted by eating and arguing. Attention focused gradually.

A woman had ridden into the clearing, bareback and bridleless, on a white horse.

LI

Helvetius grabbed my arm. 'I'm betting that's the prophetess.'

'No takers, man.'

Two of the lanks who carried messages for visitors walked either side of the skittering horse. Had it not borne a rider I would have said the creature was unbroken. It was undersized, with a shaggy coat and a manic eye. Each of the lanks had a hand on its mane for steerage and looked nervous, but there was no doubt who was in control of them, and of the wild horse, too.

Veleda dismounted among her people. Claudia Sacrata had said men would think her beautiful. Claudia was right. There were twenty-two men in our party; we all did.

She was tall, calm and unhesitant. She had the pale colouring that makes men seem weak and pretty but women mysterious. Her swathe of light gold hair fell to her waist. It was in perfect condition. Helena would have said that a woman who spends most of her days in a tower by herself has plenty of time with the comb. She wore a sleeveless purple gown and was sufficiently well developed for its scooped neck and loose armholes to distract the eye. Her eyes were blue. More importantly, they held the confidence of power.

I tried to detect how she had acquired her honoured position. She looked aloof but assured. She looked as if she could not only reach decisions, but make other people see that whatever she decreed was their only course. For us she spelled doom. The prophetess of the Bructeri was too old to be a young woman, yet too young to be called old. For Rome, she was the wrong age altogether. She knew too much to forgive us, and too little to tire of fighting us. I knew at once that we had nothing to offer her.

Helvetius knew too. 'Best of luck, Falco. Let's hope for

all our sakes we haven't turned up on her doorstep at a bad time of the month.'

I had five sisters and a girlfriend who all let rip when it suited them; I had learned to dodge. But I was beginning to think that this lady might call *any* day she had to deal with Romans the wrong one. A knot of tension, caused by bad food and too little sleep, was forming in my gut.

She moved among the feasting men as if she were welcoming them. As a hostess she was neither cool nor flushed with grating charm. Her manner was open, yet highly reserved. We saw her take no food (part of her aura – no need for sustenance), but once she raised a cup to the whole company, and then applause and cheerful noise broke out anew. As she went round the tables people spoke up to her as equals, but they listened to her replies very steadily. Only once did we see her laughing, with a warrior who must have brought his adolescent son to an assembly for the first time. Afterwards she spent several minutes talking quietly to the boy, who was so overawed he could hardly answer her.

People handed her gifts. The warrior who had captured me gave her my knife.

Our chief gestured to us. She must have thanked him for the donation. She looked once in our direction, and we felt as if she knew everything about us without being told.

She was moving on.

With both hands I broke the rope which tethered me to the others. I strode up to her – though not so near I earned a lance through my throat. She was taller than me. She wore a handsome torque in twisted gold alloy, less heavy than some but more intricate; it looked Hibernian. Her earrings were Greek – gold crescents with extremely fine granulation; they were exquisite. So was her fine clear skin. For a moment it was like approaching any attractive girl who has been fortunate in the heirloom stakes. Then I met the full impact of her personality. Close to, the first impression was of formidable intelligence, sharply applied. Those blue eyes seemed to have been waiting to confront me. They were utterly still. Never had I been so aware of meeting someone so markedly different.

Most dangerous was her honesty. The circus of tinkers who surrounded her might well be composed of charlatans. But Veleda held herself separate and shone, untouched by their tawdriness.

I turned to the chief. 'Tell your prophetess I have travelled all the way from Rome to speak to her.' I was surprised no one moved for a weapon, but they seemed to take their cue from her. She gave none. The chief did not respond to my request either. 'Tell Veleda,' I insisted, 'I wish to speak with her in Caesar's name!'

She made a small impatient movement, presumably at my mentioning the hated and feared word of Caesar. The chief said something in their own language. Veleda did not answer him.

Diplomacy is hard enough when people acknowledge you trying. I lost patience. 'Lady, don't look so hostile – it spoils a lovely face!' Once I had set off so irritably without bothering whether she would understand, it would have been feeble to stop. 'I came in peace. As you will see if you inspect them, my escort is extremely young and shy. We pose no threat to the mighty Bructeri.' In fact their experiences – and possibly the example of living with hard nuts like Helvetius and myself – had stiffened the recruits visibly.

Talking did seem to have aroused some contemptuous interest from Veleda, so I quickly continued: 'It's bad enough bringing a peace mission that nobody has asked for. I did hope to experience your legendary German hospitality; I'm disappointed, madam, by our present plight . . .' I gestured to the rest of my party again; they pressed closer together behind me. This time a warrior, probably drunk, misinterpreted and jerked forward aggressively. Veleda showed no reaction, though someone else held him off. I sighed. 'I wish I could say communication doesn't seem to be your tribe's strong point – but it's painfully clear what they intend. If you refuse to listen to my message, I ask you simply, let me return with my companions and tell our Emperor we failed.'

The prophetess still stared at me, without a sign. In a lifetime of hard conversations this was plumbing new depths. I let my voice lighten. 'If you really propose to make us all slaves, I warn you my soldiers are shore-bred fisherlads; they know nothing about cattle and not one of them can plough. As for me, I can manage a little light market gardening, but my mother would soon tell you that I'm useless in the house . . .'

I had done it. '*Silence!*' said Veleda.

I had achieved more than I bargained for: 'Right. I'm a good Roman boy, princess. When women speak to me firmly in Latin, I do what they say.'

We were getting somewhere now. As usual, it was down an alley where I would rather not have gone.

The prophetess smiled bitterly. 'Yes, I speak your tongue. It seemed necessary. When did a Roman ever bother to learn ours?' She had a strong, even, thrilling voice which it could have been a pleasure to listen to. I was no longer surprised. She made everything she did or said seem inevitable. Naturally, when traders came she wanted to exchange the news and ensure they never cheated her. Much the same went for any ambassadors who crept out of the woods.

I did have a smattering of Celtic from Britain, but so many miles lay between these tribes and those, it was a separate dialect and useless here.

I fell back on the normal degrading rites of diplomacy: 'Your civility rebukes us.' It sounded like a comic play translated from a poor original by some hack poet in Tusculum. 'I would be praising the lady Veleda for her beauty, yet I believe she would rather hear me compliment her skill and intellect – '

The lady Veleda spoke in her own language, quietly. What she said was brief, and her people laughed. The expression was probably much ruder, but its import was, *This man makes me feel tired.*

So much for diplomacy.

Veleda tipped her chin up. She knew her striking looks, yet despised using them. 'What,' she enquired deliberately, 'have you come here to say?'

That was straightforward. However, there was no way I

could simply answer, *Where's Munius, and will you kindly stop your warriors attacking Rome?*

I tried the frank grin. 'I'm getting the worst of this!'

Some trickster must have grinned at her like that before. 'You are getting what you deserve.' She sounded like another high-handed girl I often quarrelled with.

'Veleda, what Vespasian sent me here to say is vital to all of us. It cannot be bandied about like a cheap exchange of insults in a drunken shouting match. You speak for your nation – '

'No,' she interrupted me.

'You are the venerated priestess of the Bructeri – '

Veleda smiled quietly. Her smile was completely private, with no shared human contact. Its effect was to make her seem untouchable. She said, 'I am an unmarried woman who dwells in the forest with her thoughts. The gods have given me knowledge – '

'Your deeds also will never be forgotten.'

'I have done nothing. I merely provide my opinions if people ask for them.'

'Then your mere opinions have given you great powers of leadership! Deny ambition if you will, but you and Civilis nearly ruled Europe.' And nearly ruined it. 'Lady, your opinions lit the whole world like a lightning storm. Perhaps you were right, but now the world needs rest. The fight is over.'

'The fight will never be over.'

The simple way Veleda spoke alarmed me. Had she been a conventional power-seeker, these boisterous warriors would have sneered at her and Civilis would have seen her as a rival instead of a partner. She might have roused the rabble once or twice with furious oratory, but probably the Bructeri themselves would have seen her off. Even the hero Arminius had been defeated by his own people in the end. A leader who would not seek the trappings of leadership would be beyond comprehension in Rome. Here, her very rejection of ambition increased her strength.

'It's over,' I insisted. 'Rome is herself. To fight now is to run against bedrock. You cannot defeat Rome.'

'We did. We will.'

'That was then, Veleda.'

'Our time will come again.'

However confident I sounded, Veleda too felt secure. She was turning away once more. I refused to be silenced by a woman presenting her back to me. All my adult life women had been treating me like a bathhouse scraping-slave who hadn't earned his tip.

With nothing to lose, I tried making it personal. 'If this is the vaunted Gallic Empire, I'm not impressed, Veleda. Civilis has bunked off, and all I see here is a clearing in the forest with the kind of tawdry sideshow that turns up at every horse fair. Just another girl with a yearning for show business, trying to make a name for herself – and what's more, discovering that success means all her hangdog relations expect her to find them a job in her retinue... I'm sorry for you. Yours look even worse than my own.' From their impassive faces the lady's relations were either dumber than I thought, or had not shared her Latin tutor. She herself now faced up to me. Family feeling, I dare say. I carried on more quietly: 'Excuse the jibes. My people may be low, but I'm missing them.' She did not appear to have taken my point that Romans were human too. Still, I had her attention, probably.

'Veleda, your influence rests on your successful prophecy that the Roman legions would be destroyed. An easy feat. Anyone who watched the struggle to be emperor could see the Roman stake in Europe was at risk. With only two straws to draw, you picked the lucky answer. That won't work now. Rome has full control again. Once Rome was revived, Petilius Cerialis marched his men along the western bank of the Rhenus from the Alps to the Britannic Ocean, and Rome's enemies fell back before them all the way. Where is your triumphant Civilis nowadays? In the sea, probably.'

The official version of our own commander's fighting prowess may have pleased his urbane mistress in Colonia but it cannot have impressed a shrewd, scornful woman who could see the Cerialis flagship moored on her personal

603

landing-stage. Yet Veleda knew as well as I did that he may have been disorganised, but even Cerialis had won.

'I hear,' said the prophetess as if she hoped to enjoy my discomfiture, 'our kinsman Civilis has dyed his hair red again.'

Well that was an unexpected bonus. I had not dared hope for news. And it didn't sound as if the rebel was in hiding here.

'He's not with you?'

'Civilis only feels at home on the western bank of the river.'

'Not even on The Island?'

'Nowadays, not even there.'

'Rome will barber Civilis. The question is, resourceful prophetess, will you now have the courage to see that the legions were *not* defeated, and help reconstruct the world which we all so nearly lost?'

I ran out of appeals. The prophetess was still so calm I felt like a man eating grit. 'The decision,' she told me, 'will be made by the Bructeri.'

'Is that why they are here? Veleda, give up your fanatical life of opposing Rome. The Bructeri, and other peoples, will listen to you.'

'My life is irrelevant. The *Bructeri* will never give up opposing Rome!'

Looking around the Bructeri, I was surprised they had ever listened to anyone.

Veleda stayed as aloof as a Greek oracle or a sibyl. Her routine with the tower was just as much of a fake as their terrifying rituals at Delphi or gumae. But Greek and Roman prophets envelop destinies in riddles; Veleda used the open truth. Her best ploy, I thought, was that, like an orator who voices the people's secret thoughts, she drew on deep feelings which already existed. They believed they were making their own choices. We had seen it here: she was hosting this gathering as if she intended to play no part in the coming arguments. Yet I still believed that the prophetess would achieve the result she wanted. It would be the

604

wrong result for Rome. And Veleda's belief in it looked unshakeable.

This time my intervention was over. Veleda's rare public appearance was ending. She began to move and her supporters regrouped to protect her from being detained.

Once again she turned back to me. It was as if she read my thoughts: that if big decisions were about to be made at this gathering, we might have arrived at the right time. She took pleasure in telling me I would have no chance of affecting events: 'You and your companions are a gift to me. I have been asked to endorse a fate which you can probably guess.' For the first time she looked curious about us. 'Are you afraid of death?'

'No.' Only angry.

'I have yet to decide,' she announced cordially.

I managed to fight back one final time: 'Veleda, you demean yourself and your honoured reputation by slaughtering an old soldier, his servant, and a group of innocent boys!'

I had offended everyone. The chief who brought us felled me with a stupendous blow.

Veleda had reached her tower. Her male relations assembled at the foot of it, facing out towards the company. As the slim figure glided away alone into her retreat, the shadow of the great Roman doorway fell across her golden hair. The signal-tower abruptly swallowed her. The effect was sinister.

It roused all the more anxiety if you were lying on the grass with your pride lopped and a pain in your head, facing the thought of a grisly death in a Bructian sacred grove.

605

LII

Helvetius made a cursory attempt to help me rise. 'Didn't do too well there!'

I shook him off. 'Anyone who thinks his winning words stand a better chance than mine can go and try his luck in the tower!'

The scathing quips dried up.

Two of the lady's relations had been deputed to relocate us in a long stockade made of twiggy hurdles that still looked as if they were growing. This must be where she kept live gifts prior to their ritual butchering. They herded us over there, and penned us in. It was occupied already. The specimen we found huddled in a corner seemed unlikely to propitiate the hoary god whom Lentullus and I had seen in the grove.

'Oh look everyone, we've found Dubnus!'

Our lost pedlar had come in for a heavy battering. He must have been bruised in a rich pattern, then some days later somebody had gone over him with the deliberate aim of filling in any gaps that had shown between the previous contusions. 'What was this for?'

'Being a Ubian.'

'Don't lie! You came selling the Bructeri information about us. They must have used the information, but shown you their contempt!'

He looked as if he expected us to attack him too, but we made a point of explaining that we never hit people whose tribes were officially Romanised. 'Not even two-timing ones, Dubnus.'

'Not even runaway interpreters who skip just when we're needing them.'

'Not even Ubian bastards who sell us into captivity.'

'Not even you, Dubnus.'

He said something in his own tongue, which we did not need an interpreter to understand.

What happened next was a surprise. Hardly had Veleda's shambling adherents roped up the wattle and left us to ponder, than they were there again removing their feeble wisps of lashing and pulling open the exit fence.

'Mithras! The witch has changed her mind. We're all getting nice new cloaks and going to be guests of honour at the feast . . .'

'Save your breath to cool your gruel, centurion. That one won't change her mind.'

The lanks dragged us all out. The sight of Dubnus seemed to remind them that they might enjoy feeling big. He was too mashed already to be worth making him squeal again, so they started giving the odd thump to Helvetius and me. When we shoved them aside angrily, they joined the trend and picked on the centurion's servant instead. This time Helvetius decided he wasn't having it and squared up to defend his man. We braced ourselves for trouble – and trouble duly arrived. Not what we expected, though.

First Veleda popped back out of her stone retreat.

A trumpet sounded. 'Jupiter Best and Greatest – *that's one of ours!*'

It was a short, slow call on a clear but subdued instrument. Its mournful tremor sounded Roman, yet not quite right. It came from the forest somewhere close. It was blown on the twisted bronze horn which sentries use, and the call was recognisably the signal for the second night watch. It was four hours early tonight.

Then Tigris ran into the clearing, went straight across to Veleda, and lay down with his nose between his paws.

I hardly had time to guess that the prophetess must have spied the embassy from her signal-tower when someone else arrived. It was Helena's younger brother. I had long suspected this character of harbouring deep qualities, but it was the first time he had shown us his talent for makeshift spectacle.

He clip-clopped into the clearing with Orosius as an

outrider. Neither of them had the trumpet, which subtly implied someone else did (they must have left it propped against a tree). They looked good; one or both of them had spent all afternoon combing plumes and buffing bronze. Helena's brother was tackling the Bructeri as if he had an army of fifteen thousand waiting down the road. There was no road, but Camillus Justinus gave the impression he might have had one built for him. There was no army either; we knew that.

For a man who had spent the last month under canvas in the wilderness, his rig was immaculate. His air of restrained bravado was also pitched perfectly. He had the best of our Gallic horses. He must have raided our supplies for olive oil and burnished the beast so that even its hooves gleamed with their unorthodox marinade. If the horse was well groomed, so was he. Somehow, in the depths of the forest, he and Orosius had managed to shave. They made the rest of us look like the riff-raff with fleas and funny accents who can never get a seat at the races even when the gatekeeper has gone to lunch and left his ten-year-old brother as bouncer.

Justinus wore the entire panoply of his tribunal rank, plus a few details he had invented for himself: a white tunic hemmed in purple; spanking greaves with ornate gilding; a thrusting horsehair plume atop a helmet that had a shine which flashed round the forest every time he moved his head. The breastplate which sat over his heavily fringed leathers looked three times as bright as usual. Looped up around its heroically modelled torso our lad wore his heavy crimson cloak with a debonair swing. In the crook of one arm he was carrying – in an extremely relaxed manner – some sort of ceremonial stave, a novelty he had apparently copied from formal statues of Augustus. His expression had that Emperor's noble calm, and if the noble calm was disguising fright not even his friends could tell.

He rode halfway across the clearing, slowly enough to give the prophetess a good stare at his turnout. He dismounted. Orosius accepted his reins – and his stave – with silent deference. Justinus approached Veleda with a firm spring in his tribunal boots, then swept off his helmet as a sign of respect to her. The Camilli were a tall family, especially in triple-soled military footware; for once she was looking a Roman directly in the eyes. The eyes she would be seeing now were big, brown, modest, and momentously sincere.

Justinus paused. He coloured slightly: nice effect. Removing his gilded pot had allowed the lady to receive the full benefit of his frank admiration and boyish reserve. The sensitive eyes must be working their magic, and he matched the deep stillness of the prophetess with his own steadiness.

Then he said something. He seemed to address Veleda confidentially, yet the pitch of his voice carried everywhere. We knew the man. We knew the voice. But none of us had the slightest idea what he said to the prophetess.

Camillus Justinus had spoken in her own tongue.

He did it with the lilting fluency I remembered from his Greek. It took Veleda longer than she could have liked before she recovered; then she inclined her head. Justinus spoke to her again; this time she glanced in our direction. He must have asked her a question. She considered her answer, then abruptly replied.

'Thank you,' said Justinus very civilly, in Latin this time, as if paying her the compliment of assuming she would understand him too. 'Then I'll greet my friends first, please . . .' He was not asking her permission; it was a statement of intent. Then he turned back to her with a good-mannered apology: 'My name is Camillus Justinus, by the way.'

His face remained impassive as he walked across to us. We took our cue from him. He shook hands with every one of us, in a measured and grave style. With the eyes of the entire Bructian gathering upon him, Justinus did little more than speak our names, while we muttered as much information as we could.

'Marcus Didius.'

'She claims to be just a woman who dwells in the tower with her thoughts.'

'Helvetius.'

'Somebody should give her something else to think about!' Helvetius could not resist this typical shaft.

'Ascanius.'

'We're all due for a nasty death, sir.'

'Probus.'

'Tribune, what have you said to her?'

'Sextus. We're going to talk things over quietly; let me see what I can do. Lentullus!'

When he had greeted us all, his bright eyes met mine directly. 'Well, you've left me everything to do here! I even had to blow the bloody trumpet for myself.'

He was using the joke to hide some anxiety; behind the glint of amusement his face looked sad. I suddenly stepped up to him, pulling out the amulet I had been given in Vetera; he saw what it was and ducked his head to receive it round his own neck. 'If it's any help, a contact told me Veleda may be yearning for some decent conversation . . . That's for Helena. Watch yourself.'

'Marcus!' he embraced me like a brother, then I took his helmet from him. He walked bravely away from us.

He went back to Veleda. He was a shy man, who had learned to answer challenges alone. Veleda was waiting for him like a woman who thought she was likely to regret something.

I whipped round towards the pedlar, the only one among us whom the tribune had pointedly ignored. 'What did he say to her, Dubnus?'

Dubnus cursed, but answered me. 'He said: "You must be Veleda. I bring you greetings from my Emperor, and messages of peace . . ."'

'You're holding back! He made an offer – that was obvious.'

Without bothering to question what I had in mind, our reliable Helvetius stomped up behind the pedlar and hoicked his arms back in a wrestling hold that bit persuasively. Dubnus gasped, 'He said: "I see my comrades are your hostages. I offer myself in exchange."'

I had known it. Justinus dashed into danger with the

same offhand courage his sister showed when she decided impatiently that someone had to be businesslike. 'So what did Veleda answer him?'

' *"Come into my tower!"* '

What the pedlar said was true. The moment Justinus reached her, Veleda strode back towards her monument. He followed. Then we watched our innocent tribune walk into the tower alone with her.

I strode to the tower base. The goat-thief guards were standing about looking mystified, but they closed ranks when I appeared. I stood at the door with my head thrown back, staring up at the old Roman stonework with its rows of red brick-tile strengthening. There was nothing I could do. I returned to the troops. The tribune's dog remained behind, sitting at the entrance to the tower and watching intently for his master to reappear.

The recruits were taking bets on his chances, half terrified and half envious: 'She'll eat him!'

I wanted to concentrate on other things. 'Perhaps she'll spit him out . . .'

How was I to tell the tribune's sister about this? She would blame me, I knew.

'Why has he gone in there, sir?'

'You heard him: he's going to talk things over quietly.'

'What things, sir?'

'Nothing much, I expect.'

Fate. World history. His friends' lives. The tribune's death . . .

'Sir – '

'Shut up, Lentullus.'

I went back to the hurdles. I eased myself into a squatting position, trying to keep off the ground. It was the wrong time of year for sitting on grass; tonight would have a heavy dew. It was starting to feel like the wrong time of year for anything.

The others all fell on Orosius, then slowly joined me, settling down to wait for the unknown. Orosius had little to say for himself except that in his opinion the tribune was all right. I tweaked his ear and told him we knew that.

I should have known. He had an appetite for information. Camillus Justinus would not spend three years safeguarding the frontiers of a province without learning how to speak to its people. Now he was on his own with much more than the language.

He was so thorough it shook me. With his fresh-faced way of getting to know every soldier he commanded, this unlikely soul had even persuaded some hardbitten *bucinator* to teach him to sound a passable trumpet alarm. A month of woodcraft had depressed him, but left his ingenuity intact. Having come on this adventure in the first place, he would not give up. But he was twenty. He had never been exposed to harm. He stood no chance.

He had never been exposed to *women*, but perhaps we were safe there.

'Are foreign priestesses virgins, sir?'

'I believe it's not obligatory.' Only Rome equated chastity with holiness; and even Rome installed ten vestals at a time, in order to give latitude for mistakes.

'Is the tribune going to – '

'He's going to talk about politics.' Even so, the novel combination of the destiny of nations and the most attractive woman he had ever had to talk to might prove a heady mix.

'The witch might have other ideas!' They were bolder now. 'Maybe the tribune doesn't know what to do – '

'The tribune seems a lad who can improvise.'

But I certainly hoped I never had to tell his sister that I had let some mad-eyed prophetess make a man of her little brother at the top of a signal-tower.

When the torches had waned and the feast died down, I ordered our lads to rest. Later, I left Helvetius on watch, picked my way between the slumbering Bructeri and stole near the tower. One guard with a lance lolled asleep on the entrance steps. I could have grasped his weapon and closed his windpipe with its shaft, but I let him be. Others were inside the tower base, so entering was impossible.

I walked round outside. Moonlight draped the wall with sheaths of startling white. High above shone a faint glimmer from a lamp. I could hear voices. Difficult to tell which language they were using; the level of conversation was too low. It sounded like discussion rather than argument. It sounded more as if they were talking over a concert or the merits of a wall fresco than ascertaining the Empire's horoscope. At one point the tribune said something that amused the prophetess; she answered, then they both laughed.

I could not decide whether to groan or grin. I went back to my men.

Helvetius thumped my shoulder. 'All right?'

'They're talking.'

'That sounds dangerous!'

'More dangerous when they stop, centurion.' Suddenly I confided, 'I want to marry his sister.'

'He told me.'

'I didn't think he knew I was serious.'

'*He's* worried,' said Helvetius, 'that you may not be aware it's what his sister has in mind.'

'Oh, she's a frank woman! I imagined he thought I was just a low-life adventurer who was playing around with her.'

'No, he thinks you're the man for the business.' Helvetius clapped me on the back. 'So this is cosy – now we all know where we are!'

'True. The man I want to be my children's favourite uncle is – '

'Is likely to come back to us with a rather stiff walk and a queer look in his eye! You can't make his choices. He's not a baby.'

'No, he's twenty, and never been kissed . . .' Well, probably. With anyone else I might have wondered whether he had acquired his slick mastery of German from a girl. 'He's never had his throat cut with a sickle in a sacred grove either, centurion!'

'Get some rest, Falco. You know what he's like when he gets an interesting chat going. If the lady feels just as talkative, it's going to be a long night.'

It was the longest night I spent in Germany. When he came back, all the others were asleep. I was watching out for him.

It was dark. The moon had travelled into a deep band of

cloud, but our eyes were adjusted. He saw me stand up. We clasped hands, then spoke in whispers, Justinus in a light, excited tone.

'Lot to tell you.' His adrenalin was running at a fierce rate.

'What's going on? Are you on parole?'

'She wants time alone. I have to go back when the moon comes out, and she'll tell me if it's war or peace.' He was exhausted. 'I hope her lunar forecast is reliable . . .'

I surveyed the sky. The heaviness above was an unshed storm; I could see it would pass over. 'She's right – and like all magic, that's observation, not prophecy.'

We crouched down by a tree. He gave me something. 'A knife?'

'Yours. She had her presents on a coffer; I recognised it. I told her it belonged to my brother-in-law.'

'Thanks – which includes the compliment. It's my best knife, but if she's handing out hospitality gifts I can suggest more useful things.'

'I think she gave me the knife to show she was detached, and not influenced by presents.'

'Or on the make!'

'Cynic! What should I have asked for?'

I made a silly suggestion, and he laughed. But his task was too oppressive for jokes. 'Marcus, I've nothing to offer. We should have brought presents.'

'We brought the cash box.'

'That's to pay the recruits!' He had a strange simplicity.

'They'd rather be living than dead but paid up.'

'Ah!'

'I'll fetch the money from where you left it. Orosius can show me. Now tell me what you and Veleda talked about.'

'It was quite an experience!' That sounded ominous. 'We talked ourselves all round the forum. I've done what I could for the Emperor's mission. I told her we all ought to accept that the people on the west bank of the Rhenus have *chosen* to be Romanised, and that unless there is a threat to their security, the Emperor has no ambitions for crossing to the east.' Justinus dropped his voice. 'Marcus, I'm not so certain that will always hold.'

'It's policy. Things may change along the Danube, but don't complicate the issue with what may never happen. She's shrewd enough to draw conclusions for herself.'

'I've no training in this. I feel so badly equipped!'

Our one hope was that Veleda might trust him for his transparent integrity.

'Have faith. At least she's listening. Before you did your parade-ground stunt, I spoke to her myself – '

'I heard some of that. Orosius and I were hiding in the trees. We couldn't get close enough to catch everything, but I've tried to follow up what you said about the legions being in power again.'

'She has to be convinced that if the tribes fling themselves against the disciplined might of Rome it can only be suicide.'

'Marcus, she knows that.' He spoke quietly, as if with loyalty to her.

'That's not what she said.'

'She was in front of her people – '

'And arguing with a shyster of course . . .'

'No, I think your words went home. She seems deeply troubled. I fancy she was brooding on the future before we ever came here. That may be why she called the tribal gathering. When I urged her to tell the tribes the truth about what she foresaw for them, I could tell from her face the responsibility alarms her.'

'Use that.'

'I don't have to. Veleda is already suffering.'

'Dear gods, this is just like talking to you about the barmaid at the Medusa!'

I had meant it as a joke, but Justinus dropped his head. 'Something I should have told you. I owe you an apology.'

'What for?' Our rissole lunch at the Medusa seemed a thousand years ago.

'After you left for Colonia there was a rumpus at the tavern. Somebody noticed a funny smell, and it wasn't the dish of the day that time. They found the body of the legate's bedchamber slave buried under a floor. Regina confessed. When they were quarrelling she lost her temper and hit him too hard with an amphora.'

I said it made a change from battered barmaids anyway.

'You knew she was trouble. So Marcus, tell me about this one!'

'Use your initiative – you seem to have plenty. I keep away from prophets; my mother says nice boys don't mess with venerated girls.'

We were still giggling when the moon re-emerged.

'Marcus.'

'Justinus.'

'It's Quintus,' he offered wryly, like a someone making friends rather belatedly after going to bed.

'I'm honoured. I didn't even know your private name.'

'I don't tell many people,' he said quietly. 'Now, what am I doing? *Exchanging gifts, ending the battles* – '

'A snip! And *exercising caution*. Don't end up like Lupercus.'

'Ah! *Asking about Lupercus*.' I myself had been prepared to forget what had happened to Lupercus, in case the recollection gave Veleda bloodthirsty ideas. 'The first thing is to persuade her to release the rest of you . . . I hope you get back.' He could not disguise the crack in his voice.

'I hope we *all* do! Listen, when you climb the tower again, if you find Veleda in her best gown with her hair braided specially, my advice is forget the Empire and do a runner straight back here.'

'Don't be ridiculous!' he answered, in a rare mood of tetchiness.

At least during this absence I found an occupation. I woke Orosius and we crept off through the woods to where he and Justinus had left their tent and supplies. We packed everything and brought it nearer to the tower. Then we led forward the horse with the cash box, and I whistled an alert to the tribune.

The prophetess herself pushed out of the doors through

a clump of her relatives; Justinus was not with her. She was extremely pale, and tightly gripping a cloak around herself. We dumped the strongbox on the ground and I opened it to show her the silver. Veleda inspected the money cautiously while I tried to sound as clean-living as Justinus. 'I know: the Bructeri cannot be bought . . . That's not the intention, lady. This is a sign of the Emperor's friendship.'

'Your negotiator made that plain.'

'Where is he?' I asked bluntly.

'Safe.' She was sneering at my anxiety. 'You are Falco? I wish to speak with you.'

She led me just inside the lower portion of the tower. There was a bare octagonal basement, with stairs leading up several storeys round the neatly coursed Roman brick of the inner walls. Each storey was slightly reduced in diameter to provide stability for the tower; only the top was floored, since only the open roof had been built to be used. That, with some modifications for comfort, was where the prophetess lived. She did not invite me to ascend.

Veleda was frowning. I tried to sound sympathetic as I asked, 'Do I deduce that Luna reappeared prematurely?' I was right. Veleda had still not decided what to do. The uncertainty was knotting her like a snaggled fishing net.

'I have two things to say.' She spoke hurriedly, as if she had been pressurised into this. 'I have agreed to your departure. Go tonight. No one will hinder you.'

'Thanks. What's the other thing?'

'The death of Munius Lupercus.'

'So you do know? A woman among the Ubians told me otherwise.'

'I know now,' she said coldly. Obviously they had less in common than Claudia Sacrata had convinced herself. She handed me a small fold of crimson cloth. Inside were two more trifles from her curio cabinet – miniature silver spears of the kind legates receive as good service awards from the Emperor. Lupercus would have been due for his third at the end of his fatal tour in Vetera.

'So he did come here?'

'He was never here.' She spoke with her usual assurance,

618

perhaps relieved to be distanced from the sordid tale. 'Those were brought to me later. I am content that you should return them to the man's mother or his wife.'

I thanked her, and then she told me what had happened. Even Veleda looked subdued when she had finished. I had no sympathy with legates, but it set me back. 'Have you given this information to the tribune Camillus?'

'No.'

I understood why. She had established a friendly pact with Justinus; this could wreck it.

Civilis had sent Munius Lupercus across country with what Veleda chose to call a mixed group from various tribes. I did not press her for more detail; she was right not to provide fuel for recriminations. The legate had been wounded; he had lost his fort and seen his legion slaughtered; he had thought the Empire was disintegrating too. Whether he begged for release or for death, or whether his guards simply lost patience and wanted to be back with Civilis at the fighting, they suddenly accused Lupercus of cowardice. Then they treated him to their version of a coward's fate: he was stripped, bound, half garrotted, thrown in a swamp, and pressed down with hurdles until he drowned.

To do her justice, Veleda looked as though she hated telling it as much as I hated hearing it. 'They had deprived me of my gift, so the truth was slow to emerge.'

I buried my jaw in my hand. 'This truth were better submerged in the swamp with him.'

'If I were his mother or wife,' said Veleda, 'I would wish to know.'

'So would my mother and my future wife, but like you, they are exceptional . . .'

She changed the subject. 'That is all I can tell you. You and your men must depart discreetly; I have no wish to insult the chief who brought you here by exchanging his present too openly.'

'Where's Camillus?' I demanded suspiciously.

'Above. I still wish to talk to him.' Veleda paused, as if

she read all my thoughts. 'Naturally,' she said softly, 'your friend will say farewell.'

I was desperate. 'Does it have to be an exchange?'

'That was what was offered,' smiled the prophetess.

At that point Justinus himself came out on to the stairs above us and clattered down to the basement. 'So what happened to Lupercus?'

'The legate,' I relied carefully, thinking as I spoke, 'was executed on his way here. Too much time has elapsed for the details to be known.'

Veleda's mouth was pinched, but she went along with it. Then she passed Justinus and left the two of us together. As she climbed the stair her cloak slipped. I could not see what gown she wore, but her rich gold hair was now braided extremely neatly into a plait the thickness of my wrist. Justinus and I avoided each other's eyes.

I made a small snort of annoyance. '*Eheu!* I meant to ask her about horses . . .'

Justinus laughed. 'I asked her for what you wanted.'

She had agreed to my silly suggestion. 'Quintus, you smooth-talking devil! I hope you never come to me trying to wheedle a loan . . . Right, I gather she needs more of your verbal fluency. Don't bite your tongue off chattering! She wants us to leave quickly, but we'll have to wait until first light . . .'

'I must do what I have to here, Marcus.' He looked strained.

'Too many good men have said that, then thrown away promising careers with no public thanks. Don't be a fool – or a dead hero. Tell her the exchange is off. I'm expecting to see you before we leave, tribune. I'll load up, then we'll sit it out and wait for you.' He and I were responsible for the lives of Helvetius and the recruits. We both knew what had to happen.

'Leave at dawn,' Justinus said tersely. He seized the old wooden newel post and swung back up the stairs.

I left him, uncertain whether he intended to come with

us. I had a bad feeling that the tribune might not yet know himself.

However, I was damn sure that Veleda knew what *she* was intending for *him*.

Outside, I quietly roused everyone. They huddled round as I whispered what was happening.

'The witch is letting us steal away, but her colleagues may view it differently, so don't make a sound. Thanks to our fearsome negotiator, she's giving us new transport.' I paused. 'So the question is, how many of you horrible seaside beach bums are at home on a Liburnian?'

As I had thought, for once we had no problem. After all, the legio First Adiutrix had been formed from discards of the Misenum fleet. These were the best troops I could have chosen for bringing the general's flagship home.

PART SIX:
GOING HOME (PERHAPS)

GERMANIA LIBERA, BELGICA AND UPPER GERMANY
November, AD 71

'*After his first military action against the Romans, Civilis had sworn an oath, like the primitive savage he was, to dye his hair red and let it grow until such time as he had annihilated the legions . . .*'

Tacitus, *Histories*

LIV

We managed to board without alerting the Bructeri. At first
I refused to take the pedlar, then I relented, in order to
make quite certain by keeping him with us that he could
not inform on us again. The two mounts Justinus and Orosius had arrived on had been swiftly appropriated by our
hosts, but we did tice our remaining four up the gangplank,
probably because they could not see where we were leading
them.

Fumbling in the dark we struggled in silence to untangle
ropes and free wedged oars. Under way with an experienced
crew the Liburnian would outstrip anything in these waters,
but her condition was uncertain, we lacked manpower, and
none of us knew the craft, let alone the river we were about
to sail. A group of recruits slipped along the waterfront,
putting a spike into boats that might pursue us, but the
noise worried Helvetius and we recalled them.

The recruits were in their element. They could all sail
and row. Well, all except Lentullus. Lentullus was still our
problem boy who couldn't do anything.

The tone of the sky was lightening; I was starting to feel
desperate. 'Helvetius, if Camillus doesn't come soon, you
take the lads and get out of here.'

'You're not going ashore again?'

'I won't leave him.'

'Forget the heroics. Here he is!'

I admit, I was amazed.

We had eased the ship from her moorings and re-anchored
in the channel. Probus was waiting at the quay with a
bumboat to row the tribune out to us. We already had the
anchor up as we hauled them in.

'Is it war?'

'It's peace.'

625

It was too dark to see the tribune's face.

Justinus walked to the stern of the ship without another word. I looked at his set back, then signalled the others not to bother him. He settled himself in a black corner, leaning against the general's cabin and staring back towards the shore. His little dog lay down at his feet, whimpering as it recognised unhappiness. Seeing the tribune's despondent pose, my own heart sank.

We had plenty to do. We let the ship ride on the current at first, for quietness. As the light increased, the full extent of a year's neglect became obvious. Soon we had half our troops furiously bailing while Helvetius cursed and tried to fix a dried-out bilge pump. It had been a sophisticated apparatus once. So sophisticated, a period out of commission had left its wood and calfskin utterly defunct.

We drifted on, with no sign of pursuit. Ascanius and Sextus had found the sails. The leather had stiffened so much it was almost unmanageable, but we stamped it flat as best we could. The smaller triangular jib went up fairly soon, though the square sail took much longer to organise. Then we found our ship sheering too near the bank. A Liburnian is a big vessel to be manoeuvred by a band of novices, some of whom are also idiots, but I still shook my head when eyes were cast sternwards.

'The tribune could add his weight here!'

'The tribune's done enough.'

'Sir – '

'He wants to feel gloomy. Let him be!'

With all other hands assisting on the danger side, we just shipped the oars in time to avoid crashing them, then held our breath as the galley scraped and bumped along the shallows. Somehow we succeeded in turning her back into the channel. She limped on in the grey light of a cold November morning, while we spent another hour working on the sail. It finally jerked into position to a weary cheer. After that it was a mad rush back to bailing duty, then we took stock.

We had no weapons apart from the javelins, and little food. Only two of us had armour. We had salvaged four horses – who might well end up grilled. We no longer possessed cash for bartering. We had the Bructeri on the north bank, and the Tencteri on the south, both contemptuous of Romans in distress. Landing would be fatal until we came to the River Rhenus, which must be over a week away. The way our ship was listing and dragging foretold a week of hard work.

We were alive and free. That surprise was so pleasant we put half the recruits to rowing while the rest jettisoned lumber to lighten their burden, attended to the sails – and sang.

Helvetius screwed some thrust from the pump.

Then, at last, I let Ascanius take the rudder while I walked astern to investigate what Veleda had done to our boy.

LV

'What ho, Masinissa!' Justinus was too polite to tell me to remove my happy grin. 'I'm glad the amulet worked.'

'Oh it worked!' He said it in an odd voice.

I assumed my sombre uncle attitude: 'You look tired.'

'It's not serious.'

'Good. I was afraid it might be due to a broken heart.'

'How lucky we know that's not true,' he answered, much too quietly.

'She's too old for you, you have nothing in common, and your mother has enough to endure with Helena and me.'

'Of course,' he said. He might have argued the point about me and Helena.

'Well Quintus Camillus, I'm glad you can be philosophical. You're a decent lad and deserve some fun before you settle down to a dull old life as a senator, but we both know what happened back there had all the makings of a significant experience – the kind that has been known to bruise a thoughtful man's morale.'

'The Senate has been ruled out for me.'

'Wrong. You've rewritten that. I believe there are advantages, if you can tolerate the bores and hypocrites. You only have to attend the Curia once a month, and you get front-row seats in theatres.'

'Please don't jolly me along.'

'All right. As a matter of interest, did you escape or did the lady throw you out?'

'I meant my offer of an exchange. I said I had to stay.'

'Ah well. Some women can't stand pompous types who stick by their principles.'

He was silent.

'Do you want to talk about what happened?'

'No,' he said.

We watched the river slipping away behind us. We were

travelling slower than I liked for safety, but it was too fast for the tribune. He had been overwhelmed, then wrenched away before he could adjust. Now he felt racked by the scale of his feelings.

'Be prepared,' I advised. 'People other than me will ask you – people in high positions. A junior officer who has talked to the enemy has a duty to explain.' I was turning to go.

Justinus asked suddenly in a wry voice, 'What happened to Masinissa?'

I stopped. 'After he threw away his princess? He lived with honour for many years, devoting himself to kingship and such.'

'Ah, yes of course!' I waited. He was forcing himself to complete the day's official business. 'When I went back upstairs she had already decided. She will tell her people that a free Gallic Empire can never be established. That Rome will not in our lifetime lose the western Rhenus bank. That liberty in their own territory is worth more than pointless war . . . Can she make them listen?' He sounded desperate.

'She never uses compulsion. Leaving people free to choose sometimes pressures them into choosing the harder course.'

'Oh yes!' he said, rather heavily.

'Was she upset?' A fleeting thought assailed me that he might have been consoling her.

He did not answer my question but asked his own: 'What will happen to her?'

'She'll either become a crazy wraith, or she'll marry some thickset red-haired hulk and have nine children in ten years.'

After a silence Justinus said, 'She prophesied to me that if the eastern tribes resume their nomadic life, invading each other's territory, the Bructeri will be wiped out.'

'It's possible.'

For a long time neither of us spoke.

We heard Ascanius calling that he wanted a relief. I had ordered Helvetius to rest so that he could take a later watch;

629

I had to go. 'One thing puzzles me, Quintus. If Veleda had already decided, why did it take her until dawn to throw you out?'

His pause was almost undetectable. 'She was desperate for some decent conversation, as you said. So was I,' he added.

I laughed, then said he had a subtle knack of being rude, and that I could take a hint.

I loped back to supervise Ascanius. When Ascanius demanded for everyone, *'Did he, or didn't he?'*, I confidently answered no.

Justinus never did return to me the quartermaster's amulet. I was rather surprised he kept it. In fact sometimes, especially when he was wearing that painful expression he had brought with him to the boat, I almost thought he looked like a man who had given it away as a love token to some girl.

Fortuna had protected him. He was not in love; he had told me so. Quintus Camillus Justinus, senior tribune of the First Adiutrix, had proved himself one of the Empire's natural diplomats. Diplomacy involves a certain amount of lying – but I could not believe that Helena's brother would hide the truth from me.

LVI

We soon found ourselves short of time for speculation.

The flagship of Petilius Cerialis was as impetuous and unreliable as the general himself. Apart from the sorry effects of neglect, her rudder must have taken a bad knock while the rebels were towing her away. She steered like a wilful camel and sailed with a high old lack of regard for wind or current. All her weight seemed to lean to one side for some reason, a problem which worsened by the day. We had slipped off in a vessel of character – the kind of riotous character my elder brother Festus used to bring home after a night he could not remember in a tavern a long way from home. Taking her downriver felt like riding a horse who wanted to go backwards. She drew water with all the grace of a sodden log.

Most of the trouble derived from our scanty crew. In the right hands she would have been wonderful. But she was meant to have her double banks of oars fully manned, rigging-hands, a master, his deputy and a complement of marines – not to mention the general, who would no doubt have taken his shift on the oars in a tight corner. Twenty-five of us were simply not enough, and that was counting in Dubnus, who proved useless, and the centurion's servant, who made it plain he preferred to be counted out (the plea for a posting to Moesia had cropped up pathetically again). Then, as the days passed and the river grew wider and deeper, our food supplies dwindled. We were weakening when we most needed strength.

The Rhenus junction caught us unawares. The ship had been making water. We had hauled in her sails and many of us were below, frantically trying to stop the leaks. When Probus shouted, no one heard at first. When he threw back his head and roared, we floundered up on deck. There was some cheering before we realised our grave plight. The

631

undertow had strengthened. The flagship, still trailing a wing to starboard, was now dangerously low in the water and nearly uncontrollable. We were in no condition to tackle turbulence.

I shouted to drop anchor, but it failed to hold.

Just as safety seemed to be in sight, it was being snatched from us. The grey skies made everything seem more ominous. A chill north wind brought the smell of the ocean, cruelly reminding us we wanted to turn our backs on it. We were hoping to pass out into the main river; we had always known that without trained oarsmen we would have to turn downstream. We needed to drift across the Rhenus to the Roman bank, then wind gently down to Vetera. Tackling the upriver current would be impossible. For amateurs who were fighting to stabilise an oversized and leaky galley, things would be delicate enough the other way. At least if we managed to join the Rhenus safely we might hail a fleet vessel to tow us – or even take us off, for we would happily have abandoned any kudos which attached to reclaiming the Liburnian in favour of a quick journey home.

Fate had been generous for long enough, and now she turned her glamorous back on us. Impelled by the increased current and weighed down by a flooded bilge, the flagship slowly started to rotate. Even to us it became obvious she had decided to sink. This was desperate. In November, the river was at its lowest, but it still surged formidably and we were not exactly web-footed coots.

Helvetius shouted 'We have to put her in – *before* the Rhenus takes her!'

He was right. We were the wrong side of the river – still on the *wrong* river – but if she sank in midstream we would lose everything, and men would drown. The recruits might have grown up as harbour boys, but only the famous Batavians had ever swum the Rhenus and survived to boast. I said nothing, but at least one member of our party (me) had never learned to swim at all.

Luckily, although the cantankerous galley strongly objected to sailing nicely to safety, it was perfectly willing to run aground on a hostile shore.

We brought her in, which is to say she bumbled of her own accord up the muddiest beach she could find, with a rending crunch that told us she was now ready to rot. Although the ship was beached, her bitter crew had to wade through a spreading morass of turgid water and silt to reach what for human feet counted as land. She had chosen the Tencteri bank. At least, we hoped, they would not know we had slipped away from Veleda's tower in circumstances their Bructian colleagues might have wanted to query.

The junction of these two great rivers was a sombre scene. The air felt cold. The whole area was unwelcoming. With the ground too spongy for farming, the place seemed lonely and deserted. A sudden flock of heavy geese overhead, silent apart from the eerie swishing of their wings, startled us more than it should have done. We were on edge to the point where it could cause mistakes.

We were in sight of the Rhenus, so we despatched a small party to squelch to the riverbank and look for a Roman ship to hail. For once there were none – naturally. Our bored watch party came back, against orders, feebly maintaining that the ground was too marshy to cross, but we were too dispirited to harangue them. Helvetius being a centurion, made a tiresome attempt to revive us with action.

'What now, Falco?'

'I intend to dry my boots, then spend at least three hours sitting on a hummock and blaming other people for what went wrong . . . What does anyone else suggest?'

'Tribune?'

'I'm too hungry to have brilliant ideas.'

We were all hungry. So Helvetius proposed that since we were trapped here, and since the area was teeming with marsh birds and other wildlife, we might as well unpack our unused javelins and seek out prey with some flesh on it. I could remember what he had once said about stupid officers wanting boar-hunts in places they knew were dangerous, but the recruits were morose with starvation, so we let him lead off a forage band. I sent Lentullus out with a bucket looking for crayfish, to keep him out of our way. The rest of us unpacked the galley and loaded the horses, temporarily reprieved from the pot now that we needed them. Then we set off for drier ground where we could camp.

I had wet feet, and the prospect of sharing one eight-man tent with twenty-four other people was already causing misery. The flints in our tinder-box were now so worn nobody could start the fire. Helvetius had the knack – he was competent at everything. We were, therefore, badly in need of him just at the moment when Orosius and the others sloped into camp with a couple of mangled marsh birds but no centurion, admitting that Helvetius seemed to be lost.

It was so out of character I knew straight away that some disaster had occurred.

Justinus stayed on camp duty. I took Orosius, a horse, and our medical casket.

'Where were you last with him?'

'No one was sure. That's why we all came back.'

'Jupiter!' I hated the sound of this.

'What's happened, Falco?'

'I think he must be hurt.' Or worse.

Inevitably the lad could not remember where the party had strayed. While we were searching the marshes we seemed to hear noises as though someone was tracking us. We could have imagined it, for the sounds were intermittent, but we had no time to investigate. We came to a place where side-channels stagnated amongst giant reeds. There, on a ridge of firm turf, alongside a creek, we found our man.

He was alive. But he had not been able to call for help. He had a Roman throwing-spear piercing his throat, and another in his groin.

'Dear gods! Orosius, one of you careless young bastards will be strangled for this . . .'

'Those aren't ours – '

'Don't lie! Look at them – *look*!'

They were Roman javelins. No question about it. They had nine-inch spikes with soft iron necks which had bent on impact. That was by design. Stuck in an enemy's shield, a long wooden shaft dragging on a crooked head impedes movement and is impossible to pull out and throw back. While the victims struggle, we rush them with swords.

The centurion's eyes were pleading – or, more likely, giving me orders. I refused to meet their deep brown, agitated stare.

Somewhere nearby a bird rose, screaming.

'Keep watch, Orosius . . .'

Blood should never make you panic, a surgeon once told me. He could afford to be philosophical; there was money in blood for him. At this moment, if that surgeon had stepped out from a willow tree, I would have made him a millionaire. Helvetius moaned, proudly holding in the noise. Faced with a man who was suffering so horribly, it was hard not to be terrified. I dared not move him. Even if I could get him to camp, there was no advantage; what had to be done might as well be done here. Then we could think about transporting him.

I rolled my cloak into a bumper to support the lower spear; Helvetius, still unaffected by shock, was gripping the other himself. Breaking the wooden shafts would help lessen their weight, but with the iron stuck in those positions I dared not try . . .

Voices. Orosius, glad of the excuse, disappeared to investigate.

I was muttering, partly to reassure Helvetius, but more to calm myself. 'Don't look at me like that, man. All you have to do is lie there acting brave. It's my problem . . .' He kept trying to say something. 'All right. I'm going to do my best – you can give me your list of complaints later.'

I knew I had to work quickly, but it would have been easier if I had felt at all confident. Most of the blood was coming from the neck wound. One barb had failed to penetrate, which could mean the whole thing was extractable. I closed my mind to the thought that the other wound might be bleeding internally. You have to do what you can.

Our medical box was one item Justinus had managed to save from the Bructeri. Its contents were mainly salves and bandages, but I did find a couple of slender bronze hooks which might help me hold back the surrounding skin enough to free the barb. There was even a gadget for extracting missiles, but I had once seen one used: it had to be inserted, twisted under the point, then pulled out very skilfully. It was a skill I lacked. I elected to try without it first.

There was movement or noise in the channel to my left. Not quite a splash, more a skirling of water. It was so slight that I hardly registered it as I bent over Helvetius; I had no time for otters or frogs in the bulrushes.

'*Aurochs* . . .' Our tough old soldier was hallucinating like a fevered child.

'Don't try to talk – '

Then came a flurry in the osiers, a rush, a cry, and a group of men sprang from nowhere. They had their spears up for hurling, but thoughtfully held on to them with a tight grip once they discovered us.

LVII

It was a hunting party, led by some high-class bastard in discreetly well-woven brown wool. He had a Spanish horse, several reverent companions, two bearers bringing extra spears, and a bad case of apoplectic rage. He stared round, spotted me, and it was in perfect Latin that he spat, 'Oh Castor and Pollux – what are *people* doing here?'

I stood up. 'Existing – like yourself!'

My own Latin stopped him dead.

He hurled himself from the horse, dropped its bridle, then strode nearer – but not too near. 'Thought you were Tencteri. We've heard them about.' That was all I needed. 'I've lost my quarry. Something big – '

The haircut he was tearing at was black and cleanly layered to show the handsome shape of his head; the teeth he gnashed were even, orderly, and white. His belt was nielloed with silver; his boots were supple jobs whose tassels were affixed with bronze studs; his signet-ring was an emerald. His rage was the kind you can see any day in the Forum of the Romans after some inattentive donkey-driver has barged aside a man of note coming out of the Basilica Julia.

I was very tired. My body ached. My heart had rarely been more dreary. 'Your quarry's here,' I said quietly. 'Not quite killed yet.'

I stepped aside so the man with the ear-splitting senatorial vowels would have a better view of our centurion, lying wounded at my feet.

'This is Appius Helvetius Rufus, centurion of the legio First Adiutrix. Don't worry about it,' I said courteously. 'Helvetius is a realist. He always knew he stood in less danger from the enemy than from the crass incompetence of senior staff . . .'

'I am a Roman officer,' the leader of the hunting group

637

informed me haughtily, raising his well-groomed eyebrows under his neat black fringe.

'I know who you are.' Something in the caustic way I dared return his stare must have warned him. 'I know a lot about you. Your finances are based on a complicated debt structure; your domestic life is in turmoil. Your wife is restless, and your mistress deserves better. And both of them would *hate* to know you visit a certain party in Colonia . . .'

He looked amazed. 'Are you threatening me?'

'Probably.'

'Who are you?'

'My name is Didius Falco.'

'Means nothing,' he barked.

'It should do. I would have introduced myself six weeks ago, if you had been available. Then you would also have avoided an officeful of unanswered despatches, including Vespasian's critical letter about your legion's future.' He was about to speak. I continued without raising my voice or hurrying: 'He's also questioning *your* future. Your name is Florius Gracilis. Your legion is the Fourteenth Gemina, and we'll just have to pray they have sufficient experience to survive a legate whose attitude to command is casual beyond belief.'

'Listen – '

'No, you listen, sir!' I used the title as an insult. 'I have just found you using army-issue spears for private purposes, on the wrong side of the Rhenus, in company which the Emperor will certainly call unethical – '

One of the legate's companions made a sudden obscene gesture. I recognised the rapidity of the movement as much as his cleft chin and vivid sneer.

I looked the man straight in the eye. 'You're a very long way from Lugdunum!' I said.

638

LVIII

The Gaul I had last seen arguing with the two German potters squared up angrily. I had been in another world since I had travelled through his province on my way to Upper Germany, but the quarrel at Lugdunum and finding the potters' bodies now came back to me vividly. The big Gaul with the sneer said nothing. Just as well. It would keep. Out here, feeling vulnerable, I was reluctant to tackle him.

I sensed more than saw the faint movement from Helvetius. I knew he was warning me. Suddenly I understood why the centurion was lying on this ridge of turf with two spears in him. I remembered a conversation I had had with him before we left Moguntiacum. He too had seen the Gallic potter arguing with Bruccius and his nephew at Lugdunum; he had even seen the Gaul tailing them later. Maybe the Gaul had seen Helvetius. In court, a centurion's word would be enough to convict a provincial. Finding Helvetius alone out here in the wilderness must have seemed like a gift from the gods to a man who had killed twice already.

I wondered if Florius Gracilis knew just what kind of 'accident' had befallen the wounded man, but from his face when he first saw Helvetius I doubted it. Involving himself in corruption was one thing; murder would be too foolish.

Not knowing the full story, Gracilis opted for bluster. No doubt he believed he had covered his tracks on the tendering fraud and could fudge matters generally once we reached home. 'A tragedy,' he muttered. 'Let me know if I can help . . . Most unfortunate. Accidents will happen. Whole trip has been most inconvenient from day one. I was supposed to be meeting some pedlar who said he could show me the Varus battlefield. Hopeless crook. Took my money to equip himself, then failed to show.' Dubnus.

'If he's a Ubian with a long lip and a strong line in

639

grousing, I hijacked him,' I said. My position strengthened subtly. Dubnus was also a witness to the legate's junketing, and now I had control of Dubnus . . . I saw Gracilis narrow his eyes; he took the point. To reinforce it I added another: 'The pedlar betrayed us to the Bructeri, and it's safe to say he was planning the same fate for you.'

'Oh I doubt that!' Even after years of watching senators, this man's arrogance took my breath away.

Somehow we had to get home. I was prepared for bargaining. I set my feet more stubbornly and told the legate bluntly, 'If this Gaul is a friend of yours, you should be more careful. There are two dead men in Cavillonum he may be called to account for.' I offered him a get-out. 'The victims were local to your command. The community at Moguntiacum will look to you to deal with it.'

I had judged him correctly. 'Sounds as if I have something to investigate!' The legate distanced himself imperceptibly from the man with the cleft chin. Sharp practice has a lovely habit of working both ways eventually. 'I have no idea what you are doing here,' he challenged me. It was the cool, smooth, patrician voice of a man who expects to get away with everything on the grounds of his cool, smooth, patrician ancestry. 'I myself am engaged on a political reconnaissance.'

That was one way to describe his expenses-paid sweetener. 'Oh really?' Annoyance at the airy way he spoke made my voice rasp. 'Civilis, was it? The Island? Batavodurum? Spend much time in Vetera?'

'I was interested to sniff around the place . . .' A sightseer. Helvetius jerked restlessly.

I too was losing my temper. 'See the damage, smell the disaster, pick a stone out of the rampart to take home as a souvenir? After that a few days off for the *real* chase, and hard luck to any solid Roman veteran who is standing in the way of your loose spears . . . actually, I thought you might have gone across to negotiate with the prophetess.'

'Veleda?' Gracilis seemed genuinely shocked. 'Vespasian wouldn't want anyone to tangle with that witch!'

I chose not to disillusion him. 'And did you find Civilis?'

'No,' he said. Ah well. He was a senator. He would probably win a laurel wreath just for making the attempt.

After our own hardships, I must have lost control. I knew better than to hope Vespasian would demote this unsavoury character unless I came up with some scandal much worse than fiddling a tender award or going on a game-hunt in barbarian territory. His crimes included sex and death and money – but no sex lurid enough to startle Rome into a bout of sanctimony. No bribes costly enough to hire lawyers to exact revenge. And not enough death.

'You're out of bounds, legate.' Out of bounds in every way. But at my feet Helvetius was weakening all the time. 'I have an exhausted and half-starved group of men, and this badly wounded centurion. We have been on an imperial mission which I cannot discuss in public, and we're stuck here without transport, armour or supplies. May I suggest you restore your reputation by assisting us back to base?'

I had misjudged it. The Gaul muttered something. The Fourteenth's legate cynically weighed our helpless predicament against the evidence we held that could blacken his name.

'I'll see you in Hades first!' said Gracilis.

But he had made a mistake too. His was worse than mine.

Several things happened rapidly. Helvetius let out a wretched moan that made me drop to one knee beside him. The Gaul raised his javelin. He was stopped by bright voices. At the other end of the ridge Orosius appeared through some coarse bushes with Lentullus, still carrying his shrimp bucket, and the centurion's servant. I gripped Helvetius by the wrist to warn him to keep still while I dealt with any trouble.

Then he violently convulsed.

He knocked me sideways. He meant to – he was warning me.

As I sprawled on my back, my cry of protest dried in my

641

throat. Three strides from me, snorting at the legate, stood the biggest bull I had ever seen.

LIX

I lurched upright, then clapped my arms against my sides and muttered *"Hup!"* in a pleading tone. The aurochs tossed its head disdainfully.

No byre could hold this bovine. The beast was a brownish colour with black tips to its tail fur. It had a straight back, a massive head, short legs, and shoulders that could demolish civic masonry, hung with a deep collar of heavier foxy-red pelt. Its upswept horns were strong enough and wide enough to lash a maiden to them – some Dirce who had managed to offend people who could dream up frantic punishments. Its breath rasped like a Cyclops in the last stages of pneumonia.

They are untameable. The aurochs belonged centuries before man invented placid domesticity. This one was huge, yet must have been capable of moving with great delicacy – the kind of nifty footwork that also goes with bursts of tremendous speed. Its angry eye told us the spears that were stuck in its coat like briar thorns had already maddened it and now, having tracked the perpetrators with malicious stealth, it was planning to do serious damage to anything that moved. To emphasise this, it emitted a long, strained bellow that spoke loudly of primeval rage and pain. It glared at the legate broodily, as if sizing up where it could hurt him most. Then it stamped.

We all stood very still.

Now, I hate to remember what happened to Florius Gracilis. The worst was, he saw it coming. He gurgled slightly, and broke into a run. Bellowing, the great beast swung after him so fast he stood no chance. He was gored, tossed, trampled, and then stamped to death. Some of those who had been with him tried to throw spears, but once Gracilis was on the ground terror gripped everyone. They fled.

643

I and my party stayed.

The aurochs must have liked my face; I could tell it had chosen me next.

I had to protect Helvetius. I began stepping slowly to my left. It was the only direction open, and pretty soon I had to stop, for I was nearing the edge of the creek. The bank dropped down for a foot or more, and then there was a sinister overhang of long dirty grasses. The last thing I wanted was to end up in an uncertain depth of water, wallowing helplessly while the massive creature charged.

The aurochs breathed ferociously, giving the blood-stained body of the dead legate a final contemptuous toss with one tremendous horn. It waited until I stopped, then it began to move.

The rest was fast, messy and unheroic.

Behind the aurochs my three startled comrades came to life. Orosius began whooping and reached for a dropped javelin. I saw the servant race towards Helvetius. Lentullus bravely hurled his shrimp bucket. It hit the aurochs on the nose. The aurochs flung up its head, but kept coming. It was like being rushed by a rapidly moving house.

The sting of the shrimp bucket didn't stop it – nothing could. But while it blinked, I just had time to jump somewhere. Trapped by the creek, there was only one direction: I flung myself sideways. The beast passed me, so close that I snatched in my arm.

The aurochs turned on nothing. Its head was down. If I had run it would have gored me before my second stride, but something did stop it this time: Lentullus. He had run out and grabbed it by the tail. His face was contorted with effort as by some fluke he held on. The powerful animal swung angrily away from me. With a violent shake to and fro of its shoulders it dislodged the young idiot. The whip-lash from its rump flung our boy far into the creek. By then another idiot was doing something stupid. M. Didius Falco, who had once seen a Cretan wall fresco, chose this dank German riverbank as an arena to revive the lost art of bull-dancing. While the aurochs was still bellowing at Lentullus, I skipped straight for it and leapt astride its back.

Its pelt was as coarse as nautical rope and smelt of the wild. A tail clogged with dung lashed my spine. I had only one weapon, in my boot as usual: my knife. Somehow I freed it. My other arm clamped around a horn. There was no time to think: death was reaching for one of us. I gripped with both knees, heaved with all my strength on the mighty horn, hauled up the head, leaned round a flicking ear and savage eye, then started hacking through the aurochs' upstrained throat.

The kill was neither clean nor quick. It took more time, and a great deal more energy, than anyone would ever think having stood in a sparkling white toga to watch the refined priests of Jupiter conduct a taurine sacrifice on Capitol Hill.

LX

'*Mithras!*' I thought the awed cry came from Helvetius, but it must have been his servant.

My left arm was locked so tightly where I had clung on that it was hard to free. The smell of the beast seemed to permeate my own clothes and skin. I sank to the ground, shaking. Orosius rushed up and dragged me clear. Lentullus staggered from the creek, then neatly passed out. 'Must be the shock,' Orosius muttered, turning aside to attend to him. 'Finding something he could actually do . . .'

I felt disgusted – with myself, with the animal whose anger had forced me to this, and with the hot blood all over me. I dropped my forehead on to my hand, then whipped away my palm as I felt more blood on that. I managed to limp across to Helvetius. His servant, whose name was Dama, looked up at me.

'I knew I should have gone to Moesia . . .' he ranted bitterly. Then he burst into tears.

Helvetius was dead.

Hardly had I fought back my own distress when some of the legate's hunting party ventured to reappear. They were led by the Gaul with the sneer, no doubt intent on self-preservation.

It was a brief confrontation. I was still kneeling by Helvetius, gripping his hand. I said to the Gaul, 'I don't want ever to see your face in Free or Roman Germany. You've killed to protect your industry, and you've killed to protect yourself. This is where it stops.'

'Proof?' he jibed, gesturing to the dead centurion.

Suddenly Dama gave voice. He addressed himself to me, as if he could not trust himself to speak to his master's killer. 'Helvetius Rufus was a private man, but he talked to

646

me while I was arming him. He told me what he saw in Gaul.'

'Would you give evidence in court?' He assented.

The Gaul raised a spear. His intention was obvious. But we were no longer unprotected. Both Orosius and Lentullus lifted javelins themselves, ready to throw.

I stood up, covered in blood. I must have looked terrible. 'One word out of place, or a gesture I don't like, and I'll be happy to show you how the aurochs feels now it's dead!'

The men in the hunting party all backed off slowly. I waved them away with an angry gesture. They moved equally slowly out of sight, taking the Gaul from Lugdunum. I do not know what happened to them afterwards, nor do I care. As Celts, they were at far less risk in Germania Libera than we were.

That night we dined on aurochs steaks, but they had a bitter taste. We set a double watch. No one slept much. We broke camp early, then set off in a southerly direction, hoping that somewhere along the riverbank we might find the dead legate's ship.

We were going home. We had two corpses to bring with us, and more than one of us felt broken-hearted. Soon we all were.

Because, as we tramped on mournfully, we came to a wooded area. A little while after we entered it, we found there were other occupants. There were five times as many of them, and they had spotted us. They were a war band of the horse-riding, Rome-hating Tencteri.

LXI

We were surrounded before we had any inkling, but they did not attack immediately. Perhaps they were as surprised as us to find other people in their woods.

We formed up the recruits into a square – quite well, considering they had only learned the manoeuvre theoretically. Helvetius had taught them, however. As a formation the result was passable. But we all knew that we had too small a square.

The real point of a square is to lock shield-rims all around it in a protective wall. We had no shields.

Justinus was too tired and upset for a flamboyant oration, but he told the recruits to do their best. They exchanged frank glances like veterans; they understood the situation we were in.

It was late afternoon. A fine drizzle filled the woods. We were all unwashed, unfed and cold, with mist spiking our hair. I noticed that our boot-leather had set hard and was curled at the edges, with white tracery from mud and salt. The trees had turned colour in the last week or so. Winter was issuing warnings in the frosty air.

I could smell leaf-mould and fear. This was one crisis too many. It felt like a nightmare where you slither through endless ludicrous disasters, *knowing* it's a nightmare and that you must escape soon, yet unable to break free and wake safe in your bed with someone friendly soothing you.

We could not understand why the Tencteri had made no move.

Sometimes we could glimpse them between the trees. They were on horseback. Their presence was palpable on every side. We heard their mounts stamping restlessly and their harnesses chinking. Once a man coughed. If he lived in this rising river fog, it was understandable.

They were just out of spear range. For what seemed ages we stood there, straining for the first movement that would mean the end for us. We heard the shuffle of hooves in the crisp fallen leaves. We heard a shifty breeze rustle overhead.

I thought I heard something else.

Justinus and I were standing back to back. He must have sensed my tension for he looked round. I had my face raised full into the drizzle, struggling to catch sound or sense. I had nothing to tell him, but that odd quiet soul had brought back from Veleda's tower his habit of solitary action. He listened too, without comment. Then he let out a yelp and before we could stop him, he broke from the square.

He raced the ten strides to where we had left our scant baggage. Luckily he was zig-zagging, for a lance hissed out of the trees. It missed. Next minute he crouched, with some shelter from our horses. We could see him rummaging furiously. Soon he stood up. He leaned his elbows on a horse to steady himself while he held something. It was the twisted, wide-mouthed trumpet he had brought in his baggage for a lark.

When he blew, it came out as more of a waver than the notes he had produced among the Bructeri, but it still retained clear traces of the second night watch. It must have been the only call he had learned to play.

A shower of Tenctrian arrows and spears tried to silence him. Justinus dropped to the ground with his head covered. But he must have heard, as we all did, another note: clear, high, and professionally sustained. Somewhere, somewhere not far away, a second bronze Roman trumpet had sweetly answered his.

We never saw them leaving. The Tencteri must have silently melted away.

Not long afterwards a vexillation of legionaries from the Fourteenth Gemina marched out of the woods. They were all volunteers. The force had been put together and brought downriver on the initiative of the man who was leading them. Despite my prejudice I have to admit that he was Sextus Juvenalis, the prefect of the camp.

649

They were looking for their missing legate, but the
Fourteenth have always boasted about being thorough, so
as well as claiming his body they also rescued us.

LXII

A bridge, a tollbooth, a ridiculous column – and the girl I was longing to see.

The journey had taken sufficient time for us to start readjusting to the real world. However, it might take the world longer to adjust to us savages. Along the river had been civilised towns with baths and Roman food. Civilised contact, too, with men we understood, though for most of the journey we had found ourselves clinging in a tight clique of our own, quarantined by an adventure that seemed too big to discuss.

When we finally landed and returned to the fort we had started from, we took the centurion's ashes to rest in the Principia shrine. As we left the parade-ground, the recruits said goodbye. I would certainly be leaving soon, and their close contact with their senior tribune must also end when Justinus resumed the normal loftiness that was expected from his rank. Our tattered band left us on the Via Principia almost tearfully, but just then a group of passing comrades called out a welcome; we watched a swagger hit them, and they went off visibly boasting. Only Lentullus turned back at the last minute, with a shy wave.

Justinus was having some trouble with his throat. 'I hate to say I'll miss them.'

'Don't worry.' Even I felt subdued. 'You're back in harness, Quintus. There will be plenty of other annoyances . . .'

He swore cheerfully, in one of the several languages he had picked up for chatting to women.

He had the good idea of sending a message to his legate's secretary that there was so much to report he needed a proper appointment – later. This dodge left us free to go off to his house, pretending to stroll lazily as if we had nothing special in mind.

Helena was in the garden. It was too cold for her to be there, but it had ensured her solitude. She was grieving for us. Her brother and I came out into the portico side by side. Her face seemed to light with excitement almost before she heard our steps; then her only dilemma was which of us to rush to first.

We both held back, to let the other have her. I won in the politeness stakes. I intended to. I meant to let Quintus hug her once, then when he passed on the bundle I would feel free to keep hold of her afterwards. But Helena Justina careered past her brother and fell on me.

He had the grace to smile, before he sadly turned away. 'Stay, friend . . .'

Helena was very quick. As if she had always intended it, she broke from me and threw her arms round him joyfully. 'Falco, you horror, what have you done to my brother?'

'He grew up,' I said. 'An affliction most people manage to avoid, but when it does strike it tends to hurt.'

She was laughing. I had forgotten just how much I loved that laugh. 'How did this accident happen?'

'Don't ask. It must have been so terrible he won't say.'

Helena assumed the stillness that said young Quintus should resign himself because she had in mind that he soon would confess. She held him off for one of her fierce inspections. 'He looks taller!'

Quintus only smiled again, like a man who could keep his own council, and intended to do so.

That was when I realised I might have made a small mistake about the tribune's adventure in Veleda's tower. I had no chance to ask him, because my horrid niece and Little Flaxen Pigtails must have heard of our arrival. They galloped out screaming in a way that passed for greetings, then the tribune's dog made himself at home by biting a servant, and after that a message came that the First's legate was so delighted at our safe return he had cancelled the rest of his schedule and wanted to see Justinus straight away . . .

After he left, I waited for Helena to ask pertinent questions, but although he was her favourite and I knew she loved him dearly, for some reason she only wanted to involve herself with me.

I could have argued, but the girl was evidently set on hauling me off into a dark corner for a bout of something shameless, so rather than disappoint her I went along with it.

I had taken my mission as far as I could – and further than Vespasian had a right to expect, though I knew better than to persuade myself that that unreasonable tyrant would agree. The old miser expected to extract his full money's worth before he let me home; I still had coercing Civilis on my rosta for one thing. But I had done well enough to earn my fee. My curly mop would not be welcome back on the Palatine until the last possible moment now that more than basic expenses would be called for from the Treasury.

For reasons of my own I was in no hurry to shift from here. Decisions were looming painfully, all the worse because I already knew what the answer had to be. Since she refused to make her own decisions, I had to force the right ones on Helena.

I pretended I was staying on at the fort to complete my report on the Fourteenth. I made out that it was difficult. A credible plea. I hate reports. I was perfectly capable of producing it, but lacked the will to start.

I spent a lot of time in the tribune's study chewing the end of a stylus while I watched Helena Justina playing draughts against herself. I wondered how long it would be before she realised I had noticed she was cheating. In the end I felt forced to mention it. She flounced off in a huff, which was annoying because I much preferred dreaming and watching her.

I struggled on. The stylus was a digit shorter now. Bits of soggy wood kept breaking off and splintering my tongue. As I spat them out I registered that my niece and her friend were hanging round the door engaged in secret whispering. There had been efforts at obvious mystery ever since I had arrived back. I was so bored with the report that this time I crept up, jumped out with a roar, and grabbed the pair of them. Then I dragged them into the study and sat them down, one on each knee.

'Now you're captured. You'll sit there until you tell nice Uncle Marcus why you keep peering round the architrave. Are you spying on me?'

At first it seemed like nothing. I was today's suspect. They spent a lot of time playing at being informers. It was not a compliment; it was for the same reasons that Festus and I had always wanted to be rag-pickers: a dirty, disreputable existence, and our mother would have hated us doing it.

'But we're not going to tell you anything we've seen!' Augustinilla boasted.

'Suits me. That saves me having to do anything about it.' She seemed satisfied. It fitted the family view that her sordid Uncle Marcus would sooner lie in bed all day than exert himself turning an honest denarius. I grinned evilly. 'You'd have to be clever to produce anything useful. Most informers spend weeks on a stake-out and still never find out anything . . .'

I could see Pigtails feeling torn. Unlike my niece, she was clever enough to want to have her intelligence recognised – though not enough to hide it and make full use of her advantage. 'Tell him about the boy with the arrows!' she burst out.

Something struck a chord. I was interested now, so I tried looking bored. Augustinilla dealt with that. She shook her head vigorously. I asked Arminia directly where they had seen this boy.

'Augusta Treverorum.'

I was shocked. 'Whatever were you doing there?' My niece opened her mouth and pointed to a reddened hole where a tooth had been. 'Stop fooling. I can see what you had for breakfast wriggling through your gut. Who had you gone to see?'

'Mars Lenus,' she informed me, as if talking to an idiot. 'Mars who?'

'Mars the Healer,' Arminia consented to explain.

This was hard work. I filled in some gaps myself: 'Augustinilla had toothache – I remember that from before I went away.' The ladies looked unimpressed by this subtle reference to the forests full of fog and ferocious animals I had just endured. 'So Helena Justina took you to a shrine – '

'The tooth fell out before we went,' Arminia told me with some disgust. 'Helena made us go there anyway.'

'I wonder why that was.'

'To look around!' they chorused.

'Ah yes. How obvious! Did she see anything worthwhile?' No. Helena would have mentioned it, though she would not trouble me with news of a pointless trip. Not while I had my report to write. She regarded that as serious. 'But you saw this boy?'

'He was shooting at us. He said we were Romans and he was in the Free Gallic Empire, with permission from his father to kill us dead. So then we knew,' Arminia said.

'Tell me, Arminia.'

'Who he was.' That was more than I knew. She whispered nervously, 'The chieftain's son. The one who shoots real prisoners!'

I resisted the urge to grab them closer protectively. These were two tough women; neither needed me. 'I hope you ran away?'

'Of course,' Augustinilla scoffed. 'We knew what to do. He was pathetic. We shook him off, then doubled back and followed him.'

They cackled with delight at the ease with which they had bamboozled him. No boy was safe with these young hags on his tail. In different ways, they were both destined to be man-eaters.

I let them see me swallow. 'And then?'

'We saw the one-eyed man.'

'The man with the red beard. The beard that's *dyed*,' the little flaxen treasure specified. Just in case I had not realised what completely brilliant sidekicks I had somehow attracted to work with me.

Helena said she would write my report.

'You know nothing about the subject!'

'So what? Most men who write reports know less. How about: "The Fourteenth Gemina Martia Victrix are a sound operative unit, but they need a firmer hand than they received from their recent command structure. The appointment of a new legate with strong supervisory talents will no doubt be a priority. The Fourteenth appear amenable to relocation in Germany on a permanent or semipermanent basis. This option enables closer control of them; it will also permit full exploitation of their considerable experience with Celtic peoples, which should be particularly appropriate in the delicate political climate that exists in the Rhenus corridor . . ."

'This is rubbish!' I interrupted.

'Exactly. Just what a secretariat wants to hear.'

I left her to it. She reckoned she could rattle off and stitch together several pages on the same pretentious lines by my return. Her handwriting was neater than mine too.

I would have liked to take Helena with me, but Augusta Treverorum was ninety miles away and I had to ride hard if I wanted to be back at Moguntiacum by the Emperor's birthday and the coming parade.

A man needs a travelling companion, however, so I took someone else instead. Xanthus, who so loved to see the world, was the obvious candidate.

LXIII

Augusta Treverorum, capital of Belgica.

It had been founded by Augustus, who had taken an empty site at a strategic crossroads on the River Mosella and begun with a bridge, like any sensible man. His bridge was a decent affair, with seven pillars of ashlar set on piles. The whole structure was built on a massive scale because the river is changeable there. The town had been planned neatly. There were new vineyards struggling to establish themselves, as well as cereal crops, but the local economy thrived on two staples: ceramics and wool. The sheep supplied official mills that wove cloth for army uniforms, and the redware pots also went under contract to the legions. As a result, I was not surprised to find that the fat cats of Augusta Treverorum had managed to provide themselves with some of the largest and best-appointed villas I had seen since leaving Italy. This was a town that would attract the attentions of anyone who had learned to appreciate Roman life in its most civilised aspects (wealth and show). Someone like a high-ranking, Romanised Batavian, say.

The Temple of Mars Lenus honoured both our own god and his Celtic equivalent, *Tiw*. This was not Mars the warrior, but Mars the healer – a natural corollary, since the god of soldiers needs to mend their wounds also if he wants to bump them back into the battleline as soon as possible. Mars the god of youth (young spear fodder) was also represented.

The temple was the centre of a flourishing shrine for the sick. There was a high quota of slack taverns and sour-smelling rooms for hire, plus booths and bothies where sellers of trinkets and trifles were also grimly trying to get rich quick before their custom literally died. It had the usual depressing hangers-on selling votive models of every anatomical part from sexual organs (both sexes) to feet (left

657

or right) and ears (indeterminate), plus the whole grasping range of apothecaries, quack dentists and doctors, dieticians, fortune-tellers and money-changers. These characters all flocked to the shrine, feeding on hope and despair in equal measure while they raked in their usual sharp percentages. Occasionally I did spot somebody who was actually lame or ill, but they were encouraged to keep out of sight. Pale, sad faces are bad for trade.

Like all these places the turnover in shady entrepreneurs must be fast. People could come and go without much explanation. Few questions would be asked by those who preferred to remain unobtrusive themselves in case an official came round asking questions about licences. A man who wanted to hide could live among this shanty town more or less openly.

I never saw his son, the child with the arrows. It was just as well. I was intending to give him a thrashing, for not shooting straighter at my niece.

I found Julius Civilis looking like a man on his uppers, sitting on a stool at a shack outside town, whittling uneasily. He was keeping an eye out for trouble but he only had one eye to look out with. My informants had been efficient: I knew which dusty track he lived down, and I had a personal description. I circled round in the local fields and silently approached him on his blind side.

'The game's up, Civilis!'

He spun round and saw me standing there. I took my sword out slowly and laid it on the ground between us. It served to establish a truce for us to talk. He must have guessed I still had my knife, and since Civilis had been a cavalry commander I had no doubt he was hung about with daggers for cutting stones out of hooves – or carving notches on imperial agents' ribs. To catch me out he would have to be first into action, and quick with it; he looked too dispirited to try.

He was older than me. Taller and much more solid. Probably even more depressed than I was. He wore leather trousers to just below the knee and a cloak trimmed with strands of raddled fur. He was heavily scarred and moved stiffly, like a man who had fallen from a horse once too often. His missing eye looked as if it had been taken out by something like an artillery bolt, leaving a deep twisted seam. His good eye was sharply intelligent. He had a beard down to his cloak-brooch and long strands of wavy hair; both were red. Not the bold red I had been promising myself, but a sadder, more faded colour that seemed to mirror what was left of the rebel's life. That too was showing grey at the roots.

He let me introduce myself. 'So this is what it feels like meeting a footnote to history!'

'Less of the footnotes!' he growled. I found myself liking him. 'What do you want?'

'Just passing through. I thought I'd look you up. Don't be surprised. A child could find you here. In fact a child did – a mere eight-year-old, and not very bright, though she had help from a much cleverer Ubian. Worried?' I asked gently. 'You know what it means. If a child can find you, so can any smouldering legionary whose mate you killed at Vetera. Or any disgruntled Batavian, come to that.'

Julius Civilis told me what he would like me to do with myself; it was wittily devised and succinctly phrased. 'You say that in much the same terms as the famous Fourteenth Gemina, who also think I stink. Must be the Roman influence. Do you miss all that?'

'No,' he said, but jealously. 'The Fourteenth? Those braggarts!' He himself had commanded an auxiliary detachment in Germany before he had tried for glory; he would have heard about their parent legion from his kinsmen in the eight famous Batavian cohorts who deserted. 'I suppose we have to talk. Do you want the story of my life?'

He had the right background; this interview would be businesslike. I could have been dealing with one of our own. Well, I was really. 'Sorry.' I hoped he could hear that my regret was genuine. I would have given a lot to hear the full story from the rebel's own lips. 'I'm due in Moguntiacum for the Emperor's birthday parade. I've no time to listen to the drivel about twenty years in the Roman camps, then your only reward being Imperial suspicion and the threat of execution . . . Let's get down to it, Civilis. You took the money. You enjoyed the life. You were grateful to be exempt from taxation and gain the benefits of a regular income and a structured career. If things had been different, you would have taken your discharge diploma and retired as a Roman citizen. Right up to the moment when Vespasian became Emperor you could have basked in his friendship and been a great force locally. You threw it away for a dream that became pointless. Now you're stateless and hopeless too.'

'That's pretty bilge! Have you finished?' His single eye regarded me with more good judgement than I liked.

'No, but you have. Events have passed you by, Civilis. I see here an exhausted man. You're saddled with a large family; so am I. Now that your stand against fate is in tatters I can guess how you must be being nagged. You're suffering earache as well as backache and heartache. You're sick of trouble and tired of the campaign – '

'I'd do it again.'

'Oh I don't doubt that. In your shoes, so would I. You saw a chance, and made the most of it. But the chance is over. Even Veleda accepts that.'

'Veleda?' He looked suspicious.

I said smoothly, 'Imperial agents have just interviewed the lady in her signal-tower. Incidentally, my own view is we ought to charge her rent for that . . . She concedes the peace, Civilis.'

We both knew the Batavian's independence movement was nothing without support from Free Germany and Gaul. Gaul had long been a lost cause for rebellion: too comfort-loving by half. Now Germany was opting out too.

'So much for freedom!' murmured the red-haired man.

'Freedom to run wild, you mean? Sorry. I sound like every father there ever was berating a child who wants to stay out late in unsuitable company.'

'You can't help that. Rome,' he replied drily, 'is a paternalist society.' It felt strange to be addressed in refined, lightly satirical Latin by a man who looked as if he had spent a month huddled up against a gorse-bush on an open moor.

'Not always,' I confessed. 'My father ran away from home and left the women to get on with it.'

'You should have been a Celt.'

'Then I'd be fighting with you.'

'Thanks,' he said. 'Thanks for that, Falco. So it's parole again?' He was referring to the times other emperors had pardoned him. I hoped he realised this emperor was here to stay. 'What am I required to do?'

'You and your family will live in Augusta Treverorum at a fixed address. Protection will be arranged at first, though I reckon you should soon be assimilated into the local community.' I grinned. 'I don't feel Vespasian will want to offer you a new legionary command!' He was too old to care. 'Apart from that, here comes somebody whom I asked to meet us specially . . .'

A familiar figure had approached, incongruous among the run-down hovels where Civilis had lain up. He had a haircut that shrieked quality, and unacceptable shrimp-pink shoes. Undeterred by his own dramatic turnout, he scrutinised Civilis with visible pity.

'Falco! Your friend has a florid crop of foliage disfiguring his pediment!'

I sighed. 'This character has developed a putrid line of rhetoric since he met me . . . Julius Civilis, prince of Batavia, may I introduce to you Xanthus, one-time barber to emperors – and the best barber on the Palatine at that. He has shaved Nero, Galba, Otho, Vitellius, and probably Titus Caesar, though he never reveals the names of current clients. He has something in common with Celts, I think; he collects celebrity heads. Xanthus,' I announced gently to the rebel chief with the ghastly locks, 'has come to Augusta Treverorum all the way from Rome in order to give you a snappy trim and shave.'

LXIV

I managed to speak to Helena Justina during the parade. I hoped that in a public place politeness would oblige her to restrain her reaction to what I had in mind. Well, it was worth a try. I expected trouble anywhere I broached the tender issue. She would never like what I now had to say, even though I told myself she would have to accept that I was right.

The Fourteenth had made it pretty plain that this, like everything else at Moguntiacum, would be their show. It was the usual tiresome business. Lack of cash and too much cynicism meant there were hardly ever decent spectacles, even in Rome. Here we were in Europe, and seventeen days into November was no time to be holding outdoor festivities. It ought to be a rule that no one can qualify for emperor unless they can claim a midsummer birthday. The only exemption might be for people born on the Aventine thirty years ago in March . . .

As I expected, both the crowd and the glitter were spread far too thinly; the weather was freezing; and the catering was terrible – where you could find any. The formalities took place on the parade-ground, which unlike a decent amphitheatre had no easy exit gates. The few women of Roman extraction who attended were of course subject to strict public conventions. Three of them, along with a couple of guests, had to sit on a dais wrapped in jewelled silks while twelve thousand hairy males stared at them pointedly. Nice work, if they liked it. I knew one lass who was hating it.

The event was due to last all day. I only felt obliged to stay for the presentation of the Hand. Once we had dealt with that, I intended to say my piece to Helena – assuming I could get near her – then slip away.

Both legions were actually taking part, which slowed things to a leaden pace. Patterned marching, even by men in dress uniforms with helmet plumes, has never been my idea of stimulating theatre. The action drags, and the dialogue is terrible. The promoter here had even failed to provide an orchestra; all we had was military silver and brass. Seeing everything twice over so that both sets of troops could affirm their loyalty to the Emperor increased the tedium to torture. I had been miserable enough in the first place.

It started to rain.

This was what I had been waiting for. The ladies on the dais were shrieking with alarm in case their dresses shrank or their face-paint ran. The group of slaves who were supposed to raise a canopy above them were making a splendid mess of it. I could see Helena losing her temper, as she did when other people became disorganised and it was not her place to interfere. Knowing she would excuse me if I saved the situation, I leapt up on to the dais, grabbed one of the supporting poles, and helped the slaves to lift the canopy.

The women we were protecting were the legate's wife of the Fourteenth, Maenia Priscilla, an older more sensible body who must be the mother hen of the First Adiutrix, Helena Justina, another visitor who was a schoolfriend of the mother hen, and Julia Fortunata. Presumably she had been invited because her status was too high to ignore and her position in the life of the late Gracilis too low to acknowledge. In any event, Maenia Priscilla, clad fetchingly in mourning white, was making the most of her role, while Julia took every opportunity to pet and comfort her. No public statement was to be made about the ex-legate's non-exemplary behaviour, but his women had both been told. As a result neither felt obliged to mourn him too sincerely. I was pleased to see that widowhood, or its equivalent, was bringing out the best in them. Their bravery was wonderful to watch.

It stopped raining. The ladies relaxed. We furled the temporary roof, then I crouched down at Helena's side, ready to spring to attention on awning duty if disaster struck again.

I thought her ladyship shot me a curious look.

Out in the field they were reaching a climax in the elaborate ceremonial. Cohorts of auxiliary cavalry came out to stage a mock battle. The First Adiutrix now came into their own, for the Fourteenth had not yet had their lost Batavians replaced, which at last gave the First an opportunity to sneer as they fielded theirs. These were Spaniards I think. Their small sturdy horses were well matched, and tricked out in full parade regalia with winking discs on their leatherware, gilded eye pieces, and huge roundels on their chests. The riders wore indigo uniforms that contrasted with the brilliant scarlet saddle-cloths. They swept round in ceaseless whorls and circles, shaking feathered spears and brandishing round shields with pointed bosses centred on exotic patterns alien to Rome. The air of mystery was compounded by their formal parade helmets, which covered their faces like calmly expressionless theatrical masks. For half an hour this noble equestrian chorus rode the windy parade-ground like haughty gods, then they suddenly swooped out through the great gates to the Via Principia, leaving all the spectators bereft and dismayed.

Warm drinks were supplied on the dais.

Not before time.

I wondered rather pitifully whether I should speak to Helena now. She was enjoying her refreshments, so I chose to let the moment pass.

'There's Julius Mordanticus!' Helena called to me, waving at the local crowd. One of the huddled group of pointed hoods raised an arm back to her. He and his friends were happy. I had been interviewed by the provincial governor about the ceramics franchise fraud, and afterwards I had been able to bring the local potters good news. 'I meant to say,' Helena told me guiltily, 'while you were in Augusta Treverorum he gave us a present of a superb set of dinner bowls. What a pity,' quipped my insensitive sweetheart, 'we have no dining-room to use them in!'

We never would have now. I looked away.

The pause in formalities was lingering as people clutched

hot refreshments tightly, trying to warm their hands. Helena continued chattering. 'Is it true when Xanthus shaved the rebel, you brought the trimmings away in a little bag to impress the Emperor?'

'It's true.'

'How did you persuade Xanthus to take part?' Xanthus would do anything for me nowadays; I had given him a *genuine* aurochs' horn. If he had it made into a drinking-cup, he would drown himself, it was so big. I had told him to take great care, because apart from the one I owned myself, there would be no repeats. 'He seems an odd choice to supervise a rebel,' hinted Helena.

'Xanthus is looking to settle down and make his pile in a town where Nero's name will give him massive prestige, but he can rise above his past existence as a slave. Augusta Treverorum fits: refined, but not too snobbish. He'll be shaving the cream of Belgican society on his portico, while poor women queue up at his back door to have their golden tresses sheared to make expensive wigs for society dames in Rome.'

'I don't think I approve of that.'

'They could sell worse things, love. Anyway, I bet our lad with the puce shoelaces will end up a substantial citizen, donating temples and civic columns with the best.'

'And Civilis?'

'Xanthus gave him an ebony rinse to stop him being recognised. He'll be safe from assassins, and secure for us. The barber will be visiting his house to shave him every day. If Civilis absconds, his disappearance will be noted immediately.'

It was the perfect bail. And the unfortunate chief would never get a chance to rabble-rouse, now that he would be battened under hot napkins listening to gossip most of the day.

Helena smiled. I loved her smile. 'Marcus, you're wonderful.' The mockery was fairly delicate.

Out on the parade-ground the provincial governor, his head covered, was preparing to take yet another set of auguries. He was assisted on behalf of the Fourteenth by their senior tribune, Macrinus, who was standing in for the dead legate. I could see Maenia Priscilla getting excited. She stood no chance now. Ambition had superseded all else. Given this chance to show off as a substitute, Macrinus was rapt in pursuit of his public career.

I did not need to peer at a sheep's sickly liver to know the omens were bad for me. 'What's the matter?' asked Helena quietly.

'There is something I have to say to you.'

'Well then, you had better get on with it.'

The standard-bearers were carrying their poles to the central arena. Giant men with bearskins or wolfskins, the animals' heads resting upon their helmets, and the paws crossed on their chests. They walked with their sombre pace to surround the governor, then speared the ground with the stout spikes of their carrying poles. The spikes held – the gods were in favour. So there the standards of the Fourteenth Gemina Martia Victrix stood. The golden eagle with the legion's number. The individual markers for each cohort of foot-soldiers, and the fringed square flags used by the cavalry. The Emperor's portrait taking pride of place. Battle honours from half a century. Their statue of Mars. And now, presented to the legion before the entire assembled company palm outwards as a symbol of either power or friendship, their mighty Hand.

Still kneeling beside Helena, I stared hard at the ceremony. 'I have finished my mission. It's time for me to leave. I've been thinking. Some women can achieve more good for the world than men.' Her finger was tickling the back of my neck; in a moment she would know it was inappropriate and she would stop. I forced myself to speak: 'Helena, for the sake of Rome you ought to marry Titus. When you answer his letter – '

A blaze of trumpets interrupted me.

Brilliant. My life's big gesture shattered by a misplaced musical blast.

The standard-bearer with the Hand received the governor's approval, then began to pace through the entire legion to display Vespasian's gift. He approached the cohorts. At each one their particular signal party went through a short routine of acknowledgement before he set off to the next. Throughout his slow march all the trumpets in the legion brayed.

Helena's hand lay completely still against my neck. To lose her sweet consoling touch would be unbearable. But I was tough. I would do it. I would make myself. If Helena Justina chose the Empire as her duty, I would send her back to Rome alone, while I opted for permanent exile, roaming the wilder edges of the Empire, or even beyond it, like a miserable ghost . . .

Just as I was about to spring from the dais and depart like a hero, Helena bent down to me. Her hair brushed my cheek. Her perfume enveloped me in a cinnamon haze. Her lips moved softly right against my ear: 'You can stop looking so pathetic. *I wrote to him the day you left Colonia.*'

Helena sat back. I crouched where I was. We watched the standard-bearer stamp his way decisively round two more infantry cohorts, then the trumpets stilled.

I looked up. Helena Justina tapped me gently on the nose with her knuckle, the one wearing the silver ring I had once given her. She did not look at me. She was gazing across the parade-ground with an expression of refined interest like any other high-born lady wondering how soon she could go home. Nobody but me could realise how obstinate, and how beautiful, she was.

My girl.

The chief standard-bearer of the XIV Gemina represented their senior tribune with the Emperor's Iron Hand. It was a handsome item, two feet high, and the man in the bearskin must be breathless from the weight. An armourer had regilded the chips in its decoration, but I happened to know that it had a dented thumb where I had bashed it against a bedstead in some crummy travellers' doss-house on my journey across Gaul.

'Are you staying with me, Helena?' I dared to ask meekly.

'No choice,' she said (after pausing to think about it). 'I

667

own a half-share in your samian dinner service, which I don't intend relinquishing. So stop talking nonsense, Marcus, and watch the parade.'

POSEIDON'S
GOLD

Extract from the Family Tree

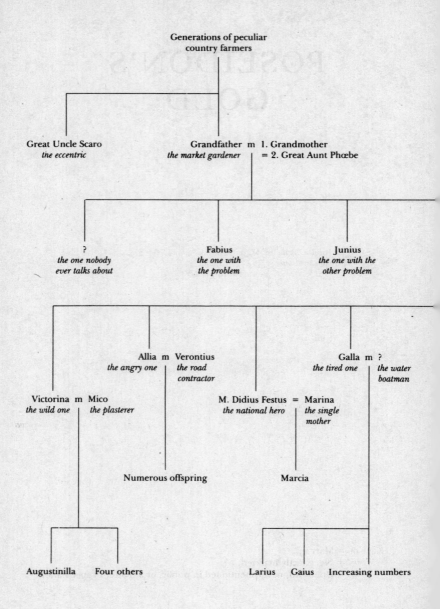

# of Marcus Didius Falco

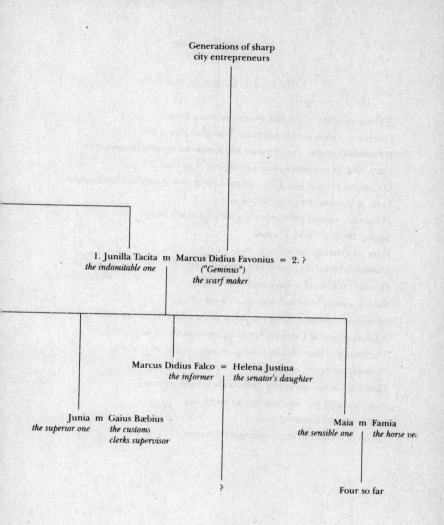

Generations of sharp
city entrepreneurs

1. Junilla Tacita m Marcus Didius Favonius = 2. ?
the indomitable one   ("Geminus")
                                    the scarf maker

Marcus Didius Falco = Helena Justina
the informer   *the senator's daughter*

Junia m Gaius Bæbius
the superior one   *the customs
              clerks supervisor*

Maia m Famia
the sensible one *the horse ve*

?

Four so far

Key: 'm' = Married;
     '=' = Not exactly married;
     '?' = Unknown, never mentioned in public, or a matter of speculation.

Other Characters in the Story

T Censorinus Macer *a soldier who once believed a hot tip*

Laurentius *a centurion who knows that fortunes are there to be lost*

L Petronius Longus *a watch captain who does his best in trying circumstances*

Marponius *an encyclopaedia salesman: the trial judge to avoid*

D Camillus Verus & Julia Justa *nice parents with normal problems (their children)*

Lenia *a laundress with terrible taste in men*

Epimandos *a waiter who tries to please (on a hiding to nothing)*

Stringy *the cat at Flora's Caupona*

Flora *who probably does not exist*

Manilus & Varga *two painters with short memories*

Orontes Mediolanus *a much sought-after sculptor*

Rubina *a model whose measurements are worth taking*

Apollonius *a geometry teacher who fails to get the measure of the real world*

A Cassius Carus & Ummidia Servia *discerning patrons of the (lost) arts*

The Aristedon Bros *shippers to the discerning (sailing in tricky waters)*

Cocceius *an 'honest' auctioneer*

Domitian Caesar *a ruler who claims he has to follow the rules*

Anacrites *a spy who maintains that it's not his fault*

Ajax *a dog with a criminal record*

Group of Jewish Prisoners *building the Colosseum*

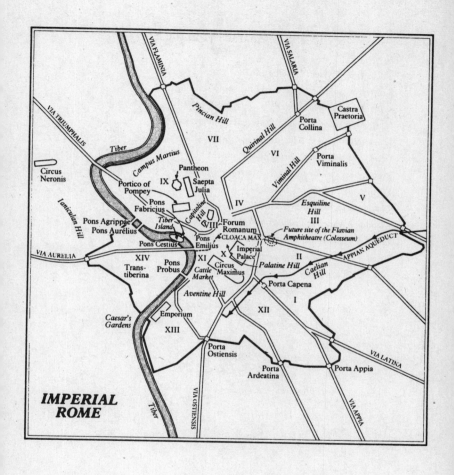

VIA FLAMINIA

VIA SALARIA

VIA TRIUMPHALIS

Castra
Praetoria

Pincian Hill

Porta
Collina

VII

Quirinal Hill

Tiber

VI

Porta
Viminalis

Campus Martius

Circus
Neronis

Pantheon

Viminal Hill

V

IX

Saepta
Julia

*Esquiline
Hill*

Portico of
Pompey

IV

III

Janiculan Hill

Pons
Fabricius

Capitoline Hill

Forum
Romanum

Future site of the Flavian
Amphitheatre (Colosseum)

Pons Agrippae
Pons Aurelius

*Tiber
Island*

VIII

APPIAN AQUEDUCT

Pons Cestius

Pons
Emilius

CLOACA MAX.

Imperial
Palace

VIA AURELIA

XIV

Pons
Probus

X

XI

*Circus
Maximus*

Palatine Hill

II

*Caelian
Hill*

Trans-
tiberina

*Cattle
Market*

Porta Capena

I

Aventine Hill

XII

*Caesar's
Gardens*

Emporium

XIII

Porta
Ostiensis

Porta
Ardeatina

VIA LATINA

Porta Appia

VIA OSTIENSIS

VIA APPIA

Tiber

IMPERIAL
ROME

ROME; CAPUA; ROME

March–April, AD72

I

A dark and stormy night on the Via Aurelia: the omens were bad for our home-coming even before we entered Rome.

By that time we had covered a thousand miles, making our journey from Germany in February and March. The five or six hours on the last stint from Veii were the worst. Long after other travellers had tucked themselves up in wayside inns, we found ourselves alone on the road. Electing to press on and reach the city tonight had been a ridiculous option. Everyone in my party knew it, and everyone knew who was responsible: me, Marcus Didius Falco, the man in charge. The rest were probably expressing their views fractiously, but I couldn't hear. They were in the carriage, thoroughly damp and uncomfortable, but able to see that there were colder and wetter alternatives: I was on horseback, completely exposed to the driving wind and rain.

Without warning, the first dwellings appeared – the tall, crowded apartments that would line our way through the unsavoury slums of the Transtiberina district. Run-down buildings without balconies or pergolas stood pressed together, their grim ranks broken only by black alleys where robbers normally lay in wait for new arrivals to Rome. Maybe tonight they would prefer lurking safe and cosy in their beds. Or maybe they would be hoping the weather would put travellers off guard; I knew the last half-hour of a long journey can be the most dangerous. In the apparently deserted streets our hoofbeats and rattling carriage wheels announced our presence resonantly. Sensing threats all around us, I gripped my sword pommel and checked the knife hidden in my boot. Sodden thongs were trapping the blade against the swollen flesh of my calf, making it difficult to extricate.

I wound myself deeper into my waterlogged cloak, regretting it as the heavy folds constricted me clammily. A gutter collapsed overhead; an icy sluice doused me, frightened my horse and knocked my hat askew. Cursing, I fought to control the horse. I realised I had missed the turn that would have taken us to the Probus Bridge, our quickest route home. My hat fell off. I abandoned it.

A single gleam of light down a side-street to my right marked what I knew to be the guard-post of a cohort of the Vigiles. There were no other signs of life.

We crossed the Tiber on the Pons Aurelia. In the darkness below I could hear the river at full surge. Its rushing water had an unpleasant energy. Upstream it had almost certainly overflowed its banks on to all the low ground around the foot of the Capitol, yet again turning the Campus Martius – which could be spongy at the best of times – into an unhealthy lake. Yet again turgid mud the colour and texture of sewage would be oozing into the basements of the expensive mansions whose middle-class owners jostled for the best waterfront views.

My own father was one of them. At least thinking of him having to bale filthy floodwater out of his entrance hall cheered me up.

A huge gust of wind stopped my horse dead in its tracks as we tried to turn into the Cattle Market Forum. Above, both the Citadel and Palatine Hill were invisible. The lamplit Palaces of the Caesars were drowned out of sight too, but I was now on familiar ground. I urged my horse past the Circus Maximus, the Temples of Ceres and Luna, the arches, fountains, baths and covered markets that were the glory of Rome. They could wait; all I wanted was my own bed. Rain cascaded down a statue of some ancient consul, using the bronze folds of his toga as gullies. Sheets of water swept off pantiled roofs whose gutters were quite unable to cope with this volume. Cataracts tumbled from porticoes. My horse struggled to press under the sheltered walkways against the shopfronts, while I pulled his head round to keep him on the road.

We forced a passage down the Street of the Armilustrium. Some of the undrained side-lanes at this lower level looked knee-deep in water and quite impassable, but as we turned off the high road we were going steeply uphill – not flooded, but treacherous underfoot. There had been so much rain sluicing the Aventine lanes today that not even the normal stinks rose to welcome me home; no doubt the customary reek of human waste and unneighbourly trades would be back tomorrow, steamier than ever after so much water had swilled around the half-composted depths of middens and rubbish tips.

A gloomy throb of the familiar told me that I had found Fountain Court.

My street. This sour dead end looked bleaker than ever to a stranger returning. Unlit, with shutters barred and awnings furled, the alley had no saving grace. Unpeopled even by its normal throng of degenerates, it still ached with human grief. The wind whooped into the cul-de-sac, then came straight back in our faces. On one side my apartment block reared like some faceless republican rampart built to withstand marauding barbarians. As I drew up, a heavy flowerpot crashed down, missing me by no more than a digit's width.

I dragged open the carriage door to shepherd out the exhausted souls for whom I was responsible. Swathed like mummies against the weather they stiffly descended, then discovered their legs as the gale hit them and fled into the quieter haven of the stairwell: my girlfriend Helena Justina, her waiting woman, my sister's young daughter, and our carriage-driver, a sturdy Celt who had been supposed to help guard us. Hand-picked by me, he had trembled with terror for most of the way. It turned out that he was as timid as a rabbit off his home ground. He had never been out of Bingium before; I wished I had left him there.

At least I had had Helena. She was a senator's daughter, with all that entails, naturally, and more spirited than most of them. She had outwitted any mansio-keepers who tried to withhold their most decent rooms from us and made short work of villains claiming illegal bridge tolls. Now her expressive dark eyes were informing me that after the last hours of today's journey she intended to deal with me. Meeting those eyes, I did not waste effort on a cajoling smile.

We were not home yet. My rooms were six floors up.

We tackled the stairs in silence and in the dark. After half a year in Germany where even two storeys were a rarity, my thigh muscles were protesting. Only the fit lived here. If invalids in financial straits ever hired an apartment over Fountain Court, they were either cured rapidly by the exercise or the stairs killed them. We had lost quite a few that way. Smaractus the landlord ran a profitable racket selling off his dead tenants' effects.

At the top, Helena pulled a tinder-box from under her cloak. Desperation gave me a firm hand, so I soon struck a spark and even managed to light a taper before the spark died. On my doorpost the faded tile still announced that M. Didius Falco practised his trade here as a private informer. After a short, hot quarrel while I tried to remember where I had stowed my latch-lifter and failed to find it, I borrowed a dress pin from Helena, tied it to a piece of braid ripped from my own tunic, dropped the pin down the hole and waggled.

For once the trick worked. (Normally you just break the pin, earn a swipe from the girl and still have to borrow a ladder to climb in.) This time there was a reason for my success: the latch was broken. Dreading the outcome, I pushed open the door, held up my taper and surveyed my home.

Places always look smaller and scruffier than you remember them. Not normally this bad, though.

Leaving home had carried some risks. But the Fates, who love picking on a loser, had thrown every lousy trick at me. The first invaders had probably been insects and mice, but they had been followed by a particularly filthy set of nesting doves who must have pecked their way in through the roof. Their excrement spattered the floorboards, but it was nothing to the filth of the vile human scavengers who must have replaced the doves. Blatant clues, some several months old, told me none of the people to whom I had been giving houseroom had been nicely brought up citizens.

'Oh my poor Marcus!' Helena exclaimed in shock. She might be tired and annoyed, but faced with a man in complete despair she was a charitable girl.

I handed back her pin with a formal gesture. I gave her the taper to hold. Then I strode in and kicked the nearest bucket right across the room.

The bucket was empty. Whoever had broken in here had sometimes made an effort to throw their rubbish into the container I had provided, but they had had no aim; besides, sometimes they hadn't even tried. The rubbish that missed had stayed on the floor until decay welded it to the boards.

'Marcus, darling – '

'Hush, lass. Just don't speak to me until I've got used to it!'

I passed through the outer room, which had once served as my office. Beyond, in what was left of my bedroom, I found more evidence of the human trespassers. They must have fled only today when the old hole in the roof broke open anew to let in a spectacular deluge of pantiles and rainwater, most of which was still soaking my bed. A further inflow of dirty drips was joining the party. My poor old bed was beyond all help.

Helena came up behind me. 'Well!' I made a grim attempt to sound bright. 'I can sue the landlord if I want to give myself a *really* bad headache!'

I felt Helena's hand entwine in mine. 'Is anything stolen?'

I never leave pickings for thieves. 'All my movables were stowed with my relatives, so if anything's missing I know it's gone to family.'

'Such a comfort!' she agreed.

I loved that girl. She was inspecting the wreckage with her most refined distaste, yet her gravity was meant to make me burst into desperate laughter. She had a dry sense of humour that I found irresistible. I threw my arms around her and clung on to her for sanity.

She kissed me. She was looking rueful, but her kiss was full of tenderness. 'Welcome home, Marcus.' The first time I ever kissed Helena she had had a cold face and wet eyelashes, and then, too, it had been like waking from a deeply troubled sleep to find somebody feeding you honey cakes.

I sighed. Alone, I might just have cleared a space and curled up exhausted in the filth. But I knew I had to find a better roost. We would have to impose ourselves on relatives. Helena's parents' comfortable house lay on the other side of the Aventine – too far and much too risky. After dark Rome is a heartless, unethical city. That left either divine aid from Olympus – or my own family. Jupiter and all his associates were steadfastly chomping ambrosia in some other fellow's apartment; they ignored my pleas for help. We were stuck with my lot.

681

Somehow I chivvied everyone downstairs again. At least the night was so terrible the usual thieves had missed their chance; our horse and carriage still stood forlornly in Fountain Court.

We passed the shadow of the Emporium, which was bolted up but even on a night like this exuded a faint whiff of exotic imported timbers, hides, cured meats and spices. We reached another apartment block with fewer stairs and a less bleak exterior, but still one I could call home. Already encouraged by the expectation of hot food and dry beds, we scrambled up to the familiar brick-red door. It was never locked; no Aventine burglar was brave enough to invade this dwelling.

The rest were keen to be first inside, but I pushed ahead of them. I had territorial rights. I was a boy coming home to the place where he grew up. I was coming home – with an inevitable feeling of guilt – to the house where my little old mother lived.

The door opened straight into her kitchen. To my surprise an oil-lamp stood lit; Ma's habits were normally more frugal. Perhaps she had sensed we were coming. It was quite likely. I braced myself for her greeting, but she wasn't there.

I stepped inside, then stopped dead in astonishment.

A complete stranger was taking his ease with his boots up on the table. No one was allowed that luxury if my mother was in the vicinity. He eyed me blearily for a moment, then let out a deep and purposely offensive belch.

II

Like any self-respecting mother, mine had made her kitchen the command post from which she aimed to supervise her children's lives. We had other ideas. That turned Ma's kitchen into a lively arena for people to eat themselves sick while complaining about one another loudly in the vain hope of sidetracking Ma.

Some things here were fairly normal. There was a stone cooking bench partly set into the outside wall with a view to spreading the weight; in front of it the floor bowed disastrously. Ma lived three floors up and her apartment had an attic, but my sisters used to sleep up there as children, so by tradition the cooking smoke was fanned out of a window downstairs by anybody who was hanging about; the fan hung on a shutter catch.

Above the bench gleamed a row of copper pans, paterae and frying skillets, some second-hand and bearing several lifetimes' knocks. On one shelf stood bowls, beakers, pitchers, pestles, and a motley batch of spoons in a cracked vase. Nails that would hang half an ox carcass held ladles, graters, strainers and meat mallets. A cranky row of hooks supported a set of giant cooking knives; they had evil iron blades bound on to cracked bone hafts and each was scratched with Ma's initials: *JT* for Junilla Tacita.

The highest shelf held four of those special pots for cooking dormice. Don't misunderstand that: Ma says dormice are nasty things with no meat on them, only fit for snobs with poor taste and silly habits. But when it's Saturnalia, you are already half an hour late for the family party and are desperately buying your mother a present to excuse the last twelve months of neglecting her, those dormice coddlers always look exactly what she needs. Ma accepted each graciously from whichever offspring had fallen for the sales pitch this time, then let her unused collection grow reproachfully.

683

Bunches of dried herbs scented the room. Baskets of eggs and flat platters heaped with pulses filled any empty space. An abundance of besoms and buckets announced what kind of spotless, scandal-free kitchen – and family – my mother wished spectators to believe she ran.

The effect was being spoiled tonight by the ill-mannered lout who had belched at me. I stared at him. Bushes of wiry grey hair sprang out either side of his head. Like his uncompromising face, the bald dome above was tanned to a deep mahogany gleam. He had the look of a man who had been in the Eastern desert; I had a nasty feeling I knew which bit of boiling desert it must have been. His bare arms and legs had the permanent leathery musculature that comes from long years of hard physical activity rather than the fake results of a training programme at the gymnasium.

'Who in Hades are you?' he had the nerve to demand.

Wild thoughts that my mother had taken a lover to brighten her old age flashed into my mind, then scuttled away sheepishly. 'Why don't you tell me first?' I answered, giving him an intimidating glare.

'Get lost!'

'Not yet, soldier.' I had guessed his profession. Though his tunic was faded to a thin pink, I was closely inspecting the two-inch-thick studded soles of military boots. I knew the type. I knew the garlic breath, the scars from barracks squabbles, the cocksure attitude.

His mean eyes narrowed warily but he made no attempt to remove those boots from my mother's hallowed work surface. I dropped the bundle I was carrying and pushed back the cloak from around my head. He must have recognised the wet tangle of the Didius family curls.

'You're the brother!' he accused me. So he had known Festus. That was bad news. And apparently he had heard of me.

Acting like a man visitors certainly ought to have heard about, I sought the upper hand. 'Things seem to have grown slack around here, soldier! You'd better clear the table and straighten up, before I kick the bench from under you.' This subtle psychology worked. He swung his boots to the ground. 'Slowly!' I added, in case he planned on jumping me. He eased himself upright. One good thing about my brother had been that people respected him. For at least five minutes (I knew from experience) associated respect would attach to me.

'So you're the brother!' he repeated slowly, as if it meant something.

'That's right. I'm Falco. And you?'

'Censorinus.'

'What's your legion?'

'Fifteenth Apollinaris.' It would be. My surly mood deepened. The Fifteenth were the unlucky outfit my brother had graced for several years – before he made himself famous by flinging his handsome carcass over a hot Judaean battlement into a thicket of rebels' spears.

'So that's how you knew Festus?'

'Agreed,' he sneered condescendingly.

While we talked I was aware of restless movements behind me from Helena and the others. They wanted their beds – and so did I. 'You won't find Festus here, and you know why.'

'Festus and I were good mates,' he declared.

'Festus always had a lot of friends.' I sounded calmer than I felt. Festus, rot his eyes, would enter into a drinking pact with any skunk which had mange and half its tail missing. Then, generous to the last, my brother would bring his new friend home to us.

'Is there a problem?' the legionary enquired. His air of innocence was suspicious in itself. 'Festus said any time I was in Rome –'

'You could stay at his mother's house?'

'That's what the boy promised!'

It was depressingly familiar. And I knew the Fifteenth Legion had been redeployed recently from the Judaean war zone back to Pannonia – so presumably large numbers of them would now be asking for a spell of leave in Rome.

'I'm sure he did. How long have you been here?'

'A few weeks . . .' That meant months.

'Well I'm glad the Fifteenth Apollinaris has been augmenting Junilla Tacita's budget!' I stared him out. We both knew he had made no contributions at all to my mother's housekeeping. What a home-coming. First my wrecked apartment, now this. It seemed that while I was away Rome had filled up with unscrupulous losers all looking for rent-free beds.

I wondered where my mother was hiding. I felt an odd nostalgia to hear her nagging me while she spooned hot broth into my favourite bowl and pulled me out of my sopping clothes like when I was a child. 'Right! Well, I'm afraid I shall have to unstick you from your billet, Censorinus. It's needed by the family now.'

'Of course. I'll shift as soon as possible . . .'

I stopped smiling. Even my teeth were tired. I gestured to the pathetic band I had brought with me. They were standing in silence, too exhausted to join in. 'I'd be glad if you'd make your arrangements fairly briskly.'

His glance went to the shutters. Outside we could hear the rain splashing as hard as ever. 'You're not going to turn me out on a night like this, Falco!'

He was right, but I owed the world a few punches. I grinned evilly. 'You're a soldier. A bit of wet won't hurt you . . .' I might have gone on amusing myself, but just at that moment my mother came into the room. Her beady black eyes took in the scene.

'Oh you're back,' she said, as if I had just come in from weeding a carrot patch. A small, tidy, almost tireless woman, she brushed past me, went to kiss Helena, then busied herself prying free my sleepy niece.

'Nice to be missed,' I muttered.

Ma ignored the pathos. 'We had plenty you could have been doing.'

She did not mean picking ticks off a dog. I saw her glance at Helena, plainly warning that there was bad news for later. Unable to face whatever crises had befallen the Didius clan, I dealt with the problem I knew about. 'We need a refuge. I gather big brother's old bed has already been claimed?'

'Yes. I thought you might have something to say about that!'

I could see Censorinus starting to look nervous. My mother peered at me expectantly while I tried to work out what I was supposed to do. For some reason she seemed to be playing the helpless old soul whose big tough son had emerged from his warren to defend her. This was quite out of character. I handled the situation delicately. 'I was merely commenting on a fact, Ma —'

686

'Oh I knew he wouldn't like it!' Ma announced to no one in particular.

I was too tired to resist. I squared up to the legionary. He probably thought he was tough, but he was easier to tackle than a devious mother with complicated motives.

Censorinus had grasped that the game was over. Ma was now making it plain that she had simply let him lodge there while she waited for someone else to argue about it. I was back: her agent for the dirty work. There was no point fighting my destiny.

'Listen, friend. I'm worn out and chilled to the bone, so I'll be blunt. I've travelled a thousand miles at the worst time of year to find my apartment wrecked by intruders and my own bed full of rubble from a leaking roof. In ten minutes' time I intend to be flat out in the alternative, and the fact that my alternative is where you've been making yourself at home is just fortune's way of warning you that the gods are fickle friends – '

'So much for hospitality to strangers!' Censorinus scoffed at me. 'And so much for comrades who tell you they're mates!'

Uneasily I noticed a threat in his tone. It had nothing to do with what we seemed to be discussing. 'Look, I want the spare room for me and my lady, but you're not being turned out into the night. There's a dry attic that's perfectly liveable – '

'Stuff your attic!' the legionary retorted; then added, 'And stuff Festus, and stuff you!'

'Whatever makes you feel better,' I replied, trying not to sound as if for this family, the one good aspect of Festus's death had been that we did not have to dole out free food and lodging to an endless succession of his colourful friends.

I saw Ma pat the legionary's shoulder. She muttered consolingly, 'I'm sorry, but I just can't have you here upsetting my son . . .'

'Oh Jupiter, Ma!' She was impossible.

To speed things up I helped Censorinus pack. As he left he gave me a malevolent glare, but I was too preoccupied with the joys of family life to wonder why.

III

Helena and Ma combined efforts to allocate space to my party. Our servants were briskly rushed off to the attic. My young niece Augustinilla was tucked up in Mother's own bed.

'How's Victorina?' I forced myself to ask. We had been looking after the child for my older sister whilst she was ill.

'Victorina died.' Mother gave the news matter-of-factly, but her voice was tense. 'I wasn't going to tell you tonight.'

'Victorina's gone?' I could hardly take it in.

'In December.'

'You could have written.'

'What would that have achieved?'

I dropped my spoon on to the table and sat cradling my bowl, taking comfort from the warmth that remained in the pottery. 'This is unbelievable . . .'

Wrong. Victorina had had an internal problem, which some quack Alexandrian doctor who specialised in prodding the female anatomy had convinced her was operable; his diagnosis must have been false, or more likely he bungled the surgery. It happens all the time. I had no business to be sitting there, feeling so surprised that she had died.

Victorina was the eldest in our family, tyrannising the other six of us who had somehow struggled alive through infancy. I had always stayed fairly remote from her, a matter of choice since I hated being bruised and terrorised. She was in her teens when I was born, and even then had a terrible reputation: an eye for the boys, a saucy green parasol, and the side-seams of her tunic always revealingly unstitched. When she visited the Circus, the men who held her parasol for her were always repugnant types. In the end she picked up a plasterer called Mico and married him. I finally stopped speaking to her at that point.

They had five surviving children. The baby must be not yet two. Still, childhood being what it was, he could well be joining his lost mother before he was three.

Helena was missing this conversation. She had fallen asleep, crushed against my shoulder. I half turned, easing her into a kinder position; one where I could gaze down at her. I needed to see her, to remind myself the Fates could spin a sound thread when they chose to. She was completely at rest. No one ever slept so deeply as Helena with my arm around her. At least I was some use to somebody.

Ma draped a blanket over both of us. 'So she's still with you?' Despite her contempt for my previous girlfriends, Ma reckoned Helena Justina was much too good for me. Most people thought that. Helena's own relatives were first in the queue. Perhaps they were right. Even in Rome, with its snobbery and tawdry values, she could certainly have done better for herself.

'Seems like it.' I caressed the soft hollow of Helena's right temple with my thumb. Utterly relaxed, she looked all sweetness and gentleness. I didn't fool myself that was her true nature, but it was a part of her – even if that part only showed when she was sleeping in my arms.

'I heard some tale she had run away.'

'She's here. So the tale's obviously wrong.'

Ma intended to find out the whole story. 'Was she trying to get away from you, or did you scram and she had to chase after you?' She had a good grasp of how we ran our lives. I ignored the question, so she launched off another: 'Are you any nearer settling things?'

Probably neither of us could answer that. Our relationship had its volatile moments. The fact that Helena Justina was the daughter of a millionaire senator while I was an impoverished informer did not improve our chances. I could never tell whether every day that I managed to hold on to her took us one step nearer our inevitable parting – or whether the time I was keeping us together would make us impossible to separate.

'I heard Titus Caesar had his eye on her,' Ma continued inexorably. That was best left unanswered too. Titus could pose a tough challenge. Helena maintained she had rebuffed his overtures. But who could really tell? She might privately welcome our return to Rome and the chance to impress further the Emperor's son. She would be a fool if she didn't. I should have kept her in the provinces.

To claim my fee for what I had done in Germany, I had had to come back and report to the Emperor; Helena had come with me. Life must go on. Titus was a risk I had to face. If he wanted trouble, I was prepared to put up a fight. 'Everyone says you'll let her down,' my mother assured me happily.

'I've avoided it so far!'

'There's no need to get snappy,' commented Ma.

It was late. Ma's apartment block hit one of the rare occasions when all its tenants had fallen quiet at once. In the silence she fiddled with the wick of the pottery oil-lamp, scowling at the crude bedroom scene embossed on the redware – one of my brother's joking household contributions. Being a present from Festus meant the item was impossible to throw out now. Besides, the lamp had a clean, steady burn despite the pornography.

The loss of my sister, even the one I had had least time for, brought my brother's absence to the surface again too.

'What was all that with the legionary, Ma? Plenty of people knew Festus, but not many of them turn up on the doorstep nowadays.'

'I can't be rude to your brother's friends.' No need, when she had me to do it for her. 'Maybe you shouldn't have evicted him like that, Marcus.'

My turning out Censorinus was what she had plainly intended from the moment I arrived; yet I was getting blamed for it. After knowing my mother for thirty years the contradiction was predictable. 'Why didn't you give him the twiggy end of a besom yourself?'

'I'm afraid he'll bear a grudge against you,' murmured Ma.

'I can handle that.' The silence carried ominous overtones. 'Is there a particular reason why he might?' My mother remained mute. 'There is!'

'It's nothing.' So it was serious.

'You'd better tell me.'

'Oh . . . there seems to be some trouble over something Festus is supposed to have done.'

All my life I had been hearing those fatal words. 'Oh here

690

we go again. Stop being coy, Ma. I know Festus, I can recognise one of his disasters from a hippodrome's length away.'

'You're tired, son. I'll talk to you in the morning.'

I was so weary my head was still singing the rhythms of travelling, but with some doom-laden fraternal mystery hanging in the air there was little hope of sleep until I discovered what I had come home to – and probably no sleep then.

'Oh cobnuts, I'm tired all right. I'm tired of people dodging the issue. Talk to me now, Mother!'

IV

Festus was three years in the tomb. The writs had mainly dried up, but promissory notes from debtors and hopeful letters from abandoned women still trickled back to Rome from time to time. And now we had a military interest; that might prove harder to deflect.

'I don't expect he did anything,' Ma comforted herself.

'Oh he did it,' I assured her. 'Whatever it is! I can guarantee our Festus was right in there, beaming cheerfully as usual. Ma, the only question is, what am *I* going to have to do – or more likely, how much will it cost me – to get us all out of whatever trouble he's caused this time?' Ma managed to find a look that implied I was insulting her beloved boy. 'Tell me the truth. Why did you want me to kick out Censorinus the minute I came home?'

'He had started asking awkward questions.'

'What questions?'

'According to him, some soldiers in your brother's legion once put money into a venture which Festus organised. Censorinus has come to Rome to reclaim their cash.'

'There is no cash.' As my brother's executor I could vouch for it. When he died I received a letter from the will clerk in his legion that confirmed everything I could have guessed anyway: after paying his local debts and providing a funeral there was nothing for them to send home to me but the comfort of knowing I would have been his heir, had our hero been able to keep any cash in his arm-purse for more than two days. Festus had always spent his quarterly pay in advance. He had left nothing in Judaea. I could find nothing in Rome either, despite the labyrinthine complexity of his business schemes. He ran his life on a marvellous talent for bluff. I thought I knew him as closely as anyone, but even I had been deluded when he chose.

I sighed. 'Give me the full story. What was this sticky venture?'

692

'Some scheme to make a lot of money, apparently.' Just like my brother, always thinking he'd hit upon a fabulous idea to make his fortune. Just like him to involve everyone else who had ever shared his tent. Festus could charm investments from a dedicated miser whom he'd only met that morning; his own trusting pals had stood no chance.

'What scheme?'

'I'm not sure.' Ma looked confused. I wasn't fooled. My mother's grip on facts was as strong as an octopus entwining its future dinner. She undoubtedly knew what Festus stood accused of; she preferred me to find out the details for myself. That meant the story would make me angry. Ma wanted to be somewhere else when I blew up.

We had been talking with lowered voices, but my agitation must have made me tense; Helena stirred and woke, instantly alert. 'Marcus, what's wrong?'

I squirmed stiffly. 'Just family troubles. Don't worry; go back to sleep.' Immediately she forced herself awake.

'The soldier?' Helena correctly deduced. 'I was surprised you sent him packing like that. Was he a confidence trickster?'

I said nothing. I liked to keep my brother's indiscretions to myself. But Ma, who had been so wary of telling me the tale, was prepared to confide in Helena. 'The soldier is genuine enough. We are in some trouble with the army. I let him lodge here because at first he seemed to be just somebody my elder son had known in Syria, but once he got his boots under the table he began to pester me.'

'What about, Junilla Tacita?' Helena queried indignantly, sitting up. She often addressed my mother in this formal way. Oddly, it marked a greater intimacy between them than Mother had ever allowed my previous female friends, most of whom had had no acquaintance with polite speech.

'There is supposed to be a money problem with something poor Festus was involved in,' my mother told Helena. 'Marcus is going to look into it for us.'

I choked. 'I don't remember saying I'd do that.'

'No. Of course you're bound to be busy.' My mother changed tack adroitly. 'Will you have a lot of work waiting?'

I was not expecting an eager stream of clients. After six months away I would have lost any initiative. People always

693

want to rush ahead with their foolish manoeuvres; my competitors would have grabbed all the commissions for commercial surveillance, gathering court evidence and finding grounds for divorces. Clients have no concept of waiting patiently if the best operative happens to be busy in Europe for an indefinite period. How could I avoid it if the Emperor up on the Palatine expected his affairs to take priority? 'I doubt if I'll be stretched,' I admitted, since my womenfolk were likely to overrule me if I tried to fudge the issue.

'Of course you won't,' cried Helena. My heart sank. Helena had no idea she was taking the cart into a cul-de-sac. She had never known Festus; she could not possibly imagine how his schemes had so often ended.

'Who else is there to help us?' urged Ma. 'Oh Marcus, I did think you would have an interest in clearing your own poor brother's name . . .'

Just as I had known it would, the mission that I refused to accept transformed itself into a mission I could not refuse.

I must have muttered some grudging noise that sounded like assent. Next thing, Ma was declaring that she would not expect me to give my precious time for nothing, while Helena was mouthing at me that in no circumstances could I send my own mother a daily expenses sheet. I felt like a new length of cloth receiving a fuller's battering.

Being paid was not my worry. But I knew this was a case I could not win.

'All right!' I growled. 'If you ask me, the departed lodger was just playing on a slight acquaintance in order to clinch a free billet. Suggesting foul play was just a subtle lever, Ma.' My mother was not a person who gave in to leverage. I yawned, pointedly. 'Look, I'm not going to waste a lot of effort on something that happened so many years ago anyway, but if it will make you both happy, I'll have a word with Censorinus in the morning.' I knew where to find him; I had told him that Flora's, the local caupona, sometimes hired out rooms. He would not have travelled much further on a night like this.

My mother stroked my hair, while Helena smiled. None of their shameless attentions improved my pessimistic mood. I knew before I started that Festus, who had got me into trouble all my life, had now forced me to commit myself to the worst yet.

'Ma, I have to ask you a question – ' Her face did not alter, though she must have seen what was coming. 'Do *you* think Festus did whatever his cronies are asserting?'

'How can you ask me that?' she exclaimed in great affront. With any other witness, in any other enquiry, that would have convinced me the woman was pretending to be offended because she was covering up for her son.

'That's all right then,' I responded loyally.

V

My brother Festus could walk into any tavern in any province of the Empire, and some wart in a spotty tunic would rise from a bench with open arms to greet him as an old and honoured friend. Don't ask me how he did it. It was a trick I could have used myself, but you need talent to exude such warmth. The fact that Festus still owed the wart a hundred in local currency from their last acquaintance would not diminish the welcome. What's more, if our lad then progressed into the back room where the cheap whores were entertaining, equally delighted shrieks would arise as girls who should have known better all rushed up adoringly.

When I walked into Flora's, where I had been drinking on a weekly basis for nearly ten years, not even the cat noticed.

Flora's Caupona made the average seedy snack shop look chic and hygienic. It squatted on the corner where a dingy lane down from the Aventine met a dirty track up from the wharves. It had the usual arrangement, with two counters set at right angles for people in the two streets to lean on reflectively while they waited to be poisoned. The counters were made from a rough patchwork of white and grey stone that a man might mistake for marble if his mind was on the elections and he was virtually blind. Each counter had three circular holes to take cauldrons of food. At Flora's most of the holes were left empty, out of respect for public health perhaps. What the full cauldrons held was even more disgusting than the usual brown sludge with funny specks in it that's ladled out to passers-by from rotten street food shops. Flora's cold potages were off-puttingly lukewarm, and their hot meats were dangerously cool. Word had it a fisherman once died at the counter after eating a portion of slushy peas; my brother maintained that to avoid a long legal dispute with his heirs, the man was hastily processed and served up as spicy halibut balls. Festus had always known such stories.

Given the state of the kitchen behind the caupona, that one could be true.

The counters enclosed a cramped square space where really hardened regulars could sit down and have their ears knocked by the waiter's elbow as he went about his work. There were two sagging tables; one had benches, the other a set of folding camp-stools. Outside, blocking the street, lolled half a barrel; a feeble beggar permanently sat on it. He was there even today, with the remnants of the storm still producing showers. No one ever gave him alms because the waiter lifted anything he received.

I walked past the beggar, avoiding eye contact. Something about him had always looked vaguely familiar, and whatever it was always made me feel depressed. Perhaps I knew that one wrong move professionally could have me ending up sharing his barrel stump.

Indoors, I took a stool, bracing myself as it wobbled disastrously. Service would be slow. I shook today's rain out of my hair and looked around the familiar scene: the rack of amphorae, misty with spiders' webs; the shelf of brown beakers and flagons; a surprisingly attractive Greek-looking container with an octopus decoration; and the wine catalogue painted on the wall – pointlessly, because despite the impressive price list that claimed to be offering all styles of drink from house wines to Falernian, Flora's invariably served one dubious vintage whose ingredients were not more than second cousins to grapes.

Nobody knew if 'Flora' had ever existed. She could be missing or dead, but it wasn't a case I would volunteer to solve. Rumour reckoned she had been formidable; I thought she must be either a myth or a mouse. She had never put in an appearance. Maybe she knew what kind of vittles her lax caupona served. Maybe she knew how many customers wanted a word about diddled reckonings.

The waiter was called Epimandos. If he had ever met his employer he preferred not to mention it.

Epimandos was probably a runaway slave. If so he had hidden here, successfully evading pursuit, for years though he retained a permanently furtive look. Above a skinny body, his long face sunk slightly on the shoulders as if it were a theatrical mask. He was stronger than he looked, from heaving heavy pots about. He had stew stains down his tunic, and an indelible whiff of chopped garlic lurking under his fingernails.

The name of the cat who had ignored me was Stringy. Like the waiter, he was in fact quite sturdy, with a fat brindled tail and an unpleasant leer. Since he looked like an animal who expected friendly contact, I aimed a kick at him. Stringy dodged disdainfully; my foot made contact with Epimandos, who failed to utter a protest but asked, 'The usual?' He spoke as if I had only been away since Wednesday instead of so long I couldn't even remember what my usual used to be.

A bowl of vivid stew, and a very small wine jug, apparently. No wonder my brain had blotted it out.

'Good?' asked Epimandos. I knew he had a reputation for uselessness, though to me he had always seemed keen to please. Maybe Festus had something to do with it. He had made a habit of hanging around Flora's, and the waiter still remembered him with evident affection.

'Seems well up to standard!' I broke off a chunk of bread and plunged it into the bowl. A tide of froth menaced me. The meaty layer was much too brightly coloured; above it floated half a digit of transparent liquor, topped with sluggish blobs of oil where two shreds of onion and some tiny scraps of dark green foliage were wriggling like bugs in a water-butt. I took a bite, coating the roof of my mouth with grease. To cover the shock, I asked, 'Is there a military tyke called Censorinus lodging here since yesterday?' Epimandos gave me his normal vague stare. 'Tell him I'd like a word, would you?'

Epimandos ambled back to his pots, which he started poking with a bent ladle. The greyer potage glopped like a swamp that was about to swallow the waiter head first. An odour of overstrong crabmeat swam around the caupona. Epimandos gave no indication he intended to pass on my message, but I held back the urge to nag. Flora's was a dump that took its time. Its clients were in no hurry; a few had something they were supposed to do, but they were intending to avoid it. Most had nowhere to go and could barely remember why they had wandered in.

To disguise the flavour of the food I took a swig of wine.

Whatever it tasted of wasn't wine. At least it gave me something different to think about.

For half an hour I sat pondering the brevity of life and the ghastliness of my drink. I never did see Epimandos make any effort to contact Censorinus, and he was soon busy with lunchtime customers who turned up to lean on the counters from the street. Then, when I was risking my second wine jug, the soldier abruptly appeared at my side. He must have come out from the back space where stairs ran up past the cooking bench to the tiny rooms that Flora's occasionally hired to people who didn't know anywhere more sensible to stay.

'So you're looking for trouble, are you?' he sneered nastily.

'Well, I'm looking for you,' I replied as best I could with my mouth full. The dainty I was toying with was too sinewy to be hurried; in fact I felt I might be chewing this gristle for the rest of my life. Eventually I reduced it to a lump of tasteless cartilage which I removed from my mouth with more relief than decorum, and placed on the rim of my bowl; it promptly fell in.

'Sit down, Censorinus. You're blocking the light.' The legionary was induced to plant himself on the edge of my table. I kept my tone fairly civilised. 'There's a nasty rumour flying about that you've been slandering my famous brother. Do you want to talk about your problem, or shall I just thump you in the teeth?'

'There's no problem,' he sneered. 'I've come to claim a debt. I'll get it too!'

'That sounds like a threat.' I abandoned the stew but carried on with my wine, not offering him any.

'The Fifteenth don't need to make threats,' he boasted.

'Not if their grudge is legal,' I agreed, applying an aggressive edge myself. 'Look, if something's bothering the legion, and if it involves my brother, I'm prepared to listen.'

'You'll have to do something about it!'

'So tell me straight out what's griping you – or else we'll both forget about it.'

Both Epimandos and Stringy were listening. The waiter was leaning on his pots and picking his nose while he stared at us quite openly, but the cat had enough delicacy to pretend to be licking a dropped bread roll under the table. Flora's was not a place to arrange your elopement with an heiress or buy a vial of poisonous green jollop to wipe out your business partner. This caupona had the nosiest staff in Rome.

'Some of us lads who knew Festus,' Censorinus informed me self-importantly, 'chipped in with him in a certain venture.'

I managed not to close my eyes and sigh; this sounded horribly familiar. 'Oh?'

'Well, what do you think? We want the profits – or we want our stakes back. Straight away!'

I ignored the heavy-handed bit. 'Well so far, I can't say I'm either interested or impressed. First, anybody who knew Festus will fully expect to hear that he didn't leave overflowing jars of coinage under every bed he slept in. If there was a pot there he pissed in it, that's all! I was his executor; he gave me a zero legacy. Second, even if this fabulous venture was legitimate, I would expect to see documentation for your debt. Festus was an airy beggar over most things, but I've got all his business chits, and they were immaculate.' At least, the set I found scratched on bone blocks at Mother's were. I was still waiting to discover other more dubious accounts hidden away somewhere.

Censorinus eyed me coldly. He seemed very tense. 'I don't like your tone, Falco!'

'And I don't like your attitude.'

'You'd better be prepared to pay.'

'Then you'd better explain.'

Something was not right. The soldier seemed strangely reluctant to come out with the facts – his only hope of persuading me to contribute. I could see his eyes dart, with more agitation than seemed called for.

'I mean it, Falco – we expect you to cough up!'

'Olympus!' I lost my temper. 'You haven't told me the date, the place, the scheme, the terms, the venture's outcome, or the amount! All I'm getting is bluster and blather.'

Epimandos came nearer, pretending to wipe down tables and flicking chewed olive stones about with the end of a mouldy rag.

'Get lost, garlic seed!' Censorinus shouted at him. He appeared to take note of the waiter for the first time, and

Epimandos was overcome by one of his nervous fits. The waiter jumped back against a counter. Behind him other customers had started to peer in at us curiously.

Keeping an eye on Epimandos, Censorinus crouched nearer to me on a stool; he lowered his voice to a hoarse croak: 'Festus was running a ship.'

'Where from?' I tried not to sound alarmed. This was a new item in the canon of my brother's enterprises and I wanted to know all about it before any more debtors appeared.

'Caesarea.'

'And he cut some of you in?'

'We were a syndicate.'

The big word impressed him more than me. 'Shipping what?'

'Statues.'

'That fits.' Fine art was the family business on our father's side. 'Was the cargo from Judaea?'

'No. Greece.' That fitted too. There was a voracious appetite in Rome for Hellenic statuary.

'So what happened? And why are you only calling in your debt three years after his death?'

'There's been a damned war in the East, Falco – or hadn't you heard?'

'I heard,' I replied grimly, thinking of Festus.

Censorinus took more of a grip on himself. 'Your brother seemed to know what he was doing. We all put in with him to buy the stock. He promised us high percentages.'

'Then either the ship sank, in which case I feel sorry for both him and you but there's nothing I can do about it – or else you should have received your money long ago. Festus lived on the wild side, but I never saw him cheat.'

The soldier stared at the table. 'Festus said the ship did sink.'

'Hard luck. Then why in the name of the gods are you bothering me?'

He didn't believe it really had sunk; that was obvious. But he still had enough loyalty to Festus not to say so outright. 'Festus told us not to worry; he would see we didn't lose by it. He would get us the money back anyway.'

'That's impossible. If the load was lost – '

'It's what he said!'

'All right! Then he must have meant it. I'm not surprised that he was offering to make good; you were his mates. He wouldn't have let you down.'

'Better not!' Censorinus was incapable of keeping quiet, even when I sympathised.

'But whatever plan he had for recouping the loss must have involved further deals. I don't know about them, and I can't be responsible for arranging them at this stage. I'm surprised you're even trying it on.'

'He had a partner,' Censorinus grouched.

'It wasn't me.'

'I know.'

'Festus told you?'

'Your mother did.'

I knew about my brother's business connection. I didn't want anything to do with him, and more particularly neither did Ma. The partner was my father, who had abandoned his family years before. Festus had kept up with him, though Ma could hardly bring herself to mention his name. So why had she discussed him with Censorinus, a stranger? She must have been deeply concerned. That meant so was I.

'You've answered your own question, Censorinus. You need to negotiate with the partner. Have you seen him? What does *he* have to say for himself?'

'Not a lot!' That didn't surprise me. Pa had always been bad news.

'Well, that's it then. I can't improve on the story. Accept it. Festus is gone. His death's robbed us all of his joyful presence, and it's robbed you of your cash, I'm afraid.'

'That's no good, Falco!' Desperation had entered the soldier's voice. He leapt to his feet.

'Calm down!'

'We've got to have that money back!'

'I'm sorry, but that's fate. Even if Festus did produce a cargo to make a profit from, I'm his heir and I'd be the first in the queue – '

Censorinus grabbed my tunic to haul me from my seat. I had sensed trouble coming. I flung my bowl in his face, cracked his arm sideways, and broke free. As I sprang up I

702

pushed the table back at him, clearing space to move. The waiter let out a bleat of protest; he was so surprised the elbow he was leaning on slipped and he lurched into a cauldron, armpit-deep in gravy. The cat fled, yowking.

Censorinus lashed out. I parried, more in annoyance than anything else since this all seemed so pointless. He went for me in earnest, so I fought back. Epimandos jumped up on the counter to avoid damage to his person; the other customers leaned in from the street, cheering raucously. We had a short, ungainly bout of fisticuffs. I won. I threw the soldier out into the lane; he picked himself up and slunk off muttering.

Peace resumed in the caupona. Epimandos was wiping his arm with his rag. 'What was that all about?'

'Jove only knows!' I flipped some coppers at him for the bill, then set off home.

As I left, Epimandos picked up the bread roll that Stringy had been licking earlier, and replaced it in the customers' bread basket.

VI

The following morning, I started re-establishing my normal life in Rome.

I stayed in bed long enough to prove that I wasn't a client who needed to leap out and grovel for favours at some rich patron's house. Then I showed myself to the eager populace in the Forum, though most were looking the other way. I dodged my banker, a girl I preferred not to recognise, and several of my brothers-in-law. Then I sauntered into the men's baths at the back of the Temple of Castor for a complete physical overhaul. After a fierce exercise and massage session with Glaucus my trainer, who was in one of his sarcastic moods, I bathed, invested in a shave and haircut, told some jokes, heard some gossip, lost a denarius in a bet about how many flea-bites were on some stranger's leg, and generally began to feel like a civilised Roman again.

I had been away six months. Nothing had changed in politics or at the racing stables, but everything cost more than when I left. The only people who seemed to have missed me were the ones I owed money.

I borrowed a toga from Glaucus and made my way up to the Palatine for an audience with the Emperor. My report made an adequate impression on the old man, though I should have remembered to leave it until after dinner when his mood would be more generous. But my mission in Germany had gone well; Vespasian liked to quibble, yet he always acknowledged success. He was fair. He sanctioned my fee and expenses. There was, however, no attempt to offer me another job. That is the risk with freelancing: the constant threat of unemployment and bankruptcy, then just when you've trained yourself to enjoy lots of free time, they offer you some mission even Hercules would baulk at.

Even so, I picked up a satisfactory bag of silver at the Palace, returned to the Forum, greeted my banker with a happy smile and watched him open my rather small bank box.

The coins made a sweet chink as they were stowed. There was still not enough there to force me to make tricky investment decisions, let alone the huge amount I would require if I ever decided to approach Helena Justina's senatorial father in the role of hopeful son-in-law. Luckily the noble Camillus was not expecting it to happen, so never bothered me with pressing questions about my plans.

After that, I diddled away the rest of the afternoon making excuses not to look for private clients.

I ought to have known that while I was out taking the air so aimlessly, the spinning Fates would be preparing to snag my thread.

That morning Helena had shouted in my dozing ear that she and my mother were going to my old apartment to begin clearing up. Eventually I strolled along there. Around Fountain Court the streets all smelt of drains, because in that sector of the city they *were* the drains. The inhabitants looked as drab and despondent as ever. This was the hole I had found for myself six years ago, when I came home from the army and felt that unlike my brother who still lived at home with a mother, *I* was too big a boy for that. Festus had said I was crazy – which made me all the more stubborn.

Another reason for leaving home had been to avoid pressure to go into the family business – either breaking my back market-gardening out on the Campania, or auctioneering, which would involve getting even more dirt on my hands. I can earth up a leek or tell lies about an antique lamp. But I had thought myself a sociable, easygoing character, so, naturally, the solitary, cynical life of an informer had seemed ideal. Now I was thirty, fending off family responsibilities on all sides, and stuck with my disastrous choice.

Before I went upstairs I paused to pay my respects to Lenia, the haggard virago who owned and ran the laundry that occupied the ground floor. Thunder was still growling about, so not much was going on because nothing they bothered to wash would ever dry. A very tall man draped in a rather short toga was standing in silence while his wife harangued Lenia about sending back wrong laundry. Lenia was getting the worst of some tense issue about a stain, so when I popped my head indoors she left them at once and came to be rude to me.

'Falco, you half-arsed donkey-drover! Who let you back into Rome?'

'Public demand for my civilising influence.'

'Hah! Good trip?'

'Wish I had stayed there – my apartment's wrecked.'

'Oh really?' Lenia, who had connections with the snail slime I called my landlord, assumed an expression as though she would love to talk further, but must urgently dash to the pie shop before the ovens cooled.

'You know it is!' I retorted. In a dispute with the landlord there was no future; still, raising my voice eased the knot that was strangling my liver.

'Don't involve me. Speak to Smaractus . . .'

'I'm looking forward to the pleasure!'

'He's out of town.' That parasite Smaractus had probably heard I was back and arranged himself a six-month stay at his holiday home on Lake Volsena. Yachting would be a cold sport in March. 'So people got in, did they?' Lenia must have spotted the interlopers every time they took the stairs. In fact, they had probably stuffed a silver coin in her fist to find out where there was an empty roost. 'That's terrible!'

I gave up the struggle. 'Are my womenfolk here?'

'There's been some toing and froing. Your sister dropped in earlier.' That could have meant any one of five – no, four now. Victorina was gone.

'Maia?' Only Maia would put herself out for me.

Lenia nodded. 'Oh, and that bastard Petronius was looking for you.'

This was better news. Petronius Longus, captain of the Aventine Watch, was my closest friend. I was looking forward to swapping insults while regaling him with lurid lies about my foreign trip.

'How are the wedding plans?' I shouted at Lenia as I bounded for the stairs.

'Progressing!' That was bluff. Lenia and Smaractus were supposed to be linking fortunes, only somehow neither could bring themselves to the point of sharing their money bags. 'What about yours?' she retaliated.

'Oh, at about the same wonderful stage . . .'

I nipped for the stairs before this line of questioning bit too hard.

707

VII

I guessed that my rooms had reached the point of getting worse before they could be improved. On the landing outside there was hardly room to squeeze through the mounds of broken furniture and swag bags of jetsam in order to reach the front door.

Helena Justina met me coming out. She was carrying a heavy bale of rubbish, wrapped in what was left of a cloak with its corners knotted. She looked exhausted. Helena was stubborn and courageous about the squalor she had to live in alongside me, although she had been delicately reared. I could see her strength was failing. She knocked into the discarded frame of my bed, bruised herself badly, and spoke a word no senator's daughter should have known; she must have picked it up from me.

'Here – give me that!'

She edged away from my outstretched hand. 'I have to keep going. Don't upset my balance, or I'll drop.'

'Drop on me,' I murmured temptingly. Using my strength I took the bundle from her; Helena drooped against me, letting her full weight collapse while she held on around my neck.

Manfully I supported both my lass and the bundle of rubbish, pretending it was effortless. When she had made her point, she tickled my neck unfairly so I had to let go of the bundle. It crashed downstairs for a couple of landings. We watched, though with no interest in chasing after it.

'Ma gone?' I asked hopefully. She nodded. 'That's all right then!' I murmured, starting to kiss her while we still stood amidst the chaos on the landing. Mine was the only apartment on the sixth floor, so we were assured of privacy. Revived by a day in Rome, I didn't care who saw us anyway.

After a while I stopped, held Helena's hot, tired face between my hands and gazed into her eyes. I watched peace making itself at home in her soul. She smiled slightly, while she let me take the credit for calming her. Then her eyes half closed; she hated me to know the effect I had. I hugged her and laughed.

We went into the apartment holding hands. The place was virtually empty, but now clean. 'You can sit on the balcony,' Helena told me. 'We washed it out – and scrubbed the bench.'

I took her with me. It was nearly dark and pretty cool, but that made a good excuse for huddling close. 'The apartment has never been so clean. It's not worth it. Don't wear yourself out over this dump, fruit.'

'You won't want to stay long at your mother's.' Helena knew me.

'I can bear living at Ma's if I have you to protect me.' That was surprisingly true.

I kept her there, looking at the view while she rested. Ahead of us an aggressive wind was driving clouds at a fast pace above the Tiber and a dull threat of rain darkened our normal vista across to the Ianiculan. Rome lay below, sullen and muted, like a disloyal slave whose sins had been found out.

'Marcus, you never told me properly what happened when you saw the soldier yesterday.' That's the trouble with gazing at views; once people start feeling bored, gluey issues may be raised.

My attention lingered on the winter scenery. 'I didn't want to worry Ma.'

'She's not here; worry me.'

'I wanted to avoid that too.'

'Keeping things to yourself is what worries me most.'

I gave in. She was badgering, but I like being badgered by Helena. 'I saw Censorinus at the caupona, but we got nowhere. He told me some of my brother's cronies in the legion lost money on importing Greek statues.'

'So what's their point?'

'Our Festus gaily assured them all he would see them right for the loss.'

'He failed though?'

'He promptly dropped off a battlement. Now they want me to square matters, but Censorinus refused to come clean about the original deal . . .'

As I tailed off Helen's interest sharpened. 'What

709

happened?' She knew I was hiding something. 'Was there trouble at the caupona?'

'It ended in fisticuffs.'

'Oh Marcus!'

'He started it.'

'I hope so! But I bet you were digging your heels in?'

'Why not? Nothing else they can expect if they choose to be secretive.'

Helena had to agree. She thought for a moment, then asked, 'Tell me about your brother. I used to have the impression everyone approved of him. Now I can't decide *what* your feelings are.'

'That's it. Neither can I sometimes.' He had been eight years older than me. Distant enough for an element of hero worship – or for the other thing. Part of me hated him; though the rest loved him much more. 'He could be a trial. Yet I couldn't bear losing him. That sums him up.'

'Was he like you?'

'No.' Probably not.

'So are you taking this any further?'

'I'm waiting to see.'

'That means you want to give up.' It was a reasonable comment. But she didn't know Festus. I doubted if I could escape; even if I tried doing nothing, the situation was out of control.

Helena was starting to hunch against the cold. I said, 'We need some dinner.'

'We can't keep imposing on your mother.'

'How right – let's go and see *your* parents!'

'I thought you might say that. I brought a change of clothes. I ought to bathe first . . .'

I surveyed her; she looked filthy, but full of fight. Even a layer of grime could not smother her resourceful character. Being covered with dust enhanced the brightness of her great dark eyes, and when her hair was slipping out of its pins I only wanted to help dismantle it . . . If there had been a bed, we would have gone no further that evening. There was no bed, and no reasonable substitute. I grinned ruefully. 'My darling, it may not be a bright idea to bring you to your parents looking as if you've spent all day working like a slave in a furnace-house. On the other hand, bad treatment is all your noble relatives expect from me, so let's go and use your papa's private bathhouse for free.'

I had a double motive in this. If Helena's parents were about to reveal that Titus Caesar had been sniffing around while we were abroad, the worse Helena looked on arrival, the easier it would be for them to accept that I had won her first. It had been pure chance, but as the one piece of luck in my sordid life I intended clinging on to it. Once Helena threw herself at me, no one could expect me to refuse the gift – any more than they ought to hope the son of a deeply conservative emperor would take her on after me.

That was *my* hope, anyway.

The Camillus family lived in one half of a private two-house block just off the Via Appia near the Capena Gate. The next-door house was empty, though they owned that too. It was deteriorating while it stood unoccupied. Theirs was no worse than the last time I saw it, a modest spread that bore the marks of a permanent cash shortage. Poor paint in the interior had faded badly since the house was built; mean fittings in the gardens failed to match the standards of grandeur originally set by the rest of the house. But it was comfortably furnished. Among senators they were an unusually civilised family – respectful to the gods, kind to children, generous to their slaves, and even gracious with underprivileged hangers-on like me.

There was a small bath suite, served by water from the Claudian Aqueduct, which on winter evenings they kept fairly hot. Struggling or not, they had the right domestic priorities. I scraped Helena down, enjoying the delicate bits. 'Hmm, I've never yet made love to a senator's daughter in the senator's own bath-house . . .'

'You're versatile; you'll come to it!'

Not then, however. Noises way off announced company. As her father turned up for his pre-dinner soak, Helena threw a towel across my lap and disappeared. I sat on the side of the plunge bath trying to look more respectful than I felt.

'Leave us alone, please,' Decimus Camillus commanded the slaves who came in with him. They went, but made it clear that giving instructions was no business of the master of the house.

Decimus Camillus Verus was a friend of Vespasian's and therefore on the up at present. He was tall, with uncontrollable hair and vivid eyebrows. Relaxing in the steam, he had a slight stoop; I knew he made an effort to exercise but he preferred to lurk in his study with a pile of scrolls.

Camillus had taken to me – within limits, of course. I hated his rank, but liked him. Affection for his daughter had partly bridged the social abyss between us.

But he was in a tetchy mood. 'When are you and Helena Justina planning to make yourselves legitimate?' So much for thinking he wasn't expecting it. An extra load of pressure descended on me. It was measured in sesterces, and its exact weight was four hundred thousand of them – the cost of my joining the middle rank so that marrying me would not entirely disgrace Helena. I was making little progress in collecting so much money.

'You don't need an exact date? Quite soon, I should think,' I lied. He always saw through me.

'Her mother asked me to enquire.' From what I knew of Julia Justa, 'asked' was putting it mildly. We let the subject drop like a hot boiled egg.

'How are you, sir? What's the news?'

'Vespasian is summoning Justinus home from the army.' Justinus was his son.

'Ah! I may have had a hand in that.'

'So I gather. What have you been telling the Emperor?'

'Only to recognise talent.'

'Oh that!' scoffed the Senator, in his wry way. A shy man's mischievous wit sometimes broke through his diffident manner. Helena's sense of humour came from him, though she threw her insults about more lavishly.

Camillus Justinus was the younger of Helena's two brothers; we had been living with him in Germany. 'Justinus has been building a fine reputation,' I encouraged his father. 'He deserves the Emperor's favour, and Rome needs men like him. That's all I told Vespasian. His commanding officer should have put in a good report, but I don't rely on legates.'

Camillus groaned. I knew his problem; it was the same as

my own, though on a much grander scale: lack of capital. As a senator Camillus was a millionaire. Yet there was no slack in his bank account. Providing the trappings of public life – all those Games and public dinners for the greedy electorate – could easily wipe him out financially. Having already promised a career in the Senate to his elder son, he now discovered his younger boy had rather unexpectedly fixed himself a notable reputation. Poor Decimus was dreading the expense.

'You should be proud of him, Senator.'

'Oh I am!' he said glumly.

I reached for a strigil and started to scrape the oil off him. 'Is anything else on your mind?' I was probing in case there were developments on the Titus front.

'Nothing unusual: modern youth, the state of trade, the decline in social standards, horrors of the public works programme . . .' he said self-mockingly. Then he confided, 'I'm having trouble disposing of my brother's estate.' So that was it.

I was not the only Roman whose sibling had caused him embarrassment. Camillus had had a brother, now disgraced, whose political plotting had blighted the whole family. That was why the house next door still stood empty, and apparently why Decimus looked tired. I knew the brother was dead – but as I also knew, things don't end there.

'Did you approach the auctioneer I recommended?'

'Yes. Geminus is very helpful.' That meant very un-demanding about provenance and probate.

'Oh he's a good auctioneer,' I agreed wryly. Geminus was my absentee father. Apart from his habit of running off with redheads, he could pass for an excellent citizen.

The Senator smiled. 'Yes. The whole family seems to have an eye for quality!' That was a gentle poke at me. He pulled himself out of his gloom. 'That's enough about my troubles. How are you? And how is Helena?'

'I'm alive. Can't ask for more. Helena is herself.'

'Ah!'

'I'm afraid I brought her back fractious and full of foul language. It hardly fits the decent upbringing you and Julia Justa have given her.'

'Helena always managed to rise above that.'

I smiled. Helena's father enjoyed a quiet joke.

Women are supposed to behave demurely. They can be manipulating tyrants in private, so long as the good Roman myth of female subservience is sustained. The trouble with Helena Justina was that she refused to compromise. She said what she wanted, and did it too. That sort of perverse behaviour makes it extremely difficult for a man who has been brought up expecting deceit and inconsistency to be sure where he stands.

I liked it. I liked to be kept jumping. I liked to be shocked and astonished at every turn, even though it was hard work.

Her father, who had had no choice in the matter, often looked amazed that I had volunteered to take her on. And there was no doubt, he enjoyed seeing some other victim on the jump.

When we went into dinner we found Helena glittering in white, with golden hems on elaborate swags of drapery; oiled; scented; necklaced and braceleted. Her mother's maids had as usual conspired to make their young mistress look twice my rank – which she was – and twenty times my worth.

For a moment I felt as if I had tripped over my boot-thong and fallen headlong on the floor mosaic. But one of the necklaces was a string of Baltic amber that her mother had not seen before. When the noble Julia asked about it in the course of her scratchy small talk, Helena Justina announced in her own brisk fashion, 'That was my birthday gift from Marcus.'

I served Helena's mother to the best delicacies from the appetisers with rock-steady decorum. Julia Justa accepted with a politeness she had honed like a paring knife. 'So some good did come out of your trip to the River Rhenus, Marcus Didius?'

Helena spoke up for me quietly. 'You mean some good in addition to securing peace in that region, rooting out fraud, rallying the legions – and providing the opportunity for a member of this family to make his name as a diplomat?'

Her mother waived her sarcastic objection with a tilt of the head. Then the Senator's daughter gave me a smile whose sweetness was as rich as the summer stars.

The food was good, for winter fare. It was a friendly meal, if you like your friendship of the formal, surface kind. We all knew how to be tolerant. We all knew how to make it plain we had rather a lot to tolerate.

I had to do something about it. Somehow, for Helena's sake, I had to scramble into the position of a legitimate son-in-law. Somehow I had to find four hundred thousand sesterces – and I had to find them fast.

VIII

Petronius Longus caught up with us that same evening.

We had been on the verge of turning in. Ma usually went to bed early, because at her age she needed to build up her stamina for the next day of furiously organising the family. She had waited up for our return – one of the restrictive practices that made me prefer to live elsewhere. After dinner at the Senator's I had chosen to come home, partly to reassure Ma but also because I knew if I stayed, as Helena's father offered (though her mother was markedly cooler), the Capena Gate house steward would give Helena and me separate rooms and I could not face a night of creeping along strange corridors trying to find my lass. I told Helena she could stay behind in comfort. 'They'll give you a softer pillow – '

She thumped my shoulder. 'That's the pillow I want.' So we both came back, which made two mothers happy – or as happy as mothers ever like to feel.

When they saw Petro shambling into the kitchen even Ma and Helena decided to stay up longer. Women took to him. If they had known as much about him as I did they might have been more disapproving; then again, they would probably have blamed me for the wild episodes in his past. For some reason Petro was a man whose indiscretions women excused. For some other reason, I was not.

He was thirty years old. He arrived dressed in various shapeless brown woollen garments, his usual unobtrusive working uniform, plus winter additions of fur in his boots and a hooded cloak so voluminous he could have been hiding three loose women and their pet duck under it. Stuck through his belt he carried a thick cudgel for encouraging quiet behaviour on the streets; these he supervised with a light, reasonable hand, backed up by well-aimed bodyweight. A twisted headband rumpled the straight brown hair on his broad head. He had a placid mentality he certainly needed

716

when picking through the grime and greed at the low end of Roman society. He looked solid and tough, and good at his job – all of which he was. He was also a deeply sentimental family man –a thoroughly decent type.

I grinned widely. 'Now I know I'm really back in Rome!'

Petronius slowly lowered his large frame on to a bench. His expression was sheepish – presumably because he had a wine amphora under one arm, the usual credential he offered when visiting me.

'You look tired out,' Helena commented.

'I am.' He never wasted words. I cracked the wax of his amphora to save him the effort, then Ma produced winecups. He poured. He sloshed the liquor into the beakers with careless desperation, paused briefly to chink his cup on mine, then drank fast. He had trouble written all over him.

'Problems?' I asked.

'Nothing unusual.' Ma topped him up, then found a loaf and some olives to cosset him with. Petro was another friend of mine who was reckoned to be a cut above what I deserved. He rubbed his forehead wearily. 'Some tourist who managed to get himself slashed to ribbons by a maniac, or several, in a hired room . . . I can't say he should have used the door-bolt, because in that flea-pit so much luxury wasn't available.'

'What was the motive? Robbery?'

'Could be.' Petro sounded terse.

In winter the rate of muggings among strangers usually fell. Professional thieves were too busy counting their winnings from the summer season. Actually killing the victim was a rare event. It attracted attention, and was normally unnecessary; there were pickings enough from idiots who came to see Rome, their pouches bursting with spending money, and then stood around the Via Sacra like curly little lambs waiting to be fleeced.

'Any clues?' I asked, trying to encourage him.

'Not sure. If there are, I don't like them. They made a disgusting mess. Blood everywhere.' He fell silent, as if he could not bear to talk about it.

Helena and Ma came to a mystical decision. They both yawned, patted Petro on the shoulder, ignored me, and made themselves scarce.

717

Petronius and I drank some more. The mood relaxed – or I assumed it did. We had known each other a long time. We had been best friends throughout our army careers; those had both been short (we helped each other fake reasons for leaving), but the province we had been allocated to was Britain, during a fairly lively period. Not something to forget.

'So how was the famous German trip, Falco?'

I told him something about it, though saved the best; his mind was clearly unreceptive to anecdotes. I saw no point in enduring the mishaps of travel and the trials of dealing with foreigners unless I could entertain my friends with them afterwards. 'Gaul seems as lousy as we remember it.'

'So when did you get back to Rome?'

'Day before yesterday.'

'I must have missed you around – been busy?'

'Nothing special.'

'I was looking for you earlier today.'

'Lenia told me.'

'So where were you?' Petro had a stolid insistence when he wanted to exert himself.

'I told you – nowhere special!' I was laughing at him cheerfully. 'Listen, you curious bastard, this conversation seems to be taking an odd tone. If I was a provincial sightseer you had stopped on the Via Ostiana, I'd be frightened you were going to demand a peek at my docket of citizenship on pain of five hours in your lock up . . . What's the game, Petro?'

'I wondered what you were up to this morning.'

I was still grinning. 'That sounds as if I need to consider it carefully. Jupiter, I hope I'm not being asked to produce an alibi.'

'Just tell me,' Petronius insisted.

'Bumming about. What else would I be doing? I've just come home after a foreign trip. I need to assert my effervescent presence on the streets of home.'

'Who saw you?' he asked quietly.

That was when I first realised the inquisition must be serious.

'What's up, Petro?' I heard my own voice drop several tones.

'Just answer the question.'

718

'There's no way I'm going to co-operate with a legal officer – any officer, Petro – unless I know why he's latched on to me.'

'It's better if you answer first.'

'Oh rot!'

'Not at all!' Petro was growing heated now. 'Listen, Falco, you've placed me between Scylla and Charybdis – and I'm in a very flimsy boat! I'm trying to help you; that ought to be obvious. Tell me where in Hades you were all morning, and make it good. You need to satisfy Marponius as well as me.' Marponius was a judge on the murder panel whose aegis included the Aventine. He was an interfering halfwit whom Petro could hardly tolerate; that was usual with officialdom.

'Right!' Anxiety made me speak angrily. 'Try this. This evening Helena and I gorged ourselves with luxury at the home of the most excellent Camillus. Presumably His Honour's word will be acceptable? You know Glaucus; Glaucus is straight. I was in the Forum; I saw my banker and Sattoria, not to mention Famia and Gaius Baebius, but I made sure they didn't see me, so that's no help. Perhaps they noticed me skulking behind a pillar, trying to avoid them,' I added with increased restraint, since Petro was looking at me mournfully.

'Who's Sattoria?' he asked, having recognised the other names.

'No one you know. No one *I* know any longer.' Not now I had a respectable girlfriend who took a sombre view of·my bachelor past. Nice to have somebody bother about you. Nice, but occasionally things grew tense.

'Oh her!' Petro commented matter-of-factly. Sometimes I wondered about him. He looked henpecked, but occasionally gave the impression that he led a double life.

'You're bluffing, you beggar. You've no connection with Sattoria . . . After that I was up at the Palace for an hour or two, so surely even Marponius will say I'm in the clear for that period – '

'Skip the Palace. I've already covered that angle.' I was amazed. The sneaky bug must have been sleuthing round Rome as tenaciously as a clerk after promotion. 'I want your whereabouts earlier on.'

719

'Can't help you. I was tired out after travelling. Helena and Ma went to clean up my apartment. They left me here in bed. I was asleep, so I wasn't up to anything, but don't ask me to prove it – the classic useless excuse . . . Petro, I can't stand this! What in the name of the Capitoline Triad is fretting your tiny worried mind?'

Petronius Longus stared at the table. I could tell we had reached the crunch. He looked as lonely as a gold piece in a miser's pocket. 'Try this. The corpse I had to look at this morning', he informed me in an unsteady voice, 'was a centurion called Titus Censorinus Macer. He was done in at Flora's Caupona – and every time I ask if he had upset anybody recently, people rush at me with lurid tales of some blazing row he had with you.'

I groaned. Not too loudly; a murder suspect needs to beware of bad acting.

'Lucius Petronius, I can hardly believe I'm hearing this . . .' I believed it all too easily. From the moment my brother's business life had become an issue yet again, I had expected deep trouble on the next throw of the dice. This was the worst yet, however.

'Believe it!' Petronius advised.

'Oh gods, Petro, I'm standing on a real midden heap of shit. You know Marponius hates informers. Now my name's written on a tablet in the denouncing jar! Just the chance he needs to interfere with my free movement and slander me at Pincian Hill dinner parties. Still!' I cheered up. 'Since you're the investigating officer, Marponius doesn't need to know.'

'Wrong, Falco!'

'Don't worry about it. I'll help you track the killer down.'

Petro sighed. 'Marponius knows already. He's having one of his "social responsibility" fits. Every five minutes he wants me to show him round a brothel or introduce him to a professional gambling cheat. I was with him discussing another case when they turned up to fetch me to Flora's. Coming along to have a squint at a genuine body was the highlight of the judge's year. Well,' he added reminiscently, 'it was until he actually set eyes on the mess.'

'I get it.' I had gathered this was a murder that would deeply affect a judge's shockable mind. 'Having seen the gore, and thrown up his breakfast on the doorstep of the action, His Honour feels personally involved in the whole damned enquiry? You'd better tell me everything. I suppose all the hangers-on at Flora's who normally wouldn't pass the time of day with their own lice, couldn't wait to talk with the great man?'

'Exactly. Your name took about three seconds to surface. We hadn't even forced a passage through the throng. I was still trying to get upstairs to inspect the remains.'

'This looks bad.'

'Smart, Falco!'

I knew Marponius was the impetuous type who would expect the first suspect he heard about to be condemned. Much neater than complicating life with other possibilities. He was probably already drawing up a jury list for my trial in the Basilica. Assuming he reckoned I rated the Basilica.

'So what's the situation, Petro? I'm a wanted man; Marponius thinks you're looking for me. Have you found me now, or do I get leeway to search for evidence myself?'

Petronius Longus gave me the straight look he normally kept for women; it meant he had no intention of being straight. 'Marponius wants this tied up speedily. I told him I couldn't find you at your apartment. I may have forgotten to mention I might be seeing you later on here.'

'How much to go on forgetting?'

'I'm sure you'll manage to persuade me!' There was nothing corrupt in Petronius. On the other hand, he would reckon any favours he notched up voluntarily ought to be accounted for in kind at a later date.

'Thanks.'

'You'll have to move fast. I can't keep it up for ever.'

'How long?'

'I can probably bluff for a day.' I thought I would be able to stretch him to three. We were pretty close friends. Besides, Petro hated Marponius too much to give an inch to his requests for speed. Watch captains are elected by the populace; Petronius took his authority from the plebeian electorate.

That said, he liked the work, he enjoyed his local status, and with a smart wife and three young daughters to keep he needed his public salary. Upsetting a judge would be a bad idea. Not even I could expect that of him; if it came to dilemma-time, I wouldn't even ask.

Petronius excused himself; discord always went to his bladder. While he was otherwise occupied I spotted his note tablet lying alongside his cloak on the table. Like everything he owned, it was solid and heavy, four or five reusable waxed boards bound with a criss-cross of leather thongs between two square wooden protectors. I had seen him use it on numerous occasions, unobtrusively scratching details about some luckless suspect, often at the same time as he talked to them. The tablet had a substantial, well-aged look that made it appear reliable. Produced in court, to be read from in his sombre tones, Petro's memory-jogger had secured many a conviction. I had never expected to be listed there myself among the reprobates. It gave me a feeling I didn't like.

I flipped the top cover and found he had been assembling a timetable of my own movements that day. Suppressing my indignation, I inserted the missing events for him in a neat, bitter script.

X

When he came back he immediately recaptured his notes. He noticed my additions but said nothing.

I moved the amphora aside, then set Petro's winecup well out of his reach.

'Sobriety-time. You'd better go over all you've found out so far.'

I saw an uneasy look on his face. Maybe telling the chief suspect exactly what evidence had been amassed against him struck a wrong note, even when I was the suspect. But habit won. He opened up. 'All we have is an extremely bloody corpse.'

'When was he done?'

'Marponius thinks last night, but Marponius just likes the idea of unspeakable crime at midnight. It could have been early this morning.'

'It would be!' The one period for which I had no alibi. 'I'll have to dodge Marponius while I try to prove what really happened. Let's cover every possibility. Any chance of suicide?'

Petro guffawed. 'Not with those wounds. Self-infliction can be ruled out. Besides,' he informed me reasonably, 'the victim had paid in advance for his room rent.'

'Yes, that would be stupid, if he knew he was depressed! And he was badly hacked, you say? Was some villain trying to prove a point?'

'Could well be. Are you going to suggest what? Or tell me *who* is trying to make their mark?'

I had no idea.

Together we considered alternatives. Censorinus could have picked up a bedmate – of either sex – who had turned spiteful at some point. 'If so, no one at Flora's saw the paramour,' Petro said. 'And you know Flora's!' A curious hovel, as I was remarking earlier.

'Had he been robbed?'

'Probably not. All his kit appeared to be present and correct.' I made a private note to try and get a look at it some time.

'What about a disappointed debtor?' Even as I said it, I could hear the false note. Censorinus was *collecting* debts. Petro stared at me. The details of my quarrel must have whistled all along the Tiber's southern bank. Petronius certainly knew at least as much as I did about why the soldier had been in Rome, and what he had wanted here.

'I met him a couple of times when I came over to see your mother while you were away. I had already formed the impression he might be leaning on your family for more than a free bed. Would I be right in assuming your wonderful brother was at the back of it?' I did not reply. 'With the greatest respect, Marcus Didius,' Petro began, employing only slight reproach, 'there do seem to be one or two aspects which you could help clarify!' He said it as if he were loath to embarrass me. That meant nothing. He was tough; which meant tough on his friends too. If my foolish behaviour made an arm lock or a knee in the groin necessary, Petro would not flinch from it. And he was bigger than me.

'Sorry.' I forced myself to unwrap the parcel from him. 'Whatever you want. Yes, there is some problem over a project Festus was involved with. No, I don't know what it was. Yes, I did try to extract details from Censorinus. No, he wouldn't tell me. And most certainly, no, I don't want to be involved if I can help it – but yes, as sure as the little goddess likes pomegranates, I'll get to the bottom of this mystery rather than let myself be sent to the public strangler for something my fabled brother failed to square!'

'I'm rather assuming,' said Petronius, smiling slightly, 'someone else killed the soldier at Flora's. I presume even you would have had more common sense than to quarrel with him so publically first.'

'True, but with Marponius on your back you'd better keep me on your list of suspects until I'm formally cleared.' Marponius would agree eventually with Petro's view of my innocence; he would appropriate Petro's verdict and claim it as his own. Until that happened life for me could be extremely difficult. 'If the dead man's grouse against Festus was legitimate, I might have had a motive for removing him.'

'Everyone who saw you fighting at Flora's was quick to admit that Censorinus never explained to you what his bugbear was.'

'Good of them! But he did walk part of the way along the sandy track. He was telling me that Festus had owed money to a gang of his old pals for some galley that foundered.'

'If I know you,' Petro argued loyally, 'they only had to prove it and you would have robbed your own savings coffer to put the golden Festus in the clear.' Petro never shrank from swimming against the tide of public opinion; my brother, whom so many people adored, had not been wildly popular with my old friend. They were different types.

Petro and I were different too, but in another, complementary way that made us friends.

'I do use a knife.'

'Neatly!'

Petronius had seen me use my knife.

I knew now that Petronius Longus must have stood up to the judge Marponius and insisted that the soldier's killing lacked my personal style. Even so, I could see they had no choice but to harry me until something else turned up.

'Just for routine,' Petronius asked me levelly, 'where is your knife at present?'

I produced it from my boot. I tried not to feel harassed. He examined it, carefully looking for blood. Of course he found none. We both knew that proved nothing; if I had killed someone I would have cleaned my weapon scrupulously after the event. Even if the occasion had been legitimate, that was my normal good housekeeping routine.

After a time he returned it, then warned me, 'You're liable to be stopped and searched on sight. I presume I can trust you not to carry an offensive blade inside the city boundary?' Going armed in Rome is illegal, a neat trick which means that the law-abiding have to walk down dark alleys undefended, just waiting to have their throats cut by wicked types who ignore the rules. I said nothing. Petro went on insultingly, 'And Falco, don't take your ugly hide *beyond* the city boundary – or any temporary amnesty is cancelled at your first step.'

'Oh that's rich!' I was highly annoyed with him. He could become extremely irritating when he exerted his official role.

'No, it's fair!' he retorted. 'It's not my fault if you start throwing punches at an off-duty legionary who next minute gets himself sliced up. Think yourself lucky I'm not measuring you for manacles. I'm freeing your reins, Falco, but I want a return. I need to know what this business with your brother was, and you stand more chance of discovering the details than anyone, including me.' That was probably right. And I was going to start digging in any case; I was now irresistibly curious about the statues scam.

'Petro, if the body is all we have to go on, I'd like to take a look at it. Is the carcass still at Flora's?'

Petronius looked prim. 'The body's off limits. And keep away from Flora's, if you don't mind.'

There were moments in this conversation when our old friendship started coming under too much strain. 'Oh cobnuts! Holding a public post goes to your head sometimes. Stop treating me like a tired husband whose nagging wife has just been found laid out lifeless on a public compost heap.'

'Then you stop giving me orders as if the whole bloody Aventine was yours under private lease!'

'Try being a mite less officious!'

'Just try growing up, Falco!'

Petronius rose to his feet. The lamp guttered nervously. I refused to make an apology; so did he. It didn't matter. Our friendship was too close to be blown apart by this condescending exchange of personal views.

At least I hoped it was. Because without his help, my witless implication in the murder of Censorinus could have fatal results for me.

He was stomping off in a huff, but turned back from the doorway.

'Sorry about your sister, by the way.'

With so much else on my mind, I had forgotten about Victorina. I had to think hard to realise what he was saying.

I opened my mouth to remark that he must be more sorry than I was, then stopped. I did pity her children, left to the mercy of their feeble father the plasterer. Besides, I had never been quite sure about relations between Victorina and

Petronius. But one thing was certain: when women were involved, Lucius Petronius Longus had never been as shy as he appeared.

XI

After he left I sat where I was. I had a lot to think about. It was the proverbial case with no easy solutions. In fact, as was normal for me, no solutions at all.

Helena Justina came to see what I was doing (or how much I was drinking). Perhaps she had heard me quarrelling with Petronius. Anyway, she must have guessed there was a problem and that the problem might be serious. At first she tried to pull me gently by the arm, attempting to lure me to bed, but when I resisted she gave way abruptly and sat down alongside.

I went on thinking, though not for long. Helena knew how to handle me. She said nothing. For several moments she simply stayed with me, holding my right hand between both of hers. Her stillness and silence were comforting. As normal, I was completely disarmed. I had been intending to keep the situation from her, but pretty soon I heard myself saying despondently, 'You had better know. I'm a suspect in a murder case.'

'Thank you for telling me,' Helena remarked politely.

Immediately my mother popped out from somewhere near at hand. She has always been shameless about listening in.

'You'll need something to keep your strength up then!' exclaimed Ma, banging a patera of broth on to the embers of her cooking bench.

Neither of them seemed the least surprised – or at all indignant – that I had been subjected to such a charge.

So much for loyalty.

XII

Next day the weather continued to be abysmal, and so did my own mood. I was faced with far more than investigating my shady brother's past for family reasons, a hard enough task. But if I was to escape a murder charge, within the next day or so I had to find out why Censorinus had died and name the real murderer. Otherwise the best I could hope for was exile to the ends of the Empire, and if I came up before a judge who hated informers – as most of them did – there might even be the threat of crucifixion beside a highway like any common criminal or being turned into bait for an arena lion.

Only my own family seemed likely to offer any clues as to what Festus and his army pals had been about. Forcing my relatives to sit still and answer questions like witnesses was a dire prospect. I tried my sister Maia first. Maia was my favourite, but as soon as I spread myself out on a couch she upset me by commenting, 'I'm the last person you should be asking. Festus and I never got on.'

She was the youngest surviving child in our family, and in my opinion had the best looks and character. We had barely a year between us, while a gap three times as long divided me from our next sister, Junia. Maia and I had stuck together ever since we shared a nursery beaker and took turns learning to stagger about in a little walking-frame on wheels. In most ways she was easygoing. We rarely squabbled, either when we were children or later on.

Most women on the Aventine look like hags from the moment they have their first baby; Maia, with four behind her, still appeared younger than her thirty years. She had dark, extremely curly hair, wonderful eyes, and a round, cheerful face. She had picked up a good dress sense when she worked for a tailor, and had kept up her standards even after she married Famia, a sozzled horse vet with a bulbous nose and minimal character. Famia was attached to the Green faction, so sporting discernment was not his gift; his brains

730

seemed to have run out once he latched on to my sister. Luckily she had enough apples in the basket for both of them.

'Give me some help, Maia. The last time Festus came home on leave, did he say anything to you about being in partnership with some people from his unit importing art from the East?'

'No. Marcus, Festus would never have talked about anything important in front of me. Festus was like you were in those days. He thought women were just for being rammed from behind while they were bent over a cooking bench preparing dinner for him.'

'That's disgusting.' I felt upset.

'That's men!' she retorted.

One reason Maia disapproved of Festus was the effect he had had on me. He had undeniably brought out my own worst side, and she had hated having to watch it. 'Maia, don't do him down. Festus had a sunny nature and a golden heart — '

'You mean he always wanted his own way.' Maia remained implacable. She was normally a treasure to deal with. On the rare occasions when she took against someone she enjoyed letting rip. Excess was our family's strong point. 'There's one obvious person you ought to talk to, Marcus.'

'You mean Geminus?' Geminus, our father. Maia and I shared views on the subject of Father. They were not complimentary.

'Actually,' she scoffed, 'I was thinking of ways you could avoid trouble, not walk right into it! Marina, I meant.' Marina had been my brother's girlfriend. For various highly emotional reasons I did not want to go and see Marina either.

'I suppose there's no escaping it,' I agreed gloomily. 'I'll need to have things out with her.' Talking to Marina about the last time we both saw Festus was something I dreaded.

Maia misinterpreted. 'What's the problem? She's dim, but if Festus ever said anything that her soppy brain actually remembers, she'll tell you. And Juno, Marcus, she certainly owes you some favours!' After Festus died I had made an effort to keep Marina and her young daughter from starving while Marina was out enjoying herself with the fellows who eventually replaced Festus in her disordered life. 'Do you want me to come with you?' Maia demanded, still trying to push me into it. 'I can make sense of Marina – '

'Marina's no problem.'

My sister seemed to have no idea why I wanted to steer clear. That was unusual, because the scandal was no secret. My brother's girlfriend had made sure the entire family knew that she and I had a sordid connection. The last time Festus was home on leave in Rome, in fact the night before he departed back to Judaea, he had left her and me together, with results I preferred to forget.

The last thing I wanted nowadays, especially while I was living with Helena at my mother's, was to have that old story raked up again. Helena Justina had high moral standards. A link between me and my brother's girlfriend was something Helena would not even want to understand.

Knowing my family, Helena was probably being told all about it even as I sat glumly in my sister's house trying to put the saga out of my mind.

XIII

Maia lived on the Aventine, not two streets from Mother. Not far away was another group of my relatives whom I needed to visit; my dead sister Victorina's household. It was unlikely to help my enquiries, but as nominal head of our family it was my duty to pay my respects. With a murder sentence hanging over me, I went along as soon as possible, feeling like a man who might soon be arrested and deprived of the chance.

Victorina and her depressing husband Mico had made their nest on one side of the Temple of Diana. Victorina, with her long career of dirty assignations at the back of the Temple of Isis, had never appeared to realise that living next to the chaste huntress might be inappropriate.

As addresses go, it occupied a glamorous site, but had few other selling-points. They existed in two rooms among a warren of dingy apartments at the back of a large copper shop. The constant clanging of mallets on metalware had left the whole family slightly deaf. The tenement they rented had slanting floors, frail walls, a rotten ceiling and a strong odour from the giant vat of urine in the stairwell which the landlord never emptied. This polluting dollium leaked slowly, which at least made room for refills. Hardly any light could penetrate to the apartments – an advantage, since seeing their homes too clearly might have led to a long queue of suicides on the Probus Bridge.

It was some time since I had needed to pay a visit to my sister's place. I could not remember exactly where she lived. Treading gingerly because of the leaky dollium, I made a couple of false attempts before I identified the right apartment. Hastily avoiding the neighbours' curses and lewd propositions, I dived through what remained of a coarsely woven curtain and found my destination. There could have been no greater contrast than that between the neat apartment where Maia was successfully bringing up her children and the humid hole, with its fragrance of cabbage and

733

children's damp tunics, in which this other feckless family lived.

Mico was at home. Inevitably, he was out of work. As a plasterer my brother-in-law had no skill. The only reason he was allowed to remain in the Plasterers' Guild was pity. Even when contractors were desperate for labour, Mico was the last man they called in.

I found him attempting to wipe honey from the chin of his youngest but one. His eldest daughter, Augustinilla, the one we had been looking after in Germany, glared at me as if the loss of her mama was all my fault, and stalked from the house. The six-year-old boy was systematically hitting the four-year-old with a small clay goat. I prised the baby off a distinctly grubby rug. He was an antisocial tyke who clung to his perch like a kitten putting out its claws. He burped, with the evil relief of a child who was choosing his moment to throw up now that a visitor had provided a respectable cloak for him to throw up on.

In another corner of the room a slack bundle of flab clothed in unappealing rags cackled at me amiably: Mico's mother. She must have slid in like fish oil the minute Victorina died. She was eating half a loaf but not bothering to help Mico. The women in my own family despised this placid old dame, but I saluted her without rancour. My own relations were born interferers, but some folks have the tact to sit by and merely act as parasites. I liked her style. We all knew where we were with Mico's mother, and it wasn't being harried out of doors by a broom or having our guilty consciences probed.

'Marcus!' Mico greeted me, with his usual effusive gratitude. I felt my teeth set.

Mico was small and swarthy. He had a pasty face and a few black teeth. He would do anyone a favour, provided they were prepared to accept that he would do it very badly and drive them wild with incessant chat.

'Mico!' I cried, slapping him on the shoulder. I reckoned he needed stiffening. Once his balance was upset for any reason, depression set in. He had been a long river of gloom even before he acquired the excuse of five motherless children, his mother at home, no work, no hope, and no luck. The bad luck was his real tragedy. If Mico tripped over a bag of gold bits on his way to the baker's, the bag would split open, the aurei would scatter – and he would watch every one of them drop down a manhole into a sewer at full flood.

My heart fell as he drew me aside with a purposeful air. 'Marcus Didius, I hope you don't mind, but we held the funeral without you . . .'

Dear gods, he was a worrier. How Victorina ever stood him I don't know. 'Well of course I was sorry to miss the formalities . . .' I tried to look cheerful since I knew children are sensitive to atmosphere. Luckily Mico's tribe were all too busy pulling at each other's ears.

'I felt terrible about not allowing you a chance to do the eulogy . . .' Apart from the fact I was delighted to be spared it, this idiot was her husband. The day they married, Victorina had become his charge in life and death; it was Mico's duty to dredge up something polite to declaim at her funeral. The last thing I would have wanted was for him to step aside in my favour as some misplaced compliment to me as head of the Didius family. Besides, Victorina had had a father living; we all did. I was just the unhappy soul who had had to shoulder the responsibility when our shirking, self-seeking father chose to do a moonlight flit.

Mico invited me to a stool. I sat, squashing something soft. 'I'm really happy to have this chance for a chat, Marcus Didius . . .' With his normal unerring judgement he had chosen as a confidant a person who could hardly bear to listen to five words from him.

'Pleased to help . . .'

Things went from bad to worse. Mico assumed I had come to hear a full commentary on the funeral. 'A really good crowd turned out for her – ' Must have been a quiet day at the racecourse. 'Victorina had so many friends . . .' Men, mostly. I can never understand why fellows who have tangled with a good-time girl acquire such peculiar curiosity if she passes on. As Victorina's brother I would have resented it.

'Your friend Petronius was there!' Mico sounded surprised. I wanted to be surprised myself. 'Such a decent fellow. Good of him to represent you like that . . .'

'Lay off, Mico. Petronius Longus is on the verge of locking me up in jail!' Mico looked concerned. I felt a renewed surge

of my own anxiety about Censorinus and my deadly predicament. 'How are you managing?' I changed the subject
abruptly. Mico's nasty-tempered baby was kicking my left
kidney. 'Is there anything you need?' My brother-in-law was
too disorganised to know. 'I've some New Year presents from
Germany for the children. They're still packed, but I'll bring
them round as soon as I can get at them. My apartment's
wrecked – '

Mico showed a genuine interest. 'Yes, I heard about your
rooms!' Great. Everyone seemed to know what had happened, yet not one of them had tried to do anything about it.
'Do you want a hand putting things straight?' Not from him, I
didn't. I wanted my old place to be liveable, and by next week
not next Saturnalia.

'Thanks, but you have enough to think about. Make your
ma look after the children while you get out a bit. You need
some company – you need some *work*, Mico!'

'Oh something will come up.' He was full of misplaced
optimism.

I gazed around the sordid room. There was no sense of
absence, no silence left by Victorina's loss. It was hardly
surprising. Even in life she had always been off somewhere
else having her own idea of a good time.

'I see you're missing her!' Mico remarked in a low voice.

I sighed. But at least his attempts to comfort me seemed to
cheer him up.

Since I was there I decided to get a few questions in: 'Look,
I'm sorry if this is not the right time, but I'm making some
enquiries for Mother and I'm seeing everyone about it. Did
Festus ever say anything to you about a scheme he was involved
in – Greek statuary, ships from Caesarea, that sort of thing?'

Mico shook his head. 'No. Festus never talked to me.' I
knew why that was. He would have had more luck trying to
dispute the philosophy that life is a bunch of whirling atoms
with a half-naked, barely sober garland girl. 'He was always a
pal, though,' Mico insisted, as though he thought he might
have given the wrong impression. I knew it was true. Festus
could always be relied on to throw crumbs to a stranded
fledgling or pat a three-legged dog.

736

'Just thought I'd ask. I'm trying to find out what he was up to on his last trip to Rome.'

'Afraid I can't help you, Marcus. We had a few drinks, and he arranged a couple of jobs for me, but that's all I saw of him.'

'Anything special about the jobs?' It was a forlorn hope.

'Just normal business. Plastering over brickwork . . .' I lost interest. Then Mico kindly informed me, 'Marina probably knows what deals he had on. You ought to ask her.'

I thanked him patiently, as if the thought of speaking about Festus to his girlfriend had never occurred to me.

XIV

If I was ever to solve the soldier's murder I needed to take a more direct hand. Petronius Longus had warned me to keep away from Flora's. I had no intention of obeying him. It was lunch-time, so I turned my feet straight towards the caupona.

Wrong move: I was compelled to go past. One of Petro's troopers was sitting outside on a bench beside the beggar on the barrel. The trooper had a pitcher and a dish of soggy stuffed vine leaves, but I knew what he was really doing there: Petro had told him to make sure I didn't get in. The man had the nerve to grin at me as I passed by, faking a nonchalant expression, on the far side of the street.

I went home to Ma's house. My second mistake.

'Oh Juno, look what's straggled in!'

'Allia! What have you come for – a bodkin or a pound of plums?'

Allia was my second-eldest sister; she had always been Victorina's closest ally, so I was as low in Allia's affections as the grit in an empty amphora, and she had never featured at all in mine. She must have been here to borrow something – her normal occupation – but luckily she was leaving just as I arrived.

'Before you start on about Festus – don't!' she informed me with her regular brand of truculence. 'I know nothing about it, and I really can't be bothered.'

'Thanks,' I said.

There was no point in attempting to argue. We parted company on the threshold. Allia lurched off, big-boned and slightly ungainly, as if she had been mishandled during the birth process.

Helena and Ma were sitting at the table, both fairly straight-backed. I threw myself on to a coffer, ready for the worst.

'Allia has been telling us some interesting stories,' Helena

738

announced bluntly. That would be the Marina incident. It had been useless to hope she would never find out.

I said nothing, but saw Helena lock her teeth on the left-hand side with an angry overlap. I was angry myself. Encountering Allia always felt like reliving several hours of childhood – the dreariest part that normal memory sensibly wipes out.

Looking tired, Mother left me alone with Helena.

'Stop looking so shifty!' At least she was speaking.

I drew a long breath, surreptitiously. 'You had better ask me.'

'Ask you about what, Marcus?'

I wanted a chance to explain things away. 'Ask about whatever poisoned thistle Allia planted in the melon field.'

'I'll find you some lunch,' said Helena Justina, pretending she had not heard this magnanimous offer.

She knew how to punish me.

XV

The lunch Helena provided was adequate, though no more. I shuffled off afterwards, looking as if I had useful work to do. In fact I spent the afternoon exercising at the baths. I wanted a chance to brood over the Censorinus killing – and to get myself in shape for whatever problems lay ahead of me.

When I first appeared at the palaestra Glaucus gave me a sideways look. He said nothing, but I guessed he had been interviewed about me by Petronius.

I was in no hurry to return to Mother's house. As I dawdled along the Ostia Road the rain finally stopped. A pale sun forced itself through the clouds, touching roof finials and awning-poles with a cheerful gleam. I risked pushing my cloak back from my head. When I breathed, the air smelt cold but no longer full of storms. It was simply winter in Rome.

The city half slept. The streets felt lonely. A few people who had no option scuttled here and there, but it was hardly the glad place I knew in warmer days. No one walked for pleasure in Caesar's gardens, no one sat out on balconies shouting across to their neighbours, no one drowsed on stools in doorways, no one went to the theatre and filled the evening air with distant rumbles of applause. I heard no music. I saw no partygoers. The acrid smell of bathhouse smoke crawled sluggishly on the still air.

Lights began to be lit. It was time to be going somewhere positive, even if the somewhere was not home. Wandering aimlessly could attract the wrong attention. Besides, it makes a man depressed.

With nothing to lose, I had another go at Flora's.

This time there were no visible representatives of the watch. I had to be careful, since Petronius sometimes dropped in on his way home to dinner. I won't say he needed to strengthen his resolve before he faced his wife and their three raucous children, but Petro was a man of habit, and Flora's was one of his habitual haunts. I had a swift

740

look round both outside and in before I let my feet come to a halt.

I had timed it just right. Petro's operative had done his job and reported back to the guardhouse. There were no other customers. The day's wastrels had drifted off. It was just too early for the evening trade. Flora's was all mine.

I leaned on the counter. Epimandos, the shabby waiter, had been scraping out bowls, but the minute he saw me he dropped his spatula.

'The usual?' he let out before he could stop himself, but then he froze in panic.

'Skip the food. I only have time for a half jug of house red.' I was keeping him on tenterhooks. For once he leapt into action. The jug appeared so rapidly I nearly put my palm in it as I turned back from a quick survey of the street behind. Still no sign of Petronius.

Epimandos was staring at me. He must be well aware I was chief suspect in the Censorinus case. He must have been amazed even to see me when the whole Aventine was waiting to hear I had been arrested.

Still stringing him along, I took a huge swig of wine like a man intent on getting horribly drunk. Epimandos was bursting to ask questions, yet petrified what I might say or do. I amused myself bitterly wondering how he would react if I had actually done the deed; if I did get drunk; if I sobbed on his welcoming shoulder and confessed my crime like an idiot. He ought to be grateful I was here, providing a scene to thrill the customers with when he told them about it afterwards. Mind you, saying 'Falco came in, drank a half-pitcher, then left quietly,' would hardly grab their attention.

I paid up, then made sure I had finished the wine, in case Petro appeared and I had to abscond hastily.

Fear that I might be leaving without providing any gossip must have helped the waiter find his tongue. 'People are saying you're going to be arrested.'

'People love to see someone else in trouble. I've done nothing.'

'The men from the watch told me you'll have a hard time getting out of it.'

'Then I'll be serving some slander writs.'

Epimandos tugged at my tunic urgently. 'But you're an investigator! You can prove you're innocent – ' he had a touching faith in my skills.

I interrupted his agitated mutterings. 'Epimandos, how much to let me have a look at the room upstairs?'

'What room?' he gasped feebly.

'Why, just how many nasty secrets are you hiding at Flora's?' The waiter blenched. This place had certainly been used by antisocial characters more than once. 'Settle down. I'm not prying into the caupona's murky past.' He still looked terrified. 'I mean the room where your lodger signed off from the legions before his time.' Epimandos did not move or speak. I began more sternly: 'Epimandos, I want you to take me up to the room Censorinus hired.' I thought he was going to pass out. He had always been easily unnerved. It was one of the reasons I summed him up as a runaway slave.

'I can't!' he finally whispered desperately. 'They've roped it up. There was a guard here until ten minutes ago . . .' He seemed to be thinking up excuses.

'Oh Hercules! You're not telling me the body's still in your pigeon loft?' I glanced up expressively. 'That's a bit inconvenient. You'll be losing trade if blood starts dripping through the ceiling.' The waiter looked more and more uncomfortable. 'Why can't they drag the corpse away on a cart?'

'It's because he was a soldier,' Epimandos croaked. 'Petronius Longus said the army had to be notified.'

That was rubbish. Most unlike my disrespectful friend Petronius. I frowned. Petro would always override what others regarded as proper formalities. I even wondered for a wild moment if he was stalling on the removal order so as to give me a chance for a squint . . .

'Got any oysters tonight?' I asked Epimandos.

'No.'

'I think I'll have some.'

He found a slight increase in confidence now I had stopped talking about corpses. 'We never have oysters, Falco.' He was used to dealing with people who were deaf or drunk or both. 'You'll get oysters at the Valerian.' The Valerian was the caupona on the opposite corner. It was neat and clean, but always empty. For no obvious reason the locals had decided to ignore the Valerian as steadfastly as they patronised Flora's, even though Flora's was overpriced and gave you gut-ache.

'I can't be bothered to shift. Epimandos, run over and get me a bowlful, will you?'

Whether he grasped the idea or not, Epimandos let himself be bullied into running over the road. I hoped he had the sense to dally for a long chat with the Valerian's waiter.

I nipped through the kitchen area and up the back stairs. I knew where lodgers were installed, because when Ma's Campania relations descended we sometimes bedded them out here. There were three rooms – two tiny cubicles over the kitchen and a larger one above the bar. Censorinus had had the biggest. I knew because its door was tied up.

Petronius had returned my knife after his inspection, so I already had it out to slice through the rope, which had been wound on to two large nails by his men. Their efforts were pretty feeble, however. The web of heavily stranded hemp looked impressive at first glance, but a pantomime dancer could have made a forced entry without breaking a fingernail. I managed to drag one knot right off, which meant I would be able to replace it intact when I left. If I was fast, I might be able to come and go undetected.

Without pausing to wonder any further about the pathetic attempt to deter entry, I opened the door gently on the room where the soldier's murder had taken place.

XVI

Don't ask me to describe it.

You never expect what you find. Sometimes – the lucky times – any evidence that a violent crime has occurred seems hardly noticeable. So little shows that quite a few crimes must entirely escape discovery. At other times, the violence is horrendously clear. You reel back, amazed that anyone could wreak such savagery on another human being. This was one of those.

This murder had been committed in a frenzy. Even my warning from Petronius had failed to prepare me. Petronius apparently believed in Greek understatement.

We had talked about villains 'making their mark', as if Censorinus's death might have been a syndicated killing ordered by some magnate in the underworld. As soon as I saw the room I gave up the idea. Whoever killed Censorinus Macer was acting under devastating stress.

It had to have been a man. Impassioned women can achieve vindictive damage, but this act had taken brute strength. Blow after crazy blow, long after death had occurred. The face, when I forced myself to look at it, was difficult to recognise. Petro was right: there was blood everywhere. Even the ceiling was splashed. To clean the room properly would entail dismantling the furniture and swabbing the surfaces several times. Olympus knows what the killer must have looked like when he left.

I felt reluctant to move around even now, after the gore had dried.

But there was no point in having come unless I used the opportunity. I forced myself into routine activity.

The place was roughly eight feet square. A small room. It had one small, high window, deeply recessed. A small bed. One blanket; no pillow. The only other furnishings were a cloak hook, beneath which a faded scarlet uniform item had dropped to the floor, perhaps during the murder, plus a stool

744

that stood by the rickety bedhead. On the stool I saw one of Flora's stained wooden trays with a full pitcher and a winecup that had been knocked on its side. The rich liquid gleam of the red wine in the pitcher mocked the dried and caking bloodstains everywhere else.

Military kit had been neatly stowed at the foot of the bed. To reach it meant passing close by the dead soldier, whose remains lay half sprawled on the bed. I knew Petro and his men had managed to search the kit. I, with an indictment hanging over me, had to get there and do likewise.

The man's boots were lying just under the bed; I stumbled over one of them and barely avoided contact with the corpse. I gagged, managed to recover myself, then carried on.

His boots were off; he must have been going to bed, in bed, or getting up. Someone else might have been joining him under the blanket for social reasons, but in my opinion an intruder did this. Censorinus was not dressed for company. Soldiers put their boots on before they answer a knock at the door. Soldiers always want to be able to kick out if they hate your face.

Anyway, there was only one winecup on the tray.

The rest of his stuff, as Petronius had said, appeared to be complete. I had seen it all before when I helped Censorinus pack to leave my mother's house. Sword, dagger and belt; helmet; vine staff; knapsack of the usual small tools; spare red tunic and underwear. As he was on leave, he was not carrying spears or a shield. An old mansio bill was the only document. (From the Via Appia out on the Campagna, a place I knew.)

The weapons were all stowed tidily. It confirmed my theory that he was caught completely off guard. He must have been attacked unexpectedly, making no attempt to reach his gear and defend himself. He must have died after the first ferocious blow.

Had he been robbed? At Mother's he had kept his financial arrangements from me. I could see an arm-purse on him now, unopened; that alone would not have held enough funds for his journey to Rome. The mattress looked as if somebody had pulled it askew looking for money, but that could have been Petronius. Until the body was removed there was no scope to investigate the bed properly. Censorinus would have to be lifted off first. I was desperate – but not that desperate.

With the room in such a sorry condition, I was not prepared to ferret under floorboards either. There were practical problems. I was short of time, minus a jemmy, and unable to make noise. Petro would probably come back to do it. Better for him to find anything that was there.

I tried to memorise everything so I could brood on it later. Later, something that meant nothing now might suddenly make sense.

Averting my gaze, I eased my way past the body and escaped.

I had to fight for self-control before I replaced the ropes, and when I turned round from doing that a figure standing in the gloom below frightened the wits out of me.

'Epimandos!'

We stared at one another. Even with the length of the stairs between us, I could see he looked petrified.

I descended slowly until I reached him; the horror from above came after me, fingering my neck.

He was standing in my way. He was carrying a whole earthenware pot of oysters, holding it in the crook of his arm quite easily; years of heaving great food containers from the fire to their counter-holes had given him muscle.

'Forget it, I lost my appetite.'

'Do you know who did it?' he burst out in a frightened whisper.

'I know it wasn't me!'

'No,' Epimandos said. He was high in customer loyalty.

I would have preferred time to recover, but while we were out there in the kitchen, away from other eyes and ears, I asked him about the night the soldier died. 'I told the watch captain all that.'

'You're very public-spirited. Now tell me.'

'The same as I told Petronius?'

'Only if it's true! After Censorinus and I had had our little disagreement, when did he reappear?'

'He came back in the evening.'

'By himself?'

'Yes.'

746

'You sure of that?'

Epimandos had been sure until I asked him; insisting he thought about it frightened him into doubts. His eyes moved rapidly as he quavered, 'He was alone when he had supper here anyway.'

'Did he stay in afterwards?'

'Yes.'

'Drinking?'

'He went upstairs.'

'Did he say anything?'

'Like what?' demanded the waiter suspiciously.

'Anything at all?'

'No.'

'Did anyone come to see him afterwards?'

'Not that I saw.'

'Were you busy that night?'

'Well . . . More than the Valerian was.' That meant normal trade.

'That evening, could anyone have gone indoors past you without you noticing?'

'It's possible.' With the tight internal arrangements, front entry would be difficult for anyone avoiding notice. But the waiter could never watch the back end of the caupona, which we locals used as our private way out if we saw debt-collectors approaching down the street. Sharp bailiffs and their bully-boys came in that way.

'Did you go out on any errands?'

'No. It was pouring with rain.'

'Were you working all night?'

'Till we closed.'

'Do you sleep here?' Epimandos nodded reluctantly. 'Show me where.'

He had a cabin on one side of the kitchen. It was a dreary burrow. The occupant slept perched on a ledge with a straw pillow and a sludge-coloured coverlet. I noted few personal possessions – just an amulet on a nail and a woollen cap. I remembered my brother had given him the amulet, probably as a pledge for an unpaid bill.

He ought to have heard anyone who got in after he closed the caupona, whether they forced the sliding doors at the

747

front or secretly used the back entrance. But there were five empty amphorae lolling on their points against one wall: knocking back the ends of them must be the waiter's perk. I guessed he normally turned into bed dead drunk, a habit that might well be known by local villains. That night he could have been in such a stupor he failed to hear the violent struggle overhead.

'So did you notice any odd noises that night?'

'No, Falco.' He sounded pretty definite. Such certainty worried me.

'Are you telling me the truth?'

'Of course!'

'Yes, of course you are . . .' Did I believe him, though?

Customers were shouting for attention. Epimandos edged towards the main area of the shop, eager to get away from me.

Suddenly I sprang on him: 'Who found the body? Was it you?'

'No, the owner, going up to get his rent . . .'

So there was an owner! I was so surprised I let the waiter slip away to face the raillery in the bar.

After a moment I let myself out through the back way: a slatted stable door on rusty pins that led to an alley full of dead fish-pickle jars and olive-oil flagons. There were about fifteen years of empties, lurking below a corresponding smell.

Anyone like me who had been coming here for half a lifetime would have known about this unsecured, unsecurable exit. Any stranger could have guessed its existence too.

I paused for a moment. If I had emerged straight after seeing the body I would have thrown up drastically. Controlling myself while I questioned the waiter had helped put it off.

I turned back, looking closely at the stable door in case the killer had left bloodstains to mark his retreat. I could find none. But inside the kitchen area stood pails of water. A murderer could have washed, at least partially, before he left.

Walking slowly, I went round to the main street. As I passed the caupona heading homewards, a tall figure, plainly not a customer, hovered in the shadows outside the Valerian. I took no notice. There was no need for the usual caution. The sinister individual was neither a robber nor a marauding pimp. I recognised that bulky shape, and I knew what he was doing there. It was my friend Petronius, keeping a suspicious eye on me.

I called a mocking goodnight and kept going.

It failed. Petro's heavy footfall pounded after me. 'Not so fast!'

I had to stop.

Before I could start grumbling at him he got in first in a grim tone, 'Time's running out, Falco!'

'I'm dealing with the problem. What are you doing, wearing out the pavements on my tail?'

'I was looking at the caupona.' He had the tact not to ask what I had been up to there myself. We both glanced back. The usual dismal crowd were leaning on their elbows arguing about nothing, while Epimandos applied a taper to the tiny lamps that were hung above the counters at night. 'I wondered if anyone could have made a forced entry to the lodger's room from out here . . .'

I could tell from his tone he had decided that was unlikely. Looking up at the frontage of Flora's we could see that while the place was open, access would be impossible. Then once the shutters were drawn for the night there would be a blank face on the street side. Above the bar were two deeply recessed window openings, but it would take a ladder to reach them and then climbing in through such a small opening would be awkward. Censorinus would have heard anyone trying to do it well before they were on to him.

I shook my head. 'I think the killer went up the stairs.'

'And who was he?' demanded Petro.

'Don't nag me. I'm working on it.'

'You need to work fast then! Marponius has summoned me to a conference tomorrow about this stinking case, and I can tell you in advance, the conclusion will be that I have to haul you in.'

'I'll keep out of your way then,' I promised, as he growled and let me go.

Only when I had turned the corner did I remember meaning to ask him about the caupona's owner, the mystery rent-collector whom Epimandos told me had discovered the corpse.

I made it back to Mother's in a sombre mood. I seemed no further forward, though I now had some feeling for events the night the soldier died. How his death connected with Festus was a mystery. Censorinus had been killed by somebody who hated him. That depth of emotion had nothing to do with my brother; Festus had been friends with everyone.

Or had he been? Maybe somebody had a grudge against him that I wasn't aware of? And maybe that was what had brought disaster on a man who had been known as one of my brother's associates?

The ghastly scene in the room still hovered on the edge of my consciousness as I went indoors.

I was already hemmed in by problems, and when I entered the apartment I discovered another: Helena Justina was waiting for me, alone.

Mother was out – probably gone to see one of my sisters. She might stay the night. I had an idea things had been arranged that way. Our driver from Germany had already taken his pay, such as it was, and left us. Helena had lent her maid to her mother. Nobody on the Aventine has a maid.

So we were alone in the apartment. It was the first time we had been on our own like this for several weeks. The atmosphere was unconducive to romance.

Helena seemed very quiet. I hated that. It took a fair amount to upset her, but I frequently managed it. When she did feel hurt I lost her, and she was hurt now. I could tell what was coming. She had been thinking all day about what Allia had told her. Now she was ready to ask me about Marina.

XVII

Things began quietly. Helena let me kiss her cheek. I washed my hands. I pulled off my boots. There was dinner, which we set about in virtual silence. I left most of mine.

We knew each other too well for preliminary skirmishes. 'Want to talk about it?'

'Yes.' Always direct, this one.

After what I had witnessed that evening, it was the wrong time for an argument, but if I tried to dodge, even temporarily, I was afraid that it could be the end of everything.

I gazed at her while I tried to clear my head.

She was wearing a long-sleeved dark blue dress, winter-weight wool, with agate jewellery. Both suited her; both went back to before I met her. I remembered them from when I first knew her in Britain; then she had been a haughtily independent young woman, recently divorced. Though her confidence had been eroded by the failed marriage, defiance and anger were what I most recalled from those days. We had clashed head-on, yet by some divine metamorphosis that had turned into laughing together, followed inevitably by love.

The blue dress and agates were significant. She may not have thought about it. Helena despised premeditated drama. But I recognised in her appearance a statement that she could be her own woman again any time she chose.

'Helena, it's best not to quarrel at night.' It was honest advice, but came out more like insolence. 'You're proud and I'm tough; it's a bad combination.'

During the day she must have withdrawn into her private self. Helena had given up a great deal to live with me, and tonight she must be as near as she would ever be to throwing that back in my face.

'I can't sleep beside you if I hate you.'

'Do you?'

'I don't know yet.'

751

I reached to touch her cheek; she leaned away. I snatched back my hand. 'I've never cheated you, sweetheart!'

'Good.'

'Give me a chance. You don't want to see me grovelling.'

'No. But if what I've heard is only half right, I'll be seeing you squirm soon!'

Helena's chin came up. Her brown eyes were bright. Maybe we both felt a thread of excitement, sparring like this. But Helena and I never wasted time inventing pretexts. Any accusations that were about to be flung would carry as much weight as wet sandbags.

I leaned back a little. I felt breathless. 'So what's the procedure? Are the questions to be specific, or shall I just warble cheerily?'

'You seem to be expecting a crisis, Falco.' That 'Falco' was bad.

'I do keep an eye on what you're finding out about me.'

'Have you something to say about it?'

'My darling, I've spent most of the afternoon thinking up explanations to win you round!'

'Never mind the explanations. I'm well aware you can invent wildly and phrase it like a barrister. Tell me the truth.'

'Ah that!' I always told her the truth. That was how I already knew the truth sounds more insincere than anything.

When I made no effort to respond further, Helena seemed to change the subject. 'How are you getting on with your mother's business?'

'It's my business now. I'm a murder suspect, don't forget!'

'What have you done today?' It appeared oblique, but I knew it would be relevant.

'Spoke to Maia; Mico; Allia. Got nowhere with any of them. I talked to the waiter at Flora's – and I inspected the corpse.'

I must have looked drawn. 'Did you have to do that?' Helena asked in a changed voice.

I smiled wryly. 'So you still have some heart?'

'I have always treated you reasonably!' That was a fierce dig. 'I think you have been wasting time, Marcus. It's obvious there were two people you ought to have seen immediately. You've spent a whole day dodging the issue, and contacted neither. The situation's too serious for this.'

'There is time.'

'Petronius only gave you today!'

'So you've been listening to private conversations?'

She shrugged. 'Thin walls.'

'Who are these people I'm supposed to be ignoring?'

'You know who. Your brother's old girlfriend for one. But first you should have gone straight to your father.'

I folded my arms. I said nothing; Helena fought me silently. 'Why do you hate your father?' she demanded eventually.

'He's not worth hating.'

'Is it because he left home while you were just a child?'

'Look, my childhood is none of your business.'

'It is,' snapped Helena, 'if I have to live with the results!'

Fair comment. And I could not object to her interest. Helena Justina's main criterion for living with a man was that he let her read his thoughts. After thirty years of keeping my own council, I went along with it. Being an informer is a lonely profession. Allowing Helena free access to the inner sanctum had come as a relief.

'All right. I can see I have to suffer.'

'Marcus, you're trussed up like a bird in a braising pan – '

'I'm not done for yet. Mind you don't get pecked.'

Her eyes glimmered; that was promising. 'Stop prevaricating! Tell me the truth.'

'You won't like it.'

'I realise that.'

'You win.' I faced the inevitable. I should have told her all this a long time ago. She must have half guessed it anyway, while I had nearly forfeited the right to give her my version. 'It's quite simple. I don't know what went on between my parents, but I've nothing to say to any man who walks out on his children. When my father took a stroll I was seven. Just about to assume the toga praetexta. I wanted my papa to be there watching at my first big ceremony.'

'You don't approve of ceremonial.'

'I don't now!'

Helena frowned. 'Plenty of children grow up with only one

753

parent present. Still, I suppose the lucky ones at least get a stepfather to despise or stepmother to hate.' She was teasing, and on this subject I object to being teased. She read my face. 'That was bad taste . . . Why did your parents never divorce formally?'

'He was too ashamed to do it; she was, and is, too stubborn.' I used to wish I was an orphan. At least then I could have started again, without the constant hope or dread that just when everything had settled down our paterfamilias might reappear, upsetting everyone with his old blithe smile.

Helena was frowning. 'Did he leave you without money?'

I began to answer angrily, then took a deep breath. 'No, I can't say that.'

When my father ran out with his redhead we never saw him for several years; I learned afterwards that he had been in Capua. Right from the start there had been a man called Cocceius who brought money to my mother on a fairly regular basis. It was supposed to be coming from the Auctioneers' Guild. For years I accepted that story, as Mother appeared to do. But when I grew old enough to work things out I realised that the Guild was acting as agent – a polite excuse for my mother to accept my father's money without lessening her disgust for him. The main clue was that the weight of the coin bag increased with time. Charitable hand-outs tend to tail off.

Helena was looking at me for more answers. 'We just about escaped being destitute. We were barely clad and fed. But that applied to everyone we knew. It sounds bad to you, love, with your privileged upbringing, but we were the swarming mass of the great Roman poor; none of us expected any better from life.'

'You were sent to school.'

'Not by him.'

'But your family did have benefactors?'

'Yes. Maia and I had our school fees paid.'

'She told me. By the lodger. Where did he come from?'

'He was an old Melitan moneylender. My mother found space for him so the rent money would help out.' She only let him have a fold-up couch and a shelf for his clothes in a corridor. She had assumed he would hate it and leave, but he clung on and lived with us for years.

'And your father disapproved? Was the lodger a cause of arguments?'

This was all wrong. *I* was supposed to be the intruder who went round asking awkward questions, forcing long-hidden secrets to bubble to the surface of other people's ornamental ponds. 'The Melitan did cause a lot of trouble, but not the way you mean.' The Melitan, who had no family, had wanted to adopt Maia and me. That had caused some tumultuous rows. To Helena, who came from a civilised family where they hardly seemed to wrangle over anything more serious than who beat the Senator to the best bread roll at breakfast, the riots among my own tribe must sound harsh and barbaric. 'I'll tell you about it some day. My father's disappearance was directly related to his flamboyant girlfriend, not the lodger. Times were hard and he wasn't prepared to endure the struggle with us. The Melitan was irrelevant.'

Helena wanted to argue, but accepted it. 'So your father suddenly walked out one day – '

'It seemed unexpected, but since he left with a red-haired scarf-maker, maybe we should have been prepared.'

'I've noticed you hate redheads,' she said gravely.

'Could have been worse: could have been a Macedonian; could have been a blonde.'

'Another colour you loathe! I must remember to stay dark – '

'That means you're not leaving me?' I threw in lightly.

'Even if I do, Marcus Didius, I shall always respect your prejudices!' Helena's gaze, which could be oddly charitable, met mine. A familiar spark tingled. I let myself believe that she would stay.

'Don't go!' I murmured softly, with what I hoped were pleading eyes. Her mood had changed again, however. She looked back as if she had just spotted mould on a best table napkin. I kept trying. 'Sweetheart, we haven't even started yet. Our "old times" have yet to be enjoyed. I'll give you things to look back on that you cannot even dream – '

'That's what I'm afraid of!'

'Ah Helena!'

'Ah nuts, Marcus!' I should always have spoken to her in formal Greek, and never have let her pick up my own slang.

'Stop bluffing,' commanded the love of my life. She had a sharp eye for fraud. 'So your father started a new life as an auctioneer in Capua; he eventually reappeared in Rome, the man I know as Geminus. Now he is a rich man.' She had met my father briefly. He had made sure he steamed in like Lars Porsena of Clusium to inspect the high-born madam who had picked me up. I still felt good whenever I remembered his amazement. Helena Justina was not some enamelled old baggage I was chasing for her money. He found her presentable, apparently rational, and genuinely fond of me. He never got over the shock and I never stopped gloating.

This sibyl could also be too shrewd for her own good: 'Is it his wealth you resent?'

'He can be as rich as he likes.'

'Ah! Is he still with the redhead?'

'I believe so.'

'Do they have children?'

'I believe not.'

'And he's still there twenty years later – so he does have *some* staying power!' Without intending to let her see a reaction, I ground my teeth. Helena queried thoughtfully, 'Do you think you inherited that?'

'No. I owe nothing to him. I'll be loyal to you of my own accord, princess.'

'Really?' Her light inflection belied the sharp whip in the insult. 'You know where he is, Marcus; you recommended him to my own father. Sometimes you even work with him yourself.'

'He's the best auctioneer in Rome. One of my professional specialities is recovering stolen art. I deal with him when I have to – but there are limits, lass.'

'Whereas,' she started slowly. Helena could use a word like 'whereas' not merely to shade her argument, but to add hints of moral stricture too. Her conjunctions were as piquant as anchovy. 'Whereas your brother seems to have worked with Geminus on a much more frequent footing . . . They were close, weren't they? Festus never felt the anger that obsessed you after your father left?'

'Festus never shared my anger,' I agreed bleakly.

Helena smiled slightly. She had always thought I was a

broody beggar. She was right, too. 'The two of them had a long and regular partnership on a straightforward father-and-son basis?'

'It seems like it.' Festus had had no pride. Maybe I had too much – but that was the way I liked it.

'Don't you know, Marcus?'

'I am forced to that conclusion. Festus never mentioned it.' Sparing my feelings, I suppose. Mother's too. 'There was a hiatus in relations when my father was living out of Rome, but Festus must have resumed contact pretty soon afterwards.' Sometimes I wondered if they had even stayed in touch throughout the time when Father was hiding up in Capua. 'Certainly by the time Festus died they shared a lock-up in the antiques quarter, over at the Saepta Julia.' Where my mother could not see them. 'And then they were as close as two termites.'

'So your father will know about the statues and the ship that sank?'

'He should. If it was one of their joint ventures.' She had dragged the words out of me like crusted amber oozing from an old pine tree. Before Helena could capitalise on the achievement, I said sternly, 'I left him until last deliberately. I am going to see Geminus tomorrow.'

'I think you're afraid to face him.'

'Not true – but you have to understand, my father can be a very tricky customer. I wanted to assemble as many facts as possible before I tried talking to him.' She was closer to the truth than I admitted. I had never discussed family affairs with Father, and I hated the thought of starting now. 'Helena, just leave me to get on with it!'

Very manly. Asking for trouble, in fact. That glimmer in her eyes was quite dangerous now.

'All right.' I hate reasonable women. 'Don't scowl,' she complained. 'Anybody would suppose I interfered.'

'May I be eaten alive by ravens if I thought it . . . Is that the end of the marathon grilling?'

'No.'

I thought not. We still had Marina to upset our evening. The grilling had hardly started yet.

757

XVIII

I made one last attempt to restore peace. 'I'm in serious trouble, sweetheart. I may be under arrest soon. Don't let's spoil our evening with any more home truths.'

Helena Justina listened almost demurely, her hands lightly folded in her lap. Anyone who had never met her might suppose she was a woman of quality interviewing a cushion-stuffer who was seeking outwork. I knew her better. She looked sad, which meant she was angry — *more* angry than if she had merely looked annoyed.

Soon she would be sad too.

'Marcus, when people are so eager to tell me that you seduced your brother's girlfriend, I would like to assure them I have already heard the full story from you.'

'Thank you,' I said, pretending to assume it was a compliment. The full story posed some problems. Only Festus knew that. 'To start with, Helena, if I did seduce my brother's girlfriend, Marina did not object to it — and as for Festus, it was probably his plan.'

'Maybe she seduced you?' suggested Helena, almost hopefully.

I smiled. 'No, that's your privilege.'

Then I told her about that long and dreadful night in Rome.

My brother Festus was thirty-five years old when he died. Frankly, we had not been prepared to lose him to a hero's death. An accident during a prank seemed more his style.

Being older, he had always seemed to me to belong to another generation, though by that time the gap between us was closing. People used to say how alike we looked. That was only because we had the same rampant curls and silly grins. He was shorter and more thickset. More athletic and with a sweeter temperament. More gifted in business, luckier with women, smarter, sharper, more easily accepted as a treasure by the family. It was always pretty clear to me that both my parents and most of my sisters made Festus their favourite. (However, I had my share of being spoiled; my childhood place was as the family baby since Maia, who really owned that position, would not stand for the fuss.)

Like a good Roman citizen who saw his chance to eat, drink and fart at the Empire's expense while using its unrivalled facilities for world travel, Festus enlisted in the legions as soon as he looked old enough.

'So he *must* have been in touch with your father,' Helena commented. 'He would need the signed release from his family.'

'True. Just one aspect of public life where having a missing father causes painful embarrassment.'

'You were in the army later. What did you do about that?'

'My Great-Uncle Scaro stood in as my guardian.'

'You liked him?'

'Yes.' Uncle Scaro, a friendly old scallywag, had always given me the place in the world that my father had taken away.

Entrepreneurs do well in the army. After all, regulations exist to exploit. Whereas I had had to serve five years in the bitter Northern provinces, Festus had easily wangled himself supremely cosy billetings: a brief spell in Spain, Egypt with the Fifteenth Apollinaris, then posted East with them once the civil war broke out in Judaea. This last could have proved a miscalculation, but since the whole Empire was about to erupt then, Festus would have been fighting wherever he was. With expert precision he had placed himself under the command of the future emperor, Vespasian. His legion was led by Vespasian's own son, doubly convenient as my brother had somehow made it to centurion, so was visible to Titus Caesar daily at his war council.

In the year that the Jewish Rebellion began, when Nero sent Vespasian to deal with it and the Fifteenth Legion were posted from Alexandria to help, Festus had come home on sick leave. He had organised one of the wounds in which he specialised: it looked vicious enough to gain a pass for convalescence in Italy, though once he set foot at Ostia he seemed able to do pretty well whatever he wanted, especially if it involved girls. Other people's girls, mostly. Festus

759

believed it was non-combatants' patriotic duty to lend home-leave centurions their women. Women went along with this.

The army was less free and easy. With the legions being so stretched out in the desert, they needed every man. After six weeks in Rome, Festus was annoyed to receive an urgent recall to Judaea.

'Festus struck us as one of life's eternal survivors. None of us imagined he was going back to be killed.'

'Festus presumably imagined it least of all,' Helena said. 'Is this where I start feeling annoyed?'

'Afraid so . . .'

On his last night in Rome, the last time I ever saw him, we went to the Circus Maximus. Festus had always been a keen attender at the Circus, mainly because of the saucy women he could sit next to in the unsegregated seats. He was a devoted frequenter of girls who frequent the few places where girls exhibit themselves accessibly. In the proximity of Festus women showed off eagerly. I used to watch with astonished fascination. It happened even when, as on that night, his long-term girlfriend Marina had been brought along.

Festus saw nothing unusual in spending the last night of home leave with both his younger brother and his girl. It made us an awkward party. He simply never noticed it. Just as he never seemed to notice me lusting after the girl.

'Was Marina attractive?'

'Distinctly.'

'Don't bother to describe her,' Helena snarled.

Festus had always liked women who drew the crowds. Even when Marina was sulking because Festus was leaving Italy heads turned as we took our bench at the Circus, and later when Festus was dragging us round a series of dimly lit bars, she made us a highly conspicuous party. She had known Festus for years. As a fixture she could rightly feel more confidence than the various kittens who succumbed to a few days of passion then found themselves airily waved goodbye. It was assumed, probably even by Festus himself, that one day he would marry her. Only Mother had doubts. She said to me once it was more likely he would outrage everyone by bringing home an exotic little doll he had only known a fortnight and announcing that he had found true love. Festus certainly had a romantic streak. However, he died before he got round to it. That saved Mother from having to train some moppet who thought herself too pretty to help in the home. It left me with the task of shocking the family with an unlikely girlfriend, and it left Marina unmarried but unassailable. She was one of the family. Because by then Marina had honoured us by producing my niece Marcia.

Little Marcia was assured of lifelong support from the Didius clan. If anyone ever hinted to Marina that Festus might not be Marcia's father, Marina snapped back swiftly that if Festus was not responsible, it had to be me.

Helena forced out, 'I asked you once if Marcia was yours. You denied it.'

I had hardly known her then. I had been trying to impress her. Explaining Marcia had been too difficult to tackle. Maybe I should have done it anyway. It was worse now.

'Let's say the subject carries a question mark . . .'

What had happened was that in the early hours of the morning, when Festus, Marina and I were all too drunk to be cautious, my big-hearted brother had fallen in with some sozzled artists in a down-market tavern below the Caelian Hill. His new friends were well up to standard for Festus: all badly pickled gherkins who had no cash in their frayed tunic pockets but an easy habit of joining another party's table and calling loudly for more wine. I was tired. I had been very drunk, but was recovering enough to feel sullen and foul-mouthed. By now drink seemed unattractive. Even putting up with Festus had temporarily lost its sparkle. I said I was leaving. Marina announced she had had enough too. Festus asked me to take Marina home for him.

He promised to follow immediately. He was bound to forget her. In fact I had a strong suspicion the bold brunette who had sat next to him at the Circus was now awaiting him on some balcony. Marina had noticed the brunette too. Since this was her own last chance of seeing him, Marina took it badly. When we arrived at her apartment she complained that he mistreated her. I felt hard done by too; it was *my* last chance of seeing him. He might for once have stood up some dismal strangers and stuck with us. Waiting for him to let us down while we trailed after him on the wine-bar crawl had built up a fine old head of self-righteousness.

I made the foolish comment that it was lucky for Festus that I was not the type to try and put one over on him; so Marina said, '*Why not?*'

Afterwards, Marina made it plain the occasion had given her small pleasure. There was no chance of me enjoying myself either. Drink, guilt and confusion ruined it.

Some time during the next morning, I found myself back at my apartment with no idea how or when I got there. I knew Festus would have left for the port several hours before, provided he was capable. (He was, and he did.) So we never even said goodbye.

For weeks I avoided Marina. I found excuses to leave town as much as possible. Later I heard that she was pregnant, but everyone assumed Festus had fathered the baby; it suited me to think the same.

Then a year later came the day when I returned from a visit to Great-Uncle Scaro, who lived at the family homestead on the Campagna. I went to take Mother news of her relatives. I found the whole family assembled. I remember noticing a document that lay on the table. And when none of the women wanted to speak (for once), one of my brothers-in-law threw the news at me: Festus had led a sally over a battlement at some parched town called Bethel in Galilee, and had been killed as he turned back to call his men up after him. He was awarded the Mural Crown for being the first to cross an enemy rampart, and his heroic ashes had been scattered in Judaea.

At first I could not believe it. Even now I sometimes thought it must be a dream or trickery.

It emerged that Marina and Festus had never made a habit of writing to each other, and she had seen no reason to change that simply to tell him he had acquired a daughter. Why worry him? When he came home Marina would introduce him to the gurgling child and Festus would immediately adore her. (This was correct. Apart from the fact that Marcia was a good-looking baby, my brother was a deep sentimentalist.)

Losing my brother was bad enough. It was at the same family gathering, after I came back from the Campagna, that people thrust at me Marina's sudden public declaration about our night of what is so thoughtlessly called love. She had made a wild statement announcing that I had to look after her because our misguided fling was when she had conceived little Marcia.

My family reacted to this news in their usual good-natured fashion. Not one disbelieved it. I had shown a marked fondness for the new baby, and on his last visit Festus had, after all, been a wounded man.

'Was he wounded in that area?' Helena interrupted. She had been listening with a dazed expression, not entirely unsympathetic towards me.

'Look, this is about my family: it's a mad story. Festus,' I said quietly, 'had stabbed himself in the foot.'

'Sorry. I forgot people are not logical. What happened?'

'What do you think? I was greeted with torrents of invective, and instructed to marry the girl.'

Helena looked even more numb. She thought I was telling her that I had been concealing a wife.

It had nearly occurred. Under the influence of even more guilt and confusion, and seriously drunk, I heard myself agree to do it. At that, Marina, who had a hard streak of self-preservation, counted up the lives we were about to ruin and even she panicked. She restored Festus as Marcia's father, and backed out hastily. For me it brought many more insults, though at less cost.

That left the present situation.

'What exactly is the present situation?' sneered Helena.

'Only what you think.'

'I think it's appalling.'

'Quite.'

Obviously I had to care for the child. I had to do that for my brother's sake. There was no chance of shedding my responsibility for the mother either. Conscience is a terrible thing. Marina had a hold over me that I would never break. She might have gone off and married, but why should she bother when she was free to enjoy herself with me paying the bills? Meanwhile, I had made myself a target for every kind of abuse whenever my relatives cared to exert their talent.

There was no abuse from Helena. She looked upset, though not vindictive. I would have preferred to see jugs being hurled. Understanding always makes me miserable.

Unable to bear the tension any longer, I sprang up and paced about. Helena was leaning her elbows on Ma's kitchen table; her head was bowed in both hands. Eventually I stood behind her with my hands on her shoulders. 'Helena, don't judge the present by past events. You ought to know something tremendous happened to me when I met you.'

She allowed both the contact and the comment without reacting.

Helpless, I moved away. Helena got up, stretching, then left the room, evidently going to bed. I had not been invited but I tagged along anyway.

We lay in the dark for what seemed like hours, not touching. I must have dozed off for I woke again unhappily. Helena lay still. I put my hand on her arm. She ignored it. I turned away from her huffily.

After a second Helena moved too. She crept behind me, knees in the crook of mine and face pressed against my spine. I waited long enough to make some sort of point, though not so long she bounced away again. Then I turned over carefully, gathering her close. For a short period I could feel her crying. That was all right. It was my fault – but she was crying from relief that we were now in each other's arms. We were friends. We would be friends for a long time.

I held Helena until her grief subsided, then we fell deeply asleep.

XIX

It was a cold night. After the North, where they make better preparations for winter than in Mediterranean countries, we felt it all the more. Bad weather always catches Rome by surprise. With only a brazier to take the chill off the long dark hours, my brother's old room could grow bitter by dawn. Still clinging together, we both awoke.

Helena had been planning. 'If you're going to see this Marina, I think I'll come too.'

I thought it was best for everyone if I went alone. Mentioning this point of view seemed a bad idea.

Marina made a habit of being as inconvenient as possible. (She was certainly right for our family.) She lived, as she had always done, right around the curve of the Aventine, across the Via Appia and almost at the foot of the Caelian in the quaintly named Vicus Honoris et Virtutis. This irony was too obvious to be commented upon. If honour and virtue had been qualifications for living there, it would have been an empty street.

'Is she *very* good-looking?' asked Helena, as we walked there together.

'Afraid so. Festus attracted dramatic women.'

'Unlike you?'

This sounded tricky. 'I go for character . . . To find looks in addition is a bonus, of course.' I realised she was laughing at me.

The light atmosphere ended as soon as Marina let us into her two-room hutch. I had forgotten just how striking she was. I saw Helena sigh slightly. Her fierce glance at me said she felt she had been inadequately warned. Things were not going well.

Marina was a short, dark, sultry vision with immense, wide-set eyes. She manoeuvred those eyes constantly, to nerve-racking effect. With a fine nose and high cheekbones,

765

she had a faintly Eastern appearance. This suggestion was strengthened by her manner; she thought it elegant to make gestures involving bent wrists and stagily poised fingers.

She had once been a braid-maker, but nowadays felt little need to toy with employment. Nowadays she had me. Securing an honest sucker who made no demands had left Marina free to spend her time on her appearance. Her menfriends were pretty pleased with the results. They should be. The results could have been hung up and framed. Fortune had been as generous with Marina as I was; her conquests were getting a voluptuous shape allied to a free and easy manner, attractive goods even before they discovered the permanent lien on my bank box.

She was a cracker to look at, but the air of an awe-striking goddess was wiped out as soon as she opened her mouth. She had been born common, and was making a brave attempt to remain completely faithful to her origins. 'Ah Marcus!' The voice was as coarse as hessian. Naturally she kissed me. (Well, I *was* paying the bills.) I stepped back. This only allowed more room for Helena to inspect the immaculate turnout on the breathtaking body. Marina pretended to spot Helena. 'How come you need a chaperone these days?'

'Hands off, Marina. This is Helena Justina. She thinks I'm cool and sophisticated and that my past is full of very plain girls.'

Marina became noticeably cooler herself; she must have sensed a force to be reckoned with. Helena, in the same stately blue outfit as yesterday (still registering independence), seated herself gracefully as if she had been asked. 'How do you do?' This voice was quiet, cultured, and effortlessly satirical. Marina's sense of humour was basic; basically, she didn't have one. She looked tense.

Helena made no attempt to register disapproval. It only increased the impression that she was privately sizing up the situation and intended some swift changes. Marina was known for panicking every time the sparrows cheeped; she went pale under the purplish tones of her cheek paint and flailed around for rescue. 'Have you come to see the baby, Marcus?'

There was no sign of little Marcia, so the child must be parked elsewhere. I had already had a few arguments about that habit. Marina's idea of a suitable nurse for a four-year-old was Statia, a tipsy second-hand clothes dealer married to an expelled priest. Since he had been expelled from the Temple of Isis, whose attendants had the worst reputation in Rome, his habits had to be pretty seedy. 'I'll get someone to fetch her,' Marina mumbled hastily.

'Do that!'

She rushed out. Helena sat extremely still. I managed to avoid indulging in nervous chat, and stood about looking like the man in charge.

Marina returned. 'Marcus is *so* fond of my daughter!'

'Tact has never been your strong point!' Ever since she informed my family what had gone on between us, my relationship with Marina had had formal overtones. At one point we could not afford to quarrel; now we were too remote to bother. But there was an edge.

'He loves children!' Marina gushed, this time directed even more plainly at Helena.

'So he does. And what I like,' Helena returned sweetly, 'is the way it doesn't matter whose they are.'

Marina needed time to take this in.

I watched my brother's girlfriend staring at mine: beauty in the unfamiliar presence of strong will. She looked like a puppy sniffing at a strange beetle that seemed likely to spring up and bite its nose. Helena, meanwhile, conveyed lightness, discretion and sheer class. But our hostess was right to be nervous; this was someone who could bite.

I tried to take things in hand. 'Marina, there's a problem with a dodge Festus was running. I have to talk to you.'

'Festus never told me about his dodges.'

'Everyone keeps saying that.'

'It's true. He was a tight one.'

'Not tight enough. He promised some soldiers to make them a fortune. He let them down and now they're coming on to the family to make it up to them. I wouldn't care, but one of them has been sent down to Hades and circumstantial evidence strongly points to me.'

'Oh, but surely you didn't do it!' The girl was an idiot. I used to think she was bright. (Bright enough to rook me, though she would break a logic tutor's heart.)

767

'Oh don't be ridiculous, Marina!' She was wearing saffron yellow, a colour so clear it hurt the eyes; even in this weather she went bare-armed. She had beautiful arms. On them she wore a whole rack of bracelets that rattled continually. I found the noise highly irritating. 'Be sensible!' I commanded. Marina looked offended by this advice; I thought Helena smiled. 'What do you know about Greek statues?'

Marina crossed her legs and gave me the full eye treatment. 'Offhand, Marcus, not much that I can think of!'

'I'm not asking for a lecture on Praxiteles. What do you know about any plans Festus had for importing the stuff and flogging it to rich people?'

'It was probably with help from Geminus.'

'Do you actually know that?'

'Well it sounds right, doesn't it?'

'Nothing in the story sounds right! The whole business sounds like trouble – and we're all in it. If I go to trial for murder that's the end of my funds, Marina. Put your mind on that practical issue, take a grip on yourself and think back.'

She set herself in the pose of a very attractive, fairly thoughtful woman. As a statue she would have been high art. As a witness she remained useless. 'Honestly, I don't really know.'

'He must have talked to you about something, sometimes!'

'Why? Business was business, bed was bed.' This topic was too uncomfortable.

'Marina, I'm trying to remember things myself. Was he restless on that last visit to Rome? Preoccupied? Anxious about anything?'

She shrugged.

She could. She didn't have Petronius Longus writing her name on a certificate of arrest while Marponius hopped from one foot to another just waiting to bang his seal ring on it.

'Well you were there!' smirked Marina. The implication was pointed, and quite unnecessary.

At this point a neighbour galloped in, carrying my niece. Marina seized the child with a relieved glance of thanks, the neighbour fled, and we all prepared for trouble. Marcia looked around, assessed the audience like a professional, then threw back her head and screamed.

768

Marina was bluffing madly as she tried to soothe her offspring. 'See what you've done, Marcus.' She was a fond, though vague mother, who suffered unreasonably at Marcia's hands. Marcia had never been one to co-operate. She had a keen sense of occasion. She knew exactly when a tormented wail could make her mother appear like a monster. 'She was perfectly happy. She likes going to play at Statia's – '

'She's showing off as usual. Give her here!'

As Marina weakly passed the child to me, Helena intercepted. Marcia fell into her arms like a galley hitting dock, then stopped screaming and settled on Helena's lap looking blissfully good. It was a fraud, but well timed to make both her mother and uncle feel inadequate. 'Let me see what I can do with her,' Helena murmured innocently. 'Then you two can talk.' She knew Marcia. They made a fine pair of conspirators.

'She loves it at Statia's,' Marina muttered again defensively.

I was annoyed. 'You mean she loves dressing up in filthy cast-off rags, and being allowed to eat the musical bars out of the ex-priest's sistrum!'

'You don't know that they neglect her.'

'I do know I've seen Marcia do an impressive imitation of Statia falling over drunk!' She also liked singing obscene hymns to Isis and mimicking suggestive rites. The child was a natural for the low life.

Marcia gazed lovingly at Helena, as if all this was news to her. Helena kissed her curly head consolingly. 'Don't worry, darling. It's only Uncle Marcus having one of his quaint fits.'

I growled. No one was impressed.

I sank on to a stool, burying my head in my arms.

'Uncle Marcus is crying!' giggled Marcia, intrigued. Helena whispered something, then put her down so Marcia could run to me. She flung her fat arms round my neck and gave me a smacking wet kiss. A worrying smell of wine lees hung around her. 'Uncle Marcus needs a shave.' She was a frank, open-hearted child. Maybe that was why I worried about her. She would be a frank, open-hearted woman one day.

I picked her up. She always seemed tougher and heavier than I expected. Marina had hung a tawdry bead anklet on one chubby foot and let Marcia paint red spots on her cheeks. Somebody, probably at Statia's, had given her a grotesque amulet. I had to close my mind to these details or I would have really lost my temper.

Holding my brother's oddly solid child, I tried reconstructing his last night in Rome yet again. Marina had said it: I was there all right. Any clues should be apparent to me, if only I could remember them.

'I do reckon he was edgy.' I was trying to convince myself. Marina only shrugged again in her distant, disinterested way. With those shoulders and that bust, she went in for shrugs on principle. The principle was: knock 'em dead. 'Old Festus was skipping on his toes that last night. Olympus knows what caused it, though. I doubt if it was the thought of going back to Judaea. He didn't care if the arrows were flying; he thought he could duck. Marina, do you remember that gang of ghastly wall artists he picked up?'

'I remember the girl at the Circus Max!' Marina said, with force. 'I'm damned sure he picked *her* up!'

'Can't say I noticed,' I mumbled, trying to avoid a scene. Helena was watching us with the tolerant expression of an intellectual at Pompey's Theatre enduring the ghastly farce while awaiting a serious Greek tragedy. If she had had a handful of almonds, she would have been eating them one at a time with the tips of her teeth. 'Marina, think about those graffiti merchants. They were gruesome. Where did they come from? I assumed he didn't know them, but are we sure?'

'Festus knew everyone. If he didn't know them when he went into the bar, he would know them by the time he left.'

Making cronies of a barful of people was his signature. 'He had his moments, but normally he drew the line at slaves and wall painters. He was making out to us that those posers were strangers. Did you know them yourself?'

'Just some tricksters at the Virgin. Their usual ghastly clientele – '

'The *Virgin?*' I had forgotten the name. Festus would have thought it a great joke. 'Is that where we ended up?'

'It's a terrible place.'

'That part I remember.'

'I'd never seen them before.'

'It must be quite near here. Do you still hang around there?'

'Only if somebody pays me to go.' Marina was as frank as her winsome child.

'Have you ever seen those artists again?'

'Not that I recall. Mind you, if I was desperate enough to be in the Virgin, I was probably too tipsy to spot my own grandmother.'

'Or you wouldn't want your granny to spot you.' Even at eighty-four Marina's old granny would have made a good Praetorian Guard. She liked hitting first and asking questions afterwards. She was three feet high, and her right upper-cut was legendary.

'Oh no! Granny drinks at the Four Fish,' Marina solemnly put me right.

I sighed, gently.

XX

Helena could see I was growing exasperated at the way this conversation jerked about.

'What we need to ascertain,' she intervened, in a tone so reasonable I felt my left foot kick out angrily, 'is whether Didius Festus was contacting somebody in particular on his last home leave. Somebody who can tell us what his plans were. Why are you asking about the artists, Marcus? He could have been arranging business at any time during his leave. Was there really something special about his last night – and about that group?'

Suddenly Marina declared, 'There certainly was!' I started to feel hot. She was oozing indiscretion, though it did not come immediately. 'For one thing,' she said, 'Festus was jumping like a cat on a griddle. You noticed that – you just said so, Marcus. That wasn't like him. Normally he breezed into places and stirred everyone else up, but he let the excitement flow over him.'

'That's true. And he could hardly wait to drag us on from one bar to the next. Normally once he got comfortable he wouldn't shift. That night he kept dodging on to new squats every five minutes.'

'As if he was looking for someone?' suggested Helena quietly.

'For another thing,' Marina pressed on inexorably, 'there was the little matter of him sending me off with you!'

'We don't need to resurrect that,' I said. Well, I had to try.

'Don't mind me,' smiled Helena. The knives were out all round.

'Suit yourself,' sniffed Marina. 'But Marcus, if you really want to know what he was up to that evening, I think this little incident needs considering.'

'Why?' Helena asked her, bright with unhealthy interest.

'It's obvious. It was a blatant fix. He annoyed me over the brunette, then he got up sunshine's nose as well.'

'Doing what? What offended sunshine?'

'Oh I can't remember. Just Festus being himself, probably. He could behave like a short-arsed squit.'

I said, 'Looking back, I can see he was trying to get rid of both of us – despite the fact it was our last chance of seeing him, maybe for years.'

'You were both very fond of him?'

Marina threw up her hands elegantly. 'Oh gods, yes! We were both planning to stick to him like clams. He had no chance of keeping secrets. Even getting us to leave the Virgin was not safe enough. We would both have been back. Well, I would. If I had gone home and he hadn't turned up soon afterwards, I would have stormed out again looking for him – I knew where to look, too.'

Helena glanced at me for confirmation. 'Marina's right. Festus was often elusive, but we were used to it. She had dragged him away from drinks counters in the early hours of the morning on many occasions. It was their natural way of life.'

'What about you?'

'As it was his last night, once I sobered up a bit I might well have gone back to toast his health again. I knew his haunts as well as Marina did. If he wanted any privacy, then he had to shoot us off somewhere, and make it stick.'

'So he annoyed both of you deliberately, then threw you together?'

'Obvious!' Marina said. 'Marcus had always been jealous of Festus. This loon had been eyeing me up for years – so why did Festus suddenly present him with the goods after all that time?'

I felt surly. 'I seem to be coming out of this as weak, cheap, and sly.' They both looked at me in silence. 'Well thanks!'

Marina patted my wrist. 'Oh you're all right! Anyway, he owed you enough; no one could say otherwise. What about that business with your client?'

She genuinely puzzled me with that one. 'What client?'

'The woman who hired you to find her dog.' I had forgotten the damned dog. The female client now returned to mind quite easily – and not only because she was one of the first I ever had after I set up as an informer.

773

'It was a British hunting hound,' I told Helena hastily. 'Very valuable. Superb pedigree and could run like the wind. The daft creature was supposed to be guarding the woman's clothes at some bathhouse; a slave stepped on his tail accidentally and he ran off like stink down the Via Flaminia. The young lady was heartbroken . . .' It still sounded an unlikely tale.

'Well you've been in Britain!' Helena Justina said gently. She knew how to cast aspersions. 'I expect you have a special affinity with British dogs.' Oh yes. Lovely work for a professional; every informer ought to learn how to call 'Here boy!' in at least twelve languages. Five years later the jobs I was taking on seemed just as motley. 'Did you find him?' Helena pressed.

'Who?'

'The dog, Marcus.'

'Oh! Yes.'

'I bet your lady client was really grateful!' Helena understood more about my business than I liked.

'Come off it. You know I never sleep with clients.' She gave me a look; Helena had been my client once herself. Telling her she was different from all the others somehow never carried weight.

The woman in search of the lost doggie had had more money than sense and astounding looks. My professional ethics were of course unimpeachable – but I had certainly considered making a play for her. At the time big brother Festus had convinced me that tangling with the moneyed classes was a bad idea. Now Marina's words cast a subtle doubt. I gazed at her. She giggled. She obviously assumed I had known what was going on; now I finally saw the reason Festus had advised me to steer clear of the pretty dog owner: he had been bedding her himself.

'Actually,' I told Helena gloomily, 'it was Festus who found the bloody dog.'

'Of course it was,' Marina piped in. 'He had it tied up at my house all along. I was livid. Festus pinched it from the baths so he could get to know the fancy skirt.' My brother, the hero! 'Didn't you twig?'

'Ah Marcus!' Helena soothed me, at her kindest (not so kind as all that). 'I bet you never got your bill paid either?'

774

True.

I was feeling abused.

'Look, when you two have finished mocking, I have things to do today – '

'Of course you have,' smiled Helena, as if she was suggesting I should hide in a barrel for a few hours until my blushes cooled.

'That's right. Repolishing my grimy reputation won't be a quick job.' It was best to be straight with her, especially when she was sounding facetious but looking as if she was trying to remember where she last put the vial of rat poison.

I kissed Marcia resoundingly and gave the child back to her mother. 'Thanks for the hospitality. If you remember anything helpful, let me know at once. I'm due for the public strangler otherwise.' Helena stood up. I put my arm round her shoulders and said to Marina, 'As you see, my time should really be being taken up by this lovely girl.'

Helena permitted herself a complacent sniff.

'Are you two getting married?' Marina asked sympathetically.

'Of course!' we both chimed. As a couple we lied well.

'Oh that's nice! I wish you both every happiness.'

One thing must always be said for Marina: she had a good heart.

XXI

I informed Helena I had had enough supervision for one day and was going to my next appointment alone. Helena knew when to let me make a stand. I felt she acquiesced too graciously, but that was better than a fight in the open street.

We were virtually at her parents' house, so I took her for a daughterly visit. I made sure I escorted her to within sight of the door. Stopping for goodbyes gave me a chance to hold her hand. She could manage without consolation, but I needed it.

'Don't hate me, sweetheart.'

'No, Marcus.' She would be a fool not to view me with caution, however. Her face looked guarded. 'I always knew you had a colourful life behind you.'

'Don't judge me too harshly.'

'I think you're doing that yourself.' Maybe somebody had to. 'Marina seems a nice girl,' Helena said. I knew what that meant.

'You're hoping someone some day will snap her up.'

'I don't see why not.'

'I do. The men she hangs around with know she's not looking for a husband. It makes it easier for them – not having to worry about the fact they all have wives!'

Helena sighed.

We were standing on a corner of the great Appian Way. It was about as public as the Forum of the Romans on a quiet day. Brown-clad slaves with baskets and amphorae on their bent shoulders butted up the street in both directions trying to get in the way of five or six litters carrying ladies from refined homes. Workmen were chiselling unconvincingly at the dark bulk of the old aqueduct, the Aqua Marcia. A cart laden with marble slabs came by, struggling to mount the raised pavement as it lurched out of control. Three donkey-drovers waiting to overtake it, two old women with a goose, and the queue on a bench outside a barber's had tired of watching the cart and started to notice us.

To make the day memorable for everyone, I slid my arms around Helena Justina and kissed her. Rome is a city of sexual frankness, but even in Rome senators' daughters are rarely grappled on street corners by creatures who are obviously only one rank up from woodlice. I had caught her off guard. There was nothing she could do to stop me, and no reason for me to stop of my own accord. A small crowd collected.

When finally I let her go Helena became aware of the crowd. She remembered we were in the refined Capena Gate sector, home of her illustrious parents. 'There are rules, Falco!' she muttered hotly.

I had heard that in patrician circles husbands had to make appointments three days ahead if they wanted to embrace their wives. 'I know the rules. I felt like changing them.'

'Do it again, and I'll jab my knee somewhere painful.'

I kissed her again, so she applied the knee, though her nerve failed and it was too gentle to do damage. The crowd applauded anyway.

Helena looked upset; she thought she had hurt me. 'Goodbye Marcus!'

'Goodbye, my darling,' I responded in a pained croak. Now she suspected me of feigning.

Helena strode to her father's house in her most frosty style. I watched her right to the door, with my arms folded. While she waited for the porter, whose attentions at the door were always haphazard, she turned back furtively to check that I was gone. I grinned and then left, knowing she was safe. Her family would lend her an escort of slaves when she wanted to go back to the Aventine.

After the tension at Marina's I felt stiff and in need of action. I made a detour for some weight training. There was plenty for a man to do at the gymnasium. I managed to linger for hours.

'We're seeing a lot of this customer lately,' Glaucus commented in his wry way.

'You guessed it; the customer is trying to avoid his family!'

Calmer, I nearly put off further investigation. But kissing Helena publicly in the street had reminded me of my preference for kissing her more privately. If Petronius decided to arrest me there would be no point struggling to rehouse us, but if I could manage to keep out of jail, new furniture for my wrecked apartment was a priority.

'Petronius was looking for you,' Glaucus warned me. My trainer had a restrained way of speaking that could play on my worst fears.

'Skip it. I'm avoiding Petro as well . . .'

I didn't care whether or not I interviewed my father, but Petronius Longus would never expect to find me in his company, so a visit to Geminus promised me some breathing-space. Besides, where my father was I might find a cheap bed. So I set off for the Saepta Julia.

With my cloak around my ears, I emerged from the bathhouse into the Forum, skulked past the Temple of Fortune below the Citadel, and furtively made for the Theatre of Marcellus, my starting-point for a hike into the Campus Martius. Everyone I passed seemed to look at me twice, as if my tunic had a foreign cut or my face was a suspicious shape.

Now that I was going to see Geminus my sour mood returned. I still felt restless. Little did I know I was heading for a chance to expend real energy.

Many public buildings have been inflicted on the Campus by men who thought they ought to be famous – all those pompously named theatres, baths, porticoes and crypts, with the occasional temple or circus to keep the tourists agape. I passed through without noticing them; I was too busy looking out for officers of the watch, in case Petronius had instructed them to look out for me.

The Saepta Julia lay between the Baths of Marcus Agrippa and a Temple of Isis; it had the Temple of Bellona at the end nearest my approach. I took a long detour round the Flaminian Circus, partly to stay unobtrusive. I was too bored to go straight up the road which reaches the Saepta the simple way. I came out near Pompey's Theatre, facing the long Porticus in front of it. I could hear a lot of noise, so I turned my boots that way.

The Porticus of Pompey was the usual impressive enclosure. Heavy architecture on four sides formed a secluded interior space where men could hang about pretending to admire works of art while they hoped some-

778

thing more lively would turn up: an invitation to dinner, a quarrel, an expensive boy with a body like a Greek god, or at least a cheap female prostitute. Today the interior was stuffed with goods and people. No need for me to walk further: an auction was being held there, supervised by none other than my loathed papa.

The goods he was shifting looked authentic from a distance and only mildly dubious from closer to. He knew the trade.

I could hear him up on his trestle, trying to cajole bids. He had a slow, unsensational voice that carried effortlessly round the inner quadrangle. From his vantage point above the crowd I presumed he would soon see me. I made no attempt at contact. We would be face to face and quarrelling soon enough.

He was trying to rustle up interest in a mixed batch of folding stools. 'Look at this one: pure ivory; beautifully carved. Probably from Egypt. The noble Pompey himself might have sat on it – '

'Pompey had his noble head cut off in Egypt!' a heckler called out cheerfully.

'True, sir, but his noble arse was left intact – '

Pompey's stool was part of a house clearance. Someone had died and the heirs were selling up so they could divide the cash. On inspection these relics of a departed life were faintly sad: half-used flagons of ink and rolls of untouched papyrus, lidless grain jars still part full of wheat, baskets of old boots, bales of blankets, the bowl they used to feed the watchdog from. There were pans with loose handles and oil-lamps with broken noses. Lazy bidders settled their backsides against couches with chipped legs and shredded material: signs of long wear that an owner stops noticing but which stood out pathetically here.

That said, it had been a middle-class household; to me that hinted of bargains, for the family money was probably recent and the chattels had a modern air. I adopted a casual attitude, while scanning the lots eagerly.

No sign of a bed, of course; the one thing I wanted. I could see some good outdoor stoneware (I had no garden, but in Rome dreams are cheap). The outstanding piece in the sale was a pedestal table with a huge citron-wood top that must have cost thousands; even in the open air on a dull winter's day its grain shimmered lustrously. Geminus had had it polished up with oil and beeswax. I drooled, but moved on to a group of neat bronze tripods of various sizes. One, with lion's feet and a nicely scrolled lip to stop things rolling off the top, involved a fascinating device for adjusting its height. I had my head underneath, trying to work out how to move it, when one of the porters nudged me.

'Don't bother. Your old fellow's slapped a huge reserve on that. He wants it himself.'

Trust him.

I glanced at Pa on his trestle, a short but commanding figure with untidy grey curls and a straight, sneering nose. Those dark eyes of his missed nothing. He must have been watching me for some minutes. Gesturing at the tripod, he gave me a derisive wave to confirm that I would be overbid. For a wild second I would have given *anything* to get the adjustable tripod – then I remembered that is how auctioneers grow rich.

I moved on.

The heirs were determined to milk their inheritance. A pair of folding wooden doors that probably once graced a dining-room had been lifted off their pivots. The bronze dolphin from a fountain had been wrenched from its plinth, grazing the poor creature's beak. The looters had even cut handsome painted panels from interior walls, shearing them off on thick rectangles of plaster. Geminus would not approve of it. Neither did I.

Other things were not quite right today. Being a born rifler through rubbish, at first the sale goods held my attention and I hardly noticed the people or the atmosphere. Then gradually I began to suspect that I had walked in on a situation.

The auction would have been publicised for a week or so at the Saepta. Big sell-offs attracted a regular core of buyers, most of whom would be known to Geminus. Some I even recognised myself: dealers, plus one or two private collectors. There was little here for real connoisseurs, so those in search of serious art were already drifting off. The dealers were a shabby, peculiar lot, but they were there for a purpose and got on with it. A few passers-by could always be expected to wander in, and the Porticus had its daily quorum of unemployed intellectuals hanging about. Then there were various people looking embarrassed because they were auction novices; they probably included the sellers, trying to check up on Geminus, and curious neighbours of the dead man who had come to pick over his library and sneer at his old clothes.

Among the usual time-wasters in the cloisters I spotted five or six awkwardly large men who did not fit in at all. They stood about in separate places but wafted a clear smell of confederacy. They all wore one-armed tunics like labourers, but with leather accessories that could not have been cheap – wrist-guards, ponderous belts with enamelled buckles, the odd hide cap. Though they sometimes pretended to inspect the merchandise, none of them bid. Geminus had his regular cadre of porters bringing the lots to him, but they were an elderly squad, significant for their small size and meek manners. He never paid much; his labour force had stayed with him out of habit, not because they were growing fat on it.

It struck me that if thieves were planning to raid a sale in progress (which had been known), I had best hang around.

Hardly had I reached this magnanimous decision, when the trouble began.

XXII

More people were arriving to swell the crowd: ordinary men in twos and threes, wearing ordinary tunics and cloaks. Nothing to get stirred up about.

Geminus had moved on to the lamps.

'First lot in this section: an important piece, gentlemen – ' He was not a lamps man; big pots and carpentry were what grabbed his attention, so he was galloping through the lighting more rapidly than it deserved. 'A silver lampadarium, in the form of a Corinthian column, deft architectural detailing, four arms, one lamp chain is missing but could easily be replaced by a competent silversmith. An extremely nice item . . . Who'll start at a thousand?'

Bids were sluggish. Winter is a bad time for selling. The gloomy weather made everything, even deft architectural detailing, look dull. If people care for their heirs they should die when it's hot.

A yard from me a customer, one of the ordinary cloak men, pulled a plum-coloured coverlet from a basket. It had a loose end of fringe dangling; he gave it a disparaging tug, which was fair comment, but then turned to his companion with a laugh and deliberately ripped a yard more from its stitches.

A porter stepped forward adroitly and reclaimed the material. Most people noticed nothing. But I spotted two of the big lads moving disturbingly closer.

'Now a charming set,' Geminus was announcing. 'A pair of candelabra in the form of trees, one with a pine marten creeping up the stem to catch a bird in the branches – ' Someone to the left of me knocked the elbow of a porter who had been carrying a rack of condiment pots; little brown jars skittled everywhere, their gooey contents sticking sandals to the gravel as people tried to step away but found their feet welded to the pathway by old fish pickle. 'The other column has a household cat about to spring – ' A porter sprang, just in time to steady a pile of round silver scroll boxes that were teetering off balance.

Around me the atmosphere was altering. In a second, for no obvious reason, the mood became rough. I spotted the eldest porter swiping a large gilded urn from the centre of the big citron table; he threw the metalware into a chest and slammed the lid for safety. Above the heads of the crowd I spied one columnar lamp being wielded so that it tangled in the thicket of others waiting to be sold, knocking them down like pine trees in a hurricane. Two dealers, who realised what was happening, stepped back on their way out and accidentally fell among crates of kitchen gear. Cries of alarm went up as innocent viewers found themselves being jostled. Fine goods received rough treatment. Sensitive people took elbow jabs in delicate spots.

Near the auctioneer's raised platform the populace had thinned out fast as damage occurred on every side. Pottery was smashing all around and loose bronzes were bowling under foot. One of the large thugs was grappling another man, with dangerous results for Geminus; they swayed furiously against the trestle, which creaked and collapsed. I heard Geminus call a warning that changed into protest. After forty years of bellowing bids, his yell cut the air with a rasp that hurt, then he disappeared in a jumble of slats and spars.

The porters were doing what they were supposed to if a fracas arose: throwing themselves on the stuff, best pieces first, then hurling it back into the carts and crates in which it had been brought to the Porticus. As Gornia, their foreman, nipped past me gathering up valuables, he squawked, 'Show some filial piety, Marcus; give us a bloody hand with this!'

Filial piety was not my strong point, but I was prepared to join in a fight. I looked around for something useful. I seized a curtain-pole; it still had a curtain attached, so I wound that round hastily before whirling the whole heavy flagstaff to clear myself space. It marked me as trouble. As two of the big men in the hide caps ran at me, I swung the rod across their knees and cut off their rush like sickling corn.

Suddenly my father scrambled out of the wreckage of his stand. He was clutching the auction cash box and looked a nasty reddish colour. 'Not them! Not them!' I ignored him. (The traditional filial response.) 'Go for the other lot, you idiot – ' The big chaps I had been attacking must be muscle Geminus had hired. Things must be desperate if he actually paid for protection.

I grabbed his arm and pulled him upright while he still mithered on at me. 'Settle down, Pa. I haven't damaged your bouncers – ' Well, not much.

His frustrated cry was cut off as one of the supposedly innocent customers rammed him in the chest with a rolled carpet. Still breathless from his previous fall, he could not resist the blow.

One of the bouncers grabbed the 'customer' who had felled Geminus. Seizing him round the waist, he swung the fellow, carpet and all, so that he belted another troublemaker sideways with his woven load. Struggling to realign my loyalties I whammed my curtain-pole into the second man, and batted him back again. It cleared a path for my father to escape with the cash box (his main priority), while I launched myself into the midst of another fracas. Someone had a reading-couch completely up-ended on one of its sphinx-shaped ends and was turning it towards a group of bystanders. I managed to lean on him while another came at me. The end of my pole painfully settled that one, though I lost my weapon in the process. The couch crashed down, leaving one sphinx with a broken wing and several folk with badly squashed toes. Somebody came at me from behind. Applying my shoulder as I spun round, I knocked my assailant on to his back on the citron table; I gripped his belly and with a wild shove skidded him along the polished wood. His belt stud scoured out a livid white scar. My father, reappearing at exactly the wrong moment, hollered with anguish; he would rather have seen ten men butchered than witness fine wood being damaged.

The leather boys were slow learners. They still regarded me as part of the organised rumpus. I was fighting back, while I tried to remember to hit the big lads gently in order to lessen Father's compensation claim. Even so, if they charged him by the bruise, he would soon be digging deep.

It was no time for finesse. I aimed a large stone pestle at someone's neck; it missed, but the sensational crack as it hit the ground stopped him short in his tracks. I managed to shut another's man arm in a heavy box so that he screamed out with pain. I saw my father ramming someone against a column as if he were trying to demolish the whole Porticus. At this point the porters grew tired of protecting the silverware and raced in ready to break teeth. The little old chaps were tougher than they looked. Soon wiry arms were flailing and bald heads were butting people as the auction staff took a hand. The giants had finally grasped that I was family and lined up with me. The opposition decided their hour was up and fled.

'Do we follow them?' I yelled at Gornia, the whiskery chief porter. He shook his head.

A mop of grey curls appeared again as my father brought his presence to bear on the wreckage of his sale. 'This won't encourage the buyers. I think we'll call it a day!'

'That's shrewd!' I was busy reassembling a fold-up chair that had been unfolded rather too drastically. 'Strikes me, someone else blew the trumpet on this sale . . .' When I got the chair back together, I sat down on it like a Persian king surveying a battlefield.

Geminus had clapped a consoling arm around one of the muscle-men; he was holding his eye after a particularly well-aimed blow from me early on in the fight. Several of the others had shines that would be glowing by tomorrow. I was well bruised myself, come to that. They gave me what I hoped were admiring looks; I started to feel exposed.

'Those are big lads. Do you buy them by the yard?'

'Trust you to attack the hired help!' grumbled Geminus through a split lip.

'How was I to know you had your own cohorts? I thought your old lads were on their own with it. I'd have stepped aside if I'd realised these lummoxes were being paid to get their knuckles grazed!'

Coughing with exertion, Geminus fell on to an unsold couch. He was showing his age. 'Jupiter, I could do without all this!'

I stayed silent for a while. My breathing had already stabilised, but my thoughts were running fast. Around us the toughs made a feeble show of helping the porters tidy the mess, while the old chaps worked with their usual uncomplaining zeal. If anything, the fight had perked up their spirits.

My father let them get on with it in a way that made me think this had happened before. I gazed at him, while he pointedly ignored my interest. He was a solid man, shorter and wider than I always remembered him, with a face that could pass for handsome and a nature some folk found attractive. He annoyed me – but I had been brought up by schoolmasters who declaimed that Roman fathers were stern, wise and models of humane ethics. This high-minded philosophy made no allowance for those who drink, play draughts and womanise – let alone for mine, who did most of those things sometimes, and never seemed to have read the elegant grammarians who said a Roman boy could expect his papa to spend all day thinking noble thoughts and sacrificing to the household gods. Instead of taking me down to the Basilica Julia to explain what the barristers were arguing about, mine took me to the Circus Maximus – though only when the ticket gate was being manned by his cousin, who gave us cheap rates. When I was a child, sneaking into the Games at a discount was a source of deep embarrassment to me.

It never happened to Livy.

'You were expecting trouble,' I tackled my father. 'Want to talk about what's going on?'

'All in a day's work,' replied Geminus, through his teeth.

'This was a set-up – organised disruption. Is it a racket? Who's responsible?' I had been drawn into the argument, and I wanted to know its cause.

'Somebody, no doubt.' Dear gods, he could be an awkward mule.

'Well sort it out yourself then!'

'I will, boy. I will.' Wondering how such a miserable old groucher could have fathered such a reasonable character as myself, I leaned back my head and closed my eyes. I had only just noticed I was beginning to stiffen all over, and had gone deaf in my left ear. 'Anyway,' retaliated my father, 'you took your time arriving. I expected you two hours ago.'

I opened my eyes again. 'No one knew I was on my way.'

'That right? I was told that you wanted a fatherly chat.'

'Then you were told wrong!' I worked it out. 'Helena's been here.' She was incorrigible. It was not enough to leave her outside her father's house; I should have pushed her right in through the door and told the Senator to put the bar across.

My father leered. 'Nice girl!'

'Don't bother telling me she could do better for herself.'

'All right, I won't bother to tell you . . . So how's the love life coming along?'

I grunted. 'Last time I saw her, she kneed me in the groin.'

'Ouch! Thought you'd filched a demure one!' he scoffed, wincing. 'What bad company taught her that trick?'

'Taught her myself.' He looked startled. I felt tetchy suddenly, and launched off against old grievances. 'Listen, you may live among the sleek cats now, but you must still remember what it's like to be holed up in an Aventine tenement – all men with evil thoughts and no door locks. I can't protect her all the time. Besides, if today is anything to go by, I'll never know where she is. Women are supposed to stay at home weaving,' I grumbled bitterly. 'Helena pays no attention to that.'

I had said more than I intended. My father leaned on one elbow, lolling there as if I had passed him a dish of interesting winkles but no serving spoon. 'She's still with you, anyway . . . So when is the wedding?'

'When I'm rich.'

He whistled offensively. 'Someone's expecting a long wait then!'

'That's our business.'

'Not if you make me a grandfather before you achieve the formalities.'

This was a sore point, and I reckoned he knew it. He had probably heard through the family grapevine that Helena had miscarried once, distressing us both more than either of us expected, and filling us with the usual unspoken doubts about our ability ever to produce a healthy child. Now Helena was terrified, while I was trying to delay the question for life's strongest reason: poverty. The last thing I needed was my damned father taking an interest. I knew why the old snob was so curious: he wanted us to have a family so he could boast he

787

was related to a senator. I said angrily, 'You're a grandfather already. If you want to lavish attention where it's needed, try Victorina's orphans.'

'So what's Mico doing?'

'The usual: not much.' My father heard this without a reaction, though it was possible he would help. 'Did you go to the funeral?' I asked, more inquisitive than I wanted to appear.

'No. My assistance was deemed unnecessary.' His mood was quiet, his manner uninvolved. I could not tell whether he was upset; I was not sure I cared.

'Victorina was your daughter,' I said formally. 'You should have been given the opportunity.'

'Don't break your heart over it.'

'If I had been here you would have been informed.' Playing the prig was not my style, but his air of resignation annoyed me. 'You can't blame anyone; you're not exactly famous as a paterfamilias!'

'Don't start!'

I hauled myself to my feet. 'Don't worry. I'm off.'

'You haven't tackled what you came to ask.'

'Helena was here; she asks my questions for me.'

'I don't talk to women.'

'Maybe you should try it for once.' Maybe he should have tried it when he was living with my mother.

It had been pointless even coming here. I could not face an argument over Festus; I really was leaving. My father, looking for something he could be awkward about, was furious. 'Right! We've entertained you with a scrap, now you run off and tell your ma you've got your tunic dirty playing on the Campus with the big rough boys.'

In the act of flinging my cloak round me, I paused. This was not helping me solve the Censorinus case. Besides, I did need a story to tell my mother, and I needed it fairly soon. She was renowned for her impatience with slackers. 'There is something I want,' I conceded.

Geminus swung his legs off the couch so he could sit up and stare at me. 'This is a novelty!'

'Wrong. I'm simply on the scrounge. Does your warehouse at the Saepta contain a cheap but decent bed?'

He looked sadly disappointed, but did rouse himself to take me there.

XXIII

The Saepta Julia was a large enclosed area where voting took place. It had been remodelled by the energetic Marcus Agrippa, Augustus's general and son-in-law. Since he could see he would never get a chance to be Emperor himself, he had made his mark in the next best way: by building larger and with more innovation and magnificence than anybody else. He had had a good eye for the best spots to glorify. Much of the modern Campus Martius was his work.

Agrippa had transformed the Saepta from little more than a giant sheep pen to one of the gems in his memorial complex. It now formed an architectual match with the Pantheon and the great Agrippan Baths that sprawled majestically alongside – most famous for having free public entrance. Marcus Agrippa had certainly known how to buy popularity. The space enclosed by the Saepta was big enough to be used for gladiatorial combats, and had even been flooded for mock sea fights in Nero's day, though that had proved inconvenient for the people who normally worked there. Businessmen are not impressed by having to close their premises to allow in a group of fancy triremes. The enclosing walls, two storeys high, contained a variety of shops, especially goldsmiths and bronze-founders, plus associated folk like my father, who for years had been earning a fortune from the second-hand art and antiques trade.

Because of the political connection there was another side to the place. It would have been useful for me to have my own office in the Saepta; it was where people brought my kind of work. My father's presence was the main reason I kept away from the area, though traditionally the Saepta Julia was where the informers hung out.

I mean the other informers – the ones who had given my business its bad name. Those vermin whose heyday was under Nero, skulking behind temple pillars to overhear unguarded comments from the pious, or even using

790

conversations at private dinner parties to betray their last night's hosts. The political parasites who, before Vespasian purged public life, had put fear into the whole Senate. The slugs who had empowered bad emperors' favourites, and oiled the jealousies of worse emperors' mothers and wives. Gossips whose stock-in-trade was scandal; bastards whose very oath in court could be bought for an emerald eardrop.

Right at the start of my career I had decided that clients who went to the Saepta looking for an informer were not clients who wanted me.

I lost a lot of trade that way.

Leases in the Saepta Julia were at a premium; my father had managed to acquire two. Like Festus, he knew how things were done. I suppose having cash helped, but reputation must also have come into it. Whereas some traders struggled to fit themselves into hole-in-the-wall lock-ups, Geminus had a select suite on the upper floor, where he could stroll out on to the balcony and survey the whole enclosure below, plus a large warehouse at ground level, which was obviously more convenient for delivery of large or heavy items. His office, always stylishly fitted out, adjoined the Dolabrium, where votes were counted – throbbing with life during elections, and pleasantly quiet at other times.

We started downstairs, in his main display area. After the usual attempts to palm me off with three-legged, woodwormy frames and oddly padded couches marked with dubious sickroom stains, I persuaded my parent that if he wanted me to perpetuate the family name it ought to be done on decent equipment. He found me a bed. I refused to pay what he said it was worth, so rather than lose the chance of sharing a grandchild with the illustrious Camillus, he halved the asking price.

'Throw in the mattress, will you. Helena can't sleep on just the webs.'

'I'd like to know where you acquired your cheek!'

'Same place I learned not to sob too much when auctioneers start pretending they are facing bankruptcy.'

He grunted, still fidgeting around my purchase. 'This is pretty plain, Marcus – ' The bed had a straightforward beech frame, with boxy ends. I liked the simple scallop ornament that enlivened the headboard. The mere fact it had four feet on the ground would be a luxury in my house. 'I'm having doubts. This is meant to be shoved in a wall niche,' Geminus fussed unhappily.

'I don't want silver legs and tortoiseshell. Why encourage burglars? When can you deliver?'

He looked offended. 'You know the system. Cash down, and buyer collects.'

'Stuff the system! Bring it round as soon as possible and I'll pay you when I see you. I'm still at Fountain Court.'

'That dung heap! Why don't you get a decent job and start honouring your debts? I'd like to see you install that girl of yours in a nice town house with an atrium.'

'Helena can manage without marble corridors and spare stools.'

'I doubt it!' he said. If I was honest, so did I.

'She's looking for a man of character, not libraries and a private lavatory.'

'Oh she's found that!' he sneered. 'All right, I'll have the bed taken to your flea-pit, but don't expect the favour to be repeated. It's not for you I'm doing this . . . Helena bought an item, so I'll be sending a cart up the Hill anyway.'

It gave me an odd feeling to hear my father, whom I could barely tolerate, speaking of Helena Justina with such familiarity. I had never even introduced them; not that that had stopped him presenting himself behind my back and assuming instant paternal rights. 'What item?' I growled.

He knew he had me. I could have swiped the grin off his face with the nearest besom. 'The girl has taste,' he commented. 'She pipped you on the nail . . .'

I hated to show my interest, but I had guessed. 'That tripod table! How much did you sting her for?'

He chortled annoyingly.

The porters were bringing back the unsold goods from the interrupted auction. As they hauled in the savaged wall panels I said, 'Whoever buys the house those were ripped from will need the holes repaired. You could send Mico round to offer his services to make good.'

'Make bad, you mean? All right, I'll give him the address.'

'If he's lucky the new owners won't have heard about him. Anyway, his bodging can be covered up before it's noticed. The wall plaster will need painting,' I mused, trying to wheedle out information without him noticing. 'No doubt you were already thinking of a commission for suggesting a panel artist?' My father refused to bite. Like Festus, he could be secretive about business affairs. I tried again. 'I suppose you know all the hack picture painters?'

This time the twinkle in his eye that had once drawn the women appeared. Nowadays it was dry and dark and sceptical. He knew I was prodding at something specific. 'First the bed; now renovation. Are you planning to gild your filthy doss-house like a palace? Careful, Marcus! I hate to see inappropriate ornamentation . . .'

'Just a few false perspectives,' I joked back feebly. 'A landscape with satyrs for the bedroom and a set of still lifes in the kitchen. Dead pheasants and fruit bowls . . . Nothing too elaborate.' I was getting nowhere. I had to be direct. 'Helena must have told you. I want to track down a group of daubers I once saw Festus meet at a cheap bar on the lower Caelian. It was a hovel called the Virgin.'

'She told me,' he agreed, like someone refusing to enlighten a small child as to what he might be getting for a Saturnalia gift.

'So do you know them?'

'I'm not aware of it. No jury,' declared my father, 'will convict a man for being kept in ignorance of his son's friends!'

I ignored the jibe. Angrily I burst out, 'I suppose you are also going to tell me you know nothing about the scheme Festus was running just before he died?'

'That's right,' Geminus answered levelly. 'That's exactly what I'll say.'

'You're not talking to Censorinus now!' I reminded him.

'No. I'm talking to you.' This kind of conversation only occurs in families. 'It's a waste of good air,' he grumbled, then stretched abruptly. 'This is typical of you – riding the mule backwards, staring at the tail flicking flies off its arse! I thought we would have come to the soldier half an hour ago, but you do have to dally in the byways pretending you forgot

793

what you were sent to find out – I know you were sent!' he scoffed, as I started interrupting. He knew I would not have come on my own account. 'If we have to rake over old miseries, let's start at the beginning – and let's do it respectably over a drink!'

That was when he gripped me by the elbow as if I had raised a sensitive issue too publicly, and steered me from the open frontage of his warehouse to the discreet haven of his office on the upper floor.

I felt like a man who was about to be sold a fake silver wine-heater with one foot that keeps dropping off.

XXIV

On my very occasional visits I had noticed that my father's office changed in mood and character as he sold off whatever choice pieces adorned it. To this private quarter were brought his most select customers – the ones who had to think themselves special for the next half an hour while he palmed them off with something. Here they were seated on ivory, or chased silver, or sweetly scented oriental woods, while Geminus produced exquisitely decorated cups of spicy wine and told them lies until they found themselves buying more than their budget could afford. Today he had a suite from Alexandria: delicate painted coffers and sideboards on slim legs, with horned ibis and lotus-flower patterns. To complement the Egyptian look he had dug out some tall peacock fans (permanent props, which I had seen before), and added sumptuously tasselled cushions to the odd, hard couch that had lived there for ever and was not for sale. Behind the couch hung a dark red curtain; behind that, actually bricked into the wall, was his bank box.

Before we talked, he went to the box and stashed the takings from today's auction. I knew his habits about money were methodical. He never opened the bank chest in front of the staff, let alone customers. I was treated differently – one of the few ways he acknowledged that I was family. In my presence he would quietly go to the box and unlock it with the key he kept round his neck on a thong, as if we two, like he and Festus, were in some sort of partnership. But it had only happened since my brother died.

He dropped the curtain hastily as a lad came in bringing the usual galley tray of wine and bowls of almonds. 'Hello, Falco!' grinned the youth, seeing me leaning on a wall like a spare broom. Then he looked uneasy. None of the staff knew quite what to make of me. The first few times I came here I had refused to admit to any relationship; now they all knew I was the master's son, but they could see I was not on the same easy

795

terms as Festus. No one could blame them if they found that hard to understand; faced with my father, I felt confused myself.

Since I was not a customer the lad seemed to have second thoughts about the refreshments, but Papa grabbed at the wine flask, so he left the tray with us. 'That watch captain you know was looking for you, Falco! Some judge wants to interview you.'

Surprised, I threw nuts down my throat too rapidly, then choked. Geminus assumed that knowing look of fathers, though waited for the boy to leave before he spoke: 'Is this about the unpleasantness at Flora's?'

'Do I gather you know that dump?'

I thought he gave me a wry look. The caupona was uncomfortably close to Mother's. 'I've been there a few times.' Flora's had only existed for ten or twelve years; it postdated Pa's return from Capua. But Festus was always hanging round the place. Anyone who knew Festus was bound to have heard of it. 'Helena told me you were being fingered. Sounds as if Petronius is about to step on your tail.'

'He's given me time,' I assured him, like a man of the world who was merely threatened by a creditor who had made him a new cloak and unreasonably wanted payment.

'Oh yes? I do have some influence,' he offered.

'Don't interfere.'

'By the sound of things, you will need bail.'

'It won't come to that.'

'Right.' This was our usual happy repartee. He was hating me and I was enjoying it. 'Let me know when we all have to come to court and cheer while the bastards convict you!' We were silent while he poured wine. I left mine on the shelf where he had placed the cup. 'Oh drink up and don't be so pompous. We've been here before; you're in deep trouble, but you don't want help, especially from me – '

'Oh I want your help!' I snarled. 'I don't expect to get it, but I want to know what in Hades has been going on.'

'Sit down and calm down. You're not in some cheap drinking-house.'

I refused to sit, but forced control into my tone: 'It's obvious something happened before our famous hero speared himself at Bethel. My guess is that you were in it with him, but you hoped the affair had happened too far away to bring repercussions here.'

'It was nothing to do with me.' He made no effort to avoid self-righteousness.

'Then you've no reason to avoid telling me about it! We all have to face the truth,' I said grittily. 'The Fifteenth have been restationed and all the ones we apparently owe money to are making sure they snatch home leave. One man came to stir the porridge pot, and now he's dead someone else is bound to follow. This will not go away.' My father inclined his head dourly, agreeing that point at least, so I carried on. 'Whoever knifed Censorinus may have met him by accident – or they may be in on the story too. If so, I don't fancy meeting them on a dark stair. Somebody in the past must have stepped in a very nasty cow-pat, and now the stink has reached home. At the moment it's attached to me, but you won't be surprised to hear I'm planning on a good wash-down.'

'You need more than a plan.'

I felt my chest tighten. 'Is this guesswork or fact?'

'Bit of both,' said my father.

He was ready to talk. Since the winecup was handy and I hate waste, I grasped it and attached my posterior to a low stool. I had chosen a tight corner, preferring this to greater comfort. Above me a dog-headed god sneered inscrutably down his long snout from the flank of a cupboard. 'We have to discuss Festus,' I insisted in a low voice.

Our father laughed briefly, almost to himself. 'Big subject!' He stared into his wine. We were drinking from small, stupid metal cups, fancy items designed for courtesy, not serious thirst-quenching. He held his between the tips of two fingers and a thumb; he had large hands with stubby fingers, the same shape as my brother's. On his right hand he wore a grand seal ring with a haematite stone and a smaller gold one with the head of a Claudian emperor, an oddly conventional set for a man in his trade who was constantly seeing much finer jewellery. In some ways he was a conventional man, more so than either of his sons.

On his left third finger he still wore his wedding ring; I never knew why. Maybe he never thought about it.

'Marcus Didius Festus . . .' Geminus furrowed his brow. 'Everyone thought he was special. Maybe he was. Or maybe he just could have been –'

'Don't get maudlin,' I urged impatiently. 'Festus had flair and courage. Big brother thought nothing of running a business venture from the army, from a thousand miles away. But he must have had a receiver at this end, and you must have been him.'

'We shared some joint investments,' he agreed.

'Like what?'

Geminus waved a hand. 'You're sitting on some of it.' The Egyptian furniture. 'Festus found this when the Fifteenth were in Alexandria. It came in a load that was shipped over just before he died.'

'I didn't see it the last time I was here.'

'No, I've just decided to get rid of it.' I knew selling could be a matter of mood. A man could lose heart extolling his dead partner's treasures; more so when the partner had also been his favourite son. 'When Festus died this just got left. Somehow I couldn't face dealing with it. But when that lag from the Fifteenth came round I took notice again. I don't know why I kept it so long; it's not my style, this lightweight stuff.'

'So where was it?'

'I had it at home.'

At this mention of the house he shared with the woman he had run off with, the atmosphere stiffened. I knew where he lived. I had never been inside, but presumably the dwelling bulged with enticing collectables. 'I thought you might still have a warehouse full of big brother's tasty imports?'

My father looked unreliable. 'There may be a few items at Scaro's old barn.' This was out on the Campagna, on Great-Uncle Scaro's farm, a place Pa had used for long-term storage after he married Ma. (Free use of her brothers' outbuildings was one obvious reason he first took to her.) My father stopped going out there when he abandoned home, but later on Festus took over the barn. 'When I got in touch with your Uncle Fabius he assured me it was virtually empty.'

'Fabius wouldn't recognise a box labelled *Bullion*! Mind if I take a look some time?'

'You'll go if you want to, whatever I say.'

'Thanks for the warrant!'

'Keep your hands off the stuff, if there is any.'

'I don't steal. Don't forget I'm big brother's executor. Anyway, I'll only go if I'm out of jail. I have a few serious questions to answer for Petronius before I can consider field trips. Look, tell me about Censorinus. I know he was whinging about some project that had failed, but I have no details and I certainly don't know why he was so secretive. Was Festus importing something illegal from Greece?'

Pa looked indignant. 'Why should he? Are you saying he was robbing temples or something?' I would not have put it past him. 'Greece is stuffed with desirable art,' Father demurred. 'There was no need to raid holy shrines. Anyway, it's no secret. Festus had acquired a mixed cargo of statues, giant urns and vases. He added some conventional goods from Syria and Judaea: linen, purple dye, cedar logs.'

'You sound annoyed.'

'I'm not a bloody merchant. I hate that sort of hardware. Festus fixed it up himself. Jupiter knows how he broke into the local cartels, but you know what he was like. The Tyrian Purple Guild has been officially closed to foreigners for a thousand years, but I expect they welcomed our boy like a long-lost Phoenician prince ... He hired a ship called the *Hypericon*; it sank off Crete.'

'You weren't involved in it?'

'No. I told you. The *Hypericon* was his own venture. He laid it on while he was out in the East. That was why he was using his comrades to provide capital. He had heard about this load; it clearly included top-rate items and there was no time to contact me.' I knew that in their partnership it was my brother who provided the entrepreneurial spirit; Pa was the financier. Festus was a finder; Pa bought and sold. That worked when they could make arrangements in advance, but posed difficulties otherwise. Corresponding with Judaea could take anything from fifteen days, if the tides and winds were right, up to half a year. Or infinity, if your ship sank.

I thought it through, to familiarise myself with the wrinkles. 'If Festus had access to good pickings, he would not allow sheer distance to inconvenience the scheme. Or lack of funds.

So he involved his mess-tent cronies and they lost their cash. That's a tragedy, but what's the peculiar angle? Why the big fuss now? What was odd about this load?'

'Nothing.' Geminus spoke quietly. 'As far as I know the batch was normal. What smelled was the backing money.'

'You know that?'

'I believe it.'

'So how come?'

'Work it out.'

I considered the problem. 'What are we talking about – a few old marble gods and a bunch of blackware alabastrons?'

'Not according to Censorinus. From what he said, Festus had laid hands on enough top-quality ceramics to stock a private museum. The statuary was supposed to be outstanding. That was why he needed more cash than usual; that's why he would not risk jeopardising the deal by taking time to contact me.'

'Did you and he not have banking arrangements overseas?'

'Up to a point.' For a moment I wondered whether Pa had had limited faith in big brother's probity. He smiled slightly, seeing my doubts. But he gave me the public explanation: 'I hate investing heavily in cargoes from abroad: one bent captain, one awkward customs officer, or one big storm and it's lost. Festus found that out the hard way when the *Hypericon* foundered.'

'He was a hothead. He had good taste, but airy ideas.'

'Selling bubbles,' agreed Geminus. There was a trace of admiration in his tone. His own character was cautious, almost cynical; I had inherited that. But perhaps we both yearned to be able to take wild risks with my brother's happy bravery.

'I still don't see why the Fifteenth Apollinaris have come on our tails over it now.'

'Desperation.' My father's tone grew flat. 'Apparently the best piece in this missing cargo had the legionaries' name on it. Where would a bunch of active-service centurions get the cash to purchase a Phidias?'

'A *Phidias*?' He had handed me two shocks at once. 'This is the first I've heard about Festus cornering the market in the Seven Wonders of the World.'

'So he thought big!' shrugged our pa. Not for the first time I felt second-best in the family scheme.

'When I joked about robbing temples, I didn't have the statue of Zeus from Olympia in mind!'

'He told me it was a Poseidon,' reported my father drily. 'He did say that it was fairly small.'

'That probably meant it was huge! You knew about this?' I demanded incredulously.

'Only when it was too late to be jealous. I heard the *Hypericon* had sunk. On that last leave Festus confessed he had suffered a major loss with her, and he told me about the Poseidon.' Festus must have been bursting with it, even after his plan disintegrated.

'Did you believe the story?'

'I found it hard to take seriously. Festus was drunk most of the time on that leave – though if he *had* lost a Phidias, it's understandable. I would have been drunk myself. In fact, after he told me I soon was.'

'Well the god's appropriate, Father. If Festus had the genuine article on board the *Hypericon*, it's now at the bottom of the sea.'

'And that's where his mates in the Fifteenth may wish they were,' Geminus growled, 'if my theory of why they are so agitated holds good.'

'So what is your theory?' My sense of foreboding grew steadily.

Geminus drained his cup with an angry gesture. 'That your brother's honourable comrades had bought themselves a Phidias by robbing their legion's savings bank.'

As soon as he said it, the ghastly tale made sense.

'Dear gods. If they get found out, that's a capital offence.'

'I think we can assume,' Pa told me, with the light, wry air that my brother had not inherited, 'Censorinus was hoping you and I would pay the money back in time to save their skins. The Jewish Revolt is well in hand, the Fifteenth Apollinaris have come to a pause in their glorious military task, normal military life resumes, and – '

'Don't say it. They are now expecting a visit from the Treasury auditors!'

XXV

Things were falling into place, but they made me no happier.

The room felt cold. My corner seat had become so uncomfortable I wanted to leap up and prowl about, but was held in my place by horror.

Ma had asked me to clear my brother's name. The deeper I went, the worse things appeared. If this were true, I could not believe Festus had been unaware of the source of his funding; in fact a fear was gnawing at me that big brother might well have suggested it.

Each army legion possesses a savings bank, stored in a holy of holies under the headquarters shrine. As well as the compulsory deductions from his pay that each soldier suffers for food and equipment, and the contribution to the burial club which will give him a reverent funeral, the administration ensures that if he reaches discharge after his twenty-five years of suffering, he will go into the world with some standing: half of every imperial donative is forcibly locked up for him. These are the lavish grants paid out by new emperors on their accession, or at other times of crisis, to ensure the legions' loyalty. In a full-term career every legionary must expect to have his loyalty ensured on several occasions – and it does not come cheap.

The money is sacrosanct. A batch of clerks take care of it, and of course it represents a scandal just waiting to happen, so much cash permanently sitting about in boxes, out on the wild frontiers of the Empire. But if there had ever been such a scandal, I had never heard of it. Trust my brother to involve himself in this fabulous first!

My mind raced. If the Fifteenth did now have a large hole in their coffer, there could be reasons why it had not yet been spotted. The savings banks had been frequently topped up during the Year of the Four Emperors: four new men on the throne, during a harsh civil war, had found that pleasing the armed forces became a high priority. One reason for Galba's

802

downfall was his reluctance to pay the customary grateful donative to the army when he came into the purple; his three successors learned from his bloody corpse in the Forum, and contributed promptly. With all these extras pounding in, the centurions of the loyal Fifteenth could have put some large rocks at the bottom of the legion's coffer, and got away with the deception.

But those uncertain days were over. Now their famous general Vespasian had become Emperor and was settling his backside on the cushioned throne for a long reign: a tax-collector's son, much given to cash-counting. The return of normality gave clerks more time to put money into piles and tick off lists on their papyrus scrolls. The bankrupt Treasury meant that auditors were Rome's coming profession. Eager accountants were out and about everywhere, looking for missing cash. It could not be long before somebody spotted a hole the size of even a smallish Phidias in a prestigious legion's money chest.

'This is not good news for the family name,' I commented.

My father had the expression you would expect of a man who is about to see his son the national hero publicly exposed, especially when his other son is taking the initiative. 'Looks like a straight choice between losing the family name, or losing the family fortune protecting it.' His comment was essentially cynical.

'That's your fortune then. It's a choice I don't have!'

'Fancy!' commented Geminus, unenthusiastically.

'We need to be braced for trouble. I don't give two peas for my reputation, but I don't relish finding angry soldiers lurking at Mother's house wanting to crack my head. Is there anything else I should be aware of in this mess?'

'Not as far as I know.' The way he said it told me there was more to be found out.

I had struggled enough for one day. I let it go, and moved on to other aspects: 'One thing puzzles me.' That was an understatement, but I had to be practical. Counting all the unknowns in this story would leave me depressed. 'Festus served in Egypt and Judaea. The missing cargo came from Greece. Would it be too pedantic to ask how come?'

'He was using an agent. He met a man in Alexandria – '

'That sounds like the beginning of a very sticky story!'

'Well you know Festus; he always had a lupin round himself. He got around the backstreets and shady bars.' My father meant Festus was always involved in numerous little enterprises, doing deals and supplying services.

'True. If there was a man selling counterfeit amulets, Festus always knew him.'

'That doesn't mean he bought the produce with the fishy smell,' Geminus argued, defending his lamented boy.

'Oh no!' I carolled facetiously. 'But sometimes he was taken in.'

'Not in this.'

'Well, let's keep the possibility in mind! Alexandria is a city with a dubious reputation to start with. Wherever he went, Festus could always be relied on to fall in with the man other people avoid. Do we have a name for the agent he was using?'

'What do you think?'

'No name!'

'Call him Nemo, like Odysseus. Nemo moved in the art world; he told Festus he could get hold of some exquisite Greek artefacts. Presumably he did it. That's all I know.'

'Did Festus at any point actually inspect this cargo?'

'Of course. Your brother had his head on,' insisted Pa. 'Festus saw it in Greece.'

'He got around!'

'Yes. Festus was a boy.'

'I thought the *Hypericon* sailed from Caesarea?'

'Was that the story from Censorinus? Presumably she went there afterwards so Festus could add his cedar wood and the dye. Maybe that was where he paid the agent for the vases and the other stuff.'

'Did the agent sail on with the ship?'

Father gave me a long look. 'Unknown quantity.'

'When his ship sank, did that have any bearing on the wound that brought big brother home?'

'Sole purpose of allowing the wound to happen, I should think.'

Festus had got himself home to sort things out. That meant the answer to at least some part of the problem lay here in Rome. So I did have a slim chance of finding it.

My next question would have been whether the events I had witnessed that day at the auction were also relevant. I never asked it. Our conversation was interrupted by a very hot, very tired child.

He was about twelve. His name was Gaius. He was my sister Galla's second-eldest, and an urchin of some character. Most of him was small for his age. He had the gravity of a patriarch and the manners of a lout. Gaius would probably grow up to be a man of modesty and culture, but at the moment he preferred to be difficult. He liked to wear boots that were too big for him. He had tattooed his name on his arm in Greek lettering with something that passed for blue woad; some of the letters were festering. He never washed. Once a month, on Galla's insistence, I took him to the public baths at a quiet period and cleaned him up forcibly.

Bursting into the office, he threw himself on to an empty couch, expelled a huge lungful of air, wiped his nose on the cuff of a nasty-coloured tunic and gasped, 'Jupiter, chasing you takes spunk! Don't just sit there quaking, Uncle Marcus. Give me a drink!'

XXVI

Three generations of the Didius family eyed each other warily. I ignored the plea for liquor. When I sat tight Geminus fed the urchin a small one. 'Oh Grandpa, don't be stingy!' Gaius lifted the wine jug with a deft hand and sloshed out more for himself. I retrieved the jug, then served myself a refill while there was still a chance.

Our host recaptured his jug grumpily and drained out the last trickle. 'What do you want, nipper?'

'Message for Trouble there,' he said, glaring at me.

At home he was known as 'Where's Gaius?' because no one ever knew. He roamed the city on his own in a private world of schemes and dodges: a familiar trait. He was far worse even than Festus, a complete gangster.

Still, his father was a boatman so no one could blame him. The water-flea was a womanising dead loss; even my dim sister kicked him out of their home as often as possible. In those circumstances sophistication in the children had to be ruled out.

I gazed at him benignly. Gaius was unimpressed, but gruffness would have achieved no more. There is nothing you can do, faced with a knowing sprat in an oversized and dirty tunic who behaves like a man twice your age. I felt like a pimply ten-year-old who had just heard where babies come from – and did not believe a word of it. 'Speak up, Hermes! What's the message, Gaius?'

'Petronius has offered half a denarius for the first person to find you.' I thought Petro had more sense. 'The others are all running round like bare-arsed gibbons.' Gaius prided himself on a charming vocabulary. 'Not a lead among them. I used my noddle, though!'

'How come?' twinkled Father. Gaius was acting up for him. To the grandchildren, Pa was a dangerous renegade with a deep hint of mystery. He lived amongst the glittering goldsmiths' halls of the Saepta, in a cavern full of entrancing junk; they all thought he was wonderful. The fact that my mother would go wild if she knew they came here to visit him only added to the intrigue.

'Obvious! Petro said this was one place he had covered; so I ran straight here!'

'Well done,' I observed, while my father scrutinised Galla's tricky offshoot as if he thought he might have identified a new business partner (given my own unsuitable attitude). 'You've found me. Here's a copper for bringing me the warning – now scram.'

Gaius inspected my coin in case it was counterfeit, sneered, then shoved it into a purse at his belt that looked heavier than my own. 'Don't you want the message?'

'I thought that was it?'

'There's more!' he assured me. It was meant to tantalise.

'Forget it.'

'Oh Uncle Marcus!' Robbed of his golden moment, Gaius was reduced to a child again. His thin wail filled the office as I stood up to assume my cloak. He rallied, however. 'It's about that fancy coronet you've persuaded to pay your bills for you!'

'Listen, smacker, that's the love of my life you're insulting. Don't speak of Helena Justina like a charitable foundation – and don't imply I'm hanging round the lady with a view to sequestering her cash!' I thought my father hid a grin. 'Helena Justina,' I declared, in a stately tone, 'is too shrewd to be bluffed by that sort of confidence trick.'

'She's after character!' Pa told the boy.

'So she's taken on a loser!' Gaius smirked back. 'What's the attraction, Grandpa? Is he good in bed or something?'

I pulled his ear, harder than I had meant. 'You're only jealous because Helena is fond of Larius.' Larius was his elder brother, the shy, artistic one. Gaius belched rudely at the comparison. 'Gaius, there's no need to give me the message. I'm well aware of it. Petronius wants to arrest me – and I don't want to know.'

'Wrong,' Gaius informed me, though at last he quailed somewhat. He must have known I was likely to thump him when I heard the news. His voice became much smaller as he announced rather nervously: 'Petronius Longus has arrested your Helena!'

XXVII

The judge lived in an impressive house of the type I could easily covet. Worse, his house might even convince me to aspire to his rank.

It was a detached town villa just off the Vicus Longus, not too large and not too small; it had some fine rooms for impressing public visitors, but was arranged for decent privacy. Marponius never went down to Petro's meagre guardhouse; he had felons brought here for interviews. He had a social conscience. He wanted lags like me to discover the urge to reform through seeing what could come from more legitimate types of crime. Compared to speculation and usury, mere theft and murder began to look unprofitable and quite hard work. Even being an informer seemed a dead-end job.

I presented my person at a ponderous marble portico. The elaborate studs and shiny bronze door furniture were overdone to my mind, but as an auctioneer's son I had seen that much of the world has unsubtle taste. Under the frippery, it was a solid hardwood door. The judge simply belonged to the group that likes to ruin good material.

Marponius and I would never agree on decor. I was a spare-time poet with a refined nature, whose occupation called for a sensitive, humane approach. He was a dull thug from the middle rank who had made himself rich, and therefore significant, by selling scientific encyclopaedias to New Men. By New Men I mean ex-slaves and foreign immigrants; people with overflowing coffers but no education who want to appear cultured. They could afford to buy literary works by weight – and more importantly, they could fit themselves up with ranks of literate slaves to read the works aloud. In the shifting social strata of Rome there was plenty of scope for applying gloss to upstarts. So if a treatise was Greek, incomprehensible and came in twenty scrolls, Marponius had his team of scribes copy it out. He used best-quality papyrus, black gall ink, and highly scented sandalwood for the end-pieces. Then he supplied the slaves with refined voices too. That was where the money lay. It was a neat trick. I wish I had thought of it.

I was kept waiting for some time. When I was finally let into the party, I found Marponius, Petro and Helena sitting together somewhat awkwardly. The first thing they all saw was my bruised face from the auction fight: an unimpressive start.

We were in a bright red and gold salon. The wall panels were a short series of the adventures of Aeneas, shown as rather a stodgy, bow-legged chap – the artist's diplomatic allusion to the owner's own physique. The judge's wife was dead, so Dido was spared such indignity and could appear as a highly voluptuous, handsome young piece having trouble with her drapery. The artist considered himself a dab hand at diaphanous veils.

Like his Aeneas, Marponius had a flat-topped head and a lather of light curly hair, receding each side of his rather square brow. His backside was too large, so he tended to strut like a pigeon with too much tail. As I came in he was just telling Helena he was 'a man of ideas'. A female slave was present for propriety, and she had Petro for extra protection, but Helena knew what men's ideas were like. She was listening with the usual calm expression she applied to stressful situations, though her pale face told me everything.

I crossed the room and kissed her formally on one cheek. Her eyes closed briefly, with relief. 'I'm sorry, Marcus . . .'

I sat alongside on an elaborately gilded couch, and held her hand in a light grip. 'Never apologise!'

'You don't know what I've done!'

I said to Marponius. 'Hail, Judge! I gather from the smell of new paint there is still money in scientific tomes?'

He looked torn. He wanted to slap me down, but had trouble resisting the urge to discuss business. He was proud of his efforts. Unfortunately he was also proud of being a judge. 'Pity it still leaves you time to indulge an interest in criminology. What's the charge against my wench?'

'You're both in this, Falco!' He had a sharp voice, its effect as subtle as dragging a sword across a ceramic plate.

I noticed that Petronius Longus was looking embarrassed. This depressed me. He rarely made a lot of noise, but he was perfectly capable of treating Marponius with the contempt he deserved. When Petro stayed quite so silent things must be bad.

I nodded to him as he picked up on my scrutiny. 'You owe my disreputable nephew Gaius a finder's fee. But I want it on record that I came here voluntarily.' Petro's stare remained unhelpful. I tackled his glib superior. 'So what's going on, Marponius?'

'I am waiting for someone to appear as a spokesman for the lady.'

Women possess no judicial identities; they are not allowed to appear in court, but must have a male relation representing them.

'I'll do it. I act for her father.'

'A message has gone to the Senator,' Marponius fussed. Helena pursed her lips while even Petronius winced. I hoped Camillus Verus was missing at some unknown public baths.

'Falco will speak for me,' Helena said coldly, adding, 'if I must have a male mouthpiece!'

'I require your guardian,' Marponius corrected. He was a pedantic nuisance.

'We regard ourselves as married,' said Helena. I tried not to look like a husband who had just been told the household bills were three times what he thought.

The judge was shocked. I murmured, 'Socially, it's a future fixture in the calendar, though a man with your grasp of the Twelve Tables will appreciate that the mere agreement of two parties that a marriage exists brings the contract into effect – '

'Don't get clever, Falco!' Marponius knew the legal tables backwards, but rarely met women who broke the rules. He glanced at Petronius for help, though was obviously remembering he distrusted Petro's loyalties. 'What am I supposed to make of this?'

'I'm afraid it's true love,' Petronius pronounced, with the sombre air of a public works engineer reporting a cracked sewer in the vicinity.

I decided against upsetting the judge's middle-class ethics with further wit. He was more used to threats. 'Marponius,

Helena Justina is an innocent party. Camillus is very public-spirited, but having his noble child wrongly arrested may offend his tolerance. Your best plan is to establish the facts before the Senator arrives, and greet him by restoring his daughter with a public apology.'

I could sense that the others present were sharing an awkward moment. Agitation flickered in the wondrous dark depths of Helena's eyes, and her grip on my hand felt tense. More was wrong here than I yet knew.

A slave came in and informed the judge that the messengers had failed to find Camillus Verus. People were still looking, but his current whereabouts were unknown. Good man. My future father-in-law (as it seemed best to regard him while we were pretending to be respectable) knew when to lie low in a ditch.

His sensible daughter forced herself to be gracious to the judge: 'Ask your questions. I do not object in principle to answering in the presence of Didius Falco, and that of Lucius Petronius Longus, who is a valued family friend. Ask me what you want. If they advise me to defer my response on a particular matter, we can stop until Father arrives.'

I loved her. She was hating herself for sounding so meek – and hating Marponius for swallowing the act. 'Alternatively,' I told him, 'we can all sit around a finger-bowl of honey cakes, and while we wait for her furious parent you can try to sell the lady thirteen scrolls on natural philosophy in a filigree library box.'

Helena boasted prosaically, 'If it's concerned with fiery particles, I think I've read that one.'

'Tread gently,' I teased Marponius. 'The watch captain has apprehended an educated girl!'

'I'll expect a rapid batch of injunctions!' he quipped wryly, taking a grip on himself. Marponius could be an objectionable prig – but he was no fool. If a man had any sense of humour at all, Helena was likely to bring out the best in him.

'Actually, it lets her out of the murder,' I smiled. 'She never gets into trouble; she's always curled up on all the cushions in the house, with her nose in a scroll . . .' As we joked, those eyes of hers were still sending me agonised messages. I was desperate to find out the cause. 'Sweetheart, perhaps the man you regard as your marriage partner can properly ask why you are sitting in a stranger's house with a distressed expression and somewhat lightly chaperoned?'

'This is a formal examination,' Marponius interrupted, stiffly reacting to the implied criticism. 'It is a private session of my court! The lady knows I am a judge attached to the permanent tribunal relating to the Cornelian Law against assassins and drug-making –'

'Poisons, knifings and patricide,' I interpreted for Helena. The special murder tribunal had been established by the dictator Sulla. After a hundred and fifty years it had signally failed to stamp out death in the streets, but at least killers were processed efficiently, which suited Rome. The praetor had a whole panel of locally elected judges he could call on to hear cases, but Marponius had set himself up as the expert. He enjoyed his duties. (He enjoyed the status.) When he took an interest in the early stages of a particular investigation, he could rely on being chosen for the hearing afterwards if the officers of the watch ever caught someone.

Now they had caught me. Helena's distress made me attack Marponius. 'Under that legislation is there not a penalty by fire and water for inciting a judge falsely to bring a capital charge?'

'That is correct.' He had replied too calmly. He was too sure of his ground. Trouble was licking its fangs at me. 'No charge has been brought yet.'

'Then why is the lady here?'

'A charge does seem likely.'

'On what accusation?'

Helena answered me herself. 'Acting as an accessory.'

'Oh cobnuts!' I looked across at Petronius. *His* eyes, which were brown, honest and always frank, told me to believe it. I turned back to Helena. 'What's happened today? I know you went to the Saepta and visited my father.' I felt annoyed at having to mention Geminus, but making Helena sound like a girl who devoted her attentions to the family seemed a good idea. 'Did something occur afterwards?'

'I was going home to your mother's house. On the way,' she said rather guiltily, 'I happened to pass Flora's Caupona.'

I was starting to worry. 'Carry on!'

812

'I saw the body of Censorinus being taken away. The street was blocked temporarily, so I had to wait. I was of course in a carrying-chair,' she inserted, having grasped that some niceties were called for. 'The bearers talked to the waiter from the caupona while we were stuck there, and he happened to be bewailing the fact that he now had to tidy up the rented room.'

'So?'

'So I offered to help.'

I let go of her hand and folded my arms. The bad memory of that bloody room where Censorinus was murdered forced itself back into my mind. I had to repel it. Petronius knew I had been there, which was damning enough; admitting it to Marponius would be my key to a jail cell. Sending my girlfriend looked like the act of a desperate man.

I knew why she had done it. She wanted to scour the place for evidence that might clear me. But any stranger would assume she had gone there to *remove* clues that would convict. Marponius was bound to think it. Even Petro would be failing in his duty if he ignored the possibility. His deep sense of unhappiness filled the room almost like an odour. I had never before been so conscious of putting our long friendship under strain.

'It was stupid,' Helena spoke crisply. 'I offered on the spur of the moment.' I sat dumbstruck, unable to ask if she had got as far as the ghastly scene upstairs. She looked so white it seemed probable. My throat closed helplessly. 'I only reached the downstairs kitchen,' she said, as if I had transmitted my agony. 'Then I realised my presence there could only make things appear worse for you.'

'So what happened?' I managed to croak.

'The waiter seemed desperate for company. I suppose he was frightened to enter the murder room alone, even after he knew the body was no longer there. I was trying to think of an excuse to leave, without being rude to the poor man, when Petronius Longus arrived.'

I stared at him. He spoke to me at last. 'Encouraging your nicely bred girlfriend to visit the gory scene looks black, Falco.'

'Only if I'm guilty!' He must have known how closely I verged on losing my temper. 'And I did not send her.'

'A jury may not believe you,' Marponius commented.

'Juries are notoriously stupid! That's why the praetor will expect you to advise him on whether this charge is likely to stick before he lets things reach a court.'

'Oh I shall give the praetor good advice, Falco.'

'If justice is more than a dilettante hobby for you, your advice will be that this case stinks!'

'I don't think so.'

'Then you don't think – end of issue! I had no motive for killing the centurion.'

'He had a financial claim on you.' Without any formal signal, the atmosphere had shifted so that the judge was grilling me.

'No, he had a claim against my brother. But the claim was rocky. Marponius, I don't want to slander the brave centurions of the glorious Fifteenth Legion, but my private investigations already suggest it was a claim they could not pursue too openly. Anyway, where are your facts? Censorinus was seen alive, eating his dinner at the caupona, long after I had left and gone home to my own family. Petronius Longus has checked up on my movements the next day, and although there may be a period that I can't account for with witnesses, neither can you present anyone who will say they saw me at Flora's when the soldier lost his life.'

'The fact that you disagreed with him so violently – '

'Rules me out! We had a very strange quarrel, initiated by him, right in front of the very curious public. If you base your case on that, you are calling me a very stupid man.'

Marponius frowned. For a moment I had the illusion of controlling the situation, then the sensation altered. He made a gesture to Petronius. Some unpleasant challenge, previously arranged, was about to emerge.

Petronius Longus, with his air of misery deepening even further, stood up from his seat on the far side of the tasteful room and came across to me. He unwrapped a piece of cloth he had been guarding, and held out an object for me to inspect. He kept it just beyond my reach, and made sure that Marponius and Helena could both watch my face.

'Do you recognise this, Falco?'

I had a split second to reach the wrong decision. Delay would have answered for me. I took the honest option, like a fool. 'Yes,' I said. 'It appears to be one of my mother's cooking knives.'

Then Petronius Longus told me in a quiet voice, 'Helena Justina found it this morning amongst other utensils on the caupona's cooking bench.'

XXVIII

Criminals cut and run. For a second I knew why.

I stared at the knife. It was not one to excite a cutler. There was a gnarled bone handle, attached by a stout iron ring to a heavy blade that tapered to a solid point. The point had a small twist, as if at some time in its past the knife had been trapped and bent; such a nick at the end of a strong knife is impossible to straighten out.

It was like all my mother's other knives. They were not a true set, but they had all come from the Campagna when she was married. They were tough country items that she wielded with great force. Plenty of other homes in Rome must have similar gear. But I knew this was hers. Her initials were scratched on the handle: *JT*, for Junilla Tacita.

The room was quite large, but suddenly felt close and full of smoke from the braziers heating it. There were high square windows; I could hear a squall beating on the expensive glass, and one casement rattled. Squat slaves with straight-cut hair moved about constantly. Here was I, under threat of exile or far worse, while these ninnies came and went removing empty bowls and attending to the lamps. Helena dropped her hand back over mine; hers was icy cold.

Marponius was doing everything strictly now. 'Petronius Longus, have you shown this knife to Didius Falco's mother?'

'Yes, sir. She admits it must have been hers originally, but claims she lost this one at least twenty years ago.'

'How can she be sure?'

'She recognised the misshapen point.' Petro's quiet patience as he answered the judge's questions only depressed me more. 'She remembered it being caught in a cupboard door when her children were small.'

'Has she any explanation as to how it reached the caupona?'

'No, sir.'

'Describe how it was found.'

Petronius now had a set face. He gave his report with

816

impeccable neutrality: 'I had ordered the removal of the body this afternoon. Later I entered the caupona with a view to completing my search of the scene. The soldier's corpse had been impeding a full investigation previously. I saw Helena Justina talking to the waiter at the foot of the stairs that run up from the kitchen to the rented rooms.'

'I remember!' said Marponius importantly.

'At my approach, Helena turned towards me, and appeared to notice this knife on the work bench; she picked it up. Both of us have eaten at Falco's mother's house on many occasions. We both recognised the pattern and initials. Helena made no attempt to hide it, but handed it to me immediately. As you see, it has been washed, but is stained around the shaft junction with traces of reddish colouring.'

'You take that to be blood?'

'I am afraid so.'

'What is your interpretation?'

Petro dragged out the words slowly. 'I asked the waiter about the knife. I didn't tell him I knew where it came from. He maintained he had never seen it before; it was not one he used at Flora's.'

'Is this the weapon which killed Censorinus?'

Petronius answered reluctantly. 'It may well be. If the waiter is telling the truth, the killer may have brought his own weapon to the caupona. When he came down from the bedroom he washed it in one of the buckets of water that are always in the kitchen area; then he threw the knife among the other utensils.'

'You're looking for someone intelligent,' I said dryly. 'It was a good place to hide a domestic implement. Pity it was recognised!'

Helena murmured in anguish, 'I'm sorry, Marcus. I just saw it and picked it up.'

I shrugged. 'That's all right. I never put it there.'

'You cannot prove that you didn't,' said the judge.

'And you cannot prove that I did!'

Helena demanded of Marponius, 'Are you really convinced that knowing someone had been stabbed upstairs, the waiter would not notice a strange knife among his tools?'

'Epimandos is pretty vague,' I said. Marponius looked

817

unhappy, knowing it was bad practice to produce a slave in court. (Worse still if my pet theory was right and Epimandos was a runaway.)

Petronius agreed with me: 'He keeps a jumble of kitchen tools lying about at the back of the caupona. He's dreamy, untidy, and he was hysterical after the corpse's discovery. He could have missed anything.'

I was grateful for his help, but had to go on. 'Petronius, I still cannot accept unequivocally that this knife killed the centurion. Flora's is not renowned for hygienic practices; the red stains may not be blood at all, or if they are, it may be left from cutting up meat. What I'm saying is, you cannot actually prove that this is the murder knife.'

'No,' he replied levelly. 'But it's about the right size for the wounds.' It seemed too small, lying in his great hand. 'It's sharp enough,' he added. All my mother's knives were. They looked clumsy, but she used them a lot. They would slice through a cabbage stalk quite easily, taking any careless fingertip with them.

'The knife could have been anywhere since Ma lost it. It's not tied to me.'

'You are her son,' Petronius pointed out. 'Junilla Tacita is famously defensive. I cannot altogether take her word that the knife had been lost.'

'She would not lie, even for me.'

'Would she not?' Marponius asked, checking with me, Helena, Petronius. In fact none of us was sure. Attempting to appear reasonable, the judge said to me, 'If you ever brought me a suspect with this amount of evidence, you know you would expect me to order a trial.'

'I wouldn't do it. I would not be convinced myself.'

Marponius sniffed. My views were unimportant; he had too high an opinion of his own place in the world. I had my own thoughts on where he belonged: face down in a wet gulley with a rhinoceros standing on top of him.

I glanced at Petro. Slowly he said, 'Falco, I don't want to believe you did this, but no one else is a suspect, and all the circumstantial evidence indicts you.'

'Thanks!' I said.

I was feeling tired. This was hopeless. There was nothing I

could say or do to extricate myself – or Helena, who looked like my accomplice in a bungled cover-up. The judge had completed his questions. He decided to hold both of us in custody.

Normally I would have appealed for assistance to Petronius. As he was the arresting officer, I had to wait for somebody else to come forward with our bail.

Somebody would. Helena Justina's family would adore the chance to berate me for getting her into this.

We were to be kept at the judge's house temporarily. He had us locked in separate rooms, but as soon as the house quietened down I picked my way out of mine and into hers. Only the fact that Helena was also trying to break her lock with a brooch pin held me up.

XXIX

I came in and leaned against the door, trying to look debonair. Helena had stepped back. Still clutching the brooch, she gazed at me. Guilt and fear were in her eyes; they were brighter than ever with anxiety now I had arrived. Mine were smiling. Probably.

'Hello, sweetheart. Are you breaking out to find me?'

'No, Marcus. I'm trying to escape before I have to face your wrath.'

'I never get angry.'

'Well you never admit it.'

I could never be angry with Helena Justina when she was fighting back with that determined glint. We were in serious trouble, however, and we both knew it. 'I am merely perplexed at how to extricate us from this mess, to which you must admit you have contributed . . .'

'Don't try being reasonable, Falco. The effort makes your ears go red.'

'Well, if you wanted to get back at me for my fling with Marina, I could have suggested less drastic ways – ' I stopped. There were tears welling in her eyes. Helena had made a terrible mistake and under the show of pride she was desolate. 'I'll get us out of this,' I said, more gently. 'Just brace yourself for some bad jokes from your father when he has to come here grovelling to Marponius while he coughs up your surety.'

'Yours has been sent for too.'

'Mine won't come.'

She would not be consoled, but we were on friendlier terms now. 'Marcus, what happened to your face?'

'It hit somebody's fist. Don't worry, fruit. Marponius hasn't enough evidence against us to name a date for a hearing in court. That means he has to release us. If I'm free on bail I shall at least be able to pursue my enquiries without constantly having to dodge Petronius.'

Helena looked rueful. 'Your best friend – who now knows you're living with an idiot!'

I grinned at her. 'He knew that already. He thought you were insane to take me on.'

'He told the judge it was true love.'

'And is he wrong?' I reached for the brooch she was still holding, and pinned it back on her neatly. 'Marponius believed him enough to lock us up in separate cells to prevent collusion. Well, then – ' A tremulous smile from Helena answered my broad grin. I held out my arms to her. 'So, my darling, let's collude!'

XXX

It took so long for Helena's papa to rally round, I began to dread that he was leaving us to stew. He might have refused to pay a judicial ransom to release me, but I did think he would rescue Helena. Her mother would insist on it.

Helena's conscience was tormenting her. 'It's all my fault! I just noticed the knife and took hold of it because I wondered whatever something of your mother's could be doing there . . .'

Holding her close I soothed her. 'Hush! All the family go to Flora's. Any one of them could have decided to take their own bread-cutter to attack the week-old rolls. And they are all daft enough to leave it behind afterwards.'

'Maybe one of them will remember . . .'

My money was on Festus as the culprit, so that was out.

We were lying on a couch. (Purely for convenience; I had more tact than to seduce my girlfriend under the nose of a 'man of ideas'.) Anyway, it was a hard couch.

The room was dark, but noticeably more high-class than where I had been locked up. As a cell for a senator's daughter, it passed. There was a gilt footstool for the couch. An apple log smoked in a fire-basket. We had dim lamps, a small Eastern carpet on one wall, side-tables bearing curios, and vases on shelves. It was cosy. We had privacy. There was in fact no reason why we should rush to decamp.

'Why are you smiling, Marcus?' She had her face buried in my neck, so I was surprised she realised.

'Because I'm here with you . . .' Maybe I was smiling because we had squared the odds.

'You mean, we're in terrible trouble as usual, but this time it's my fault . . . I shall never forgive myself for this.'

'You will.'

The house had fallen quiet. Marponius was the type who dined alone then retired to his study to reread Cicero's defence of Sextus Roscius. If ever he hired himself a dancing girl, it was so he would have an audience when he practised snippets of fine oratory.

Caressing Helena's head, I let my mind wander back over the day. Then my thoughts meandered even further, through childhood and youth, trying to make sense of the complex fiasco that had brought me here.

So far I had established that my brother, the eternal entrepreneur, had probably connived with some of his fellow centurions to rob their legion's savings bank; that he had purchased what might be a rare antique statue; and that his ship had sunk.

I had not actually established, but I strongly suspected, that the agent employed by Festus might have absconded with the statue before the ship foundered. That was good, possibly. I might be able to track down the agent and make a quick denarius from the Phidias myself.

Perhaps the agent had had nothing to do with it.

Perhaps the ship had not really sunk.

Then a more ugly possibility faced me. Maybe it had never sunk – *and maybe Festus knew that*. He could have lied about the *Hypericon*, then have sold the goods privately and run off with the money. If so, my role now was impossible. It was too late to cash in on the Phidias, I had no money to pay off the legionaries, and I could not clear my brother's name for Ma.

Almost everything I had discovered so far was dubious. It looked as if we had stumbled across the worst-ever crisis in my brother's fabled 'lupin round': his business ventures in the grey economy. Those had usually failed – usually a day after Festus himself had safely pulled out of them. He always trod a sticky path, like a wasp on the rim of a honey jar. Maybe this time he had overbalanced and fallen in.

Helena moved so she could see me. 'What are you thinking about, Marcus?'

'Oh, the Golden Age – '

'The past, you mean?'

'Correct. The long-lost, glittering, glorious past ... Probably not so glorious as we all pretend.'

'Tell me. What aspect?'

'It's possible you have allied yourself with a highly dubious family.' Helena laughed ironically. She and I were such close friends I could tell her the unthinkable: 'I am beginning to wonder if my brother the hero in fact ended his days as a thief and a candidate for cashiering.' Helena must have been expecting it, for she simply stroked my brow quietly and let me take my time. 'How can I ever say that to Ma?'

'Make quite sure of the facts first!'

'Maybe I won't tell her.'

'Maybe she already knows,' suggested Helena. 'Maybe she wants you to put the record straight.'

'No, she asked me to clear his name! On the other hand,' I argued unconvincingly, 'perhaps all this only looks like a scandal – but appearances deceive.'

Helena knew my opinion: that is not how scandals work.

She changed the subject, trying to ease my introspective mood by asking about what had happened to me earlier that day. I described the disrupted auction, then told her what I had learned from Geminus about my brother's last business scheme, including the Phidias Poseidon. I ended with how I had been summoned by that ghastly urchin Gaius and had left my father in his office, surrounded by flotsam like some old sea god in a cave.

'He sounds like you,' she commented. 'Hiding away from the world at the top of your sixth-floor apartment on the Aventine.'

'It's not the same!'

'You don't like people going there.'

'People bring trouble.'

'Even me?' she teased.

'Not you.' I grimaced at her. 'Not even today.'

'Perhaps,' Helena suggested thoughtfully, 'your elder brother also had a secret den somewhere?'

If so, it was the first I knew of it. Yet behind his open, cheery attitude, Festus had been full of secrets. He had lived with his mother; he certainly could have used a hideaway. Jupiter knew what would be waiting there if ever I discovered it.

We stopped discussing the issue because just then Marponius came in person to inform Helena that her father had arrived to free her. The judge was wearing his best toga for entertaining such splendid company, and a big grin because the surety he had demanded from the noble Camillus before he would release his dangerous daughter was extremely large. When he saw me in the same room he looked annoyed, though he said nothing about it. Instead, he enjoyed himself announcing that I too was to be set free on recognizance.

'From whom?' I demanded suspiciously.

'From your father,' grinned Marponius. He obviously knew I found the thought unbearable.

Produced for our parents as a murderer and his accessory, we managed not to giggle inanely, but felt like bad teenagers being hauled off home from the town jail after some prank in the Forum that would horrify our ancient great-aunts when they heard of it.

By the time we appeared, our two rescuers were close allies. They had met before. Now they had a disgrace in common and thanks to the judge's ingratiating wine steward, they were both slightly drunk. Geminus was down on one knee having a good look at a large urn from southern Italy that was pretending to have Athenian origins. Camillus Verus had kept slightly more control of his manners, though only by a thread. He gave me a whimsical salute, while commenting loudly to my own father, 'I suppose this makes a change from having to complain about their expensive hobbies, wild parties and shocking friends!'

'Never have children!' Pa advised Marponius. 'And by the way, Judge, your urn's cracked.'

Marponius rushed to inspect his flawed property. While he was crouching on the floor, he managed to speak a few hurried words about releasing us into family custody, the fathers' duties of supervision, et cetera. In return, Pa gave him the name of a man who could make the crack invisible (one of a horde of such dubious craftsmen known at the Saepta Julia). The judge then scrambled upright, shook hands all round like some theatrical pimp restoring long-lost twins, and let us escape.

As we struggled out into the winter night, our happy fathers were still congratulating themselves on their generosity, making jokes together about how to supervise our parole, and wrangling about which of their houses we should be dragged off to dine in.

Rome was cold and dark. It was late enough for the streets to be growing dangerous. Helena and I were hungry, but we had endured enough. I muttered that if they wanted to check up on us we would be with Ma, then we both fell into the chair they had brought for Helena and made the bearers set off at a cracking pace. I gave a loud instruction for Mother's house, then once we got around the first corner I changed the directions to Fountain Court.

Now I had an impossible mission, an indictment for murder – and two highly indignant fathers chasing me.

But at least when we reached the apartment the new bed had arrived.

XXXI

Next morning Helena was startled when I jumped out of bed at first light.

This was not easy. The new bed was successful in various ways that are private, and it had given us a most comfortable night's sleep. We awoke under a huge feather-filled coverlet which we had brought home from Germany, as warm as chicks in a nest. Beside the bed, in pride of place, stood the adjustable bronze tripod Helena had acquired from Geminus – as a present for me, apparently.

'Is this for my birthday? It's not for three weeks.'

'I remember when your birthday is!' Helena assured me. It was partly a wry joke, because of an occasion when I had somehow missed hers, and partly nostalgia. She knew the date because that was the first time I ever kissed her, before I realised the frightening fact that I was in love with her, or could believe she might be in love with me. We had been at a ghastly inn in Gaul, and I was still amazed at my bravado in approaching her – not to mention the consequences. By the way she smiled, Helena was also thinking about the occasion. 'I felt you needed cheering up.'

'Don't tell me how much he stung you for it; I don't want to be depressed.'

'All right, I won't tell you.'

I sighed. 'No, you'd better. He's my father. I feel responsible.'

'Nothing. When I said how much I liked it, he gave it to me.'

That was when I sprang out into the cold.

'Dear gods, Marcus! What's this?'

'Time is running out.'

Helena sat up, huddled in our German coverlet and staring at me from amidst a tangle of fine dark hair. 'I thought you said the enquiry would be less pressing now you didn't have to dodge Petronius?'

'This has nothing to do with the enquiry.' I was pulling on more clothes.

'Come back!' Helena launched herself across the bed and locked her arms around me. 'Explain the mystery!'

'No mystery.' Despite fierce resistance, I pushed her back into bed and tucked her in tenderly. 'Just an unpaid bill of four hundred thousand big ones that suddenly fell due.' She stopped struggling, so I managed to kiss her. 'First, I found out yesterday that a certain rash young lady is prepared to state in public – before a judge – that we are virtually man and wife . . . and now I've discovered my relations at large are sending us gifts to set up home! So forget the enquiry. Compared with the urgent need to assemble a dowry, a little matter of being a murder suspect fades into insignificance.'

'Fool!' Helena burst out laughing. 'For a moment I thought you were serious.'

She did have a point. When a man of my meagre standing has fallen for a senator's daughter, however much he adores her he takes a risk in hoping for something to come of it.

I let her enjoy the hilarious prospect of marriage to me, without bothering to worry her with the news that I meant what I said.

As I walked down the Aventine and towards the Emporium the warm glow of having reached a decision about Helena kept me going for about two streets. After that normality descended. Bad enough was the problem of trying to pluck four hundred thousand sesterces from thin air. If I wanted Helena I had to pay the price, but it was still far beyond my reach. Even more depressing was the next task I had set myself: seeing another of my brothers-in-law.

I tried to find him at his place of work. He was not there. I should have known. He was a bureaucrat; naturally he was on holiday.

My sister Junia, the superior one, had married a customs clerk. At seventeen, this had been her idea of moving up in society; now she was thirty-four. Gaius Baebius had progressed to supervising other clerks at the Emporium, but Junia undoubtedly had grander dreams in which a husband who merely hung around the docks collecting taxes did not feature. I sometimes wondered if Gaius Baebius ought to start testing his dinner on the dog.

They did own a dog, mainly because they wanted to have a door-tile warning people to beware of him. Ajax was a nice dog. Well he had been once, before life's troubles got him down. Now he set about his duties as a watchdog as seriously as his master fulfilled his important role at the customs-house. Ajax's friendly greeting for tradesmen was to tear the hems off their tunics, and I knew of at least two lawsuits brought after he removed chunks of visitors' legs. I had actually given evidence for one of the plaintiffs, for which I had not yet been forgiven.

Ajax did not like me. When I appeared in his slightly smelly doorway innocently trying to gain admittance, he strained at his leash until his kennel began to slide across the floor. I managed to hop past, with his long snout an inch from my left calf, cursed the dog in an undertone, and shouted a somewhat tense welcome to whoever was inside the house.

Junia appeared. She shared Ajax's view of me. In her case it was legitimate, since my birth had supplanted her as the youngest in our family. She had maintained a thirty-year grudge against me for loss of privilege, even before I told a magistrate she kept a vicious dog.

'Oh, it's you! If you're coming in, take your boots off. They're covered with mud.' I was already unstrapping them; I had been to Junia's house before.

'Sort out your hound, will you? Good boy, Ajax! How many travelling onion-sellers has he killed today?'

My sister ignored that, but called her husband. It took two of them to drag the dog and his kennel to their proper position and calm the wild creature down.

I greeted Gaius Baebius, who had come out from his breakfast licking honey from his fingers. He looked embarrassed to be found relaxing in his second-best tunic, clearly unshaven for the past few days. Gaius and Junia only liked to be seen in public in full formal dress, with her leaning submissively on his right arm. They were spending their lives practising for their tombstone. I felt sombre every time I came within two yards of them.

They had no children. This perhaps explained their tolerance of Ajax. He ruled them like a spoiled heir. Had the law allowed it, they would have adopted him formally.

Being the only childless female among our highly fecund family had left Junia enjoying her right to bitterness. She kept herself very smart, her house so clean flies died of fear, and if asked about offspring said she had enough to do looking after Gaius Baebius. Why he caused so much work was a mystery to me. I found him about as exciting as watching a bird-bath evaporate.

'I hear you're on holiday?'

'Oh it's just a few days,' warbled Junia offhandedly.

'Of course you'll have four months at your private villa in Surrentum once the weather bucks up!' I was joking, but my sister blushed because that was what they liked to imply to people who knew them less well. 'Gaius Baebius, I need to talk to you.'

'Have some breakfast, Marcus.' My sister probably hoped I would say no, so although I had bought myself a bread roll on the way to their house, I accepted on principle. Some folk when they acquire money spend it avidly; Junia and her husband belonged to the other type, and were painfully mean in some ways. They were always changing the furniture, but hated to waste money on starving relatives.

Junia led the way to their dining-room. It was about three feet wide. Their apartment was the usual small rental, but Gaius Baebius had recently improved it with some odd partitioning. It stayed up, provided no one leaned against the walls, and enabled them to pretend they had a separate triclinium where banquets could take place. In fact people now ate squashed on stools in a row against a low table. Unfortunately, my brother-in-law's interior-design scheme meant if you had the table there was no room for even one proper eating-couch. I squeezed in without comment; he was really proud of their superior living style.

Junia served me a small chunk of loaf – making sure I got the black bits – and a sliver of pallid, tasteless cheese to help it down. Meanwhile Gaius Baebius carried on munching a mound of cold meats.

'New plates?' I asked politely, since much of mine was visible.

'Yes, we thought it was time we invested in Arretine. Such a wonderful gloss – '

'Oh these are not bad. We bought some ourselves,' I countered. 'Helena and I wanted something just a little more original. We hate to go out to dinner and find the same service we dine off at home . . . Ours was a present from a friendly potter at a little place I discovered when we were staying in Germany.'

'Really?' Junia had always been impossible to tease. She did not believe my foray into fancy dinnerware.

'I'm quite serious.' On the rare occasions when I managed to surpass these snobs I liked to make it known.

'Fancy that!' Junia rattled her bracelets and applied her gracious air. 'What did you want to ask Gaius Baebius?'

Insulting my hosts paled, so I settled down to business. 'I'm being forced to unravel a muddle our beloved Festus left behind.' I saw them exchange a glance; word of my mission had run ahead of me. Junia surveyed me as if she knew Festus was about to be exposed as a villain and she blamed me for everything. 'Did you meet the soldier who was camping out at Mother's house? He's dead – '

'And you're supposed to have done it?' Trust Junia.

'Anyone who thinks so needs a new head, sister!'

'We didn't like to say much.'

'Thanks, Junia! Leaving things unsaid until the pot boils over is a fine art in our family, but this time it won't work. I'm desperate to clear myself before I'm in court on a murder charge. It all seems to hang on Festus and his business network. Gaius, the soldier came up with some story about imports. Can you tell me this: when Festus was sending items to Italy from abroad, did his ships land at Ostia?'

'As far as I know. I expect,' offered Gaius Baebius prudishly, 'Festus thought that having a brother-in-law in customs meant that he could dodge his harbour dues.'

I grinned. 'He certainly thought it! No doubt he was wrong?'

'Of course!' exclaimed Gaius Baebius. No doubt it was sometimes true.

'Would your records show whether a particular ship landed? I'm talking about the year he died, so we have to go back a bit.'

In between large mouthfuls of breakfast, Gaius Baebius addressed the subject in his slow, pedantic way. 'Is this the ship that's supposed to be missing?' More of this story must be current than people had previously acknowledged.

'The *Hypericon*, that's right.'

'If she did land, someone would have her listed. If not, no.'

'Good!'

'If she fully unloaded at Ostia, Ostia will have the records. If her cargo went into barges and came up to be sold at the Emporium, it would be recorded here in Rome. Festus wasn't selling through official channels though, so you probably want Ostia.'

'Well, Ostia's close enough,' I replied airily. 'What if she was beached somewhere else in Italy?'

'The only way to discover that would be to visit every possible port and check their lists – if the local officials are willing to let you look at them. And always assuming,' Gaius Baebius added heavily, 'the *Hypericon* behaved in a legitimate fashion.' Something we both knew must be open to doubt. 'And paid the proper duty.'

'If not,' I agreed despondently, 'she could have slipped into land anywhere and had the cargo smuggled ashore.'

'And it was years ago.' He liked to be optimistic.

'And she may really have sunk, so I'm wasting my time.'

'Sinking was certainly the story. I remember the fuss Festus made about it.'

'At last somebody seems to know something about the problem!' I flattered him. 'I think we can assume the *Hypericon* never came into Ostia. Either she did sink – or she would have been hidden away. But would you be prepared to do something for me, old son? To help the family?'

'You mean check up on her?'

'Not only her. I want you to examine the lists for that whole year.'

'I'd have to go to Ostia.'

'I'll pay your mule hire.' He would pinch official transport anyway, if I knew him.

I could see he was prepared for the inconvenience; probably it was a good excuse to escape from Junia. As for her, she would let him go off on the trip because Festus had been her brother too. Junia must have been watching this possible scandal unfolding with more horror than the rest of us; after all, she was the one who had refined ideas.

'Let's get this straight, Falco. You want to see if Festus had any *other* commissioned vessel that came into Ostia?' Gaius Baebius loved that. 'Oho! You think he transferred the goods?'

'I've no idea. I'm simply looking into every possibility. I should have done this before, as his executor. Even if this cargo was submerged, there may be something else worth looking for. What I'm hoping is that I may discover a cache of property belonging to Festus that I can sell to get his legion off our backs.' What I was hoping was to find more than that.

'Why don't you just tell them there is nothing?' demanded Junia angrily.

'I've already done that. Either they don't believe me, or they intend to be paid regardless of whether it ruins the whole family.' I held my tongue about the savings-bank theory. 'Gaius Baebius, are you prepared to help me? Will the lists still exist?'

'Oh they should exist all right. Have you any idea, Falco, how many vessels come into Rome in a season?'

'I'll help you look,' I volunteered quickly.

'It will still be a job and a half,' Gaius grumbled, but it was plain he would do it. 'I could go out to the coast today and see my pals at the port. I can have a look at what we're letting ourselves in for.' Gaius Baebius was a true bureaucrat; he loved to think he was so important he had to ruin his holiday by rushing back to work. Most people would baulk at a round trip of twenty miles, but he was ready to gallop off to Ostia immediately. 'I'll be back by the end of the morning.' The man was an idiot. If I carried out enquiries at such a dash, I would be worn out. 'Where can I find you later?'

'Let's have a late lunch. I'll be at a wine bar near the Caelian.'

Junia pricked up her ears. 'I trust this is not a place with a bad reputation, Marcus?' My sister kept her husband out of trouble; not that he exerted himself getting into any.

'It's not called the Virgin for nothing.' Junia looked reassured by the name of the drinking-house and told Gaius he could go.

'There may be one other problem,' I confessed. 'Any ship Festus chartered could be registered in the name of an agent he was using. Unluckily, no one I have been able to speak to – '

'He means Father!' snapped Junia.

'Is able to supply the agent's name.'

Gaius Baebius bristled. 'Well, that's a blow!'

'All right, all right! I'll sort it out somehow – '

'Gaius Baebius will have to help you,' my sister told me snootily. 'I do hope there is not going to be any unpleasantness, Marcus!'

'Thanks for the support, dearest!' I lifted a slice of veal sausage from my brother-in-law's laden plate as I took my leave.

Then I had to go back for another, to use for distracting the dog.

XXXII

My next task was trickier: I went to see my mother to ask about the knife.

She was being extremely vague on the subject. I learned no more than she had already told Petronius. 'Yes, it looked like mine. I really can't be expected to remember where something disappeared to when I probably haven't seen it for twenty years . . .'

'Somebody must have walked off with it,' I told her grimly. 'Allia's the prime candidate.'

Ma knew my sister Allia was always popping into someone else's house to borrow half a loaf or a set of loom weights. She was famous for not bothering to have her own possessions while there was anybody else she could count on to supply her needs.

Not that I was suggesting Allia was implicated in the soldier's death.

'I suppose you're right.' Whilst apparently agreeing, Ma managed to put mysterious doubts into her tone.

Under strain, I could hear myself getting annoyed. 'Well, will you ask all the family what they know about this thing? It's important, Ma!'

'So I gather! I heard you were arrested, but you let yourself be bought out!'

'Yes, my father released me,' I answered patiently.

'Last time you were in prison, *I* was good enough to bribe the jailer!'

'Don't remind me about that.'

'You ought to have more pride.'

'Last time had been a stupid mistake over nothing, Ma. This time a murder-court judge happens to have a pressing case against me. The position is rather different. If they haul me in front of a jury, your precious boy may be lost. The surety cost heavily, if that's any consolation. Geminus will be feeling the gap in his purse.'

835

'He'll feel it even more if you run off!' My mother clearly saw me as even more of a ruffian than Pa. 'So how are you getting on?'

'I'm not.'

Ma gave me a look as if she thought I had deliberately arranged my arrest to escape having to exert myself on my brother's behalf. 'So where are you dashing off to now?'

'A wine bar,' I said, since she already thought the worst of me.

It was true, anyway.

Finding a seedy bar I had visited only once before, five years earlier, at the end of a long night's entertainment, when I was depressed and drunk, took time. I spent nearly an hour roaming alleys round the Caelian. When I finally came across the Virgin, Gaius Baebius was already there. He looked tired, but smug.

'Ho there, my travel-stained *amicus*! How did you manage to arrive so promptly? I've been wearing myself out looking everywhere. Do you know this place?'

'Never been here, Falco.'

'How did you find it so quickly then?'

'I asked someone.'

After working off his breakfast and working up another appetite with his mad gallop to Ostia, he was tucking into a substantial lunch. He had bought and paid for it; there was no offer to include me. I called for a small flagon and decided to eat later on my own.

'The records still exist,' mumbled Gaius, chewing happily. 'It will take a few months to wade through them.' He was a slow worker. I could speed him up, but I knew in advance it would frustrate me.

'I'll help if they will allow me in. Can I look at them with you?'

'Oh yes. Any citizen with a legitimate reason can inspect the shipping lists. Of course,' he said, 'you have to know the procedures.' From Gaius Baebius this was a message that he was doing me a favour, and would remind me about it in future at every opportunity.

'Fine,' I said.

My brother-in-law started making elaborate arrangements for meeting me tomorrow, while I groaned inwardly. I hate people who complicate life with unnecessary paraphernalia. And I was none too pleased at the prospect of spending days in his dreary company. Lunch was bad enough.

I was looking around. The place was as grim as I remembered. Gaius Baebius sat eating his bowlful of beef and vegetables with the impervious calm of an innocent. Maybe my eyesight was better. I was filled with unease by the dark corners and sinister clientele.

We were in a dank cellar, a hole cut half into the Caelian Hill, more a burrow than a building. Beneath its filthy arched roof stood a few battered tables lit by tapers in oily old jugs. The landlord had a lurching gait and sported a viciously scarred cheek, probably acquired in a bar fight. His wine was sour. His customers were worse.

Since my last visit one of the rough-cast walls had acquired a crudely drawn pornographic picture in wide swathes of murky paint. It involved some mightily furnished manly types and a shy female who had lost her guardian and her clothes but who was gaining some unusual experience.

I summoned mine host. 'Who did your striking art work?'

'Varga, Manlius and that mob.'

'Do they still come in here?'

'On and off.' That sounded useless. It was not a den where I wished to hang around like a critic or a collector until these flighty artists deigned to appear.

'Where can I look them up while I'm in the neighbourhood?'

He made a few desultory suggestions. 'So what do you think of our frescos?'

'Fabulous!' I lied.

Now that the wall-painting had been drawn to his attention, Gaius Baebius was staring at it so fixedly I felt embarrassed. My sister would have been seriously annoyed to see him studying it so closely, but she would be more furious if I abandoned him anywhere so dangerous. Out of brotherly regard for Junia I had to sit there fuming while Gaius slowly finished his lunch-bowl as he perused the brothel scenes.

'Very interesting!' he commented as we left.

Shedding my inane relation, I followed up the landlord's suggestions for finding the fresco painters, but had no luck. One place the man had sent me was a rented room in a boarding-house. I could go back there at a different time and hope for better results. Any excuse was welcome. Needing food fairly urgently, I took myself off somewhere that by comparison was highly salubrious: back on the Aventine, to Flora's Caupona.

838

XXXIII

Flora's was in a greater state of misery than usual: they had the decorators in.

Epimandos was hovering outside, robbed of his kitchen but making an attempt to serve drinks and cold snippets to people who did not mind lunching in the street.

'What's this, Epimandos?'

'Falco!' He greeted me eagerly. 'I heard you had been arrested!'

I managed a grunt. 'Well I'm here. What's going on?'

'After the problem upstairs,' he whispered tactfully, 'the whole place is being done up.'

Flora's had been there for at least ten years and never seen a painter's brush before. Evidently a murder on the premises was good for trade. 'So who ordered this? Not the legendary Flora?'

Epimandos looked vague. He ignored my enquiry and burbled on. 'I've been so worried about what was happening to you – '

'So have I!'

'Are you going to be all right, Falco?'

'I've no idea. But if I ever catch up with the bastard who really did kill Censorinus, he won't be!'

'Falco – '

'Don't flap, Epimandos. A whimpering waiter kills the lively atmosphere!'

I looked for a seat. Outside they were limited. The objectionable cat, Stringy, was sprawled over one bench displaying his revolting belly fur, so I perched on a stool beside the barrel where the beggar always sat. For once it seemed necessary to nod at him.

'Afternoon, Marcus Didius.' I was still trying to think of a polite way to ask if I knew him when he introduced himself resignedly: 'Apollonius.' It still meant nothing. 'I was your schoolteacher.'

'Jupiter!' Long ago this hopeless soul had taught me geometry for six years. Now the gods had rewarded his patience by making him destitute.

Epimandos rushed up with wine for both of us, apparently pleased that I had found a friend to take my mind off things. It was too late to leave. I had to converse politely; that meant I had to invite the ex-teacher to join my lunch. He accepted my invitation timidly while I tried not to look too closely at his rags. I sent Epimandos across the road to fetch me a hot meal from the Valerian, and another for Apollonius.

He had always been a failure. The worst kind: someone you could not help but feel sorry for, even while he was messing you about. He was a terrible teacher. He might have been a snappy mathematician, but he could not explain anything. Struggling to make sense of his long-winded diatribes, I had always felt as if he had set me a problem that needed three facts in order to solve it, but he had only remembered to tell me two of them. Definitely a man whose hypotenuse squared had never totalled the squares of his other two sides.

'What a wonderful surprise to see you!' I croaked, pretending I had not been ignoring him every time I had come to Flora's over the past five years.

'Quite a shock,' he mumbled, going along with it as he devoured the broth I had supplied.

Epimandos had nobody else to serve, so he sat down by the cat and listened in.

'So what happened to the school, Apollonius?'

He sighed. Nostalgia was making me queasy. He had had the same dreary tone when he was lamenting some stubborn child's ignorance. 'I was forced to give up. Too much political instability.'

'You mean too many unpaid fees?'

'Youth is the first to suffer in a civil war.'

'Youth suffers, full stop,' I answered gloomily.

This was an appalling encounter. I was a tough man doing a swinish job; the last thing I needed was a confrontation with a schoolmaster who had known me when I was all freckles and false confidence. Around here people believed I had a shrewd brain and a hard fist; I was not prepared for them to see me

840

doling out free broth to this scrawny stick insect with his sparse hair and shaking, age-mottled hands while he flapped over my forgotten past.

'How's your little sister?' Apollonius enquired after a time.

'Maia? Not so little. She worked for a tailor, then she married a slovenly horse vet. No discernment. He works for the Greens, trying to keep their knock-kneed nags from dropping dead on the track. He has a nasty cough himself – probably from pinching the horses' liniment.' Apollonius looked puzzled. He was not in the same world as me. 'Her husband drinks.'

'Oh.' He looked embarrassed. 'Very bright, Maia.'

'True.' Though not in her choice of husband.

'Don't let me bore you,' the schoolmaster said courteously. I cursed him in silence; it meant I would have to carry on with the chat.

'I'll tell Maia I saw you. She has four children of her own now. Nice little things. She's bringing them up properly.'

'Maia would. A good pupil; a good worker; now a good mother too.'

'She had a good education,' I forced out. Apollonius smiled as if he were thinking, *Always gracious with the rhetoric!* On an impulse I added, 'Did you teach my brother and the other girls? My eldest sister, Victorina, died recently.'

Apollonius knew he should be saying he was sorry but lost himself answering the first question. 'Some I might have done, from time to time . . .'

I helped him out: 'The elder ones had a problem getting any schooling. Times were difficult.'

'But you and Maia were always signed on every term!' he cried, almost reprovingly. He was bound to remember; we were probably the only regular attenders on the whole Aventine.

'Our fees were paid,' I acknowledged.

Apollonius nodded fiercely. 'By the old Melitan gentleman,' he insisted on reminding me.

'That's right. He thought he was going to be allowed to adopt us. He paid up every quarter in the hope he was improving two shiny-faced heirs.'

'*Did* he adopt you?'

841

'No. My father would not hear of it.'

This set me off reminiscing. For someone who so clearly had little interest in children once he had produced them, my father could be a ferociously jealous man. If we misbehaved he would happily threaten to sell us as gladiators, yet he took pride in rejecting the Melitan's pleading overtures. I could still hear him boasting that free-born plebeians got their children as a trial for themselves, and did not breed for others' convenience.

The rows over sending Maia and me to school occurred not long before Pa lost his temper and left us. We felt it was our fault. We had the blame hanging over us; it made us a target for bullying from the rest.

After that fatal day when Papa left for an auction as usual but forgot his way home, Mother still strung the Melitan along – until even he finally twigged that no adoption would occur. He fell sick with disappointment, and died. With hindsight, it was rather sad.

'Do I sense, Marcus Didius, that all was not well?'

'Right. The Melitan caused some trouble.'

'Really? I always thought you and Maia came from such a happy family!' That just shows, teachers know nothing.

I cradled my winecup, caught up again in the anxieties the Melitan had imposed upon our house: Pa raging against him and all moneylenders (the Melitan's occupation), while Ma hissed back that she had to have the lodger's rent. Later Pa took to suggesting that the reason the old man was so keen on acquiring rights in Maia and myself was that we were his by-blows anyway. He used to roar this out in front of the Melitan as a hollow joke. (One glance at us disproved it; Maia and I had the full Didius physiognomy.) The Melitan was trapped in a stupid situation. Since he was so desperate for children, sometimes he even persuaded himself we were his.

Impossible of course. Ma, looking on like thunder, left us in no doubt.

I hated the Melitan. I convinced myself that had it not been for the anger he caused in my father, my Great-Uncle Scaro would have adopted me instead. Knowing about the quarrels that had already occurred, Scaro was far too polite to suggest it.

I wanted to be adopted. That is, if I was never claimed by my real parents. For of course I knew, as children do, that under no circumstances did I belong to the poor souls who were bringing me up temporarily at their house; someday my palace awaited me. My mother was one of the Vestal Virgins and my father was a mysterious and princely stranger who could materialise in moonbeams. I had been found on a river-bank by an honest old goatherd; my rescue from the toil and turmoil surrounding me had been foretold in a sibylline prophecy . . .

'You were always the dreamy one,' my old schoolmaster informed me. 'But I thought that there was hope for you . . .' I had forgotten he could be satirical.

'Still the same academic assessments: cruel, but fair!'

'You were good at geometry. You could have been a school-teacher.'

'Who wants to starve?' I retorted angrily. 'I'm an informer. It makes me just as poor, though I'm still being set puzzles, in different ways.'

'Well that's pleasing to hear. You should do work that suits you.' Nothing disturbed Apollonius. He was a man you could not insult. 'What happened to your brother?' he mused.

'Festus was killed in the Judaean War. He died a national hero, if that impresses you.'

'Ah! I always supposed that one would come to no good . . .' That dry humour again! I was expecting a long stream of anecdotes, but he lost interest. 'And now I hear you're contemplating a family of your own?'

'Word flies round! I'm not even married yet.'

'I wish you good fortune.' Once again the force of other people's premature congratulations was pushing Helena and me into a contract we had hardly discussed. Guiltily, I recognised that I was now committed both in private and in public to a plan that *she* saw quite differently.

'It may not be that simple. She's a senator's daughter, for one thing.'

'I expect your charm will win her round.' Apollonius only understood the simplicity of shapes on a slate. Social subtlety eluded him. He had never grasped why my father, a Roman citizen, should be outraged by the thought of having two of his children taken over by an immigrant. And he could not see the immense pressures that now kept me and my lady apart. 'Ah well, when you do have your own little ones, you know where to send them to learn geometry!'

He made it sound easy. His assumptions were too tempting. I was letting myself be won over by the pleasure of meeting somebody who did not see my marriage to Helena as utterly disastrous.

'I'll remember!' I promised gently, making good my escape.

XXXIV

Back at the apartment I found Helena sniffing at tunics. They were ones we had worn for travelling, just fetched back from the laundry downstairs.

'Juno, I hate winter! Things you send to be washed come back worse. Don't wear those; they smell musty. They must have been left too long in a basket while damp. I'll take them to my parents' house and rinse them out again.'

'Oh, hang mine over a door to air for a bit. I don't care. Some of the places I've been in today were not fit for pristine whites.'

I kissed her, so she took the opportunity to sniff teasingly at me.

One way and another that kept us busy until dinner-time.

According to custom in our house, I cooked. We had half a chicken, which I sizzled in oil and wine, using a rattly iron skillet over a grill on the brick cooking bench. There were no herbs, because we had been away at the time when we should have been collecting them. Helena owned an expensive collection of spices, but those needed picking up from her parents' house. All in all, things at the apartment were even more disorganised than normal. We ate sitting on stools, holding our bowls on our knees, since I still had to obtain a new table. My boast to Junia had been true: we did possess an impressive dinner service in glossy red Samian pottery. For safety I had stored it at Mother's house.

Suddenly I felt overwhelmed by despair. It was thinking about the dinnerware that did it. Problems were building up all around me, and the prospect of having our only civilised possessions packed away, perhaps for ever, was just too much to bear.

Helena noticed how I was feeling. 'What's the matter, Marcus?'

'Nothing.'

'There's something niggling you – apart from the murder.'

845

'Sometimes I think our whole life is buried in straw in an attic, awaiting a future we may never arrange.'

'Oh dear! It sounds as if I should fetch out your poetry tablet, so you can write a nice morbid elegy.' Helena took a mocking view of the melancholy stuff I had been trying to write for years; she preferred me to write satires for some reason.

'Listen, fruit, if I did manage to acquire four hundred thousand sesterces, and if the Emperor was willing to include my name on the middle-rank scroll, would you actually be prepared to marry me?'

'Find the four hundred thousand first!' was her automatic response.

'That's me answered then!' I muttered gloomily.

'Ah . . .' Helena put her empty bowl on the floor and knelt at the side of my stool. She wrapped her arms around me, spreading her warm red stole across my knees comfortingly. She smelled clean and sweet, faintly perfumed with rosemary, which she used to rinse her hair. 'Why are you feeling so insecure?' I made no reply. 'Do you want me to say that I love you?'

'I can listen to that.'

She said it. I listened. She added some details, which cheered me up slightly. Helena Justina had a convincing grasp of rhetoric. 'So what's wrong, Marcus?'

'Maybe if we were married I would be sure you belonged to me.'

'I'm not a set of wine jugs!'

'No. I could scratch my name on a jug. And also,' I continued doggedly, 'you would then be certain that I belonged to you.'

'I know that,' she said, smiling rather. 'Here we are. We live together. You despise my rank and I deplore your past history, but we have foolishly chosen to share each other's company. What else is there, love?'

'You could leave me at any time.'

'Or you could leave me!'

I managed to grin at her. 'Maybe this is the problem, Helena. Maybe I am frightened that without a contract to honour I might storm off in a temper, then regret it all my life.'

'Contracts exist only to make arrangements for when you break them!' Every partnership needs someone sensible to keep its wheels in the right ruts. 'Besides,' Helena scoffed, 'when you do run off, I always come and fetch you back.'

That was true.

'Do you want to get drunk?'

'No.'

'Maybe,' she suggested, with a hint of asperity, 'what you do want is to sit in your shabby apartment, alone, scowling over the unfairness of life and watching a solitary beetle climb up the wall? Oh, I do understand. This is what an informer likes. To be lonely and bored while he thinks about his debts, and lack of clients, and the scores of scornful women who have trampled all over him. That makes him feel important. Your life is too soft, Marcus Didius! Here you are sharing a small but tasty dinner with your rude but affectionate sweetheart; it obviously spoils your act. Maybe I should go, my darling, so you can despair properly!'

I sighed. 'I just want four hundred thousand sesterces – which I know I cannot get!'

'Borrow it,' said Helena.

'Who from?'

'Someone else who has got it.' She thought I was too mean to pay the interest.

'We're in enough trouble. We don't need to expire under a burden of debt. That's the end of the subject.' I tightened my arm around her and stuck out my chin. 'Let's see if you're a woman of your word. You've been rude to me, princess – now how about being affectionate?'

Helena smiled. The smile itself made good her boast; the sense of well-being it brought to me was uncontrollable. She started tickling my neck, reducing me to helplessness. 'Don't issue a challenge like that, Marcus, unless you are sure you can take the consequences . . .'

'You're a terrible woman,' I groaned, bending my head as I feebly tried to avoid her teasing hand. 'You make me have hope. Hope is far too dangerous.'

'Danger is your natural element,' she replied.

There was a fold at the top of her gown which gaped slightly from her brooches; I made it wider and kissed the warm, delicate skin beneath. 'You're right; winter's dreary. When clothes come back from the laundry, people put on too many of them – ' It did provide entertainment when I tried taking some of them off her again . . .

We went to bed. In winter, in Rome, with neither hot air in wall-flues nor slaves to replenish banks of braziers, there is nothing else to do. All my questions remained unanswered; but that was nothing new.

XXXV

Gaius Baebius had not exaggerated how many records of incoming ships we would have to scrutinise. I went out with him to Ostia. I was not intending to stay there, only to provide initial encouragement, but I was horrified by the mounds of scrolls that my brother-in-law's colleagues happily produced for us.

'Jupiter, they're staggering in like Atlas under the weight of the world! How many more?'

'A few.' That meant hundreds. Gaius Baebius hated to upset people.

'How many years do you keep the records for?'

'Oh we've got them all, ever since Augustus dreamed up the import duty.'

I tried to look reverent. 'Amazing!'

'Have you found out the name of the agent Festus used?'

'No I haven't!' I barked tetchily. (I had forgotten all about it.)

'I don't want to find myself having to read this mountain twice –'

'We'll have to ignore that aspect and do the best we can.'

We settled that I would run my thumb down looking at the ships' names, while Gaius Baebius slowly perused the columns of whoever had commissioned them. I had a nasty feeling this method of splitting the details was likely to lose something.

Luckily I had left instructions with Helena that I would return home for any emergency – and to define 'emergency' liberally. Only next morning word came that I had to go back to see Geminus.

'Sorry. This is a fiendish nuisance, Gaius, but I must go. Otherwise I'll be breaking the conditions of my bail – '

'That's fine, you go.'

'Will you be all right carrying on for a while?'

'Oh yes.'

I knew Gaius Baebius had decided that I was flicking through the documents too casually. He was glad to see me depart, so he could plod on at his own dire pace. I left him playing the big man among his gruesome customs cronies while I fled back to Rome.

The request to visit Geminus was genuine. 'I would not send a false message when you were working!' cried Helena, shocked.

'No, my love . . . So what's the urgency?'

'Geminus is afraid the people who disrupted that auction are planning to strike again.'

'Don't say he's changed his mind and wants my help?'

'Just try not to get hurt!' muttered Helena, hugging me anxiously.

As soon as I reached the Saepta, I had the impression the other auctioneers were greeting my appearance with knowing looks. There was a disturbing atmosphere. People were gossiping in small groups; they fell silent as I passed.

The rumpus had happened, this time right in the ware-house. Overnight intruders had vandalised the stock. Gornia, the chief porter, found time to tell me how he had discovered the damage that morning. Most of it had already been cleared up, but I could see enough smashed couches and cabinets to guess the losses were serious. Potsherds filled several buckets on the pavement, and glass fragments were rattling under someone's broom. Bronzes stood covered in graffiti. Inside the wide doorway, what had been a garden statue of Priapus had now, as they say in the catalogues, lost its attribute.

'Where's himself?'

'In there. He should rest. Do something with him, will you?'

'Is it possible?'

I squeezed between a pile of benches and an upturned bed, stepped over some bead-rimmed copper pans, knocked my ear on a stuffed boar's head, ducked under stools hung lopsidedly from a rafter, and cursed my way to the next division in the indoor space. Pa was on his knees, meticulously collecting up pieces of ivory. His face was grey, though he applied the usual bluster once I coughed and he noticed me. He tried to stand up. Pain stopped him. I grabbed him with one arm and helped him ease his stocky frame upright.

'What's this?'

'Kicked in the ribs . . .'

I found two feet of free wall he could lean on and propped him there. 'Does that mean you were here when it happened?'

'Sleeping upstairs.'

'Helena said you were expecting a racket. I could have been here with you, if you had warned me earlier.'

'You have your own troubles.'

'Believe me, you're one of them!'

'What are you so angry for?'

As usual with my relatives, I had no idea.

I checked him over for ruptures and fractures. He was still too shaken to stop me, though he did protest. There was one monstrous bruise on his upper arm, a few cuts on his head, and those tender ribs. He would live, but he had taken all he could. He was too stiff to make it to the office upstairs, so we stayed there.

I had been in the store enough times before to realise that despite the clutter there was more empty space than usual. 'I see a lot of gaps, Pa. Does that mean you had the stuff smashed to ruins last night, or are you generally losing custom nowadays?'

'Both. Word gets around if you're having liveliness.'

'So there is something wrong?'

He gave me a look. 'I've called for you, haven't I?'

'Oh yes. Times must be bad! And I thought you just wanted to check that I hadn't jumped bail.'

'No chance of that,' my father grinned. 'You're the cocky sort who is bound to think he can clear himself of the charge.'

'As it's murder, I'd better.'

'And as it's my money bailing you, you'd better not skip!'

'I'll repay the damned money!' We were hard at it quarrelling again. 'I never asked you to interfere! If I'm desperate Ma will always assist with a judicial bribe – '

'I bet that stings!'

'Yes, it hurts,' I admitted. Then I threw back my head in disgust. 'Dear gods, how do I get in these messes?'

'Pure talent!' Pa assured me. He too breathed heavily and

calmed down. 'So when will you be solving the murder?' I merely grimaced. He changed the subject: 'Helena sent word she had to bring you back from Ostia. Did you scavenge a bite on the journey, or can you finish off my lunch for me? I couldn't face it after the punch-up, but I don't want her-at-home to start . . .'

Some traditions continued, regardless of the personnel. Ma had always sent him out with his midday meal in a basket. If he was sleeping away while he guarded some particularly valuable hoard, she doggedly despatched one of us with the bread, cheese and cold meat. Now the redhead was supplying him with his daily snack – probably no longer to keep him out of expensive foodstalls, but simply because he had been trained to the routine.

I hated to be drawn into these new domestic arrangements. However, Helena had pushed me off without sustenance, and I was starving. I ate his meal. 'Thanks. Not up to Mother's standards, she'll be glad to hear.'

'You always were the charming one,' sighed Pa.

He lived in style, actually. After I had chewed through the cold kidneys rolled in bacon, with slices of must cake soaked in a piquant sauce, my father roused himself enough to say, 'You can leave me the beetroot.'

That took me back. He had always been a beet addict. 'Here, then . . . Your bacon's filled a hollow, but I could do with something to wash it down.'

'Upstairs,' said Pa. 'You'll have to go yourself.'

I made my way to the office. Here there was no evidence of the vandals, so perhaps Pa's intervention had stopped them reaching this far. Presumably they would have tried to break into the money chest. There was a possibility they would come back again for it, I reflected anxiously.

I was still poking around for a wine flask when Geminus staggered up behind me after all. He found me looking at that week's special.

It was one of the pots he loved, painted in a warm amber, with darker reliefs in several earthy tones. He had it set up on a none-too-subtle plinth. It appeared to be extremely old and Ionian, though I had seen similar at sales in Etruria. It had panache. There was a pretty striped foot, then a base decorated florally, above which the wide body carried a scene of Hercules leading the captive Cerberus to King Eurystheus, the king so terrified he had leapt into a large black cooking pot. The characters were full of life: Hercules with his lionskin and club, and Cerberus every inch a hound from Hades, his three heads distinguished by different shades of paint. Apart from his wriggly entourage of spotted snakes, Cerberus reminded me of Junia's dog, Ajax. The vessel was beautiful. Yet somehow I felt dissatisfied.

Geminus had come in and caught me frowning. 'Wrong handles!'

'Ah!' The oldest story in the world of fakes. 'I knew something was odd. So your repair man needs a lesson in art history?'

'He has his uses.' The noncommittal tone warned me not to pursue this; I was intruding on the profane mysteries.

I could guess. Sometimes an article comes up for sale with an uncertain history or unconvincing provenance. Sometimes it is better to adapt the said item before it appears publicly: change a bronze palmette to an acanthus leaf; swap the head on a statue; give a silver tripod a satyr's feet instead of a lion's claws. I knew it was done. I knew some of the handy adaptors who did it. Sometimes I had been the frustrated member of an auction audience who suspected the changes but could not prove deceit.

It was part of my informing job to be aware of these procedures. I had a sideline tracing stolen art, though it never paid well. Collectors always expected a bargain, even for normal services. I grew tired of presenting an expenses bill, only to be asked if that was the best I could do on it. Most people who had treasures thieved were full of cheek, but they were novices. Giving them a ten per cent discount 'for trade' was an insult to the real connoisseurs at the Saepta.

'It's not what you're thinking,' my father told me suddenly. 'I got it for nothing. The whole top was missing. My man re-created it, but he's an idiot. With a wide neck, it should have body loops – ' He gestured to make two lugs set below the shoulders. The repair had its two handles carried up and hooked on to the throat, like an amphora. 'He can't tell a vase from a bloody jug, that's the truth of it.' Catching my sceptical look, he felt obliged to add, 'It's for sale "as seen". Naturally I'll mention what's been done – unless I really take against the customer!'

I restricted myself to saying, 'Strikes me the demigod has tied Cerberus on a rather thin piece of string!'

Then Pa produced the ritual wine tray, and we sat around with the silly cups again.

I tried to take a firm filial grip. 'Now stop behaving like a bonehead. This time you're going to tell me what is going on.'

'You're as bad as your mother for having a rant.'

'Somebody doesn't like you, Father,' I said patiently. 'Somebody other than me!'

'Someone wants some money,' sneered my honourable parent. 'Money I refuse to give.'

'Protection?'

I saw his eyes flicker. 'Not in essence. Paying up would protect me from this aggravation, certainly; but that's not the dispute.'

'Oh there is a dispute then?' I demanded.

'There was.'

'Is it not settled?'

'Temporarily.'

'So they will leave you alone for now?'

'For the time being.'

'How did you achieve that?'

'Simple,' said Geminus. 'While they were kicking seven bells out of me yesterday evening, I told them the person they really needed to argue with was you.'

XXXVI

I assumed an expression of Roman steadfastness and calm.

'What's up, son? Fly gone up your nose?'

'I'm staying detached.'

'You can't. You're in this – up to your neck.'

'I'll abdicate.'

'Afraid not,' he confessed. For once he looked guilty. 'Not possible.'

This was ridiculous. Marponius was going to be planning a new trial list soon; I should have been back at Ostia seeking to clear my name.

No, I shouldn't have been in this mess at all. I should have been living with my beloved in some peaceful villa in the country where my worst concern was whether to spend the morning catching up on my correspondence, or peel an apple for Helena, or go out and inspect the vines.

'You look upset, son.'

'Believe me, even before this news I was not exactly overflowing with Saturnalian jollity!'

'You're a Stoic.' I knew my father had no time for any flavour of philosophy. A typical Roman prejudice, based on the simple concept that thought is a threat.

I blew out my cheeks in irritation. 'Let me struggle to understand what is happening. You know some violent people who have a long-standing grievance, and they have just been told by you that I'm the person they want to tackle about their debt? So good-mannered of you to warn me, Didius Geminus! Such fatherly respect!'

'You'll dodge out of it.'

'I hope so! After I've dealt with any inconvenience from the auction-busters, I'll be looking for somebody else to attack. I advise you to start getting nippy yourself.'

'Show some piety,' complained my father. 'Show some parental reverence!'

'Cobnuts!' I said.

We were both breathing heavily. The situation felt unreal. Once, I had vowed I would never speak to my father again. Now here I was, sitting in his office with curious Egyptian gods peering over my shoulder from some inconsequential red and yellow furniture, while I let him lumber me with Hercules knows what troubles.

'Was your roughing-up arranged by the legionaries?'

'No,' said Pa. He sounded pretty definite.

'So it's unconnected with the death of Censorinus?'

'As far as I can see. Are you going to help out?'

I swore, not bothering to keep it under my breath. If I had stuck to my contempt for him, I could have avoided this. I ought to walk out now.

Yet there was only one answer to give him. 'If you're having a problem, naturally I'll help.'

'You're a good boy!' Geminus smirked complacently.

'I'm a good informer.' I kept my tone low and my temper cool. 'You need a professional for this sort of work.'

'So you'll do the job?'

'I'll do the job, but while I'm trying to save my neck on the other count I can't spare much time to dabble in auction fraud.' He must have known what was coming even before I dished it up: 'If I break into my schedule to do you a favour, you'll have to pay me at top rates.'

My father leaned back and stared at the ceiling in momentary disbelief. 'He's not mine!'

Unluckily for both of us, I certainly was.

'If you don't like it,' I mocked, 'you have a father's usual remedy. Go ahead – disinherit me!'

There was a shifty pause. In fact I had no idea what would happen, on my father's death, to the proceeds of his long auctioneering career. Knowing him, he had not addressed the issue. So that was another mess for me to sort out one day. If only to avoid it, I did my duty mentally and wished him a long life.

'I gather you're short of collateral?' he smiled, immediately all smoothness again. He passed a weary hand through those uncombed grey curls. 'Ah well, what are fathers for?' More than I ever got from this one. 'I'll hire you if that seems to be the form. What are these rates we hear so much about?' I told him, making a quick calculation and trebling them. (Well, he wanted me to get married.) He whistled in outrage. 'No wonder you never have any clients. Your charges are deplorable!'

'No worse than the auction percentage – and I work a lot harder for my wages. All you have to do is bawl loudly and bluff people. Informers need brains, bodyweight, and a gripping business sense.'

'And too much cheek!' he commented.

'So that's a contract,' I said.

Whatever it was we were clinching had yet to be revealed. That did not bother me. Shyness was usual among my clients. The inquisition of the prospective customer was the first part of any job I ever did, and usually the trickiest. Compared to that, asking questions of mere villains, cheats and bullies was easy labour.

Pa poured himself more wine. 'Drink on it?'

'I'll keep sober if I'm working.'

'You sound like a prig.'

'I sound like a man who stays alive.' I reached out and grasped his wrist, preventing him from lifting the cup. 'Now tell me what the job is.'

'You aren't going to care for it!' he assured me contentedly.

'I'll deal with my emotions. Now feel free to elaborate!'

'I should never have got you into this.'

'Agreed. You should have shown restraint when those bastards were applying their boots to the apples of your Hesperides – ' I was losing my temper (yet again). '*What's the wrinkle, Pa?*'

Finally he told me, though even then extracting the details was like squeezing olives through a jammed press.

'This is how it is. Things take time in the fine-art world. When people are commissioning creative works, they don't expect quick deliveries, so the fashion is to let problems ride.'

'How long ago did this marathon start?'

'Couple of years. I received an enquiry; I put the people off. I said it wasn't my problem; they didn't believe me. This year they must have remembered to do something about it, and they came back. More insistent.'

857

I was grinding my teeth. 'More aware, you mean, that they were losing cash? On whatever it is,' I added, though I knew.

'Exactly. They became aggressive, so I threw my javelin.'

'In a manner of speaking?'

'Well I told them to push off.'

'With spicy phraseology?'

'They might have thought so.'

'Jove! Then what?'

'It went quiet for a bit. Next the auctions were invaded. Last night it was the warehouse – and me, of course.'

'You may have been lucky last night. Read the dead sheep's liver, Pa. If these people are not soon satisfied, somebody may end up damaged even more severely. From what you mentioned earlier, these bruisers may bash me?'

'You're tough.'

'I'm not a demigod! And actually, I don't enjoy spending my life looking over one shoulder for large types with nails in their cudgels who want to practise hunt-the-decoy through the streets.'

'They don't want bloodshed.'

'Thanks for the reassurance, and tell that to your kicked ribs! I'm not convinced. There was a dead soldier at Flora's Caupona who may have inadvertently stepped in these people's way. That worries me – '

'It worries me,' cried my father. 'If you're right, there was no need for that!'

'I'd rather not have people standing round a pyre next week saying the same thing over me! In a minute I'm going to start demanding names from you – but first I have a crucial question, Father.' He looked pained at my tone, as if I were being insensitive. I forced myself to keep my voice level. 'Just tell me: does this problem of yours have anything to do with big brother Festus and his missing Phidias?'

Our father found an expression of amazement from his skilled repertoire. 'However did you realise that?'

I closed my eyes. 'Let's stop acting the farce, shall we? Just come clean!'

'It's quite simple,' Pa acquiesced. 'The people who want to talk to you are called Cassius Carus and Ummidia Servia. A couple. They don't socialise in a vulgar way, but in the trade they regard themselves as persons of influence. They have a big house with a private art gallery, nice place off the Via Flaminia. They collect statues. They had been lined up by Festus to acquire his Poseidon.'

I was already groaning. 'How closely lined up?'

'As tight as they could be.'

'And persons of influence don't like to be diddled?'

'No. Especially if they intend to go on collecting – which carries some risks, as you know. People want a reputation. They don't like their mistakes to be publicly known.'

I asked, '*Were* they diddled?'

'I reckon they think so. Carus and Servia were certainly expecting to receive the property. But then Festus lost his ship, so he failed to deliver it.'

'Had they actually paid for the goods?'

'Afraid so.'

I pulled a face. 'Then they were definitely diddled – and we are rightly being chased. How much – if it's not a saucy question – are we two honest brokers being asked to find?'

'Oh . . . call it half a million,' muttered Pa.

XXXVII

When I left the Saepta Julia, the air was thin and cold. I nearly went into the Agrippan Baths, but could not face a long walk home on a winter evening after I had let myself be made happy and warm. Better to do the heavy work, then relax.

Pa had offered me a lift in his ornamental litter back to the Thirteenth Sector, but I elected to walk. I had had enough. I needed to be alone. I needed to think.

Helena was waiting. 'Just a quick kiss, my darling, then we're going out.'

'What's happened?'

'I'm really getting grown-up work! First my mother employs me to prove Festus is *not* a criminal; now my father has hired me because Festus probably is.'

'At least your brother brings in jobs,' said my beloved, ever the optimist. 'Am I coming to help?'

'No. The irrepressible Geminus has fingered me for the Phidias. Some quick-tempered creditors may be coming here to look for me. You'll have to be stowed somewhere safer until the heat's off. I'll take you to the relation of your choice.'

She chose going back to Ma again. I took her; ducked the maternal enquiries; promised to see them both when I could; then trudged off through the gathering darkness towards the Caelian.

I was now determined to track down my brother's friends, the loathsome wall painters.

I tried the Virgin, without luck.

I tried all the other places where Varga and Manlius were supposed to hang out, but they were not there either. This was tiresome, but par for the course in my work. Investigating consists mainly of failure. You need thick boots and a strong heart, plus an infinite capacity for staying awake while parked in a draughty pergola, hoping that that strange scuttling sound is only a rat, not a man with a knife, though all the time you know that if the person you are watching for ever does turn up, they will be a dead loss.

Helena had asked, 'Why don't you go straight to the art collectors and explain?'

'I will go. I hope to have something to offer them first.'

As I stood watching an extremely nasty doss-house in the worst area of a bad district in this heartless city, it did seem unlikely that a rare old Greek statue would be standing around here with its toes as cold as mine, waiting for a lift in a waggon to a more refined environment.

I must have been there on surveillance for four hours. On a cold March Thursday, that's a long time.

The street was pitch-dark. It was short, narrow, and stinking; an easy touch for comparisons with life. The night-life was plentiful: drunks, fornicators, more drunks, cats who had learned from the fornicators, even drunker drunks. Drunken cats, probably. Everyone round here had been at an amphora, and I could understand it. Everyone was lost. The dogs; the cats; the humans. Even the fire brigade, wandering up with half-empty buckets, asked me the way to Oyster Street. I gave them correct instructions, then watched their smoky flare disappear in the wrong direction anyway. They were going to a tavern for a quick one; the fire could just blaze.

A whore offered me a quick one of the other sort, but I managed to plead poor plumbing. She cackled and launched into medical theories that made me blush. I told her I was one of the vigiles, so with a vicious curse she staggered off. Beyond the corner, where the streets were wider, even the normal night-time rumble of delivery carts seemed slack tonight. Beyond that, sharp on the frosty air, I heard the call of a Praetorian trumpet sounding the watch over their great camp. Above my head, where the stars should be, only blackness loomed.

Eventually the passers-by thinned out. My feet were frozen. My legs were too exhausted to stamp. I was wearing two cloaks and three tunics, but the chill had slid right under them. This was some way from the river, but even here the Tiber fog seeped into my lungs. There was no breeze; just that still, deceptive coldness like an animal that eats your heart while you stand.

It was a night when professional burglars would glance quickly outside, then decide to stay in and annoy their wives. Heartbroken women would be hanging around the Aemilian Bridge waiting for a quiet moment to edge over the parapet and jump into oblivion. Tramps would cough to death in the gateways at the Circus. Lost children and runaway slaves would huddle against the huge black walls under the Citadel, slipping into Hades by accident when they forgot to breathe. There was no blizzard; it was not even raining. But all the same it was a bitter, baleful, dolorous night, and I hated to be out in it.

In the end I broke the rules. I strode up to the painters' lodging-house, entered by the creaking door, felt my way up five flights of stairs (fortunately I had counted the storeys when I was here before), found their room, spent half an hour trying to pick the lock, discovered the door was open anyway, and then sat in darkness waiting for them. At least I was under cover now.

XXXVIII

Manlius and Varga came swinging back home in the dead of night, arguing at the tops of their voices with a gang of other artistic delinquents as if it was broad daylight. I heard a shutter crash open and someone screamed at them; they answered with an innocent calm that hinted this was a regular occurrence. They had no sense of time. They had no sense of decency either, but having seen them cadging drinks off Festus I already knew that.

The other crowd went on, leaving my two to lurch upstairs. I sat, listening to their uneven approach. Informers dread this moment: sitting in pitch-darkness, waiting for a problem.

I already knew quite a lot about them. Anyone who broke into their room stumbled over discarded amphorae. Their room smelt sour. They owned few clothes, and paid fewer laundry bills. They lived such abnormal hours that by the time they thought of washing, even the public baths had closed. As well as their own odours, which were plentiful, they lived among a complicated waft of pigments: lead, palm resin, galls, crushed seashells and chalks, together with lime, gypsum, and borax. They ate cheap meals, full of garlic and those artichokes that make you fart.

In they fell, all paint-stains and dirty politics. The smoke from a resinous torch added itself to the other smells that lived here. It enabled me to see I was in a communal room. A small space crammed with beds for three or four people, though only these two appeared to be renting at present. The painters showed no surprise at finding me sitting there in the dark. They did not object: I had brought them an amphora. Well, I had met creative types before.

One was tall and one short, both of them bare-armed, not from bravado but because they were too poor to own cloaks. They both had beards, mainly to strike a defiant social attitude. They were aged about thirty, but their manners were adolescent and their habits puerile. Under the grime they might both have been good-looking in different ways. They preferred to make their mark through personality; a kind friend should have advised them their personalities needed sprucing up.

They stuffed their torch into a narrow oil jar: some tasteful Greek's funeral urn. I guessed the Greek was still in it. That would be their idea of fun, making a lampstand out of him.

Neither of them remembered me.

'Who's this?'

'I'm Marcus – ' I began, intending full formality.

'Hey, Marcus! Wonderful to see you!'

'How's your life, Marcus?'

I refrained from saying that only select members of my family were permitted to use my personal name. Etiquette is lost on free spirits; especially ones who are habitually drunk.

Manlius was the designer. The tall, sleepy-eyed one, he wore what had once been a white tunic and had a fringe of dank black hair. Manlius squiggled and doodled in miniature. He had drawn neat little columns, swags and flower vases all around his corner of the room.

Varga's short legs were compensated for by a wide moustache. His tunic was a brownish manganese colour, with rags of purplish braid, and he wore sandals with gold thongs. Ma would have reckoned him untrustworthy. He was the one who could paint. He preferred ambitious battle scenes with bare-chested mythological giants. He had a good line in tragic centaurs; one five feet high reared up in agony above his bed, gorily speared by an Amazon.

'I'd like to meet your model!'

'The girl or the horse?'

'Oh the horse – amazing fetlocks!'

Our quips were satirical; the Amazon was startling. I pretended to admire her sensitive skin tones so we could all leer at her shape. Her body owed something to the girl who had posed for the picture, though more to Varga's fervent lust. He had improved her until she was almost deformed. I knew that. I knew his model; had seen her, anyway. His painted fighting maid was based on a luscious bundle whose proportions in real life would make a man gulp, yet not despair. The Amazon was for wild dreams.

The original model was a ripe brunette with wide-set daring eyes, eyes that had fallen on my brother once, almost certainly by design. She was the girl he had sat next to at the Circus, the night he dumped Marina on me. The night, I now felt certain, when he had roamed through our city on the lookout for someone though for once, I reckoned, the girl was only a messenger.

'Who owns the body?'

'Rubinia – though I made some adaptations! She often sits for us.'

I was in the right place. That night, Rubinia must have told Festus he would see the painters at the Virgin. (She had probably told him her address too, though that was now irrelevant.)

I laughed, easily. 'I think she knew my brother.'

'More than likely!' chortled Manilus. He must be commenting on the girl; he had not asked me who my brother was.

Maybe he knew.

Probably not yet, I thought.

While I wondered how to work around to my enquiry, we lay on the beds with our boots on, drinking steadily. (Artists do not have mothers who bring them up nicely – or at least, they do not have to acknowledge them.)

My reference to Festus was forgotten. The painters were the casual type who would let you mention an acquaintance, or a relation, without further curiosity. They knew everyone. If he was carrying an amphora or sitting in a bar with a full purse on him, any stranger was their friend. Trying to remind them of one past patron among so many could prove difficult.

Our encounter tonight became as bad as I expected: they started talking about politics. Manlius was a republican. I was one myself, though wary of mentioning it in this loose-tongued company. Too serious a hope of restoring the old system implied removing the Emperor. Vespasian might be a tolerant old buffer, but treason was still a capital offence, and I try to avoid such hobbies. Being set up for a soldier's murder was unpleasant enough.

Manlius definitely wanted to dispose of Vespasian; Varga hated the entire Senate. They had a plan to turn Rome into a

865

free public gallery, stocked by grabbing patrician collections and raiding the public porticoes, and financed from the Treasury. The plan was highly detailed – and completely impractical in their hands. These two could not have organised an orgy in a brothel.

'We could do it,' declaimed Varga, 'if the establishment were not protected by the mailed shirts and hidebound mentality of the Praetorian Guard.'

I decided against mentioning that I sometimes worked as an imperial agent, in case I was found decapitated in a public square. Artistic people have no sense of proportion – and drunks have no sense.

'This is a city run on fear!' Manlius slurred. 'For instance – here's a for instance, Marcus – why do slaves all wear the same clothes as the rest of us? Why do their masters make sure of that?'

'Because they work better if they're warm?'

My answer produced a huge guffaw. 'No! Because if they all wore a slave uniform, they would realise that there are *millions* of them, controlled by a mere handful of bastards they could easily overthrow if they put their minds to it – '

'Thank you, Spartacus!'

'I'm serious,' he mumbled, making serious efforts to pour himself another drink.

'Here's to the republic,' I toasted him gently. 'When every man tilled his own furrow, when every daughter was a virgin, and every son stayed at home to the age of forty-nine, saying "Yes, Father" to everything!'

'You're a cynic!' commented Varga, evidently the astute one of this rollicking pair.

I mentioned that I had a nephew who had apprenticed himself to a fresco painter on the Campanian coast. Actually Larius was on my mind now because I was thinking he might have attached himself to some useless degenerate like these two. He was embarrassingly sensible, but I should have checked before I left him there.

'Campania's a dump!' Manlius grumbled. 'We were there; it was dreadful. We went for the sun and the women and the precious grapes – plus the stupendously rich clients, of

866

course. No luck. All snobs, Marcus. Nobody wants you unless you're a Greek or a local. We came home again.'

'Are you in work at the moment?'

'Surely. Good commission. Varga's doing The Rape of the Sabine Women for aristos to gaze at while they stuff themselves silly on peacocks in aspic. He creates a nice rape, Varga . . .'

'I can believe it!'

'I'm doing them a pair of rooms: one white, one black. Either side of the atrium. Balanced, see? Balance appeals to me.'

'Doubles your fee?' I grinned.

'Money means nothing to artists.'

'This generous attitude explains why you had to descend to painting rude sketches at the Virgin – settling a bill, I presume?'

Varga winced. 'That thing!'

'You were slumming,' I said, looking at the quality of what he painted for himself.

'We were, Marcus. The need to drink is a terrible thing!'

I was tired of this. My feet had warmed up enough to start hurting; the rest of me was stiff, tired and bored. I was sick of drinking; sick of holding my breath against the unsavoury atmosphere; sick of listening to drunks.

'Don't call me Marcus,' I said abruptly. 'You don't know me.'

They blinked at me blearily. They were a long way from the real world. I could have tripped them up merely by asking for their names or when their birthdays were.

'What's up, Marcus?'

'Let's go back to the beginning: I am Marcus Didius Falco,' I resumed, from an hour earlier. Thanks to the effects of my amphora their bravado was extinguished and they let me finish this time. 'You knew Marcus Didius Festus. Another name; another face; believe me, another personality.'

Manlius, the one who rescued them from trouble perhaps, waved a hand, managed to place it on the bed, and propped himself half upright. He tried to speak, but gave up. He lay down flat again.

'Festus?' quavered Varga, staring at the ceiling. Above his head, nicely positioned for gazing at while nearly insensible, he had painted a small, exquisite Aphrodite Bathing, modelled not by Rubinia but some small, exquisite blonde. If the painting was accurate, he would have done better luring the blonde to bed, but they do expect regular meals and a supply of glass-bead necklaces. No point investing in the hair dye otherwise.

'Festus,' I repeated, struggling to organise something sensible here.

'Festus . . .' Varga rolled himself sideways so he could squint at me. Somewhere in those puffy eyes a new level of intelligence seemed to glimmer. 'What do you want, Falco?'

'Vargo, I want you to tell me *why*, on a certain night five years ago when I saw you with him at the Virgin, Marcus Didius Festus wanted to meet with you?'

'He can't remember who he met at the Virgin five *days* ago!' Manlius responded, gathering the shreds of his critical faculties. 'You don't want much!'

'I want to save my neck from the public strangler,' I retorted frankly. 'A soldier called Censorinus has been murdered, probably for asking just this sort of question. Unless I can shed light on events, I'll be condemned for the killing. Hear that, and understand me: I'm a desperate man!'

'I know nothing about anything,' Varga assured me.

'Well you know enough to lie about it!' I rasped good-humouredly. Then I lowered my voice. 'Festus is dead; you cannot harm him. The truth may even protect his reputation – though I'm honestly not expecting it – so don't hold back to avoid offending me.'

'It's a complete fog to me,' Varga repeated.

'I hate people who pretend to be idiots!' I spun off the bed where I was lying, and got hold of his right arm. I twisted it enough to hurt. As I sprang at him I had whipped out my knife; I laid it against his wrist so the slightest movement would make him cut himself. 'Stop messing me about. I know you met Festus and I know it's relevant! Come clean, Varga, or I'll slice off your painting hand!'

Varga went white. Too drunk to resist, and too innocent to know how to do it anyway, he stared up at me in terror, hardly able to breathe. I was so frustrated by the enquiry, I almost meant what I said. I was frightening myself, and Varga could tell. A vague sound gurgled in his throat.

'Speak up, Varga. Don't be shy!'

'I can't remember meeting your brother – '

'*I* remember you meeting him,' I declared coldly. 'And I wasn't even in on the conspiracy!'

His friend shifted anxiously. At last I was getting somewhere.

'There was no conspiracy involving us,' Manlius burst out from the other bed. 'I told that to the soldier when he came!'

XXXIX

'This is news to me!' Varga pleaded.

I pressed the knife harder against his arm, so he could feel the edge of the blade, though in fact I had it turned so it did not yet pierce the skin. 'Careful. You're very drunk, and I'm not entirely sober. One wrong move, and you've painted your last tantalising nipple . . .' I stared at Manlius. 'Carry on. I'm versatile. I can manage to threaten one man while the other does the talking!'

'Tell him,' Varga urged faintly. 'And I wouldn't mind knowing myself . . .'

'You weren't here,' Manlius explained. They had peculiar priorities. His main concern seemed to be convincing his pal that there were no secrets at the lodging-house. 'It was one of your days for taking Rubinia's measurements . . .'

'Cut the ribaldry!' I grated. 'What happened with Censorinus?'

'Laurentius,' corrected Manlius.

'Who?'

'He said his name was Laurentius.'

I released Varga, but sat back on my heels, still holding the knife where they could both see it. 'Are you certain? The soldier who died was called Censorinus Macer.'

'Laurentius was what he told me.'

If Censorinus had had a crony with him in Rome, I was very relieved to hear it; this Laurentius would be a prime suspect. Cronies fall out. They sit in a tavern having a drink, then they quarrel about money, or women, or political philosophy, or simply about whether their boat home leaves on Tuesday or Thursday. Then it's natural that somebody gets stabbed and his pal legs it . . . Or so I tried to convince myself, overlooking to some extent the violence with which the centurion had been attacked.

'So tell me about this Laurentius. What was his rank and legion, and when did he come to see you?'

'A while ago – '

'Weeks? Months?'

Being specific was not a habit here. 'A month or two . . . possibly. I don't know the other details.'

'Oh come on, you're a damned painter, aren't you? You're supposed to be observant! Did he carry a vine staff?'

'Yes.'

'Then he was a full centurion. He would have been close friends with Festus. Did he tell you that?' Manlius nodded. 'Good. Now take a deep breath and tell me what he wanted.' There was no flicker of rational thought below the painter's long untidy fringe of hair. 'Did he,' I spelled out, 'ask you about the *Hypericon*, for instance – or did he go straight to the matter of the Phidias?'

Manlius smiled finally. It was a gentle, undeceptive smile. I did not place a scruple of trust in that soft grin – but the words he uttered rang true enough: 'I don't know what you're talking about, Falco. The soldier was asking about someone. I remember,' he told me quietly, 'because it was the same person Festus was so stirred up about on that night in the Virgin.'

'Who?'

'Orontes Mediolanus.'

'The sculptor,' Varga contributed.

This was the part that did make sense.

I kept my voice as steady as possible. 'And where in Rome can I find this Orontes?'

'That's the point!' Manlius burst out, with relaxed and unvindictive triumph. 'Orontes has disappeared from Rome. In fact he vanished years ago.'

I had already guessed the sequel. 'He had vanished when Festus was after him?'

'Of course! That was why Festus came looking for us. Festus wanted to ask us where in Hades Orontes was.'

I went back a step. 'How did you know Festus?'

'He noticed models,' Varga said, convincingly. We all glanced at his Amazon and imagined Festus taking notice of Rubinia.

'And why did he think you could track down Orontes?'

'Orontes used to lodge with us,' Varga explained. 'In fact, earlier this evening, you were lying on his bed!'

871

I stared at it. The hard, lumpy mattress was covered with a thin blanket. Unwashed food bowls were piled underneath, and these two untidy idiots kept paint-kettles on one end, encrusted with copper oxides and enamels. Perhaps the bed had gone downhill since the sculptor lived here, but if not I could see why he might have left: maybe he was just fastidious.

'So what happened to Orontes?'

'Disappeared. One morning we went out and left him snoring; when we came back he had taken himself off. He never came back.'

'Wandering feet! Sounds like my father ... Did you worry?'

'Why? He was grown up.'

'Were his things missing?'

I had asked the question casually. The painters half exchanged a glance before one said yes and the other no. 'We sold them,' Varga admitted. I could believe it. Their guilty expressions were right, since the property had not been theirs to sell. All the same, I sensed an atmosphere, which I noted. They could well be lying about this.

I went over all the ground a second time, confirming the facts. There was little to add. I learned only that the centurion Laurentius had gone away as dissatisfied as I was. Manlius had no information about where this soldier had been staying in Rome. Neither of them knew what Festus had wanted the sculptor for.

Or if they knew, they were not admitting it to me.

I poured what remained of the amphora into their winecups and formally saluted them.

'Farewell, boys! I'll leave you to contemplate how fine art can save the civilised world from its sterility.' From the doorway I grinned at the squalor they inhabited. 'Own up. This is just a sham, isn't it? Really, you're two hard-working citizens who love the Empire and live like lambs. I bet you say a prayer to the hearth goddess every morning and write home to your mothers twice a week?'

Manlius, who was probably the sharper one of the disreputable pair, gave me a shamefaced smile. 'Have a heart,

Falco! My mother's eighty-one. I have to show devotion to such age.'

Varga, who lived among more private dreams, studied his Aphrodite mournfully, and pretended he had not heard.

XL

In Fountain Court everything lay still. That was worrying. Even in the dead of night there was usually some husband receiving brain damage from an iron pot, a pigeon being tortured by delinquent youths, or an old woman screaming that she had been robbed of her life savings (Metella, whose son regularly borrowed them; he would pay her back, if the string of prostitutes he ran worked double shifts for a fortnight).

It must be nearly dawn. I was too old for this.

As I reached the laundry, the tired trudge of my feet brought more trouble: Lenia, the drab proprietress, flung open a half-shutter. Her head flopped out, all tangles of madly hennaed hair. Her face was white; her deportment unstable. She surveyed me with eyes that needed an oculist and screeched: 'Oi, Falco! What are you doing up so late?'

'Lenia! You put the scares on me. Is Smaractus there?'

Lenia let out a pathetic wail. She would wake the whole street, and they would blame me. 'I hope he's at the bottom of the Tiber. We had a terrible row!'

'Thank the gods for that. Now kindly close up your dentistry – ' We were old friends; we could dispense with compliments. She knew I despised her fiancé. It had something to do with him being my landlord – and more with the fact he was as savoury as a pile of hot mule-dung. 'Is this goodbye to the wedding?'

'Oh no.' She calmed down immediately. 'I'm not letting him off that! Come in, come in – '

Resisting was useless. When a woman who spends her life heaving around monstrous troughs of hot water grabs your arm, you fly in the direction she pulls or lose a limb. I was dragged into the sinister cubicle where Lenia fiddled her accounts and accosted her friends, then pushed on to a stool. A beaker of cheap red wine fixed itself in my fist.

874

Lenia had been drinking, like the whole of Rome this wintry night. She had been drinking on her own, so she was hopelessly miserable. With a cup banging against those awful teeth again, she cheered up, however. 'You look rough too, Falco!'

'Been boozing with painters. Never again!'

'Until the next time!' Lenia jibed raucously. She had known me a long while.

'So what's with Smaractus?' I tried her wine, regretting it as much as I had feared. 'Cold feet about the matrimonial benefits?'

I was joking, but of course she nodded mournfully. 'He's not sure he's ready to commit himself.'

'Poor soul! Pleading his tender youth, I suppose?' Whatever age Smaractus was, his notorious life had left him looking like some desiccated hermit half dead in a cave. 'Surely that miser can see that he'll make up for what he's losing as a bachelor by gaining a prosperous laundry?'

'And me!' Lenia retorted snootily.

'And you,' I smiled. She needed someone to be kind.

She gulped at her cup, then ground out vindictively, 'How are your own affairs moving along?'

'Perfectly, thanks.'

'I don't believe that, Falco!'

'My arrangements,' I stated pompously, 'are moving to their conclusion with efficiency and style.'

'I haven't heard about this.'

'Quite. I'm keeping clammed up. If you don't let people interfere, things don't go wrong.'

'What does Helena say?'

'Helena needn't be bothered with details.'

'Helena's your bride!'

'So she has enough worries.'

'Gods, you're a mad devil . . . Helena's a nice girl!'

'Exactly. So why warn her she's doomed? This is where you went wrong, Lenia. If Smaractus had stayed blissfully ignorant of your approach with the sacrificial pig, you could have forged his name on a contract one night when he was sleeping off a flagon and he would never have felt the pain. Instead you've put the wind up him, and given him a thousand opportunities to wriggle free.'

'He'll be back,' Lenia cracked morbidly. 'The careless prick left his beryl signet-ring.'

I managed to steer the subject away from marriage and cheap jewellery. 'If you want to upset me, try my arrest by Marponius.'

'News spreads!' Lenia agreed. 'We all heard you stabbed a soldier and ended up in manacles at a judge's house.'

'I did not stab the soldier.'

'That's right, one or two crazy types do reckon you might be innocent.'

'People are wonderful!'

'So what's this fable, Falco?'

'Bloody Festus has landed me in it as usual.'

I told her the tale. Anything to stop her drinking. Anything to stop her pouring more for me.

When I finished she hooted with her usual grating derision. 'So it's a fine-art mystery?'

'That's right. I strongly suspect that most of the statues and all of the people are fakes.'

'You do talk! Did he find you that night, then?'

'What night, Lenia?'

'This night you've been talking about. The night Festus left for his legion. He came here. I thought I told you at the time ... Late, it was. Really late. He banged on my door, wanting to know if you had staggered home so drunk you couldn't make the stairs and were curled up in my washtub.' Since six flights do hurt after revelry, it had been known.

'I wasn't here –'

'No!' giggled Lenia, knowing about the Marina fiasco.

'He should have known where I was ... You never told me this –' I sighed. One more in a long string of undelivered messages.

'You talking about him tonight just reminded me.'

'Five years late!' She was unbelievable. 'So what happened?'

'He flaked out in here, making a nuisance of himself.'

'He had had some.' Much like us this evening.

'Oh I can handle soaks; I get enough practice. He was broody,' complained the laundress. 'I can't stand miserable men!' Since she had elected to marry Smaractus, who was a

876

long-faced, insensitive, humourless disaster, she was gaining practice in tolerating misery too – and with more yet to come.

'So what was Festus on about?'

'Confidential,' sneered Lenia. 'He groaned, "It's all too much; I need little brother's strong right arm", and then he shut up.'

'Well that was Festus.' Sometimes, however, my secretive brother would be gripped by a bacchic drive to talk. Once the mood was on him, once he decided to display his inner being, he would usually open up to anyone who got in the way. He would ramble for hours – all rubbish, of course. 'It's too much to hope he revealed any more?'

'No. Tight bastard! Most people find me easy to talk to,' Lenia boasted. I remembered to smile graciously.

'So then what?'

'He got fed up of waiting for his precious brother who had stayed out playing around with Marina, so he cursed me, cursed you a few times, borrowed one of my washtubs, and disappeared. He went off muttering that he had work to do. Next day I heard he had left Rome. You weren't around much afterwards yourself.'

'Guilt!' I grinned. 'I bummed off to the market garden until the heat died down.'

'Hoping Marina would have a convenient lapse of memory?'

'Maybe. What did he want a washtub for?'

'Juno, I don't know. It turned up again on the doorstep covered with mud or cement or something.'

'He must have been rinsing his smalls . . . Why did you never tell me this before?'

'No point. You would have been upset!'

I was upset now.

It was one of those pointless, tantalising events that sting you after someone dies. I would never really know what he had wanted. I could never share his problem; never help. Lenia was right. Better not to know these things.

I found an excuse to leave (yawning heavily) and staggered upstairs.

Six flights give you a lot of time for thinking, but it was not enough.

Both missing and hating my brother, I felt exhausted, dirty, cold and depressed. I could have dropped on the stairs, but the landings were freezing and stank of old urine. I was heading for my bed, knowing that all too soon I had to be up out of it again. Despair made my feet heavy; I was chasing a hopeless puzzle, with disasters fast closing in on me. And when I reached my own apartment I groaned even more, because more trouble was waiting for me. Under the ill-fitting door a gleam of light showed. That could only mean someone was in there.

I had already made too much noise to start creeping up and springing surprises. I knew I was too drunk for an argument and too tired for a fight.

I did everything wrong. I forgot to be careful. I could not be bothered to organise a possible escape. I was too tired, and too angry to follow my own rules, so I just walked straight in and kicked the door shut after me.

I was staring at the lamp that burned on the table quite openly, when a small voice murmured from the bedroom, 'It's only me.'

'Helena!' I tried to remember that one of the reasons I loved her was her startling knack of surprising me. Then I tried to play sober.

I snuffed the light, to disguise my state. I dropped my belt and fumbled off my boots. I was icy cold, but as a gesture to civilised living I shed a few layers of clothing. As soon as I stumbled to bed Helena must have realised my condition. I had forgotten the bed was new; in the darkness it was wrongly aligned for the path my feet knew, and the wrong height. Besides, we had moved it to avoid the great hole in the roof, which Smaractus had still not repaired.

When I finally found the bed, I fell in awkwardly, almost falling out. Helena kissed me once, groaned at my foul breath, then buried her face in the safer haven of my armpit.

'Sorry . . . had to suborn some witnesses.' Warmth and comfort greeted me alluringly as I tried to be stern. 'Listen, you disobedient rascal, I left you at Mother's. What's the excuse for this?'

Helena wound herself around me more closely. She was welcome and sweet, and she knew that I was not complaining much. 'Oh Marcus, I missed you . . .'

878

'Missing me could get you hurt, woman! How did you get here?'

'Perfectly safely. With Maia's husband. He came right up and checked the room for me. I've spent an evening going around your sisters' houses asking about the knife from the caupona. I dragged your mother with me, though she wasn't keen. Anyway, I thought you would want to know the results,' she excused herself weakly.

'Bamboozler! So what's the good news?'

I felt a small, but obvious, belch escaping. Helena shifted further down the bed. Her voice came faintly through the coverlet. 'None, I'm afraid. Not one of your relatives can remember taking that knife from home, let alone ever using it at Flora's.'

Even in the dark I could feel my head spinning. 'The day's not a total disaster. I heard a couple of things. Censorinus had a companion in Rome – Laurentius. It's good. Petro will have to find him before he can indict me.'

'Could this be the murderer?'

'Unlikely, but possible . . .' Talking was difficult. 'And there is, or was once, a sculptor called Orestes – no, Orontes. He's disappeared, but it's given us another name . . .' In the new bed, already warmed for several hours by Helena, relaxation was seeping gloriously through my frozen limbs. I wrapped myself around her more conveniently. 'Dear gods, I love you . . .' I wanted her safe, but I was glad she was here. 'I hope Famia was sober when he brought you.'

'Maia wouldn't send me home without safe protection. If she had known it was a drunk I would be waiting for she would not have let me come at all!' I tried to think up a rejoinder, but none came. Helena stroked my cheek. 'You're weary. Go to sleep.'

I was already doing so.

Hazily I heard her saying, 'Your father sent a message. He suggests that tomorrow morning he should take you to visit Carus and Servia. He says, *Dress up*. I've put a toga out for you . . .'

I wondered who in Hades were Carus and Servia, and why I should allow these unbidden strangers to bother me with

such formality. Then I knew nothing until I woke the next day
with a splitting head.

XLI

It was late morning when I lurched from the apartment. I wore my favourite worn indigo tunic, since my idea of dressing up has always been to put comfort first; my heaviest boots, since the weather looked foul; a cloak, for the same reason; and a hat, to shade my eyes from painful light. My head hurt and my internal organs felt delicate. My joints ached. An upright posture seemed unnatural.

I went first to see Petronius. He was kicking his heels at the guardhouse, pretending to write reports while he sheltered from the weather. This made him glad of any excuse to wake up and hurl insults at a friend.

'Watch out, boys. A hangover on legs just found its way in. Falco, you look like a fool who has been up all night consuming cheap drink in rough company.' He had seen me do it before; I had done it with him.

'Don't start!'

'Let's have some gravity then. I assume you've come to present me with a nicely bound set of tablets detailing who killed Censorinus Macer, what their dirty motive was, and where I can find them tied to a pergola, awaiting arrest?'

'No.'

'Stupid to hope!'

'I've got a couple of leads.'

'Better than nothing,' he answered grumpily.

'What about you?

'Oh I'll stick with nothing. I like to feel safe. Why start dicing with evidence and proof?' Luckily he settled down after this frivolity and talked plainer sense. He listed the usual enquiries. He had spoken to all the people who were in Flora's the night the soldier died, but had learned nothing useful. 'Nobody saw anyone with Censorinus, or noticed anyone go up the backstairs to his room.'

'So that's a dead end.'

'Right. I grilled Epimandos a few times. I don't like the

shifty look in his eye. He's a strange one, though I can't prove anything against him.'

'I think he's a runaway. He looks worried because of that.'

'He's been there a few years.'

'He has.' I stretched my stiff limbs. 'He always gives the impression of looking over his shoulder.' That applied to most of Rome, so Petro received the news calmly. 'Festus knew something about his past, I think.'

'Festus would!'

'Is it worth arresting Epimandos on suspicion?'

Petronius looked prim. 'Arresting people on suspicion would mean arresting you!'

'You did!'

'Who's starting now, Falco? In the damned waiter's case, I decided against it, though I still have a man watching Flora's dump. I don't think Epimandos would conceal anything if he could clear you,' Petronius told me. 'He seems too loyal to you.'

'I don't know why that should be,' I admitted honestly.

'Neither do I,' said Petro, with his usual friendly attitude. 'Have you paid him to corroborate your story?' I scowled; he relented. 'Maybe Festus had something to do with it, if they were on good terms. Whatever it is, Epimandos is really panicking that he might have caused your brush with Marponius. I told him you were perfectly capable of getting yourself hauled up on a false charge without help from a dumb stew-doler.'

'Well that should clinch a free drink for me next time I toddle into Flora's! And how is our beloved Marponius?'

Petronius Longus growled contemptuously. 'What are these leads you promised me?'

'Not much, but I've two new names to follow up. One is a sculptor called Orontes Mediolanus who knew Festus. He disappeared several years ago.'

'That sounds a dud line.'

'Yes, leave that to me, if you like. I specialise in hopeless clues ... Apart from him, there was a centurion called Laurentius recently in Rome, asking the same questions as Censorinus.'

Petro nodded. 'I'll take that on. It fits the form. I managed

882

to prod your ma into remembering that Censorinus did go out a couple of evenings, saying he was seeing a friend.'

'Ma never told me!'

'You have to ask the right questions,' Petro replied smugly. 'Leave this to the professionals, eh Falco?'

'Professional bollockers! Who was the friend?'

'Your ma didn't know. He was only mentioned casually. This Laurentius is a good candidate, though. They could have deliberately planted Censorinus with your mother to harass the family, while the other man stayed elsewhere and pursued other issues.' Petro leaned back on his stool, flexing his shoulders as if he too was feeling the effects of the damp morning. He was a big, muscular character who hated drizzly weather. Except when he went home to play with his children, he needed to be out of doors; it was one reason he liked his job. 'Did you spot that Campania mansio bill?'

His eyes were half veiled, hiding any impression of collusion over me inspecting the dead man's kit at the caupona.

'I saw it,' I confirmed, also keeping my expression bland.

'Looked to me as if it was a reckoning for two.'

'I didn't notice that.'

'It was not specific, but at country prices I'd say it covered hay for two horses or mules, and more than one bed.' His voice dropped. 'Wasn't it for some place near your grandfather's farm?'

'Near enough. I would go out there, but it would be breaking my bail.'

'Why not?' Petro grinned at me suddenly. 'After all, you went to Ostia!'

How in Hades did he know? 'Are you following me, you bastard?'

He refused to say. 'Thanks for the name of Laurentius. I'll make enquiries among the military authorities, though if he was just in Rome on leave his presence may not have been registered officially.'

'If he was here with Censorinus, pretending to be innocents on holiday,' I pointed out, 'he ought to have come forward the minute he heard about the murder.'

'True,' Petro agreed. 'Suspicious, otherwise. If I have to,

I'll write and query him with the Fifteenth, but that will take weeks.'

'Months, more likely. If his nose is clean with them, they won't necessarily answer a civil enquiry at all.'

'And if his nose is *not* clean with them,' Petro answered with gentle cynicism, 'they will disown him quietly, and still not answer me.' Soldiers only had to answer to military law. Petronius could certainly ask a centurion questions, and if Laurentius was shown to have killed Censorinus, Petro could report it formally – but if the murder had been committed by a fellow legionary, then the legions would deal with the culprit. (That meant the legions would hush it up.) For Marponius and Petro this new angle could be frustrating. 'There are better ways to proceed. My men can start checking the lodging-houses here; that's more likely to produce results. If Laurentius *is* implicated, it may be too late to stop him leaving Italy, but I'll have somebody watching at Ostia. If he's spotted, I can ask him politely to return to Rome and talk to me – '

'He won't come.'

'Does it matter? If he refuses, he looks guilty and you're cleared. By virtue of his non-co-operation, I can oppose any charges against you. Marponius would have to go along with it. So what are your plans, reprieved suspect?'

'I'm going out with my damned father for an educational talk on art.'

'Enjoy yourself,' smiled Petronius.

Relations between us had improved drastically. If I had known it would be so easy to retrieve our long-standing friendship, I would have invented a name for a suspect days ago and given him someone else to chase around after.

'To save you having to tail me,' I replied with my customary courtesy, 'I'm picking up Pa from the Saepta now, then spending the rest of the morning at some big house in the Seventh Sector, after which – if my parent sticks to his usual rigid habits – we'll be returning to the Saepta prompt at noon so he can devour whatever the redhead has stuffed into his lunch-satchel.'

'This is all very filial! When did you ever spend so much time in the company of Geminus?'

I grinned reluctantly. 'Since he decided he needed protection – and stupidly hired me.'

'Such a pleasure,' chuckled Petronius, 'to see the Didius family sticking together at last!'

I told him what I thought of him, without rancour, then I left.

XLII

Aulus Cassius Carus and his wife Ummidia Servia lived in a house whose exterior unobtrusiveness told its own tale of wealth. It was one of the few big houses built by individuals after the great fire in Nero's time; it had then managed to escape both looters and arsonists during the civil war following Nero's death. This house had been commissioned by people who flourished in hard times, and who had somehow avoided offending a half-mad emperor whose favourite subjects for execution had been anybody else who dared to proclaim artistic good taste.

Carus and Servia proved an unlikely moral: it was possible to be both Roman and discreet.

In a city where so many thousands were crammed into high-rising tenements, it always surprised me how many other folk managed to acquire large plots of land and live there in stately private homes, often virtually unknown to the general public. These two not only managed it, but did so in the classic Roman style, with blank walls apparently guarding them, yet an atmosphere of making their home available formally to anyone who produced a legitimate reason for entering. After a few words with their porter, Father and I established our business, and what had appeared from the outside to be a very private house opened all its public rooms to us.

A slave went off carrying our request for an audience. While we waited for a reaction we were left free to wander.

I had assumed my toga, but was otherwise my happy self.

'You might have combed your hair!' whispered Geminus. He eyed the toga; that had belonged to Festus, so it passed muster.

'I only comb my hair for the Emperor, or women who are *very* beautiful.'

'Dear gods, what have I brought up?'

'You didn't! But I'm a good boy, who won't ingratiate himself with thugs who kick his ancient pa in the ribs!'

'Don't cause trouble, or we'll get nowhere.'

'I know how to behave!' I sneered, subtly implying I might not draw upon the knowledge.

'No one,' decreed Didius Geminus, 'who wears a coloured tunic with his toga knows how to behave!'

So much for my indigo number.

We had passed a senatorial statue, presumably not ancestral, since our hosts were only middle rank. Also in the atrium were a couple of loyal portrait heads of the Claudian emperors, their clean-cut boyish looks at odds with the gruff and rugged features of Vespasian who ruled Rome today. The first general collection was out of doors in a peristyle garden just beyond the atrium. In March the effect was bare horticulturally, though the art showed up well. There were various columnar herms, among a rather twee gathering of hounds and hinds, winged cupids, dolphins, Pan among the reeds, and so forth. They had the inevitable Priapus (fully formed, unlike the vandalised creature at Father's ware-house), plus a gross Silenus sprawled on his back while a fountain trickled uncertainly from his wineskin. These were ordinary pieces. As a plant lover, I took more interest in the Eastern crocuses and hyacinths that were enlivening the garden.

My father, who had been here before, led me with a firm step to the art gallery. At this point I began to feel shafts of envy.

We had passed through several quiet, well-swept rooms with neutral decor. They contained a spare quantity of extremely good furniture, with one or two small but superb bronzes displayed on plinths. The entrance to the gallery was guarded by not one, but a pair of gigantic sea creatures, each bearing nereids on their threshing coils, amid fulsome waves.

We crept between the sea-nymphs and in through a majestic portal set. The alabaster door-case stood as high as my rooms at home, with huge double doors in some exotic wood studded with bronze. They were folded back, probably permanently since pushing them closed would take about ten slaves.

Inside, we were dumbstruck by a twice life-size Dying Gaul in glorious veined red porphyry. Every home should have one – and a stepladder for dusting him.

Then followed their set of Famous Greeks. Rather predictable, but these people had crisp priorities in throwing together a set of heads: Homer, Euripides, Sophocles, Demosthenes, a handsome bearded Pericles, and Solon the Law Giver. Crowding afterwards came some anonymous dancing maidens then a full-length Alexander, looking nobly sad but with a good mane of hair that should have cheered him up. These collectors preferred marble, but allowed in one or two excellent bronzes: there were Spear Carriers and Lance Bearers; Athletes, Wrestlers and Charioteers. Back with the classic Parian stone we came on a winged and sombre Eros, plainly in trouble with some mistress who had stamped her foot at him, facing a pale, even more remote Dionysus contemplating the eternal grape. The god of wine looked youthful and beautiful, but from his expression he had already realised his liver would be for it if he carried on that way.

Next came a wild jumble of delights. Plenty and Fortune; Victory and Virtue. A Minotaur on a pedestal; a caseful of miniatures. There were graceful Graces, and musing Muses; there was a colossal group of Maenads, having a ripping time with King Pentheus. There was what even I immediately recognised as a more than decent replica of one of the Charyatids from the Erechtheion at Athens. Had there been room, they would probably have imported the whole Parthenon.

The Olympian gods, as befitted their status, were lording it in a well-lit hall to themselves. Enthroned there were Jupiter, Juno and Minerva, that good old Roman triad, plus a formidable Athene, partly in ivory, with a pool to keep her humid. There was, I noted bleakly, no lord of the oceans – unless (faint hope) he was away in a workshop being cleaned.

All these pieces were astounding. We had no time to scrutinise how many were original, but any copies were so good they must be desirable in their own right.

I can only summon up a certain amount of reverence before an uncontrollable need to lighten the atmosphere sets in: 'As Ma would say, I'm glad someone else has to sponge this lot down every morning!'

'Hush! Show some refinement!' This was one of my many

quarrels with Pa. Politically, he was perfectly shrewd, and as cynical as me. Move on to culture, and he became a real snob. After selling antiques to idiots for forty years, he should have been more discerning about owners of art.

We were about to leave the Hall of the Gods when the owners thought it time to appear. They must have reasoned we would be gasping with admiration by now. On principle I tried to look too ethereal to have placed a value on the goods; no one was fooled. One of the reasons for letting folk walk around was so they could reel at the stupendous cost of what they had just seen.

The pair came in together. I already knew from Father that I was about to meet a couple where his taste and her money had made a long, successful bond. He was to speak the most, but her presence remained a force throughout. They were a firmly welded pair, welded by an inexorable interest in grabbing things. We had come to a house where the need to possess hung in the air as strong as a sickness.

Cassius Carus was a thin, mournful streak with dark curly hair. About forty-five, he had hollow cheeks, and pouched, heavy-lidded eyes. He had apparently forgotten to shave lately – too enraptured with his monumental nudes, no doubt. Ummidia Servia was perhaps ten years younger, a round, pallid woman who looked as if she could be irritable. Maybe she was tired of kissing stubble.

They both wore white, in lavishly formal folds. The man had a couple of gross signet-rings, the woman gold filigree about her, but they did not trouble much with jewellery. Their uncomfortably dignified dress was to set them up as fitting custodians of their art. Personal adornment did not come into it.

They knew Father. 'This is my son,' he said, producing a chill for a second while they worked out that I was not the fabulous Festus.

Each gave me an upsettingly limp hand.

'We've been admiring the collection.' My father liked to slaver.

'What do you think?' Carus asked me, probably sensing more reserve. He was like a cat that jumps straight on the lap of the only visitor who sneezes at fur.

889

In my role as the auctioneer's respectful son I said, 'I have never seen better quality.'

'You will admire our Aphrodite.' His slow, light, slightly pedantic voice made this virtually an instruction. Carus led the way for us to view the wonder, which they kept until last in the collection, in a separate courtyard garden. 'We had the water put in specially.'

Another Aphrodite. First the painter's special, now an even more suggestive little madam. I was becoming a connoisseur.

The Carus model was a Hellenistic marble whose sensuality stopped the breath. This goddess was too nearly indecent to be displayed in a temple. She stood in the middle of a circular pool, half undressed, turning to gaze back over one lithe shoulder as she admired the reflection of her own superlative rear. Light from the still water suffused her, setting up a gorgeous contrast between her nakedness and the rigid pleating of the chiton she had half removed.

'Very nice,' said my father. The Aphrodite looked even more satisfied.

Carus consulted me.

'Sheer beauty. Isn't she a copy of that very striking Venus on the great lake at Nero's Golden House?'

'Oh yes. Nero believed he had the original!' Carus said 'believed' with a flick of contemptuous malice, then he smiled. He glanced at his wife. Servia smiled too. I gathered Nero thought wrongly.

Putting one over on another collector gave them even more pleasure than possessing their incomparable piece. This was bad news. They would enjoy putting one over on us.

It was time to tackle business.

My father walked away around the path, drawing Carus with him while I murmured about nothing much to Servia. We had planned this. When two members of the Didius family go visiting there is always some fraught plan – usually an interminable dispute about what time we are going to leave the house we have not even arrived at. On this occasion Pa had suggested we should each try our wheedling skills on both parties, then we could adopt whichever approach seemed best. Not this variation, anyway. I was getting nowhere with the woman. It was like plumping a cushion that had lost half its feathers. I could see Pa going rather red, too, as he and Carus conversed.

After a while Geminus brought Carus back round the remaining half of the circle. Adroitly changing partners, he imposed what was left of his famous attraction for women on the woman of the house, while I attacked her spindly spouse. I watched Pa oozing masculine civility over Servia as she waddled at his side. She hardly seemed to notice his efforts, which made me smile.

Carus and I moved to stone benches, where we could admire the pride of the collection.

'So what do you know about marbles, young man?' He spoke as if I was eighteen and had never before seen a goddess undressing.

I had stared at more nude femininity than he owned in his whole gallery, and mine was alive, but I was a man of the world, not some boasting barbarian, so I let it pass.

In our introductory message, I had been described as a junior partner at the auction-house. So I played gauche and offered, 'I know the biggest market is in copies. We cannot shift originals these days even if we bundle them in fives and throw in a set of fish skillets.'

Carus laughed. He knew I was not referring to anything so important as a Phidias original. Anyone could shift that. Somebody probably had.

My father despaired of entrancing Servia even more quickly than I had, so they both rejoined us. These preliminaries had established the rules. Nobody wanted to be charmed. There would be no easy release from our debt. Now Pa and I sat side by side, waiting for our limpid hosts to put the pressure on us.

'Well, that's a sign of modern life,' I carried on. 'Only fakes count!' By now I knew that in chasing after Festus I was destined to expose another one.

'Nothing wrong with a decently done fake,' Pa opined. He looked calm, but I knew he was miserable. 'Some of the best current reproductions will become antiques in their own right.'

I grinned desperately. 'I'll make a note to invest in a good

Roman Praxiteles, if ever I have the cash and the storage-room!' As a hint of our family poverty this was not impressing our creditors.

'A Lysippus is what you want!' Geminus advised me, tapping his nose.

'Yes, I saw the fine Alexander in the gallery here!' I turned to our hosts confidentially: 'You can always tell an auctioneer. Apart from a wandering look in his eye from taking bids off the wall – inventing non-existent calls, you know – he's the one whose ugly snout bends like a carrot that's hit a stone, after years of giving collectors his dubious investment tips . . .' We were getting nowhere. I dropped the act. 'Pa, Carus and Servia know what they want to invest in. They want a Poseidon, and they want it by Phidias.'

Cassius Carus inspected me coldly in his fussy way. But it was Servia, their financier, who smoothed down the thick white folds of her mantle and broke in. 'Oh no, it's not a future investment. That piece already belongs to us!'

XLIII

I saw my father grip his hands.

Rejecting the humble role that had been imposed on me, I hardened my attitude. 'I came to this tale rather late. Do you mind if we just run over the facts? Am I right in my understanding? My elder brother Didius Festus is said to have acquired from Greece a modest statue, alleged to be a Poseidon and thought to be by Phidias?'

'Known to be bought by us,' responded Carus, obviously thinking he had put me down wittily.

'Pardon me if I'm churlish, but do you have a receipt?'

'Naturally,' said Servia. She must have dealt with my family before.

'I have been shown it, Marcus,' murmured Pa. I ignored him.

'It was made out to you by Festus?' Carus nodded. 'Festus is dead. So what has this to do with us?'

'My point exactly!' stated Pa. He drew himself up. 'I made my son Festus independent of parental authority when he joined the armed forces.' This was probably a lie, but no outsider could refute it. It sounded straight, though I could not imagine why Pa and Festus would have gone through such a formality. Acquiring emancipation from the power of his father is something that only troubles a son who feels bound by his father's power in the first place. In the Didius family this had never applied. Any pleb on the Aventine would probably grin widely and say the same.

Carus refused to accept any disclaimer. 'I expect a parent to take responsibility for his son's debts.'

I felt a strong need for irony. 'Nice to see that some people still believe in the family as an indissoluble unit, Father!'

'Bull's testicles!' Maybe Carus and Servia took this as a reference to the mystical rites of an Eastern religious cult.

Maybe not.

'My papa's upset,' I excused him to the couple. 'When somebody says he owes them half a million, he loses his grip.'

Carus and Servia gazed at me as if what I said was incomprehensible. Their indifference to our problem astonished me. It also made me shiver.

I had been in many places where the atmosphere was more sinister. Toughs armed with knives or staves have a vivid effect; there were none of those here. Yet the mood was sour and in its way just as intimidating. The message reaching us was uncompromising. We would pay up, or we would suffer; suffer until we gave in.

'Please be reasonable,' I pressed on. 'We are a poor family. We simply cannot lay hands on so much cash.'

'You must,' said Servia.

We could talk all we wanted. But however closely we argued, we would never actually communicate. Even so, I felt compelled to struggle on: 'Let's follow through what happened. You paid Festus for the statue. In good faith he attempted to import it, but the ship sank. By then you owned the statue. It is,' I declared, more boldly than I felt, 'your loss.'

Carus tossed a new nut into the mixing bowl: 'No mention was ever made to us that the statue was still in Greece.'

That was tricky. My heart lurched. I wondered what the date was on their receipt. Trying not to look at my father, I even wondered if my impossible brother had sold the Phidias to them after he already knew it was lost. Surely Pa would have noticed this detail when he saw the receipt; surely he would have warned me?

One thing was definite: I could not draw attention to our lad's fraud by asking to see the receipt for myself now. It did not matter; if Festus had deceived them, I did not want to know.

'You mean you bought the item sight unseen?' I floundered wildly.

' "*Antique marble*," ' intoned Carus, evidently quoting from this bill of sale which I preferred not to examine. ' "*A Phidias Poseidon, heroic proportions, expression of noble placidity, wearing Greek dress, heavily coiffed and bearded, height two yards four inches, one arm raised to hurl a trident . . .*" We have our own shippers,' he informed me in a biting tone. 'The Aristedon brothers. People we trust. We would have made our own arrangements. *Then* it would have been our loss. Not this way.'

Festus could have let them take the shipping risk. He would have known that. He was always well up on customers' backgrounds. So why not? I knew without even thinking about it. Festus was bringing the statue home himself because he had some extra wrinkle up his grubby tunic-sleeve.

This was not my fault. It was not even Pa's.

That would not stop Carus and Servia.

'Are you taking us to court?'

'Litigation is not our philosophy.'

I managed not to comment, *No; only thuggery*. 'Look, I only recently came upon this problem,' I began again. 'I am trying to investigate what happened. After five years it is not easy, so I ask you to be sympathetic. I give you my word I will endeavour to illuminate the issue. I ask you to cease harassing my elderly father –'

'I'll take care of myself!' scoffed the elderly Didius, ever to the fore with a pointless quip.

'And give me time.'

'Not after five years!' Carus said.

I wanted to fight. I wanted to storm out, telling him he could do his worst and we would resist everything he did.

There was no point. I had already discussed it with Father on the way here. We could provide muscle at the auctions. We could barricade the office and the store. We could guard both our homes and never step outside without a train of armed guards.

We could not do all those things, however, every day and every night, for years.

Carus and Servia had the grim insistence of people who would persist. We would never be free of the worry, for ourselves, our property – our women. We would be smothered by the cost of it all. We would never escape the inconvenience, or the public doubt that soon attaches to people who are trailing disputed debts.

And we could never forget Festus.

They were growing tired of us. We could see they were about to have us thrown out.

My father was the first to acknowledge the deadlock. 'I

895

cannot replace the Phidias; no similar piece is known. As for finding half a million, it would wipe out my liquidity.'

'Realise your assets,' Carus instructed him.

'I'll have an empty storehouse, and a naked house.'

Carus just shrugged.

My father stood up. With more dignity than I expected, he simply said, 'Selling everything I have, Cassius Carus, *will* take time!' He was no longer requesting favours, but laying down terms. They would be accepted; Carus and Servia wanted to be paid. 'Come along, Marcus,' Pa ordered quietly. 'We seem to have plenty of work to do. Let's go home.'

For once I abandoned my insistence on stating in public that he and I honoured different versions of 'home'.

He strode out with a set face. I followed. I was equally in despair. Half a million was more than I had already failed to assemble for my own most cherished purposes. It was more money than I really hoped to see. If I ever did see it, I wanted the cash so I could marry Helena. Well I could kiss goodbye to *that* idea for ever, if I became embroiled in this.

Yet even if it broke me for ever, I realised I could not leave my father to shoulder the whole burden of my feckless brother's debt.

XLIV

We had walked to the collectors' house. We walked back.

Well not quite: my father strode, at a ferocious pace. I hate to intrude upon another man's trouble – and when a man has just failed to escape paying out half a million sesterces, he is certainly in trouble. So I marched along beside him, and since he wanted to fume in complete silence, I joined in loyally.

As he steamed down the Via Flaminia my father's visage was as friendly as Jove's thunderbolt, and my own may well have lacked its usual winsomeness.

I was thinking hard as well.

We had almost reached the Saepta when he wheeled up to a wine-bar counter.

'I need a drink!'

I needed one too, but I still had a headache.

'I'll sit here and wait.' Monumental masons were removing my skull on a tombstone hoist. 'I spent last night oiling two painters' vocal cords.'

Pa paused in the midst of ordering, unable to decide which of the wines listed on the wall was sufficiently strong to create the oblivion he needed. 'What painters?'

'Manlius and Varga.' I paused, too, though in my case there was no real wrench to the brain cells; I had only been applying my elbow to the counter and staring vaguely round me like any son accompanying his father out of doors. 'Festus knew them.'

'*I* know them! Go on,' urged my father thoughtfully.

On I went: 'Well, there's a disappearing sculptor who used to lodge with them – '

'What's his name?' asked my father.

The barman was growing anxious. He could sense a lost sale approaching.

'Orontes Mediolanus.'

My father scoffed. 'Orontes never disappeared! I ought to

know; I use that idle bastard for copies and repairs. Orontes lodged with those loafers on the Caelian until at least last summer. They took your drink and twisted you!'

The barman lost his sale.

We raced off to find Manlius and Varga.

We spent most of the afternoon on the chase. My father dragged me round more sleepy fresco artists – and more of their burgeoning models – than I could bear to think about. We toured horrid hired rooms, freezing studios, teetering penthouses, and half-painted mansions. We went all over Rome. We even tried a suite at the Palace where Domitian Caesar had commissioned something elegant in yellow ochre for Domitia Longina, the dalliance he had snatched from her husband and installed as his wife.

'Nothing like it!' muttered Father. There was plenty like it actually; the Flavian taste was predictable. Domitian was only toying at that stage; he would have to wait for both his father and his brother to die before he could launch into his master plan for a new Palatine. I said what I thought about his decorating clichés. 'Oh you're right!' agreed Pa, grovelling to the inside knowledge of an imperial agent. 'And even adultery with the pick of the smart set is a convention nowadays. Both Augustus and that repulsive little Caligula acquired wives by pinching them.'

'That's not for me. When I grabbed a senator's daughter, I chose one who had divorced herself in readiness for my suave approach.'

'Quite right!' came a rather sardonic reply. 'You would hate to be publicly criticised . . .'

At last someone told us the address where our quarries were working. We made our way there in silence. We had no plan this time. I was angry, but saw no need to elaborate. I never enquired what Father felt, though I did find out quite soon.

The house in question was being done over completely. Scaffold hung threateningly over the entrance where old roof-tiles were flying down from the heavens into a badly placed skip. The site foreman must be a dozy swine. We clambered in, through a mess of trestles and ladders, then tripped over a tool-bag. Pa picked it up. When the watchman raised his head from a game of draughts scratched in the dusty base of a half-laid tessellated floor, I called out, 'Have you seen Titus anywhere?' and we rushed past, pretending to follow his vaguely raised arm.

There is always a carpenter called Titus. We used him several times to bluff our way around. Even a fat fusspot in a toga, who was probably the householder, let us evade questions, merely frowning fretfully when we barged past him in a corridor. His property had been in the hands of louts for months. He no longer complained when they knocked him aside, peed on his acanthus bed or took naps in their filthy tunics on his own favourite reading-couch.

'Sorry, governor!' my father beamed. He had the knack of sounding like an unskilled pleb who had just put his pick through a water-pipe and was shuffling off out of it quickly.

I knew Manlius would be working near the atrium, but there was too much going on there when we first arrived. We left him, and started working through the dining-rooms, looking for raped Sabines. It was a big house. They had three different feeding areas. Varga was touching up his Sabine ladies in the third.

The plasterer had just left him with a new section. For frescos, the trick is to work extremely fast. Varga was facing a huge new stretch of smooth wet plaster. He had a sketch, with several writhing bottoms on it. He had a kettle of flesh-tone paint already mixed. He had a badger-hair brush in his hand.

Then we came in.

'Whoa, Varga. Drop the brush! It's the Didius boys!' That harsh command, which startled both the painter and me, came from Pa.

Varga, slow on the uptake, clung on to his brush.

My father, who was a solid man, grasped the painter's arm with one hand. He gripped the painter bodily with the other, lifting him off his feet, then he swung him in a half-circle, so that a bright pink streak from the brush scraped right across three yards of plaster, just smoothed over by an extremely expensive craftsman. It had been a perfect, glistening poem.

'Mico could learn something here! Well don't just stand there, Marcus, let's fetch that door off its pinions. You nip into the kitchen alongside and pinch the rope they hang the dishrags on – '

Bemused, I complied. I never willingly take orders – but this was my first game of soldiers as one of the Didius boys. Clearly they were hard men.

I could hear Varga moaning. My father held him fast, sometimes shaking him absent-mindedly. On my return he threw the painter down, and helped me lift an ornamental folding door off its bronze fastenings. Gasping for air, Varga had hardly moved. We picked him up again, spread-eagled him, and lashed him to the door. Then we heaved the door up against the wall, opposite the one Varga was supposed to paint. I coiled the spare rope tidily, like a halyard on a ship's deck. The rope still had the damp cloths on it, which added to the unreal effect.

Varga hung there on the door. We had turned it so that he was upside down.

Good plasterwork is very expensive. It has to be painted while it's wet. A fresco painter who misses his moment has to pay from his wages for redoing the job.

Pa flung an arm across my shoulders. He addressed the face near his boots. 'Varga, this is my son. I hear you and Manlius have been singing false tunes to him!' Varga only whimpered.

Father and I walked across to the new wall. We sat down, either side of the wet patch, leaning back with our arms folded.

'Now, Varga,' Pa chivvied winningly.

I grinned through wicked teeth. 'He doesn't get it.'

'Oh he does,' murmured my father. 'You know, I think one of the saddest sights in the world is a fresco painter watching his plaster dry while he's tied up . . .' Father and I turned slowly to gaze at the drying plaster.

For five minutes Varga lasted out. He was red in the face but defiant.

'Tell us about Orontes,' I suggested. 'We know you know where he is.'

'Orontes has disappeared!' Varga spluttered.

'No, Varga,' Father told him in a pleasant tone, 'Orontes has not. Orontes was living at your dump on the Caelian quite recently. He repaired a Syrinx with a missing pipe for me only last April – his normal botched effort. I didn't pay him for it till November.' My father's business terms were the unfair ones that oppress small craftsmen who are too artistic to quibble. 'The cash was delivered to your doss!'

'We pinched it!' Varga tried brazenly.

'You forged the pig off his signet-ring for my invoice then – and which of you was supposed to have done my job for me?'

'Oh shove off, Geminus!'

'Well if that's his attitude – ' Pa hauled himself upright. 'I'm bored with this,' he said to me. Then he fiddled about with a pouch at his waist and pulled out a large knife.

XLV

'Oh come on, Pa,' I protested weakly. 'You'll frighten him. You know what cowards painters are!'

'I'm not going to hurt him much,' Pa assured me, with a wink. He flexed his arm as he wielded the knife. It was a stout kitchen effort, which I guessed he normally used to eat his lunch. 'If he won't talk, let's have a bit of fun – ' His eyes were dangerously bright; he was like a child at a goose fair.

Next minute my father drew back his arm, and threw the knife. It thonked into the door between the painter's legs, which we had tied apart – though not *that* far apart.

'Geminus!' screamed Varga, as his manhood was threatened.

I winced. 'Ooh! Could have been nasty . . .' Still amazed at Pa's aim, I scrambled to my feet as well, and whipped my own dagger from my boot.

Pa was inspecting his shot. 'Came a bit close to castrating the beggar . . . Maybe I'm not very good at this.'

'Maybe I'm worse!' I grinned, squaring up to the target.

Varga began to scream for help.

'Cut it out, Varga,' Pa told him benignly. 'Hold on, Marcus. We can't enjoy ourselves while he's squalling. Let me deal with him – ' In the tool-bag he had snaffled was a piece of rag. It stank, and was caked with something we could not identify. 'Probably poisonous; we'll gag him with this. Then you can really let rip – '

'Manlius knows!' wailed the fresco painter weakly. 'Orontes was his pal. Manlius knows where he is!'

We thanked him, but Pa gagged him with the oily rag anyway, and we left him hanging upside down on the door.

'Next time you're thinking of annoying the Didius boys – think twice!'

We found Manlius at the top of a scaffold. He was in the white room, painting the frieze.

902

'No, don't bother coming down; we'll come up to you . . .'

Both Father and I had nipped up his ladder before he knew what was happening. I grasped him by the hand, beaming like a friend.

'No, don't start being nice to him!' Pa instructed me curtly. 'We wasted too much time being pleasant with the other one. Give him the boot treatment!'

So much for auctioneers being civilised men of the arts. With a shrug of apology, I overpowered the painter, and pushed him to his knees.

Here there was no need to go off looking for rope; Manlius had his own for hauling up paint and other tools to his work platform. My father unwound this rapidly, hurling down the basket. Snarling horribly, he sawed through the rope. We used a short piece to tie up Manlius. Then Pa knotted the longer remaining length around his ankles. Without needing to consult one another we picked him up, and rolled him over the edge of the scaffold.

His cry as he found himself swinging in space broke off as we held him suspended on the rope. After he grew accustomed to his new situation, he just moaned.

'Where's Orontes?' He refused to say.

Pa muttered, 'Someone has either paid these nuts a fortune, or frightened them!'

'That's all right,' I answered, gazing over the edge at the painter. 'We'll have to frighten this one more!'

We climbed down to the ground. There was a plasterer's lime bath, which we dragged across the room so it was directly under Manlius. He hung about three feet above it, cursing us.

'What now, Pa? We could fill it with cement, drop him into it, let it set and then heave him into the Tiber. I think he'd sink – ' Manlius was holding out bravely. Maybe he thought that even in Rome, where the passers-by can be frivolous, it would be difficult to carry a man who was set in concrete through the streets without attracting attention from the aediles.

'There's plenty of paint; let's see what we can do with that!'

'Ever made plaster? Let's have a go . . .'

We had wonderful fun. We tipped quantities of dry plaster into the bath, poured in water, and stirred madly with a stick. Then we stiffened it with cattle hair. I found a kettle of white paint, so we tried adding that. The effect was revolting, encouraging us to experiment more wildly. We hunted through the painter's basket for colourings, whooping as we made great swirls in the mixture of gold, red, blue and black.

Plasterers use dung in their devious mysteries. We found sacks of the stuff and tipped it into our mud pie, commenting frequently on the smell.

I climbed back up on to the scaffold. Pausing only to pass a few well-informed comments on the riot of garlands, torches, vases, pigeons and bird-baths and cupids riding panthers from which Manlius had been creating his frieze, I unfastened the rope holding him. Leaning back on my heels, I let it slip slightly. Pa stood below, encouraging me.

'Down a bit! Few more inches – ' In a nerve-racking series of jerks, Manlius sank head first towards the plasterer's bath. 'Gently, this is the tricky bit – '

The painter lost his nerve and frantically tried to swing himself towards the scaffold; I paid out rope abruptly. He froze, whimpering.

'Tell us about Orontes!'

For one last second he shook his head furiously, keeping his eyes closed. Then I dunked him in the bath.

I dropped him just far enough to cover his hair. Then I pulled him out a few inches, refastened the rope, and nipped down to inspect my achievement. Pa was roaring unkindly. Manlius hung there, his once black hair now dripping a disgusting goo in white, with occasional red and blue streaks. The ghastly tide-line came up as far as his eyebrows, which were bushy enough to hold quite a weight of the thick white mess.

'Couldn't be better,' said Pa approvingly.

The painter's hair had formed itself into ludicrous spikes. Grasping his inert body, I spun him gently between my hands. He turned one way, then lazily came back. Pa halted his progress with the stirring stick.

'Now, Manlius. Just a few sensible words will get you out of this. But if you're not going to help us, I might as well let my crazy son drop you right into the bath . . .'

Manlius closed his eyes. 'Oh gods . . .'

'Tell us about Orontes,' I said, playing the quiet one of our pair.

'He's not in Rome – '

'He *was* in Rome!' Pa roared.

Manlius was cracking. 'He thought it was safe to come back. He's gone again – '

'What was he frightened of?'

'I don't know . . .' We let him swing round in another circle; being upside down must have become quite painful by now. 'Of people asking questions – '

'Who? Censorinus? Laurentius? Us?'

'All of you.'

'So *why* is he frightened? What has he done, Manlius?'

'I really don't know. Something big. He never would tell me – '

A feeling was growing. I grabbed Manlius by the ear. 'Was my brother Festus annoyed with him?'

'Probably . . .'

'Something to do with a lost statue, was it?' asked Father.

'Or a statue that was not lost at all,' I growled. 'From a ship that never sank – '

'The ship sank!' croaked Manlius. 'That's the truth of it. Orontes told me when he was getting out of Rome to avoid Festus. The ship with the statue sank; that's the honest truth!'

'What else did he tell you?'

'Nothing! Oh cut me down – '

'Why did he tell you nothing? He's your chum, isn't he?'

'Matter of trust . . .' Manlius whispered, as if he was afraid even to mention it. 'He's been paid a lot of money to keep quiet . . .' I could believe these romantic politicians would actually honour such a trust, even if the villains who bribed them were the worst kind of criminals. This lot probably lacked the moral scepticism to recognise true villainy.

'Who paid him?'

'I don't know!' His desperation told us this was almost certainly true.

'Let's get this straight,' Geminus nagged ominously. 'When Festus came to Rome looking for him, Orontes heard about it and deliberately skipped?' Manlius tried to nod. It was difficult in his position. Paint and wet plaster dribbled

905

from his hair. He blinked his eyes fretfully. 'After Festus died, Orontes thought he could come back?'

'He likes to work . . .'

'He likes to cause a heap of shit for the Didius family! And now every time anyone else starts asking questions, your wily pal does another bunk?' Another feeble nod; more turgid drips. 'So answer me this, you pathetic runt – where does the coward run off to when he leaves Rome?'

'Capua,' groaned Manlius. 'He lives in Capua.'

'Not for long!' I said.

We left the painter hanging from his scaffold, though on our way out we did mention to the watchman that there seemed to be something odd going on in the Sabine triclinium and the white reception room. He muttered that he would go and have a look when he had finished his game of draughts.

Pa and I walked into the street, kicking pebbles morosely. There was no doubt about it; if we wanted to sort out this mystery, one of us would have to go to Capua.

'Do we believe that's where Orontes is?'

'I reckon so,' I decided. 'Manlius and Varga had already mentioned that they stayed in Campania recently – I bet they went down there to visit their pal in hiding.'

'You'd better be right, Marcus!'

In March, the long flog down to Campania just to wrench some sordid tale from a sculptor held no promise that appealed to this particular member of the rampaging Didius boys.

On the other hand, with so much at stake in my promise to Mother, I could not allow my father to go instead.

LXVI

We had been in the far north of the city; we made our way gloomily south. This time we walked at merely a brisk pace. My father was still not talking.

We reached the Saepta Julia. Pa carried on. I was so used to marching alongside him into trouble that at first I said nothing, but eventually I tackled him: 'I thought we were going back to the Saepta?'

'I'm not going to the Saepta.'

'I can see that. The Saepta's behind us.'

'I was never going to the Saepta. I told you where we were going when we were at the Carus house.'

'Home, you said.'

'That's where I'm going,' said my father. 'You can please your pompous self.'

Home! He meant where he lived with his redhead.

I did not believe this could be happening.

I had never yet been inside the house where my father lived, though I reckoned Festus had been no stranger there. My mother would never forgive me if I went now. I was not part of Pa's new life; I would never be. The only reason I kept walking was that it would be a gross discourtesy to abandon a man of his age who had had a bad shock at the Carus house, and with whom I had just shared a rumpus. He was out in Rome without his normal bodyguards. He was under threat of violence from Carus and Servia. He was paying me for protection. The least I could do was to see he reached his house safely.

He let me trudge all the way from the Saepta Julia, past the Flaminian Circus, the Porticus of Octavia and the Theatre of Marcellus. He dragged me right under the shadow of the Arx and the Capitol. He towed me on reluctantly, past the end of Tiber Island, the old Cattle Market Forum, a whole litter of temples and the Sublician and Probus Bridges.

Then he let me wait while he fumbled for his doorkey,

failed to find it, and banged the bell to be let in. He let me slouch after him inside his neat entrance suite. He flung off his cloak, peeled off his boots, gestured brusquely for me to do likewise – and only when I was barefoot and feeling vulnerable did he admit scornfully, 'You can relax! She's not here.'

The reprieve nearly made me faint.

Pa shot me a disgusted look. I let him know it was mutual. 'I set her up in a small business to stop her nosing into mine. On Tuesdays she always goes there to pay the wages and do the accounts.'

'It's not a Tuesday!' I pointed out grumpily.

'They had some trouble there last week and now she's having some work done to the property. Anyway, she'll be out all day.'

I sat on a coffer while he stomped off to speak to his steward. Someone brought me a pair of spare sandals and took my boots to clean the mud off them. As well as this slave, and the boy who had opened the door to us, I saw several other faces. When Pa reappeared I commented, 'Your billet's well staffed.'

'I like people round about me.' I had always thought having too many people around him was the main reason he had left us.

'These are slaves.'

'So I'm a liberal. I treat my slaves like children.'

'I'd like to riposte, and you treated your children like slaves!' Our eyes met. 'I won't. It would be unjust.'

'Don't descend to forced politeness, Marcus! Just feel free to be yourself,' he commented, with the long-practised sarcasm peculiar to families.

Pa lived in a tall, rather narrow house on the waterfront. This damp location was highly desired because of its view across the Tiber, so plots were small. The houses suffered badly from flooding; I noticed that the ground floor here was painted plainly in fairly dark colours. Left to myself, I looked into the rooms attached to the hallway. They were being used by the slaves, or were set up as offices where visitors could be interviewed. One was even stuffed with sandbags for

908

emergency use. The only furniture comprised large stone coffers that would remain unaffected by damp.

Upstairs all that changed. Wrinkling my nose at the unfamiliar smell of a strange house, I followed my father to the first floor. Our feet trampled a grand Eastern carpet. He had this luxurious item spread on the floor in regular use, not hung safely on the wall. In fact everything he had brought home – which meant plenty – was there to be used.

We marched through a series of small, crowded rooms. They were clean, but jammed with treasures. The wall paint was all elderly and fading. It had been done to a basic standard, probably twenty years ago when Pa and his woman moved here, and not touched since. It suited him. The plainish red, yellow and sea-blue rooms with conventional dados and cornices were the best foil for my father's large, ever-changing collection of furniture and vases, not to mention the curios and interesting trinkets any auctioneer obtains by the crate. It was organised chaos, however. You could live here, if you liked clutter. The impression was established and comfortable, its taste set by people who pleased themselves.

I tried not to get too interested in the artefacts; they were astonishing, but I knew they were now doomed. As Pa walked ahead of me, sometimes glancing at a piece as he passed it, I had the impression he was secure, in a way I did not remember from when he lived with us. He knew where everything was. Everything was here because he wanted it – which extended to the scarf-maker, presumably.

He brought me to a room that could be either his private den or where he sat with his woman conversing. (He had bills and invoices scattered about and a dismantled lamp he was mending, but I noticed a small spindle poking out from under a cushion.) Thick woollen rugs rumpled underfoot. There were two couches, side-tables, various quaint bronze miniatures, lamps and log baskets. On the wall hung a set of theatrical masks – possibly not my father's choice. On a shelf stood an extremely good blue-glass cameo vase, over which he did sigh briefly.

'Losing that one is going to hurt! Wine?' He produced the inevitable flagon from a shelf near his couch. Alongside the couch he had an elegant yard-high gilded fawn, positioned so he could pat its head like a pet.

'No thanks. I'll go on tending the hangover.'

He stayed his hand, without pouring for himself. For a moment he gazed at me. 'You don't give an inch, do you?' I understood, and glared back silently. 'I've managed to get you inside the door – but you're as friendly as a bailiff. Less,' he added. 'I never knew a bailiff refuse a cup of wine.'

I said nothing. It would be a striking irony if I set out to find my dead brother, only to end up making friends with my father instead. I don't believe in that kind of irony. We had had a good day getting ourselves into all sorts of trouble – and that was the end of it.

My father put down the flagon and his empty cup.

'Come and see my garden, then!' he ordered me.

We walked back through all the rooms until we reached the stairs. To my surprise, he led me up another flight; I assumed I was about to partake in some perverse joke. But we came to a low arch, closed by an oak door. Pa shot open the bolts, and stood back for me to duck my head and step out first.

It was a roof-garden. It had troughs filled with plants, bulbs, even small trees. Shaped trellises were curtained with roses and ivy. At the parapet more roses were trained along chains like garlands. There, between tubs of box trees, stood two lion-ended seats, providing a vista right across the water to Caesar's Gardens, the Transtiberina, the whale-backed ridge of the Ianiculan.

'Oh this is not fair,' I managed to grin feebly.

'Got you!' he scoffed. He must have known I had inherited a deep love of greenery from Ma's side of the family.

He made to steer me to a seat, but I was already at the parapet drinking in the panorama. 'Oh you lucky old bastard! So who does the garden?'

'I planned it. I had to have the roof strengthened. Now you know why I keep so many slaves; it's no joke carrying water and soil up three flights in buckets. I spend a lot of my spare time up here . . .'

He would. I would have done the same.

We took a bench each. It was companionable, yet we remained distinct. I could cope with that.

'Right,' he said. 'Capua!'

'I'll go.'

'I'm coming with you.'

'Don't bother. I can rough up a sculptor, however devious. At least we know that he's devious before I start.'

'Sculptors are all devious! There are a lot of them in Capua. You don't even know what he looks like. I'm coming, so don't argue. I know Orontes, and what's more, I know Capua.' Of course, he had lived there for years.

'I can find my way round some two-mule Campanian village,' I snarled disparagingly.

'Oh no. Helena Justina doesn't want you being robbed by every low-season pickpocket and picking up floozies – '

I was about to ask if that was what had happened when he went there, but of course when Pa ran off to Capua, he took his own floozie.

'What about leaving the business?'

'Mine is a well-run outfit, thanks; it can stand a few days without me. Besides,' he said, 'madam can make decisions if any snags arise.'

I was surprised to learn the scarf-maker commanded so much trust, or even that she involved herself. For some reason I had always viewed her as a negative figure. My father seemed the type whose views on women's social role were stiff and traditional. Still, it did not follow that the scarf-maker agreed with him.

We heard the door open behind us. Thinking about Father's redhead, I looked round quickly, afraid I should see her. A slave edged out with a large tray, no doubt as a result of Pa's talk with his steward. The tray went on to a bird-bath, creating a makeshift table. 'Have some lunch, Marcus.'

It was mid-afternoon, but we had missed other refreshment. Pa helped himself. He left me to make my own decision, so on that basis I conceded the issue and tucked in.

It was nothing elaborate, just a snack someone had thrown together for the master when he came home unexpectedly. But as snacks go, it was tasty. 'What's the fish?'

'Smoked eel.'

'Very nice.'

'Try it with a drop of damson sauce.'

'Is this what they call Alexandrine?'

'Probably. I just call it bloody good. Am I winning you round?' my father asked evilly.

'No, but pass the rolls, will you.'

There were two strips of eel left; we jabbed at them with our knives, like children fighting over titbits.

'A man called Hirrius had an eel-farm,' Pa began obliquely, though somehow I knew he would be working around to discussing our own precarious position. 'Hirrius sold his eel-farm for four million sesterces. It was a famous sale; I wish I had handled it! Now you and I could do with just one pool like that.'

I breathed slowly, licking sauce from my fingers. 'Half a million . . . I'll come in with you, but that's not much of an offer. I've been trying to raise four hundred thousand. I suppose I may have collected ten per cent so far.' That was optimistic. 'I refrained from pricing up your lovely chattels, but the picture's bleak for both of us.'

'True.' My father seemed surprisingly unworried, however.

'Don't you care? You have obviously assembled a wealth of good things here – yet you told Carus and Servia you would sell.'

'Selling things is my trade,' he answered tersely. Then he confirmed, 'You're right. To cover the debt means stripping the house. Most of the stuff at the Saepta belongs to other people; selling for customers is what auctioneering is about.'

'Your personal investment is all in this house?'

'Yes. The house itself is freehold. That cost me – and I'm not intending to mortgage it now. I don't keep much cash with bankers; it's vulnerable.'

'So how healthy are you on the sesterces front?'

'Not as healthy as you think.' If he could seriously talk of finding half a million, he was filthy rich by my standards. Like all men who don't have to worry, he liked grousing. 'There are plenty of demands. Bribes and easements required at the Saepta; I pay my whack to the Guild for our dinners and the funeral fund. Since the store was raided, I've some big losses to cover, not to mention compensating the people whose auction was knocked apart that time you were there.' He could have added, *I still give your mother an annuity*. I knew he did. I also knew she spent his money on her grandchildren; I paid her rent myself. 'I'll have a bare house when I finish with Carus,' he sighed. 'But I've had that before. I'll come back.'

'You're too old to have to start again.' He must be too old to feel sure he could manage it. By rights, he should now have been able to retire to some country farm. 'Why are you doing it? For big brother's reputation?'

'My own, more likely. I'd rather sneer at a stick like Carus than let Carus sneer at me. What about you?' he challenged.

'I was the hero's executor.'

'Well I was his partner.'

'In this?'

'No, but does it matter, Marcus? If he'd asked me to come in on a Phidias I would have leapt at it. Let me handle the debt. I've had my life. You don't need to ruin your chance of making things legal with your senator's daughter.'

'Maybe I never had any chance,' I admitted dismally.

Another of the discreet house slaves paddled up, this time bringing us a steaming jug of honey and wine. He poured for us both without asking, so I accepted the cup. The drink was headily laced with Indian spikenard. My father had come a long way from the days when all we drank at home was old wine lees, well watered down, with the odd vervain leaf to disguise the taste.

Light clung to the distant sky with a fragile grip as the afternoon drew in. In the grey haze across the river I could just see the Ianiculan Hill running away to the right. There was a house over there which I once dreamed of owning, a house where I had wanted to live with Helena.

'Will she leave you?' Pa must have read my thoughts.

'She should.'

'I didn't ask what she *ought* to do!'

I smiled. 'She won't ask it either, knowing her.'

He sat quiet for a time. He liked Helena, I knew that.

Suddenly I leaned forward, resting my elbows on my knees, cradling my cup. Something had struck me. 'What did Festus do with the money?'

'The half-million?' Pa rubbed his nose. He had the same nose as me: straight down from the forehead without a bump between the eyebrows. 'Olympus knows!'

'I never found it.'

'And I never saw it either.'

'So what did he tell you about it when he was mentioning the Phidias?'

'Festus,' drawled my father, with some exasperation, 'never gave me any idea the Phidias had been paid for by the collectors! That I only learned from Carus and Servia well afterwards.'

I sat back again. 'They really did pay him? Is there any chance this receipt of theirs is forged?'

Pa sighed. 'I wanted to think so. I looked at it very hard, believe me. It was convincing. Go and see it – '

I shook my head. I hate to pile up misery.

I could think up no new queries. Now Orontes Mediolanus was our only lead.

We spent some time (it felt about two hours) arguing about arrangements for getting to Capua. By Didius standards this was fairly refined. Even so, all my sensible plans for lessening the agony of a long, tiring journey were overturned. I wanted to ride down there at the fastest speed possible, do the business, then pelt home. Pa insisted his old bones were no longer able to endure a horse. He decided to arrange a carriage, from some stable he vaguely specified as a meeting-place. We came near to agreeing terms for sharing expenses. There was some discussion about a departure time, though this remained unclear. The Didius family hates to upset itself by settling practicalities.

Yet another servant appeared, on the excuse of collecting the tray. He and Pa exchanged a glance that could have been a signal. 'You'll be wanting to leave soon,' hinted my father.

Nobody mentioned the woman he lived with, but her presence in the house had become tangible.

He was right. If she was there, I wanted to disappear. He took me downstairs. I pulled on my cloak and boots hurriedly, then fled.

Luck was against me as usual. The last thing I felt able to cope

914

with happened: not two streets from Father's house, while still feeling like a traitor, I ran into Ma.

XLVII

Guilt settled on me like an extra cloak.

'Where are you sneaking from?'

We stood on a corner. Every passer-by must have been able to tell I was a son in deep trouble. Every lax villain on the Aventine would be chuckling all the way to the next drinking-house, glad it was not him.

Honesty pays, people tell you. 'I've been enjoying the entertainments of my father's smart town house.'

'I thought you looked sick!' sniffed Ma. 'I brought you up to avoid places where you might catch a disease!'

'It was clean,' I said wearily.

'What about the little job I asked you to help sort out for me?' From the way she spoke, I was thought to have forgotten it.

'Your "little job" was what got me arrested the other day – Helena, too. I'm working on it. That's why I had to go to Pa's. I've been running around on your commission all today, and tomorrow I have to go to Capua – '

'Why Capua?' she demanded. For obvious reasons Capua had long been a dirty word in our circle. That pleasant town was a byword for immorality and deceit, though apart from having once played host to my absconding father, all Capua ever did was to overcharge holidaying tourists on their way to Oplontis and Baiae, and grow lettuce.

'A sculptor lives there. He was involved with Festus. I'm going to talk to him about that business deal.'

'On your own?'

'No. Pa insists on coming with me,' I admitted. Ma let out a terrible wail. 'Mother, I cannot help it if your estranged husband starts claiming his paternal rights belatedly.'

'So you're going together!' She made it sound like the deepest treachery. 'I would have thought you'd want to avoid that!'

I wanted to avoid the whole journey. 'At least he can

916

identify the sculptor. The man is now our only hope of sorting out this business – which I warn you, is likely to prove expensive in every way.'

'I can lend you a few sesterces – '

'A few sesterces are nowhere near enough. The price of extracting our family from this problem is about half a million.'

'Oh Marcus, you always did exaggerate!'

'Fact, Ma.' She was trembling. I would be trembling myself if I said 'half a million' too many more times. 'Don't worry. This is men's business. Geminus and I will deal with it – but you have to accept the consequences. Finding so much to clear up my brother's problem puts paid to any hope in Hades that I can marry Helena. Just so you know. I don't want any nagging on the subject. It's out of my hands – and we have our beloved Festus to blame for everything.'

'You never liked your poor brother!'

'I loved him, Ma – but I certainly don't like what he has done to me now.'

I saw my mother lift her chin. 'Perhaps the whole business would be better left alone . . .'

'Ma, that is impossible.' I felt tired and cold. 'Other people will not let us forget it. Look, I'm going home. I need to see Helena.'

'If you're going to Capua with that man,' advised my mother, 'take Helena to look after you!'

'Helena's just returned from one long journey; the last thing she wants is a trip to deepest Campania.' Not, anyway, with a raddled old auctioneer and a hangdog informer who had never in his life been so depressed.

My mother reached up and tidied my hair. 'Helena will manage. She won't want you on your own in bad company.' I wanted to say, '*Ma, I'm thirty, not five years old!*' but arguing never got me anywhere with Mother.

Most people would think that a senator's daughter who abandoned herself to a low-life informer *was* bad company.

But the thought of taking Helena on one last fling before I was bankrupt did cheer me up.

At home, Helena Justina was waiting for me.

Dinner was eel again. A vast consignment must have wriggled into market that morning. The whole of Rome was sitting down to the same menu.

Dinner was normally my province. Since I reckoned my beloved had been brought up merely to behave chastely and look decorative, I had laid down a rule that I would buy and cook our food. Helena accepted the rule, but sometimes when she knew I was busy and was afraid of not getting fed that night, out she would rush to provide us with an unscheduled treat. My ramshackle kitchen made her nervous, but she was perfectly competent at following the recipes she had once read out to her servants. Tonight she had poached her offering in a saffron sauce. It was delicious. I munched it down gallantly while she watched me eat every mouthful, searching for signs of approval.

I sat back and surveyed her. She was beautiful. I was going to lose her. Somehow I had to tell her the news.

'How was your day with your father?'

'Wonderful! We played about with some collecting snobs, had fun picking on some artists, and now we're planning a bad boys' outing. Would you like to go to Capua?'

'I may not like it, but I'll tag along.'

'I warn you, Pa and I are established as the fabulous Didius muckers – a rough pair whose very name can clear a street. You'll be coming to impose some sobriety.'

'That's a pity,' Helena told me, with a glint in her eye. 'I was hoping I could be a loose woman who keeps a gold piece down her cleavage and swears horrendously at ferrymen.'

'Maybe I like that idea better,' I grinned.

False jollity gave me away. Seeing I needed consolation she sat on my lap and tickled my chin. In the hope of this kind of mistreatment, I had been barbered in Fountain Court before I came up. 'What's the matter, Marcus?'

I told her.

Helena said she could dispense with being middle-class and married. I suppose that meant she had never expected it to happen anyway.

I said I was sorry.

She said she could see that.

I held her tight, knowing that I ought to send her back to

her father, and knowing I was glad that she would never agree to go.

'I'll wait for you, Marcus.'

'You'll wait for ever then.'

'Ah well!' She amused herself making small plaits in my hair. 'Tell me what happened today?'

'Oh ... my father and I just proved that if different members of the Didius family combine efforts to solve a problem –'

Helena Justina was already laughing. 'What?'

'Two of us can make even more of a mess of it than one!'

XLVIII

Horace once took a journey down the Via Appia. He describes it as a farrago of crooked landlords, potholes, house fires, gritty bread and infected eyes; of being packed into a ferry to cross the Pontine Marshes, then without explanation being left motionless for hours; of staying awake half the night all keyed up for an assignation with a girl who never bothered to turn up . . .

Compared to us, Horace had it soft. Horace was travelling as minutes secretary to a summit conference of Triumvirs. He had rich patrons and intellectual company; Virgil, no less, to pick the burs off his riding-cloak. He stayed in private houses where they burned pans of sweet oil to welcome him. We stayed in public inns (when they were not closed up for winter). In place of Virgil I took my father, whose conversation fell several hexameters short of epic poetry.

However, unlike Horace, I had a hamper thrust upon me by my mother with not only good Roman bread but enough smoked Lucanian sausage to last a month. And I took my own girl. So I had the comfort of knowing that had I not been completely exhausted by travel, she would have been smilingly available any night of my choice.

One thing Horace did not have to do on his trip to Tarentum was visit his Great-Auntie Phoebe and a host of morose country relatives. (If he did, he left it right out of the *Satire*; and if his relatives were like mine, I don't blame him for that.)

There were three reasons for visiting the market garden. First: Phoebe herself, who would have heard about Helena and who was overdue for an introduction if I ever wanted a bowl of her rocket soup again. Second: so we could leave Geminus at the nearby mansio where the dead Censorinus, and possibly his centurion pal Laurentius, had stayed. Pa could not nowadays visit the market garden due to what passes for tact in our family; instead he was instructed to make himself at home at the inn, buy the landlord a large one, and find out what the soldier (or perhaps two soldiers) had been up to. The third reason for going was to investigate my brother's store.

Much is made of the Great Roman country estates staffed by thousands of slaves for the benefit of absentee senators. You hear less about subsistence farms like the one my mother's brothers ran, but they are there. Outside Rome itself and many another town, poor people scrape a living for large families who swallow any profit, slogging away, year after year, with little more than bad tempers to show for it. At least on the Campania there was decent soil, with fast roads to a voracious market when anything grew.

That had been how my parents met. On a trip to Rome, Ma had sold Pa some doubtful brassicas, then when he went back to complain, she coyly let him take her for a cup of wine. Three weeks later, with what must have seemed at the time like country acumen, she married him.

I tried to explain the set-up to Helena as we drove down the track. 'My grandfather and Great-Uncle Scaro originally shared the farm; now at various times one or two of Ma's brothers run the place. They are a raggedy set of characters, and I can't say which we'll find here. They are always going off for a foreign love affair, or to recover from a fit of remorse because their cart ran over a grass-cutter. Then, just when someone is delivering twins on the kitchen table and the radish crop has failed, they arrive home unexpectedly, all eager to rape the goatherd's teenage daughter and full of mad ideas for horticultural change. Be prepared. There's bound to have been at least one ferocious quarrel, some adultery, a dead ox poisoned by a neighbour, and a fatal accident in the nuttery since I last came. Unless Uncle Fabius discovers he had an illegitimate son by a woman with a weak heart who is threatening a lawsuit, he counts the day lost.'

'Isn't it rather inconvenient on a farm with work to do?'

'Farms are lively places!' I warned.

'True! We must expect people who spend all day dealing with Nature's bounty of life and death and growth to have seething emotions to match.'

'Don't mock, woman! I spent half my childhood on this

921

farm. Whenever there was trouble at home we were sent here to recuperate.'

'It sounds the wrong place for a rest!'

'People on farms can handle trouble as easily as pulling salad leaves ... Let me continue with the briefing, or we'll arrive before I've done. At the centre of all this strife, Great-Auntie Phoebe occupies the hearth like a rock, making polenta that would halt an epidemic and holding everyone together.'

'Your grandfather's sister?'

'No, she's his unmarried second wife. My grandmother died early – '

'Worn out by the excitement?' suggested Helena.

'Don't be romantic! Worn out by childbearing. Phoebe was a slave originally, then Grandpa's comfort for years. It happens all the time. For as long as I can remember they shared one bed, one table, and all the hard work my uncles had no time for because of their fascinating social lives. Grandpa made her a freedwoman and was always intending to marry her, but never got around to it –'

'I see nothing wrong with that, if they were happy,' said Helena, in a stern voice.

'Neither do I,' I replied, suavely deleting any tone of criticism. 'Except Phoebe is ashamed of it. You'll find her very diffident.'

Helena thought all my stories a joke until we got there.

Great-Auntie Phoebe was spinning imperturbably beside the hearth. She was a small, sweet, round-cheeked woman who looked as frail as grass but had more strength than three grown men. This was just as well, since while the others were being introspective about their personal lives she had to harvest cabbage and turn a fork in the manure heap. Not so much lately. She was probably eighty, and had decreed that delivering a calf was now beyond her dignity.

She had a passionate interest in our entire family, based on the fact she had nursed most of us through colic and adolescence. Festus had been her favourite, needless to say. ('That limb!')

Uncle Fabius was away from home for dark reasons no one would specify.

'Same trouble again?' I grinned at Phoebe.

'He never learns!' she whispered, shaking her head.

Uncle Junius was here, spending his time complaining about the absent Fabius. Well, his free time anyway. His main energy was taken up with a rapidly failing carp-farm and his efforts to seduce a woman called Armilla, wife of a neighbouring, much more prosperous, landowner.

'Leading him on?' I demanded, showing Helena how to read the code.

'How did you know?' clucked Phoebe, breaking off her thread.

'Heard it before.'

'Ah well!'

There had been a third brother once – but we were not allowed to mention him at all.

All the time we appeared to be talking about my uncles, the real subject under scrutiny was my new girlfriend. It was the first time I had brought anyone other than Petronius Longus (mainly because I used to come on holiday when both the grapes and the girls were ripe, with obvious intentions to enjoy both).

Helena Justina sat, dark-eyed and gracious, accepting the ritual scrutiny. She was an educated girl, who knew when to curb her ferocious temperament or else condemn us to thirty years of the family accusation that she had never wanted to fit in.

'Marcus has never brought one of his Roman friends to see the farm before,' commented Great-Auntie Phoebe, letting it be understood that she was referring to my female acquaintances, that she knew there had been many, and that she was relieved I had finally found one who must have displayed an interest in growing leeks. I grinned amiably. There was nothing else to do.

'I'm very honoured,' said Helena. 'I've heard a lot about you all.'

Auntie Phoebe looked embarrassed, thinking this must be a disapproving reference to her unsanctioned relationship with my free and easy grandpapa.

'I hope you don't mind if I mention this,' Helena went on. 'About sleeping arrangements. Marcus and I usually share a room, though we are not married, I'm afraid. I hope you're not shocked. It's not his fault, but I've always believed a woman should keep her independence if no children are involved . . .'

'That's a new one on me!' cackled Phoebe, who apparently liked the idea.

'It's new to me,' I replied, more nervously. 'I was hoping for the safety of respectability!'

Helena and my great-aunt exchanged a witty glance.

'That's men for you – they have to pretend!' Phoebe exclaimed. She was a wise old lady whom I held in great affection, even though we were not related (or more likely because of it).

Uncle Junius grumpily agreed to take me to the store. On the way out, I noticed Helena staring curiously at the little semi-circular niche where the household gods were displayed. There was also a ceramic head of Fabius, with flowers reverently laid before it by Phoebe, who always honoured the memory of any absent uncle (except, of course, the one who was not talked about). She had another bust of Junius on a nearby shelf, ready for the honorific treatment the next time *he* flitted. Back in the niche, between the conventional bronze statues of dancing Lares bearing their horns of plenty, lay a dusty set of teeth.

'Still got those then?' I chivvied, trying to make light of it.

'It's where he always kept them overnight,' replied Uncle Junius. 'Phoebe put them there before the funeral, and no one has the heart to remove them now.'

I had to explain to Helena. 'Great-Uncle Scaro, one of life's eccentrics, once had his mouth attended to by an Etruscan dentist. Thereafter he became a passionate devotee of Etruscan bridgework – which is a high art form, if you can afford the gold wire. Eventually poor Scaro had no teeth left to attach the wires to, and no money, come to that. So he tried to invent his own false teeth.'

'Are those them?' Helena enquired politely.

'Yup!' said Junius.

'Goodness. Did they work?'

'Yup!' Junius was plainly wondering if the senator's

daughter might be a candidate for his doleful attentions. Helena, who had a fine sense of discretion, kept close to me.

'These were model four,' I reminisced. Uncle Scaro thought a lot of me; he always kept me informed on the progress of his inventive schemes. I thought best to omit that some teeth on model four had come from a dead dog. 'They worked perfectly. You could chew an ox bone with them. You could tackle nuts, or fruit with pips. Unfortunately, Scaro choked on them.'

Helena looked heartbroken.

'Don't worry,' said Uncle Junius kindly. 'He would have seen it as part of his research. Swallowing them by accident was just how the old beggar would have wanted to go.'

Uncle Scaro's teeth smiled gently from the lararium as if he were still wearing them.

He would have liked my new girlfriend. I wished he were here to see her. It gave me a pang to leave Helena standing there, solemnly dusting his teeth with the end of her stole.

There was very little of interest in the store. Just a few broken wicker chairs, a chest with its lid staved in, a dented bucket and some straw-dust.

Also, standing at the back like a row of gloomy tombstones for Cyclops, four huge rectangular blocks of quarried stone.

'What are those, Junius?'

My uncle shrugged. A life of confusion and intrigue had made him wary of asking questions. He was afraid he might discover a long-lost heir with a claim on his land, or the taint of a witch's prophecy that could blight his efforts with the neighbour's luscious wife or get him into a ten-year feud with the ox-cart mender. 'Something Festus must have left,' he mumbled nervously.

'Did he say anything about them?'

'I wasn't here then.'

'Off with a woman?'

He gave me a nasty look. 'Bloody Fabius might know.'

If Fabius knew, Phoebe knew as well. We walked thoughtfully back to the house.

Great-Auntie Phoebe was telling Helena about the time a crazy horseman whom we later discovered might have been

925

the Emperor Nero fleeing from Rome to commit suicide (a minor aspect, the way Phoebe told it), galloped too fast past the market garden and killed half her chickens in the road. She did not know what the stone blocks were, but told me Festus had brought them on that famous last leave of his. I did find out from her, however, that two men who must have been Censorinus and Laurentius had come to the farm asking questions some months ago.

'They wanted to know if Festus had left anything here.'

'Did they mention the stone blocks?'

'No. They were very secretive.'

'Did you show them the store?'

'No. You know Fabius –' I did. He was a suspicious bastard at the best of times. 'He just took them out to an old barn we have full of ploughing equipment, then he played the country idiot.'

'So what happened?'

'It was down to me as usual.' Great-Auntie Phoebe liked to be seen as a woman of character.

'How did you get rid of them?'

'I showed them Scaro's teeth on the lararium and said those were all we had left of the last unwanted stranger – then I set the dogs on them.'

Next day we set off south again. I told Pa about the four blocks of stone. We both pondered the mystery without comment, but I was starting to have ideas, and if I knew him he was too.

He told me Censorinus and another soldier had stayed at the mansio.

'Old news!' Helena and I relayed Phoebe's tale.

'So I wasted my time! It was a lousy inn,' moaned my father. 'I suppose you two were being pampered in the lap of luxury?'

'We were!' I assured him. 'If you can stand hearing about Phoebe's chickens, and listening to Junius complaining about his brother, then it's a grand place to stay!' Pa knew that.

'I expect Junius had his eye on your girl?' he hinted, trying to annoy me in return. Helena raised the elegant curves of her eyebrows.

'He was thinking about it. I nearly took him on one side and had a quiet word – but if I know Junius, warning him against it is the certain way to make him do something.'

Pa agreed. 'It's as pointless as shouting "He's behind you!" when the Spook starts looming at the Honest Old Father in an Atellan farce . . . Where was drippy Fabius?'

'Off with his old trouble.'

'I can never remember what his trouble is.'

'Neither can I,' I confessed. 'Either gambling or boils, I think. He ran away to be a gladiator once, but that was only a passing aberration when he wanted to avoid the lupin harvest.'

'Phoebe asked after you, Didius Geminus,' said Helena in a stern voice. She seemed to think we were being frivolous in our discussion of the family news.

'I suppose the actual enquiry was, "How's that useless city mollock who fathered you?" ' grunted Pa to me. He knew what they all thought.

He had always known. Being constantly despised by my mother's peculiar relatives must have been one of the trials that had eventually proved too dreary to endure.

IXL

Capua.

Capua, Queen of the central plain (and home of smart fleas).

Capua, the most spendidly flourishing city in rich Campania (if you listen to the Capuans) or even in Italy (if you get stuck with one of those who has never seen Rome).

Do not fail to view the grand Augustan amphitheatre, which stands four storeys high with its eighty great arches all capped with marble deities – though it is more recent than Spartacus, so don't get romantic political ideas. Also, while viewing this splendid edifice, keep your eyes in the back of your head and your hand on your purse. The people of Capua earn their livelihood from visitors, and they do not always ask before claiming it. Never forget: they are so flourishing because we are so stupid. What's yours can become theirs very rapidly in Capua.

When Capua opened its doors and its heart to Hannibal, it is said that its luxury sapped his men so much that he never won another battle. We could have endured some luxury of this disgraceful quality, but things have changed since then.

We drove into Capua on a wet Monday evening, in time to find all the eateries closing up. One carriage-horse went lame just as we reached the forum, giving us an uneasy sensation that it might not be possible to drive home when we wanted to escape. My father, who had come to protect us with his special knowledge of this area, had his money pinched within two minutes. Luckily, our main cash was hidden under the floor of our carriage, with Helena's sensible feet guarding it.

'I'm out of practice,' grumbled Pa.

'That's all right. I always make a mess of choosing my travelling companions and end up nursemaiding incompetents.'

'Thanks!' muttered Helena.

'You were not included.'

'My hero!'

After ten days of misery, which ought to have been a bare week of mild pain, we were all on the edge of rebellion.

I found us a lodging-house in the usual hurried rush when darkness is descending so fast you close your eyes to the drawbacks. It was right next to the market so there would be a racket in the morning, not to mention cats yowling on the rubbish and ladies of the night plying their trade under the empty stalls. The fleas were lying in wait with little smiling faces, though they at least had some tact and stayed invisible at first. The ladies of the night were out and about already: they stood in a line silently watching us unload the coach.

Looking for cash boxes their pimps could come and lift, no doubt.

Helena wrapped our money in a cloak and carried it into the boarding-house in a bundle over her shoulder like a tired child.

'Marcus, I don't like this . . .'

'I'm here to take care of you.' She was not reassured. 'Father and I will chalk up a message on the basilica saying, "*Anyone who rapes, robs or kidnaps Helena Justina, will have to answer to the ferocious Didius boys!*" '

'Wonderful,' she said. 'I hope your fame has reached this far.'

'Indubitably!' responded Pa. Long words had always been a form of bluff in the Didius family.

It was an uncomfortable night. Luckily by the time we went to bed, having failed to find an edible dinner, we were prepared for the worst.

Next day we moved to another boarding-house, providing more easy silver for another cheating landlord, and delight to another pack of fleas.

We started to visit artists' studios. All claimed they had never heard of Orontes. All of them had to be lying. Capua thought a great deal of itself but it was, frankly, not that big. Orontes must have been going round for weeks glueing up mouths on the off chance that someone or other might follow him here.

We stopped asking.

We moved to yet another lodging-house and kept our heads down, while Father and I started to watch the forum from doorways and arches where we could not be seen.

Hanging around the forum of a strange town, in the middle of winter, when there is a gap in the local festivals, can make a man depressed.

Helena told us on our return to the current doss-house that there were no fleas, but she had definitely found bedbugs and an ostler had tried to get into the room with her when we left her on her own.

He tried again that night when both Pa and I were sitting there. Afterwards we argued for hours about whether he knew there were three of us and had come hoping for a full orgy. One thing was definite; he would not try again. Pa and I had made it plain we did not welcome friendly overtures.

Next day we moved again, just to be safe.

Finally we had some luck.

Our new rooms were above a caupona. Ever one for a risk, I popped down for three platefuls of their green beans in mustard sauce, with a side order of seafood dumplings, some bread, pork titbits for Helena, olives, wine and hot water, honey . . . the usual complicated list when your friends send you out to pick up what they gaily describe as 'a quick bite'. I was staggering under an immense tray, so heavy I could barely lift the thing, let alone open the door to carry it upstairs without spillage.

A girl held the door for me.

I took up the tray, grinned at my darling, stuffed some titbits between my jaws, and grabbed my cloak. Helena and my father stared, then fell on the food tray and let me get on with it. I ran back downstairs.

She was a lovely girl. She had a body you would walk ten miles to grapple, with a carriage that said she knew *exactly* what she was offering. Her face was older than first impressions, but had only gained in character from extra years. When I sauntered back, she was still at the caupona, buying spare ribs in a parcel to take out. She was leaning on the counter as if she needed extra support for her abundant figure. Her bold expression had silenced all the street trade, while her dancing brown eyes were doing things to the waiter that his mother must have warned him not to allow in public; he didn't care. She was a brunette, if it's of interest.

I settled down out of sight, and when she left I did what every man in the place was wanting to do: I followed her.

L

Don't even think it.

I never follow strange women with that idea.

Anyway, the darling brunette was not entirely a stranger to me. I had seen her undressed (though she was unaware of it). And I had seen her at the Circus sitting next to Festus. I could have called out her name and tried to get to know her by saying, 'Excuse me, but I think I saw you with my brother once' (*that* old line!).

Her name, had I wanted to play around like a barboy, was Rubinia.

I did the decent thing. I trailed her to the love-nest she shared with the sculptor Orontes. They lived four miles outside the city and must have thought themselves safe from discovery, especially during the hours of darkness. The gorgeous model had been quite unaware that expert feet were silently slipping along after her.

I waited until they had had time to eat their ribs and quaff their liquor and knot themselves together in an intimate arrangement. Then I went in without knocking.

They were very surprised.

And I could tell they were not pleased.

LI

Nudity does not affront me. Fighting it, especially in the female version, can be disconcerting for anyone.

The outraged model came at me with a dinner knife. As she ran across the sculptor's studio she was breasting the air with the formidable panache of the famous Winged Victory of Samothrace, though less formally clad. Luckily it was a large studio. I had a good view of her provocative features – and time to defend myself.

I was unarmed and short of ideas. But a pail of cold water stood near at hand. Brought in from a well I had seen in the garden, it was the best resource available. I grabbed it and hurled the icy contents straight at the screeching girl. She let out a louder, even higher-pitched scream, and dropped the knife.

I ripped a stiff cloth from the nearest statue and flung the unwieldy material around her, pinioning her arms.

'Excuse me, madam; you seem to be lacking a stole – ' She took this badly, but I clung on to her. We swung round in a wild dance, while the lovely Rubinia called me some names I was surprised a woman knew.

The studio was in a high barn of a building, dimly lit by one taper at the far end. Dark stone shapes loomed on all sides, casting huge, peculiar shadows. Stepladders and other equipment lay everywhere, dangerous traps for a stranger with his mind on other things. Artists are not tidy people (too much time wasted on dreaming, for one thing; and in between the creative processes, too much drink).

I shook the girl angrily, trying to keep her still.

By this time a large man who must be the missing sculptor had struggled upright from the tangle of their bed in the far corner of the place. He too was completely naked, and recently aroused for a different kind of combat. He was broad-chested, no longer young, bald, with a bushy beard as long as my forearm. He cut an impressive dash as he powered across the dusty floor yelling abuse.

These artistic types were noisy swine. No wonder they lived in the country, with no neighbours to annoy.

Rubinia was still screaming, and wriggling so frantically I did not immediately notice that her lover had snatched up a chisel and a mallet. But his first wild swing missed, and his mallet hissed past my left ear. As he feinted, this time with the chisel, I turned sharply, so the girl was in front of me. Rubinia bit my wrist. I lost any inhibitions about using her as a shield.

Still dragging the girl, I dodged behind a statue as Orontes lashed out. His chisel zinged off a half-formed nymph, modelled by someone more slender than the solid wench I was trying to subdue. Rubinia's feet scrabbled on the floor as she tried to lock her legs around the nymph's haunches. I jerked sideways preventing it, though I was losing my grip on the dust-sheet and its astonishing contents. She had slithered lower; any minute I should lose Rubinia too.

The sculptor popped out from behind a marble group. I hurled myself backwards, just missing a ladder. He was taller than me, but made clumsy by drink and agitation; his domed forehead knocked into the obstruction. As he cursed, I seized what might be my only chance. I was losing my grip on the girl, so I flung her as far from me as I could, aiding the process painfully with my boot on her expansive rear. She crashed into a pediment, letting loose another mouthful of barracks invective.

I grabbed the dazed sculptor. He was strong, but before he realised what I was up to I had whirled him in a half-circle. Then I pressed him into a sarcophagus that was standing on its end as if made to receive visitors. Seizing its massive lid, I slid the thing sideways and attempted to close the coffin on the man who was supposed to be mending it.

The stone lid's weight surprised me and I only managed to jam the thing halfway across before Rubinia came at me again, hurling herself on to me from behind and trying to tear out my hair. Dear gods, she was a stayer. As I squirmed around to face her she let go of my shoulders and grabbed the mallet. Frantic blows rained all around me, though her idea of how to hit a target was fortunately hazy. Landing a blow was made more difficult by the fact she was springing about like a maddened polecat, jabbing kicks at the part of me I prefer not to have attacked.

With two of them to overpower, things were becoming desperate. I managed to lean against the sarcophagus lid to keep Orontes trapped behind me, and at the same time fastened Rubinia's hammer wrist in my hardest grip. It must have hurt her badly. For a few seconds she went on trying to murder me, while I tried to prevent it happening. Finally I broke her hold on the weapon, gave her a clout on the temple, and grappled her.

At that moment the door crashed open. In raced a familiar short sturdy shape, topped by frenetic grey curls.

'Cerberus!' exploded my father, with what I hoped was admiration. 'I only let you out on your own for a moment, then I find you wrestling with a naked nymph!'

LII

'Don't just stand there cracking witticisms,' I gasped. 'Lend me a hand!'

Pa sauntered across the studio, grinning like Festus would have done. 'Is this some new form of excitement, Marcus? Having your end away on a coffin lid?' Then he added, with glee, 'The high and mighty Helena Justina is not going to like *this*!'

'Helena's not going to know,' I said tersely – then I threw the naked model at him. He caught her and held on with rather more relish than necessary. 'Now you've got the problem, and I've got the scenery!'

'Cover your eyes, boy!' growled Geminus cheerfully. 'You're too young . . .' He himself seemed to be coping, but I supposed he was used to fine art at close quarters. Holding Rubinia's wrists together and ignoring her passionate attempts to unman him, he catalogued her attractions with a deeply appreciative leer.

I fell prey to some tetchiness. 'How in Hades did you get here?'

'Helena,' he said, enjoying the emphasis, 'felt worried when she noticed you sloping off with that nasty smirk on your face. And now I see why!' he jibed. 'Does she know what you're like when you go off amusing yourself?'

I scowled. 'How did you find me?'

'Not difficult. I was fifteen yards behind you all the way.' That would teach me to congratulate myself on my expert tracking; all that time I was hoofing after Rubinia, so pleased with myself for doing it discreetly, someone had been tailing me. I was lucky the whole of Capua had not come to see the show. Father went on, 'When you sat down on the well-head for your watchdog session, I nipped up the road for a flagon – '

Now I was furious. 'You went off for a *drink*? And are you saying that even after the ostler incident you left Helena Justina all on her own at a lodging-house?'

'Well this is no place to bring her!' minced my pa, at his most annoying. 'She's a game girl, but believe me, son, she would not like this!' His eyes wandered salaciously over both of our naked companions, pausing on the coffined Orontes with a harder glare. 'I'm glad you've put that nasty piece of work in a suitable place! Now calm down, Marcus. With three bowls of beans inside her, Helena will be a match for anyone.'

'Let's get on with this!' My voice was clipped.

'Right. Release the corpse from the stoneware, and we'll tell the nice people why we've come visiting.'

I turned round, though still applying my full weight to the carved lid of the sarcophagus. It was a dreary thing to see an inch from your nose – all badly proportioned heroes, leaning askew as if they were marching up a ship's deck.

'I don't know about releasing him,' I mused, curling my lip at Orontes. 'He can hear us from where he's standing. I think I'll find out everything we want before I let him hop out of it . . .'

My father latched on to the idea eagerly. 'That's good! If he won't talk, we can leave him there permanently.'

'He won't last long in that thing!' I commented.

My father, whose lurid sense of humour was rapidly reasserting itself, dragged Rubinia to a statue of a particularly lewd satyr, and used his belt to tie her to its hairy hindquarters in a suggestive position.

'Ah Marcus, she's started crying!'

'She likes to make an effort. Take no notice. A girl who was prepared to kick me in the privates gets no sympathy from me.'

My father told her *he* was on her side – but she had to stay there. Rubinia demonstrated more of her vivid vocabulary. Next Geminus helped me wedge a large lump of stone against the coffin lid, so it was held fast, still half covering the opening, with Orontes peering out. I was leaning on a ladder that was tilted against a wall opposite, while Pa climbed up a large enthroned goddess and settled demurely in her lap.

I stared at Orontes, who had caused us so much trouble. He was, though I did not know it yet, to cause us rather more.

With his bald top and his great curly, bushy beard he had once been handsome and still had the dramatic authority of some old Greek philosopher. Wrap him in a blanket and sit him in a portico and folk might flock to hear him straining his brain. So far he had had nothing to say to us. I would have to cure that.

'Right!' I tried to sound menacing. 'I have had no dinner, I'm worried about my girlfriend, and even though your sultry model is a glad eyeful I'm in no mood to let this take all night.'

The sculptor finally found his voice. 'Go and jump in the Phlaegraean Marsh!' It was a deep, sombre voice, made raspy by drink and debauchery.

'Show some respect, cumin-breath!' Pa shouted down. I liked to proceed with dignity; he loved to lower the tone.

I carried on patiently. 'So you are Orontes Mediolanus – and you're a lying runt!'

'I'm not saying anything to you.' He braced himself against the inside of his stone prison, managed to shove one knee through the opening, and tried to grapple off the lid. Working with stone had given him muscle, but not enough.

I went over and kicked the sarcophagus unexpectedly. 'You'll just tire yourself out, Orontes. Now be reasonable. I can lock you in the dark in this rather heavy sarcophagus and come once a day to ask if you've changed your mind yet – or if I decide you're not worth my trouble, I can lock you in there and just not bother to come back.' He stopped struggling. 'We've not met,' I went on, politely resuming the introductions as if we were lying on marble slabs in some elegant bathhouse. 'My name is Didius Falco. This is my father, Marcus Didius Favonius, also known as Geminus. You must recognise him. Another relation of ours was called Didius Festus; you knew him too.'

Rubinia emitted a high-pitched noise. It could be terror or annoyance. 'What's that squeak for?' growled my father, gazing down at her with salty curiosity. 'Hey, Marcus, do you think I should take her out the back and ask her some questions privately?' The innuendo was obvious.

'Wait a bit,' I restrained him. I hoped he was bluffing, though I was not entirely certain. Ma had always called him a womaniser. He certainly seemed to throw himself into any available form of fun.

'Let her brew, you mean . . .' I saw Father grin evilly at

Orontes. Maybe the sculptor remembered Festus; anyway, he did not look keen to see his glamorous accomplice leaving with yet another rampant Didius.

'Think on,' I murmured to him. 'Rubinia looks like a girl who may be easily swayed!'

'Leave me out of it!' she caterwauled.

I pushed myself off the ladder and ambled over to where Rubinia was tied up. Beautiful eyes, brimful of malice, sparkled at me. 'But you're in it, sweetheart! Tell me, were you swayed by Didius Festus the night I saw you at the Circus?' Whether she remembered the occasion, she coloured slightly at my brother's name and my heavy innuendo. If nothing else, I was storing up domestic strife between Rubinia and Orontes when they reminisced about our visit after we had left. I turned back to the sculptor. 'Festus was madly trying to find you. Your girlfriend here passed him on to your friends Manlius and Varga and they bamboozled him nicely . . . Did he ever find you that night?'

Inside the sarcophagus Orontes shook his head.

'Pity,' said Pa, in a clipped voice. 'Festus had his methods with traitors!'

Orontes proved as great a coward as his friends the two painters had been. All the fight was going out of him before our eyes. He groaned, 'In the name of the gods, why don't you all just leave me alone! I never asked to get into this, and what happened was not my fault!'

'What did happen?' both Pa and I demanded simultaneously. I glared at my father angrily. This would never occur with my old pal Petronius; we had a well-established routine for doing a dual interrogation. (By which I mean Petro knew when to let me take the lead.)

But as it turned out, shouting at Orontes from two directions worked the required effect. He whimpered pathetically, 'Let me out of here; I can't stand confined spaces . . .'

'Shut the lid a bit more, Marcus!' commanded Pa. I strode towards the stone coffin, looking determined.

The sculptor screamed. His girlfriend yelled at him: 'Oh tell the bastards what they want and let's get back to bed!'

'A woman with the right priorities!' I commented quietly, a foot from her entombed lover. 'Are you ready to talk then?'

He nodded miserably. I let him out. Immediately he made a dash for freedom. Expecting it, Father had slid gracelessly down the front of the vast matron who was forming his armchair. He landed in front of Orontes and punched up the sculptor's chin with a mighty blow that knocked him out.

I caught him under the hot hairy armpits. 'Oh brilliant, Pa. Now he's unconscious! This way he'll tell us a lot!'

'Well what else did you want? To see the bastard escape?'

We got him laid neatly on the floor, then threw a jug of cold water over him. He came to, to find the pair of us lolling against the statuary while I complained to my father. 'You do have to overdo everything! Settle down, will you? We want him alive at least until he's talked . . .'

'I should have hit the girl harder,' mumbled Pa, like some demented thug who liked torturing people.

'Oh she's all right – so far.'

Orontes stared around wildly, looking for Rubinia. There was no sign of her in the studio. 'What have you done with her?'

'Not too much – yet,' smiled Father.

'Missed his vocation!' I commented. 'Don't worry; she's just a bit frightened. I've managed to hold him back so far, but I can't go on doing it. Now talk, Orontes, or you get a chisel somewhere you may not expect and Jupiter only knows what this maniac will inflict upon your bit of decorative woman-hood!'

'I want to see Rubinia!'

I shrugged. Ignoring his frantic gaze, I carefully examined the statue I had chosen to lean on. It had the body of a Greek athlete in tiptop condition, but the head of a Roman countryman aged about sixty, with a lined face and very big ears. 'Ovonius Pulcher', according to its plinth. There were half a score of these monstrosities scattered through the studio, all with identical bodies but different heads. They were the latest craze; everyone who was anyone in Campania must have ordered one.

'These are horrible!' I said frankly. 'Mass-produced muscle with entirely the wrong faces.'

'He does a good head,' Pa disagreed. 'And there are some

940

nice reproductions around us here. He's a damn good copyist.'

'Where do the youthful torsos come from?'

'Greece,' croaked Orontes, trying to humour us. Pa and I turned to each other and exchanged a slow, significant glance.

'Greece! Really?'

'He goes to Greece,' my father informed me. 'Now I wonder if he used to go there and find things for our Festus to sell?'

I whistled through my teeth. 'Treasure-hunting! So this is the clod-brained agent Festus used to employ! The legendary man he met in Alexandria . . . Greece, eh? I bet he wishes he'd stayed there sunbathing on the Attic Plain!'

'I need a drink!' interrupted the sculptor desperately.

'Don't give him any,' snapped Pa. 'I know him of old. He's a drunken sot. He'll drain it and pass out on you.'

'Is that how you spent the bribe, Orontes?'

'I never had a bribe!'

'Don't lie! Somebody doled out a lot of money for you to do them a favour. Now you're going to tell us who paid you the money – and you're going to tell us why!'

'Bloody Cassius Carus paid the money!' my father suddenly shouted out. I knew he was guessing. I also realised he was probably right.

'That true, Orontes?' Orontes groaned in feeble assent. We had found some wine while he was unconscious. Pa nodded to me, and I offered the sculptor the wineskin, pulling it back after Orontes had taken one thirsty swig. 'Now tell us the full story.'

'I can't!' he wailed.

'You can. It's easy.'

'Where's Rubinia?' he tried again. He didn't care much about the girl; he was playing for time.

'Where she can't help you.' Actually we had shut her up somewhere to keep her quiet.

Pa swung closer and grasped the wineskin. 'Maybe he's frightened of the girl. Maybe she'll give him an earful if she finds out he's talked.' He took several deep swigs, then offered me a turn. I shook my head with distaste. 'Wise boy! For the heart of a wine-producing area this is dreadful vinegar. Orontes never drank for the flavour, just the effect.'

Orontes looked at his wineskin yearningly, but Pa held on to the dreadful prize. 'Tell us about the Phidias,' I urged. 'Tell us now – or Pa and I are going to hurt you much more than anyone else who's threatened you before!'

I must have sounded convincing, because to my surprise Orontes then confessed.

'I go to Greece whenever I can, looking out for bargains – ' We groaned and sneered at his hybrid statues again, to show what we thought of that. 'Festus had an arrangement with me. I had heard where there might be this Phidias. I thought we could get hold of it. Some run-down temple on an island wanted to have a clear-out; I don't think they really appreciated what they were turfing on to the market. Even so, it wasn't cheap. Festus and some other people managed to put the money together, and he also lined up Carus and Servia as eventual purchasers. When his legion left Alexandria to fight in the Jewish Rebellion, Festus wangled himself a journey to Greece as an escort for some despatches; that was how he came with me to view the Phidias. He liked what he saw and bought it, but there was no time to make other arrangements so it had to go on with him to Tyre. After that he was stuck in Judaea with the army, so I was supposed to supervise bringing it back to Italy.'

'You were to escort it in person?' Pa queried. I guessed that was the usual system he and Festus had imposed to protect an item of large value. Either one of them, or an agent they really trusted, would have stuck with it every mile of its journey.

'That was what I promised Festus. He was sending a whole load of other stuff – nice goods, but minor quality by comparison – in a ship called the *Hypericon*.'

I poked him with the toe of my boot. The sculptor closed his eyes. 'Since the *Hypericon* sank while carrying the Phidias, and you're lying here annoying us, the rest is obvious. You broke your promise to Festus, and bunked off elsewhere!'

'That's about right,' he confessed uncertainly.

'I don't believe I'm hearing this! You let a statue worth half a million travel alone?' Pa was incredulous.

'Not exactly – '

'So *what* exactly?' menaced Pa.

Orontes groaned hopelessly and curled up, hugging his

942

knees as if he was in some terrible pain. A bad conscience hurts some folk that way. 'The ship with the statue sank,' he whispered.

'We know that!' My father lost his temper. He hurled the wineskin at a Coy Nymph; it burst with a horrible squelching sound. Red wine trickled down her scanty drapes like blood. 'The *Hypericon* –'

'No, Geminus.' Orontes took a deep breath. Then he told us what we had come to find out: 'The Phidias that Festus bought was never on the *Hypericon*.'

LIII

I ran the fingers of both hands deep into my hair, massaging my scalp. Somehow this shock was not the surprise it ought to have been. Everyone had been telling us the *Hypericon* was carrying the statue; readjusting to another story took an effort. But some things which had made no sense before might now fall into place.

'Tell us what happened,' I commanded the sculptor wearily.

'There had been some mix-up. Festus and I took the Phidias to Tyre, but the rest of his stuff, things he had fixed up on his own account, had gone to Caesarea. Festus then told me he had to make himself look a bit official – '

'You don't say!' Pa was getting rattled. 'There was a war on in that region!'

'Well that's it!' Orontes exclaimed gratefully. He appeared to lack any grasp of world events. Perhaps this was understandable, when he saw my brother behaving as if the Jewish Rebellion had been arranged solely to further his own business commissions. 'Anyway, he went down to Caesarea to supervise his other stuff and to fix up a ship – what turned out to be the *Hypericon*.'

'So you were not using her before this?' I asked.

'Oh no. We were in military transports up to then.' Bloody Festus! 'I was left in charge of the statue. Festus told me before I brought it south to let one of the Aristedon brothers inspect it.' The name was familiar; I remembered Carus and Servia mentioning they used these people to ship goods for them. 'They were to verify it for the new owners, and until they did, Festus could not clear the banker's order.'

'So Festus was paid by Carus through a banker in Syria?'

'More convenient,' Pa muttered. 'He wouldn't have wanted to carry that kind of sum with him from Rome. And if his mates in Judaea had put up the stake money, he could pay them their profits straight away with less risk to the cash.'

'I see. But before Carus would cough up so much money, he wanted an agent of his own to see the goods? So how did you lose our statue, Orontes?'

He was really squirming now. 'Oh gods . . . I thought it was for the best . . . Aristedon, their agent, turned up in Tyre and approved the statue. I was supposed to take it by road to Caesarea, but with soldiers barging about on all the highways, I was not looking forward to the trip. It seemed a godsend when the Aristedon brother suggested that his clients would prefer him to ship the Phidias in his own boat, the *Pride of Perga*.'

'Did you go along with that?' demanded Pa contemptuously.

'I assume Aristedon gave you some form of receipt?' I added dangerously.

'Oh yes . . .' Something was not right there. He had gone pale, and his eyes were wandering.

'So you let him take it?'

'Why not? It meant I could stop worrying about it. And I could forget about coming home on the *Hypericon*. I wanted to go back to Greece. That way I could spend my commission from Festus buying stuff for myself.'

I weighed in: 'So you handed over the Phidias, let the rest of my brother's cargo take its chance with the *Hypericon*, flitted off to Achaea, then wandered back to Italy in your own good time?'

'That's right, Falco. And since it meant I escaped drowning, I'm not going to apologise!' It seemed a reasonable attitude – unless this clown had lost your family a small fortune. 'After I got home I discovered the *Hypericon* had sunk and Festus had lost all his gear.'

'So where in Hades is the Phidias?' grated Pa.

'I was just congratulating myself on having saved it, when I heard that the *Pride of Perga* had miscarried too.'

'Oh come on!' roared my father. 'This is too much of a coincidence!'

'It was a bad time of year. Dreadful storms everywhere.'

'So then what happened?' I put in.

'I found myself in trouble. I was visited by Carus. He made me swear I would not tell Festus about the statue swap –'

'He paid you for this deception?'

'Well . . .' The sculptor looked more shifty than usual. 'He bought something I had.'

'It can't have been one of your pieces,' my father said pleasantly. 'Carus is a shit, but he is a connoisseur!'

Orontes spoke before he could help himself. 'He bought the receipt.'

Both Father and I had to try very hard to restrain ourselves.

'How much for?' I asked, with feigned lightness of tone – my only way to avoid a burst blood vessel.

'Five thousand.' The admission was almost inaudible.

'*Is that all?* The bloody statue was worth half a million!'

'I was hard up . . . I took what I could get.'

'But whatever did you think you were doing to Festus?'

'It didn't seem so bad,' wailed Orontes. Clearly he belonged to the amoral class of artists. 'If I had not changed the arrangements, Festus would have lost the statue anyway, in the *Hypericon*. I don't see any difference!'

'*All* the difference!' my father raged. 'Half a million nice bright shiny ones that Carus now thinks he can force us to pay!'

'He was trying to squeeze Festus too,' Orontes conceded dismally. 'That was why I didn't want to meet him when he came back to Rome. I reckoned Festus knew what I had done, and was coming after me.'

Father and I looked at each other. We were both reminiscing about my brother, and we were both perturbed. Simple rage did not explain the agitation Festus had been showing on that last trip home. If he had known that this worm Orontes had cheated him, he would simply have enlisted help, either from me or from Father, to blast the fool. Instead, he had been running in circles trying to organise one of his secret plans. It could only mean he really believed that Cassius Carus had a grievance, and needed to be squared.

Orontes misinterpreted our silence. Giving his all, he went on in anguish, 'Carus must have been putting terrible pressure on Festus by then, and Carus is known as a dangerous character.'

'Too dangerous for a fool like you to meddle with!' my father told him brutally.

'Oh don't go on – ' He had no grasp of priorities. 'I'm sorry about what happened, but there seemed no way for me to get out of it. The way Carus first put it, he made me feel I had done wrong to let the statue go. He said everybody would feel better if we pretended it had never happened.'

'I cannot believe this character!' Pa muttered to me in despair.

'Can we get the five thousand off him?'

'I've spent it,' Orontes whispered. By then I was prepared for that. Nothing useful or good would ever come out of this studio. 'I spent everything. I always do. Money seems to shrivel up the minute I appear . . .' I gave him a glare that should have shrivelled something else. 'Look, I know you have a lot to blame me for. I never thought it would end the way it did – '

A bad feeling was creeping over me. Both my father and I were very still. A man with more astuteness would have shut up rapidly. But Orontes lacked any sensitivity to atmosphere. He went straight on· 'I left Rome and kept right out of the way as long as I knew Festus was prowling about. When Manlius told me he had left, I hoped he had managed to sort something out about the cash, and I just tried not to think about it. So how do you imagine I felt when I heard what had happened to him, and realised it was all my fault?' His question was almost indignant. 'I knew Carus and Servia hate to be done down, and I realised their methods could be harsh. But I never thought,' Orontes wailed, 'Carus would put the frighteners out so badly that Festus would do what he did!'

'What did Festus do?' I demanded in a low voice.

Suddenly Orontes realised he had caused himself an unnecessary predicament. It was too late. The reply came dragging out of him irresistibly: 'I suppose he had come under so much pressure, he chose to die in battle so that he could get away from it!'

LIV

When I returned to the inn where we were currently staying, Helena was in bed. She stopped there, grumbling occasionally, while I spent half an hour trying to force the door-catch: my father's idea of keeping her safe had been to lock her in. Unfortunately, he had remained at the studio to keep an eye on Orontes. I had walked the four miles back to Capua, in the dark, getting more and more cold, footsore and miserable – only to find that my aggravating father still had the key to our room stuffed down his tunic somewhere.

My efforts to break in quietly failed dismally. In the end I abandoned caution and took a run at the door with my shoulder. The lock held, but the hinges gave. There was a terrible noise. It must have been obvious throughout the building that a Roman lady of status was having her room broken into, yet nobody came to investigate. Nice place, Capua. I could not wait to get out of it.

I squeezed inside. Unable to find a tinder-box, I bruised myself squeezing back out again to fetch a lamp from the corridor. Then I puffed my way back in a second time, cursing harshly.

Helena had eaten her own bowl of beans and all the side orders. I devoured my own cold portion, plus half of Father's, while I started to tell her what had happened. Cold beans can be fine in a salad in summer, though as a main course in winter they lack panache. Oil had gelled on them unpleasantly.

'Is there any bread?'

'You forgot to bring it. Too busy,' Helena informed me from beneath the blankets, 'ogling big-busted customers.'

I carried on talking, putting in all the details about Rubinia's unclothed bust.

Helena could always be won over by a story, especially if it featured me. At first barely the tip of her nose was visible above the bedcovers, but gradually more emerged as the tale of the silly antics and hard questioning caught her interest. By the time I had finished she was sitting up and holding out her arms for me.

I climbed into bed and we wrapped ourselves together for warmth.

'So what happens now, Marcus?'

'We've told Orontes he has to come back to Rome with us. He knows he is in real danger from either Carus or us, so he's happy to wilt under whichever option lets him return where he really wants to be. The man's an idiot!' I complained restlessly. 'He has no concept that there now has to be a confrontation – and that whatever happens, it will turn out unpleasantly for him. He's just happy to stop running.'

'But have you escaped paying all that money to Carus?'

I sighed. 'This is a problem. Carus does have written evidence that he paid Festus for the statue, whereas we ourselves have nothing to prove that Orontes handed the thing over to his representative in Tyre. Aristedon and the ship's crew drowned when the *Pride of Perga* sank. There are no other substantial witnesses.'

'And as for the bribe Carus subsequently paid to the sculptor, naturally an extortionist does not give a receipt to his collaborator?'

'No, love – so we cannot prove the fraud. It's Orontes's word against Carus's.'

'Orontes could appear as a witness, though?'

'Oh yes!' I agreed gloomily. 'He can appear. If we can keep him alive, sober, and willing to testify – which Carus will try to prevent. If we can keep him more frightened of us than he is of Carus, so that when we haul him into court he tells our story. And if we can make this limp, lying, unreliable character look believable to a jury!'

'Carus will probably bribe the jury.' Helena kissed my ear. 'Orontes is a bad witness,' she added. 'He ignored your brother's instructions, then sold the receipt without a quiver. The opposing barrister only has to accuse him of perennial bad faith, and you've lost your case.'

By now I was ranting moodily. 'Orontes is completely flabby. Carus is rich and single-minded. In court he would come over as an honest citizen while our man would be quickly discredited ... But we're not giving this to the barristers. Why pay fees on top, when you're already up to your nostrils in dung? Pa and I are determined to do something, however.'

'What can you do?' Her hands were wandering pleasantly in places that liked wandering hands.

'We haven't decided. But it has to be big.'

We both fell silent. Exacting revenge from the collectors needed time and careful thought. Tonight was not the moment. But even if my own ingenuity failed me, I half hoped to lure Helena into contributing some devious invention. Something had to be done. She would understand that. She hated injustice.

She had become completely still in my arms, though I could sense busy thoughts working in that needle brain.

Suddenly she exclaimed, 'Trust you to leave a gap in the story!' I started, afraid I had passed over something significant. 'The luscious nude model went missing from the scene halfway through!'

I laughed awkwardly. 'Oh her! She was there all the time. While the sculptor was unconscious we gave her the choice of shutting up and promising to stop kicking, or being tucked out of the way while we woke him up and questioned him. She preferred to stay volatile, so we penned her in the sarcophagus.'

'Dear gods, the poor thing! I hope Orontes will be allowed to let her out of it?'

'Hmm! I don't want to make sordid suggestions,' I mumbled, 'but I strongly suspect that when my ghastly parent gets bored with discussing theories of art, he will arrange that Orontes has enough wine to knock him senseless – then Geminus may surreptitiously let out the model himself.'

Helena pretended she had no idea what sordid suggestions I meant.

'So what next, Marcus?'

'Next,' I promised her with intense relief, 'you and I and my happy father, and the sculptor, and his luscious model if he wants to bring her, are all going home ... I wonder if Smaractus will have bothered to fix the roof?'

Helena was silent again. Maybe she was contemplating

sharing a trip home with Rubinia. Maybe she was worrying about our roof.

I had plenty to think about as well, and none of it was cheerful. Somehow I had to devise a scheme to punish Carus and Servia. Somehow I had to avoid us paying out to them half a million sesterces which we had never owed them anyway. To keep myself from exile I had to solve a murder that was beginning to look inexplicable. And somehow I had to explain to my mother that her beloved son the national hero may have been no more than a failed entrepreneur who took a long stride into oblivion simply because the pressure of his bungled business commitments was growing too much for him.

'What time is it?' asked Helena.

'Jupiter, I don't know! The middle of the night – tomorrow, probably.'

She smiled at me. It had nothing to do with anything we had been discussing. I knew that, even before she said gently, 'Happy birthday, then!'

My birthday.

I had known it was coming. I thought no one else here with me had realised. Ma would be thinking about me with her own scornful reverence, but she was in Rome, so I had escaped the nostalgia and damson cake. Pa had probably never known his children's anniversaries. And Helena . . . well. A year ago, Helena had been with me on my birthday. We had been strangers then, resisting any hint of attraction between us. All the same, I had given myself a brief birthday treat and kissed her, with unexpected results for both of us. From that moment I had wanted more of her; I had wanted it all. I had started the sequence that ended with me falling in love with her, while a small, dark, dangerous voice began whispering that it might be a challenge to make this unattainable creature love me.

It was a year since the first time I held her in my arms, assuming then that it would be the only occasion she ever let me come near her. A year since I saw that look in her eyes when I risked it. A year since I fled from her, stunned by my own feelings and misunderstanding hers, yet knowing

951

that somehow I would have to hold this woman in my arms again.

'Remember?'

'I remember!'

I took a long slow breath against her hair, absorbing the sweet natural scent of her. Without moving, I enjoyed the now familiar shape of her body, cosseted against mine. Her fingers moved against my shoulder, tracing patterns that raised goose-pimples. 'Here we are in another stinking inn . . . I could never have dreamed I would still have you near me.'

'Oh Marcus, you were so angry with me.'

'I had to get angry before I dared touch you.'

She laughed. I could always make her laugh. 'You laughed me into adoring you!' she commented, as if I had spoken.

'Not that night! You locked yourself in your room, and refused to speak to me.'

'I was too terrified.'

'Of me?' I was amazed.

'Oh no! I knew that when you stopped playing iron-jawed demigods you would be a complete sweetheart . . . Of myself,' confessed Helena. 'Frightened of how much I wanted to be in your arms, how much I wanted you to go on kissing me, how much I wanted more than that – '

I could have kissed her then. Her dark eyes were soft and inviting; she was willing me to do it. But it was more fun to lean back so I could see her, and just think about it while she smiled at me.

No year of my life would ever bring me so much change. No trick of fate would ever give me anything so precious.

I put out the light so I could forget our dismal surroundings; then I ignored all the debts and disasters that were oppressing me. A man must have some comfort in his life. I said, 'I love you. I should have told you that right at the start a year ago – and this is what I should have done about it straight away . . .'

Then I let my thirty-first birthday begin with a celebration in the noblest Roman style.

LV

Our carriage-horse was still lame, so we hired a couple of litters, went across to the coast and took a ship home from Puteoli. I will pass over it briskly, though the journey seemed interminable. I spent most of it lying under a leather sail. The only times I poked my head out were when I needed to be ill.

That was often enough.

I believe the others found the weather fair, the sea air invigorating, and their various fellow passengers an enthralling mixture of types. Helena and my father got to know each other better, while they had the tact to keep the cheating sculptor and his blowzy mistress well away from me.

Even though I knew my taxes had paid for it, no sight was ever so welcome to me as the great lighthouse at Portus, the new complex at Ostia, unless it was the colossal statue of Neptune. When we sailed under Neptune's knees I knew our ship was inside the basin, and about to berth. We had to wait about before disembarking while the usual nautical business took precedence over passengers' eagerness to land. I managed to send a message ashore to the customs post, so the first sight that greeted us when our feet hit the quay was Gaius Baebius, my brother-in-law.

'You might have spared us!' muttered Father under his breath.

'I'm hoping to cadge a free ride home in official transport if we tag along with him.'

'Oh smart boy! *Gaius Baebius*! Just the man we were hoping to see . . .'

My brother-in-law was full of something – something and nothing, needless to say. He was reticent in front of strangers – and even before Helena, since a customs-clerks supervisor's attitude to women tends to be traditional, and Gaius Baebius had had seventeen years of living with my sister Junia to teach him to keep his mouth shut. Junia had the strong-willed woman's traditional attitude to men: she thought we were there to be told we were idiots and made to keep quiet.

Leaving Helena disconsolately guarding the baggage (which was *our* idea of what women were for), Father and I got Gaius on his own in a wine bar and set about grilling him. Freed from female supervision, out it poured: 'Listen, listen, I've had some luck!'

'Won at the races, Gaius?' Pa chivvied. 'Don't tell the wife then! Junia will whip it out of your hand before you can take breath.'

'Olympus, Marcus, he's worse than you for looking on the dark side ... No. I've found something you were looking for –'

'Not a trace of the *Hypericon*?'

'No, not that. I'm sure she really sank.'

'Don't you keep a list of lost vessels?' Pa demanded.

'Why should we?' Gaius Baebius gave him a scornful look. 'There's no money for the state in seaweed and silt.'

'That's a pity,' Father carried on. 'I'd like to know for certain that the *Pride of Perga* really hit bottom –'

'So what have you discovered, Gaius?' I insisted, as patiently as I could while I was tossed between this squabbling pair.

'Festus!'

I felt a sickly qualm. I was not yet ready to talk to any member of the family on that subject. Even Pa fell silent.

Gaius Baebius noticed I had lost my appetite; he lunged eagerly to grab my bowl.

'Give!' urged my father, trying not to sound subdued. 'What about Festus?' His eyes had fallen on a second spoon, with which he fought Gaius Baebius for what was left of my food.

'I found –' Gaius had his damned mouth too full of my snack to talk. We waited for him to masticate with the ponderous thoroughness that characterised his life. I could have kicked him. Rather than have to endure his pained reproach if I attacked him, I restrained myself, though the restraint was precarious. 'I found,' he let out meticulously after a long wait, 'the note of what Festus paid in excise dues when he came ashore.'

954

'When? On his last leave?'

'Exactly!'

My father's eyebrows, which had retained more blackness than his rampant hair, shot up his brow. He looked down that long, straight nose of his. 'Festus came home on a stretcher in a military supply ship!'

'Yes, he came home on a stretcher, but he damned soon hopped off it!' Gaius Baebius risked a slightly critical note. All my sisters' husbands had looked askance at my brother, as in fact they still did at me. Gaius Baebius would be full of himself if he ever found out that Festus had thrown himself into his heroic death in order to escape some bullying creditors – not to mention the messy detail that unknown to my brother the creditors were criminally fraudulent.

Having to face people like my brothers-in-law with this depressing tale was the main trial ahead.

'So Festus, despite being wounded, managed to bring something home with him on which duty was payable?' I sounded as pedantic as Gaius himself; it was the only way to squeeze sense from him.

'You're with me!' cried Gaius triumphantly. 'You're not so dumb!' The man was unbearable.

Father rescued me before I exploded. 'Come on, Gaius! Don't keep us in suspense. What was he importing?'

'Ballast,' said Gaius Baebius.

He sat back, satisfied that he had baffled us.

'Hardly seems to rate paying duty,' I commented.

'No. The tax was a small debit.'

'Sounds to me as if Festus may have made a payment to somebody at the customs post in order to get his item described as valueless!'

'That's a slur on the service!' said Gaius.

'But it makes sense,' answered Pa.

My father had a way of sounding sure of himself that could be intensely irritating. I only endured it because I thought he must be holding out on Gaius Baebius, who annoyed me even more. 'Father, we can't even guess what this import was – '

'I think we know.'

I assumed Geminus was bluffing, but he looked too calm.

'Pa, you've lost me – and Gaius Baebius is a thousand miles behind!'

'If this "ballast" is what I reckon it might be, then you've seen the stuff, Marcus.'

'I take it we don't mean a load of fancy gravel for rich people's garden paths?'

'Bigger,' said Father.

Another mystery that had long been lying at the back of my memory found its moment to rush to the fore. 'Not those blocks of stone I was shown in the store by drippy Uncle Junius?'

'I guess so.'

'Have you seen old Junius? How is he?' flapped Gaius Baebius, with his normal fine grasp of priorities.

'So what are these blocks?' I asked my father, ignoring the interruption.

'I have some ideas.'

That was all he would say, so I sprang the thrill for him: 'I'm not short of ideas myself. I bet the ship that Festus came home in discovered a sudden need to call at Paros, the Marble Isle.'

Pa chortled. He agreed with me. 'I wonder how our canny lad persuaded the captain to stop off for him?'

Gaius Baebius was squirming like a child left out of adult secrets. 'Are you talking about Festus? What would he want marble for?'

'Having something made, no doubt,' I replied offhandedly.

'Could have been anything,' Father murmured, smiling to himself. 'Copies of statues, for instance . . .'

My own thoughts exactly. Festus would reason, *Why sell only one half-million Phidias, when a sculptor like Orontes could be making you quadruplets?*

'Oh that reminds me!' uttered my sister's bright spark. 'The ballast was not all he had to pay duty on. I nearly forgot to mention – there was some sort of statue as well.'

LVI

We came up from Ostia by river. It was a cold, slow trip. We made a silent party, all lost in contemplating the mystery that Gaius Baebius had handed us.

It had stopped raining, but when we reached Rome the sky was full of unshed showers. The roads were glistening. Pools of water lapped over the pavements where careless stall-holders and frontagers had let cabbage leaves and old brick-ends block gullies. Roofs dripped occasionally. The air was damp with Tiber fog, through which our breath wreathed extra moisture trails.

As we disembarked, one of Petro's men who had been keeping an eye on the river barges came up. 'Falco!' he coughed. 'Petronius has us all looking for you.'

'I haven't skipped bail. I was with my surety – ' My laughter died. 'Problem?'

'He wants a word. Says it's urgent.'

'Mars Ultor! What's up?'

'That other centurion who's connected with the stabbed legionary made himself known. The boss interviewed him once, but he deferred a final judgement while we checked the man's story.'

'Am I cleared, or did he come up with an alibi?'

'Don't they always? Better hear it from Petro. I'll run up to the guardhouse and say you're back.'

'Thanks. I'll be at Fountain Court. Any time Petronius wants me, I'll make myself available.'

'You sound like one of his women!' remarked the trooper mysteriously.

We met at Flora's. I found Petronius Longus sitting over his lunch while he talked to the waiter and one of his own men, Martinus. Martinus stepped outside when I turned up. Another meal, previously ordered by my courteous friend, appeared at once in front of me. Epimandos served us with great diffidence, a mark of respect for Petronius, presumably.

I noticed that alongside Petro his thick brown cloak lay folded neatly on a pile of gear that I recognised as the dead soldier's kit. I ignored it politely for the time being. Epimandos, who may also have recognised the stuff, walked around that part of our bench as if the watch captain had brought a witch's cauldron into the bar.

Petronius was as placid and unperturbed as usual. 'You look depressed, Falco. Do I blame the caupona broth?'

'Blame Festus,' I confessed. He laughed briefly.

I had known Petronius long enough to tell him the worst. He listened with his usual impassivity. He had a low opinion of people with artistic interests, so the Carus deceit came as no surprise. He had a low opinion of heroics too; hearing that my brother's demise might not have been so glorious as we had all been pretending left Petro equally unmoved.

'So when were the civic crowns ever awarded to the right men? I'd sooner your Festus snapped one up than some bugger who happened to know the faces in a war council.'

'I suppose you have a poor opinion of the Didius family anyway?'

'Oh, some of you can be all right!' he replied with a faint smile.

'Thanks for the recommendation!' We had covered enough formalities. I could broach business now. 'So what's with the centurion?'

Petronius stretched his long legs. 'Laurentius? Seems a straight sucker who happened to have palled up with an unlucky one. He came to the guardhouse, saying he had only just heard the news, what could I tell him about it, and could he take charge of Censorinus's effects?' Petro patted the kitbag in acknowledgement.

'You've arranged to meet him here? What's the idea?'

'Well, probably nothing. A vague hope of unnerving him with the scene of the crime,' Petro grinned. 'It might work if he did it – if not, you and I are poisoning ourselves with Epimandos's broth for nothing, as usual!'

'You don't think he did do it.' I had deduced this from his tone. 'What's his story?'

'They both had leave. Censorinus was supposed to be

staying with a "friend's family". I haven't let on so far that I know you all. Laurentius is Roman-born, so he was at his own sister's house.'

'You checked that?'

'Of course. It matched.'

'And where was Laurentius when the murder occurred?'

'Laurentius, plus sister, plus sister's four children, were all staying with an aunt at Lavinium. They went for a month.'

'And you've now been to Lavinium?' I asked him gloomily.

'Would I fail you? I did my best, Falco! But everyone at Lavinium from the town magistrate downwards confirms the tale. The actual night in question was somebody's wedding, and I can't even make out that the centurion could have slipped away unnoticed and come back to Rome secretly. He was much in evidence at the festivities, and until halfway through the next morning he was lying in a kitchen, nicely drunk. The whole wedding party can vouch for him – except the bridegroom, whose mind was on other things. Laurentius didn't do it,' Petro confirmed in his steady voice. He picked his teeth with a fingernail. 'Actually, having met him, he is just not the type.'

'Who is?'

'Well . . .' Petronius graciously accepted that hard and fast theories, like instinctive judgements, only exist to be disproved. But I knew what he was saying. He had liked the centurion. That meant I would probably like him too – though his easily proven innocence unfortunately left me the much harder task of proving my own. I was starting to feel gloomy again – once more a suspect under threat.

I leaned my chin in my hands, staring at the filthy table. Stringy the cat jumped up onto it, but walked around my patch as if its greasy condition was too disgusting for an animal to tolerate. Petronius stroked him absently, while signalling Epimandos to bring more wine.

'Something will turn up, Falco.'

I refused to be consoled.

We were drinking in silence when Laurentius arrived.

As soon as he leaned on the outdoor counter I could see what Petro meant. He may well have killed in his professional

959

capacity, but this was no casual murderer. He was about fifty, a calm, wry, sensible type with a small-featured, intelligent face and neat strong hands that were used to practical work. His uniform was well cared-for, though the bronze studs were not ostentatiously buffed. His manner was rational and quiet.

He looked for us then ordered a drink, in that order. He came over without fuss, politely bringing his flagon with him.

Then he gave me a second look, so I would notice it, and said, 'You must be related to Didius Festus?' People who had known my brother always spotted the likeness.

I acknowledged the relationship. Petronius introduced us both, without commenting on why I was there.

'I checked your story,' Petronius told the centurion. 'Regarding your whereabouts when the murder was committed, you're in the clear.' The man moved his head, accepting that Petronius had a job to do, and that it had been done fairly. 'I've brought you your crony's kit; there's nothing we need as evidence. You gave us an affidavit. If you want to leave Rome to return to your unit, I have no objections. But I do have a few other questions,' Petro said, throwing it in unexpectedly as the centurion prepared to leave us. Laurentius sat down again.

His eyes went to me and I said, 'Censorinus had been staying with my mother.' Again he acknowledged the situation with a small turn of the head. I added quietly, 'Before he moved out to here.'

Laurentius glanced around the bar swiftly. If there was alarm in his eyes, it seemed the right sort of shock. 'Is this where . . . ?'

Petronius nodded, staring at him steadily. Realising what was going on, the centurion returned his gaze with a cool, almost angry expression. 'I have never been here before.'

We believed him.

Released from the test, he looked around again. He was simply a man whose friend had died there, showing the natural sad interest. 'What a place to go . . .' His eyes fell on Epimandos, who jumped and darted away somewhere into the back room. 'Did that waiter find him?'

'The owner discovered him,' said Petro. 'A woman called Flora. She went in to ask for his rent.'

'*Flora?*' It was the first I had heard of this detail. 'I thought "Flora" was a myth!'

Petronius said nothing, though he seemed to give me an odd look.

Laurentius was now becoming more upset. 'This trip of ours has all turned into a horror – I'm regretting we ever bothered.'

'Long leave?' asked Petro politely.

'I'm taking a break. I've asked for a new posting. The Fifteenth has been reassigned to Pannonia – I can't stand a tour in that tedious backwater.'

'Will you get a new legion?'

'Should do. I'm looking for action. I've asked for Britain.'

Petro and I, who had served there, exchanged a wry look. 'You seem confident.'

'Oh yes. The chance of a move is a bonus for those of us who held the fort in Judaea while the rest came home with Titus for his official Triumph.' Laurentius glanced at me with a slight smile. 'The Festus principle, you know – never volunteer for anything, unless you're volunteering to be left out!'

'I can see you knew my brother!' I grinned.

The military chat had relaxed the tense atmosphere. Laurentius turned back to Petro, asking confidentially, 'Have you no idea what happened to Censorinus?'

'None,' Petro said slowly. 'I'm beginning to think it must have been just one of those casual encounters that go wrong sometimes. We may solve it one day. If so, it's most likely to be solved by accident.'

'Pity. He seemed a good man.'

'Had you known him long?'

'On and off. He wasn't from my own century.'

'But you were in the same investment club?' There was no change in Petro's tone as he asked, and he appeared to be looking at his wine. But once again, Laurentius knew what was happening.

'This is about that?' He glanced from Petronius to me.

Petronius Longus adopted the frank approach: 'I asked Falco to be here because he needs the same answers as I do. Your pal had a fine old row with him, and we would like to

961

know why. Falco *needs* to know, because the quarrel implicates him in the death.'

'Wrongly?' the centurion asked me in a light, easy tone.

'Wrongly,' I said.

'Nice to be sure of these things!' Laurentius folded his hands calmly on the table. 'Anything you want to know, Watch Captain,' he said. 'If it will help find the killer.'

'Right.' Then Petronius raised a hand so his trooper Martinus, who had been hanging about at the counter, came back into the caupona and sat down with us. Laurentius and I exchanged half a smile. Petronius Longus was doing things properly. Not only was he making sure he had a witness to his own procedure when he interviewed two suspects (one of them known to him), but Martinus brought out a waxed tablet and openly took notes. 'This is Martinus, my second in command. He'll be keeping a record, if the two of you don't mind. If what we talk about is shown to be a private matter which has no bearing on the murder, then the notes will be destroyed.'

Petro skewed round to ask the waiter to step out and give us some privacy, but for once Epimandos had discreetly disappeared.

LVII

Petronius asked the questions; at first I sat tight.

'Centurion, are you now prepared to volunteer what it was you and the dead man wanted from the Didius family?' Laurentius nodded slowly, though made no reply. 'You were trying to recover your stake money from an investment which Didius Festus had organised?'

'In effect.'

'Am I allowed to ask where the money came from?'

'None of your business,' Laurentius answered pleasantly.

'Well,' said Petronius, at his most reasonable, 'let me put it this way: the dead man's quarrel with Falco over this money has been cited as a possible motive for Falco stabbing him. I know Falco personally, and I don't believe he did it. I do know that we are talking about the price of a statue by Phidias, and it could be suggested that a group of centurions on active service in the desert might have found it difficult to come up with so much ready cash?'

'It was not difficult,' Laurentius informed him laconically.

'Resourceful fellows!' smiled Petronius. This was all extremely civilised – and it did not help.

The centurion had enjoyed dodging but was not, in fact, trying to be difficult. 'The money we are trying to replace now we had gained on a previous flutter; it would have been doubled by another sale which Festus was hoping to make. I came to Rome to ascertain what happened about that second sale. If Festus went ahead, we're well in profit. If he didn't, we're back level; we'll just have to give it the gambler's shrug and start again.'

I felt obliged to intervene. 'You sound nicely philosophical! If that is your attitude, why was Censorinus so desperate when he tackled me?'

'It was different for him.'

'Why?'

Laurentius looked embarrassed. 'When he first came

into the syndicate, he was only an optio – not one of us.'

The trooper Martinus was grimacing at Petro, not understanding the reference. Unlike us, he had never been in the army. Petro quietly explained to his man. 'An optio is a soldier who has been nominated as suitable for promotion to centurion, but who is still waiting for a vacancy. It can take a long time for one to come up. He spends the waiting period acting as second in command in the century – much like yourself.' There was a slight edge in Petro's voice. I knew he had long suspected that Martinus was trying to encroach on his position – though he did not think Martinus was a good enough officer to push him aside.

'I'd better come clean on the whole story,' said Laurentius. If he had noticed the personal atmosphere, it was one he understood.

'Clarification would be appreciated,' I agreed, as mildly as I could.

'A group of friends,' Laurentius explained, 'found the money for an investment – never mind how – ' I avoided looking at Petronius; this was almost certainly a reference to raiding the legionary savings bank.

'Don't write this down,' Petronius instructed Martinus. Martinus awkwardly lowered his stylus.

'We made the investment successfully – '

'And I hope you replaced your capital?' Deliberately I let him know I had guessed where they had taken it from.

Laurentius smiled demurely. 'Relax. We did! Censorinus was not part of our syndicate then, incidentally. On that first scheme we made something like a quarter of a million profit, between ten of us. We were happy men, and Festus was already a hero in our eyes. There was no way to spend the money in the desert, so we sank it into *another* investment, knowing that if we came unstuck we could now just thank the Fates for being vindictive, and we'd lost nothing overall – though if we made our sale, we could all retire.'

'Censorinus then came in with you?'

'Yes. We had never talked about our winnings, but when people have a windfall word always gets out. Censorinus was already being considered as a candidate for promotion. He was becoming friendly with our group in anticipation of his co-option. Somehow he must have heard we were on to a good investment. He approached us, and asked to come in on it.'

Petro showed an interest: 'The rest of you were risking your profit – but he had to draw on his savings?'

'Must have,' shrugged Laurentius. Again he was revealing embarrassment. 'Obviously we expected him to match what we put into the kitty.' Since their kitty was founded on an illegal loan from the savings bank, this was wondrously unfair of them. They had pulled off a scam – and immediately overlooked their good fortune in getting away with it. 'Actually, I now realise he put in everything he had and then borrowed some, but at the time the rest of us were pretty offhand about where he was finding the cash.' Petro and I could imagine how cocky the others would have been; how insensitive to a newcomer. 'Look, there was no pressure on him to join us. It was his choice.'

'But when your project fell through it hit him much harder than the rest of you?' I asked.

'Yes. So that's why,' Laurentius said to me with a hint of apology, 'he did tend to become hysterical. He was a bit of a jumpy beggar anyway, in my opinion – ' That was shorthand for saying Laurentius himself would not have promoted him. 'I'm sorry. With hindsight, I ought to have handled the whole thing myself.'

'It might have helped,' I said.

'Did he explain?'

'Not properly. He was very evasive.'

'People like to be suspicious,' Laurentius commented.

I drained my winecup with a wry smile. 'And your syndicate is suspicious of me?'

'Festus always said he had a very sharp brother.' That was news. I set the cup down again carefully. Laurentius murmured, 'Our second investment seems to be mislaid. We did wonder if it might have been found by you?'

'I don't even know what it is,' I corrected him gently – although by then I thought I did know.

'It's a statue.'

'*Not* the drowned Poseidon?' asked Petronius. His man Martinus made a jump towards his stylus again, but Petro's great paw clamped over his wrist.

'No, not the Poseidon.' Laurentius was watching me. I think he was still wondering whether I might have found this second piece, perhaps when Festus died.

Meanwhile I myself was wondering if Festus had disposed of it deliberately, and diddled his mates.

'Everyone's keeping secrets!' I told the centurion levelly. 'You'll be glad to hear I live in squalor. The watch captain will assure you I'm not soaking in luxury with profits that should have been yours.'

'He lives in a pit!' Petro grinned, confirming it.

'This special item seems to be lost,' I said. 'I searched my brother's property after he died, and I've looked in his store since, but I haven't found your treasure. My father, who was my brother's business partner, never heard tell of a second statue. And as far as we can see, even the agent Festus was using for your business never knew it existed.'

'Festus thought the agent was an idiot.'

I was pleased to hear that. I thought so too. 'So where did this statue come from?'

'The same island as the other,' said Laurentius. 'When Festus went to Greece to inspect the Poseidon, he found out that the temple actually owned two they might sell.' I could imagine my brother giving Orontes the slip, and getting talking to the priests on his own. Festus never took agents on trust. His winning style could easily have uncovered further information that the sellers had withheld from Orontes, who lacked all my brother's charm, as I knew well. 'We only had enough cash to buy the Poseidon at first. We had to sell on – '

'To Carus and Servia?'

'Those were the names. What we got from them replaced our original stake money, and enabled your brother to go back to Greece with our profit – '

'But *without* Orontes?'

'Without Orontes.'

'And he bought?'

Laurentius smiled with resignation. 'That time he bought a Zeus.'

LVIII

Later the same day, for the first time in history, my father had himself brought over to Fountain Court. When he arrived Helena was wrapped in a blanket, reading, while I scrubbed a bucket of mussels. He expected her to vanish so we could enjoy a manly chat, as happens in normal households, but she waved to him graciously and stayed where she was. He then expected me to shove the bucket away shyly under the table, but I carried on.

'Gods! I'm killed by the stairs . . . She's got you hard at it then?'

'This is how we live. No one asked you to turn up and criticise.'

'Marcus is the cook,' said Helena. 'He likes to feel he's supervising my domestic education. But I would be allowed to make you some hot honey if you want?'

'Got any wine?'

'Only for those who are stopping to dinner,' I snapped. My father was incorrigible. 'We're nearly out. I can't feed casual inebriates; I want it for the sauce.'

'I can't stop. Expected at home. You're a hard-hearted host.'

'Have the honey. She does it with cinnamon. You'll have sweet breath, a pleasant temper, and it will ease your poor old chest after the stairs.'

'You're living with a bloody apothecary, girl!' Pa grumbled at Helena.

'Yes, isn't he wonderful? Like a human encyclopaedia,' she answered, with evil insincerity. 'I'm going to lease him to Marponius . . .' Then she smiled and made sensible drinks for all of us.

My father gazed slowly around our outer room, deduced there was another just as awful behind the curtain, dismissed the balcony as a disaster waiting to send us to an early death, and turned up his nose at our furniture. I had acquired a pine

967

table. We liked the fact it had all four legs and very little woodworm, but by his standards it was plain and pitiful. Apart from that we owned the mean stool I was sitting on, the chair Helena gave up for him, another she fetched from the bedroom for herself, three beakers, two bowls, one stew-pot, some cheap lamps, and a mixed set of scrolls containing Greek plays and Latin poetry.

He was looking for ornaments; I realised that we had none. Perhaps he would send us a chestful next time he did a house clearance.

'Olympus! Is this it then?'

'Well in the next room there's the scallop-end bed you sold me, and a rather nice movable tripod Helena picked up from somewhere. Of course our summer villa at Baiae is a haven of unconfined luxury. We keep our glass collection and the peacocks there . . . So what do you think?'

'It's even worse than I feared! I admire your courage,' he said to Helena, visibly moved.

'I admire your son,' she answered quietly.

Pa still looked wounded. The horror of my living quarters seemed a personal affront to him. 'But this is awful! Can't you get him to do something?'

'He's trying his best.' Helena sounded terse.

I went out and peed off the balcony to avoid any need to contribute. An angry shout arose from the street below, cheering me up.

When I came back in, I told my father what I had learned from the centurion about the statue of Zeus. 'It makes things neat, anyway. First we have one statue and one ship – now there are two ships and two statues.'

'But it's not quite symmetrical,' Helena commented. 'One of the statues was lost in one of the ships, but the Zeus came ashore with Festus and presumably still exists somewhere.'

'That's good,' I said. 'This one is lost, but we can find it.'

'Are you going to try?'

'Of course.'

'You've had no luck so far!' remarked my father gloomily.

'I wasn't looking until now. I'll find the Zeus – and when I do find it, even if we repay the centurions' syndicate their share of the investment, there's still a chance for the rest of us to get rich. In addition to big brother's agreed percentage of the proceeds, we have four blocks of genuine Parian marble. We can do what Festus must have been planning, and have four copies made.'

'Oh surely you wouldn't sell fakes, Marcus!' Helena felt shocked. (At least I assume she did.) Pa gazed at me with a whimsical expression, waiting for me to answer her.

'Never entered my mind! Good copies can fetch a wonderful price in their own right.' It sounded almost sincere.

Helena smiled. 'Who would make your copies?'

'Orontes – who else? We were clambering all over his stuff at the studio; he has a sure touch with replicas. It's my belief that was all Festus wanted to ask him the night he was looking for the bastard so urgently. Orontes was petrified that Festus wanted a fight with him, when in fact my het-up brother was quite innocent of the Carus fraud, and was just offering Orontes work. Festus had received his military orders. He had to go back to Judaea. It was his last chance to fix the deal.'

'And is Orontes really good?'

Pa and I consulted each other, remembering again what we had seen of his work at Capua. 'Yes; he's good.'

'And after the trick he pulled on Festus, he owes us a free commission or two!'

Helena tried it out: 'So Festus was simply wanting to say to him, "Come and look at this Phidias Zeus I've just brought home, and make me four more of them" . . .' She jumped in her seat. 'So Marcus, this means the original must have been somewhere it could be viewed! Somewhere Festus could have shown it to the sculptor that very night – somewhere here in Rome!'

She must be right. It was here. It was worth half a million, and as my brother's heir and executor, part of it belonged to me. It was here, and I would find it if it took me twenty years.

'If you can find it,' said Helena quietly, 'I have an idea how you two could get your own back on Cassius Carus and Ummidia Servia.'

Father and I pulled our seats closer, and gazed at her like attentive acolytes at a shrine.

'Tell us, my darling!'

'To make my idea work properly, you will have to pretend you believe they really did lose their money on the Poseidon. That means you will have to put together the half-million sesterces and actually pay over the cash – '

We both groaned. 'Must we?'

'Yes. You have to convince them that they've beaten you. You have to lull them into a false sense of security. Then when they are full of themselves for cheating you, we can make them over-reach and fall for this proposal of mine . . .'

That was when Helena, my father and I sat together around my table, and hatched the scheme that would give us our revenge. Father and I put forward some refinements, but the basic plan belonged to Helena.

'Isn't she bright?' I asked, hugging her with delight as she explained it.

'She's beautiful,' agreed my pa. 'If we bring this off, maybe you'll use the proceeds to let her live somewhere more appropriate.'

'We have to find the missing statue first.'

We were nearer to that than we thought, though it took a tragedy to bring us near enough.

It was a good afternoon. We were all friends together. We had schemed, and laughed, and congratulated ourselves on how clever we were and how skilfully we were planning to turn the tables on our opponents. I had given in over the wine, which we poured into beakers for toasting each other and our scheme of revenge. With it we ate winter pears, laughing again as the juice ran down our chins and wrists. When Helena took a fruit that was going brown, my father reached for a dinner knife and cut off the bruised portion for her. Watching him hold the fruit in one sturdy hand while he pared off the bad part, stopping the knife-blade against his blunt thumb, a pang of reminiscence took me back a quarter of a century to another table, with a group of small children clamouring to have their father peel their fruit.

I still did not know what we had done to drive him away from us. I would never know. He had never wanted to explain.

970

For me that had always been the worst part. But perhaps he simply could not do it.

Helena touched my cheek, her eyes quiet and understanding.

Pa gave her the pear, cut in slices, popping the first piece into her mouth as if she was a little girl.

'He's a demon with a blade!' I exclaimed. Then we laughed some more, as my father and I recalled how we had rampaged against the painters as the dangerous Didius boys.

It was a good afternoon. But you should never relax. Laughter is the first step on the road to betrayal.

After Father had gone, normality resumed. Life reasserted its usual grim messages.

I was lighting a lamp. I wanted to trim off the burnt wick. I was thinking about nothing as I tried to find the knife I normally used. It was missing.

Pa must have walked off with it.

Then I remembered the knife that had stabbed Censorinus. Suddenly I understood how a knife which had once been my mother's had arrived at the caupona. I knew how my mother, who was so careful, could have lost one of her tools. Why when Petronius Longus had asked her about it, she had chosen to seem so vague – and why when Helena tried to question members of the family, Ma had almost feigned disinterest. I had seen her being vague and unresponsive on the same subject scores of times. Ma knew exactly where that 'lost' knife had gone twenty years ago. Its discovery must have placed her in a terrible dilemma – wanting to protect me, and yet aware that the truth itself would not spare our family. She must have put the knife in my father's lunch-basket, on the day he left home. Either that, or he had simply picked it up for some job or other and carried it away with him the way he had mine today.

My father had been in possession of the murder weapon.

Which meant that the main suspect for killing Censorinus would now appear to be Didius Geminus.

971

LIX

It was a wild idea. Those are the ones that always seem the most believable once they strike you.

This was one thing I could not say to Helena. Not wanting to let her see my face, I stepped on to the balcony threshold. Ten minutes ago, he had been here, joking with the two of us, more friendly than he and I had ever been. Now I knew this.

He could have lost that knife, or even thrown it away, a long time ago. I did not believe he had. Pa was famous for collecting cutlery. When he lived with us, the decreed system was that every day he was given a knife in his lunch-basket; he usually pinched the daily knife. It was one of the irritating habits by which he made his presence felt. He was always in trouble about it, one of the endless wrangles that colour family life. Sometimes he needed a sharp blade to prod a suspect piece of furniture, testing for worm. Sometimes he had to swipe through the cords tied around a bale of new stock. Sometimes he palmed an apple from a fruit stall in passing, then wanted to cut slices as he walked. We children bought him a fruit-knife for a Saturnalia present once; he just hung it on the wall of his office, and went on exasperating Mother by filching the picnic tools.

He must still do it. I would bet he was driving the redhead to distraction with the same little game – still on purpose, probably. And the day Censorinus died, maybe the knife in his pouch had been that old one.

So my father could have killed the soldier. Why? I could guess: Festus again. Rightly or wrongly, Geminus must have been trying to protect his precious boy.

I was still standing there, lost in desperate thoughts, when we had another visitor. It was so close to my father's departure, and Geminus was so much on my mind, that when I heard feet on the stairs I thought it must be him again, coming back for a forgotten cloak or hat.

They were old feet, but they belonged to someone lighter and more fragile than my hefty pa. I had just worked that out, with great relief, when the new arrival staggered in. Out of context, it took me a moment to recognise his troubled voice as he asked for me. As I came in from the balcony I saw Helena, who had been full of concern for the old man, grow suddenly still as she noticed my own frowning face. The light I had meant to attend to was flaming up madly; she strode across and blew it out.

'Oh it's Apollonius! Helena Justina, this is the man I was telling you about the other day; my old teacher. You look terrible, Apollonius. Whatever's wrong?'

'I'm not sure,' he gasped. It was a bad day for elderly folk at Fountain Court. First my father had arrived whey-faced and coughing. Now the six flights of stairs had nearly finished Apollonius as well. 'Can you come, Marcus Didius?'

'Get your breath! Come where?'

'Flora's. Something has happened at the caupona; I am sure of it. I sent a message to Petronius Longus, but he hasn't appeared, so I thought you might advise me what to do. You know about crises – '

Oh I knew about those! I was up to my neck in them.

Helena had already fetched my cloak from the bedroom. She stood holding it, staring hard at me but keeping her questions to herself.

'Stay calm, old friend.' I felt a strange, deep, gentle care for other people who were in trouble. 'Tell me what has disturbed you.'

'The place has been shuttered since just after lunch-time – ' Flora's never closed in the afternoon. So long as there was a chance of extracting a copper from the public for a lukewarm stuffed vine leaf, Flora's never closed at all. 'There is no sign of life. The cat is scratching at the door, crying horribly. People have been beating on the shutters, then just walking away.' Apollonius himself probably had nowhere else to go. If he found the caupona unexpectedly closed he would just sit outside on his barrel hopefully. 'Oh please come, if you can, young Marcus. I feel something is dreadfully wrong at that place!'

I kissed Helena, grabbed my cloak and went with him. The

old man could only go slowly, so when Helena decided not to be left out, she soon caught up with us.

We saw Petronius arrive at Flora's just ahead of us. I was glad of it, although I would have gone in on my own otherwise. But Apollonius was not alert to the sensitivities. I was still under suspicion for what had happened to Censorinus. If there was some new upset at the scene of his murder, it was better to have official company.

The caupona was as the old man had described. Both huge shutters had been drawn across the wide entrances in front of the counters; both were securely locked from inside. It looked as I had rarely seen it except at the dead of night. Standing in the street, Petronius and I tossed up pebbles at the two small windows in the upper rooms, but nobody responded.

Stringy was gnawing at one doorpost miserably. He rushed up to us, hoping we might give him some dinner. A caupona cat does not expect to find himself hungry; he was thoroughly indignant. Petronius picked him up and fussed him while he stared at the locked building thoughtfully.

Across the street at the Valerian there were more customers than usual. People, some of whom would normally have been wasting a few hours at Flora's, turned on their elbows to watch us, while eagerly discussing the unusual activity.

We told Apollonius to wait outside. He sat down on his barrel; Helena stopped with him. Petronius gave her the cat, but she put it down fairly swiftly. Even though the poor girl had fallen for an informer, she did have some principles.

Petro and I walked round to the back alley. There was the usual stink of kitchen rubbish; the usual seedy atmosphere. The stable door was locked – the first time I had ever seen that. It was of flimsy construction; the lower portion was weaker and gave way to a hard shove from Petronius. He reached in and fiddled with the bolts on the upper half, eventually giving up and simply ducking underneath. I followed. We emerged inside the kitchen area. Everywhere was completely still.

We stood, trying to see in the dark. We recognised that silence. We knew what we were looking for. Petronius always carried a tinder-box; after several attempts he struck sparks, then managed to find a lamp to light.

As he held up the little lamp he was standing ahead of me, his bulk blocking my view. His shadow, that great head and the raised arm, sprang up to the side of me, flickering alarmingly on the rough caupona wall.

'Oh shit, he's dead!'

I assumed it was another murder. Still locked in my own preoccupations, I thought drably, *Geminus must have come here and killed the waiter just before he turned up at Fountain Court so full of concern for us, so full of laughter and fun* . . .

But I was wrong. I had hardly begun to feel angry with my father when Petronius Longus moved aside for me.

I noticed another shadow. By the single flame of the feeble lamp, its slow motion attracted attention as a long, dark, slanted shape turned slightly with some changing air current.

In the well of the stairs was Epimandos. He had hanged himself.

LX

Petronius had the longer reach. He cut the body down, not even needing the stool Epimandos had used. We were far too late; the corpse was cold. We carried him into the deep dark of the interior, and laid him on a counter. I fetched the thin blanket from his bed and covered him. Petronius unlocked and partly pushed open a shutter. He called in the others.

'You were right, Apollonius. The waiter's topped himself. It's all right; don't be afraid to look. He's decent now.'

The old teacher came into the caupona, showing no excitement. He looked at the covered body with compassion. He shook his head. 'Saw it coming. Only a matter of time.'

'I must talk to you,' Petronius said. 'But first we all need a drink – '

We looked around, but then gave up. It seemed tactless to raid Flora's. We all went over to the Valerian. Petronius told the other customers to make themselves scarce, so they wandered across to Flora's and stood outside in huddles. Rumours had spread. A crowd collected, though there was nothing to see. We had locked up after us. Petronius, who had his soft side, even brought away the distressed cat.

The Valerian had a quiet atmosphere and quite good wine. The waiter allowed Petro to feed Stringy, which was sensible because Petronius was looking for an excuse to start a fight over nothing just to ease his feelings. He always hated unnatural death.

'This is a tragedy. What can you tell me?' Petro asked the teacher wearily. He was stroking the cat and sounded as if he was still looking for trouble. Apollonius blanched.

'I know a little about him. I'm at the caupona frequently . . .' Apollonius left a small, tactful pause. 'His name was Epimandos; he had been a waiter there for five or six years. Your brother,' he said, turning to me, 'arranged the job for him.'

I shrugged. 'I never knew that.'

'There was some secrecy surrounding it.'

'What secrecy?' demanded Petronius. Apollonius looked shy. 'You can speak freely. Was he a runaway?'

'Yes, he had been a slave, I believe,' agreed my old geometrist.

'Where did he come from?'

'Egypt, I think.'

'*Egypt?*'

Apollonius sighed. 'This was told to me in confidence, but I suppose now the man is dead . . .'

'Tell me what you know!' Petro commanded bluntly. 'That's an order. This is a murder enquiry.'

'What? I thought the waiter had committed suicide?'

'I don't mean the waiter.'

Petro's angry manner was making Apollonius clam up. It was Helena who reassured him, asking gently, 'Please tell us. How did a slave from Egypt end his days serving in a caupona here?'

For once my terrible teacher managed to be concise. 'He had had a bad master. I understand the person was notorious for his cruelty. When Epimandos ran away, Didius Festus found him. He helped him come to Italy, and to obtain work. That was why Epimandos had a special regard, Marcus, for members of your family, and for you.'

I asked, 'And do you know why Epimandos killed himself today?'

'I think so,' Apollonius responded slowly. 'His cruel master was the medical officer in your brother's legion.'

'This all happened when Festus and the Fifteenth Legion were stationed at Alexandria?'

'Yes. Epimandos worked in the infirmary, so everybody knew him. After he escaped and came to Rome he was terrified that one day somebody would walk into Flora's, recognise him, and send him back to that life of torment. I know there was an occasion recently when he thought he had been noticed – he told me so one evening. He was in great distress and had got himself extremely drunk.'

'Was that Censorinus?'

'This he did not actually say,' Apollonius replied carefully.

977

Petronius had been listening in his fatalistic way. 'Why have you never mentioned this before?'

'Nobody asked.'

Well he was only the beggar.

Petro stared at him, then muttered to me, 'Censorinus was not the only one who noticed the waiter. Epimandos probably killed himself because he guessed he had also been recognised by Laurentius. It happened when we ourselves invited the centurion to Flora's earlier today.'

Remembering how the waiter had shot out of sight when Laurentius looked at him, I believed it and was appalled. 'Do you know this for certain?'

'Afraid so. After we all left the place, Laurentius was puzzling over why the waiter had seemed familiar. He finally remembered where he had seen Epimandos before, then realised its implication regarding the death of Censorinus. He came straight to see me. That was one reason why I was delayed when Apollonius sent his message.'

I had been feeling grey before this news, which was deeply depressing. It did solve some of my problems. For one thing, it showed my brother Festus in a better light (if you approve of helping slaves escape). It also meant I could stop panicking over Geminus. This reprieve for my father had hardly sunk in; I must still have looked dreadful. I was coming to terms with just how relieved I felt.

I suddenly realised that Helena Justina was gripping my hand fiercely. Saving me mattered to her so desperately she could no longer hold back: 'Petronius, are you saying that the waiter must have been the soldier's murderer?'

Petronius nodded. 'I reckon so. You're cleared, Falco. I shall tell Marponius I am no longer looking for a suspect in the Censorinus case.'

Nobody gloated.

Helena had to be certain about all this. 'So what happened the night he died? Censorinus must have recognised the waiter, possibly while he was in the midst of quarrelling with Marcus. Later perhaps he had a confrontation with the waiter. When Epimandos realised the trouble he was in, the poor soul must have been in despair. If Censorinus was spiteful, maybe he threatened Epimandos with returning him to his master, and then – '

She was so unhappy Petro finished it for her. 'Epimandos took him up a drink. Censorinus obviously failed to realise the danger he was in. We can never know if he really did threaten the waiter – and if so, whether the threats were serious. But Epimandos was clearly terrified, with fatal results. Desperate, and more than likely drunk, he stabbed the soldier with a kitchen knife which he snatched on his way upstairs. His terror of being returned to the medical orderly explains the ferocity of the attack.'

'Why did he not run away afterwards?' Apollonius asked thoughtfully.

'Nowhere to run,' I answered. 'No one to help him this time. He tried to discuss it with me.' Remembering Epimandos's pathetic attempts to get my attention I was furious with myself. 'I dismissed him as just curious – the usual sensation-seeker who hangs around after a murder. All I did was brush him aside and threaten vengeance on whoever had committed the crime.'

'You were in a difficult position personally,' Apollonius consoled me.

'Not as bad as his. I should have noticed his hysteria. After he killed the soldier he must have frozen. I've seen it before. He just acted as if it had never happened, trying to blot the event right out of his mind. But he was almost begging to be discovered. I should have recognised that he was appealing for my help.'

'There was nothing to be done!' Petro pointed out harshly. 'He was a runaway slave, and he had murdered a legionary: nobody could have saved him, Marcus. If he hadn't taken this action today, he would have been crucified or sent to the arena. No judge could have done otherwise.'

'It was very nearly me who ended up in the dock!' I answered hollowly.

'Never! He would have stopped it,' Apollonius broke in. 'His loyalty to your family was too strong to let you suffer. What your brother had done for him meant everything. He was desperate when he heard they had arrested you. He must have been in anguish, hoping you would clear yourself and yet not discover his own guilt. But from the start his position was hopeless.'

'He seems a very sad character,' Helena sighed.

'After what he had suffered in Alexandria, his quiet life here was a revelation. That was why he exploded at the thought of losing it.'

'Yet to kill someone!' protested Helena.

Again it was Apollonius who answered her: 'The caupona looks dreadful to you, maybe. But nobody beat or whipped him, or subjected him to worse abuse. He had food and drink. The work was easy and people talked to him like a human being. He had a cat to fondle – even me at the door to look down on. Within this small world at the crossroads, Epimandos had status, dignity and peace.' From a man in beggar's rags himself the speech was heartbreaking.

We all fell silent. Then I had to ask Petronius. 'What's your theory about that knife?'

Helena Justina glanced at me quickly. Petro had an unfathomable expression as he said, 'Epimandos lied when he claimed he had never seen it. He must have used it often. I have just managed to trace the knife to the caupona,' he admitted, surprising me.

'How?'

'Leave it alone.' He sounded embarrassed. He could see I wanted to argue. 'I am satisfied, Falco!'

I said quietly, 'No, we ought to get this sorted out. I think the knife left my mother's house with my father – '

Petro cursed under his breath. 'Exactly!' he told me. 'I know it did. I didn't want to mention it; you're such a touchy beggar on some subjects – '

'What are you saying, Petro?'

'Nothing.' He was trying to hide something; that was obvious. It was ridiculous. We had solved the murder – yet we seemed to be plunging deeper into mystery. 'Look, Falco, the knife was always part of the caupona's equipment. It's been there ever since the place first opened ten years ago.' He looked shiftier than ever.

'How do you know?'

'I asked the owner.'

'Flora?'

980

'Flora,' said Petronius, as if that ended everything.

'I didn't think Flora existed.'

'Flora exists.' Petronius stood up. He was leaving the Valerian.

'How,' I demanded emphatically, 'did this Flora acquire the knife if Pa had it?'

'Don't worry about it,' said Petro. 'I'm the investigating officer, and I know all about the knife.'

'I have a right to know how it got there.'

'Not if I'm happy.'

'Blow you, Petro! I was damned nearly sent to trial because of that implement.'

'Tough,' he said.

Petronius Longus could be an absolute bastard when he chose. Official posts go to people's heads. I told him what I thought of him, but he simply ignored my rage.

'I must go, Falco. I'll have to advise the owner that the waiter's dead and the caupona's empty. That crowd outside is looking for an excuse to break in and smash up the furniture while they help themselves to free wine.'

'We'll stay there,' Helena volunteered quietly. 'Marcus will keep the thieves and looters out until a watchman can be sent.'

Petro glanced at me for confirmation. 'I'll do it,' I said. 'I owe Epimandos something.'

Petronius shrugged and smiled. I did not know the reason, and I was so annoyed with him I did not care.

LXI

I told Helena to go home; rebelliously she came with me.

'I don't need supervision.'

'I disagree!' she snapped.

The waiter's body still lay where we had left it in the main part of the building so we hovered about in the back. Helena marched into the little cubicle Epimandos had slept in, and sat on his bed. I stood in the doorway. I could see she was furious.

'Why do you hate your father so much, Falco?'

'What's all this about?'

'You can't hide from me. I do know!' she rampaged. 'I understand you, Marcus. I can see what perverted suspicions you were harbouring about who had used your mother's knife!'

'Petronius was right. Forget the knife.'

'Yes, he's right – but it took a long argument to convince you. You and your stubborn prejudices – you're hopeless! I really did think that after Capua and your meetings with Geminus in Rome these past few weeks, you and he had at last reached an accommodation. I wanted to believe you two were friends again,' she wailed.

'Some things don't change.'

'Well you don't, obviously!' I had not seen Helena so angry for a long time. 'Marcus, your father loves you!'

'Settle down. He doesn't want me, or any of the rest of us. Festus was his boy, but that was different. Festus could win anybody over.'

'You are so wrong,' Helena disagreed miserably. 'You just won't see the truth, Marcus. Marriages do fail.' She knew that; she had been married. 'If things had been different between your parents, your father would have had just as strong a grip on you and all the others as your mother has today. He stands back – but that doesn't mean he wants to. He still worries and watches over what you all do – '

982

'Believe that if it pleases you. But don't ask me to alter. I learned to live without him when I had to – and that suits me now.'

'Oh you're so stubborn! Marcus, this could have been your chance to put things right between you, maybe your only chance . . .' Helena rounded on me pleadingly: 'Listen, do you know why he gave me that bronze table as a gift?'

'Because he likes your spirit and you're a pretty girl.'

'Oh Marcus! Don't always be so sour! He took me to see it. He said, "Look at this. I had my eye on it for Marcus, but he'll never accept it from me".'

I still saw no reason to change my own attitude because these two had palled up. 'Helena, if you have come to an arrangement, that's charming and I'm delighted you get on so well – but it's between you and him.' I did not even object to Helena and Pa manipulating me, if that thrilled them. 'I don't want to hear any more.'

I left her sitting on the waiter's bed, below the amulet Festus had once given Epimandos. It had not done the waiter much good.

I stalked away. The main bar, with its sad contents, still repelled me, so I lit another lamp and stomped upstairs.

I looked in the two small rooms that lay above the kitchen area. They were furnished for thin dwarves with no luggage who might be prepared to spend their free time at Flora's sitting on rickety beds staring at spiders' webs.

Gruesome fascination drew me to the other room again.

It had been scrubbed and rearranged. The walls had been washed over with a dark red paint, the only colour that would hide what had been underneath. The bed was now below the window, instead of by the door. It had a different blanket. The stool where the soldier's wine tray had been placed by Epimandos on that fatal night had been changed for a pine box. As a gesture to decor, a large Greek pot with a lively octopus design now stood on a mat on the box.

The pot used to be in the bar downstairs. I remembered it there; it was a fine item. I had always thought that. However, when I went to have a closer look, I noticed that the far-side rim was badly chipped. The pot would not repay mending. All the owner could do with the thing was shove it somewhere and admire the octopus.

I was thinking like Pa.

I always would.

I lay on the bed gloomily.

Helena could no longer bear to be at odds with me, so she came upstairs too. Now it was her turn to stand in the doorway. I held out my hand to her.

'Friends?'

'If you like.' She stayed by the door. Friends we might be, but she still despised my attitude. However, I was not intending to change it; not even for her.

She looked around, realising this was where the soldier died. I watched her quietly. Women are not supposed to think, but mine could and did, and I liked to watch the process. Helena's strong face changed imperceptibly as she considered everything here, trying to imagine the last minutes of the soldier's life, trying to comprehend the waiter's demented attack. This was no place for her. I would have to take her downstairs again, but too soon a move would offend her.

I was watching Helena, judging my moment, so the puzzled thought caught me unawares: 'There's something wrong about this room.' I stared about me, wondering what had worried me. 'The size is odd.'

I did not need Apollonius to draw me a geometric sketch. As soon as I thought about it, I realised the floor plan here upstairs was much smaller than the ground-floor area. I swung myself upright and went out on to the landing to check. The other two guest rooms, which were so tiny they hardly counted, occupied the space above the kitchen and the waiter's cubicle. The staircase used up a few more feet. But this eight-foot-square room where Censorinus had died was only about half the size of the caupona's main room downstairs.

Behind me Helena had entered the soldier's room. 'There's only one window here.' She was acutely observant. As soon as I went back to her I understood what she meant. When Petronius and I stood in the street throwing pebbles up, there had been two square openings above our heads. Only one lit this room. 'There must be another bedroom up here, Marcus – but there's no door into it.'

'It's been blocked up,' I decided. Then a possible reason struck me. 'Dear gods, Helena, there may be something hidden up here – another body, for instance!'

'Oh really! You always have to dramatise!' Helena Justina was a sensible young woman. Every informer should have one as his associate. 'Why should there be a body?'

Trying to withdraw from the ridicule, I defended myself. 'Epimandos used to be terrified of people asking questions about these rooms.' I heard my voice drop, as if I were afraid of being overheard. There was nobody here – or if there was, they had been sealed up for years. I was remembering a conversation I must have misconstrued at the time. 'There is something here, Helena. I once joked about hidden secrets and Epimandos nearly had a fit.'

'Something hidden by him?'

'No.' I was drowning in a familiar sense of the inevitable. 'Someone else. But someone Epimandos respected enough to keep the secret – '

'Festus!' she exclaimed quietly. 'Festus hid something here that he did not tell even you about – '

'Ah well. Not trusted, apparently.'

Not for the first time I fought off a wild pang of jealousy as I faced the fact that Festus and I had never been as close as I had convinced myself. Maybe nobody had known him properly. Maybe even our father only touched him in passing. Not even Pa knew about this hiding-place, I was sure of that.

But now I knew. And I was going to find whatever my brother had left in it.

LXII

I ran downstairs, looking for tools. As I went, I checked again the layout of the small landing. If there was indeed another room, it had never been accessible from the corridor; the stairs were in the way where its door ought to be.

Bringing a cleaver and a meat-hammer from the kitchen, I ran back. I felt mad-eyed, like a butcher who had run amok in the August heat. 'People must have entered through this room here . . .' In Rome, that was common. Thousands of folk reached their bedrooms through at least one other living area, sometimes a whole string of them. Ours was not a culture that valued domestic privacy.

Feeling the wall with my open hand, I tried to forget how it had been splashed with the soldier's blood. The construction was rough lath and plaster, so rough it could have been my brother-in-law Mico's work. Maybe it was. Now I remember Mico telling me that Festus had arranged work for him . . . But I doubted whether Mico had ever seen what was bricked up in the missing room. Somebody else must have filled in the doorway secretly – almost certainly someone I knew.

'Festus!' I muttered. Festus, on his last night in Rome . . . Festus, rolling away from Lenia's laundry in the dead of night, saying he had a job to do.

That must have been why he wanted me; he needed my help with the heavy work. Now I was here without him, and about to undo his labours. It gave me an odd feeling, which was not entirely affectionate.

A few inches from the cloak hook I found a change in the surface. I walked the width of the wall, tapping it with a knuckle. Sure enough, the sound altered, as if I was passing a hollow area, slightly more than two feet wide. It could have been a doorway once.

'Marcus, what are you going to do?'

'Take a risk.' Demolition always worries me. The caupona was so badly built, one wrong move could bring the whole place crashing down. Doorways are strong, I told myself. I bounced on my heels, testing the floor, but it felt safe enough. I just hoped the roof stayed up.

I felt for a crack, applied the cleaver like a chisel, and tapped it gently with the meat-hammer. Plaster shattered and dropped to the floor, but I had not been fierce enough. I had to use more force, though I was trying to be neat. I did not want to crash into the hidden room in a great shower of rubble. What was there might be delicate.

By pulling off the upper skim of plaster, I managed to trace the edge of the lintel and frame. The doorway had been blocked with fireclay bricks. The infill had been poorly done, hurriedly no doubt. The mortar was a weak mix, most of which crumbled easily. Starting from near the top, I tried to remove the bricks. It was dusty work. After much effort I freed one, then lifted out more, bringing them towards me, one at a time. Helena helped pile them to the side.

There certainly was another room. It had a window, matching the one where we were, but was pitch-black, unlit and filling with dust. Peering through the hole, I could make out nothing. Patiently I cleared a space in the old doorway that would be wide enough and tall enough to step through.

I stood back, recovering, while the dust settled a little. Helena hugged my damp shoulders, waiting quietly for me to act. Covered with dirt, I grinned at her excitely.

I took the pottery lamp. Holding it ahead of me, I squeezed an arm through the narrow gap and stepped sideways into the tomblike stillness of the next room.

I had half hoped to find it full of treasure. It was empty, apart from its single occupant. As I pulled my shoulders through the gap and straightened up, I met the man's eyes. He was standing by the wall exactly opposite, and staring straight at me.

987

LXIII

'Oh Jupiter!'

He was not a man. He was a god. The lord of all the other gods, unmistakably.

Five hundred years ago a sculptor with divine talent had breathed life into a massive marble block, creating this. The sculptor who was later to ornament the Parthenon had, in the days before his greatest fame, made for some small anonymous island temple a Zeus that must have excelled all expectations. Five hundred years later, a gang of cheap priests had sold it off to my brother. Now it stood here.

It must have been an awesome task hauling this upstairs. Some of the tackle my brother had used lay abandoned in a corner. I wondered if Epimandos had helped him. Probably.

Helena had ventured into the room after me. Clutching my arm, she gasped, then stood with me staring in rapture.

'Nice piece!' I whispered, aping Geminus.

Helena had learned the patter: 'Hmm! Rather large for domestic consumption, but it does have possibilities . . .'

Zeus, naked and heavily bearded, surveyed us with nobility and calm. His right arm was raised in the act of hurling a thunderbolt. Set on a pedestal in the darkened inner sanctum of some high Ionic temple, he would have been astonishing. Here, in the silent gloom of my brother's abandoned glory hole, he quelled even me.

We were still standing there, lost in admiration, when I heard noises.

Guilt and panic struck us both. Somebody had come into the caupona below us. We became aware of furtive movements in the kitchen area, then feet approaching up the stairs. Someone looked into the soldier's room, saw the mess and exclaimed. I dragged my attention from the statue. We were trapped. I was trying to decide whether there was more to be gained by extinguishing the lamp or keeping it, when another light was thrust through the gap in the brickwork, with an arm already following.

The arm wriggled frantically, as a broad shoulder jammed in the narrow space. Someone cursed, in a voice I recognised. The next minute loose bricks tumbled inward as a sturdy figure forced its passage, and my father burst through into the hiding-place.

He looked at us. He looked at the Zeus.

He said, as if I had just produced a bag of apples, 'I see you've found it then!'

LXIV

His eyes devoured the Phidias.

I asked quietly, 'What are you doing here?' Pa let out a small groan of ecstasy, ignoring my question as he lost himself in admiration of the Zeus. 'Did you know this was here, Pa?'

For an instant Geminus blinked unreliably. But he cannot have known for much longer than I had, or the statue would not have been left here. He must have been starting to guess as he came up the stairs. I tried not to believe he had run into the caupona at top speed, intent on breaking down the wall himself.

He walked around the Zeus, admiring it from all sides. I amused myself wondering whether, if he had found the statue first, he would ever have told me.

My father's expression was inscrutable. I realised he looked just like Festus, and that meant I shouldn't trust him.

'We should have known, Marcus.'

'Yes. Festus was always hanging around this place.'

'Oh he treated it like home!' agreed Pa, in a dry tone. 'We should have guessed. And what's more,' he declared, 'this won't be the end of it. Your precious brother must have had hideaways packed with treasure everywhere he ever went. We can find them,' he added.

'Or we can tire ourselves out looking!' I commented. Euphoria dies very quickly. I felt tired already.

'He will have had a list,' said father, hanging his lamp on the statue's thunderbolt and coming back round to us.

I laughed. 'That would be madness! If it was me, the details would be locked only in my own head!'

'Oh me too!' agreed Pa. 'But Festus was not like us.'

I saw Helena smile, as if she enjoyed thinking that my father and I were alike. With half a million sesterces' worth of Phidias standing opposite, I allowed myself to smile back at her.

We all stood about for as long as possible, gazing at the

Zeus. Then, when it became ridiculous to stay in that dark empty space any longer, we squeezed back to the comparative luxury of the furnished room beyond.

Pa surveyed the rubble from my demolition work. 'You made a right mess here, Marcus!'

'I was as tidy as I could be, in a hurry and without proper tools – ' While the others gawped and marvelled, I had been planning. 'Look, we need to move fast. We'll have to cover up this rubble as best we can. It would be better to remove the statue before anybody sees it. Horrible – but we must shift it. *We* are sure it belonged to Festus, but explaining that to the owner of the building may not be so easy – '

'Relax,' interrupted my father graciously. 'Nobody's coming here tonight.'

'That's where you're wrong. Will you listen to me? I've been left here on guard while the owner is informed by Petronius that the waiter's dead. Any moment we're expecting to be joined by the mysterious Flora, and she won't be pleased to discover this great hole in her wall – '

Something made me stop. Nobody else was coming. Pa had said it in a flat voice. Even without a reason given, I understood.

'Thanks for looking after things,' my father chirruped wryly. I was still trying to ignore the implications, though already aghast. He reassumed his shifty look. 'Flora's not coming. Acting as watchman is man's work; I volunteered.'

Then I groaned as I realised what I should have worked out weeks before. I knew why my brother had always treated this place as if he owned it; why he had found jobs here for runaways; why he had made free with the rooms. It was all in the family.

Petronius was right. Flora existed. And right, too, that I would have preferred not to discover it. Flora's Caupona was the business my father had bought for the woman who now lived with him, to stop her interfering in his own. *Flora* was Pa's ladyfriend.

LXV

The first part of our plot against Carus and Servia was the most painful: my father raised half a million sesterces by auctioning his chattels. A friend of his called the bids on the day, with Gornia from the office supervising the rest of the sale. Father went to Tibur for a couple of days while it happened, presumably taking the redhead. I had gone to the Campagna, to fetch one of our blocks of Parian stone.

We closed the caupona, on the excuse of Epimandos's death. We made a space in the kitchen area, installed the marble block, brought Orontes over from his lodging with the painters on the Caelian, and set him to work.

'Can you do it?'

'If it will get you awkward beggars off my back . . . Oh I'll do it; just leave me in peace to get on with it!'

Using the Zeus as a copy, together with his memory of its brother the Poseidon, Orontes was to redeem his betrayal of Festus by making us a new Phidias.

While this was in hand, we lulled the collectors into a false sense of security by paying off our supposed debt.

It was just before dawn.

We drove up the Via Flaminia in an open cart, during the last hour that wheeled vehicles were allowed into Rome. Mist hung above the Campus Martius, clothing all the silent public buildings with a wintry chill. We passed the grey stone of the Pantheon and the Saepta, heading towards the elegant gardens and mansions up in the north of the city.

All the streets were still. The revellers had gone home; the robbers were busy hiding their swag under floorboards; the prostitutes were sleeping; the fire brigade were snoring. Door-porters were so deeply asleep visitors could have banged for half an hour and still been left out on the step.

We were ready for that.

When we reached the peaceful middle-class lane where

Cassius Carus dwelt with his lady, we backed our cart up against their front portal. As if on cue, one of our oxen lowed. My father sat up on the cart, blurred in the light of smoking torches, and solemnly began to bang an enormous copper bell. A great cloud of starlings rose like a dark curtain from the pantiled roofs and circled anxiously. I and two helpers walked along the street pounding massive gongs.

It was a refined middle-class area where the inhabitants liked to keep their heads down on their pillows whatever excesses were going on outside, but we roused them. We kept up the noise until everyone took notice. Shutters flew open. Watchdogs were barking. Tousled heads appeared everywhere while we carried on banging in a slow, deliberate manner as if it were some dread religious rite.

Finally Carus and Servia burst from their front door.

'At last!' roared my father. The helpers and I gravely made our way back to him. 'The vultures appear for the reckoning!' Pa informed the audience. 'Now hear me: Aulus Cassius Carus and Ummidia Servia maintain that my son Didius Festus – who died a national hero, in possession of the Mural Crown – owed them half a million sesterces. Never let it be said that the Didius family reneged!' It was brilliant. After years of observing puzzled punters in the auction ring, he had the knack of sounding like a man who believed he had probably been cheated, though he could not quite see how. 'Here's the cash then! I call on all those present to be my witnesses.'

He walked to the edge of the cart. I joined him there.

'Here's your money, Carus! It's been counted!'

We raised the first lid together, up-ended the chest on the edge of the wagon, and let its contents spill out on to the roadway. The first consignment of our half-million tumbled at the collectors' feet. With an anguished cry they fell on it, vainly trying to catch up the cash as the coins bounced and spun over pavement and gutter. We shoved aside the empty chest and heaved forward another. Helped by our companions we continued this until a mound of twinkling coinage filled the entrance to the Carus home, chest-high, like a great pile of winter grit left beside a steep road.

It was all in small change. Box after box of mixed coppers,

ancient bronze bits and silver fell like the mica chips that spangle the sand in the Circus Maximus. We emptied the entire amount into the road. We had no need of a receipt: the whole street could bear witness to our delivery. In fact, as we turned the cart and drove away, many of the collectors' extremely helpful neighbours were rushing up, still in their slippers and nightwear, eager to help gather up the money from the road.

'Enjoy it, Carus,' was my father's parting shot. 'That little lot should see you all right at a few public latrines!'

LXVI

Some weeks later, the fine-art world was humming with news of a forthcoming private sale.

At the gallery of Cocceius stood an interesting marble.

'I can make *no* claims,' said Cocceius, who was an honest kind of dealer, 'for its artist, or its antiquity.'

Collectors soon heard about the statue's striking features, and flocked to gawp. It was a Poseidon: nude, one arm poised and throwing a trident, and with a rich curly beard. Very Greek – and quite magnificent.

'It has an intriguing history,' Cocceius informed enquirers in his comfortable way. He was a quiet, reassuring man, a pillar of the Auctioneers' Guild. 'The illustrious Senator Camillus Verus found this rather nice piece in the attic when going through his late brother's house . . .'

That old tale!

People all over Rome went rushing home to look in their attics.

Nobody else had one.

Two people, a man and a woman heavily wrapped in cloaks and veils, came to view the statue incognito. Cocceius gave them a familiar nod.

'What's the provenance, Cocceius?'

'None, I fear. We can make no guesses. Though it's certainly Parian marble, as you can see.' That was evident. This was no Roman copy in limestone. Even fine Carrara would be noticeably more grey in the vein . . .

'What's the reason for selling?'

'It seems a convincing story. I understand the Senator is trying to raise cash to put his second son into the Senate. I dare say you can ask around their neighbours for confirmation. The bright young thing has made an unexpected name for himself, and with Daddy having Vespasian's ear, his path is now clear to the top. Finance is their only problem. So offers are invited for this rather handsome sea god, though you'll have to use your judgement as to what it is . . .'

'Where did it come from?'

'Absolutely no idea. The noble Senator's brother imported things. But he's dead, so we can't ask him.'

'Where did he trade?'

'All over. North Africa. Europe. Greece and the East, I believe . . .'

'Greece, you say?'

'There does appear to be some minor damage to one shoulder . . .' Cocceius was completely open, a model of neutrality.

'It's excellent. But you make no claims?'

'I make no claims.' Cocceius was certainly honest; such a refreshing change.

There are many ways of making claims – and not all of them involve direct lies.

The closely swaddled collectors went away to think about it.

Next time they came, the owner was apparently considering withdrawing the statue from sale. Alarmed by this news, the cloaked man and woman stood in the shadows and listened. Maybe other people were in other shadows, but if so they were invisible.

The Senator's noble daughter was explaining to Cocceius that her father might be having doubts. 'Of course we do need the money. But it's such a lovely thing. If it commands a large price, that's wonderful. But we're tempted to keep it and enjoy it at home ourselves. Oh dear! Father doesn't know what he should do for the best . . . Could we ask an expert to have a look at it?'

'Certainly.' Cocceius never pushed his clients to sell against their will. 'I can arrange for an art historian to give you an authoritative opinion. How much are you prepared to pay?'

'What can I get?' asked the noble Helena Justina.

Cocceius was honest, but a humorist. 'Well, for a small fee I can get you a man who will close his eyes and say the first thing that comes into his head.'

'Forget the small fee,' she answered.

'For a little bit more I can get you a *proper* expert.'

'That's better.'

'Which sort would you like?'

Helena looked surprised – though not so surprised as she might have looked before she met me. 'Which sorts can I have?'

'Either Arion, who will tell you it's genuine – or Pavoninus, who will maintain it's a fake.'

'But they haven't seen it yet!'

'That's what they always say.'

Apparently Helena Justina was now growing tense. 'How much,' she demanded at her most crisp (which was about as crisp as toasted bread when you answer the door and forget it until you smell smoke), 'how much would we have to pay for the very best?' Cocceius told her. Helena drew a sharp breath. 'And what will we get for that exorbitant amount?'

Cocceius looked embarrassed. 'You will get a man in a slightly peculiar tunic who stares at the statue for a very long time, drinks some herb tea in a thoughtful manner, then tells you both of the possible verdicts and says that frankly he cannot say for certain which is correct.'

'Ah I see! He,' said Helena, collapsing with a smile, 'is the really clever one.'

'Why is that?' asked Cocceius, though he knew all along.

'Because without putting his own reputation at risk, he leaves people to convince themselves of what they want to hear.' The noble Helena reached a decision in her usual swift manner. 'Let's save our cash! I can speak for Papa.' Obviously they were a free-thinking, liberal family. (And the women were *very* forceful.) 'If we can establish my brother's career the sale will be worth it. People will recognise quality. If anybody offers a good figure, Papa will sell.'

The collectors in the cloaks hurriedly sent both Arion and Pavoninus to look at the Poseidon; then they also paid for the man in the odd tunic, who had very peculiar diction too, and who said that they must make up their own minds.

They decided their need for the Poseidon was desperate.

The question of money was discreetly raised.

Apparently, in order to put young Justinus into the Senate,

the illustrious Camillus would need a very large amount. 'The figure which has been mentioned,' said Cocceius in a hushed voice, like a doctor announcing a fatal disease, 'is six hundred thousand.'

Naturally the collectors offered four hundred. To which the owner replied that that was an outrage; he could not possibly settle for less than five. The deal was struck. Half a million in gold aurei (plus the commission to Cocceius) was exchanged for the unknown statue.

Two hours later people were being invited to a viewing at the private house of Cassius Carus and Ummidia Servia, who had acquired a Poseidon by Phidias.

We were even. We had got them off our backs, then retrieved our money. We had fooled them: we had sold them our fake.

We still had the Zeus. We were rich.

Father and I bought an amphora of the best well-aged Falernian. Then we bought two more.

After that, before we touched a drop but knowing we were on the verge of becoming extremely drunk, we went along together to the caupona for a fond look at our Zeus.

We went in through the back lane. The stable door had been properly locked by Orontes when he left. We opened up, amid happy exclamations. We banged the door behind us and lit lamps. Then slowly our celebrations died.

In the cleared space where I had placed the marble block for Orontes to carve still stood – a marble block. A chunk of it was missing, however. Clean stone gleamed with Parian whiteness where this piece had been removed: a neat rectangle, taken off the top. Most of the marble that was supposed to have been transformed into the Poseidon remained untouched.

We walked upstairs. By then we both knew what had happened, but we had to see the proof.

In the room where our Phidias Zeus had been left for Orontes, all that remained now was a severed arm holding a thunderbolt.

'I'm dreaming this . . .'

'That lazy, cheating, dissolute bastard! If I catch him – '

'Oh he'll be far away . . .'

Instead of bothering to carve a whole new statue, Orontes Mediolanus had simply adapted the existing one, giving it a new right arm. Now the Zeus had a trident instead of a thunderbolt.

Instead of a fake, we had sold Carus and Servia our genuine Phidias.

LXVII

It was April, and not as far as I knew an official black day in the Roman calendar, though it would be for ever in mine. In the old republican period New Year began on the Ides of March, so this was the first month of the year. The Senate went into recess to brace itself. To tackle April, you needed to be fit. April was packed with celebrations: the Megalensis and the Floral Games, the Games and Festival of Ceres, the Vinalia, the Robigalia and the Parilia, which was the birthday of Rome itself.

I was not sure I could sustain so much civic joy. In fact, at the moment I hated the thought of any jollity.

I walked through the Forum. At his request I had taken my father to the Saepta and dumped him in his office, stunned, though sober at that point. He wanted to be alone. I, too, could not face seeing anyone. My entire family would be gathering at Mother's, including Helena. Being greeted with garlands, when in fact I was bringing them nothing but my own stupidity, would be unbearable.

I should have checked up. Orontes had told me he preferred to work uninterrupted. I had been taken in by that simple lie.

Creation is a delicate process. Deceit is a fine art.

The Fates had a fine way of deflating our arrogance. I walked through Rome, driving myself on until I could accept what I had done, the chances I had lost. I needed occupation, or I would lose my sanity.

There were still questions to pursue. In all this, I had not forgotten the original commission from my mother. We had solved a murder, and almost pulled off a vengeful coup on behalf of the whole family, but one subject remained open even now: my elder brother's reputation.

Maybe his had been a flawed judgement. Carus, with the aid of Orontes, had defrauded him. I could hardly blame

Festus for that any longer, since Orontes had done the same to me. One commercial transaction had gone awry, the only one I knew about. Even without possession of the facts, Festus had been taking steps to put it right. Only his death had intervened. Only the fact that he had trusted no one – not even Father, not even me – had prevented his plans from being followed through.

Was Festus a hero?

I did not believe in heroics. I did not believe he had made some glorious, selfless sacrifice for Rome. Being honest, I had never believed it. He was romantic – but if he had ever, for some unimaginable reason, *chosen* that path, then he would have clinched his deals first. Festus could not have borne the thought of leaving an unfinished scheme. That Phidias, bricked up in Rome where it might never have been found; those blocks of marble abandoned on my sleepy uncles' farm; they told me absolutely: he was expecting to come back.

Did he think I would finish the business? No. I was his executor, but only because the army had forced him to make a will. It was a joke. There was nothing to bequeath formally. There had never been plans for me to adopt those transactions that were my brother's pride and joy. He had wanted to do it; he had intended to complete them himself.

My only legacy was to decide, now, what kind of name I should allow him to keep.

How could I decide?

All I could do was miss him. There was nobody like him. Anything I had ever done that was bad had had its origin in his encouragement. The same went for anything affectionate or generous. I might not believe he was a hero, but that still left plenty to believe in: that great heart, that great colourful, complicated character which even three years after he had died still dominated all of us.

I had continued for too long simply wondering. Tonight, if it existed anywhere, I was going to find the truth.

I had entered the Forum down the Gemonian Steps from the Capitol. I walked from the Rostra and the Golden Milestone, the whole length of the Basilica Julia to the Temple of Castor, where I thought about attending the baths, then abandoned the thought. I was in no mood for the attentions of slaves and conversation with friends. I passed the Vestals' House and Temple, emerging into the area the republicans called the Velia.

All of the district around me, from the Palatine behind me to the Esquiline ahead, taking in both the Oppian and Caelian hills, had been destroyed by fire and then taken over by Nero for the abomination he called his Golden House.

House was the wrong word. What he had created here was even more than a palace. Its lofty structures leapt between the crags, a feast of fabulous architecture. The interior decor was unbelievable, its richness and imagination surpassing anything artists had previously created. In the grounds, he had achieved another wonder. If the architecture was amazing, despite representing such blatant megalomania, even more dramatic was this entire landscape surrounding the halls and colonnades: a natural countryside within the city walls. Here there were parks and woodlands where wild and tame animals had roamed, all dominated by the famous Great Lake. It had been the tyrant's private world, but Vespasian, in a calculated propaganda coup, had thrown it open to everyone as a vast public park.

Smart move, Flavians! Now we had an emperor who treated his own divinity as an irony. He talked of pulling down the Golden House, though he and his sons were currently living there. The lake, however, had already been drained. It was the best-placed site in Rome, right at the end of the Sacred Way, on the main approach to the Forum. There Vespasian intended to use the cavern left by the drained lake to build the foundations and substructures of an immense new arena that would bear his family name.

It was the glory of the city long before the Emperor laid the first stone with his golden trowel. Sightseers regularly came and stood around it. This was the place in Rome to spend a peaceful hour, or several, watching someone else at work. The site of the Flavian Arena had to be the biggest- and best-ever hole in the ground.

I had last stood here looking at it in the company of the centurion Laurentius. After the waiter's death at Flora's

Caupona, Petronius and I had sought him out. Rather than talk at his sister's house, amidst the clamour of her young children, we had walked through Rome until we ended up at this building site. Here we had told Laurentius what had happened to Epimandos, and of our belief that Epimandos must have murdered Censorinus.

Laurentius had been prepared for it. Recognising the runaway had already suggested the whole story. Nevertheless, its confirmation, and hearing about the waiter's lonely end, had made us all dispirited.

Laurentius was a sensible type, but even he began to philosophise gloomily.

'Look at those, for instance!' he had exclaimed, as we passed a group of Eastern prisoners. They were digging foundations, though not very busily. Construction sites have their moments of frantic activity, but this had not been one of them. 'We legionaries flog ourselves in the burning sun with our brains boiling in our helmets,' Laurentius complained bitterly, 'while this lot calmly get captured and take their ease in Rome . . . What's it all for?' he demanded. The old cry.

That was when I had asked him about Festus. He had not been present at Bethel. 'I was off with a detachment under Cerialis, in bandit country further south. We were clearing the ground around Jerusalem in preparation for the siege, while the old man himself tackled the towns in the hills – ' He was referring to Vespasian. 'Is there a problem, Falco?'

'Not really.' I felt obliged to show some diffidence. To criticise a campaign hero is to take issue with the whole conduct of the campaign; nailing Festus as less than glorious would diminish the survivors too. 'I did wonder what exactly happened.'

'Did you not receive a report?'

'Who believes reports? Remember, I've been in the army myself!'

'So what are you thinking?'

Somehow I had laughed, almost dismissively. 'Knowing what I do now, I wonder whether when Festus overstretched himself commercially, your own syndicate might have chucked him off the ramparts in disgust at their financial loss?'

'Not an issue!' replied the centurion. He was terse. 'Trust the report . . .' There was nothing else I would learn from him.

Yet as he turned away, in the act of leaving us, he threw back over his shoulder, 'Believe the story, Falco.' Those hard bright eyes glared at me from that quiet, trustworthy face. 'You know what happens. These things are all the same when you get down to it – what took Festus off was probably some stupid accident.'

He was right, and if so, he was right that we all had to forget it. I could believe that angle. Yet it was not enough. For my mother there had to be more than mere belief.

I could go to Pannonia. I could find people who had been present – the men from my brother's own century who had followed him on to the battlement. I already knew what they would tell me. They would say what the army had said.

I could get them very drunk, and they would then tell me another story, but that would be because drunken soldiers all hate the army, and while they are drunk they blame the army for a lot of lies; those lies become truths again as soon as they sober up. His comrades had a vested interest in my brother's official fate. Dead men have to be heroes. Nothing else applies.

Dead officers even more so.

The Judaean campaign was now famous: it had produced an emperor. That was an accident which nobody had expected in the months when Festus died. Festus was lost in March or April; Vespasian was not hailed emperor anywhere until July, and it had taken him a great deal longer than that to complete the process of gaining the throne. Until then, the Jewish Rebellion was nothing. Just another political foul-up in a terrible spot where we pretended to be taking the gifts of civilisation to the wild men, in order to keep a toe-hold in a lucrative trade arena. Unlike most of his colleagues, Festus at least knew at firsthand about the dyes and the glass and the cedar wood, and the links with the silk and spice routes which we needed to protect for ourselves. But even with that knowledge, nobody would fight there – not for a baking desert full of nothing but goats and squabbling religious zealots – unless they could believe at least the promise that their corpse would achieve some glory. Being first man over the battle-ment of some faded hill town had to count.

It had to count for the mother he had left behind in Rome too.

So since she had asked me, I did what I could. This niggle had been dogging us all for three years now, and the time had come to settle it.

The Flavian Arena was to be built by a workforce which the conquests of Vespasian and Titus had conveniently provided: captured Judaean slaves.

I had come to see them.

LXVIII

It was late afternoon when I started my search. I had to tackle one after another of the grisly gang foremen, whose demeanour was worse than the prisoners they guarded. Each passed me on to some other filthy lout with a whip. Some expected money just for saying no. Most were drunk and all of them were nasty. When I finally found the right group of prisoners, talking to them was quite pleasant by comparison.

We spoke in Greek. Thank the gods for Greek – always there to help an informer dodge paying the price of an interpreter.

'I want you to tell me a story.' They stared at me, anticipating violence. It was giving me bad memories of a time I once disguised myself as a hard-labour slave. I found myself scratching reminiscently.

These were prisoners of war, nothing like the millions of nice, clean, cultured fellows Manlius and Varga had ranted about, the secretaries, stewards, toga-folders and wine-mixers who filled the streets of Rome looking just the same as their kempt masters. These were the few male survivors of various Judaean massacres, hand-picked to look good in Titus Caesar's Triumph. Most of the thousands of prisoners had been sent to forced labour in Egypt, the imperial province, but these shaven-headed, dirty, sullen youths had been carried off to Rome first to be paraded as a spectacle, then to rebuild the city in Vespasian's '*Roma Resurgans*' campaign.

They were fed, but thin. Building sites start work at dawn and pack up early. It was late afternoon. They were sitting around braziers now, outside their crowded bivouacs, their faces dark and hollow in the firelight as the winter darkness fell. To me they looked foreign, though I dare say I myself was being regarded by them as an exotic from a culture where everyone had dark jowls, unsavoury religious beliefs, strange culinary habits and a big hooked nose.

'Bear up,' I consoled them. 'You're slaves, but you're in Rome. It may seem hard for hill-farmers to find themselves brought here for endless mud-shovelling, but if you survive this hard labour through to the stonecutting and construction work, you're in the best place in the world. We Romans were hill-farmers once. The reason we clustered here among our theatres, baths and public venues is quite simple – we noticed that hill-farming stinks. You're alive, you're here – and you have access to a better life.'

Jests were not required. Even well-meant stoicism failed. They were desolate and dreaming of their goats.

They let me talk, however. Anything different is welcome to men on a chain-gang.

I knew from their foreman that these hailed from the right area. I explained what I wanted. 'It happened about this time of year, and about three years ago. There had been a hiatus since the autumn before, after Nero died; you may remember a period of uncertainty when hostilities ceased. Then came spring. Vespasian decided to revive his campaign. He climbed into the hills – where you come from – and he occupied your towns.'

They stared at me. They said they did not remember. They said it like men who would lie to me even if they did.

'What are you?' they asked me. Even prisoners of war are curious.

'An informer. I find things for people. Lost things – and lost truths. The mother of this soldier has asked me to tell her how he died.'

'Does she pay you for this?'

'No.'

'Why do you do it?'

'He matters to me too.'

'Why?'

'I am her other son.'

It was as pleasing circuitous as a riddle. The slight shock drew a dry cackle of laughter from these demoralised men whose days were confined to digging foreign mud from a giant foreign hole.

A prisoner rose from his haunches. I never knew his name. 'I remember,' he said. Maybe he was lying. Maybe he just felt

I had earned some sort of tale. 'Vespasian was placing garrisons in all the towns. He took Gophna and Acrabata. Bethel and Ephraim came next.'

'Were you at Bethel?' He swore that he was. Maybe he was lying now. There was no way I could really tell. 'Was it a stiff fight?'

'To us, yes – but probably, no.'

'Not much resistance?'

'Little. But we were going to fight,' he added. 'We gave up when we saw the fierceness of the Roman charge.'

Evidently he thought this was what I was wanting to hear. 'That's gracious of you,' I said politely. 'Did you see the centurion?'

'The centurion?'

'The officer. Mailed shirt, metal on his legs, fancy crest, vine stick – '

'The officer who led the charge?'

'He led it?'

'From the front!' smiled the prisoner, certain I would like that. Maybe he had been a soldier too.

'But he fell?'

'He was unlucky.'

'How?'

'An arrow squeezed in somehow between his helmet and his head.'

I believed that. This man had seen our boy.

Helmet not strapped properly. Trust him. Always unlaced, unhooked, half-belted. He hated feeling trapped. Loved sauntering into battle with his chin-strap waving free, as if he had just paused to dint the enemy on his way to somewhere else. Jupiter knows how that man got promoted.

Well I knew how. He was bloody good. Our Festus, with even only half his mind on a problem, could outstrip most of the dull plodders he was up against. Festus was the charismatic kind who soars to the top on talent that is genuine, easy and abundant. He was made for the army; the army knew its man. Stupid enough to show he did have that talent. Placid enough not to offend the establishment. Bright enough, once he was in position, to hold his own against anyone.

Yet still dumb enough to leave his helmet loose.

'Is this satisfactory?'

It was what I had come to hear.

Before I left they gathered around me with more questions about my work. What did I do, and who did I act for? I repaid their description of Bethel with some tales of my own. They were starving for stories, and I had plenty. They were fascinated by the fact that anybody from the Emperor down could hire me and send me out into the world as an agent; they even wanted to take me on for a commission of their own. (They had no money, but we were on good terms by then and I had mentioned that half my 'respectable' clients forgot to pay.)

'So what's your quest?'

'A retrieval.'

They began a long rambling saga involving a sacred item.

I had to break in. 'Look, if this involves the treasures that the conquering Titus lifted from your Temple at Jerusalem and dedicated on the Capitol, I'll stop you there! Robbing trophies from Rome's most sacred altar lies outside my sphere of activity.'

They exchanged furtive glances. I had stumbled on some much older mystery. Intrigued, I pressed for details. What they had lost was a large ship-like box of great antiquity, surmounted by two winged figures and supported on two carrying-poles. The Judaeans wanted to find it because it had magical properties which they believed would help them overthrow their enemies. Ignoring the fact that I didn't want my fellow Romans struck by lightning or smitten with fatal diseases (well not many of them), I was tempted. I love ridiculous stories. But explaining such a peculiar commission to Helena was more than I could face.

I grinned. 'Sounds as if you need a real daredevil for this job! I do divorces, which are hard enough, but I don't think I can undertake to find Lost Arks . . .'

I repaid their information about Festus with hard currency, and we parted friends.

As I picked my way from the bivouac, the unknown

prisoner called out after me, 'He was heroic. His whole heart was in the matter. Let his mother be told, the man you seek – your brother – was a true warrior!'

I didn't believe a word of it. But I felt prepared to tell the lie.

LXIX

I can't say I was feeling happy, but I did feel sufficiently improved to give myself a minor treat: I walked from the Forum up the Via Flaminia to the collectors' house. Then I joined the throng who were congregating in their gallery, viewing the Phidias.

Smart people were standing around with that air of constipated fright people have when gazing at great art without a proper catalogue. The women were wearing gold sandals that hurt their feet. The men were all wondering how soon they could politely leave. Silver salvers with very small pieces of almond cake were handed round to reward those who had come to do reverence. As usual on these occasions there had been wine earlier, but by the time I arrived the waiter with the tray had disappeared.

Poseidon looked good. Among the other marble gods, ours held his own. I felt a certain glow of pride. I felt even better when Carus wafted up, his mournful face almost happy for once, with Servia bundling along on his arm.

'Looks impressive.' I popped in an almond slice. 'What's the provenance?'

They dwelt lightly on the tale of the illustrious senator and his brother who imported from the East. I listened thoughtfully. 'A brother of Camillus? Not the one with the cloud attached to his name? I've heard a few shady stories about that one – wasn't he a merchant who handled dubious commodities, and died in mysterious circumstances?' I stared back at the statue. 'Well, I'm sure you know what you're doing!' I remarked. And then I left.

Behind me, I had left an insidious worm of distrust already gnawing morbidly.

LXX

The party at my mother's house which I had wanted to avoid was over. 'We heard about your disaster so I sent them home.' Ma sounded gruff.

'Geminus sent a message about what happened,' Helena explained in an undertone.

'Thank you, Papa!'

'Don't grouch. The message was mainly to warn us to look after you. When you didn't turn up we were worried sick. I've been looking for you everywhere – '

'That makes you sound like Marina drag-netting the bars for my brother.'

'The bars were where I looked,' she confirmed, smiling. She could see I was not drunk.

I sat down at Ma's kitchen table. My women surveyed me as if I were something they ought to catch in a beaker and put out on the back steps. 'I had a job to do, remember. A certain party commissioned me to investigate Didius Festus.'

'And what did you find out?' Mother demanded. 'Nothing good, I dare say!' She seemed to be her old self.

'Do you want to know?'

She thought about it. 'No,' she said. 'Let's leave it alone, shall we?'

I sighed gently. That was clients for you. They come pleading with you to save their skins, then when you've given up weeks of hard effort for some pitiful reward, you take them the answer and they stare at you as if you're mad to bother them with these puny facts. A case that was all in the family made things no better, though at least I knew the parties from the start, so I was prepared for it.

A bowl of food appeared before me. Ma ruffled my hair. She knew I hated that, but she did it anyway. 'Is it all sorted out?' This was a purely rhetorical question, meant to soothe me by pretending to show an interest.

I took a stand. 'All except the knife!'

'Eat your dinner,' said my mother.

Helena muttered to Ma apologetically, 'I'm afraid Marcus has a fixation with tracing your old cooking knife – '

'Oh really!' snapped my mother. 'I don't see the problem.'

'I think Pa took it.'

'Of course he did.' She was perfectly calm.

I choked. 'You could have said that in the first place!'

'Oh I thought I did . . .' I would get nowhere trying to pin her down. Now everything was my fault. 'What are you making so much fuss for?'

I must have been exhausted, because I came straight out with the question everyone had been too sensitive to pose to her: 'If Pa pinched the knife when he left home, how did it reach the caupona?'

My mother appeared to be offended she had reared such a fool. 'Surely it's obvious! It was a good knife; you wouldn't throw it out. But that woman of his wouldn't want someone else's equipment in amongst her own kitchen tools. First chance she got, she gave it a decent home somewhere else. I would have done the same,' said Ma, without vindictiveness.

Helena Justina looked as if she were trying not to laugh.

After a silence it was Helena who risked an even braver question: 'Junilla Tacita, what went wrong between you and Geminus, all those years ago?'

'Favonius,' replied my mother, rather shirtily. 'His name was Favonius!' She had always said that changing his name and pretending to become someone else was ridiculous. My father (said my mother) would never change.

'What was the reason he left?'

Helena was right. My mother was tough. There was no real need to tiptoe around these dainty issues which she must have faced squarely in her time. Mother answered Helena quite freely: 'No special reason. Too many people crammed in too small a space. Too many quarrels and too many mouths to feed. Then people give up on each other sometimes.'

I said, 'I never heard you tell anyone that before!'

'You never asked.' I had never dared.

I ate my dinner, keeping my head down. Coping with family, a man needs to build up his strength.

Helena Justina was seizing her chance to explore. She

should have been an informer; she had no inhibitions about asking tactless questions. 'So what made you marry him? I imagine he must have been very good-looking in his younger days.'

'He thought so!' Ma chuckled, implying otherwise. 'Since you ask, he seemed like a good prospect, with his own business and no hangers-on. He ate well; I liked the way he cleaned up a dinner-bowl.' A rare nostalgic haze came over her. 'He had a smile that could crack nuts.'

'What does that mean?' I scowled.

'I know!' Helena Justina was laughing, probably at me.

'Well, he must have caught me in a weak moment,' decided Ma.

I did tell her what the prisoners had said about her famous son. She listened, but what she thought or whether she was pleased to know it was impossible to tell.

She must have had another weak moment after that, because she suddenly exclaimed, 'Did you leave him at the Saepta then?'

'Who? Geminus?'

'Somebody ought to get him out of there.' I felt the familiar formidable sense of pressure as once again my mother was planning an unwelcome job for me. 'He shouldn't be left there all on his own, brooding and getting drunk. It's Tuesday!' Ma informed me. 'He'll have nobody at his place.' Quite right. Pa had told me his red-headed fancy piece, Flora, would be over at the caupona, on her weekly visit, going through the accounts. 'There's a new waiter at that food stall; she'll be wanting to supervise.'

I could hardly believe what I was hearing. In connection with the family, my mother knew everything. You could never escape it; not even if you left home for twenty years.

'I'm not going to be responsible – ' I mumbled weakly.

Then, needless to say, I left for the Saepta Julia.

LXXI

The Saepta was supposed to close in the evening, but rarely did. Jewellery stalls do most of their trade at night. I always enjoyed the atmosphere after dinner. Streamers of small lamps were lit around the porticoes. People relaxed. There were faint odours of spiced meat and fried fish from itinerants selling hot food from trays. The small shops looked like glittering caverns of treasure as the lights gleamed off the metalware and gems. Trash you would never look at by day turned into highly desirable curios.

My father's office had lost its Egyptian furniture but had gained, courtesy of a forthcoming sale, an elephant's foot, some African war gear with a funny smell, a stone throne that could convert into a personal lavatory, two copper cauldrons, three tall stools, a small obelisk (suitable for a garden ornament) and a rather nice set of glass jugs.

'I see you're back on target to make a fortune out of junk! The mulberry glass could turn into a real sale.'

'Right. You should come into partnership; you could be good at this.' My father appeared to be sober: quite a surprise.

'No thanks.' We stared at each other, each thinking over the failed statue scam. The mood between us prickled savagely. 'I've done my best, Pa. I went to the Carus house tonight and planted the thought that they bought a fake. They may have the Phidias, but they'll never enjoy it.'

'This is really good!' rasped my father sarcastically. 'Some people convince the customers that fakes are real. *We* have to live the hard way – we pretend that the genuine article is a fraud!' He launched into the normal family flattery: 'This is your fault!'

'I admit it. End of subject.'

'I left you in charge,' he roared at me bitterly.

'Orontes was your contact! I'll trace him, don't worry,' I threatened, enjoying the prospect of knocking out the sculptor's brains.

'No point. He'll be miles away with that frowsty whore Rubinia.' My father was as angry as I was. 'I've not been idle either; I've been to see Varga and Manlius. He's left Rome all right.'

'I'll get him back!' I insisted. 'We still have four blocks of good Parian marble – '

'It won't work,' Pa answered rebelliously. 'You cannot force an artist to produce on command. We'd risk him splitting the stone or turning it into some crass cupid with a dimpled bum that you wouldn't stick on a bird-bath. Or a boudoir nymph!' (His worst insult.) 'Leave it with me. I'll find someone.'

'Oh that's rich. One of your hacks, I suppose. We're back in the world of putting false noses on damaged busts, distressing brand-new carpentry, adding Greek handles to Etruscan urns – '

'I'll find somebody else, I said! Someone who can do us a decent copy.'

'Nice Lysippus?' I sneered.

'A nice Lysippus,' my father agreed, not turning a hair. 'Better still, four of them. Wrestlers would be popular.'

'I've lost interest,' I complained bitterly. 'I'm not cut out for this. I know nothing about sculpture. I can never remember whether the canon of perfect proportion is supposed to be illustrated by the Spear Carrier of Polyclitus and the Discus Thrower of Lysippus – '

'Wrong way round,' said my father. Actually I knew I had it right. He was trying to unnerve me. 'And it's the Scraper, not the Discobolos, who illuminates the rule.'

'Four wrestlers then.' Defeated by his tireless villainy, I calmed down. A new sculptor would have to be paid his commission, but four good copies of fashionable originals would still bring us in a birthday present and a half.

'You want to learn how to stay peaceful,' advised Pa. 'You'll do yourself damage blowing off like that every time the Fates hand you a small reverse.' He was the world's most blatant hypocrite.

I noticed we both had our arms folded as we both seethed. With the same wild hair and our chests thrust out, we must have looked like a pair of antique warriors squaring up under the beaded rim of a cinerary vase. He remembered to ask what I had come for.

'Rumour had it you were drunk. I've been sent to shove your head under a fountain and drag you off home safely.'

'I'm sober – but I'll get drunk with you now if you like,' Pa offered. I shook my head, though I knew it was a kind of truce.

He sat back on the old couch, considering me. I stared back. Since he was perfectly sober and not visibly brooding, it seemed time to put an end to my pointless trip. Something was delaying me. There was something I had been thinking about subconsciously.

'So what are you hanging about for, Marcus? Want to have a talk?'

'There's no more to say.' There was only one chance for this sort of submission, so I waded straight in: 'I could ask you a favour, though.'

My father was startled, but managed to rally: 'Don't strain a gut!'

'I'll ask you once, and if you say no we'll forget it.'

'Let's not make a Pythian dance out of it.'

'All right. You've got five hundred thousand sesterces bricked into the wall chest behind you, am I right?'

Father looked guarded. He dropped his voice carefully. Involuntarily he glanced towards the gloomy red curtain behind his couch. 'Well yes, that's where it is – at the moment,' he added, as if he suspected me of planning to steal it. His suspicion reassured me. Some things remained beautifully normal, even though I felt sick and light-headed.

'Consider this then, Father. If we had never found the Zeus, you were so sick of having auctions disrupted we would have paid the money to Carus, with no prospect of recouping it. Your money chest and my bank box in the Forum would both be empty now.'

'If you want your contribution back – '

'I want more than that,' I apologised.

My father sighed. 'I think I know what's coming.'

'I promise this is the first and only time in my life I'll lean on you.' I took a deep breath. There was no need to think about Helena; I had been thinking about her for the past twelve months. 'I'm asking for a loan.'

'Well, what are fathers for?' My father could not decide whether to mock me or to groan. There was no suggestion of refusing, even for a joke.

Asking the question had made me feel nervous myself. I grinned at him. 'I'll let you see the grandchildren!'

'What more can I ask!' quipped Geminus. 'Four hundred thousand was it? Carus paid up in big gold ones. At four sesterces to the denarius and twenty-five denarii to the aureus, that will be four thousand – '

'It has to be invested in Italian land.'

'Land then. I dare say I can find an agent to buy us a bog in Latium or a bit of Alban scrub . . .' He rose from the old couch and pulled back the curtain, fetching out the key on its greasy thong. 'You'll want to have a look at it.'

We stood side by side as he unlocked the chest. Even before the lid came up completely I could see the soft gleam of the aurei sparkling under the heavy woodwork. The money chest was full. I had never seen so much gold. The sight was both soothing and terrible.

'I'll pay you back.'

'Take your time,' said my father gently. He knew what this had cost me. I would be in hock to him for the rest of my life – and that had nothing to do with the money. The four hundred thousand was only the start of this debt.

He closed down the lid and locked the chest. We shook hands. Then I went straight to the Palatine and asked to see Vespasian.

LXXII

Under the Flavian emperors the imperial palace was being run with an atmosphere so professional it was positively staid. Sufficient Neronian flimflam remained here to make their serious efforts appear almost ridiculous by contrast. Beneath the exquisite painted panels, stuccoed ceilings with frivolous arabesques, extravagant carved ivory and massed beaten gold, sober teams of bureaucrats now toiled to drag the Empire back from bankruptcy and make us all proud to belong to Rome. Rome itself was to be rebuilt, its most famous monuments meticulously restored while carefully chosen additions to the national heritage would be positioned at suitable spots: a Temple of Peace, nicely balancing a Temple of Mars; the Flavian Arena; an arch here; a forum there; with a tasteful number of fountains, statues, public libraries and baths.

The Palace had its quiet times, and this was one of them. Banquets were held, since a cheerful and well-run banquet is the most popular form of diplomacy. The Flavian regime was neither mean nor cold. It valued teachers and jurists. It rewarded entertainers. With luck, it would even reward me.

In normal circumstances personal petitions for social advancement would be left with the Palace chamberlains to await a decision in maybe months' time, although reviewing the Senatorial and Equestrian Lists was a Flavian priority. One of Vespasian's first acts had been to appoint himself Censor, with the aims of conducting a headcount for taxation purposes and bringing new blood to the two Orders from which public posts were filled. He had his own ideas about suitable people, but never despised the noble Roman art of putting oneself forward. How could he, after he, a rather despised member of the Senate, had put himself forward successfully for the post of emperor?

Adding my scroll to the mountain in a chamberlain's office did not suit the Falco temperament. Since I was known as an

Imperial agent I walked in, looking as if I had some sinister affair of state on my mind, and jumped the queue.

I was hoping to find the old Emperor in jovial mood after his dinner. He worked early and late; his most redeeming country virtue was simply getting things done. Evenings were when he was in good spirits, and when favours should be asked. Evening was therefore when I turned up in my toga and best boots, barbered neatly but not effeminately, aiming to remind him of successful missions on my part and old promises on his.

As usual, I left my luck with the Guard on the door. Vespasian was out of Rome.

The Flavians were famous as a family team. Having two grown sons to offer long-term stability had been Vespasian's chief qualification. He and his elder son Titus were virtually partners now; even the younger, Domitian, took a full part in public duties. The night I came to beg for advancement both imperial sons were working; the chamberlain, who knew me, told me to choose which Caesar I wanted to see. Even before I had made up my mind I knew the best choice was to walk away. But I was geared up for action, and could not back down.

Not even I could ask Titus, who had once cast interested eyes on Helena, to give me promotion so I could snatch the girl myself. There had been nothing between them (as far as I could ascertain), but without my presence there might have been. He had a pleasant mentality, but I hate to push a man beyond reasonable limits. Tact necessarily intervened.

'I'll take Domitian.'

'Best thing. He's doing the public appointments nowadays!' The Palace staff laughed. Domitian's fervour in handing out postings left and right had caused even his mild father to criticise.

Despite jumping the queue, I had to wait about. I ended up wishing I had brought one of the judge's encyclopaedias to read or my will to write. But finally it was my turn, and in I went.

Domitian Caesar was twenty-two. Handsome; solid as a bullock; curly-topped, though hammer-toed. Brought up among women while his father and Titus were away on public duties, instead of his elder brother's sweet disposition he now had the introverted, obstinate air that is more often found in an only child. In his first acts in the Senate he had made mistakes; as a result he had been demoted to organising poetry competitions and festivals. Now he conducted himself well in public, yet I distrusted him.

There were reasons for that. I knew things about Domitian that he would not want repeated. His reputation as a plotter had foundation: I was in a position to indict him for a serious crime. I had promised his father and brother they could rely on my discretion – but my knowledge was what had prompted me to choose him of the two young Caesars, and I walked into his presence tonight full of confidence.

'Didius Falco!' I had been announced by officials. It was impossible to tell from his greeting whether the young prince remembered me.

He wore purple; that was his privilege. His wreath was fairly plain and reposing on a cushion. There were no mounds of grapes or jewel-encrusted goblets, very few garlands and certainly no sinuous dancers writhing around the floor. He was attending to public business with the same seriousness as Vespasian and Titus. This was no debauched, paranoid Julio-Claudian. Yet I knew he was dangerous. He was dangerous – and I could prove it. But after so many years in the business, I should have known that did not make my own position safe.

The room was of course full of attendants. Slaves who looked as though they had work to do were, as always in the Flavian audience chamber, quietly proceeding with their business, apparently unsupervised. There was someone else there too. Domitian gestured to a figure on the sidelines.

'I have asked Anacrites to join us.' My request for an audience would have been relayed long before I was actually summoned; during the tedium of my long wait, this disaster had been arranged. Domitian thought I was there as an agent. He had sent for support. Anacrites was the Palace's official Chief Spy.

He was tight-lipped and tense; pale-eyed; obsessively neat; a man who had brought the undercover arts of suspicion and jealousy to new depths.

Of all the petty tyrants in the Palace secretariat he was the meanest, and of all the enemies I could have picked in Rome I hated him the most.

'Thanks, Caesar. We need not detain him. My business is personal.' Nobody reacted. Anacrites stayed.

'And your business is?'

I took a deep breath. My palms were sweating unaccountably. I kept my voice low and even. 'Some time ago your father made me a wager that if I could produce the financial qualifications, he would make me a member of the middle class. I have recently returned from Germany where I completed various actions on the state's behalf. I now wish to marry and settle to a quieter life. My elderly father agrees with this decision. He has deposited four hundred thousand sesterces with a land agent, for investment in my name. I have come to beg the honour which your father promised me.'

Very neat. So restrained. Domitian was even more restrained. He merely asked me, 'You are an informer, I believe?'

So much for polite rhetoric. I should have said, *'You're a rat and I can prove it. Sign this scroll, Caesar, or I'll spew the dirt from the Rostrum and finish you!'*

His Caesarship did not look at Anacrites. Anacrites did not need to speak to him. Apart from the fact that everything must have been settled between them before I had even crossed the threshold for my fatal audience, the rules were quite clear. Domitian Caesar stated them: 'In reforming the Senatorial and Equestrian Orders, my father is concerned to provide reputable, meritworthy groups from whom he can draw future candidates for public posts. Are you,' he asked, in that measured tone with which I could not quarrel, 'proposing that *informers* should be regarded as reputable and meritworthy men?'

I opted for the worst kind of salvage: telling the truth. 'No, Caesar. It's a seedy, disgusting occupation, picking over secrets at the worst end of society. Informers trade in betrayal and misery. Informers live off other people's death and loss.'

Domitian stared. He had a tendency to be morose. 'Nevertheless, you have been useful to the state?'

'I hope so, Caesar.'

But the upshot was inevitable. He said, 'That may be. But I do not feel able to grant this request.'

I said, 'You have been most courteous. Thank you for your time.'

He added, with the diffidence that characterised the Flavians, 'If you feel an injustice has been done, you may wish to ask my brother or the Emperor to re-examine your case.'

I smiled bitterly. 'Caesar, you have given me a reasoned adjudication which conforms with the highest social principles.' Once Domitian had stacked the odds against me there was no point in exclaiming. Titus would probably refuse to interest himself. I knew without exposing myself to more sorrow that Vespasian would support his boy. As my own would say, what are fathers for?

I scoffed, 'Injustice I cannot accuse you of, Caesar – merely ingratitude. No doubt you will inform your father of my views, the next time he wants me for some stinking mission that exceeds the capabilities of your normal diplomats?'

We inclined heads politely, and I left the audience.

Anacrites followed me out. He seemed shocked. He even seemed to be calling upon some brotherhood of our trade. Well, he was a spy; he lied well. 'Falco, this had nothing to do with me!'

'That's good.'

'Domitian Caesar called for me because he thought you wanted to talk about your work in Germany – '

'Oh I do like that,' I snarled. 'Since you had nothing at all to do with my achievements in Germany!'

The spy was still protesting. 'Even freed slaves can buy their way into the middle rank! Are you accepting this?' Spies are simple people.

'How can I quibble? He followed the rules. In his place, Anacrites, I would have done the same.' Then, knowing that Anacrites was probably a freedman, I added, 'Besides, who wants to rank with slaves?'

I walked from the Palace like a prisoner with a life sentence who had just heard he was to benefit from a national amnesty. I kept telling myself the decision was a relief.

Only as I plodded to collect Helena from Mother's did I

gradually allow my spirits to sink under the knowledge that my losses today, which already included dignity and pride, now had to include ambition, trust and hope.

LXXIII

Not knowing how to face Helena Justina, I went to get drunk. At Flora's Caupona there were lamps along both counters. The new waiter was presiding with a care and attention which must already have lost several of the old lackadaisical customers. Not a crumb marred the mock-marble counters, which he flicked every few seconds with a cloth, while waiting eagerly for requests to serve the few nervous inebriates. What the caupona had gained in cleanliness it now lacked in atmosphere.

Still, that would change. The old dismal standards were too ingrained to stay under for long. After ten years, mediocrity would reassert itself.

I was pleased to see this new waiter was a man I recognised.

'Apollonius! Just filling in until you get the call back to education?'

'On the house!' he said proudly, placing a cup two inches from my elbow and following it with a neat little dish of exactly twenty nuts.

There was no way I could get drunk in such a pristine environment. Good manners forbade forcing this enraptured soul to hear my pathetic ramblings, let alone mop up after me. I managed a minute of small talk, then drained my cup. I was just leaving when a woman came in from the back room with her sleeves rolled up, drying her hands on a towel.

For a moment I thought it was Mother. She was small, tidy, and unexpectedly grey-haired. Her face was sharp, her eyes tired and suspicious of men.

I could have left even though she had seen me. Instead, I took a deep breath. 'You must be Flora.' She made no reply. 'I'm Falco.'

'Favonius's younger son.' I had to smile at the irony of my preposterous father running away to a 'new life' when even the woman he took with him insisted on using his old name.

She must be wondering whether I posed some sort of

1025

threat. Probably Festus when he was around had worried her; possibly she understood that I was different.

'May I ask you to give a message to my father? It's bad news, I'm afraid. Tell him I went to the Palace, but was turned down. I'm grateful, but his loan won't be required.'

'He will be very disappointed,' the redhead, who was no longer a redhead, commented. I fought off my anger at the thought of the two of them discussing me.

'We'll all survive,' I told her. Speaking as if we were one glorious united family.

'Perhaps you will have another opportunity,' Flora offered me quietly, like any distant female relation consoling a young man who had come to announce a failure on the worst day of his life.

I thanked Apollonius for the drink, and went home to my mother's house.

Too many voices greeted me; I could not go in.

Helena must have been waiting. As I reached the foot of the stairs again, heading off by myself, her voice called out, 'Marcus, I'm coming – wait for me!'

I waited while she seized a cloak, then she ran down: a tall, strong-willed girl in a blue dress and an amber necklace, who knew what I had come to tell her well before I spoke. I did tell her, as we walked through Rome. Then I gave her the other dreary news: that whatever I had said to Anacrites, I did not intend to stay in a city which broke its promises.

'Wherever you go, I'll come with you!' She was wonderful.

We went up on the Embankment – the great ancient rampart built by the republicans to enclose the original city. Rome had long outgrown these battlements, which remained now as a memorial to our forefathers and a place to climb to view the modern city. Helena and I came here in times of trouble, to feel the night air blowing around us while we walked above the world.

From the Gardens of Mycaenas on the slopes of the Esquiline arose a soft springtime odour of damp soil stirring with new life. Dark, powerful clouds were thrusting across the skies. In one direction we could see the stark crag of the Capitol, still lacking the Temple of Jupiter, lost to fire in the civil wars. Curving round it, outlined by small lights on the wharves, the river took its meandering course. Behind us we heard a trumpet from the Praetorian barracks, causing a raucous surge of drunken noise from a drinking-house near the Tiburtina Gate. Below, monkeys chattered among the disreputable booths where fortune-tellers and puppeteers entertained the cheap end of society who even in winter took their fun out of doors. The streets were full of waggons and donkeys, the air rent with shouting and harness-bells. Exotic cymbals and chanting announced the begging priests and acolytes of some unsavoury cult.

'Where shall we go?' demanded Helena as we walked. Respectable girls are excited so easily. Brought up to be chaste, staid and sensible, naturally Helena Justina now kicked up her heels at the first promise of a jape. Knowing me spelt ruin for her parents' dreams of curbing her, just as knowing her spelt disaster for my own occasional plans to reform into a sober citizen.

'Give me a chance! I have just reached a wild decision in a moment of despondency; I don't expect to be taken up on it.'

'We have the whole Empire to choose from – '

'Or we can stay at home!'

Suddenly she stopped in her tracks, laughing. 'Whatever you want, Marcus. I don't mind.'

I threw back my head, breathing slowly and deeply. Soon the damp winter odours of the soot from a million oil-lamps would be giving way to summer's scents of flower festivals and spicy food taken in the open air. Soon Rome would be warm again, and life would seem easy, and taking a stand would become just too much agony.

'I want you,' I said. 'And whatever life we can make for ourselves.'

Helena leaned against my side, her heavy mantle wrapping itself around my legs. 'Can you be happy as we are?'

'I suppose so.' We had paused, somewhere above the Golden House, near the Caelimontana Gate. 'What about you, sweetheart?'

'You know what I think,' said Helena quietly. 'We reached the decision that mattered when I first came to live with you. What is marriage but the voluntary union of two souls?

1027

Ceremony is irrelevant. When I married Pertinax . . .' She very rarely referred to this. 'We had the veils, nuts and the slaughtered pig. After the ceremony,' said Helena baldly, 'we had nothing else.'

'So if you marry again,' I replied gently, 'you want to be like Cato Uticensis when he married Marcia?'

'How was that?'

'Without witnesses or guests. Without contracts or speeches. Brutus was present to take the auguries – though maybe you and I should dispense even with that. Who wants their failures to be prophesied in advance?' With me, she could be certain there would be failures. 'They simply joined hands, communing in silence, while they gave their pledge – '

Romantic moments with a girl who is well read can be difficult. 'Cato and Marcia? Oh that's a touching story. He divorced her!' Helena remembered angrily. 'He gave her away to his very rich best friend – while she was *pregnant*, mark you – then when the lucrative second spouse dropped dead, Cato took her back, acquiring the fortune. Very convenient! I see why you admire Cato.'

Gamely I tried to laugh it off. 'Forget it. He was full of weird ideas. He banned husbands from kissing their wives in public – '

'That was his grandfather. Anyway, I don't suppose anyone noticed,' Helena snapped. 'Husbands ignore their wives in public; everyone knows that.'

I was still living with a mass of prejudice derived from Helena Justina's ex-husband. Maybe one day I would dispel her bad memories. At least I was willing to try. 'I won't ignore you, love.'

'Is that a promise?'

'You'll see to it!' I said, holding off a moment of panic.

Helena chuckled. 'Well I'm not the incomparable Marcia – and you're certainly not Cato!' Her voice dropped more tenderly. 'But I gave you my heart a long time ago, so I may as well add my pledge . . .'

She turned towards me, grasping my right hand in hers. Her left hand lay upon my shoulder, as always with that plain band of British silver which she wore on her third finger to mark her love for me. Helena made a good stab at the pose of adoring submissiveness, though I am not sure whether I quite pulled off the frozen look of caution which is often seen in married men on tombstones. But there we were, on that April night on the Embankment, with nobody to see us, yet the whole city assembled around us had we wanted the presence of witnesses. We were standing in the formal Roman matrimonial pose. And whatever communing in silence entails, we were doing it.

Personally I have always thought that Cato Uticensis has a lot to answer for.

ONE VIRGIN TOO MANY

The latest Falco Bestseller

A frightened child approaches Roman informer Marcus Didius Falco, pleading for help. Nobody believes Gaia's story that a relation wants to kill her – and neither does he. Beset by his own family troubles, by his new responsibilities as Procurator of the Sacred Poultry, and by the continuing search for a new partner, he turns her away. Immediately he regrets it. Gaia has been selected as the new Vestal Virgin, and when she disappears Falco is officially asked to investigate. Finding Gaia is then a race against time, ending in Falco's most terrifying exploit yet...

'She brings Imperial Rome to Life'
Ellis Peters

'Davis' books make old Rome sound fun...
it is all so enjoyable'
The Times

'Wonderful, great fun all round'
Daily Telegraph

TWO FOR THE LIONS

Lumbered with working alongside reptilian Chief Spy Anacrites, Marcus Didius Falco has the perfect plan to make money – he will assist Vespasian in the Emperor's 'Great Census' of AD73. His potential fee could finally allow him to join the middle ranks and be worthy of long-suffering Helena Justina.

Unexpectedly confronted with the murder of a man-eating lion, Falco is distracted from his original task, uncovering a bitter rivalry between the gladiators' trainers. With one star gladiator dead, Falco is forced to investigate and the trail leads from Rome to the blood-soaked sand of the arena in North Africa.

THREE HANDS
IN THE FOUNTAIN

Back in Rome after a dangerous mission to the Roman province of Baetica, Marcus Didius Falco is enjoying a drink of ill-travelled Spanish wine when he makes a gruesome discovery in the local fountain: a severed human hand.

Inevitably he is drawn into a search of the water supply and Rome's hundreds of miles of sewer and aqueduct. There he finds evidence of a whole series of murders. Each killing has taken place during a public festival, and the Roman Games are only days away: Time is running out if he is to prevent the murderer striking again.

'Uniquely entertaining'
Time Out

'Bizarre, funny and satisfying'
Irish Times

'One of the best of the current writers in this field'
Sunday Times

'As always, Davis wears her research lightly. bringing Ancient Rome to vivid life in a series of delicious vignettes'
Manchester Evening News

A DYING LIGHT
IN CORDUBA

Nobody was poisoned at the dinner for the Society of Olive Oil Producers of Baetica, though in retrospect this was quite a surprise…

Inimitable sleuth Marcus Didius Falco is back with a vengeance. On one night, a man is killed and Rome's Chief of Spies left for dead. Naturally there is no one except Falco to conduct the investigation. Soon he is plunged into the fiercely competitive world of olive oil production. Political intrigue, an exotic Spanish dancer and impending fatherhood, all add to Falco's troubles.

'With the passing of Ellis Peters, the title Queen of the Historical whodunnit is temporarily vacant. Lindsey Davis is well suited to assume it – and she is funnier than Peters … Davis' books make old Rome sound fun … it is all so enjoyable'
The Times

'The cast of characters is as various, corrupt, nasty and gnarled as the best of Dickens, described with similar scope and loving attention'
Mail on Sunday

'Highly readable, funny and colourful'
Times Literary Supplement

TIME TO DEPART

'I still can't believe I've put the bastard away for good!'
Petro muttered. Petronius Longus, captain of the
Aventine watch and Falco's oldest friend, has finally
nailed one of Rome's top criminals. Under Roman law
citizens are not imprisoned but allowed 'time to
depart' into exile outside the Empire. One dark and
gloomy dawn Petro and Falco put the evil Balbinus
aboard ship.

But soon after, an outbreak of robbery and murder
suggests a new criminal ring has moved into Balbinus'
territory. Petro and Falco must descend into the
underworld of Vespasian's Rome to investigate...

'Non-stop action, excitement and astonishments
– a real cracker'
The Good Book Guide

'Absolutely smashing'
Daily Telegraph

'Davis' writing zings with fun'
Daily Mail

LAST ACT IN PALMYRA

AD 72: Marcus Didius Falco leaves Rome on his most dangerous mission yet.

A commission to find a missing water organ player and an Imperial order to spy out the Lands of the East send Falco and his aristocratic girlfriend, Helena Justina, across the sea to Petra.

But the rose-red city turns out not to be so rosy after the couple discover a murdered Roman playwright and they flee with the man's erstwhile employers, a group of travelling actors.

Falco, naturally, feels obliged not only to take up his stylus to fill the dead man's role in the company, but also to investigate the murder. Soon another murder, several accidents and the dangers of the desert are making him wish he'd stayed at home...

THE COURSE OF HONOUR

The love story of the Emperor Vespasian, who brought peace to Rome after years of strife, and his mistress, the freed slave woman Antonia Caenis, this book recreates Ancient Rome's most turbulent period – the reigns of Tiberius, Caligula, Claudius and Nero, and Vespasian's rise to power.

As their forbidden romance blossoms, she is embroiled in political intrigue, while he embarks on a glorious career. Years pass, then Vespasian risks all in the climactic struggle for power – bringing hope for Rome, but a threat to the relationship that has endured so long.

The Course of Honour will delight not only the fans of Lindsey Davis's bestselling Falco novels, but anyone with an interest in the era that inspired Robert Graves's classic *I, Claudius*.

'Like reading Pliny rewritten by Raymond Chandler'
Sunday Times

'Extremely good…as well as being
a convincing love story'
Daily Mail

LINDSEY DAVIS IN ARROW